Pe

re (Bernard) Chocarne

The Inner Life Of The Very Reverend Pére Lacordaire

Pe

re (Bernard) Chocarne

The Inner Life Of The Very Reverend Pére Lacordaire

ISBN/EAN: 9783741127458

Manufactured in Europe, USA, Canada, Australia, Japa

Cover: Foto ©Andreas Hilbeck / pixelio.de

Manufactured and distributed by brebook publishing software
(www.brebook.com)

Pe

re (Bernard) Chocarne

The Inner Life Of The Very Reverend Pére Lacordaire

THE INNER LIFE

OF THE

VERY REVEREND

PÈRE LACORDAIRE, O.P.

Translated from the French of the REV. PÈRE CHOCARNE, O.P.,
by the Author of "*Knights of St. John*," "*St. Dominic and the Dominicans*," *&c., etc.*

. (*With the Author's permission.*)

WITH PREFACE

BY THE VERY REV. FATHER AYLWARD,
PRIOR PROVINCIAL OF ENGLAND.

Second ☙ Thousand.

LONDON:
R. WASHBOURNE, 18 PATERNOSTER ROW.
1878.

PREFACE.

IT is not without reserve and hesitation that I have consented to write a preface to this translation of the "Life of Lacordaire." For I cannot but feel that anything I can say must derive its interest solely from my recollection of his visit to me during his brief stay in England ; and the shortness of that visit, and the merely adventitious circumstance of my holding the office of provincial at the time, will scarcely, perhaps, in the reader's judgment, entitle me to assume that familiar style which a writer of personal reminiscences is supposed to claim as his right.

It was in the spring of 1852 that he arrived at Hinckley. I had scarcely had notice of his coming, and the short time during which I had expected him, the reader may well suppose, was not passed without emotion on my part. Nor need I say how subdued and reverent I felt when I stood in our little front parlour in the presence, for the first time, of that great and illustrious brother—and he, too, at my feet and asking my blessing—whose name for nearly twenty years before had always had greater power than any other to awaken my enthusiasm, and who, as an orator and champion of religion, had won a place which, in the estimation of many Frenchmen, had remained unoccupied since the time of Bossuet.[*] He had shortly before preached the sermon at St. Roch which brought his work in Paris to a close ; a result which, as I gathered from subsequent conversation with him, although he alluded to it with great reserve, seemed to surprise him. He appeared to be unaware that he had said anything of a particularly strong kind, and seemed to think he might justly have said things much stronger.

"From that day, however," says M. de Montalembert, "it became impossible for him to preach in Paris." He therefore took advantage of the respite to make a tour of the northern provinces of the Order. He thus writes in one of his "Letters to Young Men" (Letter xxxv.) : "I write to you from Ghent, where we have a house. I came intending to visit our convents in the northern provinces, namely, in Belgium, Holland, England, and Ireland. They are provinces upon which we count for the general restoration of our Order, and I thought it very useful to get an accurate knowledge of them, especially as we are just about holding our first provincial chapter in France."

Much therefore that we had to commune upon had

---

[*] "When I look around for one greater, one more eloquent than he, I can only think of Bossuet."—(*Montalembert, Memoir of Lacordaire,* p. 311.)

reference to the interests of the Order, its discipline, its doctrinal traditions, its studies, its prospects for the future. He spoke with great interest of the little course of homilies on the Scripture text, which he had commenced not long before in our church of Carmes, Rue de Vaugirard, and mentioned with signs of great pleasure the attraction which the simple display of the riches of the Bible seemed to exercise upon the crowds who came to listen. Father Chocarne alludes to this course in chap. xviii. Now and then in the midst of his conversation a gleam of gaiety would break out, and when the delivery of his thought demanded two or three minutes of uninterrupted talk, one remarked all the rapidity and decision which characterise his style. But, on the whole, the idea with which he impressed you, at least for the first day or two, was one of pensiveness and reserve. I thought at the time this might be occasioned by the sense of wrong under which he was suffering; I now see, from his life and letters, it was part of his nature. " Despite myself I weigh what I say, in order not to appear too simple and too loving " (Letter xxxii.).

We had much free and happy conversation upon a variety of questions, very disconnected, and for the most part ending in nothing. I could not at all times agree with him—(may I not unpresumptuously say it ?)—nor he with me. Of several of these questions I have a vivid recollection. For instance : How easy it is to misinterpret St. Augustin, taking him *ad literam*, and to make it *appear* that the doctrine of the "Augustinus" is deducible from his works; whether (speaking of matters within the limits of Catholic teaching) if Molina verges to one false extreme, *some* of our Thomists do not seem to tend towards the other; whether there may not be a natural beatitude, such as Catherinus understood it; what was the effect of strict observance on the health and working powers of our students and brethren at Woodchester, particularly in the points of perpetual abstinence and midnight rising. Next to these things, he was chiefly inquisitive concerning the English constitution; and in the interchange of thought on this subject I had to express my doubts as to the success of most of the continental experiments in constitutional government, as being sudden, violent, and revolutionary, the work of men *intent* on change, discarding national tradition, breaking up old kingdoms, and endeavouring to piece them together again in accordance with a pre-formed theory. To all which he seemed either to demur, or to give only a very cold and silent assent. He appeared interested in hearing it maintained that England could not serve as an example herein to other nations, because its constitutional liberties and representative system are the slow growth of many centuries, originating in our Saxon times, and rooted in our Saxon habits; checked under the early Plantagenets; stimulated into rapid development under the leadership of De Montfort; surviving the despotism of the Tudors, and the fanaticism and exclusiveness of the Puritans; and passed on through the Revolution of 1688, with changing fortune down to our own times ; extending to every portion of our public society, and regulating every portion of our public business, from the Imperial Parliament to the municipal council and the village vestry. He asked what book could be recommended as containing a good treatise. on our Constitution ? which, as he did not understand English, was a difficult question to answer; for, with the exception of Guizot, with whose writings on our constitution and history he was already well acquainted, I could not then call to mind any French author who had written professedly about it. I could only therefore mention a few English books ; but as I knew of no translations of them into French, my answer did not serve for much.

He repeatedly mentioned his surprise and disappointment at the apathy shown, as he thought, to the memory of O'Connell. And on my expressing my conviction that posterity would do him justice, and that his fame would grow greater as time went on, he would only reply by confessing again and again his inability to understand how the *present* generation of English and Irish Catholics, the very ones he had raised up and emancipated, should seem to have forgotten his life and services. He little knew that men would arise claiming the leadership of his countrymen, and owing everything to him, who would confess no love for his name, but would glory in discarding his plans, disowning for themselves all part

with him in his loyalty to the Church and in his allegiance to the principles of a true Catholic politician,
and treating them with open derision.

We had to touch upon the freedom of the press.
The Catholic body were still undergoing the persecution which licentious journals had not ceased to inflict
upon us from the time of the re-establishment of our
hierarchy.   But I forget just now what, and upon
what subjects, were the attacks which seemed then
particularly intended to wound our minds, and to add
to the bitterness and mistrust of our neighbours.   I
could not help complaining to him of the want, on the
part of our governing authorities, of reasonable powers
of repression ; for if I remember rightly, those attacks
were of a *quasi-personal* kind.   I was driven by stress
of argument to urge that the fact of the press being
perhaps (but not surely) open to you for defence, as to
others for aggression, signified little ; that you were
still kept under a powerful tyranny, hostile or favourable to you according to caprice, or accident, or the
expediency of those who undertake to create and to
tutor public opinion ; that there was an essential
immorality in subjecting men to the action of a vast
and mysterious kind of being, arbitrary and irrespon-
sible, a *corporate intelligence*, invisible, ever present,
powerful of intellect, but refusing to own a conscience.
As I have already said, we were chafing under a sense
of unfairness, and were all, of course, very angry (as
the reader will doubtless have already perceived), and
as men are likely to be when "leading journals" agree

to make you unhappy, and try to write you down. None felt this more keenly at times than our late great Cardinal. I was wishing that Father Lacordaire would be on my side. But, although I know I used my best French, I could get no hearty response from him; naught but a grave, tender, and patient look, which seemed to me to show that he *endured* the expression of my views.

This, I remember, was whilst I was driving him to Desford, a village about five miles from Hinckley, on our way to M. de Lisle's, of Gracedieu Manor, the friend of his friend Montalembert. He was much interested with his visit to Gracedieu, the resort, in years past, of so many eminent Catholics, whether foreigners or Englishmen, converts or others. I well remember the varied talk which all took part in, as well in the house, as during our walk through the woods to St. Bernard's Abbey, and on our return by the way of the little mountain chapel of the " Calvary." He was struck with everything ; and almost everything suggested a topic of conversation—the wild scenery of Charnwood Forest—the foundation, only a few years before, of the abbey—the progress of the Catholic religion in the neighbourhood, and throughout the kingdom generally—the politics of the day, and the rumour of what Louis Napoleon was said to be contriving against England.

But I fear the reader will hardly pardon all this personal gossip, which, however, although it is trifling, will not be without interest for those who approach

this charming book of Père Chocarne to try and gain
a closer acquaintance with that noble and engaging
character whose intimate life it professes to reveal.

Lacordaire himself has said something of the impression made upon him during this visit. In one of
his Letters (Letter xxxvii.) he writes: "I spent the
last ten days in visiting very beautiful things : first of
all, two of our monasteries, one situated at Hinckley,
a little town in Leicestershire, and the other in
Leicester itself; then a mansion in which I received
hospitality, the Cistercian convent called Mount St.
Bernard, Alton Towers, belonging to Lord Shrewsbury, Cheadle Church, a Passionist monastery not far
from there, the town of Birmingham, and lastly, the
Catholic College of St. Mary's, Oscott. All this,
which says but little to you, said much to me, and
taught me a great deal touching the marvellous
growth of the Catholic Church in England. You can
form no idea of the magnificence of these establishments, of the beauty of their situation, nor of the
touching sight afforded by this resurrection of the works
and arts of the faith upon a heretical soil. This, you
are told, is a church built by a converted minister ; this
monastery was built in the solitude by such and such
a gentleman ; this chapel upon a rock contains a picture of our Lord's Passion, and Protestants themselves
come here to sing hymns ; this cross is the first which
has appeared for three centuries upon a high road."

I am sorry to say I could not accompany him to
Oxford, whence the above letter is dated. He was not

one who *could* be insensible to the charm of such a
place ; accordingly, there is great beauty of manner in
his expression of the thoughts and feelings which
possessed him whilst walking through the streets and
colleges of that wonderful city, unequalled for many
things by any other in Europe, and which, of all non-
Catholic cities, is the one which interests a Catholic
mind the most. "After ten days thus employed, I
came alone to Oxford to rest, and to write in peace to
those I love. What a sweet and lovely place this
Oxford is ! Picture to yourself, in a plain surrounded
with hills, and watered by two rivers, an assemblage of
Gothic and Greek monuments, churches, colleges,
quadrangles, porticoes, scattered about, profusely but
gracefully, in noiseless streets terminating in vistas of
trees and meadows. All these monuments devoted to
science and letters have their gates open ; the stranger
may walk in just as into his own house, because it is
the resort of the beautiful for all who appreciate it.
One crosses silent quadrangles, meeting here and there
young men wearing the cap and gown ; no crowd, no
noise ; a gravity in the air as well as in the walls
darkened by age, for it seems to me that nothing is
repaired here for fear of committing a crime against
antiquity. And still the most exquisite cleanliness is
visible from top to bottom of the buildings. I never
saw anywhere such well-preserved monuments with
such a beautiful air of decay. In Italy the buildings
look young ; here it is time which shows without
dilapidation, simply in majesty.

"The town is small, and still it does not seem to want in size : the number of the monuments makes up for houses, and gives it a look of vastness. How my heart yearned for you, as I walked solitary amidst these young men of your own age! Not one of them knew or cared for me : I was. to them as though I did not exist, and more than once tears started into my eyes at the thought that elsewhere I should have met friendly looks."

This sense of loneliness would have been relieved had there been some one to trace out to him the situation and boundaries of the well-known "island," (no longer an island,) which were also, formerly, the situation and boundaries of our famous Oxford schools, convent, and church, but of which, I believe, scarce a vestige now remains. He who knew so well the power of the love, "far brought from the storied past," with which a man loves his land, and a religious (no less laudably) loves his ancient Order, would have felt additional emotion on having the spot pointed out where stood those halls which had heard of old the voices of our most famous men, Fishacre and Robert Bacon, Bromyard, Stubbs, Kilwardby, Joyce, Holkot, and Trivet. Had there been a Catholic Oxford in his days, no voice would have had greater power of fascination than his over such minds as those amongst whom he felt as an alien and one unknown. For his peculiar gift from God seems to have been to bring his very soul to play on all the higher and purer feelings of educated young

men ; that soul " which," as Montalembert says, " like
Almighty God Himself, loved *souls* above all things :
'*Domine qui amas animas*' (Sap. xi. 27) ; that soul in
which austerity and firmness were blended with such
a wonderful sweetness, in which tenderness and
loftiness went hand in hand, in which the candour of
the child was allied to such intense manliness"
(Memoir, p. 9).

The Count de Montalembert, his old associate and
brother in arms, has expressed in manly and affecting
language the tenderness and truth of his love for
Lacordaire. It reminds you of David's lamentation
for the death of *his* friend : "*Doleo super te, frater mi
Jonatha, decore nimis, et amabilis super amorem
mulierum. Sicut mater unicum amat filium suum, ita
ego te diligebam*" (II. Reg. i.). He thus concludes his
Memoir :—"What neither time, nor the injustice of
man, nor the 'treachery of glory,' will ever take from
him, is the greatness of his character, the honour of
having been the most manly, the most finely tempered
and most naturally heroic soul of our times."

The reader is now going to be introduced to an
intimate acquaintance with this great character, this
"heroic soul," through Père Chocarne's delightful
pages. His "*Vie Intime et Religieuse de Lacordaire*"
has had extraordinary success in France and elsewhere. And this is not to be wondered at, considering
the subject of the book, and the charm with which
the writer has invested it.

I cannot conclude without saying that, but for the

suggestions and kind importunity of the Very Rev.
Dr. Russell, O. P. Provincial of Ireland, whose taste
as a man of letters is only surpassed by his love for
his Order, this translation would not have been
undertaken. Père Chocarne himself was good enough
to write from America a word of approval and
encouragement. He also wrote to the Paris publishers (Mme. Poussielgue et Fils), to whom all rights
of republication were reserved, and they kindly
granted the necessary permission. As to the translation itself, every intelligent reader will acknowledge
the ability with which it has been executed. It is due
to a writer who has already enriched our English
Catholic literature with many original works, the
interest of which, both for matter and style, is confessed and appreciated by every one.

J. D. A.

St. Andrew's, Newcastle-on-Tyne,
   October 2, 1867.

CONTENTS.

CHAPTER V.

1830-1832.

CHAPTER VI.

CHAPTER VII.

1833-1836.

CHAPTER VIII.

1836-1838.

CHAPTER IX.

1838, 1839.

CHAPTER X.

1839, 1840.

CHAPTER XI.

CHAPTER XVIII.

1849-1854.

CHAPTER XIX.

CHAPTER XX.

1860, 1861.

CHAPTER I.

T happened, in the year 1793, that the parishioners of Recey-sur-Ource, a small village near Chatillon-sur-Seine in Burgundy, rose in revolt against their curé. The Abbé Magné, who had been called on once before to accept the civil constitution of the clergy, had hitherto contented himself with keeping silence, and had continued the discharge of his sacred functions. This time the malcontents returned to the charge, and were resolved to have their way.

All the revolutionary, as well as all the timid inhabitants of the parish collected round the presbytery, and, tumultuously forcing their way in, obliged the curé to repair to the church. There, before the altar, they called on him to take the oath. The Abbé Magné, whose disposition, though naturally gentle, showed itself firm and intrepid in the presence of danger, endeavoured to explain his conduct. He reminded his people of the law of God, of the rights of conscience, and his own duty as a priest; and appealed to the religious sentiments of those around him, and their affection, which had been so often

tried. But his words were drowned in a clamour of
threats and blasphemies. Guns and sabres were
pointed at his person. The abbé bared his breast;
"Kill me," he said, "if that be your pleasure, but
know that I will never take a sacrilegious oath."
There was a moment's hesitation, then a voice made
itself heard above the tumult, crying out, "Let him
go! but woe be to him if he come back again!"

The crowd drove before them the pastor of whom
they were not worthy, accompanying him to the end
of the village with their yells and hisses. Then they
returned to the presbytery, in order to satisfy their
rage by sacking and pillaging its humble contents.

Meanwhile the curé journeyed on, abandoned to
the care of God, with his head bowed down, and his
heart drowned in sorrow, when, at a turn in the road,
he suddenly came upon a group of children, who surrounded him, weeping and kissing his hands. They
were those whom, a few months previously, he had
received to their first Communion. Guided by their
hearts they had come by different roads to this spot
in order to bid adieu to their pastor. The tears of
the old man and of the children mingled in a last
embrace. It was a simple and sublime leave-taking,
which, to the desolate heart of the poor priest, was
at once his reward and the viaticum of his exile, and
in the midst of so dark a night gave him a gleam
of hope for the future.

The Abbé Magné wandered for a long time in
the neighbourhood of Langres, living almost on
nothing, and hiding himself among the rocks and
forests. His retreat being at length discovered, he
crossed over into Switzerland, with a soldier's knapsack on his back, and thence found his way into
Italy, and lived for some years at Rome. But
Rome was not his parish; the dome of St. Peter's
could not make him forget the steeple of his own
church; and one evening he re-entered Recey, with his
knapsack on his shoulders and his stick in his hand.

The popular excitement was by this time quieted; nevertheless, there still existed no little danger for the proscribed priest, as well as for those who should offer him an asylum. He went to the house of M. Nicolas Lacordaire, the village doctor of Recey. He well knew his liberal opinions, but he knew him also to be the friend of order, and to possess a generous heart. He was not deceived in his expectations. The door was opened to him, and the priest was kindly welcomed and carefully concealed. An altar was raised in a retired part of the house; and there, for three months, those Christians who still remained faithful were enabled to assist at the Holy Sacrifice, to have their children baptized, and to listen to the Word of God.

Three years after these events, the Abbé Magné baptized John Baptist Henry Lacordaire. It was on the 12th of May, 1802, the same year in which France beheld her churches re-opened, and restored to the service of public worship. If the Abbé Magné could at that moment have rent the veil which conceals the future, and have foreseen what the child was one day to become, he would not have failed to recognise the blessing of God which had rested on this house, in recompense for the protection granted to the persecuted priest—Jesus Christ thus rewarding in the son the father who had given him shelter under his roof—and, whilst returning thanks to the good Providence which had at last restored to the faithful their desecrated temples, he would also have thanked God for sending an apostle who was one day to fill those same temples with wondering and enraptured crowds.

In 1806, M. Lacordaire removed to the village of Bussières, where he died of a chest complaint, leaving his widow with four sons, of whom Henry was the second. Madame Lacordaire, who was a native of Dijon, was the daughter of an advocate in the Parliament of Burgundy; her name was Anna Maria Dugied. Left thus alone, with the care of her children's educa-

tion, and with a moderate fortune, which, if it raised
her above poverty, was yet far from ample, she was
not dismayed. A strong and courageous Christian,
she placed her confidence in God, and desired before
all things to make her children Christians also. She
cultivated within them the germs of that faith which
all were to lose, but to which all were also one day to
return. In spite of her narrow means, she desired to
give them a first-rate education. But it was especially
on their will that this admirable woman succeeded in
stamping the impress of her own soul, conveying to
them that singular quality of masculine strength and
decision which was her own most characteristic feature.

On the death of her husband, Madame Lacordaire
went to reside near her family at Dijon. Henry was
then four years of age. He had hardly, therefore,
known his father. At a later period, his affectionate
heart felt this as a wound from which he secretly
suffered ; and the pain was renewed from time to time,
when the chance spectacle of paternal joys, or a word
from one of his father's friends, would call up a breath
of old childish memories. One old man, who had
formerly been intimate with M. Nicolas Lacordaire,
and had often held Henry in his arms when a child,
came to see him a few years since, at the convent in
the Rue de Vaugirard at Paris. Father Lacordaire
was never weary of hearing him relate those thousand
trifles which complete in our hearts the imperfect
sketch of a portrait which has been interrupted by
the stroke of death. He evinced visible signs of
emotion, and when this friend prepared to take his
leave, " I entreat you," said Father Lacordaire to him,
affectionately taking his hand, " let us talk a little
longer of my father."

A sincerely good man, animated with an inexhaustible fund of charity for the poor, M. Nicolas
Lacordaire had been the simple village doctor of
Recey-sur-Ource. His family had earnestly pressed
him to settle in the capital, where his merit could

hardly have failed to have earned for him a distinguished position ; but his taste preferred a country life. His son Henry inherited this predilection. " No one would believe," he wrote one day, " how happy it makes me to think that I was not born in a town." Somewhat above the middle height, with a lofty forehead, and large sparkling eyes, in which there sometimes appeared a slight expression of melancholy, M. Nicolas Lacordaire was a man of cultivated mind and simple tastes, and possessed the talent of graceful and engaging conversation. Whenever he spoke, a circle of listeners was sure to gather around him ; he had the same gift of charming his audience which his son exercised to so high a degree of fascination. In his features Henry bore a remarkable resemblance to his father ; from him also he inherited his intellectual gifts, as from his mother he received the qualities of his soul—his indomitable strength of will—his almost Spartan austerity — his love of simple, sober, and regular life—and, above all, his early impressions of the faith.

In one of his journeys he made a long round, in order that he might go and kneel at his father's grave. He wished once more to see his paternal home, that house which for three months had been the house of God. All his memories of his childhood then returned upon him. Though fifty years had elapsed since then, nothing had been changed. He felt himself at home again ; everything was the same—even the old hangings remained on the walls. He expressed his astonishment to the person then owning the residence. " Ah, my Father," replied the latter, " this house has a priceless value in my eyes for the sake of the name which it recalls. As long as I live, I shall not allow any of the objects associated with such memories to be disturbed."

No doubt, when he bade farewell to his old home, and gave it a last look, he felt those sentiments arise in his heart which he elsewhere expressed in words :

" O home of our fathers, where, from our earliest years, we drew in together with the light of day the love of everything holy ! It is in vain that we grow old—we return to you with a heart for ever young ; and were it not eternity that calls us, and removes us from you, nothing could console us for the grief of seeing your shadows lengthen, and your sun grow pale !"[1]

His mother loved him more than any of her other children. He wrote at a later period : " Of my mother's four children, her heart clung to me more than to the rest. The gentleness of my temper won me this preference."[2] He was, in fact, a child of charming beauty, in whom sweetness was united to petulance, and quiet tastes to the sallies of a lively and ardent temperament. By a sort of presentiment of his future vocation, he liked in his childish play to imitate a priest. His mother had arranged a little chapel for him, in which nothing was wanting. Henry used to officiate at the altar, and his brothers served his Mass. It was a fine opportunity for preaching, and he did not at that time require much pressing. He preached to everybody who came, but particularly to his nurse, who was his most willing listener.[3] " Sit down, Collette," he would say, " the sermon will be long to-day." And, in fact, he would preach with so much force and vehemence that the nurse was sometimes terrified, and, clasping her hands, she would exclaim, " But, Master Henry, that's enough ; you will do yourself harm ! Don't make yourself so hot !" " No, no," he would reply, " people commit too many sins. It is no matter being tired ; I could preach for ever." And then he would recommence his tirades on the decay of faith and the loss of morals. " Persons remember having seen him, when only eight years old," says

---

[1] XXXIV. Conférence de Nôtre Dame.
[2] Unpublished Letter, Nov. 1849.
[3] Collette Marquet, whose married name was afterwards Crollet, died on the 20th November, 1862. She delighted in relating these anecdotes to a good priest, by whom they were repeated to us.

M. Lorain, in his excellent biographical notice,[1] "reading aloud to the passers-by the sermons of Bourdaloue, and imitating, at a window which served him as a pulpit, the gestures and declamations of the priests whom he had heard preach."

He has himself related in his Memoirs his first childish recollections. These have already been given to the public, in the " Letters to Young Men," published by M. l'Abbé Perreyve ; but they naturally find a place here, and we shall therefore be pardoned for reproducing them. I do not know if anything like them has ever been written of a similar kind. For myself, I have never read anything which went more directly to my heart—I know nothing more touching, more eloquent, or more simply sublime ; and when we remember that he dictated these lines on what was a few days later to be his death-bed—when we call to mind in the midst of what agony his soul preserved this serenity, this freshness and fulness of ideas —we are no doubt filled with admiration for his genius, but far more are we moved to render homage to God, who, after having bestowed on one of His creatures such gifts, consecrated and immortalised by the service they rendered to the truth, left him the full use of them up to his last moment, and commanded death to respect them to the end, even as He has often protected from the corruption of the tomb the bodies of those saints whose virginity has never been tarnished.

"My personal recollections," he writes, " begin to grow clear about the time when I was seven years old. Two events have served to grave that epoch in my memory. My mother at that time sent me to school to begin my classical studies, and she took me to the curé of the parish to make my first confession. I passed through the sanctuary, and found a kind, venerable old man all alone in a fine large sacristy. It was the first time I had ever spoken to a priest ; hitherto I had only seen him at the altar,

[1] Correspondant, tom. xvil. p. 817.

surrounded by religious ceremonial, and in a cloud
of incense. The Abbé Deschamps—for that was his
name—was sitting on a bench, and made me kneel
beside him. I quite forget what I said to him, and
what he said to me; but the remembrance of this
my first interview with the representative of God
left on my soul a pure and most profound impression. Since then I have never entered the sacristy
of St. Michael's at Dijon, or breathed its air, without
the scene of my first confession reappearing before
my eyes, with the forms of that beautiful old man,
and myself in the ingenuous simplicity of childhood.
Indeed, the entire church of St. Michael's is bound up
with holy associations, and I have never seen it without experiencing a certain emotion with which no
other church has since inspired me. My mother,
St. Michael's church, and my first religious ideas,
form in my soul a picture, the earliest, the most
touching, and the most durable of all. At the age of
ten, my mother obtained for me a *demibourse* at
the Lyceum of Dijon. I entered there three months
before the end of the scholastic year. There, for the
first time, I felt the hand of sorrow, which, while it
afflicted me, made me turn to God in a more earnest
and decided manner. From the very first day, my
schoolfellows selected me as a kind of plaything or
victim. I could not take a step without being
pursued by their brutality. For several weeks they
even deprived me by violence of any other food
than my soup and bread. In order to escape their
ill-treatment, I used, as often as possible, to get
away from them during the time of recreation, and,
going into the schoolroom, conceal myself under a
bench from the eyes alike of my masters and companions. There, alone, without protection, abandoned
by every one, I poured out religious tears before God,
offering Him my childish troubles as a sacrifice, and
striving to raise myself, by tender sentiments of piety,
to the cross of His divine Son."

We must interrupt this narrative to dwell for a moment with pious emotion on these *religious tears*, this first revelation of God to a child's heart by suffering, this first vision of his salvation in the cross of Jesus Christ. This little sufferer, hidden under a bench in the college of which he was afterwards to be the honour, and taking refuge at the feet of the Great Victim, gives the key to the entire life of Father Lacordaire. He was not to be raised by God until he had been abased. He was to know glory, but only at the price of hard humiliations and bitter disappointments ; and in the hour of success, as in that of trial, his refuge, his resource, his life, his very passion, was to be the cross, the cross of Him who sought the little schoolboy hidden under his bench. " Brought up," he continues, " by a strong and courageous Christian mother, the sentiment of religion had passed from her bosom into mine like a sweet and virgin milk. Suffering transformed that precious liquor into the manly blood which made me, whilst still a child, a kind of martyr. My persecution came to an end, however, when the holidays began and when school recommenced, either because they were tired of tormenting me, or because it may be I earned their goodwill by sacrificing something of my innocence and simplicity.

" About this time there came to the Lyceum a young man of twenty-four or twenty-five years of age, who had just left the normal school, whence he had been summoned to undertake the direction of an elementary class. He took a great fancy to me, though I was not one of his pupils. He occupied two rooms in a separate part of the house, and I was allowed to go there and work under his care during part of the study hours. There for three years he gratuitously lavished on my education the most assiduous attention. Although I only belonged to the sixth form, he made me often read and learn by heart, from one end to the other, the tragedies of Racine and Voltaire, which

he had the patience to make me recite aloud. As a
lover of letters, he tried to inspire me with similar
tastes; and as a man of honour and integrity, he
endeavoured, at the same time, to make me gentle,
chaste, sincere, and generous, and did his best to
master the effervescence of a somewhat indocile nature.
But as to religion, he was a stranger to it. He never
spoke to me on the subject, and I observed the like
silence in my conversations with him. Had he not
been wanting in that precious gift, he would have been
the preserver of my soul, as he was the good genius of
my intellect ; but God, who had sent him to me as a
second father and a true master, was pleased in His
providence to permit that I should fall into the abyss
of unbelief, in order that I might one day the better
understand the glory of revealed truth. My revered
master, then, M. Delahaye, suffered me to be swept
along in the same current which bore my schoolfellows far away from all religious faith ; but he fixed
in my soul the love of literature and the love of
honour, which had been the guiding principles of his
own life. The events of 1815 deprived me of him
unexpectedly ; and he entered the public service as a
magistrate. I have always associated his memory with
everything good that has since befallen me.

"I made my first Communion in the year 1814,
being then twelve years of age. It was my last religious joy, the last ray which my mother's soul was
to shed on mine. Ere long the shadows thickened
around me, a dismal night surrounded me on every
side, and no longer did I receive from God in my
conscience any sign of life.

"At school I was considered but a middling sort
of scholar. My understanding deteriorated with my
morals; and I proceeded along the path of degradation, which is the chastisement of unbelief, and the
very reverse of reason. But suddenly, in my course of
rhetoric, the seeds of literature sown in my mind by
M. Delahaye began to spring up and blossom, and at

the end of the year prizes without number came to
rouse my pride far more than they rewarded my labour.
My classical studies ended with a very indifferent
course of philosophy, which had neither breadth nor
depth."

The years passed by Henry Lacordaire at the
Lyceum of Dijon left a lasting impression there. His
earnest and studious disposition, his very countenance,
with its thin, regular features, his large eyes, broad
and open brow, and, above all, the prodigious success
of the closing years of his school-life, left a deep impression on the minds of his young companions. He
was cited on all occasions as a diligent worker and
an unexampled prize-man. They used to relate how,
in his time, when the day-scholars collected under the
portico before the opening of the classes, the children
would climb the bars of the enclosure, in order to see
the pupils defile into the court, and would cry out,
pointing to Henry Lacordaire, "See! there he is!"[1]

The Memoirs continue as follows :—

" On entering the school of law at Dijon I returned
to my mother's house and the unspeakable charms of
domestic life. In that house there was nothing super-
fluous, but a severe simplicity, a strict economy, the
fragrance of those antique times so different from our
own, and a certain sacred character which clung to the
virtues of the widowed mother of four sons, who saw
them grouped around her already growing out of boyhood, and who might hope to leave behind her a
generation of good, perhaps even of distinguished,
men. Yet sadness often clouded the heart of that
excellent woman, when she felt that among her sons
there was not one who was a Christian, not one who
could accompany her to the holy mysteries of her
religion.

" Happily, among . the two hundred pupils who

---

[1] Recollections drawn up by the Abbé Joseph Reignier, who entered
the Lyceum of Dijon a year after Henry's departure, and was his
fellow-student at Saint-Sulpice. These notes have been inserted in the
Année Dominicaine for July, 1865, p. 281.

frequented the school of law, about a dozen were to
be found whose understandings penetrated a little
farther than the civil code, who wished to be something more than *avocats de murs mitoyens*, and to
whom patriotism, eloquence, glory, and the virtues
of citizens, furnished more powerful incentives than
the vulgar chances of fortune. They soon became
known to each other by that mysterious sympathy
which, if it unites vice to vice, and mediocrity to
mediocrity, sometimes also brings together souls of
higher aspirations. Almost all these young men owed
their natural superiority to Christianity. Though I
did not share their faith, they were disposed to
acknowledge me as one of themselves ; and before
long, in our social meetings or long walks, we discussed
together the highest questions of philosophy, politics,
and religion.   Naturally enough I neglected the study
of positive law, absorbed in pursuits of a higher intellectual interest, and as a law-student, I was no
more distinguished than I had been as a pupil at
college."[1]
  The above is all that Father Lacordaire has told
us of this interesting period of his life. Happily,
one of the friends of his youth, a fellow-student, and,
like him, a member of the Dijon Society of Studies,
has preserved some records of this time, written
during the lifetime of Lacordaire.   M. Lorain paints
in warm colours the enthusiasm which animated the
young men of that time with regard to all the exciting questions then agitating the world ; and the
ardour with which Henry engaged in these discussions,
wherein politics and literature, philosophy and religion, were handled by turns, and judgments passed
by the young critics, who were more absolute in their
views from the fact that their decisions went no
further than their conference room.   He calls to mind
the distinguished position held by Henry Lacordaire
among this select society, and takes pleasure in relating

[1] Mémoires.

his triumphs, both of written and oral eloquence. He analyses with precision the most striking features of his genius, and it is easy to distinguish in the speeches of the student of Dijon the future orator of Nôtre Dame. Whilst describing the unbelief and the exaggeration which appeared in his political doctrines, he points out their precise nature, and measures their tendency with just moderation. Let us quote a few passages which throw great light on the character of the man, and on his religious opinions at the period of his first entrance into life.

" In all these discussions," says M. Lorain, " Henry Lacordaire took a leading part. In spite of his extreme youth, he gained at once the first place among all his equals.

" We still seem to hear those brilliant bursts of eloquence, those arguments so full of skill, of rapidity, of ready and delicate wit ; we seem to see that eye so fixed and sparkling, so penetrating and so motionless, that looked as though it would pierce into the most secret depths of our thoughts : and we seem once more to listen to that voice, clear, vibrating, full of emotion, intoxicated with its own richness, attentive to its own echoes alone, abandoning itself without reserve or constraint to the quenchless fulness of its poetic inspiration. O beautiful years ! too quickly flown ! O precious and magnificent outpourings of genius, full well did you predict the incomparable orator who was one day to be gained to the cause of God !

" The literary compositions which the young law-student read to the Dijon Society of Studies in 1821 and 1822 prove still better the progress and the tendency of his mind. In one of them he relates with much richness of imagery the story of the siege and ruin of Jerusalem by the Emperor Titus. In another he speaks of patriotism, and gathers out of Biblical, Greek, and Roman antiquity, as well as from modern history, the most touching recollections, the most

3

pathetic sorrows, which have ever been inspired by exile or regrets for lost national independence. Finally, in a third he treats of liberty after the manner of Plato's Dialogues, and the speaker whom he introduces is no other than Plato himself, conversing with his disciples on the promontory of Sunium, and exclaiming—' Liberty is justice !'

"In these first essays of a yet untried intellect, in the very choice of subjects at once so grave and so noble, might be recognised the best characteristics of the orator of Nôtre Dame.

"Were we still in the age of antithesis, I should say that the character and the genius of Henry Lacordaire abounded in singular contrasts. That mind which so often surprised one by its sudden and brilliant success, was capable also of continued, obstinate, and daily work : his nature was as patient as it was energetic—it united at one and the same time vivacity and gentleness. With his lively and impatient imagination he was still capable of maturing a profound design ; to promptness of views he joined cool reflection and deliberate calculation. By the side of his glorious youth you saw the anticipated gravity of age ; and a rattling gaiety, which even verged at times on childish buffoonery, was mingled with the meditations of the deep thinker. Together with a temperament full of ardour and passion, he had a natural liking for order and method, for the nice arrangement of small matters, for a simple elegance and a studied neatness and exactitude. Whether in verse or prose, he could stop at will in the midst of a phrase or a measure. When a friend looked into his study, symmetry of arrangement met his eye on every side. There was no disorder in the books ; the paper, the pens, the desk, the very penknife, were all disposed with a sort of correct art on the little black table, forming no disagreeable angle. The same neatness and regularity were observable in his manuscripts, in his writing, in everything he did or touched ; in a word, there was in all things a kind of material symbolism of that prudence of the serpent joined to the simplicity of the dove, which, in one of his finest Conferences, he declares himself to possess, adding with a charming grace, that, like St. Francis of Sales, he would willingly give twenty serpents for one dove."[1]

Father Lacordaire has related how it was that he came to lose his faith, and on this point the testimony of his friends agrees with his own. He had so often publicly confessed his errors, and proclaimed aloud in the pulpit how impossible it is to preserve purity for any length of time without the supernatural help of grace, that it is unnecessary for us to dwell here on the share which independence of mind, and the effervescence of the passions, always have in the apostasy of a lad of fifteen. But if he bade adieu to his mother's faith, it was only because there was no one at the Lyceum to keep it alive. "Nothing," he said, "supported our faith." He did not renounce his faith, it rather died within him. He drank, like so many others of his generation, at the poisoned sources of the preceding age, but he was not intoxicated by them. His incredulous mind took pleasure in objections, but hatred was foreign to his soul. His natural sympathies so fully harmonised with the gospel, his sincere love of truth and candour of soul were such, that Catholicism even then must needs have appeared to him as the solitary Pharos of life in the midst of that chill night which surrounded him on every side.

"I love the gospel," he said at this time, "for its morality is incomparable ; I respect its ministers, because they exercise a salutary influence on society ; but I have not received as my share the gift of faith."[2]

"I left college at the age of seventeen," he writes in his Memoirs, "with my faith destroyed, and my

---

[1] Lorain ; Correspondant, tom. xvii. p. 823.
[2] Ibid. p. 822,

morals injured, but upright, open, impetuous, sensible
to honour, with a taste for letters and for the beautiful, having before my eyes, as the guiding star of my
life, the human ideal of glory. This result is easily
explained. Nothing had supported our faith in a
system of education in which the Word of God held
but a secondary place, and was enforced neither with
argument nor eloquence, whilst at the same time we
were daily engaged in studying the masterpieces and
heroic examples of antiquity.

" The old pagan world, presented to us in these
sublime aspects, kindled within us a love of its virtues,
while the modern world created by the gospel remained entirely unknown to us. Its great men, its
saints, its civilisation, its moral and civil superiority,
the progress made by humanity under the influence of
the Cross, totally escaped our notice. Even the history
of our own country, scantily studied, left us wholly
unmoved ; and we were Frenchmen by birth without
being so at heart. I am far, however, from joining in
the condemnation which some in our own time have
passed on the study of the classics. We owed to
them the sense of the beautiful, many precious natural
virtues, great examples, and an intimacy with noble
characters and memorable times ; but we had not
climbed high enough to reach the summit of the
edifice, which is Jesus Christ ;—the friezes of the
Parthenon concealed from us the dome of St. Peter's."[1]

"There are both exaggeration and falsehood," says
M. Lorain, "in the view which represents Henry
Lacordaire as a sort of impious tribune and atheistic
democrat. That the Deism of the student was tinged
with something of Voltairian raillery, or rather with
the philosophy of Rousseau, which better suited the
conscientious gravity of his mind, cannot be denied ;
for we must make the sad avowal, it was through this
phase that all France at that time passed. But
farther than this he never went. The beardless philo-

[1] *Mémoires, p. 386.*

sopher already said, in his own beautiful style:
'Every one is free to engage in a combat against
order, but order can never be overcome. It may
be compared to a pyramid which rises from earth to
heaven : we cannot overthrow the base, for the finger
of God rests on the summit.'

" At another time he wrote : ' Impiety leads to de-
pravity, corrupt morals give birth to corrupt laws, and
licentiousness plunges a people into slavery before
they can raise an alarm. Let us be on our guard ;
there is no question here of the life of a day, of an
apparent tranquillity, of an accidental vigour which
sports with its triumphs, and is soon expended. Sometimes nations die out in an insensible agony, which
they love as if it were some sweet and agreeable repose ; sometimes they perish in the midst of feasts,
singing hymns of victory, and calling themselves immortal !'

" He who wrote thus was not yet twenty. By what
an immense interval was he already separated from
vulgar sceptics and foolish revolutionists !"[1]

In fact, we already see, in this young thinker and
writer, all the lineaments of that grand character
which was soon to develop its magnificent proportions
before God and man. He has lost his faith, it is true;
but he is perplexed to know what shall replace it as
the guide of his life ; he measures at a glance the consequences of religious indifference for individuals as
for nations, with an astonishing maturity of judgment, and he is already honestly seeking the truth.
He might easily be drawn into the errors of a lively
imagination, of an ardent temperament which spurns
restraint ; had he not felt himself held back by the
earnest side of that same nature, by his love of work,
and by a certain natural humility and distrust of self,
which make him avoid the vortex where so many un-
ripe minds are lost—the facility of their genius. He
chooses his ordinary and exclusive society amongst

1 Lorain.

studious young men ; and though he is not insensible
to their warm applause, he nevertheless prefers the
charm of those generous friendships, many of which
will survive through all the vicissitudes of his life,
and be to him a living memory of those happy years
at Dijon, on which he so loved to dwell. Who will not
be touched at the affectionate homage which he
rendered on his death-bed to the memory of his old
master ? Who will not there recognise the faithful
evidence of a heart which forgot nothing but injuries,
and was never able to understand that deformity of the
soul which is called *ingratitude ?*

Paris was soon to develop all these germs of promise;
Paris was to restore to him what it causes so many
others to lose—his religious faith.   It was to give him
the vocation from on high, and was to point out to
him his future path.   For this great battle-field is the
arena of the strong ; and the fire which dissolves and
decomposes all metal of baser alloy does but test
and purify gold.

CHAPTER II.

*He goes to Paris—His first appearance at the bar—His character—
His return to religious belief.*

ATHER LACORDAIRE continues thus the
narrative of his early years, and his arrival
at Paris: " My law studies ended, my
mother, in spite of her narrow means, determined to send me to Paris, that I might go into
residence there, with the view of entering at the bar.
She was urged to this by her maternal hopes in
my regard; but God had other designs, and she
was in reality, without knowing it, sending me to the
gates of eternity. Paris did not dazzle me. Accustomed to an exact and laborious life, I lived there
as I had lived at Dijon, with one sorrowful exception,
that I was no longer surrounded with friends and
fellow-students, but found myself in a vast and profound solitude where no one cared for me, and
where my soul fell back on itself without finding
there either God or faith, but only the pride of
anticipated glory. Introduced by M. Riambourg,
one of the presidents of the royal court of Dijon, to
M. Guillemin, an advocate of the council, I worked
in his office with patient diligence, occasionally attending the bar, and attached to a society of young men,

called the *Society of Good Studies*, which was at once
Catholic and royalist and where, therefore, I found
myself on both accounts a stranger. Having become an unbeliever, at college, I had become likewise
a liberal in the school of law, though my mother
was devoted to the Bourbons, and had given me in
· baptism the name of Henry, in memory of Henry
IV., the dearest idol of her political faith. But all
the rest of my family were liberals, I was so myself
by natural instinct, and scarcely had I caught the
echoes of public affairs than I belonged to the age
by my love of liberty, as entirely as I had already
been identified with it by my ignorance of God and
of the gospel. It was M. Guillemin who had introduced me to the *Society of Good Studies*, in the
hope that there I should change my views, which
differed from his own. But he was disappointed.
No light came to me from that quarter, and no friendship either. I lived poor and solitary, labouring in
secret at twenty years of age, without exterior enjoyments, or agreeable ties in society, without attraction for the world, or enthusiasm for the theatre; in
fact, without any passion of which I was conscious,
unless it were a vague tormenting desire of renown.
Some slight success in the Court of Assize moved me
a little, but without taking any great hold on me."[1]

Here, then, the inner life of Father Lacordaire
begins to reveal itself. This period contains no exterior fact worthy of notice. The whole progress is
interior, the whole interest is concentrated on this
dialogue of the soul with itself, in which it is faithfully portrayed. We find here none of the brilliant
strokes, whether in speaking or writing, which distinguished the young law-student; as yet we see
neither the priest, the orator, nor the religious; we
see only the man. The drama is limited to the
struggles of this soul thrown back on itself, and

[1] *Mémoires*, p. 383.

anxiously inquiring what it is, and towards what unknown shore it is led by destiny.

If, then, we wish to know the man in Father Lacordaire, it is here, in his little advocate's chamber at Paris, that we must study him. Never, perhaps, has he let fall expressions truer or more eloquent, or which throw a clearer light on the depths of his singular nature. He speaks neither from the tribune nor the pulpit; it is not a book that we are reading, nor even a correspondence; he writes to his friends at that age which is generally so unreserved; but his friends do not understand him, and do not know what to reply. It is a soul wrestling with itself and with God; a soul which has gone unarmed into the combat, and which, without knowing it, struggles on the confines of eternity. It is the hour of Divine vocation; that grave and solemn hour when a man, "left in the hand of his own counsel" (Eccl. xv. 14), hears himself called from on high, and required to choose his future path,—an hour yet more grave and solemn for the soul whom God predestines to great things. He hears himself called, but whence comes the voice? Is it from heaven? Alas! he no longer believes in the God of his mother, the only One to whom man dares to speak, and Who deigns to reply. Voices of earth likewise call him, and seek to hold him back. One of his dreams is friendship. He seeks for friends, and when he finds them, believes them perfect. He writes letters to them, in which his tender and ingenuous nature opens with transport to the most delightful prospects, and gives itself for eternity without hesitation or calculation. The next day the light breaks in, and the charm vanishes. He shares neither the religious faith nor the political views of those whom he seeks to love; he perceives, when he is disenchanted, that true friendship is impossible without unity of belief, and he sinks back with regret into his former sad isolation. Glory likewise calls him, but, hidden under the form of this phantom robed in purple, his calm reason displays to him only emptiness and death. Solitude attracts him; but without God or friends, it is a barren desert. He is fond of reading, but finds no enjoyment in his books : everything wearies and disgusts him, and he understands that there are some wants which earth is powerless to satisfy. The world, in fact, is too little for him. He requires the Infinite, he aspires after It, but heaven is closed against him ; and on this side also there is neither sign, nor answer, nor certainty, nor repose.

Worn out by his wanderings in this bitter void, his soul is cast down and exhausted. He avows his own incapacity ; he seeks for light in good faith, and prays God to take pity on him. Then it was that he found God waiting for him. The clouds then began to break, truth unveiled herself before him, and as she did so drew to herself this wandering and suffering soul. It was the second revelation of God to His beloved child by the way of suffering, and it was not the last. There was no middle stage for him between belief and devotion. On the day of his conversion, he was already in heart a priest.

Such is an abstract of the history of those two years which decided the career of Henry Lacordaire. The numerous extracts from letters of this epoch, collected by M. Lorain, throw light on the interior progress of this soul, so uncertain of its future course, agitated with anxiety *under the Etna of life.*

He lived at this time in the Rue Mont-Thabor, in a small attic chamber. Accustomed from childhood to a life directed by reason, and regulated by duty, he knew how, in the midst of the fire that devoured him, to compel himself to diligent and monotonous labour of a nature contrary to all his tastes. But he suffered from it. "This fire of enthusiasm and imagination which consumes me," he writes, "was certainly never given that it might be quenched under the ice of the law, or stifled in positive and arduous meditations.

But I am detained in my present position by that
force of reason which convinces me that to try everything, and to be always changing one's place, is not
the way to change one's nature."[1] Here, no doubt,
we see one feature of his character. His was pre-
eminently a practical mind ; he was, more than anything else, a man of duty. No one, as he acknowledges, might have been capable of more follies, on one
side of his nature ; but imagination, passion, restless-
ness, in a word, all the inferior powers, were held
tamed and docile under his powerful hand, like so
many foaming coursers.

"There are in me," he says, "two contrary principles always at war, which sometimes make me
very unhappy : a cold reason opposed to an ardent
imagination ; and the one disenchants me from all
the illusions which the other presents." This victory
of reason over imagination, however, was often dearly
purchased.

We must remember what the times then were, in
order to understand how much of their teaching
Henry Lacordaire accepted, and how much he rejected. France had not then, as now, reached a
precocious maturity by paths sown with disappointed
hopes and sad experiences, nor had she withdrawn
from public affairs out of very weariness. All was
then young : the world, liberty, and poetry, were all
full of vigour and enthusiasm. The ruins heaped up
by the preceding generation—the broken fragments
of arms and banners which the early years of the
present century had scattered over our soil—lay on
the heart of France like an immense and stifling
weight of bloody memories and humbled glories.
At the first dawn of liberty and public life, the powers
so long forcibly repressed woke once more to vigour,
and opened in a sunshine which was destined, it is true,
to see more flowers than fruits, yet for all that the
flowers were beautiful and radiant with life. A soul

[1] Lorain—Correspondant, tom. xvii. p. 825.

like that of Henry Lacordaire could not remain indifferent when, arriving at Paris in this season of
universal spring, he heard the most harmonious voices
singing, in numbers too quickly forgotten, the awakening of a great people. He beheld the grand spectacle
of social reconstruction in which enthusiasm, and
hatred, aspirations, and regrets, together with dreams
which, if wild, were yet often generous, were mingled
pell-mell together. To those who had more taste
for the invisible revolutions of the soul, there came
from the savannas of America enchanting perfumes,
breathing of a dreamy life of freedom, which intoxicated
many young minds. Henry drank of this cup, like
so many others; but he knew how to stop where ex-
travagance begins; and whilst his imagination was
wandering among the enchanting solitudes of the new
world, his patient pen was copying memoranda and
drawing up consultations. " Who among us," he exclaimed, thirty years later, " has not fancied in the
days of his youth that he was wandering free in the
solitudes of the new world, with no other roof than
the heavens, and no drink save the water of unknown
rivers—no other food than the fruits of the earth and
the game he has killed in hunting—no law but his
own will—no pleasure save the sense of independence,
and the chances of a life without constraint on a soil
without a possessor ? Such dreams were ours also.
Our heart bounded, recognising its own portrait, when,
in a celebrated book, we came upon that passage in
which the man of civilisation says to the man of the
wilderness : 'Chactas, return to your forests : resume
that holy independence of nature of which Lopes will
not deprive you—for myself, were I young, I would
follow you.' It seemed to us, as we read these words,
that we were listening to ourselves : our oppressed
soul escaped to these ideal regions, and came back
with regret to the monotonous burden of reality."[1]

His imagination cradled him in these dreams of

[1] Conférence, li. p. 600.

excessive independence, which agreed so well with
his nature, his college education, and the atmosphere
he inhaled in Paris. "The child of an age which
scarce knows how to obey," he says, "the love of independence had all my life been my nurse and guide."[1]
Moreover, in that agitated atmosphere he felt ill at
ease, and was tormented by vague desires, in which
already God lay concealed in the fictitious tears of
Réné. "Where is the soul that can comprehend me,
and will not be surprised, when I say that the very
name of Grande-Grèce makes me weep and shudder?
. . . . But the minds of other men are not made to
understand mine : I sow my seed on a slab of polished
marble."[2] What he especially sought and desired to
find was some friendship which should people for him
the vast desert of Paris. He hoped to meet with such
in the society of young men to which M. Guillemin
had introduced him ; and about a year after he came
to Paris, he wrote to one of his young comrades at the
bar the following unpublished letter, in which his
soul, his heart, his judgment, and his mind all discover
themselves in an interesting manner :

"PARIS, *November* 10, 1823.

"MY DEAR FRIEND,—When I saw you this morning,
I felt more than ever how far off from you I was, and I
felt with pain that our meetings would be merely
passing ones, and would never assume that intimate
character which long habit, and the reciprocal interchange of mind and heart, establish between two
persons. Nevertheless, I acknowledge to you that one
of my favourite ideas, and one of those which most
delighted me in looking forward to my residence at
Paris, was the hope of uniting myself to you by very
strong ties. I consoled myself for the loss of friends
who could only love me at a distance by the thought
that I had found one who would take their place, and
supply for the want of their daily intercourse, and that

[1] Mémoires.   [2] Lorain—Correspondant, tom. xvii. p. 826.

sweet goodwill which all men require to give and to receive. I took pleasure in saying to myself that, like them, you had religious principles which I love, without being as yet able to adopt them ; that, like them, you had sound political opinions, without joining to them that asperity and narrowness of views by which the truth is too often dishonoured ; and that, like them, you were pure in your life and in your tastes. I loved in you the living memory of my friends, and I drew a happy presentiment for my future life, from the fact that I am always meeting with people better than myself. The mere thought of your friendship, therefore, peopled for me the vast desert of Paris, and I waited there for you in order to complete my existence. But we are so far apart, that if I were to leave it to chance, our souls might journey on side by side without ever touching ; and really there are so many amiable men who live unknown in this world, that it seems wrong to let those escape from you who do fall into your hands. Then, again, the time of life will soon be passed at which we can hope to form such friendships : in riper age it is interest rather than affection which binds men together, for there is a certain effusion of heart which expires with our youth. As we are still both of us young, and as you understand me and know me well enough to appreciate all that there is in me, whether good or bad, I offer you what will be a lasting friendship, entreating you to grant me yours in return. See, now, I will try and paint myself to you a little, in order to give you a first mark of confidence ; it shall be the earnest of my affection.

" There are in me, then, two contrary principles, which are always at war, and which sometimes make me very unhappy — a cold, calm reason, opposed to a burning imagination—and the first disenchants me of all the illusions which the second presents. Nobody would commit more follies than I should do on one side of my being, were I not withheld by a habit of reflection which presents things to me in all their aspects. I have played the game of the material interests of this world, and, without having much enjoyed its pleasures or been intoxicated with its delights, I have tasted enough to be convinced that all is vain under the sun ; and this conviction comes both from my imagination, which has no limits save the Infinite, and from my reason, which analyses all it touches. I have a most religious heart, and a very incredulous mind ; but, as it is in the nature of things that the mind must at last allow itself to be subjugated by the affections, it is most likely that I shall one day become a Christian. I am alike capable of living in solitude, and of plunging into the vortex of human affairs : I love quiet when I think of it, and bustle when I am in it, sometimes making my castle in the air to consist in the life of a village curé, and then saying good-bye to my day-dream as I pass the Pont-Neuf—held in my present position by that force of reason, which convinces me that to try everything and to be always changing one's place is not to change one's nature, and that there are wants in the heart which earth is powerless to satisfy. I possess great activity and quick powers of conception, of which I often make a bad use. I have loved some men, but I have never yet loved women, and I do not think I ever shall love them in the ordinary way. I think you might write my epitaph thus : ' He had his faults, but he was worth as much as anybody else.'

"There, dear N——, is a sketch of my character. See if it suits you, and believe that I shall love you as long as I live, with a frankness and a warmth which may procure you some moments more of happiness during your life. That is always something. Let us dine together this evening if you are not engaged ; I shall expect you at five o'clock."

After reading this letter, one asks how he could have said, when speaking of the society of young men among whom he was thrown, "No friendship came to me from that quarter. . . . . I lived alone, unsupported by any friendship."[1] Those to whom he wrote such charming letters, and who are still living, will certainly not accuse his heart; they knew him too well. They knew that what he was seeking was not so much friends as a friend. But it may be that those who thought they knew him will see in this complaint that escaped him a new proof of that apparent insensibility which seemed to take possession of him.

In fact, many of those who saw him nearest, deceived by a reserved, almost an icy exterior, have said to themselves that he was a man who lived in his intellect alone. It would be difficult to preserve such an impression about him now, after the many, though still incomplete, revelations which have been made by his best friends of this hidden fold of his soul. But then, whence arose that coldness, that silence, which no one carried to such an audacious excess as himself?"[2] Was it pride? No, nothing was more contrary to his nature. Was it dulness or obstinacy? Neither one nor the other. Father Lacordaire had a most tender soul, and a heart of exquisite feeling. To sum up his character in a single phrase, we might borrow his own words, and say that he was "strong as the diamond—more tender than a mother;" and we know none that would be nearer the truth. And were we called on to say whether of the two, strength or tenderness, predominated in him, we should have to think long before giving a reply. These words will, I know, find many unbelievers; let me, therefore, explain myself.

There are some souls whose sensibility easily appears outside—betraying itself in the physiognomy, pouring itself out in tears, communicating itself in word and deed; like rivers which roll along with their waters full to the brink, ever ready to overflow and

---

[1] Lorain.   [2] Le Père Lacordaire, by Montalembert, p. 178.

fertilise their banks. And there are also other rarer souls, whose sensibility, lying hidden in the very depths of their being, fears the look which seems to guess its existence, is ashamed of tears, and shrinks at the slightest touch. Such souls are devoured by the interior fire, but careful to let nothing of it appear; they are as timid in public, as they are expansive in private intercourse, and are so much the more generous in the gift of themselves as they bestow it on a very small number—like streams shut in by high banks, sometimes forcing their way underground, useless apparently to the lands through which they flow, until one day we discover that some lake far away, which reflects the sunlight in its pure and tranquil depths, is fed from the hidden source of such a river.

Father Lacordaire was one of these souls. Few men knew how much and in what way he loved. Of the many friends who surrounded his life, very few entered in and gauged its depths. He had so high an idea of friendship, that in the human order of things all the rest went for nothing. He valued one moment of free outpouring of heart far above an hour of triumphant oratory. He whom he called his *brother* —the first and most illustrious friend whom Paris, a little later, was to give him—thus bears witness to this side of his character:

"It was he," he writes, "more charmed with the joys of Christian friendship than with the far-off echoes of renown, who made me understand that we are never more than half moved by great struggles; that they leave us the power of giving ourselves up, above all things, to the life of the heart; and that our days begin and end according as an affection dawns or dies out in a soul. It was thus he spoke to me; and he added, 'Alas! we were created to love only the Infinite, and this is why, when we love, that which we love appears so perfect to our heart."[1]

He would have sacrificed everything to the happiness

[1] Le Père Lacordaire, p. 14.

of being loved, yet he scarcely allowed any one to
guess it. "It is a strange thing," he writes, "people
believe me to be without feeling. At the very moment
when I feel most, I am thought cold. They do not
sufficiently distinguish the real man from the apparent
—what I am from what I choose to appear. Like
Sterne, I cannot weep before spectators. I am
ashamed of tears."[1]

He depicts himself again in a beautiful passage in
his book on St. Mary Magdalen. "Friendship," he
says, "is born in the soul, and of the soul. When
once we meet each other there, everything else disappears—just as some day, only in a far higher way,
when we meet in God, the whole universe will be for
us as a thing forgotten. But it is not easy thus to
meet in a sanctuary so impenetrable as the soul—so
hidden behind the ocean which surrounds it, and the
clouds that cover it. Holy Scripture says of God
that He dwells in light inaccessible : we may say of
the soul that it abides in an impenetrable darkness.
We think we touch it, and our hand has scarcely
seized the fringe of its garment. It withdraws and
retires at the very moment when we think ourselves
sure of possessing it—sometimes like a serpent, sometimes like a timid dove, fire or ice, a torrent or a
tranquil lake—yet, whatever may be its form or its
image, it is always the rock on which we are most
often wrecked, the port into which we most seldom
enter. Friendship, then, is a rare and divine thing,
the certain sign of a great soul, and the highest visible
reward attached to virtue."[2]

Even with those who possessed the key of the
sanctuary, and to whom he gave out of his treasury
his words old, yet ever new, he was still timid. "I
always want solitude," he writes, "to say how much
I love."[3] He reproached himself for expressions in
which his affectionate heart betrayed itself. He would

[1] Lorain—Correspondant, tom. x.::. p. 826.
[2] Le Père Lacordaire—Montalembert, p. 30.   [3] Ibid. p. 32.

have liked to have adopted a child whose heart he could have formed, and whose education he could have entirely directed. "I would have made him the son of my heart," he writes. "I would have bestowed on him the gift of myself . . . . but I feared ingratitude . . . . I should have loved him so much that had he proved ungrateful to my love for him in God, he would have inflicted too deep a wound on the weakness of my human nature."[1] Here, then, we see the gleam of lightning on the dark abyss! His heart may shut itself up now, it may conceal itself, if it will, behind the ocean and the clouds, but it has betrayed itself. Had he uttered no other words than these, those who knew him could never more have been deceived.

The course of this biography will shed some new light on this delicate point, veiled as it is by so many shadows. But it was necessary, at the outset, to point it out, and to disengage it from obscurity, in order to explain his life, to see both sides of it, "the real and the fictitious," the apparent and the hidden, to detect the man underneath the orator and the priest, to understand his silence, his desires, his regrets, his sorrowful confidences, and above all, in order to comprehend that one affection, the strongest, the tenderest, the most secret of all—his love for Jesus Christ.

On this soul, so tender, and yet so serious, so tranquil, yet so suffering, in which the germ of the future was being slowly elaborated, exterior life left its furrow, which was regular indeed, but of little depth. He pleaded causes, he drew up memoranda, he loved solitude far more than the bar, and was following his career rather than forming it. "I amused myself this morning by pleading a cause," he writes : "the cause was a detestable one : but I wanted to make sure that I could speak before a tribunal without fear,

---

[1] *Revue de Toulouse,* January 1862. From the notes of a conversation furnished by M. F. Lacointa.

and that my voice would be strong enough. I have satisfied myself by this experiment that the Roman senate could not daunt me. I don't know how I was able to utter a word." He pleaded, in fact, without being as yet authorised to do so by age, but that did not disconcert him. "Were I cited for this before the Court of Discipline," he says, "it would be a fine opportunity for making a speech, and that would be all. A young advocate who, after having pleaded with some success, should be condemned by the Court, would be honoured by his condemnation."[1]

These first efforts made him remarked; his friends encouraged him, and M. Berryer assured him that he might rise to the first rank at the bar if he would avoid the snare of his too ready eloquence. It was after one of these pleadings that the First President, M. Séguier, passed on him a eulogium which sounded like a prophecy. "Gentlemen," he said, "this is not Patru: it is Bossuet." But these successes, which might have satisfied the ambition of many men, with him only glided over the surface, and but ill protected him against the progressive assaults of a melancholy of which most of his letters at this time bear the trace. "My mind," he writes, "is older than they think: I feel its wrinkles under the flowers with which my imagination covers it. I care little for life, my imagination has laid waste its charms. I am satiated with everything without having known anything. If you could but know how sad I am growing—I love sadness, and often make it my companion. They talk to me of the glory of authorship, and of public life, and I have some such fancies. But to speak frankly, I feel a contempt for glory, and I have ceased to understand how we can take so much trouble in running after the little fool. To live quietly at one's fireside, without show and without ostentation, seems sweeter to me than to fling one's peace of mind to the mercy of fame, merely that in return she may cover you

[1] Lorain—Correspondant, p. 825.

with gold spangles. . . . I shall never rest satisfied till I have three chestnut trees, a potato-garden, a cottage, and a cornfield at the bottom of some Swiss valley."[1] It was in this way that his imagination wandered away to America, to Greece, to Switzerland. But through it all the goodness of God, by means of that reason " that analysed everything it touched," made him sound the depths of these brilliant chimeras, and drew him on little by little to the only reality, which is the Infinite, to the only Truth, which is Faith. At a later period, he himself analysed this love of melancholy, and recalled it with a sort of pleasure. "Hardly have eighteen summers shed their light upon our lives," he writes, " when we begin to suffer from desires which have for their object neither love, nor the senses, nor glory, nor anything with a form or a name. Whether wandering in secret solitudes, or in the gay thoroughfares of a splendid capital, the young man feels himself oppressed by aspirations which have no aim ; he escapes from the realities of life as from a prison, where his heart is stifled, and he asks from all that is vague and visionary, from the evening clouds, from the autumn winds, from the falling leaves of the forest, for some feeling which, whilst it wounds, may also satisfy his heart. But it is in vain; the clouds pass, the winds are hushed, the leaves fade and wither without telling him why he suffers, and without satisfying his soul any more than his mother's tears and his sister's tenderness have done. O soul, exclaimed the prophet, why art thou sad, and why art thou disquieted ? Hope thou in God. It is God, in fact, it is the Infinite, which thus stirs in our youthful hearts, those hearts that, touched by Christ, are yet carelessly wandering away from Him, and in which the Divine unction, no longer producing its supernatural effect, raises nevertheless an emotion which God alone can appease."[2]

His "religious soul" was every day gaining the

---

[1] Lorain—Correspondant, tom. xvii. p. 826.   [2] Conférence, lx.

victory over his "unbelieving mind;" and at the beginning of 1824 he wrote as follows to a friend : "Would you believe it, I am every day growing more and more a Christian ? It is strange, this progressive change in my opinions: I am beginning to believe, and yet I was never more a philosoph*er*. A little philosophy draws us from religion, but a good deal of it brings us back again—a profound truth!"[1] This was not full daylight, but it was at least the dawn. Three months before his final adieu to the world, he wrote again :—" They all predict for me a beautiful future, and yet I am very often tired of life. I can no longer enjoy anything—society has no charms for me public entertainments only weary me, I feel no attraction whatever for the material order of things. I have now no enjoyments save those of self-love, and for these I am beginning to feel disgust. Each day I feel more and more that all is vanity. I cannot leave my heart in this heap of mud." Then he adds, " *Yes ! I believe !* . . . how is it that my friends do not understand me ? How is it that they still doubt and ridicule my religious conversion ? Can I be the only man who is in earnest ? for nobody understands me.'[2]

His friends, in fact, were very far from having any suspicion of the progress which his mind had made in a few months. Not that there was any manifest want of harmony between his life and his new belief. His morals had become irreproachable, and of such an integrity as to astonish even his Christian friends. Gay by disposition, full of wit, and easily carried away in conversation, he nevertheless disliked licentious words, and when any such were uttered in his presence, he showed his displeasure by silence. One of those who knew him best at this period, has assured us that he regarded the conversion of his friend, and his entrance at Saint-Sulpice, as the reward of his purity of life. And he adds, that he had so little doubt

[1] Lorain—Correspondant, tom. xvii. p. 827.
[2] Ibid.

of the uprightness of his mind, and the candour of his soul, that later on, when he saw him engaged in the dangerous affair of the *Avenir*, he did not hesitate to predict that his faith and his honour would come out safe and sound, and that God could never abandon him.

But if his friends had remarked the cloud of sadness on his brow, they had either not understood or not believed in its cause. They saw him more rarely ; and then he appeared grave, preoccupied, and anxious. Sometimes a friendly eye surprised him on his knees in a church, hidden behind a pillar, motionless, and absorbed in profound meditation.[1]   One day one of his companions—the same to whom he had offered his friendship in the letter which will not have been forgotten by our readers—came to see him in his little room in the Rue Mont-Thabor   He was alone, sitting at his desk, leaning with his head between his hands ; on his table was neither book nor paper. " Henry," said his friend, " you are sad : you know my affection for you, I do not come to inquire your secret ; I desire to know only so much as you choose to tell me." " Thank you," replied Henry Lacordaire ; " but suffer me to tell you nothing just now.   The project I am meditating is not yet perfectly determined on in my mind.   If it comes to anything, I promise that you

[1] The circumstance here alluded to is related in a letter, quoted by the Abbé Reignier in his notice of Père Lacordaire, which is to be found in the July and August numbers of the *Annèe Dominicaine*, 1865. " Henry Lacordaire," says the writer to his friend, " is to me the *angel of the schools*, or, at least, the guardian angel of those principles with which you have endowed me ; the guide of my judicial studies, the master of my social life.   His lessons, however, are confined to example. Does he practise his religion? you will say.   Not yet ; but the other day I reproached myself for my own neglect of God, and as I passed by St. Germain des Prés, I entered, and who should I see kneeling behind a pillar, with his head half hidden in his hands, wrapt in meditation, and still as a statue, but Henry, my *bijou* of a Henry !   What could he have been doing there? . . . . Either I am much deceived or he will not content himself with this, and when he betrays the secret which is fermenting in his brain, it will not be told to me only, but to all the world."—*Translator's Note.*

shall be one of the first to know it." A few days later, the young advocate received a visit from Henry. "Well!" he said to him, "my mind is made up. I am going to enter the seminary." At these strange words, the first thought of his friend was to ask himself whether the ardent imagination of the speaker had not disordered his reason. And then Henry began to unfold to him the secret ways in which Truth had regained possession of his mind, and of his heart.

CHAPTER III.

E was converted. And now he felt the necessity of pouring out his emotions of joy and gratitude towards God to those among his friends who were able to understand him. On the eve of his entrance into the seminary, the 11th of May, 1824, he wrote : " It needs few words to say what I have to say, and yet my heart would fain say many. I am giving up the bar ; we shall meet each other there no more. Our dreams for the last five years will not be accomplished. To-morrow morning I am about to enter the seminary of Saint-Sulpice. . . . . Only yesterday, as it were, my soul was still full of the chimeras of the world ; although religion was even then present there, fame and glory were still the future towards which I looked. But to-day I place my hopes higher, and ask for nothing here below but obscurity and peace. I am greatly changed, and I give you my word that I do not know how the change has come about. When I examine the progress of my thoughts during the last five years —the point whence I set out, the gradual stages I have gone through, and the final result of this course

of reflection, which was slow and bristling with obstacles—I am myself astonished, and experience an emotion of profound adoration of God's goodness. My dear friend, all this can only be thoroughly understood by one who has passed from error to truth—who has a full consciousness of all his foregoing ideas—who can seize their different relations, their unaccountable connexion, and all the successive links of this wonderful chain, and who compares them all at the different periods of his convictions. It is indeed a sublime moment when the last ray of light penetrates our souls, and attaches to a common centre truths which till then lay scattered and apart. There is always such an immense interval between the moment which precedes and that which follows *that* moment, between what one was before and what one is after, that the word *grace* has been invented to express that stroke of magic, that lightning flash from on high. I seem to see a man who is making his way along, as it were, by chance, and with a bandage over his eyes ; it is a little loosened—he catches a glimpse of the light—and, at the moment when the handkerchief falls, he stands face to face with the noonday sun."[1]

This touch of grace was in him so vivid that he never lost the memory of it. On his death-bed he described this *sublime moment* with just the same emotion : " It is impossible for me to say the precise day or hour when my faith, which had been lost for ten years, reappeared in my heart like the flame of a torch which had never been quite extinguished. Theology teaches us that there is another light than that of reason, another impulse than that of nature, and that this light and impulse, emanating from God, act without our knowing whence they come or whither they go. 'The Spirit breatheth where He will,' says the Apostle St. John, 'and thou hearest His voice, but thou knowest not whence He cometh, or whither He goeth.'[2]

---

[1] Lorain, p. 828.   [2] St. John iii. 8.

An unbeliever one day, a Christian the next—certain with an invincible certitude—it was not the abnegation of my reason, suddenly brought into a state of incomprehensible slavery; it was rather, on the contrary, the expansion of reason—a view of all things under a broader horizon and a more penetrating light. Neither was it any sudden abasement of the will, under some strict and icy rule, but the development of all its energies by means of an act which came from a higher source than nature ; and, finally, it was not the abnegation of the affections, but their plenitude and their exaltation. The whole man was left untouched, only there was added to him the God who had created him.

" He who has not known such a moment in his life has hardly known life ; its shadow only has passed into his veins with the blood of his fathers, but the real life-blood has not swelled and palpitated there. It is the sensible accomplishment of those words of Jesus Christ in St. John's Gospel: " If any man love me he will keep my words : and my Father will love him, and we will come unto him, and make our abode with him."[1] The two great blessings of our nature, truth and beatitude, blend together in the centre of our being, engendering one another, supporting one another, and forming there a mysterious kind of rainbow which tinges with its hues our every thought and feeling, all our virtues and all our acts, up to the last great act of death. Every Christian knows this state, more or less, but it is never more vivid, or more full of emotion, than on the day of conversion ; and this is why we may say of unbelief, when it is conquered, what has been said of original sin, ' *O felix culpa!* O happy fault !' "

What, then, had taken place ? How was it that he who in the evening of one day had been an unbeliever, had the next morning arrived at invincible certitude ? Over what bridge had he crossed the abyss, and how,

[1] St. John xiv. 23.

at one bound, had he gained the threshold of the
sanctuary? Had ambition, through the voice of some
friend in the circle to which he belonged, pointed out
to him that honours would be more easily accessible
in the Church? For a moment his family thought it
had been so. Surprised and hurt at a determination
which had been taken without consulting them, they
saw in it only the calculations of self-interest. Henry
Lacordaire had informed his mother and obtained her
consent, though not without difficulty; but he had
said nothing of his resolution to the other members of
his family. "I was sure to be blamed," he said to
them afterwards, "and it was less painful to me not
to ask your advice than to ask and not to take it."
Thank God, the memory of the priest and the religious
is above this reproach of ambition; and hardly had
he left the seminary than an opportunity offered itself
of showing how little such considerations of worldly
honours weighed in his esteem.

But how had he regained his faith? Conversion,
that phenomenon of light to the intellect and of persuasion to the heart, is not ordinarily produced in the
way of sudden illumination, like a flash of lightning
in a dark night, but rather under the form of growing
daylight, like that which precedes the sunrise. The
first work of truth in a soul is to dissipate clouds, to
chase away the darkness, and to prepare a dwelling
worthy of itself. We have seen the mind of the young
advocate restless and agitated, seeking the corner-
stone of his life and unable to find it—asking it from
friendship, from glory, from an obscure privacy, from
impossible dreams, and everywhere receiving as his
only reply, sadness and weariness, "that inexorable
weariness which," as Bossuet says, "lies at the bottom
of our life." Believing in God and in His invisible
nature, but "cast back, like St. Augustine, into the
profound darkness of his soul by something which
did not suffer him to contemplate the Infinite, and to

enjoy It,"[1] he offered to this hidden and unknown
God the most beautiful prayer which a man who does
not see can make—he sought Him. He sought Him
in good faith, with an earnest desire of being enlightened, and not with the secret wish of disputing
with Truth, and treating with her as an equal. " My
dear friend," he wrote, " I have always sought truth
sincerely, setting pride on one side, and that is the
only way to find her."[2] He sought it not only with
an honest mind, but with a pure heart. He was not
one of those of whom the prophet says, they will not
understand that they may do right.[3] His religious
soul was wonderfully prepared and predestined for
faith. They, therefore, judged him very ill, and knew
him very imperfectly, who saw in his conversion only
the result of a hasty conviction, arrived at without
reflection, with no roots in the present, and no security
for the future. The child of an age puffed up with
pride and athirst for pleasure, he had received the
gift, and known the merit of a simple and upright
heart in an honest and candid soul. There was no
need for Truth to speak to him in thunder, as it
spoke to St. Paul, nor to tear him, like St. Augustine, from the slavery of the senses. He was a
wanderer who had for a brief moment lost his way
among strangers, but who returned to his Father so
soon as he heard that Father's voice calling to His
son. " I had grown old for nine years in unbelief,"
he wrote, " when I heard the voice of God calling me
to Himself. If I seek in my memory for the logical
causes of my conversion, I can find no others than the
historic and social evidence of Christianity—an evidence which appeared incontrovertible to me so soon
as my age enabled me to clear up the doubts which I
had drawn in with the very air of the university. I
point out the origin of my scepticism, though I am
resolved never to let an unkind word drop from my

---

[1] Conf., lib. vii. cap. xx. [2] Lorain—tom. xvii. p. 328.
[3] Psalm xxxv. 3.

pen, because, being early deprived of a Christian father, and brought up by a Christian mother, I owe it to the memory of the one, and the affection of the other, to declare that I received religion from them, together with my life, and that I lost it only among strangers."[1]

We see, then, that this was not one of those half conversions, one of those ill-achieved conquests, in which the vanquished, whilst they yield, never wholly surrender, but enter the camp of the victor with their arms and baggage, and strive to the end to reconcile opposite principles. Everything in his life drew him to the Catholic Church ; his reason, which proved to him its divinity ; his heart, which bade him seek there for Him Who created a type of friendship unknown to the pagan world ; his soul, which made him love its sublime morality. His conversion was therefore complete, absolute, irrevocable. Truth once known, he hastened, by embracing the priesthood, to place an abyss between himself and the world ; it was not enough for him to be the disciple of the Church : he felt that he must also be her apostle.

Let us say rather that God made him a priest in order that he might lead back, by the road which he had himself first followed, a multitude of souls wandering and wounded like his own. What were, in fact, what he calls the *logical* causes of his conversion ; that is to say, those which, apart from his natural predispositions, rationally demonstrated to him the divinity of the Catholic Church ? He has just named them : they were the social and historic superiority of the Catholic religion over every other. He expresses this more clearly in a letter written about this time to a friend :—" I have reached Catholic belief," he says, "through social belief ; and nothing appears to me better demonstrated than this argument.[2] Society is

---

[1] Considerations on the System of M. De Lamennais, chap. x.

[2] He often in his letters recurs to this mental process, which puzzled some of his friends :—" Many think it unaccountable that I should have

necessary, therefore the Christian religion is divine ; for it is the means of bringing society to its true perfection, adapting itself to man, with all his weaknesses, and to the social order in all its conditions."

Now, if no demonstration could be better founded in reason than this, none was also better fitted to meet the evils of our own time and country, or to prepare the new apostle for the mission with which God was one day to intrust him. To his observing eye, the great work and want of the day was to build up and establish modern society, just set free from a state of tutelage. And what use was made of the Church in all this fever of organisation and new systems ? *Absolutely none ;* it was an understood thing that the world could do without her. She had had her day. Men no longer attacked her in her dogmas, her morality, or her practice, as in the times of Luther and the eighteenth century ; but they put her aside among old-fashioned and worn-out institutions, and judged her unfit to be used in the work of emancipating the future. This multitude of sects which had been generated in the universal fermentation, Saint-Simonists, Phalansterians, Fourierists, socialists, communists, and equalitarians, were all seeking for some new basis of society. The laws which had hitherto governed the family, the city, and the state, were declared to be obsolete, and men were racking their brains to find out new ones. There was also to be a religion of the future, for nothing stopped the enterprising spirit of these innovators. It is easy for us now to smile at the simplicity of these attempts ; but it is less easy to be optimist enough not to recognise their traces as they still exist in society at the present day, and to believe it entirely cured of these terrible fantasies. At least, we must allow that in the midst of this general effervescence of ideas and

---

been led back to religious ideas by means of political ideas. The further I advance, the more natural does this, however, seem to me. For the rest, *we may reach Christianity by many different roads, because it is the centre where all truths meet.*"

systems, there was some merit in a young man, generous and enthusiastic, conscious of his own talent, and without any other religion save patriotism, and faith in the future of France, suddenly casting himself into the camp of the past, and exchanging the toga for the humble soutane, not much envied in our own day, but far less so then. The merit of the young philosopher lay in his judging with so just a sense, and so keen a penetration, that society, which had been so completely overthrown in the process of its enfranchisement, could only recover its balance, its true laws, its progress, and its perfection, in and through the Catholic Church; it lay in his conviction that the Church, though rejected by the builders, must still be the headstone of the corner. His merit lay in his seeing, at the age of twenty-two, what Chateaubriand consigned to the last page of his Memoirs as his religious and political testament—" *The principles of Christianity are the future of the world.* Of all my projects, my studies, and my experiences, nothing remains to me save a complete disenchantment of everything that the world pursues. My religious convictions, as they have grown and developed, have swallowed up all other convictions; on the whole earth there is not a more believing Christian, and a more incredulous man, than myself. Far from having reached its final term, the religion of the Great Deliverer has scarcely entered its third, or political period. The gospel, which contains our sentence of acquittal, has not yet been read by all. . . . . . Christianity, so stable in its dogmas, is ever changeful in its lights : its transformation includes the transformation of all things. When it shall have attained its highest point, the darkness will be entirely cleared away : liberty, crucified on Calvary with the Messiah, will thence descend with Him ; and she will restore to the nations that New Testament which was written in their favour, and which has hitherto been fettered in its operation."[1]

<hr>

[1] Chateaubriand.

Had he entered St. Sulpice two years earlier, he would have met there the man who was one day to be his brother-in-arms, and who was to fall on the field of battle just two years before him—Xavier de Ravignan. God had withdrawn him from the magistracy, that high school of talents and characters, at the very moment when the First President Séguier was saying of him: "Let that young man advance; my chair of office is waiting for him." God had chosen them both to be orators, that they might plead His cause before a people who, beyond all others, are the most sensible of the power of eloquence. Both, after passing a brief space among the secular clergy, were to find their way at last into the religious life, as though to authorise the new tone of their teaching by the silent eloquence of a more generous and devoted life. They were different in race, in origin, and in habits of mind; but, cordially knit in a love of the same cause, and the pursuit of the same end, they were destined for twenty years to bestow on their generation the gift of a pulpit eloquence so brilliant, that to find anything like it we must go back through Bourdaloue and Bossuet to the days of St. Ambrose or St. Chrysostom.

Before entering the seminary, Henry wished to inform his mother, and obtain her consent. He foresaw how much the news would sadden her heart, even while it rejoiced her faith. "To know me a Christian," he says, "was of course an unspeakable consolation to her; but to hear that I had entered the seminary would, I well knew, overwhelm her with a grief all the more poignant, from the fact of my being the object of her special affection, the one on whom she had reckoned as likely to be the comfort of her old age. She wrote me six letters, expressing the struggle between her sadness and her joy. But seeing that I was not to be moved from my determination, she at last consented that I should quit the world."[1]

Having been presented to the Archbishop of Paris

[1] *Mémoires.*

by M. Borderies, the Vicar-General, the young convert was received by Monseigneur de Quélen with much kindness. "You are welcome," said the prelate, extending his hand to him: "at the bar you pleaded causes of perishable interest ; now you are going to defend one, the justice of which is eternal. You will see it differently judged of among men ; but there is a Court of Appeal above us, in which at last we shall gain the day."

He entered at St. Sulpice, therefore, and on the 12th of May, 1824, the anniversary both of his birth and his baptism, he was sent to Issy, a country-house belonging to the seminary, which also bore the name of the Solitude. He was exactly twenty-three years of age. He found himself in his true sphere, and he was happy. A senior student, now an archbishop, was appointed to initiate him into the rule and usages of the house. He still remembers the cheerful and almost simple gaiety of the young advocate on the day of his arrival at the Solitude. The grass, the flowers, the trees in their early foliage, all filled him with delight. By his side walked one of his friends and former colleagues at the bar, with a grave, earnest, and rather sorrowful air. And when M. Guillemen introduced the two young men to the seminarist just named, and asked him to guess which of them was the future priest, he did not hesitate to point to the graver of the two, to the great amusement of Henry Lacordaire.

That which most struck him on his first entrance into this holy retreat, and which he always loved to dwell on as forming one of his sweetest remembrances, was the calm, the peace, the serenity, the divine something so hard to describe, reflected on the countenances around him. It was the living expression of a joy that the world cannot give. Suddenly withdrawn out of the bustle of a great city into the calm of a sort of cloister, he felt himself touched and penetrated by the religious silence which

reigned everywhere—in the courts, the gardens, and
the corridors—a silence, however, which was far removed from melancholy. Nothing could have better
harmonised with his present mood. He had quitted
the world, not without a struggle indeed, yet without
regret. None of his hopes there had been fulfilled.
Everything had ceased either to charm or to deceive
him. He had passed the severe winter of his youth
in the fever of doubt and the gradual failure of all his
dreams. But now the winter was past; the sun, a
new sun, had arisen on his intellect, his heart, and his
whole life. He once more breathed freely. His profound and Christian sense of the beauties of nature
made him delight in the harmony he found between
the renewal of his soul's youth and the reawakening
to life of the woods and fields under the balmy sky
of May. The kindness of the masters, the hearty
welcome he received from his new friends, the sweet
quiet of the place, combined to lift him into an
ethereal atmosphere, wherein his soul rose to God,
that it might share in the joy of the Father of the
family as He exulted over the son who had been lost,
but who now was once more found.

Men are indeed strangely mistaken when they weep
over the convert who bids farewell to the world, as
they would weep over one dead. They believe him
to be full of regret for what he is abandoning, whilst
he is tasting an inexpressible delight in his sacrifice ;
they see him giving up a few perishable goods, but
they do not see the Sovereign Good with which God
supplies the loss, and under the charm of which his
happy heart overflows with tenderness and grateful
love. His best friends tremble at the idea of the
sacred and irrevocable engagements he is about to
assume before he has had sufficient experience of the
world or of himself ; but they do not see the Eternal
Beauty which has seduced him, which captivates and
draws him sweetly to Itself. So it was with Lacordaire. His friends hardly understood him when he

replied to them in his own beautiful language, "I hope, indeed, to be one day espoused to a fair, chaste, and immortal Bride, and our marriage, celebrated on earth, will be consummated in heaven. I shall never say, *Linquenda domus et placens uxor.*"[1] But they will perhaps believe his own testimony, given in the words which relate his first impression of the seminary: "One evening I was standing at my window gazing at the moon as her beams fell softly on the house; a single star came out in the heavens, shining in what seemed an impenetrable depth. I know not how it was, but I fell to comparing our humble little dwelling with the immensity of that vault, and as I reflected that in a few poor cells of that house there were a small number of men, servants of Him, the Lord and Creator of these wonders, whom the rest of men despised and regarded as fools, I felt disposed to pity this poor world, that does not know how to lift its eyes above its head."[2]

It is even so: the walls of the cloister or the seminary are not, as men suppose, the walls of a prison, within which unhappy victims groan and suffer; they are gardens of delight, where blooms the only happiness that exists without shadow and without alloy—the happiness that springs out of victory over the passions, often purchased at a costly price, and out of friendship with God and the sweetness of fraternal charity.

Fénélon has said of the Society under whose direction the Abbé Lacordaire had just placed himself, "I know nothing more venerable than the Congregation of St. Sulpice." Since receiving that eulogium the holy Congregation has not degenerated, and those who know its spirit feel well assured that it will continue to deserve the same praise even to the end. It was not, we venture to think, without a providential design that Père Lacordaire received his first

---

[1] Lorain, *Correspondant*, tom. xvii. p. 835.
[2] Ibid., p. 831.

formation in the ecclesiastical spirit at St. Sulpice. Called as he was to the difficult mission of one day restoring in France a religious order of preachers and teachers, it was during his life at the seminary that he received his first impulse towards his future destiny, and he never lost the impression. It will therefore not be out of place to say something here of what he owed to the time passed by him at St. Sulpice, and of its influence on his after character as a priest and a religious; and also to explain how it was that the superiors of the Congregation did not at first thoroughly comprehend the richly-gifted nature which God had sent to them to be transformed.

The Catholic Church, the great link uniting heaven and earth, time and eternity, is clothed with a double aspect and character. On one hand she is stable and immovable, as eternal as the God from Whom she proceeds; and on the other she is changeful and progressive like the humanity she disciplines in order to lead it to God. Changeless in her divine constitution, she yet adapts herself to the varied habits of the nations whom Jesus Christ has given to her to baptize, to educate, to civilise and to direct. Without creating anything new, she draws out of the inexhaustible fecundity of her vital principle the power of new transformations, suited to different manners and fresh exigencies,—*non nova, sed nove.* Thus, at the period of the barbaric invasions, the Church cheerfully assumed many new responsibilities rendered necessary by the infant state of society. Thus, too, at a later period, having succeeded, with the help of the races whom she had trained, and who were not ungrateful for her care, in founding the great social and religious institution which we call Christendom, she created for its defence a new militia of knightly monks. Now, of these two aspects of immutability and of change, of limitation in what is essential, of breadth and progress in what is merely accidental, the first may be described as more peculiarly represented by the secular, and the second, by the regular clergy. The secular clergy never alters its form, or moves out of the circle of its mission. Its form, of a directly Divine origin, remains ever the same. The hierarchy is supported on the supreme Pontiff, the bishops and the priests, and this order of things must always and infallibly continue. Its mission, which is to give Jesus Christ to the world through the channel of the sacraments, never changes : there always have been, and there always will be, priests, exclusively given up to the care of souls, in order to communicate to them the grace of God. But this essential ministry, which is the sacred inheritance of the secular clergy, at the same time restricts its action. There are times and circumstances which create new positions and new wants. And at such times the Church rather addresses herself to the monastic orders. Those orders possess on one hand in the priesthood the same Divine source of graces as the secular clergy ; whilst, free from the ties of the pastoral office, and prepared by the practice of the religious vows for a larger measure of self-sacrifice, they lend themselves in a wonderful way to all the exigencies of the moment, and to the wants of a particular time or country. Thus they have successively produced the contemplative monk, labouring and teaching orders, the monastic soldier, student, and missionary. When, therefore, the Church, through her prelates assembled at the Council of Trent, decreed the foundation and organisation of seminaries, with the view of perfecting the education of priests, she naturally sought to impress such institutions with her own essential and unchangeable character. She desired that her seminaries should be fitted to produce not merely the priest of the sixteenth century, but the priest at all times ; not the French, the German, or the Italian priest, but simply, the priest.

It was reserved to the Church in France to raise up a man who was not only admirably inspired with this idea, but who knew also how to carry it out through the instrumentality of a Congregation which has nowhere found its equal. The one exclusive object of the Congregation of St. Sulpice is to form the priest. Its founder, M. Olier, refused every other ministry ; he would undertake none but this. His ideal was the priestly character, and he beheld in the priest that which is his most essential office in the Church—the Pastor. The universality of the type naturally made him little solicitous about what in our day are called specialities. As he himself avows, he cared far less to form learned doctors and eloquent preachers than good parish priests.

The three virtues most indispensable to the secular priest make up the peculiar spirit of St. Sulpice— namely, detachment from the world, a love of holy things, and respect for the hierarchy. This venerable Congregation, which for three centuries has formed and animated the body of the French clergy, and which has ever preserved its original character, re- maining so weak in appearance, and in reality so strong, does not rest on the irrevocable engagement of religious vows. The Sulpician knows no other yoke than that of the Church, no other promise save that which every priest makes to his bishop, in order that this spectacle of a will ever free, yet ever subject, might serve as an example to the priest who, living in the midst of the world, must be a rule to himself. The statutes of the Sulpician are few, simple, and easily observed, so that every priest may find in them the model of his own life, and may draw from this kind of *Presbyterium* a taste for community life, so far as the parochial ministry renders it possible or practicable. Hence one of the signs by which we recognise a holy priest is the care he takes faithfully to keep up the practices taught him in the seminary ; and hence in part the honour and esteem which have ever been enjoyed by the French clergy, formed by the rule or the spirit of St. Sulpice.

As to that other more human aspect presented by

the Church, which exhibits her to us adapting herself
to the varying needs of race and country, St. Sulpice
does not possess it, and does not wish to possess it.
This is at once the strength and the weakness of the
institute.   It takes little pains to study or develop in
its pupils special aptitudes for special needs ; it does
not occupy itself in forming doctors, learned men, or
scholars for an age intoxicated with scientific discoveries, and it aims in a very moderate degree at
kindling the fire of eloquence in any subject who gives
promise of becoming a fine orator.   The work of
St. Sulpice lies not in things like these ; and it gladly
leaves the care of them to other institutes which were
more numerous in M. Olier's time, and which are now
only slowly rising from their ashes.

From what has been said, it will be easy to understand both the benefits which St. Sulpice afforded to
the Abbé Lacordaire, and the want of which he was
nevertheless conscious ; we perceive both what he im-
bibed from her training, and what he was left to desire
and seek elsewhere.   The predispositions he brought
with him from his former life, his taste for work and
solitude, his veneration for everything that regarded
the priesthood or Divine worship, and his extreme
reserve in all his relations with the world, received
their crown and consecration in the seminary.   In
these particulars, therefore, he found no difficulty in
throwing himself into the spirit and usages of St.
Sulpice.   On one occasion he even undertook its
defence, with that slight tinge of exaggeration with
which he chose sometimes to colour his statements.
Whilst at the Solitude he tried to induce one of his
friends to remain there, who, having like himself come
from the world into the seminary, had not been able
to adapt himself to the new régime.   "Believe me,
my dear friend," said Lacordaire, "a priest who has
not passed through the seminary will never acquire
the ecclesiastical spirit."

But there were other sides of his character which,

as he himself confesses, often led him, without meaning it, to depart from the exterior habits uniformly adhered to by the other students. "I had quitted the world suddenly," he says, "without any interval which might gradually have initiated me into the secrets of Christian life, and before I had become trained to that humble and simple reserve which a young neophyte ought to cherish as his most precious treasure in so holy a place as a seminary. I felt that my new masters were good and pious men, wholly devoid of intrigue or ambition; but, without intending it, I often went contrary to the ordinary habits of their pupils. Sure of the intention which had brought me among them, I was not sufficiently careful to repress the sallies of an intellect which had been too much used to dispute, and a temper which had not as yet been brought entirely under command. Before long, therefore, my vocation began to be suspected."

But owing to his candour, and the purity of his own intention, he himself was the last to perceive the doubts with which he inspired his superiors; and he gave free vent to his attraction for prayer and study, without dreaming of the trials that were in store for him.

He began to study the Holy Scriptures, and the Divine light that had dawned on his mind soon discovered to him their mysterious beauty. "Oh, what a book, and what a religion!" he wrote; "what a marvellous chain connects the first word of the Old Testament with the last of the New!"[1] This study became habitual with him, and was numbered among those few daily practices which he seldom or ever omitted. He clung to it from a kind of instinct; not out of a mere habit of routine, but because the soul hungered after its daily food. He wrote again about the same time: "You ask me what I am doing in my solitude? I am giving myself up to the studies and meditations I have always loved. Every day I

[1] Lorain, *Correspondant*, tom. xvii. p. 831.

see more plainly that there is no truth out of religion, and that it alone resolves the endless difficulties which philosophy is powerless to overcome. My thoughts ripen all the more quickly, from the fact that I am not required to pour them forth, and so to expend what I am gradually amassing. My mind is like a field which lies fallow, but is watered with the dews of heaven."[1]

He delighted in the calm retreat of Issy, and liked its ways. The alternation of solitude with community life had a charm for him, as well as the union of strict rule with liberty. The students rose at five, and, after an hour's meditation, went to the chapel, which was situated in the midst of the garden ; and he felt a pleasure in watching the long procession of white surplices as they passed among the flower-beds and covered alleys, fragrant with the early morning air. Returning to his cell at seven o'clock, he made his own bed and arranged his chamber, like the greater number of his fellow-students, often sighing as he did so to think of the number of poor people who in their miserable garrets were occupied with the same cares. After dinner followed an hour's recreation, during which he always displayed an agreeable gaiety. It sometimes happened, however, that his lively and original nature, not yet under much control, betrayed itself in sallies which manifested something of the *gallica levitas*, seasoned with Burgundian love of fun. The good directors were astounded, and hastened to repress this boisterous levity. He never could accustom himself to the square cap, that strange head-dress, the shape of which is so grotesque that one dares not call it by its true name. Against these caps Lacordaire declared war, a war at first carried on by epigrams, but which soon became one of extermination. He would snatch them out of the hands of his friends and throw them into the fire. This gave rise to a great commotion, and very lively

[1] Lorain.

discussions ensued, some declaring in favour of the square cap, and others for the biretta, which was then a novelty. But novelty and argument were two things which St. Sulpice held in equal abhorrence. In the evening, therefore, at the hour of spiritual reading, the superior addressed them a grave reproof, and order was once more restored.

The Abbé Lacordaire always displayed perfect submission to his directors; and if they were sometimes puzzled by the contrasts of his singular character, they never had occasion to complain of his want of humility, modesty, or obedience. He was beloved by all his companions : his deep and earnest nature, wholly given up to his new and sacred duties, was adorned with a certain freshness of poetry, with the fragrance of worldly refinement, and the grace of a character long pent up within itself, but now freely poured forth ; and all this gave an indescribable charm to his personal intercourse, which made him generally loved and sought after. All his masters, however, did not understand him ; the singularity of some of his ways, his liberal opinions, and his instinctive repugnance to certain points of ordinary routine doubtless now and then deceived their observant eyes, and prevented them from at once appreciating at its just value the pure gold which lay hidden at the bottom of the vessel. For ourselves, we have been witnesses of the veneration he always preserved for the seminary, the respect with which he ever named it, and the eagerness he showed on all occasions to cite as an authority, what was done at St. Sulpice. We saw him closely, and were thus able to observe how much he owed to the gradual formation he received in the seminary ; for it was thence that he derived his priestly character, his recollected manner, his religious attitude at the altar, his tender and profound love for the Holy Scriptures and the Person of our Divine Lord ; and we rejoice, therefore, in rendering public testimony to the sentiments with which he so often edified us, and which were no less honourable to the masters than to their disciple.

Those among his directors who read his soul judged him differently from those who only saw the exterior man. One morning the Abbé Garnier, then Superior-General of the Congregation, as he was walking in an avenue at Issy, came up with the young Abbé Lacordaire, who was just then finishing his first year of theology, and taking him kindly by the hand, he said : " My dear young friend, I shall expect you next year at our house in Paris. I shall make you master of the conferences, for you must study theology to its depths ; without that, the finest talent has no solid foundation. I shall also appoint you catechist, that you may have an opportunity of exercising your gift of public speaking." Then, putting his hand affectionately on the young man's shoulder, he added : "Come, let me be your confessor." Charmed by the words of the venerable old priest, who enjoyed a high reputation for learning, the Abbé Lacordaire did, in fact, choose him for his director when he went to Paris, and a lasting affection sprang up between them.

Placed as he was, face to face with himself during this long time of retreat, he gradually came to know himself better. He no longer felt those vague and sorrowful aspirations after the Unknown which had tortured him during his years of doubt. He saw clearly enough both the end at which he aimed and the obstacle that lay in his way. The end was Jesus Christ, Whom he was called to love and to make known to others ; and the obstacle was himself. . " My end," he writes, " is to make known Jesus Christ to souls who do not know Him, to contribute in perpetuating a Divine religion, to relieve as many miseries, and check as much corruption as I can ; and my snare is the desire of making myself talked about." He laboured hard, therefore, " to lay aside this mere natural life, and to consecrate himself wholly to the service of Him

Who will never show Himself either jealous or ungrateful."

Another way in which the seminary pleased him
was that it gave him friends. His nature, no longer
pent up within itself, returned into its accustomed
channels, and flowed in the direction to which he was
guided by his heart. He allowed himself, therefore, to
cultivate and gather the flowers of friendship, and
to enjoy their fragrance without scruple. "You do not
know one of my present sources of happiness," he
wrote; "it is that I am beginning my youth over
again, or I would rather say, that age which intervenes
between youth and childhood, whilst at the same time
I retain the moral strength which belongs to elder
years. At college we are too much children, we do
not yet understand the value of men and things, we
are too deficient in ideas to know how to choose our
friends and attach them to us with lasting ties. Our
souls are then too feeble, our intellects too unformed
to grasp the higher relations of friendship. Then
again, in the world we are equally unable to form any
very solid attachments, whether it be that there men
live so far apart, or that interest and self-love glide
into what seem the purest ties, or perhaps that the
heart is less at ease in the midst of bustle and social
activity. Friendship springs up more easily in the
midst of a hundred and forty young men who constantly see one another, who have so many common
sympathies, and who are almost all like so many choice
flowers transplanted into the wilderness. I take a
pleasure in gaining their affections, and in preserving
in the seminary something of worldly amenity, and a
few graces stolen from secular life. I feel more simple,
more affable, less reserved than I used to be, free from
that ambition of shining with which I was formerly
possessed, very little concerned about the future, which
will content me whatever it may be, dreaming of poverty as in other days I dreamt of making my fortune;

and so I go on, living happily with my brethren and with myself."

This sort of community life in the midst of his brethren, an ideal which had always floated in his mind, began dimly to reveal to him his future vocation. He was *dreaming of poverty* as he had heretofore dreamt of wealth. He communicated his ideas and wishes to M. Garnier, who, without seeking to turn him from his new projects, advised him to examine the question leisurely, and to determine on nothing till he should clearly discern the Will of God. He was not at that time thinking of the Dominicans, but of the Company of Jesus, the only religious order as yet restored in France.

Another desire arose in his heart about the same time, vaguely indeed, though at a later period it took a more definite shape. It was the wish to become a missionary. He thought he could not possibly give his Divine Master, or the world at large, a more generous or more manifest proof of his faith in the gospel, than by voluntary exile from his country, and the renunciation of everything to which the human heart most closely clings, which is involved in such a vocation. From that time a desire of diffusing the light which flooded his own soul inspired all his words and resolutions. That which specially struck him in the history of the missions was the testimony they afforded to the truth. "The lives of our missionaries," he exclaims, "attest, as all men feel, that the chief source of their success, humanly speaking, has been their intense certainty of faith, which they have proved by condemning themselves to a voluntary exile among barbarous nations, and by the incredible labours they have undertaken without any visible reward. The more good we would do in religion, the larger must be the pledges we give to the world of the sincerity of our faith, by the sanctity and self-denial of our lives. As a great orator, smothered in purple robes, I should do nothing; but as a simple missionary, without talent, covered with rags, and three thousand leagues from home, I should move kingdoms. The whole course of ecclesiastical history is a proof of what I say." This twofold dream of religious and missionary life took possession of him even whilst in the seminary, and lasted through the first years of his priestly career, down to the moment when his true place in France was clearly made known to him. And thus in the course of a few months the convert of yesterday had embraced, in heart at least, every separate form of devotion to the cause of God and His Church.

Nevertheless, his superiors had not yet made up their minds as to his vocation. He was not summoned to receive holy orders at the usual time, "as though they sought to weary out his patience, and to discourage the unknown motive that had drawn him out of the world, and a worldly calling, to God and the desert. They felt uneasy when they observed his ardour for debate, and the large claims which he made for reason. When he opened his lips in class to raise any objection, his words took so lively and original a turn, and his conclusions were so bold, that they often proved somewhat embarrassing to the professors. At last, in order to save time, they begged him to put off his difficulties till the end of the lecture. He forgot this sometimes ; perhaps it was to relate a story, but the story generally ended in some treacherous question, or some home-thrust at the thesis of the master. It is the custom at the seminary for the students to take it by turns to preach in the refectory during meals. It was there that the future orator of Notre Dâme first made trial of his arms. His style excited the enthusiasm of the students, but was not much relished by the masters. In a letter to a friend he thus amusingly relates one of his first attempts : "I have been preaching, that is, only in a refectory, where a hundred and thirty persons were at dinner,

<hr />

1 Lorain, p. 837.

and I succeeded in making my voice heard through
the clatter of plates and the bustle of serving. I
suppose there can hardly be any position more unfavourable for an orator than to have to address men
who are engaged in eating. Cicero could never have
pronounced his orations against Catiline at a senator's
dinner-table, unless, indeed, he had made them drop
their forks at his first sentence. But how would it
have been if he had had to speak to them of the Incarnation? Yet that is what I had to do; and I
acknowledge that when I beheld the indifferent air
that appeared on the countenances of my audience,
not one of whom seemed to be listening, and whose
entire attention seemed concentrated on their plates,
the thought did occur to me that I should like to
throw my square cap in their faces. I came down
from the pulpit thoroughly persuaded that I had
preached horribly, and, after a hasty dinner, went out
into the garden, where I soon learnt that my sermon
had had its effect, and that many had been struck by
it. I content myself with this expression, which contains quite enough self-love, and shall repeat none of
the opinions, predictions, flatteries, good advice, and
the rest"[1]

This was the impression of the students; but the
judgment of the masters was more severe, nor must
this surprise us. St. Sulpice, as we have before remarked, was perhaps hardly qualified to discern in
the young seminarist him who has since been so often
called the prince of sacred eloquence in the nineteenth century; and the superiors felt themselves
bound to warn his fellow-students against a style of
preaching, the imitation of which could not fail to be
injurious.

Whatever may have been the cause, two years and
a half passed away without his being called to receive
holy orders. When he understood the hesitation of
his superiors, he began more seriously to consider his

[1] Lorain.

project of embracing a religious life, and thought of entering among the Jesuits. He even took some steps towards carrying this idea into execution, but Mgr. de Quélen opposed the plan.

M. Garnier then felt it his duty to communicate the intentions of his penitent to the Council. On becoming aware of his perseverance under every trial, and of his aspirations after the religious life, the Council owned that they had been mistaken in the view they had taken of his singular character. All further hesitation ceased ; the entrance to the sanctuary was at once opened to him by the reception of the sub-diaconate ; and on the 22nd of September, 1827, after three years and a half spent at the seminary, he was ordained priest by Mgr. de Quélen in his private chapel. On the 25th of September he wrote as follows : " My great desire is accomplished. I have now for three days been a priest : *sacerdos in æternum secundum ordinem Melchisedech.*"

He was a priest ; but whither was God about to call him ? Was he to remain among the secular clergy, or to become a missionary or a religious ? His mind was not yet made up. But if still uncertain what to do, he was at least quite clear as to what he would not do. And this is proved by the following incident.

When M. Garnier left Paris to make his visitation of the seminaries, the Abbé Lacordaire placed himself under the direction of another Sulpician, M. Boyer, a good and holy priest, as learned as he was humble, with a touch of southern vivacity and originality which has remained proverbial at St. Sulpice. One day the Abbé Lacordaire went to see him. " You are just come at the right moment," said M. Boyer. " Sit down, my dear fellow ; I am going to make you a cardinal." " You are joking," said the Abbé Lacordaire. " Not at all, I am determined to make you a cardinal ; listen to me." He then informed him that

6

the post of Auditor of the Rota at the Court of Rome having become vacant by the nomination of Mgr. de Isoard to the archbishopric of Auch, Mgr. Frayssinous, Minister of Ecclesiastical Affairs, who, in virtue of his office, had the right of presentation, had requested him to find some young priest qualified to fill this important charge. " I want one," said the Minister, " of first-rate merit, uniting sound learning to refined scholarship ; a man, in short, worthy of representing France at the Court of Rome, and of filling those high dignities to which, as you know, this appointment opens the way." " I will think about it," replied M. Boyer. "And, in fact," he continued, " I was thinking about it when you entered. So you see, my dear friend, Providence itself opens to you this splendid career ; for with your talents, your legal experience, your knowledge of the world and habits of public speaking, no one can be better fitted for it than yourself."

The Abbé Lacordaire, surprised for a moment at this unexpected proposal, was neither dazzled nor moved by it. " When I determined on entering the priesthood," he replied, " I had but one thing in view, and that was to serve the Church by the ministry of preaching: that is my vocation. Had I desired honours I should have remained in the world. Be so good, therefore, as to think no more of me in this matter. I shall always remain a simple priest, and shall probably one day or other become a religious." " But, reflect," replied M. Boyer, warmly. " You wish to serve the Church, and where can you do so better than at Rome, near the Holy Father, and invested with so high a dignity ?" And he was about to continue, when the Abbé Lacordaire interrupted him in his turn. " No, no, sir ; I beg you not to press me any further. I have said, and I repeat it, I shall not go to Rome: I shall become a religious. I have often spoken of this to M. Garnier, who possesses my entire confidence ; he approves my intention, and, in short, it is a settled thing."[1]

Facts like these require no comment. I will only add that the modesty of Père Lacordaire left us all his life in ignorance of this touching anecdote. It only came to our knowledge after his death, and was communicated by M. Garnier himself to a Superior of the Great Seminary, from whom we ourselves received it.

[1] The persistence of M. Boyer was the more calculated to impress the mind of the Abbé Lacordaire, because the rigid and upright character of the Sulpician was incapable of being guided by any human views. His disinterestedness was above suspicion, for he had refused the post of Vicar-General at Paris. The friend, the schoolfellow, and the relation of M. Frayssinous, he nevertheless died a simple Sulpician. One day Charles X. asked the Minister where that friend of his resided, the theologian whom he sometimes consulted before answering his questions. "Sire," replied M. Frayssinous, "he lodges in a garret in the Seminary of St. Sulpice." "That is doubtless the reason," returned the king, with a smile, "that you never propose to raise him higher."

CHAPTER IV.

Mgr. de Quélen appoints him Chaplain to the Convent of the Visitation, and afterwards to the Collége Henri IV.—His life of study—He thinks of going to the United States.

FTER refusing to go to Rome with the rank of Monsignore, and the certain prospect of a bishopric,[1] the Abbé Lacordaire willingly accepted from the Archbishop of Paris the humble post of chaplain to a convent of Visitation nuns. He preferred a cell to a palace. Was this, it may be asked, simply the result of modesty? We think not. The humility of Père Lacordaire's character did not make him think himself good for nothing ; it rather moved him to render homage to God for graces received from His hands; it tended less **to**

[1] The office of Auditor to the Rota is one of those which, according to the custom of the Roman Court, is always a step to the episcopate. The Dean of the Auditors, when he resigns his office, receives the purple by right, and is promoted to an archbishopric. In 1827, when the Abbé Lacordaire declined this honour, the post had become vacant in consequence of the nomination of Mgr. Isoard, Dean of the Auditors, to the Archbishopric of Auch, with the dignity of Cardinal. Lacordaire having declined the office, Mgr. de Retz was appointed. He died in 1844, and the post then remained vacant until 1852, when it was filled by Mgr. de Ségur, who held it until 1856. The affection of the eyes from which he suffered alone prevented his promotion to the episcopate. His successors were Mgr. de la Tour-d'Auvergne, who became Archbishop of Bourges ; Mgr. Lavigerie, Bishop of Nancy ; and Mgr. Place, who is at this moment in possession of the office.

blind him to the gift, than to urge him to cultivate it as a faithful steward. Had he considered himself suited to the posts just offered to him, I believe he would have felt no difficulty in accepting them ; but finding in himself qualities incompatible with these offices, he refused them, alike unmoved by the whispers of self-love or the sophistries of reason, which in cases like these is wont so skilfully to disguise the honour of a high dignity under its burden. Neither did his refusal arise from any selfish love of repose : he sought solitude, not in order to fly from action, but to prepare himself for it the better. It was with this feeling that he wrote later on :—" I have no ambition, and I can have none, for all the higher dignities of the clergy are either pastoral or administrative, and both kinds are totally incompatible with my tastes. I shall never hold any office, nor do I desire it. Yet one must do something with one's-self, for this is an obligation of conscience."[1] In these words we see the man ; the penetrating eye so keenly observant of his own heart, the judgment which so impartially decides his own cause, his rare discretion, and, we may add, his yet rarer virtue. If on one hand we are bound to do justice to his natural qualities, it is equally important to show the influences they received from divine grace, and to exhibit the character of the man, perfected in that of the priest. In fact, what a distance already separates the young advocate, so eager for renown, from the simple catechist of little schoolgirls at the Visitation Convent!

His duties at the Visitation were limited to giving a few instructions to the school children, and hearing their confessions. The beginnings of the great orator could hardly have been humbler. He acquitted himself of these duties with the same care and exactitude which he displayed in everything else ; but the results were moderate. There was too large a disproportion between the mind of the teacher and the intelligence

---

[1] Letter to M. Montalembert, 1833.

of his young disciples; they often admired, but they did not always understand him. The good religious thought him too metaphysical, and we can readily believe that their complaint was just. His gravity and reserve, however, were so great that no one in the house remembered ever having seen him raise his eyes when addressing his pupils.

His mother came to share his retirement at the Visitation; she was astonished at the solitary life he led there, and, well knowing his affectionate nature, she would sometimes say to him, half sadly: "You have no friends!" "And, in fact," as he says in his Memoirs, "I had none, and I was doomed to have none, until events occurred which were to change the face of the world, and at the same time to alter my own destiny."

His retired life, however, gave the young priest ample opportunities of leisure, and this was precisely what he wanted. He made use of it to prepare for coming struggles. His three years' course of theology had given him only a summary and imperfect notion of that science, which he wished to sound to the bottom, both for his own sake and that of others. He resolved to study it at its fountain-head, and entered on his task with ardour. "Strength is only to be found at the source," he wrote, "and it is there I must seek it. The road will be long, and the more so as I intend to gather up on my way whatever may serve me to frame an apology for Christianity, which I have in my mind; its outline is not yet clearly defined, but I see that its materials must be furnished by Holy Scripture, the Fathers, history, and philosophy. Whatever I have hitherto read in defence of religion appears to me weak and incomplete. Modern theologians invariably take a guide: it is for all the world like a tour in Switzerland; if a celebrated traveller has followed any particular road, every one else must go the same way, and neglect paths that would lead to new beauties, which, however, are not yet made historic."[1] From the outset he knew what he was aiming at—the apology of Christianity; this was what he felt to be his mission, the centre to which all his powers converged. And in idea he had already sketched the grand outlines of the edifice which he hoped one day to raise in defence of the faith.

When his friends urged him to appear in public, either as a writer or speaker, he replied: " I am studying, not writing. . . . . Years fly swiftly, and it is full time to be reasonable, and to look on life with eyes no longer dazzled by the sunbeams of youth. Let us be just towards God. He has not created men that they may attain celebrity, a thing which few ever reach, or care for when they have reached it. God knows the littleness of the world too well to give His creatures so poor an aim as that. He created the stars in order to disgust us with it. Glory is the illusion of childhood, and of some men who never quite grow out of childish ways. A soul really capable of glory does not think about it, he is too great for that. The wise man lives within himself; he has no need to wait thirty years in order to learn the true worth of those huge coteries we call nations ; he tries to do what good he can, and attaches himself to the corner of the world where his lot is cast ; and if he be one of those vast geniuses to whom the world itself hardly suffices, this does but increase his longing after solitude. He understands his age and his fellow-men too well not to think himself fortunate if he can keep out of their way, and eat the onions of his own garden, and the wild cherries of his own woods. . . . . The mania of being somebody ruins most minds in the present day, and if a great man is ever born among us he will see daylight in some fisherman's hut, where the son of a coal-heaver has perhaps retired with a pension of twenty crowns. The highest of all glories, that of God, is born in solitude."

In fact, he was in no hurry. No man ever more

[1] Lorain.

thoroughly possessed his soul in God, none ever
waited more patiently for the hour providentially
marked out for action, as none ever threw himself
more heartily into his work when that hour struck.
He saw how much there was to be done in the world,
but his time had not yet come. The graver passages
of his correspondence at this period are occasionally
relieved by traits of that Burgundian pleasantry which
never forsook him, and which he expressed in terms
as lively as they were original. "Were glory to come
to us as an old family friend who had slighted us a
little, we would be generous, we would not turn our
back upon her. But she should not stifle us under her
wings, and on Sunday, to mark our respect for the
Sabbath, we would put her into the pot. Doubtless
there will be plenty of fine things to be done. Every
phase of glory which is yet to rise above the horizon
will be the offspring of Catholicism. You will see
this if you keep your eye on the world. Civil society
is incapable nowadays of giving birth to a single
great man. Exhausted by her vices, she fondly dreams
that liberty will restore the powers of her youth, and,
quitting the palace, she stands before the multitude
and says, 'Behold me!' But she and the multitude
have met like Death and Sin in Milton's poem. Youth
once decayed is only renewed by immortality. Virtue
and genius once extinct can be revived by faith alone.
. . . . God has given the world into the hands of
men of genius, those created gods, on condition of
their doing Him homage. Without that they are like
the Archangel traversing chaos, and always falling
back ; because they cannot find a solid spot on which
to tread, and from which to soar upwards."[1]

In 1828 he was named assistant-chaplain to the
Collége Henri-Quatre. The duties of the office, which
were better suited to his capacity, in no degree changed
that life of study and retreat which was preparing him
for the part he was to play hereafter. He read St.

[1] Lorain, *Correspondant,* tom. xvii. p. 831.

Augustine, Plato, Aristotle, Descartes, the works of
M. de la Mennais, and Church history. "You ask me
what I am doing?" he writes. "I dream, think, read,
and pray; I laugh two or three times a week, and once
or twice perhaps I weep. From time to time I get
in a passion with the University, which is certainly the
most insufferable daughter of royalty that I know . . . .
Add to all this a few simple instructions to the pupils
of the third and fourth forms, and you have my life."

Towards the close of 1829, the idea of an apostolic
life in foreign countries, the germ of which had already
manifested itself during his residence at the seminary,
seemed sufficiently ripened in his mind to determine
him on embracing that career. He thought of going
out as a missionary to the United States. In the
spring of 1830, he for the first time visited M. de la
Mennais at La Chesnaie. "I had only seen him twice
before, and for a few moments," he says in his Memoirs,
"but he was the only great man of the French Church,
and the few ecclesiastics with whom I was on intimate
terms were all friends of his. Having reached Dinan,
I plunged into the lonely paths that led through the
woods, and presently found myself before a solitary
house, the mysterious celebrity of which was disturbed
by no passing sound. It was La Chesnaie. A letter
had prepared the Abbé de la Mennais for my visit and
my adhesion to his party, and he gave me a cordial
reception. He had with him the Abbé Gerbet, his
favourite disciple, and about a dozen young men whom
he had gathered round him under the shadow of his
glory as a precious seed for the future of which he
dreamed. My visit, though it gave me more than one
surprise, did not sever the tie which had just attached
me to this illustrious writer. His philosophy had never
gained any real possession of my understanding; his
political absolutism had always repelled me; and I
had lately begun to entertain fears lest the very orthodoxy of his theology might not be altogether above
suspicion. It was too late to draw back, however, and

after eight years' hesitation I gave myself up, without much enthusiasm, yet of my own free will, into the hands of a school which until then had gained no hold either on my sympathies or my convictions."

This step in no way interfered with his missionary projects. He even had an interview, at the house of M. de la Mennais, with the Bishop of New York, who offered him the post of Vicar-General in his diocese. Neither was his plan disturbed by the Revolution of 1830, which broke out three months later. It was plainly a serious idea which had taken root in his soul: whence, then, had it arisen?

It arose from the twofold subject which constantly engaged his thoughts—the Church and Society; two things which he desired to see as closely united in fact as they were in his own affections. It was an idea which sprang up in that priestly heart of his, which began to suffer from the want of pouring itself out in unmeasured fulness for Him Who has given Himself to us without reserve. Every young priest knows something of this noble malady; the Abbé Lacordaire felt it, and desired to be cured. Whilst still in the seminary, he had said that "the more good we desire to do in religion, the larger must be the pledges of our conviction we give to the world by the holiness and self-denial of our lives." To bid farewell to France and to his friends was indeed to his patriotic and affectionate nature a grand and generous sacrifice, the heroism of which appealed to his heart and animated his courage. Together with this motive of self-devotion was mingled another, which induced him to make choice of the United States as the scene of his labours. He had reached Catholicism, as he himself has told us, through his social belief. From the necessity of society he inferred the necessity of the Church by these easy steps: There can be no society without religion, no religion without Christianity, no Christianity without the Catholic Church. Thus he held the two extreme links of the chain, but how were they to be united? Society could not exist without the Church; but on what terms were they to be associated? Were temporal interests to be subject to the spiritual, both of right and in fact, as during the middle ages? Or rather, whatever might be the right of the question, should society be made to coexist, peacefully and independently, by the side of the Church, as in the United States at the present moment? This was the problem which anxiously engaged his mind; and he was desirous of studying on the spot the solution to which he manifestly inclined, and which he was ere long to push to extremes in the pages of the *Avenir.* He was curious to examine for himself the developments, rendered possible by liberty alone, of a Church which in 1808 reckoned two dioceses and eighty churches, and which now possesses forty-five dioceses and three thousand churches. We must also confess that the position in which the Church of France was placed by the government of the period was of a nature that might well make him seek elsewhere for a more perfect ideal. He felt there was something within him held captive, and that something was Divine, unalienable, eternally free—it was the Word of God! "The ministry of preaching has been confided to me," he cries; "that Divine Word which I have been commanded to carry to the utmost extremities of the earth without any one having the right to seal my lips for a single day. I came forth from the temple of God invested with this mighty office, and I was met on the very threshold with laws that made me a slave. The laws did not permit me to teach the youth of France under a most Christian king; and had I, like my fathers, desired to plunge into some solitude, and there to raise some peaceful home of prayer, other laws would have been found to banish me thence."[1] During the two years he had been a priest, he had seen the colleges of the Jesuits

[1] Procès de *l'Avenir.*

suppressed, the teaching of the little seminaries subjected to restrictive measures most injurious to the rights of the episcopate, and a new Sorbonne erected, which was to be the *guardian* of *Gallican maxims*. The holy ark of Gallicanism was in danger, so they gave it a guard of honour. It had been proposed to render compulsory on the great seminaries the teaching of the *Four Articles*, in virtue of a decision of the minister of the interior. The Abbé de la Mennais had been summoned before the correctional police, and found guilty of provoking disobedience to the declaration of 1682, now proclaimed a law of the state.

The Abbé Lacordaire had seen all this, and he had beheld the standard of Gallicanism set up immediately after this trial by the fourteen bishops who had signed the declaration of 1826. All these facts, so contrary to his own ideas and tendencies, had naturally great weight in determining his choice, and inducing him to look out for some land where liberty was more secure. "Who is there," he exclaimed to the same judges in 1831; "who at moments when the state of his own country saddens him, has not turned his eyes towards the republic of Washington? Who has not, in fancy at least, sat down to rest under the shadow of her forests and her laws? Weary with the spectacle I beheld in France, it was on that land that I cast my eyes, and thither I resolved to go to ask a hospitality she has never refused to a traveller or a priest."[1]

These considerations may also serve, not to justify, but to explain the sort of reaction which took possession of his mind and pen against the deplorable system of state bondage which then weighed on the Church. The Revolution of 1830 had just rendered manifest the miserable consequences of this system. The unhappy concessions that had been made to the civil power, instead of proving any profit to the

[1] *Procès de l'Avenir.*

Church, had ended, then as ever, in bringing on her equal unpopularity, and involving her in the same disasters. And we must bear these facts in mind if we would impartially judge the controversy of which we shall soon have to treat. The Abbé Lacordaire, having obtained the consent both of his mother and his archbishop, repaired to Burgundy to bid adieu to his family and friends. Whilst there, he received a letter from the Abbé Gerbet, announcing to him the plan of the *Avenir,* and soliciting him, in his Master's name, to share in an undertaking at once Catholic and national, whence they might reasonably hope for the enfranchisement of religion, the reconciliation of parties, and the consequent regeneration of society. The Abbé de la Mennais had frankly accepted the political changes which had just taken place, and had given up those absolutist doctrines rejected by common consent. Nothing could have caused the Abbé Lacordaire greater joy ; it amounted to a sort of intoxication. He no longer felt himself isolated, but had found a powerful support. The ideas which he was about to study in America had unexpectedly found in his own country an illustrious defender, a French O'Connell, who was to bring them to a brilliant issue. The great question of the day was going to be discussed on a field which had been swept clear by the late storm—the question, namely, of the true relations between Church and State. Could he quit his country at a moment when such important interests were about to be discussed ? Was it not like desertion on the eve of a battle ? And could he refuse to aid in the examination of the very questions which had so long held possession of his mind ? It was not to be thought of.

And thus the same enthusiastic love of liberty which was carrying this ardent and generous soul to a country blest with a larger freedom than his own, stopped him at the very moment of his departure, and fixed him for ever to take part in the destinies and struggles of his native land.

CHAPTER V.

1830—1832.

The "Avenir" newspaper—The Abbé Lacordaire, M. de la Mennais, and M. de Montalembert—Their journey to Rome—Condemnation of the "Avenir"—Exemplary submission of the Abbé Lacordaire—Rupture with M. de la Mennais.

THE *Avenir* was begun on the 15th of October 1830, before the last echoes of that tempest which had overthrown the altar, the throne, and society, had entirely died away.

In the present day, when most of the editors of that famous journal have been called to God, and when so much light has been shed over the problems they discussed, that it needs no prophetic powers to foresee the probable and speedy revival of those great questions mooted in the *Avenir*, it would be an interesting task to study that short and singular phase of religious controversy. Such a study will not be looked for in these pages. It would distract us from our main object, which is to make known to our readers something of the interior life of Père Lacordaire. Nevertheless, it is impossible for us not to pause for one moment, in order to distinguish the share taken in this affair by the young public writer, from that in which the man and the priest took part. Our silence might otherwise appear to arise out of a fear of encountering matter injurious to the memory of him we so much revere. But this would be a mistake. We are not writing a panegyric, and whilst depicting a character full of virtues, we feel no difficulty in admitting the existence of faults and infirmities, the result of which has only been to put forth in a broader light his uprightness of intention and his profound humility both of intellect and heart.

What then did the editors of the *Avenir* propose? They declared their object plainly enough : it was to claim back for the Church of France every privilege of liberty, whilst rejecting none of its burdens. The Revolution had just made a clean sweep of all ancient traditions. Since the restoration of order and public worship at the beginning of the century, the clergy had learnt to their cost the real value of that protection granted by a power which was ill-informed as to the real nature of its relations with the Church ; they had found out by experience what they had gained in consideration under the Empire, under the Restoration, and under the recently established régime of the *bourgeoisie*. What attitude were they to assume towards the new government ? Would the old endeavours to form an alliance between the throne and the altar now recommence ? The *Avenir* was founded to preserve them from this temptation. Its programme was, respect for the charter, and for just laws ; but for the rest, an absolute independence of the civil government. It consequently advocated liberty of opinion for the press, and war against arbitrary power and privilege ; liberty of education, and war against the monopoly of the university ;[1] liberty

[1] A word of explanation on the subject of the system of State education existing in France at the time here spoken of may assist the English reader in comprehending many allusions in Père Lacordaire's life, which might otherwise perplex him. The *Code Napoleon* centralised education like everything else. By it the local ecclesiastical schools, originally founded by the bishops, and dependent on voluntary support, were almost all abolished, one only being suffered to remain in each department, and a government *lyceum* was erected in its immediate vicinity. An imperial university was placed over all, consisting of what in England we should call a Board, presided over by a minister of State, and

of association, and war against the old antimonastic laws revived in evil times; the liberty and moral independence of the clergy, and war against the Budget of Public Worship. Very vague and uncertain limits were assigned to these different liberties, and the reserves stipulated for in the declarations of doctrine disappeared often enough when the writers were carried away by the ardour of discussion, and the vehemence of invective. They were more frequently engaged, we must confess, in obtaining the thing they sought than in preventing its abuse. Far too radical in their principles, the polemics of the journal were yet more so in the course of action which they recommended. "Liberty is not given, it is taken," was a phrase continually repeated; nor did they scruple to add example to precept. Every morning the charge was sounded, and every day witnessed some new feat of arms. The clergy were addressed as an army drawn up in battle array. Every means was tried to kindle their ardour; the zeal of the tardy was stimulated, and deserters were set in the pillory. The chiefs of the party were harangued, the plan of campaign indicated beforehand, the enemy pointed out and pursued to death. Philosophers, enemies of religion, ministers, miserable pro-consuls, members of the university, citizens, and Gallicans were all attacked at once. Resistance did but rouse the spirit of the combatants; it seemed as though the sun always set too early on their warlike ardour. Patience and discretion were not much regarded in their system of tactics; they wanted to have everything at once, and could not wait for to-morrow, and what was not granted with a good grace was to be snatched by force, and at the point of the sword. This haughty and antagonistic attitude, this want of experience in

exercising absolute power over the rectors of academies and Lyceums. Without a licence from this university no one could open a school. It was against this State monopoly of education that Lacordaire and his friends so manfully did battle.— *Translator's Note.*

men, and things, more excusable in the young disciples than it was in their master, formed, in our
opinion, the greatest fault of the *Avenir.* Its errors
and exaggerations of doctrine might have been corrected with time, good advice, and the practical
teaching of facts. But those haughty accents, so
strange when heard from the lips of priests, alarmed
even their friends, and created a certain consternation
at Rome—Rome ever calm as truth, and patient as
eternity. The responsibility of this false attitude
must be charged chiefly on the Abbé de la Mennais,
and the Abbé Lacordaire. It was the latter who
drew up the most incendiary harangues, and opened
the most difficult questions. The articles on the suppression of the Budget of the clergy were from his
pen. Later on, it is true, he took pains in the *Ere
Nouvelle* to refute his own arguments. He there defended the very opposite thesis to that which called
for the suppression of the Budget of Public Worship;[1]
but if right and justice were on the side of the journal
of 1848, it is not to be doubted that warmth and eloquence were all on that of the journal of 1830. This
may be seen from the following extract, which, at the
same time, gives some idea of the key to which the
voices of the speakers were attuned :

" We are paid by our enemies, by those who look
upon us as either hypocrites or fools, and who are
persuaded that our very existence depends on their
money. They are our debtors, no doubt, but the
worst of it is, that although our debtors, they have
come to believe that they are bestowing an alms upon
us, and an alms which it is absurd to pay. Thus their
treatment of us grows so injurious that they who put

---

[1] By the Budget of Public Worship is meant the sum of money voted
by the French Government every year for the payment of the clergy.
The Church property seized at the great Revolution was never restored,
and on the restoration of the Catholic worship, the 14th Article of the
Concordat between Napoleon and Pius VII. provided that the government should pay a certain fixed salary to every bishop and parish priest,
by way of compensation.

up with it must necessarily fall below contempt. Just imagine a debtor, who, meeting his creditor, should fling a few coins into the mud, saying, ' Go and work, you idle rascal, go and work !' Yet this is how our enemies treat us, and it is now thirty years and four months since we have been contented to stoop down and pick up the money. . . . .

" Catholic priests ! the question is of your blood, a thing we cannot despise. We are as poor as you ; our only salary is our independence. We know nothing more of to-morrow than this, that Providence will rise much earlier than the sun. How, indeed, could we treat the blood of our brethren with in-difference ? Their people is our people, their God our God, their life is ours, and more to us than our own. But we deeply feel your state of servitude, and we believe that poverty is a hundred times more honourable than the insults of a prefect or the ruin of the Church. Have men ever been treated with greater contempt ? They ridicule your prayers, and then order you to sing them. If you do not obey, you are seditious men, to whom, of course, the treasury is closed ; and if you do obey, you become so vile in their eyes that language has no terms to express what they think of you. And yet all the while the only relation in which they stand to the Church is that of her *debtors !*

" Catholic priests ! we, for our part, protest against this martyrdom of disgrace. So long as we have breath we shall call heaven and earth to witness that we are pure from the blood which they are drawing drop by drop from your veins. Some among you may hate us if they will, they may accuse us of drawing down misery on their heads. Some day, perhaps, we shall go forth into the world with their malediction, a little foreign earth will cover our despised ashes ; but at the hour of awakening we trust that God will find in our bones that love for you that will never have been extinguished !"[1]

[1] *Avenir,* t. L, p. 251, 1—58.

But whilst pointing out the errors of doctrine, and the declamatory inflation of tone exhibited by these writers, we must do justice to their sincere good faith, the purity of their aims, the uprightness of their intentions, and, above all, their perfect docility to the chair of St. Peter. The editors always protested that they desired to submit their doctrines to the Holy See, and to abide by its decision. Three months after the commencement of the journal they all signed a declaration containing their principal theories, which terminates as follows :

" If in the principles which we profess there should be anything contrary to the Catholic faith or doctrine, we implore the Vicar of Jesus Christ to warn us of it, renewing to him the promise of our perfect docility. Our first principle, the vital principle of all our writings, the very soul of our intellect, is that Truth is not a good peculiar to ourselves; and from our teaching on the subject of reason up to our faith in the Eternal Chair of Peter, we are, as it were, enveloped on all sides in a net of obedience. With the grace of God we shall end as we have begun. After passing our days full of trials and combats, when our last sigh shall have marked the end of our labours, the world may, as we trust, without fear of being contradicted by any memory of our former lives, engrave on our tombs those words of Fénélon, 'O Holy Church of Rome! if I forget thee, may I forget my very self!'"

We must also notice many extenuating circumstances ; the chaos of opinions which followed in the wake of the Revolution, the division of parties, the new situation of the clergy, the ill-will of the government, the equivocal choice of several bishops, priests insulted, religious expelled, and churches violated for a refusal of ecclesiastical sepulture. It was a pitched battle, in which the whole line was engaged, and we must not look for much calm or moderation from men standing under the fire of the enemy.

7—2

Nor, finally, let us forget the real services rendered by this journal to the cause of religion ; how it animated the clergy to the defence of their rights; humbled Gallicanism, and vindicated, if it did not actually conquer, the right of association and free education, with a tenacity of purpose which presaged sooner or later an infallible triumph. Nothing could be weaker or more thoroughly disarmed than the French clergy of that period in face of public opinion. Despots, small and great, had promised themselves the satisfaction of striking without mercy at these detested remains of fanaticism and superstition. But without their permission, a tribune had been erected in the name of religion and liberty, whence every morning some fresh abuse was denounced by eloquent writers, who took the victims of despotism under the shelter of their ægis, scourged the guilty without mercy, and demanded justice from the Executive. This tribune was, in fact, a power, and put a stop to more than one petty vexation. If the tidings came that a sub-prefect of the government had broken open the doors of a church in order to introduce a corpse (to which the ecclesiastical authorities had for certain reasons refused Christian burial),[1] that a capuchin had

---

[1] Reference is here made to the celebrated article from Lacordaire's pen on occasion of the violation of the church at Aubusson, which was broken open by order of the sub-prefect, in consequence of the parish priest having refused to give ecclesiastical sepulture to the body of a notorious and impenitent sinner.

"Your brother," he says, "has done well ; but this feeble shadow of a pro-consul thought that so much independence was unsuitable in so vile and contemptible a person as a Catholic priest. He issued orders, therefore, that the corpse should be brought into the church, even were it necessary for that purpose to use violence, and to break open the doors of the asylum, where, under the protection of the laws and of liberty, reposes the God of the universe and of the majority of Frenchmen.

"His will was accomplished ; a handful of national guards carried the coffin into the church ; and by orders of the government, force and death violated the sanctuary of God, and that without any popular *émeute*. The dwelling of a citizen cannot be thus broken into without the intervention of justice ; but justice was not so much as appealed to on this occasion when they bade religion veil her face before their

been arrested at the gates of his own convent for
wearing an illegal costume ; that six hundred soldiers
and gendarmes had, at the order of a minister, gutted
a house of Trappists as though it were a besieged
fortress, and had turned out the religious like so many
bandits, the *Avenir* raised its voice. It was always
the Abbé Lacordaire who, on these occasions, undertook the defence of the oppressed parties, and that
with so cutting and terrible an eloquence that the
aggressors long after bore the marks of his blows.

Every cause that was at the same time just and
unprotected, both within and without the French territory, found in the *Avenir* a ready defence. It is in
an article from the pen of the Abbé Lacordaire that
we find a passage on the temporal power of the Pope,
which one might think had been written in reference
to present events.

"Neither the East nor the West has been able to
take Rome out of the hands of a priest, since the day
when the Roman eagle took its flight from Italy to

---

swords. A simple sub-prefect, a paid official, liable at any moment to
be removed from his office, sitting quietly in his own home, which was
guarded from the insults of arbitrary power by thirty millions of men,
thought fit to send a corpse into the house of God. He did that whilst
you were relying tranquilly on the faith which had been sworn in the
charter of the 7th August, and whilst they were requiring your prayers
to bless the head of a great nation in the person of the king. He did
that in defiance of the law, which declares all forms of religious worship
to be free ; and how can any worship be free if its temple and its altar
be not free, and if they are able to bring in their dead clay with arms in
their hands? He offered this insult to one half the people of France,
&c, this sub-prefect !"

In another passage he gives expression to his extreme views on the
subject of the separation between Church and State, which he then
advocated. "Now the man who thus braved so many Frenchmen in
their religion, and who has treated one of their places of worship with
less respect than he should treat a stable, this man is still seated in his
chimney-corner, tranquil and self-satisfied. But you would have made
him turn pale if, staff in hand and with covered head, you had taken
your dishonoured God and carried Him into some poor hut of fir
branches, vowing as you did so never again to expose Him to the disgrace of reposing in one of the temples of the State."—*Avenir* for Nov.
20, 1830.—*Translator's Note.*

the Bosphorus ; and events seemingly incredible have, age after age, made a throne of the Apostolic Chair, and an Eternal City out of nine generations of ruins. 'We may well believe,' says Fleury, 'that it is by a particular effect of Divine Providence that the Pope finds himself independent, and the master of a territory sufficiently powerful to prevent his being easily oppressed by other sovereigns.' Yes, doubtless, we may believe this. It was necessary that the paternal and independent character, which is the very soul of the Christian priesthood, should have one striking type in the world ; and everything would have been lost if any prince could have taken the Roman Church and its head into his pay. Up to the time of Constantine this danger did not exist, and Amighty God therefore provided no temporal sovereignty for the Bishop of Rome ; but as soon as an alliance had been signed between religion and the empire, we see at once the splendour of the Cæsars taking flight to the very extremity of Europe, and the Pope spared the shame of becoming their courtier.

"Nevertheless the Roman Church still remained poor ; she continued to live on alms rather than on her patrimony, in order that Christian priests might never forget that the charity of the faithful is their true source of revenue. At once the daughter and the mother of the world, Rome both receives and gives life, happy to accept the peace of her children, which she would not exchange for the gold of kings. Kings have more than once already proposed such an exchange ; they have built palaces to receive her, they have trusted to see her the slave of their Budgets, but all the world knows what has been her reply."[1]

Neither is it without a lively emotion that we have found in the pages of this journal the first salutation uttered by a generous soul to the distracted land of Poland. It is delightful to find the Count de Montalembert, then in the twentieth year of his age, expres-

[1] *Avenir,* t. i. p. 182.

sing himself with a faith and ardent enthusiasm which still move us, as they did when we first listened to his defence of a cause always heroic, and, alas ! always unfortunate !

"At last," he exclaims, "Poland has uttered her wakening cry; at last she has shaken off her chains and bids defiance to her barbarous tyrants : brave unhappy Poland, so deeply calumniated, so bitterly oppressed, so dear to all free and Catholic hearts ! May she who has so long struggled for liberty, and who has kept unstained her ancient faith, once more regain her place among the nations! The sacrilegious legacy bequeathed to us by the eighteenth century exists no longer ; its traces are effaced from the map of Europe ; the impious work of the Congress of Vienna is annihilated, and enslaved races and outraged creeds have recovered their rights. Never more shall we behold a pitiless diplomacy distributing men like so many vile cattle, and selling the faith of nations to the highest bidder. For fifteen years God has suffered His wrath to slumber, but now it is up and awake. Kings of Europe, without faith and without love, kings who have forgotten God ! you will all in turn be smitten ; you will all learn to know the weakness of those thrones on which you thought to sit without His aid. Free and Catholic Poland ! native soil of Sobieski and Kosciusko, you who in the seventeenth as in the eighteenth century were the heroine of decaying faith, we hail the new day now dawning on you, and invite you to the sublime alliance of God and liberty!" [1]

We have already mentioned the name of M. de Montalembert. On hearing of the foundation of the *Avenir*, he had hastened from Ireland in order to enter public life in defence of that twofold cause of God and liberty to which he always remained attached. There, at the house of M. de la Mennais, he for the first time met the Abbé Lacordaire. Their close and ardent friendship dates from that day. The lively picture

[1] *Avenir*, t. i. p. 403.

which M. de Montalembert has drawn of their first meeting allows us to guess something of his feelings ; and gladly would we give free vent to our own, and say all we think of that beautiful friendship from which the survivor's generous but faltering hand has lifted a corner of the veil. But the time has not come. As to the Abbé Lacordaire, he had long been hoping for such a moment as this. He had never yet found the affection for which he had always longed. But henceforth his lowliness was at an end, and his mother could no longer say to him, " You have no friends ! " Speaking of this interview, he says of his newly-found treasure, " He is a charming youth, and I love him as if he were a plebeian. I am sure that, if he lives, his destiny will be as pure as one of the mountain lakes of Switzerland, and as famous." In the little treatise on Christian friendship which he wrote in honour of St. Mary Magdalen towards the close of his life, there occurs a vivid passage describing the commencement of such an affection between two young hearts, in which it has always seemed to us he must have recalled the precious memory of this first meeting. It is as follows :

" When a young man, aided by the grace of Christ, subjects his passions under the yoke of chastity, he experiences an expansion of heart which is in exact proportion to the guard he exercises over his senses. The necessity of loving, which is bound up with our nature itself, then displays itself in the ardour with which he pours himself forth into another soul as warm-hearted and as innocent as his own. It will not be long before he finds such a soul. It will naturally present itself to him, just as plants spring up spontaneously in the soil proper to their growth. Sympathy is never refused to him who is capable of inspiring it, and he who gives it to others will always inspire it himself. Every pure heart feels it, and will therefore draw to itself other hearts. This is the case at every age, but specially in youth, when the brow is decked with its tenderest graces, and illumined with the splendour of that higher order of beauty which attracts even the heart of God. It was thus that David appeared in the eyes of Jonathan, on the day when the young champion entered the tent of Saul, holding in his hand the head of Goliath, and when questioned by the king as to his origin, he replied, 'I am the son of thy servant Isai, of Bethlehem.' '*Immediately*,' says the Scripture, '*the soul of Jonathan was knit with the soul of David, and Jonathan loved him as his own soul.*'[1] O wonderful effect of a single glance! Only yesterday David had been keeping his father's flock, and Jonathan was on the steps of the throne; and now in a moment the distance between them is annihilated, and the shepherd and the prince become, to use the expression of Holy Scripture, *one soul.* For in that youth, whose cheek still retained the bloom of boyhood, even while he bore in his manly hand the bloody spoils of a conquered enemy, Jonathan discerned the hero; and David, beholding the son of his king spring forward to meet him, free from all jealousy of his triumph and all pride of rank, saw in that generous movement a heart capable of loving, and one therefore worthy of being loved!"[2]

It was thus with Lacordaire and Montalembert. Opposite in character, yet made for one another, they understood each other at the first glance. "Would that I could paint him," says M. de Montalembert, "such as he appeared to me when still in all the charm and splendour of his youth! He was then twenty-eight years of age; he wore the lay costume, for the state of Paris at that time did not allow of priests wearing the ecclesiastical dress. His tall, thin figure, regular features, and sculptured brow, the majestic bearing of his head, his dark and sparkling eye, and an indescribable air about his person at once noble, refined, yet singularly modest—all this was

---

[1] 1 Kings xv. ii. 1.   [2] "St. Mary Magdalen," p. 35.

but the outside covering of a soul which seemed always ready to overflow, not only in the freedom of the public speaker, but in the outpourings of private friendship. His flashing glance revealed at one and the same time treasures of passion and of tenderness; it sought not merely for enemies to combat, but also for hearts to attract and overcome . . . . His voice, already so powerful and vibrating, could sometimes assume accents of surpassing sweetness. Born to combat and to conquer, he was already sealed with the double royalty of the soul and the intellect. He appeared to me at once charming and terrible, the very type of enthusiasm for Right, or of virtue armed for the defence of Truth. I saw in him an elect soul, predestined to everything which the youthful heart most worships and desires—namely, genius and glory."[1]

M. de la Mennais, on the other hand, had no influence over the Abbé Lacordaire save that of genius. As a priest, a philosopher and a man, his power hardly made itself felt. It is true that in one of the actions brought against the *Avenir*, when addressing the jury which was to judge them both, the Abbé Lacordaire saluted the illustrious master who stood beside him, as "the great man who permitted him to call him friend," but this was rather a generous movement in favour of his fellow-defendant than any real emotion of heart. Far be it from us to accuse the memory, which is, alas! already too unhappy, of a man whom God has judged! Far from us be the vile pleasure of striking an enemy already overthrown and too severely punished! The faults of men should no more have a retrospective action than their laws. But simple regard for truth obliges us to say that the Abbé Lacordaire was never more than half admitted into his master's confidence, in the same way as he never perfectly submitted to his philosophic ideas. His letters of this epoch are a proof of what we say. We shall specially quote those written

[1] Montalembert, *Le Père Lacordaire*, p. 13.

before the date of 1830, at a time when M. de la
Mennais was *the most celebrated* and *the most venerated
priest in France*,[1] when the first volume of his *Essay
on Indifference* had caused him to be proclaimed the
last of the Fathers of the Church ; and when he appeared to the young priest, surrounded by a halo of
undisputed glory. In 1825 he wrote : "I like neither
the system of M. de la Mennais, which I think false,
nor his political opinions, which appear to me exaggerated ;" and in 1827 he wrote to a friend who had
just reproduced the opinions of his master in a con-
troversial work :—" Believe me, that if ever I am
persuaded of the truth of your doctrines I will give
my life for them. But for that I shall require time,
and light from God." Another passage written in
1834, explains to us how it was that he suffered this
system to be imposed upon his acceptance rather out
of lassitude than conviction. "After my conversion,"
he writes, "I read the works of M. de la Mennais,
that celebrated man, the defender of my resuscitated
faith, and I admired them on many accounts ; but
two things deserve notice. I thought I understood
his philosophy, although in point of fact I did not
(as I discovered later on ;) and when in course of
time I came to understand it better, it threw me into
endless perplexities. I studied it for six consecutive
years, from 1824 to 1830, without ever being able to
settle my doubts, though I was much urged by my
friends, many of whom were disciples of M. de la
Mennais. It was only on the eve of the year 1830
that I at last gave in my adhesion, rather out of
weariness than entire conviction ; for even in the
thick of my labours in the *Avenir*, I was from time to
time conscious of growing ideas which were opposed
to his philosophy ; and I now clearly see the falsehood of those opinions which I embraced with so
much hesitation."[2]

[1] Montalembert, *Le Père Lacordaire*, p. 13.
[2] "Considerations on the Philosophic System of M. de la Mennais,"
chap. ix. p. 123.

If the absolute notions of M. de la Mennais were not acceptable to his young fellow-labourer, his character was hardly more attractive to him. He who on the very first day of their acquaintance had given his heart to M. de Montalembert, never felt himself drawn towards their common master. They were alike in some points of their public character, in their indomitable faith in their cause, and in the fire and passion which they brought into the struggle ; but, on the other hand, they were parted far asunder in all that regarded their interior and private life. Whilst the one hardly ever knew how to stop in a course he had once begun, the other was capable of those sudden retractations, which evince no less respect for truth than humility of heart. The first had in a supereminent degree those qualities of mind which lead to an over-fondness for systematising, and thence, when the intellect is not kept under restraint, to error and heresy ; the second, with his faculties more perfectly balanced, after having listened to the voice of reason, lent a yet more willing ear to the language of the heart, that gentle counsellor, which all the thunder-stricken seraphim have rejected. The Abbé Lacordaire at this very epoch gave utterance to words which in part explain his life :—" *Do not let us chain our hearts to our ideas.*" His admiration for his master's genius did not extend to his character as a man, and a secret sentiment of distrust took possession of him, as he watched the movements of that great and powerful mind who had climbed to the lofty eminence he held, without having a sufficient counterpoise on the side of the heart.

It was not that M. de la Mennais was wanting in kindness ; the witness who was at this time best qualified to judge, M. de Montalembert, affirms " that at certain moments he knew how to be the tenderest and most paternal of men;" but to be so, it was, perhaps, necessary for him to feel himself entirely acceptable to those on whom such testimonies of regard were lavished. Self-love did not certainly abandon its claims, and, as we have seen, the Abbé Lacordaire was never quite subdued by his master's power of fascination. Both of them tacitly felt this ; and the same authority just quoted adds, in the very same sentence :— " M. de la Mennais never showed any tenderness towards Lacordaire."

Friendship in Père Lacordaire manifested itself at once, by confidence. If his friend were a priest, his first desire and his greatest happiness was to go to confession to him. It was a true confession, but it was also an effusion of heart ; the friend mingled with the penitent, and in this close intercourse he was certainly the happiest of the two parties concerned, so delicate was his appreciation of all that is deepest and sweetest in the harmonious union of nature and grace, of the man and the Christian. But this sort of manifestation requires in him who receives it a certain goodness of heart which rendered Père Lacordaire rather difficult in his choice of confidants. Did he find such a qualification in M. de la Mennais ? in him to whom were at that time attributed those celebrated words, the suitability of which in one of his calling is somewhat equivocal?—"*I will make them see what it is to be a priest!*" We may be permitted to doubt it. Père Lacordaire said of himself :—" When I enter an assembly of priests, one of my first movements is to look out for the one to whom I would most willingly confess. I always find him, but not in everybody." I am not aware if he ever confessed to M. de la Mennais, but I am disposed to think not.

We shall not enter into any detailed account of the labours of the *Avenir*, nor of the unexpected train of events which resulted in its final suppression. All this does not enter into our subject. Moreover, M. de Montalembert has already given the narrative of these events to the public. The pages he has written will not soon be forgotten, and will furnish a prologue to the history of the Catholic and liberal movement of the nineteenth century.

Nevertheless this narrative has one fault : that of leaving too much in the shade the glorious part which the author himself took in the struggle. In the affair of the Free School,[1] for example, "the first act of that great lawsuit which was only to be gained twenty years later," in that bold and generous effort of three men who first opened the breach, M. de Montalembert disappears behind his friend, who is placed in full relief and in the front rank, and who enjoys the honours of the whole affair, whether at the school, before the Commissary of Police, or before the illustrious audience in the Chambers. He quotes that exordium known to all the world : " Noble peers, I look around me, and I am astonished." He tells of the profound and lasting impression produced on the Chambers by the marvels of that enchanting eloquence. Then he adds, " Not more than five or six of the noble peers thus addressed are yet surviving ; but they will not contradict me when I affirm that the whole Chamber, after listening *coldly and patiently* to the other pleadings, remained as it were fascinated by the words and the presence of the young orator." But the memory of the historian has here proved unfaithful. The five or six peers who still survive will certainly not contradict me, if I in my turn affirm that the judges were neither cold nor insensible to the first of these pleadings. The journals of the day, which took as much pains in describing the general

[1] In the year 1820 M. de Montalembert, M. de Coux, and the Abbé Lacordaire determined to try the question of Liberty of Teaching, by themselves opening a school, in defiance of the privileges claimed by the University, in virtue of which all private unlicensed schools were then prohibited. The Commissary of Police lost no time in affixing seals on the school door, turning out the children, and putting the key in his pocket. The trial of the three culprits took place before the Court of Peers, and the cause was decided against them. But the speech of M. de Montalembert, then a youth only twenty years of age, inflicted a severe blow on the prestige of the University : it was a victory which eventually cost the victors dear.—*Translator's Note.*

aspect of the public assemblies as in gathering up the words of the speakers, depict to us the peers in the Palais Médicis as motionless and touched to the very heart, hardly breathing as they listened to that eloquence at once so youthful yet so masculine, so haughty yet so humble, so full at once of irony, of passion, of fire, and of sound logic. The accused became the accuser; every one as he listened forgot the crime, the judges, and his own preconceived views of the cause; the bench where the defendants sat became a tribune, and all listened in religious silence to the youth of twenty who at one bound had taken his place among the first orators of the Chambers of France. On reading this discourse over again, at so great a distance of time, and when the moral temperature of society is so different, we once more experience the warm emotions of that memorable day, and call to mind the just and happy expression of a certain witty academician, who bade us observe the noble Chamber "smiling at the eloquence of one of the criminals, as some grey-haired old man might have done as he watched the mutinous vivacity of the last scion of his race."[1] We cannot resist the pleasure of quoting a few lines, were it only for the sake of reminding him on whom success has since been so lavishly poured out, of this his first, and perhaps his most brilliant triumph. "As to us," he exclaimed, "we really do not know on what ground we can inspire any terror to the minister, nor why we have appeared worthy of his ill-treatment. How was it that he did not despise us from the height of his own greatness? Nothing now remains to us of our former power or riches. The sceptre which once extended over us its envied protection has been broken, and its fragments cast into the mire. The world, we are told on all sides, is withdrawn from us. Well, we are left alone, as much alone as they can be who have eighteen centuries of past memories, and an immortal

---

[1] Le Prince de Broglie, *Discours de Réception à l'Académie.*

hope. Those who repudiate such memories and
despise such a hope, might at least leave us alone in
our abandonment and solitude; it is strange that
they should be scared at our feeble efforts, and it is
surely imprudent for them to allow their terror to betray their weakness. One of two things, either we
have truth and justice on our side, and these our
enemies are bound to respect; or we are poor
wanderers, victims of a cruel destiny, and with
nothing to hope from the future,—if so, why hasten
our last sigh? Why must your despotism conspire
against our dying struggles? If our faith must
indeed expire, suffer us at least to choose its grave,
and let it be buried with the liberty of the world! It
was our faith that first raised that noble standard
under which the whole human race is this day drawn
up in order of battle! Suffer her at least to use that
sacred banner as her winding-sheet."[1]

The issue of the trial is well known. Lost before
the High Court of Judicature, the cause was gained
before one yet higher and more sovereign, that of
public opinion; and in reference to this defeat, the
Abbé Lacordaire was able to quote those words of
Montaigne, which he often had occasion to repeat,
" There are some triumphant defeats, of which victory
herself might be jealous."

Clouds were meanwhile gathering over the head
of the *Avenir*. If it could reckon many zealous partisans, specially among the younger clergy, it had
nevertheless enemies among men of all parties. The
other journals of every shade of opinion made war
upon it; those of the democratic opposition, as well
as those which supported the government; the legitimist papers, and those of the old clerical school. The
philosophic opinions of M. de la Mennais and the
absolute theories of his journal, particularly those
which represented the State payment of the clergy as
the badge of shame and slavery, had excited a certain

[1] Article from the *Avenir*, t. vi. p. 282.

feeling of distrust among the Episcopacy, which daily increased. The young disciples of M. de la Mennais were never afraid of a combat; but their faith and loyalty could not endure the vague suspicions raised against their orthodoxy. They began to desire a clear, open explanation, and they determined to go and demand it from the judge of all ecclesiastical controversies, the successor of St. Peter.

It was the Abbé Lacordaire to whom the idea of this journey to Rome first occurred, at a moment when their exhausted funds, and the opposition raised against them by a certain party among the clergy, threatened the inevitable ruin of the journal. He saw in this plan an opportunity " of justifying their intentions to the Holy See, of submitting all their ideas to its decision, and of thus giving a striking proof of their sincerity and orthodoxy which, happen what might, would always bring a blessing on them, and would be, as it were, a weapon snatched out of the hands of their enemies."[1]

The prudence of patience, and the notion of waiting for an opportune time, are always the last ideas which ardent and impetuous minds take into account. It is their ordinary fault to forget that the logic of facts is not so urgent as the logic of ideas; that if the seed only arrives at maturity after it has lain for long months in the ground, the mind of the public is a yet colder soil, and the ideas which germinate there are plants of even slower growth; that it is much for a man to be able during his life to cast forth into the world one fruitful principle, and that we may think ourselves happy if the sun of the next generation sees it strike root and blossom. This was the grand error of the editors of the *Avenir*. Forgetting the very title of their journal, they would have everything at once. Like unmanageable children, they had already thrown themselves with naked swords across the path of the civil authority, and now they were going with

[1] Memoirs.

still less consideration to dash themselves against the power which is not of this world. They were about to demand a prompt and definitive solution from the oracle which most rarely enunciates such decisions on controverted questions, and which by so doing shows a far greater respect for true liberty than is evinced by many of her noisiest advocates.

Accordingly, the three principal editors, the Abbé de la Mennais, the Abbé Lacordaire, and M. de Montalembert, set out for Rome, where they arrived about the end of December 1831. They were coldly received. Before granting them an audience the Holy Father required them to send in a memorial on their views and intentions. The Abbé Lacordaire drew it up. Two months later Cardinal Pacca replied in a note that their doctrines would be examined, and that meanwhile they might return to France. After this Pope Gregory XVI. consented to give them audience, received them kindly, but said not one word which bore reference to the *Avenir*.

This conduct on the part of the Roman court, which so deeply wounded the pride of M. de la Mennais, opened the eyes of the Abbé Lacordaire. Removed at a distance from Paris, the field of battle, restored to himself, enlightened and purified by that calm and luminous atmosphere which one breathes at Rome, the dawn arose in his soul, and he understood the truth. He saw that not being able to give its approbation, the Holy See could do nothing kinder or more favourable than to keep silence, and say, " We will examine." And, above all, he understood Rome.

Paris is to Rome, in a religious point of view, what a frontier constantly harassed by the enemy is to a great capital standing in tranquillity behind her lofty walls ; or what the crew of a ship is to the pilot who directs her. When the head has grown grey, and we look back at the distance of thirty years over our own history, which of us cannot detect himself smiling at the remembrance of those many infallible systems,

which we were constantly constructing in our younger
years, and at that simple conviction which we had
that the world was going to let itself be transformed
according to our ideas? A journey from Paris to
Rome often produces the same effect, and dispels the
same illusions. We leave a capital where all is youth,
ardour, and eagerness, and we enter the city of old
men and sages, the city which is astonished at nothing
because she has watched all human greatness pass
away like the stream which bathes the foot of her
hills; where truth alone remains standing, impassible,
eternal. The Abbé Lacordaire went through this
salutary disenchantment. He had come from Paris
in company with a man who had made himself a
name as vast as Europe. This man was possessed of
genius, an eloquent pen, and disciples who looked on
him as the only one who could save the Church in
her struggle with society. How was the Church
about to receive him? She was going to take scarcely
the smallest notice of him. But he brings a system
which contains her salvation?—a system? the Church
has seen them all in their turn, but salvation has
never come to her from thence. But this man possesses the secrets of the future, and he comes to tell
the Church how she is to speak to kings and to nations?
The Church has received from on high the gift of
Counsel as she has received the Spirit of Truth.
Society draws its life from her, and no man can teach
her what she owes to nations or kings.

This wonderful calm of the truth which has faith
in itself, this apparent sleep of the Vicar of Christ on
his bark in the midst of the tempest, this grandeur, in
short, of Christian Rome, was a revelation to the
Abbé Lacordaire. While the pride of his master
kept him chained in his blindness, the humility of the
disciple delivered him from *the most terrible of all
oppressions, that of the intellect.* He had struggled
with a genius superior to his own, and had ended by
being conquered; this time he encountered, not the

8—2

genius of man, but that of God in His visible representative, and he joyfully bowed before its sweet and sovereign majesty. It was not without a combat, however, nor without having known " the tortures of conscience struggling with genius," as he then expressed it to his friend. But that same power, which he was beginning better to understand, came to his aid and delivered him. " I did not deliver myself," he wrote ; "when I arrived at Rome, at the tomb of the Holy Apostles, St. Peter and St. Paul, I knelt down and said to God, 'Lord, I begin to feel my weakness, my sight fails me, truth and error alike escape my grasp; have pity on Thy servant who comes to Thee with a sincere heart ; hear the prayer of the poor.' I know neither the day nor the hour when it took place, but at last I saw what I had not before seen, and I left Rome free and victorious. I had learnt from my own experience that the Church is the deliverer of the human intellect ; and as from freedom of intellect all other freedoms necessarily flow, I perceived the questions which then agitated the world in their true light."[1]

Delivered from that philosophic system of *Universal Reason*,[2] which weighed on him like a kind of remorse,

---

[1] " Considerations on the Philosophic System of M. de la Mennais," ch. xii. p. 152.

[2] This expression refers to the peculiar theory put forward by M. de la Mennais on the subject of Certainty. Certainty, he said, could only be attained by some infallible means which could not deceive us. Now the private reason of any one particular man often deceives him. It cannot therefore be this infallible means. But the united reason of many men is an authority of much greater weight, and must be held to weigh in all cases against the reason of one. Finally, the united reason of the universal body of men is the highest possible authority which we can arrive at on earth, and the surest means, therefore, of arriving at certainty. For this authority is nothing less than human reason elevated to its highest degree of probability. This united sense, or reason of all men, he called Universal Reason, or *the common sense* (*le sens commun*), in a different signification to that which attaches to the English phrase. It is obvious that this theory, however plausible, concealed within it, as Lacordaire afterwards remarked, an *anti-supernatural element*, which, in his judgment, lay at the basis of the whole system of M. de la Mennais. For it went far towards claiming a sort of *natural* infallibility for the collective reason of a number of fallible men, unsupported by any special Divine assistance. — *Translator's Note.*

and to which he referred all the other errors of his
master, he blessed God and thanked Rome in humble
and simple accents. "After ten years spent in constant efforts to understand the true position of
philosophy with regard to the Church, after agitation
of mind, the consequences of which I hardly discerned, so quickly did wave follow on wave, and
tempest on tempest, whither had I arrived? At the
convictions possessed by all those who lean on the
mind of the Church rather than on their own. Oh
how just and holy is the providence of God, Who thus
sweetly cradles her docile children in the truth!
Others make the circle of the entire world; they seek
for something beyond their own country; but the
native land of the intellect is that which gives us light,
the only place in the whole world where the thoughts
of man are at rest. With what wondering admiration
did I not then feel the superiority of the Church, that
ineffable instinct by which she is guided, that divine
discernment which protects her from the smallest
shadow of illusion! . . .

"O Rome! it was thus that I beheld thee! Seated
amid the storms of Europe, I saw no anxiety on thy
brow, and no distrust of thyself; thy glance, turned
to the four quarters of the world, followed with sublime discernment the development of human affairs in
their connection with those that are divine; whilst
the tempest that left thee calm, because the Spirit of
God breathed in thee, gave thee, in the eyes of thy
child, less accustomed to the variations of ages, a
something which rendered his admiration full of compassion. O Rome! God knows I did not mistake
thee because I found no kings prostrate at thy gates!
I kissed thy dust with joy and unutterable reverence,
for Thou didst appear to me what thou truly art, the
benefactress of the human race during past ages, its
hope for the future, the only great thing still left in
Europe, the captive of universal jealousy, the Queen
of the world. A suppliant pilgrim, I brought back

from thee, not gold, or perfumes, or precious stones, but something rarer and more unknown, the treasure of Truth."[1]

"It was at this moment, as I venture to believe," writes M. de Montalembert, "that God for ever marked him with the seal of His grace, and laid up for him the reward due to his unshaken fidelity, so worthy of a priestly soul." We believe it also. The spectacle of this young priest kneeling before the Confession of St. Peter, and pouring out to God *the prayer of the poor*, strikes us as deeply touching ; and when we remember the arduous struggle he had just been maintaining in France, and the resistance which self-love must have offered to those words which are always so hard to pronounce, "I have been mistaken," when we bear in mind the prejudices he must have received from his early education against that element of infirmity, which is to be found in the *human* life of the Church ; and then, on the other hand, consider his full, prompt, and spontaneous adhesion to the judgment of Rome ; when we see him return so great in his humility, so free in his submission, so victorious in his very defeat, we recognise that noble character of the true priest, which, in his subsequent career, we feel will never disappoint us. We see in him the workman, formed like all those souls whom God chooses and fashions for His most difficult designs ; the man whom He will henceforth conduct in all His ways, because he has known how to become a little child ; the orator who will be able to receive glory without danger to himself, because he has already tasted the purer and higher glory of voluntary humiliation ; the writer, who can love liberty and fearlessly preach its defence in doubtful points, because he has acknowledged the rights of unity in

---

[1] "Considerations on the Philosophic System of M. de la Mennais," chap. xii. pp. 150-154. This was a refutation of the system. The Abbé Lacordaire did not publish this work until 1834, after the excitement caused by the publication of the *Paroles d'un Croyant.*

things certain ; the religious, who will hesitate before no humiliation, no sacrifice of independence, because he will already have pronounced his vows on the great arena of the martyrs. In fine, the man whose steps will be reckoned by history as so many benefits, and proclaimed as so many triumphs, for "the obedient man shall speak victories."[1]

Happy indeed would he have felt could he but have communicated the like sentiments of submission to M. de la Mennais. There was nothing that he did not urge in order to convince him of the necessity of this submission, and inspire him with courage to make it. After the note from Cardinal Pacca, and the audience with the Holy Father, he conjured him to resign himself and obey with simplicity. "Either," he said, "we should never have come here, or, having come, we must submit in silence." "No," replied M. de la Mennais, "I will provoke an immediate decision, and I will wait for it in Rome ; after that I will consider what is to be done." Resolved not to have anything more to do with the *Avenir*, and not to follow M. de la Mennais in the false path on which he was entering, and the unhappy termination of which he clearly foresaw, the Abbé Lacordaire set out alone for France, in the month of March 1832, four months before his companions.

Hardly had he returned to France, pursued by secret apprehensions of an approaching catastrophe, and by the remembrance of his friend whom he had left alone with M. de la Mennais, than he wrote to him :—"No spiritual separation has taken place between us. All my life I shall continue to defend the cause of liberty ; and indeed before M. de la Mennais had uttered a single word in her defence, I had consecrated to her my thoughts and my life. If he carries his new plan into execution, remember that all his former friends and fellow-labourers will abandon him, and that led on by false liberals into a course of action which has no

---

[1] Prov. xxi. 28.

chance of success, there are no words sad enough to express what will be the result." [1]

This new plan and its disastrous consequences were but too soon made known by the acts of M. de la Mennais. He determined at all costs, to procure an explanation. The Holy See, which judges, but never discusses, continued to preserve silence. The priest, who had already in his heart revolted from her yoke, lost patience, and after six months spent at Rome, he publicly announced that he should return to France and recommence the *Avenir*. This was a first and criminal act of resistance to the tacit, but unmistakable disapproval of the Head of the Church. On receiving the news the Abbé Lacordaire, in order more manifestly to separate his cause from that of the man whom he was resolved no longer to follow, set out for Germany, in order to spend some time there in retirement. Having reached Munich, he there met by chance M. de la Mennais and M. de Montalembert. Providence seemed to have sent him in order to soften the blow that was about to strike the unhappy priest. In fact, it was at Munich that they received the first news of the famous Encyclical of the 15th of August, 1832.

"I had hardly settled myself at my hotel," relates Père Lacordaire, "when my door opened, and M. de Montalembert entered. It was the custom in those days for the German newspapers to give in their daily sheets the names and addresses of new-comers ; and it had been thus that M. de Montalembert had learnt my arrival and my whereabouts. He took me at once to M. de la Mennais, who received me with signs of resentment. Our interview, however, had something solemn about it : we entered into conversation, and for two hours I endeavoured to demonstrate to him how vain were his hopes of being able to continue the *Avenir*, and what a blow he was about to strike at once at his reputation, his honour, and his faith. At last, whether that my words had convinced him, or that my determination to separate from him made some im-

[1] *Le Père Lacordaire*, by M. de Montalembert, p. 57.

pression on his mind, he uttered these words : ' Yes, it is true ; you see things in the right light.'   The next day the most distinguished writers and artists of Munich gave us a public dinner.   Towards the end of the repast, some one came to M. de la Mennais and begged him to come out for a moment, and an envoy of the Apostolic Nuncio presented to him a folded paper sealed with the Nuncio's seal.   He opened it, and saw that it contained an Encyclical Letter from Pope Gregory XVI., dated August 15, 1832.   A rapid glance at its contents soon told him that it was on the subject of the doctrines of the *Avenir*, and that it was unfavourable to them.   His decision was taken at once ; and without examining the precise import of the Pontifical Brief, he said to us, in a low tone, as he left the room : ' I have just received an Encyclical of the Pope against us—we must not hesitate to submit.' Then returning home he at once drew up in a few short but precise lines an act of submission with which the Pope was satisfied.

"Thus it seemed as if God had brought us all together at Munich, that we might together sign our sincere adhesion to the will of the Holy Father without distinction and without restriction ; without even reserving the manner in which we understood our own doctrines, and in which they might possibly have agreed with the theological prudence displayed in the Pontifical Act.   Content with having combated for the liberty of the Church, and for her reconciliation with the public laws of our country, we passed through France like conquered men, who were yet victorious over themselves, awaiting from the future that justice which the heat of party-spirit denied us."[1]

During the few days passed by the three travellers in Paris, an eminent writer, who at that time was on rather intimate terms with the Abbé Lacordaire, paid a visit to him and to M. de la Mennais, the impressions of which he gave in a private letter.

[1] *Memoirs.*

" I remember," he writes, "that when the Abbé Lacordaire returned from Rome with M. de la Mennais, having gone to pay them a visit at the house in the Rue Vaugirard, where they lodged, I first of all saw M. de la Mennais in a room on the ground-floor. He expressed himself on the subject of Rome and the Pope with a freedom which surprised me, since ostensibly he had just made his submission. He spoke of the Pope as of one of those men who are destined to bring forward great, and hitherto despaired of, remedies. On the contrary, when I went to see the Abbé Lacordaire, who was in a room on the first story, I was struck by the contrast—he spoke with extreme reserve and submission of the check they had received, and he particularly used the comparison of the grain of wheat, which, even supposing it to be sound, has need to be retarded in its growth, and made to sleep in the ground throughout a long winter.' It was thus that even whilst admitting a mixture of truth in the doctrines of the *Avenir*, he explained and justified the severity and resistance of the Holy See. I concluded from what I heard then, that there was no great harmony between the ground-floor and the first story, and I was the less surprised when, some time after, I heard of the complete separation which had taken place at La Chesnaie."

A noble sentiment of fidelity to misfortune, and the hope of alleviating the pain of sacrifice to the heart of his master, determined the Abbé Lacordaire to accompany M. de la Mennais back to Brittany. "As for the second time," he writes, " we reached the solitary manor-house of La Chesnaie, I believed I was bringing back a noble genius saved from shipwreck, a master more than ever venerated, and one of those glorious sufferers who bear on their brow 'that nameless gift which misfortune adds to the greatest virtues,' to use the words of Bossuet.

" My illusion, however, was profound. Before long, some of the young disciples of the fallen master came to rejoin him at La Chesnaie. The house resumed its accustomed character, its mingled air of solitude and animation; but if the old silence reigned in the woods, broken only from time to time by the voices of the tempest, and if the fair sky of Armorica was all unchanged, it was far different in the heart of the master. The wound there was raw and bleeding, and the sword was turned in it every day by the hand which ought to have plucked it out, and replaced it with God's own healing balm. Terrible clouds passed and repassed over that brow which peace had abandoned. Broken and threatening words issued from those lips which had once expressed the unction of the gospel. It seemed to me sometimes as if I were gazing upon Saul; but none of us possessed the harp of David to calm these sudden attacks of the evil spirit; and the terror of sad forebodings increased day by day in my dejected heart. At last the harrowing spectacle became too much for me to bear, and I wrote M. de la Mennais the following letter:

"LA CHESNAIE, *Dec.* 4, 1832.

"I shall leave La Chesnaie to-night. I do this out of a motive of honour, being convinced that henceforth my life must be useless to you on account of the difference of our views on the Church and on society, which only increases daily in spite of my sincere efforts to follow the development of your opinions. I believe that during my lifetime, and for a long time after I am dead, it will be impossible to establish a republic, either in France or in any other country in Europe; and I cannot take part in any system, the basis of which is a contrary persuasion, without renouncing my liberal ideas. I understand, and I believe, that the Church has had wise reasons, amid the profound corruption of parties for refusing to go on as fast as we desired. I respect her thoughts and my own. Perhaps your opinions are more just, more profound, and, considering your natural superiority to me, I ought to be convinced that it is so ; but reason does not make up the whole of a man. And so soon as I felt convinced of the impossibility of getting rid of the ideas which separate us, I saw that it was only just I should bring to a close a community of life, which is all to my advantage, and the burden of which rests entirely on you. My conscience obliges me to this, no less than my honour, for I must do something with my life in God's service, and not being able to follow you, what should I do here, save worry and discourage you, put obstacles in the way of your designs, and ruin myself ?

"You will never know, save in heaven, how much I have suffered for the last year, out of the mere fear of causing you pain. I have thought but of you in all my hesitations, my perplexities, my changes of feeling ; and however hard my existence may one day become, no grief of heart can ever equal what I have experienced on this occasion. I leave you to-day free from all anxiety on the side of the Church, enjoying a higher degree of public opinion than you have ever before done, and raised so much above your enemies that they seem brought to nothing ; it is therefore the best moment that I can choose for inflicting a grief upon you, which, believe me, will spare you many much greater ones. I do not as yet know what will become of me, whether I shall pass over to the United States, or stay in France, or in what position. Whatever I may do, rest assured of the respect and attachment which I shall always preserve for you ; and I beg of you to accept this assurance from a heart that is suffering not a little.

"I left La Chesnaie alone and on foot, while M. de la Mennais was out walking, according to his usual custom after dinner. At a certain spot in the road I perceived him through the hedge in the midst of his young disciples. I stopped, and after gazing for the last time on this great and unfortunate man, I continued my flight without knowing what was going to become of me, or feeling sure how God might regard the act I had just accomplished."[1]

This separation was much blamed by those who had not come to the same judgment as he had, and who failed to discern in this unhappy man a Saul from whom the Spirit of God was departing. He suffered from these reproaches without complaint, contenting himself with pouring out his whole heart to his best friend. " They accuse me of being merciless towards M. de la Mennais! If I had ever discovered in his heart a single sentiment of tenderness or humility, anything of that touching character which is imparted by misfortune, I could not have seen him or thought of him without being pierced to my very heart. When we were together, if I thought I detected in him anything like resignation or any sentiments devoid of pride and passion, I cannot say what I experienced. But such moments were very rare, and all I can remember of that time rather bears the stamp of an obstinacy and blindness that dried up my pity."[2]

The Abbé Lacordaire wrote these lines in February, 1834. Three months later the miserable *dénouement* of this sad history broke on the world by the publication of the "*Paroles d'un Croyant*," which cast a lurid gleam along the fatal path on which the fallen archangel was about to enter.

This event justified the line of conduct adopted by the Abbé Lacordaire. He only spoke of it to his friend in order to give glory to God and to His Church, who had so wonderfully enlightened and delivered him. " I feel too well that I am not a saint ; but I bear within me a disinterested love of the truth, and although I may have sought honourably to withdraw from the abyss in which I was plunged, never for a moment did a thought of pride or ambition form

[1] Memoirs. [2] *Le Père Lacordaire*, p. 66.

the motive of my conduct on this occasion. Pride always said to me, ' Remain where you are, do not change, and expose yourself to the reproaches of your former friends.' But divine grace cried with a yet louder voice, ' Trample under foot human respect, give glory to the Holy See and to God.' My only sagacity has lain in my frank submission ; if everything has turned out as I foresaw it would, I only foresaw it by dint of forgetting my own sense. I cannot rejoice at the abyss which obstinacy has dug under the feet of a man who has rendered great services to the Church. I hope that in His own time God may yet stop him in his course ; but I do rejoice that the sovereign Pontiff, the Father not merely of one Christian soul, but of all, has at last by his sacred authority decided the questions which were tearing to pieces the Church of France, and turning out of the right path a crowd of souls *deceived in all sincerity*, and by whose dangerous fascinations I had myself been captivated. Let all personal triumph perish, if any such there be, and may the Church of France after this memorable lesson flourish in peace and unity ! May we all pardon one another the errors of our youth, and pray together for him who caused them out of an excess of imagination, over whose beauty we cannot choose but weep."[1]

After so many quotations it still remains for us to quote the most eloquent and touching page of the book which M. de Montalembert has placed upon the tomb of his friend. Certainly he could have written nothing more to the praise of the holy priest ; but to do this it was necessary that he should accuse himself. And this he has done with a simplicity and tenderness which go straight to the heart, and powerfully move our sympathies. The Christian religion alone possesses the power of raising a man by his very abasement, and this power can only be attained

---

[1] *Le Père Lacordaire*, p. 74.

by truly great souls. The following is the passage referred to :

" But among the souls thus sincerely deceived and imperilled by the fatal influence exerted over them by this master-mind, there was one dearer to Lacordaire than all the rest, and who, more than all the rest, clung with disinterested obstinacy, less perhaps to the person of the fallen apostle, than to the great idea which seemed buried in his fall. In the midst of his own struggles and personal troubles, it was on this soul that he poured forth all the ardour of his zeal, the purest and most powerful passion of his heart. It was on him that he secretly lavished all the richest treasures of his eloquence : *Vadit ad illam quæ perierat donec inveniat eam.* Why cannot I say all, and cite the numberless letters, in which, for three entire years, he pursued this thankless task ! Some day, perhaps, when all the other witnesses and actors in the struggle have passed away, these letters may furnish materials for a chapter in his glorious life, which will certainly not be the least affecting. I have just read them over again, after the lapse of many years, with an emotion no words can ever describe. I do not know whether his genius or his goodness ever shone more brightly than during the course of this long and obstinate struggle to save one beloved soul. With the vain hope of sheltering myself from the troubles of so trying a crisis, I had taken refuge in Germany, where I was pursued by the appeals of M. de la Mennais. Whilst believing himself obliged as a priest to sign formularies of retractation, the unhappy man replied to my fears and filial representations by congratulating me on the independence I enjoyed as a layman, exhorting me to maintain it at all costs. ' This Voice,' he wrote to me, ' which in old time shook the whole world, will not now so much as terrify a class of schoolboys.' But the same post that brought me these detestable letters, brought me also others far more numerous, in which the true priest, the true

friend, re-established the rights of Truth by pointing
to the ever accessible heights of light and peace. He
even came in person to seek me out, and renew his
exhortations by the tomb of St. Elizabeth. Before,
as well as after, that short journey, he was constantly
returning to the charge with inexhaustible energy and
invincible perseverance. Misunderstood and repulsed,
he nevertheless continued to lavish his warnings, which
remained as fruitless as ever, and his predictions,
which were always verified; but with what reason,
what graceful and touching eloquence, with what a
charming mixture of severity and affection, with what
salutary alternations of unsparing frankness, and a
sweetness that could not be resisted! The tenderest of providences could not have done more, or
done it better. After having placed before me Truth
in her sacred and austere majesty, he would deck her
with all the flowers of his poetic genius, and using by
turns entreaty and argument, he would mingle with
his unanswerable logic the appeals of a heart which
had no equal in its unwearied devotion. Let the
reader judge from one page taken out of a hundred
others written in the same tone:

"'The Church does not say to you, *See;* that power
does not belong to her; but she says, *Believe.* She
says to you, at the age of twenty-three, attached as
you are to certain ideas, what she said to you on the
day of your first communion: Receive the hidden and
incomprehensible God, bow down your reason before
that of God, and before the Church, which is His
mouthpiece. Why has the Church been given to us,
unless it be to bring us back to the truth, when we
have fallen into error? . . . . You are astonished at
what the Holy See requires from M. de la Mennais.
It is certainly harder to submit when we have spoken
out before men, than when all has passed between
our own hearts and God. This is the special trial
reserved for genius. The great men of the Church
have had to snap their lives in twain, *and in a certain*

sense this is the history of every conversion. . . . . Despise my warnings if you will, yet listen to them ; for who has a right to speak if I have not? Who but myself loves you well enough not to spare you? Who can apply the fire to your wounds so well as I, who would willingly kiss them and suck the poison out of them at the peril of my life?'

"I was not as rebellious as may be thought to these warm remonstrances ; I was only restless and hesitating. Whilst obstinately resisting the pressing solicitations of Lacordaire, I used my devoted affection towards De la Mennais, the most faithful of all those which he had been able to inspire, in order to win him over to patience and silence. But I was vexed with my friend for having followed another way, and one more public and more decisive. I boldly reproached him with his apparent forgetfulness of those liberal aspirations which had formerly animated us both. And when at last I yielded, it was but slowly and with regret, and not until I had given much pain to his generous heart. The struggle lasted too long. I speak of it now with shame and remorse, for I did not then do him all the justice he deserved at my hands. I wish, therefore, to expiate this fault by acknowledging it, and I desire by this avowal to do homage to the great soul who has now found the Judge Whom he invoked with so just a confidence. It was then that I saw to the secret depths of his soul with eyes, which, if then irritated and distracted, have since been often enough bathed in grateful tears. It was he who made me understand and revere the only power before which we grow greater by abasing ourselves. The slave as I then was of error and pride, I was saved and set free by one whom I even then regarded as the ideal of a priest, as he has himself defined it : 'Strong as a diamond, more tender than a mother!' "

CHAPTER VI.

N his return from Rome to Paris, in the month of March 1832, the Abbé Lacordaire found himself in the midst of the ravages caused by the cholera. The violence of the pestilence had not softened anti-religious prejudices, and it was with difficulty that he could obtain permission to be admitted into one of the hospitals established in the granaries. There he passed his days, dressed as a layman, timidly seeking for any soul who might be found there belonging to the flock of Christ. "Occasionally," he writes, "one or two offer themselves for confession. Others die without the use of speech or hearing. I lay my hand on their foreheads, and trusting in the divine mercy, I repeat the words of absolution. It is seldom that I come away without something having occurred which makes me glad that I went. Yesterday a woman had just been brought in, and by the side of her bed was a soldier, her husband. I approached, and as I wore the dress of a layman the soldier asked me in a low voice if there were no priest to be found there. I was glad to be able to reply, 'I am one myself.' It is indeed a happiness to find oneself in time to save a soul, and give comfort to a fellow-creature."[1] We are also happy in thus finding the great apologist of Christianity by the bedside of the cholera patients, preaching his faith by works before defending it by his words, preparing himself for the apostolate of eloquence by that of charity, and already showing himself worthy to become the animating spirit of that society of St. Vincent of Paul, which a year later was to commence its glorious labours.

Having returned from La Chesnaie towards the close of the year 1832, he lost no time in again presenting himself to his archbishop, Mgr. de Quélen, "who received him with open arms, as a child who had gone through some dangerous adventure, and who had returned wounded to his father's house." "You want another baptism," he said to him, "and I will give you one."[2] He accordingly restored him to the chaplaincy of the Visitation, which he had held on leaving the seminary. It offered him an asylum after the storm—a retired shelter in which he could enter into himself—a life of study and preparation for the more splendid destinies that were awaiting him. His mother, who had not left Paris, rejoined him, and he once more began to enjoy those long days of silent labour so conformable to his taste ; so necessary also for those great duties of the apostolate on which he was soon to enter. He had begged for this retirement as a privilege on his first entrance into the priesthood. It was restored to him now as a reward and refreshment after the noise and dust of the battle. He had been born with a taste for solitude, and he always returned to it with an overflowing joy, which revealed the depths of his great and beautiful soul. "I delight in feeling this solitude all around me," he writes : "it is my element, my life. One can do nothing except in solitude, that is my great axiom."

What was the character of this love of solitude, with which the whole life of Père Lacordaire is so

---

[1] *Le Père Lacordaire*, p. 84.　　　　[2] Memoirs.

deeply stamped? Was it mere natural inclination, the aspiration of a superior intellect, or the bent of a religious soul? It was something of all these: the harmonious combination of nature, genius, and grace. There are some men who are born with this taste for silence and retirement, on whom the world weighs like a heavy burden; men like Petrarch, Rousseau, or Chateaubriand, in whom solitude so elevates the mind, the heart, and the imagination, as to render the duties of common life insupportable to them; so that as one of them said, "I have thought a hundred times that I should not have found myself badly off in the Bastile had I been bound only to remain there."[1] This mere natural bias, however, leads easily enough to misanthropy, and even to suicidal mania. With Père Lacordaire it arose neither from idleness nor hatred of mankind, but from a taste for simple enjoyments, from a love of independence tempered by the sense of duty, and a natural aptitude for recollection, united to great impetuosity in action when the right moment for action had come. He might have said with Petrarch, "I fly from the world by taste, and the gentleness of my temper brings me back to it." Early disenchanted with the frivolous enjoyments of the world, and touched by grace, solitude gave him back to God, to man, and to himself. Every religious and pensive soul loves thus to turn in upon itself, and there seek for a more perfect and divine type of what is revealed in the exterior world. And even as God beholds the world of created beings not under those visible forms which are necessary to our senses, but in His Word, in His thought, in the immaterial and uncreated ideal which was their archetype, and which remains their inimitable exemplar; so the soul of the poet, the philosopher, or the saint is disposed to close the exterior eye to imperfect images, in order to form within their divine and incomparable representation. What is the world, beheld with the

[1] J. J. Rousseau.

eyes of the body, compared to the same world beheld in its spiritual aspect ? What is the real in comparison of the ideal ? or Rubens by the side of Raphael ? Thus, too, each artist soul that has been able to find within itself the fair impress of the face of God, the reflection of His beauty, is enamoured with solitude and silence ; *amant secreta Camenæ.* Père Lacordaire possessed in an exquisite degree this religious poetry of nature. " I have bid adieu," he wrote, " to the mountains, the valleys, the rivers, and the pathless forests, to create in my own chamber, between God and my soul, a horizon vaster than the entire universe."[1] On these *wings of repose,* as he called them, he rose far above the vain tumult of the world, and steeped himself in that delicious melancholy which at once wounds and intoxicates, the true home-sickness of the saints and of great souls, and a malady of which he often loved to speak. " Weak and little minds," he said, " find here below a little nourishment which suffices for their intellect, and satisfies their love. They do not discover the emptiness of visible things, because they are incapable of sounding them to the bottom. But a soul whom God has drawn nearer to the Infinite very soon feels the narrow limits within which it is pent ; it experiences moments of inexpressible sadness, the cause of which for a long time remains a mystery ; it even seems as though some strange concurrence of events must have combined in order thus to disturb its life, and all the while the trouble comes from a far higher source. In reading the lives of the saints we find that nearly all of them have felt that sweet melancholy of which the ancients said that *there was no genius without it.* In fact, melancholy is inseparable from every mind that looks below the surface, and every heart that feels deeply. Not that we must take complacency in it, for

[1] " Letters to Young Men," p. 140.

it is a malady that enervates, when we do not shake
it off, and it has but two remedies, *death, or God.*"[1]

The peculiar character of his affections also con-
duced to make him love solitude. Timid and reserved
even with his most intimate friends, absence restored
to his heart its liberty of action. " I have always
stood in need of solitude," he acknowledges, " even to
say how much I love." His retirement was peopled
with the images of those dear to him ; and free from
all scruple, set free from all restraint, his soul then
embraced the beloved soul, poured out upon it in
large floods its deep treasures of tenderness, and
spoke in silence that language of the heart which
desires, even painfully, to express itself, and to which
at the same time all real expression is denied. " I
weigh what I say," he writes, " in spite of myself, for
fear I should seem too frank and too affectionate. I
should speak to you much more tenderly had I not
passed the age when the heart pours itself out with
full liberty." He wrote to a friend from his chamber
in an Italian inn : " The thought of you fills this
lonely little chamber, where they serve me like a
master for my money, and where, when their service
is over, I remain as solitary as an owl." After one
of these moments of effusion he writes, " You have
just given me one of the happiest mornings I have
enjoyed for a long time ; here I am alive and young,
but not enough so to embrace you as I would desire,
which nevertheless I do as well as I can with the permission of God and yours."[2] It is again from one of
these cherished retreats that he writes : " Solitude
draws us together as much as a crowd separates us.
This is why there is so little real intimacy in the
world, whereas men who are accustomed to live in
solitude dig their affections deep. I have never lived

---

[1] This letter is taken from a correspondence, which is full of interest,
and which has been given to the world under the title of *Correspondance
Inédite.* The extracts given from it in this volume will be indicated by
the words, *Inedited Correspondence.*
[2] " Letters to Young Men " (*passim*).

with people of the world, and it is with difficulty that I can put any faith in those who live in a sea where one wave presses against another without any of them acquiring consistency. The best of men are losers by this continual friction, which, while it rubs off the asperities of the soul, at the same time destroys its power of forming any strong attachment. I believe solitude is as necessary to friendship as it is to sanctity, to genius as to virtue."[1]

His soul, his heart, his imagination, his entire being grew young again in the atmosphere of silence and peace through which he loved to behold God, his friends, and the world. In proportion to the embarrassment he felt in the midst of worldly bustle and business, was his love of souls, when, from the depth of his retreat, he beheld them in the light of the charity of Christ. He lived very little in the midst of men, and yet how he loved them! It was in solitude that he probed their wounds, and found their remedy in those kind and encouraging words which penetrated and healed so many souls. His solitude had in it nothing dry or severe; it was a close and intimate colloquy with God, his friends, and humanity. How many times, on entering his cell as a religious, and finding him sitting alone, with his head bent down, without even a book before him, have we not detected in the fire of his eye and the movement of his lips, the secret of that interior communion which he had been holding with invisible guests! And so, on examining his correspondence, we have often remarked that the letters which express the most perfect confidence, the sweetest gaiety, the most persuasive piety, are nearly all dated from his favourite retreats, Santa Sabina, Chalais, and Sorèze.

He delighted then in his little chamber at the Visitation, and lived there without any anxiety as to the future. "All my days resemble one another," he writes; "I work regularly during the morning and

[1] Inedited correspondence.

the afternoon : I see nobody with the exception of a few ecclesiastics of the province, who now and then come to visit me."[1]   He read St. Augustine, for whom he daily felt a warmer admiration, and who from that time became, together with St. Thomas, his favourite author.   " He was a man subtle in style rather than in matter," he wrote, "he is the one of all the Fathers who contains the profoundest thoughts on religion; besides which, being one of the latest among them, he has the advantage of resuming the teaching of his predecessors.   He was the St. Thomas of primitive times."

In vain did occasions present themselves for drawing him once more into public life.   Twice he refused to undertake the direction of the *Univers*, a journal just then founded ; and he also declined a chair in the Catholic University of Louvain.   His love of solitude preserved him in a singular way from every temptation to engage in a busy, influential career, and he quietly repeated to himself, " A man is formed *within*, not *without* himself . . . . Every man has his hour ; all he has to do is to wait for it, and to do nothing against the order of Providence."   Sometimes he even longed to find himself in some simple country parish, and pictured to himself the life of a village curé, with his little flock and his modest church and garden. "I should like," he said, "to bury myself in the heart of the country, and to live henceforth only for a little flock, finding all my joy in God, and in the face of nature.   You would soon see that I am a very simple man, and that I have no ambition."[2]

It will be seen that in these moments of passing melancholy, he fell into a delusion not only as to his real mission, but also as to himself.   The Abbé Lacordaire was no more made for absolute obscurity than he was for a narrow sphere of action.   He was seeking for himself, and the profound disgust which

[1] *Le Père Lacordaire,* p. 90.
[2] Letter to M. de Montalembert, 1832.

he experienced at a life which had been made the butt of passion and intrigue had violently thrown him back on complete isolation. And this at times was not without its danger. Happily at this juncture God provided him with a new guide, whose mind was as penetrating as her heart was devoted, and who knew both how to make him see the danger, and how to turn him from it. At Rome, in 1837, these ideas of absolute retreat from the world returned upon him; he kept dreaming of plans for flying far away, hiding himself from the eyes of men, and utterly breaking with the past. The wise and tender eye which was watching over him thus replied : " Your letter threatening me with a long separation of course occupies my thoughts. You tell me to think of it before God ; I do nothing else, nevertheless I have not as yet found myself able to share your momentary convictions. I believe indeed that solitude may be good and useful, perhaps even necessary for you ; but it must be a solitude accompanied with calm, freedom, and possession of yourself; not isolation, which at the same time that it breaks down every barrier destroys also every support. Were you to isolate yourself from the world, you would lose the habit of associating with your fellow-men, a habit truly precious to those who are made to live with them, and for them, and which would strip you, not only of your powers of severe reason, but also of your capacity of sympathy. In all states and in all places the divine word finds its application : ' It is not good for man to be alone.' Your admirable humility is willing now to acknowledge the superiority of others, but when you have become a master in your turn, when age and experience are added to yet rarer gifts, then, my dear friend, it will not be good for you to remain isolated. Whatever you do, it will be necessary for you to have disciples subject to your immediate influence, confided to you by a higher authority, or perhaps a family of religious brethren, and at their head a common father of all. In the ardent desire that I feel for your perfection, I do not, believe me, wish to give it any particular form of my own devising. Serve God, and do what you please. Life in the world, solitude, preaching, writing, ecclesiastical dignities, a renunciation of all things, all seem to me equally suitable ; anything, in short, with the exception of that absolute retirement, in which, separated from every one, you would be exposed to the greatest danger, from the impossibility in which you would find yourself of being set free from yourself."[1]

Who was it who thus spoke to him ? Who was it who had cast so penetrating a glance into that troubled heart, and had gained such empire over him as to be able to address him in this new sort of language, which revealed the delusion into which he had been betrayed by his imagination, and who, while she endeavoured to turn him away from isolation, that moral suicide, would not force him back into the strife which destroys in a noisier, but not less deadly way ? The reader has already divined the answer: it was Madame Swetchine, a name now familiar to the world, for who has not read the life and works of that remarkable woman, crowned by death with a glory all the more dazzling because during her life she so skilfully strove to conceal it ? Who is there that does not know this Russian lady, with her thoroughly French heart ? this Catholic convert, so tolerant to those of opposite creeds, this manly intellect united to such womanly affections, the mind of Joseph de Maistre linked to the soul of a Fénélon, and warmed with a piety so amiable, a charity so delicate—this woman, in short, who said of herself, " I desire to be remembered by no other epitaph than these words: ' She who believed, who prayed, and who loved !'"

Madame Swetchine was fifty years of age when the Abbé Lacordaire was first introduced to her by his friend M. de Montalembert. It was not a mere lite-

[1] *Madame Swetchine*, by the Count de Falloux, v. 272.

rary connection formed between two minds suited to understand one another; to the Abbé Lacordaire it was a happy influence given to him at the critical moment of his life; and one, moreover, so amiable that it concealed its power under the veil of an almost maternal tenderness. This providence was unique in his life; he met in course of time with other friends and other advisers; but this mixture of friendship and authority, from one who had wisdom to detect and point out a danger as well as that persuasive kindness that subdues the heart, was a rare and perfect gift he never knew but once, and it was sent him by God at a propitious moment. Nowhere could he have found one better fitted to discharge this delicate office. The Abbé Lacordaire was devoted to the cause of God, the Church, liberty, and his native land. Madame Swetchine loved all these as much as he did; like him she desired to see the Church restored to her civil rights, and society regenerated by a baptism of faith. Both were chosen souls, resembling one another in their moral stamp, jealous above all things for the claims of truth and conscience, true, loyal, and sincere. But Madame Swetchine possessed an advantage over her younger friend in her greater knowledge of the world and the human heart; he was only travelling to the goal whence she was returning. This experience she now with unparalleled goodness placed at the disposal of the poor shipwrecked navigator; with a kindness which attached him to her as to his second mother, and which was rendered yet more precious by the hardness and injustice he was to encounter at almost every step of his opening career. She was the good angel whom God had placed at this point of the road where every sort of obscurity and ambush seemed lying in wait for him; and what dangers did she not enable him to avoid! May the example of this excellent woman teach many men the powerful influence for good possessed over an ardent and sincere soul by enlarged and enlightened charity!

Père Lacordaire, after the death of his illustrious friend, thus recalls his first meeting with her, and expresses the feelings he then experienced. " I touched on the shore of her soul," he writes, "like a wreck broken by the waves, and I remember now, after the lapse of five-and-twenty years, the light and the strength which she placed at the disposal of a young man, till then altogether unknown to her. Her counsels supported me at once against discouragement and elation. One day, when she thought she detected in my words a certain tone of doubt and lassitude, she said to me, with a singular accent, the simple words, ' *Take care !*' She had a marvellous power of discovering the side to which one inclined, and where one needed help. Her mind was so perfectly proportioned, the freedom of her judgment was so remarkable, that it was long before I was able to guess what side she would embrace. And whereas with every one else I knew beforehand exactly what they were going to say to me, I could never anticipate her views, and with no one did I ever feel more thoroughly lifted out of the atmosphere of the world."[1]

Such was, without exaggeration, the real measure of Madame Swetchine's influence over the Abbé Lacordaire. He did not owe to her, as has often been asserted, the good fortune of not having followed the Abbé de la Mennais. His submission, as sincere as it was spontaneous, and his rupture with that misguided man, had both taken place before his first meeting with Madame Swetchine. But dark clouds were still hanging over his horizon. The thunderbolt of the Vatican had struck down the editors of the *Avenir*, and they bore its traces on their brows ; and public opinion did not yet distinguish those who had arisen from the ground healed and humbled, from those whose wounds had been envenomed by their pride. They were therefore generally and indiscriminately regarded with distrust. Moreover, under

[1] *Madame Swetchine*, by Père Lacordaire.

this excusable feeling, lurked other passions such as
every defeat awakens, and which hide themselves like
vile serpents in the most dangerous recesses of the
human heart. The rancour which had been held in
check so long as the pen remained in the grasp of the
combatants, but which now felt relieved from all fear
of their lash ; the easy triumphs of mediocrity, the
jealousies which superior talent too often arouses in
commonplace minds, envious of any splendid success ;
a short-sighted orthodoxy which was about to spy
out heresy in the orator of Stanislaus and Notre
Dame, and to weary the ears of the bishops with its
tiresome denunciations ; all these were to a nature
like that of the Abbé Lacordaire dangers which I
venture to call more formidable than those from which
he had just escaped in his campaign with M. de la
Mennais. There, at least, everything was great, and
the path of duty was easily discerned ; but here
everything was petty, and the road through these
obscure and winding ways was not so soon discovered. In his frank and noble love of truth and
honour he was always exposed to one of two temptations ; either to compel his enemies, whoever they
might be, to raise their masks ; or to despise them
and their manœuvres, and run away from them. He
did neither one nor the other, and it was the advice
of Madame Swetchine which supported him against
this double peril, and helped him to ascend to those
calmer heights, where the soul, drawn up to God,
breathes an atmosphere of peace and charity, and is
no longer irritated by the murmurs of ill-will, to which
it soon ceases to listen.

She wrote to him once in order to put him on his
guard against an attack that was being prepared
against him. " It is with great repugnance," she
says, " that I give you this warning ; nothing but
God and conscience ought to come between us and
our ideas, and we should strive to raise those ideas
to their highest possible standard out of a simple
love of truth, without so much as casting a glance at

the assaults of malice. My poor dear friend, how have
you been able to excite such sentiments in the heart,
I will not say of any Christian, but of any man? But
contradiction is one of the trials that has been foretold to us, and at the height where you stand it is a
prophecy which must needs be accomplished." These
generous counsels were of the greatest service to the
Abbé Lacordaire. He soon accustomed himself to
let intrigue expend itself in silence, presenting to the
teeth of envy only a soul of steel. The injustice of
man, as it detached him from the world, more powerfully attached him to God, and when his eyes grew
weary of the present, he cast them on the future,
which he called *the great refuge and the great lever.*
Before the hatred of party spirit, he said with Dante,
"*I behold it, and I pass on.*" No one had more faith
than he had in the virtue of silence, and in its power
to vanquish, and at last to ruin, the most skilful
attacks of malevolence. At first he left his cause in
the hands of God and the future; but in time his own
age did him justice, which made him say, "Silence is,
next to speech, the greatest power in the world." "I
no longer live," he says elsewhere, "save in the future,
and in eternity. All the vain passions of parties
there disappear, and one gains strength not so much
as to think of them. When the traveller crosses the
Alps there comes a moment when the first breezes
from the Italian soil announce his approach to that
beautiful land; he stops to inhale the perfume, and
forgets the icy tempests he has left behind him. Oh,
how good is God to those who truly seek Him!"[1]
Thus he knew how to render himself worthy of the
gifts of fortune which Providence from time to time
flung across his path; occasions and persons, solitude and repose, and a holy friendship disposing
him to long-suffering and forgetfulness of injuries;
and thus, without knowing it, he was preparing for
those events which were about to engage him in a
new and important career.

[1] "Letters to Young Men," p. 288.

CHAPTER VII.

1833—1836.

OWARDS the close of the year 1833, the Abbé Buquet, then prefect of studies at the Collége Stanislaus, in Paris, proposed to the Abbé Lacordaire that he should give a course of religious conferences to the pupils in the chapel of that establishment. The proposal pleased him ; he always loved any intercourse with the young, and it seemed a good opportunity for at last trying his strength on his own ground ; and he therefore gave his consent. The conferences opened on the 19th of January, 1834. They formed an important epoch in the life of Père Lacordaire, and whilst they revealed to him his true vocation—namely, apologetic teaching from the pulpit—they also made known to Paris the great orator whom she possessed. The success of these conferences was immense. After the first day the pupils had to give up their places to crowds of strangers ; tribunes were erected in the chapel, but it was still found too small to contain the auditors, and for three months their numbers continued daily to increase.

This success was doubtless partly due to the natural

gifts of the orator, shaded though they were by many
defects ; but yet more to that solid course of study
which he had so long pursued. Almost immediately
on his entrance into the seminary, when he first began
the study of theology, the Abbé Lacordaire had, as
it will be remembered, sketched out the plan of a
Christian apology, which aimed at proving the divinity
of the Catholic religion by its effects on society. He
was in doubt whether he should carry out this plan,
as a missionary, by his pen, or in the pulpit. He did
not then see his way clear, but he thoroughly understood his end. When, therefore, he found himself in
a pulpit of his own, before an audience exactly suited
to him, by one of those unlooked-for combinations of
circumstances which reveal to a man that his hour is
come, he felt himself master, with his foot on firm
ground, and sure of victory. These first outpourings
of his genius breathed the accents of a young enthusiastic soul, full of generous and patriotic emotions.
At one bound he freed himself from the cold and
formal routine of the seventeenth century, and heed-
less of those rules of sacred rhetoric, which had held
their ground for three centuries, till men had come to
regard them as inviolable, the young orator seemed
rather to have in his mind's eye the lofty freedom of
the Fathers, or those stormy days when the hearts of
Florence rose and fell like the billows of the ocean,
as they listened to the fervid eloquence of Savonarola.
His Conferences took the form neither of lecture,
homily, nor sermon, but rather of a brilliant discourse
on sacred subjects, in which all the sympathies of the
audience were in turns engaged by the appeals of his
eloquence, faith, and enthusiasm. It was not merely
the priest who spoke, but the poet, the citizen, and
the philosopher,—it was the man of the present day
speaking to men of his own time of the things of the
past, and of a religion they believed to be in its last
agony ; leading them first to admire his talent, and
finally to respect his doctrine. But the very qualities

with which he fascinated the ears of his young hearers
furnished matter for his condemnation in the judgment of certain advocates of the old traditions. They
criticised his style as too human, his exposition of
doctrine feeble and insecure, and his political and
historical episodes as far too audacious. He had even
dared to tell the partisans of the July Revolution, that
the first tree of liberty had been planted long since in
Paradise, by the hand of God Himself. The result
was that he was denounced to the Government as a
fanatical Republican, likely to upset the minds of the
youth of France, and accused to the archbishop of
being a preacher of novelties, and a man whose
example was dangerous.

The Conferences of Stanislaus College were suspended. But help came from an unexpected quarter.
M. Affre, Canon of the Cathedral, undertook his
defence with the archbishop, whom, in course of time,
he was to succeed. Of a cold, calm, positive mind,
well skilled in theology, and disposed to favour a
severe simplicity of style, M. Affre was not very sensible of the charms of eloquence, and his nature
seemed to have little in it which would be likely to
incline him toward the Abbé Lacordaire. He had
even written a work against M. de la Mennais, in
which Gallican tendencies were not concealed. But
he was a man of honour and integrity; his soul had
expanded under the influence of the priesthood, and
he took a lively interest in the existing affairs of the
Church. This simple greatness, his distinguishing
feature both in life and death, made him instinctively
recognise the noble character of the young orator.
He was grieved to see him sacrificed to unjust prejudices, and became his advocate with Mgr. de Quélen.
The following is the notice he has left on the subject
in his Memoirs:

"I had just read the retractation drawn up by the
Abbé Lacordaire, which appeared to me full of candour. It inspired me with a warm interest in him,

10

and admiring his talents, even while I could not but discern their grave defects, I saw in them certain evidence of a great soul, and intellectual gifts of a very high order.

"A short time before I first became acquainted with the Abbé Lacordaire, he had given a course of Conferences in the Collége Stanislaus, which had excited great enthusiasm among the young men. Unfortunately they produced the very opposite effect on some restless auditors, and not without reason, if we consider how much there was that was bold and extraordinary, both in the ideas and their expression. The anxiety felt by some was, moreover, the more excusable, since M. Lacordaire was known to have been one of the chief editors of the *Avenir.* If those who accused him had been free from all suspicion of jealousy, their zeal against the young preacher would probably have been somewhat less ardent ; but they were accused, doubtless unjustly, of revenging themselves for the little interest they had themselves been able to excite, by trying to stop the mouth of a rival who had been welcomed with enthusiasm.

"The archbishop, in alarm, required that the Conferences should be written and submitted to his approval before being pronounced in public. M. Lacordaire declined this, alleging that he should lose all his advantage if he were prevented from giving an *extempore* expression to his thoughts.

"I thought it my duty to plead his cause, without concealing from myself the inconveniences which might arise from extempore preaching on such subjects as those of which he treated; but it seemed to me that these inconveniences were greatly diminished by the frank and upright character of the Abbé Lacordaire. He was in fact perfectly free from all sectarian spirit, and quite disposed to listen to the advice of persons who were interested in him. I felt sure, therefore, that even should an inexact expression escape him it would not be a voluntary error, and still less an obstinate one, that it would never be made a matter of debate, but would disappear with the passing impulse which had given it birth. And an experience of four years has since confirmed this persuasion. . . . .

" I therefore spoke in his favour to the archbishop, pointing out how different the times now were, that if he had to regret having no more as heretofore, a Sorbonne, ready at any moment to condemn a false proposition, neither had we now a class of hearers who would be likely to lay hold of any incautious words that might escape M. Lacordaire. I suggested whether it might not rather be feared lest the severity shown him should afford our young men a pretext for complaining of their chief pastor, and separating themselves from him ; whilst at the same time the conduct of the accused party had for two years given hopes of great docility—a disposition wholly opposed to that of an innovator. Experience proves, in fact, that most sects would have been stifled in their birth had not their chiefs been full of pride and obstinacy. These observations did not at first produce their effect, for the permission to preach was withdrawn from the Abbé Lacordaire.

" Shortly afterwards, however, it was restored to him, and I have some reasons for thinking that the archbishop was induced to take this determination in consequence of the arguments which I have just named. The condition of writing the Conferences in full was not insisted on, but the preacher was to submit the outline of his discourses to one of the Grand Vicars of the diocese. As far as I can remember, the archbishop allowed him to choose between the Abbé Carrière, a learned theologian, and a member of the Society of St. Sulpice, and myself. He preferred me, doubtless, on account of the special interest which I had shown in him. The Conferences were no longer given in a chapel, but at Notre Dame. I feel certain that the pulpit of the cathedral was by no means desired by him who was destined to gather around it such a numerous concourse. I have reasons for thinking that the persons who judged the young preacher so severely were glad of the choice made of this church. They hoped that the trial would prove unfavourable, and that they should succeed by this not very honourable means in causing the ruin of a renown, the influence of which appeared to them so dangerous. They were deceived in their expectations, but the Abbé Lacordaire, after attaining the most brilliant success, himself discontinued the course."[1]

We can see in these incomplete revelations how painful must have been the first steps of the Abbé Lacordaire in his career as a preacher. But this opposition, which befalls every great work, purified his soul and ennobled his character. We begin to see a certain tranquil self-restraint taking possession of this nature, hitherto so prompt and fiery. The cutting accusations of jealousy did not disturb his calm, and the orders of his superiors found him humble and resigned. "I despise the tricks that are set on foot against me," he writes; " I am alone, busy, calm, and trustful in God and in the future." And again, when the Conferences of Stanislaus were interrupted: " Obedience costs something; but I have learnt from experience that, sooner or later, it is always rewarded, and that God alone knows what is good for us . . . . *Light comes to him who submits*, as to a man who opens his eyes." And in fact the reward had not long to be waited for; it was as striking as it was unexpected. We shall leave Père Lacordaire himself to give the simple and touching narrative of the circumstances which called him to Notre Dame, and of his first appearance in that pulpit which owes its glory to his genius:

"Time drew on, and I knew not on what to resolve. One day, as I was crossing the gardens of the Luxem-

[1] Mémoires of Mgr. Affre, quoted in his life, by the Abbé Castan, p. 72.

bourg, I met an ecclesiastic whom I knew tolerably
well, who stopped me, saying, "What are you doing
now? You ought to go to the archbishop and come
to an understanding with him.' A few paces farther
another ecclesiastic, with whom I was far less intimate
than the first, stopped me in the same way and said
to me, 'You are wrong not to go and see the archbishop; I have every reason for thinking that he
would be glad to have some conversation with you.'
This double suggestion surprised me, and accustomed
as I was to be a little superstitious in the matter of
providences, I slowly took my way towards St.
Michael's Convent, not far from the Luxembourg,
where the archbishop then lived. It was not the
portress who opened the door to me, but a choir-
religious who had a kind feeling for me, because, as
she said, *'every one was against me.'* She told me
that the archbishop had absolutely forbidden any one
to be admitted just then; but, she added, 'I will go
and tell him, and perhaps he will receive you.' The
answer was favourable. On entering, I found the
archbishop walking up and down his chamber with a
sad and preoccupied air. He gave me a rather distant
welcome, and I began to walk by his side for some
minutes before he spoke a single word. At last, after
a sufficiently long interval of silence, he stopped short,
turned towards me, looked at me with a scrutinising
eye, and said:

"'I am thinking of intrusting to you the pulpit of
Notre Dame; would you accept it?' This abrupt beginning, the secret of which was entirely beyond my
penetration to discover, did not cause me any intoxication. I replied that the time for preparing was
very short, that the pulpit in which I should have to
appear was an important one, and that after having
succeeded before a limited audience, I might very
easily fail before an assemblage of four thousand
hearers. The end of it was that I asked for four-and-
twenty hours of reflection. After having prayed to

God and consulted Madame Swetchine, I determined to signify my acceptance. What then had passed to cause this change? The Abbé Liautard, formerly superior of the Collége Stanislaus and curé of Fontainebleau, had for some weeks been circulating among the clergy a manuscript pamphlet, in which he warmly blamed the archiepiscopal administration. This pamphlet had been put into the archbishop's hands the very day when the scene I have described took place, and he had just finished reading it when Providence sent me to him. It must be understood that among other accusations in this paper, the Conferences of Stanislaus were not forgotten; and the archbishop was charged with weakness and want of capacity in consequence of his conduct in that affair. I am not aware if the thought of offering me the pulpit of Notre Dame had ever before suggested itself to him; but when he saw me enter at the very moment when he was disturbed by the unfavourable judgment passed on him, it is probable that this singular and unforeseen coincidence struck him as a warning from God, and that a rapid flash of light darted into his mind, and suggested to him the thought that, by intrusting me with the cathedral Conferences, he should give his own personal enemies a triumphant answer. When he made known to those around him the engagement he had entered into with me, he was surprised to find how little opposition was offered. For in fact those among my enemies who surrounded him, hoped that this triumph would be the occasion of my fall, being persuaded that I possessed neither the theological resources nor the oratorical powers necessary for supporting me in a position where both were necessary in a very high degree. They were not aware that for fifteen years I had been applying myself to the most earnest philosophical and theological studies, and that during the same time I had also practised public speaking under a great variety of circumstances. Moreover, it is with the orator as with Mount Horeb—before God strikes him he is but a barren rock, but as soon as the Divine Hand has touched him, as it were, with a finger, there burst forth streams which water the desert.

"The day having come, Notre Dame was filled with a multitude such as had never before been seen within its walls. The liberal and the absolutist youth of Paris, friends and enemies, and that curious crowd which a great capital has always ready for anything new, had all flocked together, and were packed in dense masses within the old cathedral. I mounted the pulpit firmly, but not without emotion, and began my discourse with my eye fixed on the archbishop, who, after God, but before the public, was to me the first personage in the scene. He listened with his head a little bent down, in a state of absolute impassibility, like a man who was not a mere spectator, nor even a judge, but rather as one who ran a personal risk by the experiment. I soon felt at home with my subject and my audience, and as my breast swelled under the necessity of grasping that vast assembly of men, and the calm of the first opening sentences began to give place to the inspiration of the orator, one of those exclamations escaped from me, which, when deep and heartfelt, never fail to move. The archbishop was visibly moved. I watched his countenance change as he raised his head and cast on me a glance of astonishment. I saw that the battle was gained in his mind, and it was so already in that of the audience. Having returned home, he announced that he was going to appoint me Honorary Canon of the cathedral; and they had some difficulty in inducing him to wait until the end of the station."[1]

It was at the beginning of the Lent of 1835 that he commenced these Conferences of Notre Dame, one of the greatest and most important religious works of the century. They were indeed glorious

---

[1] Memoirs.

days, in which the old cathedral, which had so long
been silent and deserted, was roused by the noise of a
multitude invading its courts, and was made to echo
under the accents of the new orator—days of triumph
which perhaps the walls of Notre Dame will never
see again. How can we speak of those feasts of eloquence to those who were not themselves present at
them ? How bring before the eye of our reader the
singular spectacle of that immense nave filled from
early morning with men of every age, of every form
of belief, and of every party, young and old, but
especially the young students of law and of medicine,
orators, advocates, men of science, soldiers, Saint-
Simonists, republicans and royalists, believers and
unbelievers, atheists and materialists ; Paris, and all
France, in short, brought there in miniature. It was
a faithful mirror of the society of the time, which
somewhat resembled the vision of Ezekiel, that vast
field of dry bones, which by degrees arose and moved
together, and resumed their flesh and their living
hues, awaiting only the mighty voice of the prophet
to breathe into them the breath of life, and form them
into an array of soldiers ranged in battle array.[1] A
new and wonderful spectacle it was, indeed, in which
more than one during the long hours of waiting must
have asked himself what all these men had come
there to do, gathered as they were from such opposite
parties ; disciples of Voltaire hanging on the lips of a
Catholic priest ; the descendants of the Revolution of
'89, now docile listeners in a temple whence their
fathers had expelled the Christ ; seekers after a new
religion standing on the steps of a pulpit whence the
ancient creed was being preached. What did they
want, and who had brought them thither ?

There was more than one cause of this extraordinary excitement. Rarely, it must be acknowledged,
had any orator been better prepared for his audience,
or more thoroughly fitted to gain their attention. He

[1] Ezech. xxxvii. 10.

was himself the child of the age which he so heartily loved; he knew its malady, he had himself suffered from it ; he had known, as he said, the *magic* of unbelief, and he brought the remedy rather as a friend than as a master, as a father rather than as a judge. Only to see that young man of thirty-three standing there, with his pale expressive countenance, above the heads of the grandest assemblage ever gathered round any pulpit, sufficed to rivet one as by a charm. There was a dead silence when he appeared. His voice, at first low, gradually assumed greater fulness and body. Nothing could be simpler than his manner of beginning ; a brief and precise repetition of the preceding Conference, and a rapid summary of the subject on which he was about to speak formed his usual exordium. Then he took his flight upwards. Beautiful, indeed, it was to behold this young apostle, still illumined with the grace of his conversion, who had been himself rescued from error, surrounded by those who were still its captives, and burning to deliver them. How he entered into all their perplexities, making light of no objection, leading them along the paths he had himself travelled, and overthrowing on the way every opposing doctrine ; till, having at last regained the summit of truth, enraptured with its beauty, he would identify himself with its cause, and exclaim, "*My Church, my doctrine, my infallibility!*" Like another St. Paul, he bid defiance to every form of power, greatness, or glory. "Are you Frenchmen? So am I. Philosophers? I am one also. Lovers of freedom and independence? I love them both, and far more than you." Every ray of truth or beauty which has descended from the heart of God into that of man, was gathered up by him and restored to the source which gave it birth. He was not satisfied with proving the existence of God, he desired to glorify Him ; he cared not to make men say, "It is true!" if he could not also make them add, "It is beautiful!" Standing there, with his eye fixed on the Spouse of

Christ, in all her dazzling splendour, his voice rose
and fell like a chant; he seemed a prophet rather
than an ordinary speaker, and his eloquence assumed
almost the character of an ecstasy; his brow, his
glance, his every gesture betraying the emotions that
filled his soul. His hearers were breathless as they
listened, they remained like men intoxicated and
carried out of themselves. It was indeed a splendid
victory!

That Church, which the eighteenth century believed
to have fallen below contempt, which she thought to
have slain with the shafts of ridicule, arose once more
before the wondering eyes of an unbelieving world,
and was suddenly displayed before them adorned
with a grandeur which commanded the admiration of
unbelief itself. True, indeed, men might still refuse
to acknowledge the divinity of the Church, but they
were forced to own that there was nothing greater in
the world; they might still attack Christianity, but
they could no longer despise her. And his arguments, at first illustrated from the facts of science and
history, were popularised by his enchanting eloquence,
and thus becoming adapted to the current opinions of
the day, acquired the force of law.

The effect of these Conferences, specially on young
men, was irresistible. How could they fail to feel the
power of such preaching? They found in it everything which they most admired and cared for, put
forth far better than they could do it themselves.
There was not one of their favourite themes on which
he did not touch,—poetry, self-sacrifice, honour, national glory, patriotism, liberty,—all those beautiful
words by turns animated his discourse, like courtiers
doing homage to truth as to the queen, and forming
her guard of honour.

But what above all distinguished his preaching, and
marked its providential mission, whilst it formed the
chief reason of his success, was its adaptation to social
needs. It gave to society what society was hungering

and thirsting after; that Living Bread, the long priva-
tion of which had brought it to the verge of death—it
spoke to the world of God, and of His Son, our Lord
and Saviour. Christianity has a social existence, not
only in the sense that it is itself a society, the most
united, the most universal, the most ancient, the most
Catholic, and the most perfect of all societies ; but also
in this, that all societies depend on and live by it, as
the body depends on the soul, and draws its life from
thence, and as man depends and lives on God. Now
the society which the Abbé Lacordaire addressed was
remarkable precisely in this, that it was *without God.*
For the first time, perhaps, since civilised nations have
had a history, men were to be seen endeavouring to
progress without the aid of any positive intercourse
with Heaven. But if it is with difficulty that an individual can live without religious faith, much more is
it impossible for a nation to do so. What, in fact, is
a nation but a great community of sufferings, miseries,
weaknesses, and maladies of mind and body ? Without religion, and, above all, without Christianity, where
is the remedy for all these evils, the consolation for
all these misfortunes ? The Abbé Lacordaire, himself brought back to Catholicism by his deep conviction that society could not do without the Church,
received as his peculiar mission the task of developing this truth to the eyes of his countrymen. "The
old state of society," he said, "perished because it
had expelled God ; the new is suffering, because God
has not yet been readmitted."[1] His constant aim,
the thought which ran through all his instructions, his
labours, and his entire career, was to contribute what
he could in order that God might re-enter into the
faith and life of the age. All his Conferences are
based on this idea. On whatever subject he treats,
whether it be the Church in her exterior or her interior
organisation, in her Author, her dogmas, or her practical effects, he always gives the preference to the

[1] Funeral Oration on Mgr. Forbin-Janson.

social view. Perpetually to put forward side by side the gospel and society, to compare the society which is united to the Church with that which is separated from it ; to show that without the gospel the family is broken up, liberty becomes license, and authority despotism ; that all the virtues of which society stands most in need, such as humility, chastity, and charity, make up Catholicism, and are produced exclusively by Catholicism—this was the prevailing idea of his whole teaching. Without directly refuting all the errors and calumnies accumulated by the eighteenth century against the Church, this scaffolding of lies crumbled away of itself before the sublime and simple spectacle of the Church peacefully pursuing her mission of redemption and salvation. She had been accused of attempting to stifle in her bosom every germ of light and life : she replied by showing in the ark of God the only means of social redemption which survived the universal deluge of beliefs and institutions. She had been declared to be dead and buried, and she replied by walking like one alive. It was a novel style of preaching, full of apt and striking illustrations. If error and vice in the individual do not infallibly bring about their own chastisement, if the apostle, in order to rouse the slumbering conscience of the sinner, has most often to point beyond the grave in order to remind him of the terrible vengeance which pursues the offender, it is not so with the vices and wanderings of a nation; their punishment is always written on the brows of the guilty party— vengeance follows immediately and infallibly on the violation of the law. For society there is no hell to be feared, unless it be the hell of a people without principles and without restraint, an abyss of permanent anarchy which offers to the apostle pictures not less terrible, though possibly less familiar: and there is no paradise to hope for, unless it be that golden age which is more or less real according as a nation becomes more or less religious. Nothing is more salu-

tary than to present such pictures to the contemplation of a society, which, even while exhibiting the
most energetic signs of vitality, is yet trembling on
its basis. The preacher of Notre Dame did this, and
he did it precisely at the right moment. The multitude gathered at the foot of his pulpit, made up of
men of every imaginable party, came there in quest
of religious instruction no doubt, but at the same
time they desired to be told what they ought to think
of their different systems, and to be shown how to
solve that great problem, which then agitated every
mind, and which is not yet set at rest, the relations
between Church and State.

During the preceding year these Conferences had
been inaugurated at Notre Dame by preachers who
wanted neither eloquence nor talent, but the great
nave had remained almost empty ; no echo had re-
sponded to their voices. But when it became known
that the orator of Stanislaus was going to preach at
Notre Dame, the gates of the old cathedral were besieged from an early hour in the morning ; every one
wanted, at any price, to hear the voice which told
them old truth: in so new an accent ; which, whilst it
pleaded an eternal cause, had hopes and consolations
for the society of to-day ; which acknowledged that
God was able to heal the nations, and believed that
the first condition for doing good was not to anathe-
matise them. Every one applauded this large and
expansive view of Christianity, wherein God and man,
the Church and society, met and embraced as old
friends, after half a century of divorce. It was a
view which aimed at reconciling the claims of faith
and reason ; which did not even exclude those of
science and industry, and which invested liberty with
her true nobility by tracing her to Calvary as to her
source. All that was great and noble here found a
place : poetry, patriotism, and all the aspirations of
ardent youth ; the war-cry was ever " Forward !" and

the victory was felt to belong to the future, and to God.

Such were the Conferences of Notre Dame; let us hear what was said of them over the tomb of the illustrious orator, by a prelate who had been his constant auditor before he became his friend.

"The Conferences of Notre Dame form an epoch in the history of Christian eloquence, and one from which dates the commencement of an immense religious movement among the youth of the time. The vaulted roofs of the cathedral of Paris now yearly behold the spectacle of thousands of men kneeling at the Holy Table to fulfil their Easter duties. Ask them who made them Christians, and many will reply that the first spark of returning faith was kindled by the lightning-flash of this man's eloquence."[1]

Indeed, it has been too often maintained that these Conferences converted nobody. If all those whom they brought back to practical faith could rise and protest against such an assertion, we should better understand how, with some souls, when the obscurities of the understanding have once disappeared, all the rest is easy. But the fact is, as he himself acknowledged, that the primary object of his preaching was not to communicate the grace which bursts the bonds of sin; "his only aim, though he often obtained more than this, was *to prepare souls for faith.*"[2] He strove to move the masses rather than individuals, and to lead them to the threshold of that Church of which they had heard so many calumnies, to make them admire its divine proportions outside, and thus inspire them with the wish to behold its interior beauties. This mission he gloriously fulfilled. The movement of a return to Catholicism in France dates from this epoch. Until then the Church had lived in a kind of ostracism, jealously guarded by hatred and

[1] Mgr. de la Bouillerie: Funeral Oration on R. P. Lacordaire, pronounced at Sorèze, Nov. 22, 1861.
[2] Preface to Conferences of Notre Dame.

contempt. Among all the voices raised in her defence, none had attained popularity, or exercised any fascination over the public at large. The work of reconciliation began at the foot of the pulpit of Notre Dame. Père Lacordaire, in his notice of Ozanam, whilst attributing the largest share in this movement to the founder of the society of St. Vincent of Paul, thus speaks of these two phases of malicious unbelief and ardent faith, which so wonderfully succeeded one another :

"Those who have not lived through both these periods cannot picture to themselves what it was to pass out of one into the other. For ourselves, who have belonged to both epochs, and who have witnessed the contempt as well as the honour of which religion has been the object, our eyes are filled with tears as we think of the change, and we involuntarily break out into thanksgiving to Him who is unspeakable in His gifts." The Conferences of Notre Dame, and the society of St. Vincent of Paul, formed the germs of that magnificent tree which now extends its boughs over the length and breadth of France. What a contrast between Lacordaire in 1832, disguised under the secular habit in the cholera hospitals of Paris, and Lacordaire at the French academy! And to those who have lived both before and during the quarter of a century that elapses between the two events, we may add, What a prodigy also! Praise be to God who has worked this miracle! As to him who was its chief instrument, it suffices for his glory, and more than suffices for his justification. We will admit, if it is insisted on, that he never converted any one ; it is enough for us that he converted public opinion— in other words, the world.

CHAPTER VIII.

1836—1838.

Interruption of the Conferences— The Abbé Lacordaire visits Rome—Letter on the Holy See—Beginning of his Dominican vocation.

THE Conferences of Notre Dame went on for two years without interruption. Their success daily increased, and the archbishop in an impulse of gratitude had publicly bestowed on the preacher the title of *the new prophet.* He was just beginning to reap the fruits of his labour, and to enjoy that intercourse with souls which is so consolatory to the heart of every priest, and the trace of which was so profoundly stamped on his life that he could not omit dwelling upon the recollection of it in his memoirs. "Until then," he says, "I had passed my days in study and controversy; I now began, by means of the Conferences, to taste something of the apostolic life. I began to enjoy that intercourse with souls which constitutes the happiness of every true priest, and which more than consoles him for every earthly sacrifice. It was at Notre Dame, at the foot of my pulpit, that many friendships and affections sprang up, such as take their rise in no natural qualities, but which bind the preacher and his hearers together by links, the sweetness, as well as the strength of which is divine. I did not personally know all these souls, united to my own by the tie of that spiritual light which had been regained or increased within them; yet I still continue to receive daily testimonials of their gratitude, the earnestness of which astonishes me. I seem like a traveller in the desert on whom a glass of refreshing water is bestowed by an unknown hand. When once we have known these joys, the fragrance of which is like the foretaste of another life, everything else vanishes away; and pride no longer mounts up into the soul, save as the fumes of some impure and noxious vapour which has no power to deceive." Such was the position of the preacher, surrounded by newly-formed ties which seemed to be binding him more closely than ever to his grand and successful mission: when suddenly, in the May of 1836, without any apparent pretext, he resigned the pulpit of Notre Dame, and set out for Rome. He has himself explained the cause of this unexpected determination. On quitting the pulpit at the close of the station of 1836, he said: "I leave in the hands of my bishop this pulpit of Notre Dame, henceforth securely founded by him and by you, by the pastor, and by the flock. For one moment their united suffrage has rested on my head, allow me myself to resign it, and to retire once more into solitude, that I may be alone for a while with my own weakness and with God." Seventeen years later, calling to mind this interruption of his Conferences in the presence of the same audience, he said again: "Here, under this pavement, close to the altar repose the ashes of my two first archbishops; he who summoned me whilst still young to the honour of instructing you, and he who recalled me to the same post when a distrust of my own strength had separated me from you." And again, in his Memoirs, he says, "I understood that I was not yet ripe for the task." He therefore retired before the consciousness of his own insufficiency; this was his first and principal motive. Exactly when the work of apologetic teaching, the dream of his life, appeared settled and founded, when the rising generation, which he had so captivated

11

was applauding his words, and passing lightly over
his defects, perhaps even loving them better than all
the rest beside, he alone hesitates ; he pauses, and
asks for three years more of recollection, study, and
prayer. It is the property of great souls thus to
possess themselves in the midst of the most intoxicating glory, coldly to judge themselves, not according
to the passing breath of human opinion, but by the
calm light of reason ; and it is the property of virtue to
know how to tear itself away from its own triumphs,
in order to acquire in retirement that profounder
science which forms the greatest doctors and saints.

But, it must be added, together with the concert
of praise, there had also been one of clamour and
blame. If the young students, for whom these
Conferences had been specially founded, loudly proclaimed their enthusiastic delight, many in the religious and ecclesiastical circles did not at all comprehend the new style of preaching. " Never before,"
they said, "had the Word of God been thus announced.
Was there no danger to the faith in a mode of teaching which so utterly departed from the beaten track,
and in which souls ran more risk of being led astray
than of being enlightened ?" Others, without going
quite so far, whilst allowing the lawfulness of new
methods when engaged with an exceptional sort of
audience, took offence at certain words and ideas
which they deemed too bold and hazardous. Under
the protection of these remarks, which were not
without a foundation of truth, ill-will and envy poured
forth all their venom. Some sought to terrify the
archbishop, the generosity of whose heart was greater
than the depth or firmness of his mind, and they did
this by perpetually repeating in his ear certain words
chosen for the purpose. Then there was the phantom
of the *Avenir* held up before him, that spectre of
republican and *La Mennaisian* ideas.[1] The Abbé

[1] "The sermons of the Abbé Lacordaire, rightly understood, may be
reduced to newspaper articles, which would very well figure in the

Lacordaire felt the effects of this sinister influence. It would have been easy for him to have explained himself, and to have shown that the partisans of M. de la Mennais were not at all on his side, but rather among the ranks of those who could not pardon his not having recognised the individual efforts of man in his reason and free-will, and who remained attached, as their master had been before 1830, to traditionalism in philosophy, and to absolutism in politics. But he also understood the inutility of defending oneself against adversaries such as these ; he judged it wiser and more Christian to withdraw until time, circumstances, and the grace of God, should effect his complete justification. He therefore went tranquilly where Providence seemed to be leading him for the purpose of bestowing on him ere long, in the restoration of an Order of Preachers, the unforeseen completion of his work at Notre Dame, the reward of his humility under reproaches, and of his self-abnegation in the presence of triumphant success. If he had no clear views as yet of what awaited him at Rome, we may be permitted to believe that he had some presentiment of it. "I knew very well why I undertook this journey," he wrote on his return ; "but I never could have believed that Providence would have poured out upon me such abundant favours." And once, on the eve of an important decision, he said to us, in a moment of unusual openness of heart, "At all the solemn epochs of my life, I have never failed to hear the voice of God interiorly urging me forwards, and telling me what I was to do. I have always followed this secret impulse, and I have never had reason to repent doing so."

---

pages of a new *Avenir*. In our judgment, they constitute the most perfect degradation of preaching, the most complete anarchy, we will not say of theological, but simply of philosophical, thought."—*Letter to the Clergy and the Audience of Notre Dame.* By the author of "The Priest before the World." Paris : Beaujouan, Rue Saint André des Arts, 1837.

He therefore took up his abode at Rome. He went
there out of a kind of instinct, as the stone falls to its
centre, as the child runs to its mother, as the ship,
tossed with the tempest, seeks its port. Once already,
after the storms of the *Avenir*, he had there found
peace, and inhaled the pure air of true liberty; and
now he came again to ask that the same blessings
might be a second time renewed. Unlike those
rationalists who see in the Holy See the oppressor of
the intellect, he knew, " he had learnt from his own
experience that the Church is the true liberator of
the human mind." He had still present in his heart
that sentiment of ineffable joy, which had made him
write, as he rose from his prayer, " I know neither
the day nor the hour when it came to pass, but I see
what before I did not see, and I leave Rome free and
victorious!" Minds that are in love with their own
ideas fly from Rome with the same eagerness as she
is sought by humble children of the truth, who ask
for a master and a counsellor to guide their steps.
He had been accused at Paris of remaining secretly
attached to the system of a man who had violently
separated from Catholic unity. And he knew no
better reply than to go and live at Rome, at the very
centre of that unity, under the eye of him who is the
sovereign judge of all controversies. These attacks
now cause us astonishment, and one really knows not
how to account for this bitter animosity against a
priest, who from the first had shown such an admirable submission; who in 1834 had replied to the
Paroles d'un Croyant by an express and public refutation of the system of *universal reason*, and who,
more completely to dissipate all doubts, had gone to
Rome, to work, so to speak, under the eye of the
Holy Father. Yet after a residence of eighteen
months in that city, when this same priest was about
to announce his purpose of re-establishing one of the
fallen Orders in France, we shall see letters written
from Paris to Rome warning the authorities to dis-

trust the enterprise, for that this proposed Order was only destined to be a citadel and place of refuge for the old friends of M. de la Mennais. These facts help us to appreciate the obstacles which he had to encounter at every step he took, and which opposed even the purest and most sacred of his enterprises: and they show us how happily he was inspired when he determined to interrupt his Conferences and make this visit to Rome, without which, perhaps, nothing of all that he afterwards achieved would have been possible.

Once installed at Rome, he set to work without delay, like a man who has his end perfectly clear before him, and who takes his time to reach it. " I am occupying myself," he writes, " with a work which requires time, and will very well fill up my days, and give me the satisfaction of contributing my share as a priest to the labours of the Church." He had only been there a few months when M. de la Mennais published a new work against the Holy See, entitled, *"Les Affaires de Rome,"*—a kind of impeachment of his former judges, which made Madame Swetchine say : —" No one but an angel or a priest could have fallen so low !" The Abbé Lacordaire, whose name was mixed up in the affair, thought it his duty to reply. He was quite prepared to do so. He was for the second time experiencing the unutterable charm exercised over the soul by that city, " where all races have passed, to which all glories have come, where all cultivated imaginations have made at least one pilgrimage,—the tomb of the apostles, and of the martyrs, the council chamber of all memories—Rome !" [1]

He replied by his admirable *Letter on the Holy See.* In it M. de la Mennais was not named. But what a refutation it was ! What a distance did it not display between the former master, now the voluntary slave of pride, and the former disciple, set free through the Truth ! Whilst the first had not

[1] Letter on the Holy See.

dreamt of representing the question, as involving anything of a higher nature than the relations of one
man with Rome, the other had viewed it as it affected
the relations of Rome with Europe, with the whole
human race, and with God. God had not only willed
to establish on earth a Kingdom of Truth; He had
from the beginning chosen one city to be the Citadel
of Truth; and that city is not Jerusalem, but Rome.
If, after man has been redeemed through the Blood
of His Son, He has made the four great rivers of
that saving Blood to flow forth over the world, it is
not from the Rock of Calvary, but from the Rock of
the Vatican that the sacred streams will for ever flow.
And finally, if Europe, if the world is to have a
future, if the nations are to retain any gleam of hope
in the midst of their present commotions, it is on
Rome that they must fix their glance; and it is
thence alone that their Life and their Hope will
come. The Providential Mission of Rome in the
past, in the present, and in the future, make up the
subject of this work, which forms one of the purest
glories of the author's genius. He gives only outlines
and sketches, but they are of wonderful grandeur;
and the justice of his conclusions is only confirmed by
time. What truth, what eloquence, there is in the
following burst of faith and love, which so admirably
concludes these beautiful pages!

"When time shall have done justice on all those
miserable theories which, by enslaving the Catholic
Church, have deprived her of a great part of her influence on society, it will be easy to know what
remedy to apply. It will then be known that the art
of governing men does not consist in giving free reins
to the power of evil, and in putting good under watch
and ward. Good will be set free, and men wearied
out with the policy of the world will be told at last,
You wish to devote yourself to God? Devote yourselves. You wish to retire from a world which is too
full, and in which intellects superabound? Well, then,

retire. You wish to consecrate your fortune to the relief of your suffering brethren? Consecrate it. You desire to spend your life teaching the poor and the young? Then teach them. You bear a name loaded with three centuries of hatred, because your virtues have appeared late in a world which is no longer worthy of them, and you are not ashamed still to bear that name? Then bear it. All you who desire good, under whatever form, all who would wage war on pride and revolted sense, come and do what you will. We have exhausted ourselves in framing new combinations of social forms, and the elixir of life has never yet flowed out of our broken crucibles. He who has life alone gives it; he who has love diffuses it abroad, he who possesses the secret can alone reveal it to others! Then will commence a new age, over which new treasures of riches will be poured out; and this wealth will consist neither of gold nor silver, nor vessels brought from the uttermost ends of the earth and containing precious and costly things; it will neither be steam nor railways, nor all that the genius of man shall be able to tear out of the bosom of nature. There is but one thing which we can truly call wealth, and that is, *Love.* Love alone unites all things and fills all things; it knits together God and man, earth and heaven; it is the beginning, the middle, and the end of all things. He who loves, knows; he who loves, lives; he who loves, devotes himself; he who loves, is happy and content; one drop of love weighed against the entire universe would bear it away as the tempest whirls away a morsel of straw."

It will be seen that his thoughts were already engaged on the plan of obtaining liberty for the religious Orders: and this page was an eloquent plea in their favour. The manuscript of this *Letter* was shown at Rome by the author to competent judges, who gave it their entire approbation. The Abbé Lacordaire might have been content with this, and have sent the work to his publisher, but he preferred, out of delicacy, first of all to apply to Mgr. de Quélin, and ask his advice. Madame Swetchine was charged with this mission ; she employed her influence in the matter with the archbishop, using her accustomed tact in the management of this sort of business, aided yet more by her affection for the author, and her admiration for his work. Strange to say, and sad as strange, this time she did not succeed. The opinion of the archbishop, or rather that of his council, was that it was better to *adjourn* the publication, a polite word, which ill concealed a yet severer decision. It was represented that this defence of the Holy See was inopportune, certain phrases were indicated as liable to censure, and it was hinted that it would be better to consult the peace of mind of the author, and so on. The Abbé Lacordaire could not be mistaken as to what was really intended by all this ; not on the part of Mgr. de Quélen, who always sincerely loved him, but by those who suggested these objections. Every part of this apology of the Holy See had been prudently measured and attentively weighed. He had taken due precautions for satisfying his adversaries in Paris, who accused him of excessively radical tendencies, and of a systematic hatred of certain forms of government : and this was remembered when in 1848 they wished to find matter in this same *Letter* for opposing his admission into the Legislative Assembly. In reply to a book full of passion and personality he had placed the policy of the Holy See in so high a point of view that all mere party questions and party cries disappeared. Rome had read his book, and approved it, but Paris disapproved. If it be remembered that Mgr. de Quélen was surrounded by men who, as M. Affre avows, had urged the archbishop to confide the pulpit of Notre Dame to the Abbé Lacordaire, in the secret hope of seeing him humbled, who by their incessant meddling had removed him from it for a time, and who, even at Rome, pursued him with their attacks in the public newspapers,[1] we shall better appreciate the humble attitude which he assumed before so unexpected a refusal. There was an exchange of notes and letters on the subject. The archbishop wished to keep the manuscript, and the Abbé Lacordaire begged him to destroy it. Happily the archbishop did not do this, and the *Letter on the Holy See* was published about a year afterwards, in the beginning of 1838, to the joy of all the true friends of Rome ; and it is needless to say without any of the fears that had been suggested being realised.

These contradictions were not of a nature to make him regret Paris. At Rome, on the other hand, he everywhere found the best possible welcome. He was offered the post of chaplain at St. Louis des Français, and everything seemed to confirm him in his resolution of prolonging his residence in the city. About the beginning of 1837 he wrote as follows : " I could not be more kindly treated than I am by everybody in Rome. I regret my friends and those excellent young men whom I love so much ; but my time here will not be lost, and we must be content to wait awhile if we desire to do any real good. . . At no period of my life was I ever more calm and happy. I feel as though I were in port. Nowhere certainly is there to be found so much liberty with so much security. Everybody does not here make dogmas of his own ideas, and a Church of his own party. Passions roused at a distance, when they seek to glide in here, die away like the foam on the seashore. . . . . I have quite renounced Paris. My furniture is all sold. The success of M. de Ravignan, so fortunate for the cause of religion, has greatly facilitated the accomplishment of my resolutions. It would have been difficult for me not to have returned to Paris had there been no one to replace me ; but Providence has provided for that, and moreover it is in itself a very desirable thing

[1] See *Madame Swetchine,* by M. de Falloux. t. i. p. 373.

that the work at Notre Dame should not in any way be personal, but should be made the occasion for bringing out various talents for the glory of the clergy and the instruction of youth. Everything is for the best."[1]

He was writing thus at the beginning of 1837, when, in the summer of the same year, one of his old friends and fellow-students at St. Sulpice, the Abbé Chalandon, canon-theologian of Metz, and since Archbishop of Aix, met him at Rome, and begged him to come to Metz to preach there during the winter. This proposal pleased him. The wise advice of Madame Swetchine, and his own experience, began to convince him that a complete isolation, "a life spent in his study, without the stimulus of action, was not his vocation." It might be useful to try and extend in the provinces the idea of a kind of instruction which is necessary for a certain class of minds. Nevertheless we find him, before giving any promise, asking the advice of his friends in Paris. It was not merely M. de Montalembert and Madame Swetchine whom he consulted, but a new name, that of Madame la Comtesse Eudoxie de la Tour du Pin, whose touching relations with Père Lacordaire, so little known to the public, have been revealed to us by a mutual friend. It is of her that he wrote in 1851: "She was for twenty years one of the strengths of my life, by the elevation of her mind, her sympathy with mine, and her admirable spirit of self-sacrifice." Often when at Paris, having to come to some decision, he hastened to Versailles to consult her, whom he called "a rare and worthy friend." To take advice was no merit with him ; it was as much a necessity of his heart as of his intellect. Distrustful of himself, from his genius and from his virtue, he willingly accepted the lights of his friends, and made it his delight to think with them and incline to their advice. "Our own notions,

[1] Letters to Madame Eudoxie de la Tour du Pin. Douniol : Paris, 1864.

are always so uncertain," he wrote to this same friend at Versailles, " that one is delighted to find them in conformity with those of persons whom one esteems and loves." He consulted her therefore on the project of going to preach during the winter at Metz with the simplicity of a child, and a sense of the pleasure he was giving his friend when he wrote : " I want your advice, and I ask it of you in confidence. Tell me what you think of all this."

The station of Metz being agreed on, he was preparing to return to France, when the cholera detained him at Rome. The crisis was short, but terrible. Almost every one abandoned the city, but he remained, and put himself at the disposition of the Cardinal-Vicar. He wrote about this time (August 30th) : " You know the state of Rome ; even if the roads were free, I could not think of leaving under such sad circumstances. My slight knowledge of the Italian language, specially as it is spoken by the people, will not allow of my being of any very great assistance ; but it is a consolation to my incapacity to be at least exposed to the same dangers with them."[1]

At the end of September, 1837, the traces of the pestilence having nearly disappeared, he prepared to depart ; and on the 24th he wrote : " I set out tomorrow at four o'clock in the morning by a *veturino*, who will take me in thirteen days to Milan, without stoppage and without quarantine, together with the Abbot of Solesmes, a young Frenchman of my acquaintance, and an English Catholic gentleman. I go, well pleased with my journey, with my residence at Rome, and with all that I have learnt here ; loving the Holy See, in spite of its misfortunes, and France better than ever. I have seen the Pope, and received some precious souvenirs from him."[2] He carried away with him from Rome another thought, of which he does not here speak, but which constantly pursued

[1] Unpublished letters.   [2] Ibid.

him; a thought which overwhelmed him with *its* weight, and under which his *soul sank down like a rider under his horse :* [1] a thought of which we find no trace in his correspondence, but which was about to transform his entire life. He was dreaming not only of becoming a religious, but of restoring some decayed Order in France. He had not yet come to any decision on the subject; but it was during these eighteen months passed at Rome that the light had arisen on his mind, and that he had received his call from on high. He alone can reveal to us the secrets of his Dominican vocation, and can explain its causes, its difficulties, its progress, and its final victory; and he has done this under circumstances which greatly add to the interest of the narrative. This "Memoir on the Re-establishment in France of the Order of Friar-Preachers" was dictated, as we have already said, on his death-bed. The chapter which we shall extract from it, and from which M. de Montalembert has already quoted a long fragment, will be, especially to his children, like a last glance on his religious family, a memorial of the most secret and hidden recesses of his life. He had never opened it before at that page; it was like the final chant, the last cry of the soul which closes a destiny and immortalises it; after which the book is shut for ever.

"My long residence at Rome gave me opportunity for many reflections; I studied myself, and I also studied the general necessities of the Church. As to myself, already in my thirty-fourth year, having been in holy orders for twelve years, and having twice attained a certain degree of notoriety in matters undertaken for the defence of religion in France, I now found myself alone again, without ecclesiastical ties of any kind; and more than once the kindness of Mgr. de Quélen had given me to understand that parochial administration was the only line in which he should be able to help me forward. Now I felt

[1] Memoirs.

no sort of vocation to that kind of work, and at the same I saw very well, that in the existing state of the Church in France, no other path seemed to promise that security and stability which every reasonable man must desire.

" If from these personal considerations I passed on to the wants of the Church herself, it seemed clear to me that since the destruction of the religious Orders she had lost one half of her strength. I saw at Rome the magnificent remains of those institutions which had been founded by the greatest saints ; and there was then sitting on the pontifical throne, as so many had sat before him, a monk who had been drawn out of the illustrious cloisters of San Gregorio. History, yet more eloquent than the sight of Rome, showed me, from the very time when the Church came forth out of the catacombs, that wonderful series of cells, of monasteries, of abbeys, of houses of study and prayer, scattered far and wide, from the sands of the Thebaid to the farthest extremities of Ireland, and from the perfumed islands of Provence to the colder plains of Poland or Russia. It displayed before me the names of St. Anthony, St. Basil, St. Augustine, St. Martin, St. Benedict, St. Columbanus, St. Bernard, St. Francis of Assisi, St. Dominic, and St. Ignatius, the patriarchs of those numberless families who have filled the deserts, the forests, the plains, and even the chair of St. Peter with their heroic virtues. On that luminous track, the true milky-way of the Church, I discerned, as the creative principle, the three vows of poverty, obedience, and chastity—keystones of the gospel's vaulted roof, and of the perfect imitation of Jesus Christ. For He was poor, living during His childhood by manual labour, and during the course of His apostolic life on the charity of those who loved Him. He was chaste also, and He practised obedience to His Father, even to the death of the cross. There was the sovereign model left by Him to His apostles, and the fruitful germ, which later on had blossomed through long ages in the souls of these holy founders. In vain has corruption, now on this side, and now on that, gnawed at these venerable institutions. Wherever the flesh left its trace, the Spirit breathed on it again, so that corruption itself was but the fading of long-established virtues, as one sometimes sees in forests where the axe has never penetrated, trees fall under the weight of a life that has lasted so long, it can no longer resist the inroads of decay. Were we then to believe that the day had come when we were no more to behold these great monuments of faith, these divine inspirations of the love of God and man? Must we then think that the wind of revolution, instead of being the passing minister of vengeance to their faults, had been the sword and the seal of death? I could not believe it. Whatever God does is of its very nature immortal, and it is no more possible for a virtue to disappear out of the world than for a star to be lost out of the heavens.

"I persuaded myself, therefore, as I wandered through Rome, praying in her Basilicas, that the greatest service which could be rendered to Christendom in our time would be to do something for the restoration of the religious Orders. But this persuasion, though to me as clear as the gospel, left me undecided and trembling, when I went on to reflect how insufficient I was for so great a work. I had no ambition for ecclesiastical honours; and indeed, even before my conversion, I had never been sensible of that ordinary ambition on which the hearts of most men are fixed. I had loved glory before I loved God, and that was all. Nevertheless, on looking into myself, I found nothing there which appeared to me to correspond to the idea of a founder or restorer of an Order. When I cast my eyes on those giants of ancient piety and fortitude, my soul sank under me like a rider under the weight of his horse. I remained prostrate on the earth, as it were, all bruised and out of heart. The mere thought of sacrificing my liberty to a rule, and to superiors, terrified me. The child of an age that knows not how to obey, independence had been at once my cradle and my guide. How should I be able suddenly to transform myself into a docile child, and no longer seek for light to direct my actions, save in humble submission?

" Then I went on to consider further, the difficulty of gathering men together, the difference of characters, the holiness of some, the mediocrity of others, the ardour of these, the icy coldness of those, the opposite tendencies of minds, and all the causes which, even among the saints, combine to render a religious community at once the most consoling and the most painful of burdens. After the spiritual difficulties which would have to be encountered, those of a temporal nature next presented themselves. How should I be able to purchase large houses, and provide for the necessities of a crowd of religious, as poor as myself? And ought I, on mere faith in Providence, to cast myself on the chances of so perilous an issue?

" Nor was this all ; all the exterior obstacles rose up before me like so many mountains. Could I expect so much as toleration from the French Government? Even if the laws of the Revolution had done no more than declare that the State no longer recognised religious vows, and deprive communities of their hereditary patrimony—even if a vow were of its nature an act of the conscience, which is free and beyond attack, and community life one of the natural rights of man, nevertheless, even within this limitation, and under this form, the government of 1830 was evidently very little disposed to allow the religious Orders to spring up again on the soil of France. It put up with the Jesuits, as being a sort of accomplished fact, yet even they had but a precarious existence, and were every moment threatened by the current of public opinion. This public opinion was the last and most difficult

obstacle which had to be overcome; it preserved all
the traditions of the eighteenth century in regard of
the religious Orders, and did not discern the funda-
mental difference which exists between communities
living by their daily labour, and those powerful associations which existed of old, recognised by the State
both in themselves and in their rights of property.
No association, even literary or artistic, being able to
establish itself in France without a formal authorisation, this extreme servitude, which was nevertheless
accepted by the nation, gave prejudice an easy means
of sheltering itself against any appeal to natural right
or public law. What was to be done in a country
where religious liberty, admitted by all as a sacred
principle of modern society, was yet unable to protect
in the heart of one of her citizens the invisible act of
a promise made to God, and where the avowal of
this promise, if forced from him by tyrannical question-
ing, might suffice to deprive him of the advantages
enjoyed by the rest of the community? When a
nation has come to this pass, and when all liberty appears to it to be the privilege of those who do not
believe, against those who do, can we ever hope to
see the reign of equity, peace, and stability, or of any
better kind of civilisation than material progress?

"My idea, therefore, as may be seen, met with
nothing but obstacles on all sides, and, less fortunate
than Columbus, I could not even discover so much as
a plank which might bear me to the shores of liberty.
My only resource lay in that audacity which animated
the early Christians, and in their immovable faith in
the Almighty power of God. I said to myself, Christianity would never have existed in the world if there
had not sprung up obscure people, plebeians, workmen,
philosophers, and senators, little and great, who were
resolved to follow the gospel in spite of the Cæsars
and their laws. The cross has never ceased to be a
folly ; *the weakness of God* has continued, according to
the words of St. Paul, *to be stronger than man.* He

who would do anything for the Church, and who does not set out with this conviction, at the same time neglecting no human means which circumstances permit him to employ, will always remain unfit for the service of God. The first Christians did not merely die; they wrote and they spoke; they laboured to convince the emperors and the people of the justice of their cause; and St. Paul preaching Jesus Christ on the Hill of Mars, made use of the most ingenious terms of human eloquence in order to persuade his hearers. There is always in the human heart, in the state of minds, in the course of public opinion, in laws, times, and, in short, in everything, a basis for God to stand on. The great heart is to discern and use this, at the same time making the principle of our courage and hope to consist in the secret and invisible strength of God. Christianity has never braved the world; it has never insulted reason and nature; it has never made its light a power which blinds by dint of irritating: but as gentle as it is bold, as calm as it is energetic, as tender as it is immovable, it has always known how to penetrate into the heart of its generation; and those souls who will be found remaining faithful to it at the last day will have been preserved or conquered by the same means.

"I encouraged myself with thoughts like these; and it came into my mind that all my foregoing life, and even my very faults themselves, had prepared a way for me into the heart of my country and my age. I asked myself if I should not be guilty in neglecting these opportunities merely out of a timidity which would be of profit to nothing but my own case, and if the very greatness of the sacrifice were not a sufficient reason for attempting it.

"After the general question came the secondary one, namely, to what order I should give myself. Religious Orders are divided into two branches, perfectly distinct from one another. Those belonging to the first are consecrated in the shadow of the cloister, to the interior perfection of the religious himself, and only enter into the public service of the Church by means of prayer and penance : while others are devoted to work for the salvation of souls by the exterior means of science, preaching, and good works, which, born in retreat, come forth from it as Jesus Christ came and passed from the desert to Thabor and Calvary. Among these last named, which were the only ones to which my choice could possibly direct itself, history pointed out to me two great institutes. The first, created in the thirteenth century for the defence of the orthodox faith against the attack of the first great Latin heresies; the other, founded in the sixteenth century, to act as a barrier against the spread of Protestantism—the last and greatest form of religious error in the West. Everywhere rivals of each other, for the precise reason that their weapons were the same, and their end identical, there were, however, some notable differences between these two institutes. St. Dominic had laid a great burden on the body, while at the same time he left considerable latitude to the mind ; St. Ignatius had restricted the mind within the narrowest limits, but, at the same time, he had set the body free from every rule which could possibly weaken it, or render it less fit for the work of teaching and preaching. St. Dominic had given to his government the form of a limited monarchy; he had made his superiors chosen by election, and his legislation to proceed from chapters; while St. Ignatius, on the other hand, had bestowed on his Order the forms of absolute monarchy. I had then to choose between the Society of Jesus and the Order of Friar Preachers ; or rather I had no choice at all to make, for the Jesuits already existed in France, and had no need of being re-established there. The force of events, therefore, left me no doubt on the second point, but, at the same time, as it brought before me face to face the necessity of becoming a Dominican, it greatly increased my fear and irresolution. The exterior austerities of this Order, such as the perpetual abstinence from flesh meat, the

long fast from Holy Cross to Easter, the singing of
the Divine Office, the rising at midnight—all presented
themselves to me as impracticable with our weakened
bodies, specially when united to the labours of the
apostolate, so prodigiously increased by the rarity in
the present day of preachers and missionaries. I knew
by experience the prostration of strength which is occasioned by a single discourse, pronounced from the
bottom of the soul before a numerous assembly, and
I asked myself how fasting and abstinence could be
compatible with such efforts of nature, and such profound exhaustion. Nevertheless, on studying the
Constitutions of the Order, I saw that they contained
resources against themselves, or rather that the general
austerity was wisely tempered by the power possessed
by superiors of granting dispensations, not only on
account of sickness, but also in case of weakness, and
even out of the mere motive of facilitating the conversion of souls. I remarked that the only limit imposed
on superiors in the use of these dispensations was, that
they must never be extended to the entire community.
This latitude made me understand that here, as elsewhere, "the letter kills, but the Spirit giveth life." I
set myself to study the life of St Dominic, and those
of the great saints who came after him, and inherited his
virtues. The saints are the great men of the Church,
and mark on the summits of her history the most
elevated points ever attained by human nature. The
more saints an Order has produced the more is it
manifest that the grace of God has taken part in its
foundation, and continues to maintain its immortality.
All this reassured me, and of the four great elements
of which every religious institute is composed, a legislation, a spirit, a history, and a grace, it seemed to me
that not one, in all its fulness, was wanting to the Order
of St. Dominic.

"Nevertheless I had not yet made up my mind
when I returned to France towards the end of 1837.
After having preached at Metz through the whole

12—2

winter of 1838, during a mission which was largely attended, I went back to Paris. There I partially opened my mind to some of my more intimate friends. Nowhere did I meet with any sort of encouragement. Madame Swetchine let me have my own way rather than she could be said to have supported me. The others saw nothing in my project but a pure chimera. According to one the time of the religious Orders had passed by; according to another the Society of Jesus sufficed for everything, and it was useless to attempt there suscitation of Orders which were no longer needed. Some saw in the Dominican Order nothing but a decrepit and worn-out institute, stamped with the obsolete forms and ideas of the middle ages, and rendered unpopular by its connexion with the Inquisition ; and advised me, if I really wished to try the adventure, to create something new. Meanwhile it was necessary to determine on something. I had lost my mother a few years before, on the 2nd of February, 1836, and I could no longer shelter myself under the protection of her age ; on the other hand there was no longer any motive for a return to Rome. Urged forward by the situation in which I found myself, and pressed by a grace which was stronger than myself, I at last made up my mind, but it was a bloody sacrifice. Whilst it had cost me nothing to quit the world in order to become a priest, it cost me everything to add to the priesthood the additional burdens of religious life. Nevertheless in the second case as in the first, when once I had yielded my consent, I felt neither weakness nor repentance, and was able to march courageously forward to meet all the trials which awaited me."

One circumstance which must have encouraged the Abbé Lacordaire in his project was the success which had attended the attempt made by the Abbé Guéranger to restore the Benedictine Order in France. They had known one another at Rome; their community of views and thoughts had established a friendship be-

tween them ; and when the sanction of the Holy See
had been obtained for the establishment of Solesmes,
the Abbé Lacordaire announced it to his friends at
Paris as a kind of triumph. "We have at last an
abbot with mitre and crosier. . . . Solesmes is erected
into an abbey, the abbot will be for life, and all the
future Benedictine establishments in France will be
dependent on him ; . . . it is a real miracle."[1] Nevertheless, the success was not yet complete, and the
Abbé Lacordaire, on his next journey to Rome in 1838,
was to have the happiness of changing and ameliorating
the position of the Abbey of Solesmes, in consequence
of a conversation he had with Cardinal Lambruschini,
and a memorial, which he presented to Cardinal
Sala. This memorial, drawn up by the Abbé Lacordaire, had its effect ; and a few days afterwards, the
general of the Jesuits said to him, "You came just in
time for that affair."

We are not therefore surprised to find him at
Solesmes during two months of the summer of 1838,
studying the constitutions of the Order of St Dominic,
and ripening his project in solitude and prayer.
"Solesmes," he writes, "offers me a very agreeable
retreat, together with leisure, books, the company of
pious and learned persons, and strict economy.[2] I am
throughly happy and contented here. I have already
in the last eight days devoured I know not how many
great volumes, treating on our affair ; and all I read
confirms me in it the more. It is rather singular, I
have just seen an ecclesiastic, a thoroughly good man,
who came here to advise me to do precisely what I am
thinking of doing, and the very same thing happened
to me at Metz. The only thought which sometimes
dismays me, is to find myself too imperfect. I recognise in myself some good things, and especially a real
advance, during the fourteen years that have elapsed
since I first entered the service of God. It seems to

[1] Letter to Madame de la Tour du Pin.   [2] *Ibid.*

me that I am disinterested, sober-minded, not particularly proud, much more detached from the world and from a care of reputation than formerly, much more capable of self-denial, inclined towards God both in intellect and heart, easily moved by divine things, and yet nevertheless my life seems so thoroughly ordinary! However, God will dispose of me as He pleases. I feel the more confidence about it all since I never undertook anything with more calm and mature deliberation. You would not believe how tranquil and patient I feel about it. I am not pressed for time, which is an uncommon thing with me. The Abbot of Solesmes thinks me very fit for the work, and encourages me greatly about it."[1]

His residence in France did not last an entire year. Having left Rome in the September of 1837, he returned thither in the July of 1838. His plans were ripe, a secret power was urging him to break the last ties that held him back, and to set his hand to the work. Henceforth his letters give us the most faithful reflection of his soul, and we shall therefore frequently allow him to relate in his own words his life, his impressions, and his interior and religious joys.

[1] Letter to Madame Swetchine, June, 1838.

CHAPTER IX.

1838, 1839.

First attempts—Memoir on the Re-establishment in France of the Friars-Preachers—Departure for Rome with Réquédat.

BEFORE setting out for Rome the Abbé Lacordaire wished to take leave of Mgr. de Quélen, and to open his heart to him. This interview is related in his Memoirs, together with some singular circumstances :

" Mgr. de Quélen as yet knew nothing of my project, and imagined I had come back to Paris in order to resume the course of my Conferences at Notre Dame. I thought it right to inform him how matters stood. He was then living at the Pension of the Ladies of the Sacred Heart. After having heard what I had to say, he replied coldly, 'Ah, this is in the hands of God, but His Will is not as yet manifested.' Now he himself was just about to make it manifest to me, and to give me at the same time the first encouragement I had as yet received. When I arose to take my leave, I said to him, that, should we reestablish the Order of Friars-Preachers in France, St. Hyacinth would no doubt be favourable to us. Hyacinth was one of his baptismal names, and is the name also of one of the greatest Dominican saints. ' No doubt,' he replied, '-and perhaps it is you who are destined to accomplish my dream.' ' What

dream, my lord ?' 'How! do you not know my dream ?'
'No, my lord.' 'Well, then I will relate it to you ; sit
down.' And then in the most charming way, and quite
like another man, he related the following narrative :
" 'I had just been named Coadjutor of Paris with
the title of Archbishop of Trajanopolis. In the month
of August, 1820, the Cardinal de Perigord wished to
give a private retreat in his palace, exclusively to the
curés of Paris, and on this occasion I occupied an apartment in the archbishop's house. In the night of the
3rd of August, being the eve of the feast of St. Dominic,
as the clock of Notre Dame struck two in the morning,
it seemed to me that I was in the gardens of the palace,
opposite to that little arm of the Seine which flows
between the buildings of the Hôtel-Dieu. I was seated
in a chair. After a minute or two I saw a great crowd
gathered on the brink of the river, and looking up to
heaven. The sky was clear and cloudless, but the sun
appeared covered with a black veil, through which its
rays found their way, tinted of the colour of blood ; i's
course was rapid, and it seemed to be hastening to
wards the horizon. Soon it disappeared beneath it,
and all the people fled, crying out, "Ah ! what a misfortune !" Left alone, I saw the waters of the Seine,
swollen by a tide which flowed in from the sea, its
great waves entirely filling up the narrow channel.
Various marine monsters also, brought in by the flood,
stopped in front of Notre Dame and the archbishop's
house, and tried to cast themselves from the river on
to the quay. Then my dream changed ; I seemed to
be transported into a convent of nuns clothed in black,
where I remained for a very long time. At the end of
my exile I found myself at the same place where my
dream had begun. But the archiepiscopal palace had
disappeared, and in its place there stretched before my
eyes a flowery lawn. The waters of the Seine had resumed their natural course. The sun shone with its accustomed splendour. The air was fresh and perfumed
with the sweet scents of spring, summer, and autumn,

all combined ; it was something which I had never before seen or felt in the whole course of nature. Whilst I was enjoying it in a sort of intoxication of delight, I perceived to the right of me ten men all clothed in white ; they plunged their hands into the Seine, drew out the marine monsters I had seen there, and laid them on the grass, now transformed into lambs. You see,' he added, 'that the whole of this dream of 1820 has been faithfully accomplished. The monarchy, represented by the sun covered with its black veil, has suddenly fallen into the very midst of the rejoicings caused by the taking of Algiers ; and the insurgents attacked both Notre Dame and my palace. The palace was destroyed, and a lawn, planted with trees, now covers its site. I have for a long time inhabited, and still inhabit, here in this very place, a house belonging to nuns dressed in black. What now remains in order that the whole of my dream should be accomplished, save that I should see at Paris these men *clothed in white*, occupied in converting the people ? Perhaps it will be you who will bring them here.'

" Singular to relate, some months afterwards when I had taken the habit of the Friars-Preachers at the Convent of the Minerva at Rome, I wrote to acquaint Mgr. de Quélen with the fact, in a letter full of gratitude and respectful affection. Contrary to his usual custom, he remained two months without replying to me ; at last I received a line from him, in which he told me that the very day after my letter reached him he had been seized with a serious illness, from which he was still suffering ;—and of which he actually died at the close of the year 1839.

" Thus, in the dream of 1820, he had seen all the chief events of his episcopal career, and its end had been indicated to him by the apparition of these white-robed religious, who were shortly, in my person, and from the pulpit of Notre Dame, to evangelise his flock."

Having left Paris on the 31st of July, 1838, the Abbé Lacordaire reached Rome on the Feast of the Assumption. We shall let him relate, in his own private letters, the history of this important journey, the new cloistral life which was revealing itself to him, and his gratitude to God for the rapid success of his enterprise. No other pen than his could do justice to the lively picture, or paint the joy which overflowed his heart even under the new restraints of community life, or the tears of tenderness shed by the old friars at the Minerva at the unexpected arrival of this new scion of their race.

In the most insignificant circumstances he sees the hand of Providence leading him on. Our readers will pardon us, then, for respectfully and affectionately preserving the trifling details recorded in these pages. After some great battle had been gained, the historian cares to gather up the smallest incidents of the day, and to relate all the marches and counter-marches of the troops engaged. He notes down the names of every little strip of land, or obscure rivulet. Now for us this journey of our Father was his Italian campaign, and each one of its bivouacs must therefore have a place in our annals.

He thus writes from Spoleto on the 31st of August :

"How is it that I can be already at Spoleto? Nevertheless, here I am, writing to you on some vile paper, belonging to the inn, with a detestable pen, and the very worst forebodings, to tell you that I shall not be at N—— till Wednesday evening. I shall go there without passing through Rome, exactly like a conspirator who has his passport in his pocket. I should like to have written to Cardinal Lambruschini before entering Rome, in order to acquaint him with the state of affairs, and to make sure of being well received by him. All this will occupy some days. I am much touched with the hospitality you offer me on this occasion, which is one of such great interest to me. For the rest, my heart is full of the sentiments which your kindness calls forth.

" I left Paris on the 31st of July, and reached Genoa quickly enough, travelling partly by diligence, partly by courier. At Genoa the sea was so calm and the passage so short, that I ventured as far as Leghorn by the steam vessel, and hardly suffered at all. The courier took me on from Florence to Foligno, where, the conveyance to Bologna being providentially full, a thing which had not occurred to me before during my entire journey, I understood that what I had to do was to take a *veturino*, pass the walls of Rome, and travel on to N—— *incognito*." [1]

On the 22nd of August he gave an account to Madame Swetchine of his first proceedings. "The day after that which followed my arrival at Frascati I wrote to Cardinal Lambruschini to beg an audience of him, wishing to do nothing without support at headquarters. Yesterday, Mgr. Capaccini sent me word that the cardinal had gone to his abbey of Poggio-Mirteto; that he had received my letter before his departure, and that he would see me either on Saturday, Sunday, or any other day I might choose. Mgr. Capaccini's note was written in the kindest terms. I have just replied to him, and next Saturday I shall see him and the cardinal, after which, according as they may advise, I shall introduce myself at the Minerva. So you see, my dear friend, how things now stand. As for me, I am calmer and more resolved than ever. My plan has greatly ripened in my mind; pray much for me. Adieu, I cannot sufficiently entreat you to tell me your opinion as bluntly as possible. With my friends I am as hard as bronze." [2]

Five days later he announces to Madame Swetchine the result of these proceedings in a bulletin of victory. " You have certainly been praying hard for me, my dear friend, for never has battle been more completely

---

[1] Unpublished Letters.   [2] August 22, 1838.

gained than this. I wrote to you from Frascati that I had an audience fixed for the 25th with the Secretary of State. I arrived in Rome early, and went first to Mgr. Capaccini. After I had explained my plan, of which I think he had already heard, he told me there would be no kind of difficulty about it. We talked together for a long time, and he spoke very openly. He told me that the cardinal was going to the Church of St. Louis, and that I should do well to put off seeing him till the following Tuesday, which is to-morrow, when I should have finished my business at the Minerva. I understood from this that the cardinal knew everything, and that they had agreed as to the reply. So I went at once to the Minerva and called on Père Lamarche. He welcomed me as if I had been a messenger from Heaven, and made an appointment for me with the Father-General for the evening of the following day, the 26th. The present General is named Ancaroni. He has just been elected for six years, and thinks of nothing but the reform of the Order. I cannot tell you what a delightful conversation I had with this good and holy old man. I seemed to hear St. Simeon chanting his *Nunc Dimittis.* To be brief, they will give us Santa Sabina, to make our noviciate there alone, and will send elsewhere the novices who are now there, so we shall be none but Frenchmen. The noviciate will last a year, after which the colony will return to France, with myself as Provincial, or perhaps even Vicar-General, with *carte blanche.* All the necessary modifications of the rule will be granted ; we shall be allowed to found colleges, and shall have three sorts of houses, noviciates, professed houses, and colleges, thus uniting the life of the clerks-regular to that of the monastic orders ; this is a great but necessary novelty which they grant us.[1] It is sufficient of itself to secure our

---

[1] It will be seen that this plan, which would have demanded too great an alteration of the rule of the First Order, was realised later by the creation of a Third Order exclusively devoted to teaching. This passage, however, is not the less remarkable as showing how fully Père

life and practical utility. Finally, I have obtained everything without opposition, and beyond what I could have desired—all has been granted with a good grace, a joy, and kind feeling that delighted me. Every one I have seen, moreover, Mgr. Capaccini, Mgr. Acton, Cardinal Odescalchi, and others have given me the warmest welcome, and shown me the fullest confidence. Mgr. Capaccini has presented me to an auditor of the legation of Vienna, who tells me that he has often heard M. de Metternich speak in my praise. I remark everywhere a great increase of kindness.

"The Jesuits go on admirably. I said Mass in their church the first of all, and the General invited me to take chocolate with him, when we had a long talk, which satisfied me that they will treat us as friends. Père Rosaven has received your letter.

" As soon, therefore, my dear friend, as I shall have had my audience with his Holiness, and finished my visits, I shall set out on my return to France. I shall spend the winter there, looking out for five young men of faith and courage, capable of giving themselves to one another with unbounded self-devotion and true humility. That is the grand point. After Easter, which falls on the 31st of March, we shall return to Rome, and it is probable that in the beginning of May, 1839, we shall take formal possession of Santa Sabina. I am very glad now that I opened my project in 1837; it has given everything an air of maturity. . . . . May God be praised! I begin to be afraid of all He has done for me !"

It will be seen from the above that the convent of Santa Sabina at Rome had been placed at the disposal of the new French religious. Afterwards, changing this first resolution, Cardinal Sala, prefect of the congregation of bishops and regulars, formed

---

Lacordaire was occupied even from the first with plans for the benefit of youth, never separating teaching from preaching in the work to which he had devoted himself.

the idea of sending them to make their noviciate in Piedmont. The Abbé Lacordaire, foreseeing fresh obstacles, clung to the wish of having a support at Rome. He therefore caused it to be represented to the cardinal, through an influential person, that "public opinion in France would not favour the notion of the religious going to be trained in Piedmont, a foreign country by no means sympathetic with France ; and that the centre of Christendom was the only place whence they would see religious arrive in France without much surprise." He added : " It is of importance, moreover, to the Holy See, that we should set out from under her wings. *Rome and public opinion,* that is what I have always built on." Things being thus arranged, he returned to France ; and announced his coming to Madame Swetchine in the following letter :

"To-morrow evening, my dear friend, at midnight, I shall set out for France by the courier of Bologna. I have nothing new to tell you since the letter which announced to you the success of my journey, except that this success is daily more and more confirmed. I have seen the Holy Father, who received me with the greatest kindness. I leave Rome, therefore, as contented and tranquil as it is possible for a man to be in this world. . . . . Your reflections on my vocation are excellent. I assure you that in such matters human respect has never once made me either advance or draw back. The disagreeables of my position in Paris had nothing to do with my resolution, for I had never so much loved Paris, had never been more sensible of the good I might possibly do there, and never received more testimonies of esteem and confidence. My power then appeared greater than ever it had done before. It was precisely the sense I had of all this that made me hesitate to accomplish the sacrifice which God interiorly demanded of me. My career, I said to myself, is open, my course of action is plain ; why begin afresh ? Doubtless the gossip of my opponents served also as a motive to help on my determination, but it was only a feeble one. I thought of such things only to help the grace of God, and to overcome my cowardice. God knows, in this affair I have had but one combat to fight, and that has been with my own weakness at the sight of so great a sacrifice. I was happy, contented, and without anxiety, and I was about to take on my shoulders, not merely a woollen habit and a hard life, but the weighty anxiety of a family to feed and nurture. I who knew not a want was going to surround myself with children, who would look to me for their daily bread! Self-love said to me : 'Remain as you are;' Jesus Christ said to me : 'When glory and ease were offered to Me I chose the life and the death of the cross!' Here you see my entire soul during these last months. But at last I have trampled on the enemy; I no longer feel a shadow of human cowardice, and this is what assures me of success even more than the encouragements I have hitherto met with. When I entered the seminary fourteen years ago, I experienced exactly the same feelings : first of all there was a struggle in which I said just the same things to myself; then, when my decision was taken, I felt a firmness and a certainty which nothing was able to shake for a single moment. At both these great epochs of my life I have sacrificed a state of life on which I had already entered for another uncertain state—one with which I was satisfied, for one the thought of which terrified me. As to the residence in Italy of which you speak, I have never looked on it except as a *pis aller*, a refuge, a sort of hospital, in case God permitted my complete ruin—the morsel of bread which the Divine goodness leaves to the rich man who has lost his all."[1]

Who will not admire the beauty of this soul which thus lays itself bare in an analysis so exact and so profound, and with a candour which tells the good as simply as the bad ? To explain this strange attraction to the cloisteral life, the world, which never

[1] Rome, Sept. 14, 1838.

understands the things of God, will talk about ambitious views, the glory of being the head of an Order, and the desire of escaping from miserable interference. It was simply the contrary of all this. All these voices cried out to him to remain as he was. God alone commanded him to go forward, and to cast himself blindly into his act of sacrifice. He obeyed, not without a struggle, but with manly fortitude; and he sees with reason in this victory over himself the first and surest proof of divine vocation. He travelled by way of Bologna, in order to pray there at the tomb of his new Father, St. Dominic, and then returned to France, passing through Turin and Geneva. Scarcely had he returned to Burgundy, and to his own family, before the publicity which his project had attained brought him several fellow-labourers. He tried and encouraged them, but did not seek to press them. He writes to one of them : "My dear friend, I assure you I am not astonished at the interior trials which you experience. They are only natural, and what man, what saint is there who has not at one time or other felt his spirit fail him when meditating on some sacrifice which had to be made for God ? Only give free way to the empire of grace, without impetuosity and without seeking that it should be to-day or to-morrow. For my own part I spent nearly eighteen months in coming to a resolution, and several times I nearly gave up the thought. I shall simply confine myself, therefore, my dear friend, to giving you the explanations you ask." Here follow some instructions on the Dominican rule, to which we shall have occasion to refer more fully by-and-by. Then he adds : "I do not exactly know your age ; but St. Augustine did not become a priest till he was thirty-five or thirty-six, and that did not prevent his afterwards writing ten folio volumes on religious subjects, and becoming a great and powerful bishop. The only difficulty is to know how much you love Jesus Christ and His Church, and what sacrifice you are capable of making—all the rest is nothing.

Think of it before God, and write me your decision when you shall have taken it. I shall be ready on my part to receive you with open arms and open heart."[1]

Meanwhile the affair of the restoration of the order went on apace. It was noticed in the public journals, and spoken of both at Paris and Rome. People were in a state of expectation about it. What would the irreligious press say of it? What would the government do? At Rome, particularly, the friends of the future religious were anxious; and in their anxiety, not understanding the reason for the kind of publicity which he solicited, they secretly accused him of hastiness and imprudence. Informed of these fears, the Abbé Lacordaire reassured them by explaining his conduct and his plan.

"Your letter gives me an opportunity of explaining the reasons which have induced me to render public the object of my journey to Rome. The best, the most spiritual, and the most devout Romans generally fall into one great error in any question which affects France. The *government* always holds the first place in their eyes, whereas, in reality, it is *public opinion* which, before all things, we have to consider. Without the support of public opinion one can do nothing in France; but with it, and with patience, one ends in obtaining from the government whatever concurrence is necessary. Now let us see what my position was. My journey to Rome was talked about, and people began to whisper the reason which had sent me thither. For a fortnight several journals had entertained their readers with speculations on the subject. What should I have gained under such circumstances by silence? My friends took the initiative by saying out loudly and sincerely what could no longer be concealed. They discharged their volley a minute before they were fired upon, and thus gave me the credit of not fearing publicity. This has been felt as so much in my favour, that except the *Semeur*, a

[1] Aisey-le-Duc, Oct. 18, 1838.

Protestant newspaper, no journal has thought fit to attack me ; and even the attacks in the *Semeur* were not in any way disrespectful. At present, therefore, my position with the public is a good one. It has not condemned me beforehand ; it suspends judgment : and I shall be careful not to return to Rome without giving a few words of explanation.

"As to the government, my position is neither better nor worse. It is possible even that government may have been struck by the silence of the public journals, in this sense that it gives the less fear of a universal explosion. But as yet I know nothing positive. I shall do all I can to secure the goodwill of the public authorities, without, however, submitting my work to their approbation. It is the right time for us to act, and if thirty years be needed in order to restore the Dominicans in France, I trust that if it please God to leave things to their natural course, those thirty years will not be wanting to me. If I must begin by being the only French Dominican, I will be the only one. I will take my new habit into the French pulpits, and will earn for that habit the favour which may be yielded to my person. All this is new, because the position of France is new. Under the Empire and the Restoration, they introduced a congregation into France, unknown by every one under the equivocal protection of power, until power, overwhelmed by public opinion, again expelled its *protégé.* Nowadays, the progress of political and religious ideas is great enough for us to try and choose a stronger support in the public opinion itself of France. I do not say that the attempt will be without danger, specially at certain moments ; but the experiment is at least possible, and the times are in favour of it. Has not the Holy See itself, in the great affair of Germany, taken its stand on public opinion ?[1] If

[1] Reference is here doubtless made to the affairs of Cologne, which were then causing great excitement in Germany ; and the controversy which arose led the Sovereign Pontiffs Pius VIII. and Gregory XVI. to blame the conduct of the Prussian Government in their Bulls with great freedom.

this had been attempted ten years ago, would it have been possible? The great art is to know what constitutes real power in the days in which we live. It is certainly not out of vain glory that I have given my consent to this publicity. It was inevitable, and I gain nothing by it, save having been able to endure it for a month without being crushed. . . . . What support then remains for me? I reply, *Rome and public opinion.* This is what I build on, and indeed I know no other ground : it is there I shall stand or perish. But how many chances may fall out in thirty years! What powerful antecedents there are already in my favour! A certain amount of persecution will even be useful to me ; public opinion will be sure to take the part of any one who is unjustly attacked. Any way, I am full of confidence and tranquillity ; God has hitherto protected me : I am doing His work, and not my own, and obstacles have never been wanting to the best and most successful enterprises. I do not think I shall preach anywhere this winter. I shall be too busy. I am working at a *Memorial,* which must appear before my return to Rome."[1]

Some weeks afterwards he wrote to the same person, " You will hear all about me from Père de Géramb. Everything is going on well, better than I could have ventured to hope. Every one encourages me. I think the press is favourable, and the government, which is not hostile, appears only anxious as to the way in which the public and the newspapers may take it up. The archbishop has received me most graciously. Nevertheless, I am pretty sure that some have written to Rome against me. The substance of the letter will be that it is dangerous to allow the establishment of an Order which may become, and is perhaps intended to become, a refuge to the former partisans of M. de la Mennais. This is always the phantom with which they seek to terrify people. I have not yet written to Cardinal Lambruschini on the subject, because I feel myself sufficiently well

[1] Unpublished Letters, Chatillon-sur-Seine, November 3, 1838.

understood at Rome to prevent their paying any attention to this nonsense. But I should be glad if you would speak to the cardinal when you see him, and let him know that none of the friends of M. de la Mennais have taken part in the work, and that it is impossible to express how absurd such an imputation appears to any one who really knows the state of things in France. A whole century may be said to have already passed over the tomb of poor M. de la Mennais, and there is no honest man to whom he now causes any alarm.

"Forgive me for troubling you thus with my defence, but you wish me to make use of you, and really it is not myself alone who am interested in this, but in some measure the whole state of religion in this country. I am more and more struck by the disposition of minds in favour of the Church; all Europe seems preparing for events in which religious questions will play an important part. The earth revolves, and continually brings men back to God as their end and object."[1]

The moments were precious. New intrigues might have created serious difficulties for him both at Rome and Paris, which might have compromised his position. It is often an advantage, when undertaking a bold enterprise, to surprise the enemy before giving him time to reconnoitre. He knew this, and his wonderful activity proved of good service to him. These few winter months sufficed for him to draw up the "Memoir for the Re-establishment in France of the Friars-Preachers,"[2] which appeared in the spring of 1839.

It is divided into two parts. In the first he frankly tells his countrymen what he is going to do, the motives which have determined him, and his right to follow the road along which he felt himself called.

---

[1] Unpublished Letters, Paris, Nov. 21, 1838.

[2] Not the Memoirs quoted a few pages back, which were dictated on his death-bed, but one prefixed to the later editions of his life of St. Dominic ; and which is a sort of apology to the French nation for the step he was about to take.

Addressing himself less to law than to good sense, he expresses his astonishment at finding himself obliged to assume the part of an advocate in so just a cause. "But," he says, "we live in times when a man who wishes to become poor, and the servant of all, has more difficulty in carrying his wish into execution than in amassing a fortune and making himself a great name. Nearly all the European powers, whether kings or journalists, partisans of absolutism or of liberty, are leagued against the voluntary sacrifice of self, and never has the world been more terrified at a man going barefoot, and wearing a poor woollen cassock."[1]

He expresses his wonder and astonishment at finding that after having had liberty to do whatever he liked, the day when for the first time he met with chains should be that when he determined to serve God more generously. "How!" he cries, "when we, the ardent lovers of our age, asked its leave to believe in nothing, it freely granted us the permission we sought. When we demanded liberty to aspire after every office and every honour, it was not denied us. When, in our young days, we asked for liberty to influence the destinies of the world by freely treating on every question, however serious, this, too, was permitted. When we asked to be suffered to live at our ease, nothing was held to be more reasonable. But now, when, penetrated by those divine principles which are making themselves so powerfully felt in this age, we ask for liberty to follow the inspirations of our faith, no longer to aim at any dignity, to live poorly with a few friends touched with kindred desires as ourselves, *now* we find ourselves stopped short, put at the ban of I know not how many laws ; and nearly all Europe unites, if need be, to overwhelm us."[2]

He then goes on to show in what consists the essence of the religious life ; explains very clearly its harmony with the best instincts of the human heart, and shows that the attempt to destroy it must prove

[1] Page 3.   [2] Page 4.

as impossible as the effort to annihilate one of those germs dropped by the hand of God into the fertilising bosom of the earth : " Oaks and monks," he says, " are immortal." ." What is the dream of politicians and economists, if it be not the perfection of society ? And is not that perfection ranked among the chimeras of Utopia, which aims at establishing equality of rights, liberty in obedience, and universal fraternity ? And yet, what else but this is a religious community? There, the prince and the swineherd eat at the same table, all freely obey the master of their own choice, and all, whether masters or subjects, love one another as one is loved nowhere else." Moreover, he adds, " we have returned once more ; monks and nuns, brethren and sisters of every denomination, . . . we are come back again, as the harvests once more cover the fields which the plough has turned up, and where the seed has been cast by the winds of heaven. We do not say this out of pride ; pride is not the sentiment which animates the traveller returning to his native land, and knocking at the door of his old home to ask for help. We have come back because we could not do otherwise, because we have been conquered by the life that was in us ; we are as innocent of being the causes of our own immortality, as the acorn which lies at the foot of some aged oak is innocent of that sap which compels it to strike root and shoot up towards heaven. It is neither gold nor silver that has raised us to life, but that principle of spiritual germination which has been planted in the world by the hand of its Creator, and which is as indestructible as natural germination. Neither the favour of government, nor that of public opinion, has protected our existence, but that secret power which supports everything that is true."[1]

In the second part he traces a broad outline of the Order which he is about to restore in France. Having sketched in a masterly way the beautiful figure of St. Dominic, he surrounds him with an aureola of the

[1] Page 20.

illustrious members of his family; its apostles, St. Hyacinth in Poland and the north, St. Vincent Ferrer in Europe, and Bartholomew de las Casas in America; its doctors, Albert the Great and St. Thomas Aquinas; its artists, Fra Angelico da Fiesole and Fra Bartolomeo della Porta, the friend of that "Jerome Savonarola, whom an ungrateful people vainly burnt alive, since his virtue and his glory have risen higher than the flames of his funeral pile."

"If we are asked," he adds, "why we have chosen the Order of Preachers in preference to any other, we reply, because it best suits our nature, our mind, and our aim: our nature, by its government; our mind, by its teaching; and our aim, by its means of action, which are principally preaching and sacred science. . . We may perhaps be asked, furthermore, why we have preferred reviving an ancient Order to founding a new one; we reply, for two reasons: first, because the grace of being the founder of an Order is the highest and rarest that God grants to His saints, and one which we have not received; secondly, even were God to give us the power of creating a religious Order, we feel sure that after much reflection we could find nothing newer, nothing better adapted to our own time and our own wants, than the rule of St Dominic. It has nothing ancient about it but its history, and we do not see any necessity of torturing our minds for the simple pleasure of dating from yesterday."[1]

The "Memoir" produced its effect. Authority, that *queen of the world*, to which he addressed himself, was surprised by the boldness of his undertaking and the freedom of his language, and felt itself favourably disposed towards the singular man who possessed the gift of pleasing it and the courage to bid it defiance. The Abbé Lacordaire had reason to congratulate himself that he had had faith in his country. No attack from the press or the platform held the book up to contradiction; no enemy arose

[1] Pages 45—47.

before the new champion of religious liberty. "And
yet, nevertheless, the question was of St. Dominic and
the Dominicans! it aimed at reviving on the French
soil an institution long calumniated both in its founder
and his posterity! Certainly, for twenty-five years,
religion had been making great progress in France;
and yet, if such a work had been publicly announced
in a printed advertisement one year before, who
would have dared hope that the plan would have
been welcomed with silence and the safe-conduct of
public favour?

The four or five young men of courageous faith whom
he had come back to France to seek, were attracted
to him by the Memoir. We shall soon see the first
French Dominicans present themselves in succession,
at first few in number, but all chosen men. The first of
all, and the one who was likewise destined to be the first
called to heaven, was Hippolytus Réquédat. "I do
not know who gave him my 'Memoir' to read," say
Père Lacordaire, "but he read it with eagerness, an
passing at a bound from intellectual speculation i
divine things to the desire of the apostolate, he can
to find me out. I welcomed him as a brother se
from God; no question was asked, no explanati
demanded, no fear manifested; he seemed like a p
senger perfectly ready at once to embark in my fil
vessel, and who did not so much as give a glance t
the unknown ocean he was about to cross. Oer
similar souls were afterwards given to me, but me
more beautiful, more pure, or more devoted, ne
whose brows were stamped with the seal of a rer
predestination. He had the special glory of bng
my first companion; and death, by soon strikingim
a premature blow, left his memory in my soul claed
with a virginity which nothing can ever tarnish.

"It was now the spring of 1839; and in conany
with Réquédat I once more made the journeyrom
Paris to Rome, which I had already travelledhree
times. But on former occasions my mind hadeen
sorely tried by doubt and anxiety. This time. was

as luminous as the heavens beneath which we passed.
The outlines of my future existence were clear before
me ; I had nothing to do except to close the conference at Nôtre Dame, and restore in France the Order
I was about to enter. My travelling companion,
moreover, soothed my heart by the serenity of his
manners and the intrepidity of his self-devotion.
And thus this journey was a sort of continual feast."

His letters present a lively picture of this journey
and of his arrival, and it was always Madame Swetchine who was made the first sharer of his new
joys.

"ROME, *March* 27, 1839.

" How grateful I feel to you, my dear friend, for
your little word of the 16th! I received it the day
after my arrival at Rome, and it did me so much
good. Here also I find much consolation. You
would not believe what a welcome we have received,
nor what kind and excellent men our Fathers are.
For the first time in my life I see Christian fraternity,
the true expression and resemblance of Jesus Christ
among men. Had we lived together fifty years they
could not be more simple, more full of cordiality, and
what is more, the physiognomies of these good Fathers
are in perfect keeping with their words. Yesterday
we dined with old Father Olivieri, the Commissary of
the Inquisition, who wept like a child when he read
my chapter on St. Thomas, and wishes to see us a
second time. Cardinal Pacca, Secretary to the Congregation of the Inquisition, was charmed with the
'Memoir,' and with the manner in which I have treated
the Inquisition in it. All the Dominicans who have
read it approve, and consider its exactness above the
reach of reproach. On this they are unanimous. On
the other hand, what you tell me about it, my dear
friend, greatly comforts and reassures me. I see, too,
that as yet no journal has attacked us, and that is a
good augury. I must now tell you exactly how things
stand.

"No opposition has been evinced on the part of the French embassy, nor the secretaryship of state. Cardinal Sala continues to wish that the noviciate should be made out of Rome, and it has been agreed that we should make it at Viterbo, one day's journey from Rome, in a magnificent convent that the Dominicans have there. We have joyfully agreed to this modification of our plan, for we shall be much quieter there, more out of the world, and in a better air than that of Rome, during the summer. I look on this apparent contradiction as a new benefit of Providence, and one so much the more important, as we shall take the habit in Rome before going to Viterbo, and shall receive the blessing of the Holy Father; it is not yet fixed when, but there will be no very long delay. They are busy getting our habits ready. Meanwhile, I am distributing copies of the 'Memoir,' and assisting with my friends at the ceremonies of Holy Week. We are nearly always together, delighted with the inside and the outside of Rome, and the convent of the Minerva. We have the most beautiful weather possible, and this has been the case ever since our departure from Paris, with the exception of two days at Milan, and one day at Rome. Adieu, my dear friend, if you do not love the Dominicans you must have the heart of a tiger. At Viterbo, as elsewhere, you will have a son and a friend."

"ROME, *April* 6, 1839.

"Next Tuesday, the 9th of April, at seven o'clock in the evening, my dear friend, we shall receive the habit of St. Dominic from the hands of the Father-General, in the chapel of St. Dominic, within the church of the Minerva. Since my letter of the 29th of March, things have become much clearer. I have seen Cardinal Sala, who received me very kindly, and told me expressly that he would seize any occasion that might present itself of serving us. Cardinal Lambruschini also has welcomed me with his usual kindness. He is a little frightened at the state of

France, and before our departure from Paris had advised the General to wait. But this cloud was dispersed by our arrival. The Pope granted us all three a very favourable audience last Thursday. We know from Père Vaurès, the French penitentiary, that he has often spoken of our business, and always with the greatest interest, showing no other anxiety than a fear lest we should not at once succeed, in consequence of the state of France. This is also what he said to us. In reply, we told him that with time and patience we should find the favourable occasion ; that revolutions do not last for ever, and that if another tempest were to burst over France, fair weather would afterwards reappear. He had our 'Memoir' on his table, and showed it to us. I have received much praise on its account from several cardinals, among others, from the Cardinals Polidori, and Castracani. Cardinal Orioli, the former friend of poor M. de la Mennais, spoke to me very openly about him, and told me several incidents of his conduct in 1824. This morning we went together to see the General of the Jesuits; he was very cordial, and spoke much of the future union between the Dominicans and the Jesuits. We are going, before our departure, to say Mass in the chamber of St. Ignatius.

"This departure will take place the day after we have received the habit. The convent in which we shall live is called La Quercia, from a forest of oak-trees, in which was discovered a picture of Our Lady, which still exists. It is a place of pilgrimage. The convent contains thirty-five religious, of whom nine or ten are professed students, and only two novices. It is thought well of in Rome, and every one has spoken to us of it as a very holy house, in which strict observance is kept up. This is a great happiness for us.

"This is all I have to tell you that is new. You will observe that the 9th of April is the feast of St. Vincent Ferrer, which ought to be kept on the 5th, but has been transferred on account of the Octave of

Easter.   Farewell! pray much that our hearts may
be changed with our habits ; but they will never be
changed in your regard.   These are the last lines I
shall ever address you under my secular garb ; I hope
they will give you pleasure, and tell you all I feel, and
all I am for you.

" H. LACORDAIRE "

CHAPTER X.

"LA QUERCIA, *April* 15, 1839.

" T will be a week to-morrow, my dear friend, since we received the habit of St. Dominic, and to-day is the fourth which we have spent within the Convent of La Quercia. It would be difficult for me to tell you the sentiments of joy and tenderness which were excited in my soul on the evening of the 9th of April. The remembrance of my ordination is very vivid in my mind, and I can recall all its happiness; but what was then wanting I tasted in all its intoxicating fulness on the present occasion; I mean the effusion all around us of a delightful spirit of fraternity. Never did I receive such affectionate congratulations! All the Frenchmen who were there in like manner loaded me with expressions of friendship, and the same scene was renewed next day until noon, when we set out for Viterbo. We were satiated without being wearied of it. On Thursday, at eleven in the morning, we reached the Dominican Convent of Gradi, near the gates of Viterbo, and dined there with the provincial of Rome, and all the Fathers of the convent. In the evening the provincial took us on to La Quercia,

which is about half a league from Gradi, and made
known to us that our noviciate had begun, in a little
address delivered in the presence of the community.
After this we each went to our cell. It was cold; the
wind had shifted to the north, and we had only a
summer habit in a room without a fire. We knew
nobody; all the *prestige* and bustle had vanished;
friendship followed us from afar, but was no longer
close at our side. We were alone with God in presence
of a new life, the practice of which was utterly unknown to us. In the evening we went to matins, then
to the refectory, and then to bed. Next day the cold
was even more severe, and we only half understood
the course of our exercises. I felt a moment's weakness; I turned my eyes on all I had left: a clear
course of life with certain advantages, tenderly beloved friends, days full of useful conversations, my
warm fireside, my pleasant little chambers, and the
thousand enjoyments of a life on which God has
poured out so much exterior and interior happiness!
It was paying dearly for the pride of carrying out a
strong resolution, to lose all this for ever! But I
humbled myself before God, and begged Him to give
me the strength I needed. By the end of the first
day I felt He had heard me, and for three days past
consolations have been increasing in my soul, as
sweetly as the sea which caresses her shores with the
same waves with which she covers them."

How touching and beautiful is this confession!
Madame Swetchine, who received these confidences,
might well say that he could be known only by his
letters. These are not the things which a man says
of himself to the public. But what an accent of
truth they breathe! What a light they shed on
those secret recesses of his soul which we most care
to study!

The religious life, in fact, to which he was consecrating himself, had two forms and two aspects: that
of the exterior and of the interior. Seen outside, it
was the life of a man who, having quitted the world

for the gospel, had found himself too much isolated in the great family of the Church, and felt the need of making himself a smaller and more intimate family. It shows us this priest, wandering through the streets of Rome, passing over in his mind the many services rendered to the Church and the world by the religious orders, and forming dreams for restoring to his native soil, long stripped of this glory, a sucker of one of those ancient and immortal plants. It shows him to us praying in the Basilicas, gazing on the sculptured forms of all those religious founders, ranged in their places of honour, under the cupola of St. Peter's, and resolving to choose among this aristocracy of sanctity for that one which shall be most adapted to his nature, his mind, and his end. It shows him to us at last realising this dream after he had conceived it, passing the twenty last years of his life in establishing this new colony, and in dividing it into two branches; one destined for education, and the other for the apostolate, and then returning to God with the consolation of having left this young tree, if not beyond the shock of the tempests which form its life, at least sufficiently strong, and in a soil sufficiently generous, to do henceforth without the hand of any visible guardian.

Such is the aspect of this beautiful life that is best known, and I may add, it was the only one of which Père Lacordaire ever consented to speak to the public. But there was also another more private, more hidden, more wonderful life, that of his soul in its secret intercourse with God—it was the soul alone with God alone. The religious community, the apostolic labours, exist indeed, but they only hold a second rank, and do but radiate, as it were, from the first. It is God creating in a human heart the torment of eternal love, the hunger and thirst after the Infinite, and presenting Himself to heal that ineffable wound ; it is the human soul clasped in the Divine embrace. An espousal at once rapturous and agonising ; for it is the love of a just God, Who pursues with His hate the least vestiges of evil in the soul; of a holy God, Who will have nothing defiled in the Moses who is to ascend His burning mountain; of a jealous God, Who will admit none to share His love. One day, in the profound solitude of its exile, the elected soul hears itself called by God. "Man of desires! come forth, and thou shalt behold Me! *Egredere!* come forth out of thine own country, thine own family, thine own self! All these affections are innocent, yet tarnished with corruption, ambition, or self-love. Thou hast a country; come, and I will give the world for thine inheritance: thou hast friends and a family; quit them, and I will give thee friends as numberless as the stars of heaven, or the sands of the sea-shore. But, above all, come forth out of *thyself!* Unroot thy life, that thou mayest transplant it into a better land; for the obstacle is *thyself*, the enemy is thine own flesh and thine own pride. Thou art a Christian, and a priest, and thou hast a yet higher ambition; well then, go and sell all that thou hast, and come into the Promised Land, as the voluntary victim of My love, shorten that trial of absence which is imposed on the less generous victims of My justice. Instead of waiting till the hand of death shall purify thee, tear aside the veil, and open heaven now; do in thyself each day the work of death, accomplish in thyself all justice by the sword of penance; and instead of waiting till the tide shall waft thee from the shore, push boldly out and plunge into the vast abyss: *duc in altum!*"

In this colloquy wherein God, as it were, provokes the human heart to love, first steps are not the most difficult. God takes those first steps with the soul, and rather carries it than accompanies it. But once arrived half-way, He suddenly retires and disappears, leaving to man the honour of a free and disinterested choice. Like a new Abraham, the religious has quitted Chaldea, but he has not yet entered Canaan. At the summit of those hills which divide his life in two, at the moment of consummating his sacrifice, alone, between a Past which he abandons, and a

Future which is yet unknown, he turns to cast one last look on all those he leaves behind him ; his country, *his friends so tenderly beloved, his warm fireside, and the thousand enjoyments of a life which God has crowded with blessings.* It is, indeed, an hour of cruel suffering! Even to give up all this at twenty years of age, when as yet we do not know life, when as yet our life has nowhere struck root, to leave behind us a father's and a mother's cheeks bathed in tears, to feel that we have given their hearts a wound that can never be healed, even this is a sacrifice for which God alone can give the courage, and the merit of which he alone can measure. But to snap one's life in two at the age of forty, to begin it over again as it were in the dark, to tear one's self while still alive from an existence full of the most enviable realities, and the sweetest hopes, to risk a certain present for a future wrapped round about with darkness and danger, with the chance, even if the work should succeed, of being accused of ambition ; and if it should not succeed, of passing for a fool—this is what Père Lacordaire rightly called the greatest act of faith he had ever accomplished.

And yet, except the difference of position, a religious vocation is nothing if it be not this, and it would be greatly to mistake this new phase in the life of Père Lacordaire if we did not, above all, regard it from this point of view. "There are in the world," says St. Augustine, "but two loves, the love of God extending to the contempt of self, and the love of self extending to the contempt of God."[1] All other loves are but the degrees between these two extremes. The religious is he who makes it his business, if not to attain, at least to tend always to the highest degree—*the love of God,—reaching to contempt of self.* All religious discipline rests on this great law of the covenant which is established by sacrifice between God and man. The world which sees the sacrifice, but not the reward, which sees the sword, but not the

[1] De Civit. Dei, lib. xiv. cap. xxviii.

14

Hand which inflicts the wound, is astonished or scandalised : it can never understand this mystery, for "Thou hast hid these things from the wise and prudent." But those who have been initiated into the scandal and the folly of the Cross judge of the degree of intimacy which the disciple enjoys with his Master, by that passion for penance, "that thirst for immolation which is the generous half of love."

The last part of the letter quoted above gives an abridgement of the new novice's life in the Convent of La Quercia. The rule, in which fasting and abstinence hold a large place, may appear tolerably severe. We shall, however, see Père Lacordaire, on returning to France, founding his first convents on a yet more rigorous observance of the primitive constitutions.

"I will now tell you our manner of life. At a quarter past five in the morning the bell summons us to rise. A quarter of an hour later we assemble in a little inner choir at the door of the noviciate, where we sing prime, hear Mass, and make our meditation. After this we say our own Mass. Before noon we go to the choir in the church to sing tierce, sext, and none, and a high Mass on all greater feasts, and on the feasts of the chief saints of our Order. At noon we dine ; every day we keep abstinence from meat, unless in case of special dispensation, and every Friday is a fast day. On the other days we eat a piece of bread in the morning. But from the 14th of September to Easter, the fast is continued, except in case of dispensation. After dinner we recreate in common, or have a *siesta* in our own cells, as we choose. About three o'clock we have vespers and compline, compline being always sung. From four to eight, our time is free, and we can take a walk out of doors if we please. At eight we sing matins and lauds ; and at a quarter to nine have supper, followed by a conversation in the community room, and go to bed at ten. Besides this we have a little chapel in the noviciate, where morning and evening we make a short meditation at any hour most convenient to ourselves. The other exercises are made with the community, with the exception of those Fathers who are exempt from choir duty, from the nature of their offices. In the free time, that is, when not engaged in community exercises, we may meet in the common room of the noviciate to study together and speak on serious things. Every one shows us the greatest kindness and liberality. Once a week we sing the Office of the Dead, and every day the novices recite a very short Office of the Blessed Virgin, as they go from one place to another. For the Fathers the Divine Office does not take up more than two hours a day; it is less time than is occupied by the canons.

"The community is composed of professed religious, of whom several are Spaniards, professed students to the number of eight or nine, and finally, our three selves and two other Italian novices, who are going on very well.

"La Quercia is a magnificent convent, formed of two square cloisters, one of which is a masterpiece; with other courts of smaller dimensions, and a church which is grand, simple, elegant, and full of *ex-voto* offerings. The high altar, opposite the choir, contains the miraculous picture of the Blessed Virgin, and the trunk of the oak in which this picture was found. A good many people come here to visit it. From the gate of the church a magnificent avenue leads to the gate of Viterbo, which opens on the road to Tuscany. It was by this gate that I entered Viterbo in 1836, and turning my eyes to the left, I perceived the portal and bell-tower of La Quercia, without knowing its name. The neighbouring country is most delightful. On the south, quite close to the convent, there rises the summit of Monte Cimino; on the north, on the hill, is the town of Montefiascone; on the east, the Apennines; and on the west, the hills melt away as they descend to the sea, allowing it to be seen by any one who climbs it a little higher up, in order to catch a distant view of its expanse. Within this framework of mountains is a rich valley, the beauty

of whose smiling cultivation is increased by the magnificent forests which clothe the slopes of Cimino.
It is a perfect paradise. Here we are then for a year,
all three well satisfied, and sure of one another. You
remember the holy and beautiful countenance of
Réquédat; it is assuming a new and religious beauty,
so that I am never weary of admiring it. He is
indeed an admirable young man, and were I to die
now, I should feel sure in him of the restoration of
the Dominicans in France. Immediately after our
profession, he will be ordained priest, in virtue of a
privilege granted to religious; and the Bishop of
Viterbo, who has been to see us, together with the
delegate of the province, of his own accord offered to
ordain him after his profession. We shall thus all
three be priests when we return to France.

"Now, my dear friend, it is your turn to give me a
good long letter full of news. Remember I am in complete solitude here, ignorant of everything. Give me
the chief political gossip; it may be told in few words,
and I do not want to lose sight of the state of France.
I create you my journalist, with the pay of a hundred
Hail Marys per month.

"Continue still, my dear friend, to give me your
esteem: if I have ever given you pain, now is the
time to forgive me. Nothing of the old man shall
survive in your regard save the remembrance of your
affection, and the constant fidelity of my heart. Your
place is marked for ever in my life, by the moment
when you took possession of it, and by all the good
you have done me. Adieu; the Madonna of La
Quercia salutes your own Madonna.

"F. HENRI-DOMINIQUE LACORDAIRE,
of the Friar-Preachers."

We have but few details on this early part of Père
Lacordaire's religious life. He who received his first
and closest confidence, F. Peter Réquédat, is no more.
However, we have consulted his old novice-master,
Padre Palmegiani, a venerable old man, who died

about two years since (in 1863), at the age of eighty-
five years, leaving his memory in benediction by all
those who knew his kindness and his amiable holiness. He had worn the Dominican habit for more
than sixty years, and had passed the greater part of
his long career in the post of novice-master at La
Quercia. Among the illustrious religious whom he
numbered among his children, he liked to name Père
Lacordaire, Cardinal Guidi, and the Most Reverend
Père Jandel, since Master-General of the Order. The
following is the letter which, a year before his death,
he sent in reply to a French religious, who had also
been his disciple after Père Lacordaire :

"DEAR AND MUCH ESTEEMED FATHER IN JESUS
CHRIST,—I have felt the greatest consolation, after
the lapse of so many years, in once more seeing your
name under my eyes, and in reading the tender expression of your filial affection, which time has not
been able to extinguish. Let your charity, I beg of
you, continue these kind sentiments in my behalf,-and
recommend very much to Our Lord, a poor old man
who has more need than ever of the prayers and love
of his brethren, being on the verge of appearing before the tribunal of God. For myself, I assure you, I
always remember with pleasure and paternal tenderness that little band of young Frenchmen who were
the first fruits of your province, and who, after edifying our convent with their virtues, left there the germ
of regular observance and community life.

"To speak now of the blessed memory of the
reverend Père Lacordaire, I regret not to be able to
satisfy what would be both your and my desire by
the recital of many incidents. But the course of
years have weakened my strength of body, and with
it the faculties of my mind, and consequently of my
memory. I shall therefore content myself with saying
that Père Lacordaire, during his noviciate, was a perfect model of regularity and religious perfection.
Among the great and numerous virtues which dis-

tinguished him, one was dear to him above all the rest, and that was humility. Regarding himself as the last of the novices, he read at table as the others did, swept the corridors, drew water, trimmed the lamps, and in a word, willingly undertook the meanest services, without seeking any sort of distinction or dispensation. He even refused an exemption from six months of the noviciate, which was offered to him by the Master-General.

"He was never heard to speak of himself nor of what concerned him, and he would not allow any one else to do so. On this subject I remember that one day a novice asked him if it were true that at his Conferences the crowd was so great that the chairs were let out at the high price commonly reported. The humble Father appeared not to hear, and turning to his next neighbour, passed on in a pleasant manner to another subject.

"This, my dear Father, is all that I am able to tell you of a life so beautiful in the eyes of God. Do not be surprised at this; for not to speak of my own almost failure of memory, Père Lacordaire, in his great modesty, was like those stars which, while they cast forth floods of light into the heavens, only allow a few pale and feeble rays to reach our earth.

"I have been obliged, in writing to you, to make use of the hand of another, my great age not permitting me to write myself. Accept, &c.,

"FR. V. PALMEGIANI."

This letter, the touching testimony rendered by an old man about to appear before God, shows us the humble, submissive, and regular religious, an enemy to all distinctions and all dispensations in his own favour; but it leaves in shadow that closer and more secret life of which we have spoken above, the secret spring which set all these virtues in motion; in a word, the love of Jesus Christ crucified. It could not be otherwise. The religious life-blood which flowed in the veins of Père Lacordaire was but in part to be

revealed in Italy ; and only found its full expansion
in France. In his opinion, there was the same difference between a French Dominican and an Italian
Dominican, as existed between the moral situation of
the French and Italian Churches : the habit and the
rule were the same, but the ideas, the manners, the
men themselves, were totally dissimilar, and consequently, also, their spirit and their ways of acting. It
was therefore only at a later period, and in his relations with his French religious, that we shall see in
what way Père Lacordaire understood the religious
life, and what he chiefly sought for in it. With his
brethren of La Quercia, he did not the less display a
kindness and charity, the remembrance of which is
still preserved in Italy. Never did he utter a word
of blame or criticism on customs which he respected,
without, however, adopting them for France. Later
on, no one showed himself less disposed than he to
admit foreign religious into the French houses. But
this rule of government, which he made a law to himself, was made to harmonise with the greatest personal esteem and affection for individuals, so that his
name has remained loved and venerated by all those
who knew him in Italy.

Some fragments of his letters at this epoch will tell
us whither his thoughts habitually turned.

"The manner in which we are making our noviciate
without any sort of mitigation has made an excellent
impression at Rome. The Pope is more than ever
disposed in our favour. He has received several
letters from French bishops supporting the restoration of the religious orders in our country ; some
others have written in a contrary sense, but without
directly attacking us. On the other hand, I receive
many letters from young men and ecclesiastics, who
wish to take part in our enterprise. . . .

"My young companion Réquédat is a saint, and at
the same time a most tender and devoted friend to
me ; truly a precious gem among all the beautiful

souls whom God has up to this time given me the grace to know and to love.

"I am happy and hard at work, very rarely disturbed with the thought of our adversaries; I see more and more the nothingness and the pride of my past life; I hope I am more humble; I better understand the general plan of Christianity; it seems to me that I am approaching maturity, and that I shall commit fewer faults than I have done in the past. The enemies whom we shall have to encounter will be very useful to us, and will help to finish purifying our hearts: that is real penance. A few strokes of the rod on our flesh are soon effaced, although there be merit in receiving them and in feeling that one deserves them; but incessant persecution from people who understand nothing about you, and who are envious, is the real crucifixion of the Christian. Pray God that He may give us courage to bear this cross without bitterness, and to find our triumph in it as Jesus Christ found His. Years flow on, and our hair grows grey; it is time to labour seriously for eternity. . . .

"Considering how much impetuosity I have in my intellectual nature, I am astonished at finding I have been so slow in arriving at a full view of Christianity. Like a navigator who is bold and fortunate in detail, but who makes long voyages without discovering the land of which he is in search, I have touched on a shoal of islands which were not the continent. How is this?

"I have a young man with me here who, like myself, has passed through many errors; but having once become a believer, he joined me at a single bound, though I had the advantage over him of fifteen years. It is true that he found questions more advanced than they were in my time. What I have always wanted has been a man superior to myself, and in whom I had perfect confidence, some one who could introduce me into the faith, and its unnumbered applications. I have had to perform my voyage all alone, landing where I could, sounding the shoals, escaping them by a sort of miracle, and gaining something new at each fresh attempt. It has been this progress through the midst of tempests that has deceived and will deceive my adversaries; they always take me at a point of view beyond which I have long since passed, and the goodness of God always carries me farther than their malice. I am like a stag who has bounded on ahead of his pursuers. Thus, in spite of my imperfections, my faults, and my want of fervour, I feel no anxiety about the future; the difficulties you speak of do not terrify me. A single bishop would be enough for us in France, and we have several who are really and sincerely on our side."[1]

Sometimes out of this poor friar's cell, there shone forth flashes of the highest eloquence. The folly of princes who persecuted Christianity in the plenitude of its power, as they had persecuted it in its cradle, and obstinately dashed themselves against that stone which is finally to crush them all, filled his soul with holy indignation, and made him exclaim, " God and the strength of things are more than ever the only supports of Christianity, and of all the works which its spirit inspires. We are returning to the times of the apostles, and the breaking up of the Roman empire. Catacombs, the desert, ruins, and revolution, are all here to serve as asylums to the oppressed, to all those strong souls who devote themselves to the service of God and the human race. Woe to those who reckon on anything else! See how Asia, Africa, Turkey, and England are opening themselves to the propagation of Catholicism! Listen on all sides to the rising of the wind which is about to burst over our blinded kings and nations, in order to overthrow every power which opposes itself to charity and truth! Madmen that they are! Egotism devours them, pauperism gnaws at them, the mob, aroused by their impiety, swells like a furious ocean; and all that they trouble themselves

[1] Letters to Madame de la Tour du Pin. xiii. and xiv.

about is how to check the progress of Christian self-
devotion ; how they may prevent souls from embracing poverty, chastity, and all the good things of which
they stand in need ! What we have seen is nothing
in comparison of what we shall see. Society just now
is like a shipwrecked mariner, who stabs the man
that is coming into the midst of the waves to deliver
him. We shall return to France in time, and claim
our right as men, citizens, and Christians ; if she
rejects us, we shall go elsewhere ; or we shall write,
or come one by one to evangelise her. God has
never suffered liberty to be without resources in this
world. Do not therefore concern yourself on this
head, it is not worth the trouble; whoever bestows
much thought on such matters, does but slumber in
the sun of fortune."[1]

It will be seen that the cloister was not enervating
this powerful mind, and that, on the contrary, the
sober and austere life of recollection he led there,
grafting itself on a soul of masculine vigour, was
raising him to that firm and ardent faith which is the
sign impressed by God on men of His election.

It was during this year of his novitiate that he
wrote the *Life of St. Dominic.* He employed on it
only the moments left free by his religious exercises,
and would never be dispensed on this account from
any of the duties imposed on the other novices. The
life did not appear till 1841, and we shall speak of
it when treating of that period. Chateaubriand said
of this book that it contained some of the most beautiful pages in modern French literature. We will only
here quote a single page, one of those, no doubt,
which were alluded to by Chateaubriand, and which,
while describing a convent, gives a charming picture
of the house he was then inhabiting :

" A cloister is a court surrounded by a portico. In
the middle of the court, according to ancient traditions, there ought to be a fountain, the symbol of that
living water of which Scripture speaks, as " flowing

[1] Unpublished Letters.

forth unto life eternal." Under the flags of the portico are engraved funereal inscriptions, and on the arches formed by the vaulted roof are depicted the acts of the saints of the Order or the monastery. This place is sacred. The religious themselves always preserve silence while passing through it, calling to mind the thought of the dead and the memory of their Fathers. The sacristy, the refectory, and other larger rooms used by the community, are ranged round this solemn gallery, which also communicates with the church by two doors, one entering into the nave, the other into the choir. A staircase leads to the upper stories, which are built over the portico and on the same plan. Four windows, which open from the four angles of the corridors, give abundance of light, and during the night-time four lamps shed forth their beams. Along these wide and lofty corridors, whose only luxury is their cleanliness, the eye discovers to the right and left a symmetrical row of doors exactly alike. In the spaces that separate them hang old pictures, maps, plans of towns and old castles, the list of the monasteries of the Order, and a thousand simple memorials of earth and heaven. At the sound of the bell all these doors open with a certain gentleness and respect. Calm and grey-headed old men, others of precocious maturity, and some in whom youth and penance combine to produce a blended form of beauty unknown in the world—every age in life appears together under the same garb. The cells of the friars are poor, large enough to contain a couch of straw or hair, a table, and two chairs ; a crucifix and a few pious pictures form their only ornament. From this tomb, which he inhabits during his mortal life, the religious passes to the tomb which precedes immortality. Even then he is not separated from his brethren, living and dead. He is laid to rest, wrapped in his habit, under the pavement of the choir ; his dust mingles with the dust of his forefathers, whilst the praises of God, sung by his contemporaries and his successors in the cloister, move what might be thought still sensible in his remains. O dear and holy houses ! Many august palaces have been built on earth ; many magnificent mausoleums have been raised ; but art and the human heart have never gone further than in the creation of a monastery."[1]

In the midst of these labours as an historian and of his convent life, time flew swiftly by. At the end of December, 1839, he wrote : " Our novitiate draws rapidly to its close. Before Easter we shall pronounce our vows. Great consolations have come to us from every quarter during these eight or nine months, from France, from England, from Belgium, and from Rome. We have often had our hearts filled with joy when seeing the blessings poured out by God over our enterprise. How true it is that no one ever gave himself utterly to God without finding fathers and mothers, brethren and sisters, in exchange for the little that he gives up.

" I have a favour to ask of you. Our church of La Quercia, which dates from the end of the fifteenth century, possesses a celebrated and miraculous picture of the Blessed Virgin, who is the patroness of the Friar-Preachers, and fills a place of immense importance in the history of our Order. The church, built by the inhabitants of La Quercia, to give shelter to this picture, which for a long time hung in the open air among the branches of an oak, was given to the Dominicans in consequence of an event in which France had the chief share. The Senate of Viterbo did not know to what Order to give it. It was resolved to send a deputation to the gate which opens on the road to Florence, and to give the keys to the first religious who should enter. The first who entered was the Frenchman, Martial Auribelli, General of the Order. Three centuries later Providence led us hither, and we have resolved to take for our patroness the Madonna of La Quercia. One of our friends who is a painter, a Frenchman, and a most holy man,

---

[1] Vie de St. Dominique, chap. viii.
[2] He is speaking of Père Hyacinth Besson, who was at that time pursuing the study of painting in Rome.

is about to make a copy of the picture, which we shall leave in the sanctuary until our departure. We shall then take it away with us, and it shall accompany us everywhere, until the day when we shall be able to install it solemnly in our first French convent, under the title of Our Lady of La Quercia. The favour I ask of you is to attach a remembrance of yourself to this picture by giving us a frame for it."[1]

This idea of placing the restoration of the Order in France under the patronage of Our Lady reveals something of the tender and delicate piety of Père Lacordaire. Mary, the Protectress of France, and of the Order of St. Dominic, and the special Patroness of the Convent of La Quercia—all these were happy presages for the future. She was then to be also the guardian of the first house of the Order, re-established in France. And, in fact, the copy of the Madonna della Quercia, made by Père Besson, the young and saintly French artist, was solemnly placed on the altar of the Convent of Nancy, the first erected in France. It is there still, looking down on the choir of the religious, and recalling to them the tender confidence of their father in the Blessed Virgin. Later on, he desired to make her a yet more solemn consecration of his work at Paris, and after having offered the Holy Sacrifice at the altar of Our Lady of Victories, surrounded by all the brethren of the Third Order, full of joy, he offered to the Blessed Virgin a heart of silver on which were engraved these words : " Consecration to Our Lady of Victories of the re-establishment in France of the Order, and of the Third Order of St. Dominic, January 15, 1854."

As may well be supposed, they had not long to wait for their frame. Père Lacordaire, whose thoughts spontaneously ascended from the most trivial little incidents to the grandest views of faith, wrote as follows, whilst thanking the giver : " Last Sunday evening I received the magnificent frame which you have sent for the Madonna della Quercia, and I hasten

[1] Unpublished Letters, Dec. 21, 1839.

to thank you for it. Many brethren, many friends, and many children will kneel before the picture and its frame. The other day I showed a French gentleman, not yet much of a Christian, the canvas on which for four centuries the Madonna della Quercia had been painted, and I said to him : 'There is what has built the church that you see here, with the houses and cloister that surround it ; that has cleared the neighbouring fields, dug that road by which you came to Viterbo, founded two crowded fairs, and drawn to this spot millions of men !' I hope our copy may be as fortunate as the original, and I have great confidence that it will be even more so, not in consideration of my unworthy self, but of the course of events which bears us on, and which is visibly urging the world to a great Christian revival.

"In four days I shall pronounce my vows before this picture which you have adorned. Who would have told us such a thing in the autumn of 1837 ? Who could have prophesied that so many old ties would have been broken, and so many new ones contracted ? But all these mysteries have one lucid end, towards which we are moving. All the separations of time are but *rendezvous* in eternity. One day we shall behold in our true and holy country, that sacrifice is only the shortest road which conducts to reunion."[1]

We know not how better to conclude this chapter than by giving a page of sacred mysticism and of incomparable beauty. It is a letter of consolation which he wrote, a short time after first coming to La Quercia. It may be read after the finest meditations of Bossuet on the "Christian Mysteries." It is itself a meditation on the mystery of suffering. I know not if the matter or the style be most elevated. The prince, to whom these words of consolation were addressed, and who was worthy of receiving them, had just lost by successive blows his wife and two young children. We would willingly reveal his name, but if

[1] Unpublished Letter, April 7, 1840.

we are bound to respect the sentiment of reserve, behind which this noble sufferer chooses to hide himself, we may at least be permitted to thank him for for allowing us to publish so beautiful a letter :

"PRINCE,—I learned yesterday the new blow by which you have been struck, and I cannot resist the desire, under such painful circumstances, of bringing my own heart near to yours. It is not that I have the least hope of being able to comfort you. If faith did not teach me that God is Almighty, I should hardly dare to say that even He could console you. But perhaps I may be permitted to say something that may be of use to you. In sufferings like those with which you are touched, men are sometimes anxious as to the cause, at the same time that they are overwhelmed by the effects. I have asked myself in the presence of God why you have been so rapidly plunged into such an abyss of sorrow ; I have sought for the origin of your woes with the anxiety of a friend, and the conscience of a religious. Suffer me now, my prince, to tell you what I think.

" Holy Scripture presents us in many places with examples of sudden and terrible catastrophes. We never see that there were any other causes for such things than these two—the punishment of great crimes, or the reward of great virtues. Neither you, nor your family, nor your ancestors, permit us to pause at the first supposition ; but it is easy for us to explain everything by the second. You had united your lot in life to one who was too perfect for God to fail to call her prematurely to Himself. It was necessary that she should die in the flower of her age and her beauty, because there was nothing but such a death which could add to her crown. Can man himself allow a perfect flower the time to open more fully ? Alas ! we always forget that what we love is beloved by another beside ourselves, and that God is called in the Scriptures a *jealous* God ! In our love we forget One Who loves more than all creatures put

together, and Who, in order to take from them every
right of ever complaining of Him, has chosen, all
eternal as He is by nature, to die for them. Lift up
your eyes, my prince, to those regions of boundless
love ; it is there that you will learn to know the
secret of your tears. It is there that you will see in
the embrace of God the soul that was shared in so
just a measure between you and Him, that even the
delights of heaven would not have torn her from you
had not an all-powerful decree been sent to call her.
There you will see the reasons of that decree which
appears to you so cruel, and you will see how the
spotless beauty of a Christian soul conquers the heart
of Him Who in baptism was her earliest spouse. Unhappy as we are, we hardly believe these divine
mysteries ! They only hold the second place in our
intelligence, blinded as it is with the shadows of the
world ; and when the true spouse enters the nuptial
chamber, we do not even recognise Him ; we call life
and birth by the name of death ; we make a tomb of
what is the entrance into heaven, and we weep over
it as men who are without hope.

"But if it be true that it is we who are deceived
and not God, judge, my prince, of what passes in the
heart of a wife and mother, when she reads the gospel
in God Himself, and there beholds the world with all
she has left behind her. Ah ! if we could but understand the sublimity of that transformation, we should
better understand that to which we now give the
name of suffering ! What is the world when seen by
the side of the Infinite ? What is the world when
we behold it from the summits of charity and chastity?
What is the world beheld from the choir of saints and
angels? What is the world, seen from the bosom of the
Father, of the Son, and of the Holy Ghost ? There,
down below, far below, in inexplorable darkness and
misery, under the but half-crushed empire of the
devil, the soul that is just crowned, but is still trembling at the perils from which death has snatched her,
beholds her home, her husband, and her children.

Will she judge them according to the glory which now fills her, or according to the false lights of the world ? Will she weigh their happiness in the balance of men or in that of God ! A father begged a saint to obtain a long life for his son. The child died, and when the father fell into doubt and discouragement, the saint appeared to him and said : ' Could I obtain for your child a longer life than life eternal ?'

"Your beloved wife has shared between you and herself the fruits of your mutual love. She asked two of them for herself and two for you. Half of your family has gone to heaven : the other half remains on this earth, so full of thorns, in order to acquire more laborious virtues. We shall live in hard times, and shall often have occasion to think that it would be easier to die than to live. Turning your eyes towards the sorrowful horizon that every day will remove further from you, you will perhaps feel that there have been more sorrows spared than joys denied to the objects of your affection, and you will bless the incomprehensible hand that always blesses when it is extended over its servants and elect.

"These, my dear prince, are the thoughts which have suggested themselves to me whilst thinking of your affliction. Powerless as they may be to console you, they may at least bring you the assurance of an attachment which is already well known to you, but which could not have held its peace when you were so much to be pitied without doing itself a cruel violence."

If a man paints himself in his style, who is there who will not admire in these lines, not merely the genius of the writer, but the heart of the priest and the religious ! Here we see the man, the inner man, so little known ; and here, too, we see the religious, and the sublime regions in which his soul, now set more at liberty, was beginning to breathe and to live. This one page consoles us for all the details which we could have wished to have collected regarding his first year of monastic life.

15

CHAPTER XI.

ÈRE LACORDAIRE pronounced his solemn vows at the Convent of La Quercia on Palm Sunday, the 12th of April, 1840, and on Easter-day he preached at St. Louis-des-Français at Rome. His sermon opened with these words: "We have conquered, we have conquered!" What he said of Christ, the Head of the Church, he could also have said of his own work. Henceforth it was living and established. This work was now about to develop, and the life of Père Lacordaire to embrace a larger sphere of action. God from the very beginning gave him children and fellow-labourers; and we may perhaps be permitted to pause one moment in order to make known to the reader the first generation of them. For we find the workman once again in his work, the Master in his disciples, the tree in its fruit! Besides the charm which always attaches to the history of first beginnings, and besides the fragrance of piety, the poetry, the sublime self-devotion of these first flowers chosen by the hand of God, which are found nowhere else in such perfection, it will not be without its interest to show how this work was formed, who were the men first called to share it, by what motive they were animated, how they understood their mission, and loved it, and consecrated themselves to it. Père Lacordaire always expressed joy and gratitude to God for this peculiar blessing ; and we may freely speak of it here, for of his five first companions, all save one are dead. They were Brothers Réquédat, Piel, Hernsheim, and Besson, with the Most Reverend Père Jandel, who survived them all, and who for so many years governed the entire Order.

The first of these is already known to our readers. They know the affection borne by Père Lacordaire for Réquédat, but they do not yet know how truly he was worthy of it. Père Lacordaire had said of himself : " Before loving God, I had loved glory, and nothing else ;" it might have been said of Réquédat, that " before loving God, he had loved France, and nothing else." The love he felt for his country was a passion, a worship. He wished to see France great, free, and happy, and first in everything. This passion absorbed all his faculties ; his own personality was effaced in presence of the exclusive affection which entirely possessed him, and which would not suffer him to entertain any other. For himself he was insensible alike to ambition, glory, or the seductions of sense. This fever of patriotism may nowadays seem strange, and not a little extravagant ; and in fact it is a malady of which the youth of our own time are pretty well cured, but which was serious enough then, and at which nobody then thought of laughing. It was, we grant, but the effervescence of young and generous hearts, but one which was salutary to many, harmless to all, and certainly more beneficial than the selfish indifference of the present day. Possessed of a cultivated mind, surrounded by his family and all the means of success, Réquédat could not resolve on embracing any profession. He found none which corresponded to the ideal of his political faith. Meanwhile he employed himself in studying social questions, specially those which aimed at ameliorating the condition of the suffering classes, and applied his theories in his own way by exhausting his purse for the benefit of the poor. Of all the money with which his father supplied him for the purpose of maintaining his position or gratifying his tastes, he reserved to himself no more than was strictly necessary, living like a true Spartan, and buying his clothes at the Old Temple ; all the rest went to the poor. The real secret of his singular character was this : his soul was as passionately addicted to self-sacrifice as others are to self-love. To love was his life ; but to love in order to give, rather than to receive : the desire of giving himself always, and to the greatest possible number, made up the dream of his life, his heart-sickness, his interior martyrdom. His very passion for his country had no other motive than this. He wished at all costs to banish every cause of trouble and unhappiness, and to make men into one family of brothers. It was an illusion, no doubt, but the illusion of a generous heart, which merited for him two graces : that of soon becoming acquainted with a yet nobler passion, the passion for saving souls, and the yet rarer grace of preserving himself pure in the midst of the most contagious temptations. Devoted to the burning pursuit of good, tyrannised over by this noble affection, he had not so much as time to behold evil ; and this youth, only twenty years of age, rich, handsome, master of himself and his own liberty, was able to kneel at the feet of a priest, and open to him his entire soul, without having to discover to him one of those fatal stains, which are too often the cruel tribute exacted by the rebellious senses from the early years of manhood. Born at Nantes in 1819, of a family who had made their wealth by commerce, Hippolytus Réquédat, at the age of eighteen, already made one of a party of earnest and enthusiastic young men who met twice a week to discuss questions of philosophy and religion. St. Thomas Aquinas was their oracle, sometimes attacked, it is true, but always triumphant. How had St. Thomas understood progress? What were the ideas and principles of St. Thomas on the subjects of natural rights—slavery, property, or sovereignty? Such were the theses debated in this juvenile circle. Réquédat did not take the least active part in these animated controversies, the judge and doctor of which was a certain learned Italian, an ardent Catholic, who knew his *Summa*, as it is now only known on the other side of the Alps, and showed himself merciless on those who imprudently contradicted the authority of the great Dominican master. It was in these meetings that Réquédat became acquainted with Piel, who was to be the first to follow him in taking the habit of the Friar-Preachers, and the first also to rejoin him in heaven.

Piel was born at Lisieux in 1808. After having tried various professions, without fancying any, at the age of twenty-four, he suddenly declared to his father his firm resolve to be an architect. To his father's objections he replied, "I will either be an architect, or I will be nothing." It was a true vocation. Possessed of a most energetic soul, he had received, I know not whence, the artist's sacred inspiration; he set to work with ardour, and in spite of his age and his preference for the Gothic style, then held in little esteem, he soon succeeded in making himself a name in his profession.

Summoned to Nantes by a curé of that city for the purpose of constructing a Gothic church, he succeeded in getting his design approved in preference to that of his rival, in spite of the resistance and prejudices of local authorities, the administrative powers, and the judges, who had already made up their minds. He lived there a year, seeing much of his new friend, working with him, and on his side preparing, by a serious study of Christian art, for the high mission which he believed himself called to fulfil. "This is pretty nearly the life that I lead," he wrote

about this time. "Besides my plans and my esti-
mates, I have written several articles for the 'Ency-
clopœdia :' I have drawn up one on Vitruvius, and I
shall very soon send it to my dear *Européen*."[1]   I am
also preparing another paper on the uneven numbers
of the Old Testament, which I shall develop later on
into a symbolism of numbers, from all the ancient
traditions, and which will help to unveil some of the
mysteries still concealed in the synthesis of our
Gothic Cathedrals.   In order not to lose the habit of
writing, I put down on paper any good thoughts as
they suggest themselves.   Sometimes, as an exercise,
I translate from Latin into French, or from Italian
into Latin.   I am engaged in this way on some trea-
tises of Origen, translated from the Greek by Rufinus,
who has also left us some Lives of the Fathers of the
Desert.   For my Italian studies, I have selected
some verses out of the *Purgatorio* and *Paradiso* of
Dante.   This is nearly how my time is employed."[2]

In this progress of Christian ideas, and these grave
and lofty studies, the two friends were drawing near
to the full light, but they had not yet reached it.
They called themselves Catholics, and exteriorly they
lived worthy of the name, but in their hearts they did
not conceal from themselves that there was a last step
which had yet to be taken.   Réquédat, tired out with
theories, sought for action ; Piel, less virtuous than
his friend, was simply thinking of being converted.
"How difficult it is," said Réquédat, "to choose any
special end or object, now that the future seems so
obscure ; and yet without some one great end we can
do nothing that is of any value.   I see this every day,
when I have never any other answer to make in the
evening to the question, 'What have you done to-
day'? than this, 'Nothing, or almost nothing.'"   As
to Piel, we must now see what were the sentiments
inspired by the example of his friend, and of what

[1] The Journal of the School of M. Buchez.
[2] Notice sur Piel, par A. Teyssier.   Paris, Debécourt, 1843.

stamp was the character of his soul. He wrote from Nantes to his father after some reverses of fortune : "We shall never be rich, and so much the better; our duties will be all the less heavy to fulfil, since more will be required of those to whom more is given. But we have within us one treasure which is inexhaustible even to the most prodigal ; I mean charity,—not only that which clothes and feeds, but the charity also which teaches, which redresses injuries, and which consoles ; that Christian charity which ennobles and aggrandizes the soul, which renders precious the most simple acts, which prevents the faculties of the soul from remaining barren or from leading to aberration or madness. I hope we may always be rich in this treasure, the rest will be sure to be added. May God give you all health, and bless you as you love Him ; and grant you sweetness of patience and firmness of will. If tears of repentance next to the joys of innocence have a price in His eyes, if He is willing to listen to a man who was never wicked even when most guilty, He will hear me, for my prayer comes from a humble and contrite heart."[1] This day of complete reconciliation with God was close at hand.

In 1838 the two friends were at Paris, and they did not again separate. Both had the same thoughts, the same end, the same aspirations. Piel, of a more powerful intellect, and born to command, was unable, nevertheless, to resist the gentle influence of Réquédat's more tender and generous heart. Piel lodged opposite to Nôtre-Dame, in order constantly to have before his eyes that masterpiece of a so-called barbarous age ; he knew it by heart, and had constituted himself its officious defender, denouncing without delay to the authorities the shameful desecrations which he daily witnessed. He might long have remained content with admiring the exterior structure of the holy edifice without thinking of taking his place in

[1] Notice sur Piel, p. 37.

the interior among the ranks of the worshippers, had
not his friend set him the example. Réquédat was
the first to understand that the best means of making
good proselytes is to submit in everything to the
Church ; it was not enough to buy a hundred copies
of the Gospels and distribute them to all comers, or
to bring back to the simple teaching of the Catechism
such of his friends as had lost themselves in the
vague theories of Platonic spiritualism ; it was necessary at the same time to do what the Catechism com-
mands. One day, then, he entered the Church of St.
Etienne-du-Mont, and seeing some women kneeling
round a Confessional, he knelt there too, and waited
his turn. When it was come, the priest, hearing this
young man, who had never confessed since the time
of his first Communion, accuse himself of having
wished evil to the enemies of France, and reply in the
negative to all his other questions, could not believe
in his sincerity, and refused to give him absolution.
It was only after repeated proofs, that he understood
the astonishing innocence of this chosen soul, and
saw how precious a pearl God had put into his
hands.

Under the influence of Divine grace, this heart,
already so generous, enlarged yet more. His patriotism grew purer. "My God," he said, "I beseech
Thee, let the French nation freely receive Thy divine
Word, and may I have some share in the work.
Make me humble, charitable, chaste, laborious, and
patient." He said to the Blessed Virgin, "Obtain
for me the grace of finding out my vocation, of knowing the way in which I shall be able to do the greatest
possible amount of good, and bring back the greatest
number of souls to the Church, and of becoming the
most chaste, the most humble, the most charitable, the
most active, and the most patient of all men." He
wrote this petition whilst yet in the world, and recited it
every day. He would have wished to have seen all his
friends follow his example, and share his joy. "If it

were a question of logic," he wrote, "the weakness of their arguments would make me think that the day was not far off. But no ; what is wanting is humility. The individual has to submit before that society to which the Divine help has been promised to the end of days, and this to some is a difficult thing." Piel was the first to follow his friend. On the day when he made his Communion, his sister wrote to their father, "What a day! my dear father, and how good are all those who follow Him! If you could but see what rapid steps he makes in the way of the perfect!"

This was towards the close of 1838. The Abbé Lacordaire had returned from Rome, having made sure of the favourable dispositions of every one there regarding his project. It was spoken of in Paris. The *Memoir* had not yet appeared, and the field was left open to many conjectures. But by none was the idea more warmly welcomed than by the two young converts and their circle of friends. Réquédat was deputed to pay a visit to the Abbé Lacordaire, and to hear from him all that was to be said of the new plan. They quickly came to a mutual understanding, and the conclusion had not long to be waited for. The Abbé Lacordaire explained all his views. The Church, France, the apostolic work of preaching, possibly even martyrdom—all these words went like fiery darts from the heart of the priest to that of the neophyte ; his *speciality* was discovered at last, and his life seemed about to find its fulfilment. He fell at the feet of his new master, and conjured him to accept him as his first child. It is more easy to guess than to describe what must have passed at that moment in the soul of Lacordaire ; we can but feebly picture the demonstrations of ardent feeling which marked the meeting between these two souls, so well suited to understand one another.

Réquédat returned full of joy to announce to his friends that he should set out with the Abbé Lacordaire. No one was surprised, and no one tried to stop him. This sudden vocation inspired no doubts in the minds of those who knew him. Every one congratulated and encouraged him, consoling themselves for his departure with the thought that they should soon see him again in the midst of them, under the habit of a Friar-Preacher. As to Piel, he once more fell under the irresistible fascination of his friend's influence, and received the first glimpse of his own vocation. But this attraction, in which friendship, perhaps, might have had the larger share, required to be ripened by time and reflection; and it was decided that he should wait in the world for a more distinct call from Heaven. As they took leave, Réquédat said to him, "In one year's time, brother Piel, I shall expect you as a novice."

A few days after their separation Piel wrote—" We are still sad at the departure of our best friend. If you had seen with what simplicity he has accomplished all that God has demanded of him, you would have been as convinced as ourselves of the truth of his vocation, and like us, you would have been touched by the singleness of purpose with which he has obeyed it. Not one voice among those of all his friends here has been raised to detain him, and yet not one of those who love him as he deserves to be loved has been able to see him go without shedding tears. . . . . It will be an excellent thing for us to have a friend who loves France more than anything after God ; and that this friend should be so placed that light will never fail him. . . . . They have all three set out on a journey which I pray God to bless. I only left them at the last moment. We embraced for the last time, and then separated. May they very soon return to us !"

The generous soul of Piel was profoundly moved by the resolution taken by his friend. Without in any way changing his manner of life as an architect, all his thoughts were now turned towards Italy. He often spoke to his friends of his intention of following Réquédat. To prepare himself for it, he began to hear Mass daily, to go to confession every week, and to labour with courageous perseverance to correct the natural asperity of his temper.

The two French religious at La Quercia did not leave him idle. Père Lacordaire had been surrounded at Rome with young French Catholic artists, and had formed the idea of commencing his Dominican apostolate by their means, and of strengthening them in their religious and artistic convictions by the power of association. A confraternity was, therefore, set on foot, under the title of St. John the Evangelist, and Père Lacordaire, in his novice's cell, drew up its rules. The first article ran as follows :—" The end of the confraternity of St. John the Baptist is the sanctification of art and artists by the Catholic faith, and the propagation of the Catholic faith through the instrumentality of art and artists." Piel was charged with the task of carrying out the same idea in Paris, and he was named the first prior of the confraternity. Réquédat, who, under his friar's frock, was devoured with the thirst for doing good, stimulated his friend's zeal with numerous letters. Nothing better paints this enthusiastic nature, animated at once with the fire of contemplation and of action, than this correspondence. It also gives us some new and interesting details as to the first beginnings of the Dominican Restoration. On both these accounts we shall give a few extracts, from which our readers will better understand the hopes that Père Lacordaire had founded on this youth of twenty, and the inexpressible grief which he felt at his early death.

Réquédat wrote thus from Rome to his beloved brother Piel, two days before taking the habit:—

" CONVENT OF THE MINERVA,
ROME, *April* 7, 1839.

" In two days' time we shall for the first time put on the white robe of innocence and the black mantle of penance. If my prayers be heard, this day will also rise for you, my dearest brother, and then under the rule and habit of St. Dominic we shall continue a brotherhood which has left me the sweetest memories after having cost me many tears. The Friar-Preacher keeps his family name, and chooses a new patron among the saints of his Order. We had to choose among the four greatest saints, St. Dominic, St. Peter of Verona, St. Thomas, and St. Vincent Ferrer. Père Lacordaire took the name of Dominic, Père Boutaud that of Vincent, and I placed myself under the protection of St. Peter. When I chose this name I only knew the conclusion of this great saint's history, of which I now know something more; but an interior impulse, which I could not explain to myself, urged me to make this choice. When you read his life, and think of the prince of the apostles, and of many other things which you will perfectly understand without my pointing them out, you will readily understand how it was that I took this name rather than any other. The religious memories with which Rome abounds have greatly served to prepare us for the reception of the habit. It is not that the luxury and grandeur of the churches here dazzle me : that only seems to prove to me that Rome possesses a great deal of fine marble, and has given a great deal of gold to her churches ; but I have not yet seen one that is able to make me forget Nôtre-Dame of Paris. But there are so many precious remembrances here, so many holy relics, that the honour which is shown them increases one's own confidence in the saints. He who prays sincerely, loves to find repose from the difficulties of the world in the grand intercessions of Heaven. What riches does not this holy city possess ? It leans upon St. Peter and St. Paul. One alone of its many catacombs recalls the death of 60,000 martyrs ; but I must stop, for time presses.

"We have been very well received here by every one, and our project has met with enthusiastic sym-

pathy. Many difficulties, indeed, have also arisen
against us. Everybody here is terrified at the thought
of France. Our plan seems something fabulous when
they think of the revolution with which she is
threatened; no one can understand how, in so stormy
a time, one can be thinking of making foundations.
All the world has its eyes fixed on France, it is the
only nation with which men occupy themselves. And
France has left behind her here such sad remembrances,
that at the least movement on her part people expect
once more to see her soldiers, as brave as they are
irreligious. Many obstacles also are created for us in
the minds of those who will look on the French
Government as absolute. And to this must be added
certain enmities, both French and Italian, which do
not the least exist because they keep themselves in
the shade. But after all, what are difficulties like these
when we compare them to the helps which we must
derive both from the special blessing, which the Holy
Father has given us in an interview which we obtained
yesterday, and from the prayers of all our friends,
whether French or Italian, secular or religious ; when
we compare them also to our own sincerity, and finally
to the entreaties which we cease not to offer to God,
that He may grant our enemies every grace, both
temporal and spiritual, needful for their salvation. Do
you also pray for them, my dear friend, for they are
more to be pitied than we are. On Tuesday, then, we
shall take the habit, and, with the grace of God, in one
year more we shall return to France.

" The Dominicans behold a fair future opening
before them. They are already at St. Petersburg in
Russia, where they have a parish with more than
30,000 souls; at Constantinople, in Turkey, in Ireland,
in England, in Belgium, and in Poland. They have
just been re-established in Holland. The repugnance
of the emperor in their regard has been overcome;
they will soon see themselves restored at Milan ; and
to-morrow a Dominican Convent will be opened at

Venice, at the very time when three Frenchmen will be taking the habit of the Friar-Preachers, in the name of their country.

"I have already told you that the Holy Father granted us a special audience; he received us very affectionately, specially Père Lacordaire, who had already seen him five or six times. In the morning the Father-General had been to him to tell him of our taking the habit, and the Pope had replied to him, 'It is a brave and noble project, let them go on with it.' The cardinals have also heartily welcomed Père Lacordaire; one of them is to offer the Holy Sacrifice for the success of our design. What will perhaps astonish you the most, is the good-will shown us by the religious orders. The Benedictines tell us that the Order of Friar-Preachers is that which they have always liked the best after their own. The Franciscans remind us of the interview between St. Francis and St. Dominic. We have been to see the Father-General of the Jesuits; he received us most kindly, and was pleased to speak to us of the future union of the Dominicans and Jesuits foretold by a St. Macrina of Spain. Let us therefore pray that the holy Will of God may be fulfilled.

"Père Lacordaire spoke truly when he said that the Dominican Order had in it a great deal of the French character. If you were to see the good fathers at the Minerva, you would think you saw so many Frenchmen. All are more or less enthusiastic over our project, and there are already several, who, were it possible, would beg the favour of coming to consecrate their lives to the restoration of the Order in France. There exists the greatest frankness among them, and the lay brothers are treated with the utmost friendship and equality; all this is French, and we may glory in it, because it is Catholic, and our duty is to render it universal. And do not think that it is a mere thoughtless feeling of nationality which makes me proud of being a Frenchman. No, it is as a

Catholic that I consider my nation as the first and greatest of all nations. It is because I believe that God grants His graces rather to the most fervent, than to the most numerous prayers, to emotions of the heart rather than to devotions of habit, that I look on the French as the best Catholics in the world. In Piedmont, in Lombardy, and in fact all over Italy, the churches are much more frequented, the prayers much longer, the religious exercises much more numerous than in France; but in this religion of habit there is so much resemblance to the religious state of France before 1789, that one asks one's self if Providence may not have reserved for this country revolutions similar to that which overthrew the faith in our own. Not that we must be exclusive in these preferences; doubtless in all countries there are very many good and holy Catholics; nor need we lend any faith to those tales of scandal about the Roman clergy which fill so many mouths, and which are heard by so many ears, while no human eye has ever beheld them. All I mean is that in France we do not think ourselves good Catholics unless we obey the gospel, both as members of the Church, of the nation, and of our family; whilst elsewhere a man too often believes himself a good Catholic if he goes often to church, whilst he gives no thought at all to the duty of conforming his exterior life to her teaching.

" The French artists who have flocked to Rome for many years past have rendered a very bad service to their country, by keeping up in the minds of many Italians, specially ecclesiastics, the bad reputation of atheism which France earned at the time of the Revolution. This sad observation has moved Père Lacordaire to propose to Besson, to C——, and to M. Cartier, to found a society at Rome, the end of which will be to sanctify and instruct its members, and to prove to France that she has some children who know the Apostles' Creed. You know Besson, his goodness, and his devotedness. C—— is a painter, a friend of Père Lacordaire and of all those who know him. He lives with Besson ; they are two angels sheltered under the same roof. M. Cartier is a young French painter, a friend of Besson and of C——, and a good Catholic. They have accepted the proposal with delight, and are to assemble every Sunday to hear Mass together, not merely as Catholics, but also as French artists. They will then collect some small funds, in order to establish a library, and to set on foot besides certain works of charity. It is their intention to admit all Catholic artists who shall offer themselves, particularly French ones. This holy society will, moreover, have the immense advantage of supplying the young men who come to Rome with a charitable and numerous family; and these poor fellows are too often completely abandoned in time of sickness and distress. But, my dear brother, this work, undertaken by the children of France, and for her rehabilitation, will not be complete unless it has representatives in Paris. I beg and conjure you therefore immediately to communicate with Besson, in order to found this society in Paris. It will be well that a future Dominican should close his worldly career by such a work, suggested to him by a Father, who will soon be his own Father, and who already loves to call himself his friend. . . . We reckon too much on your activity, and on those good friends, the Catholic artists who surround you, to doubt of the success of this project. I embrace you heartily as a brother.

H. RÉQUÉDAT.

"*P.S.*—We have just come up from the refectory, where, according to custom, it was put to the vote whether or no we should be accepted. The good brothers would not follow the ordinary custom, which is to vote ; they determined to await our arrival in order to give us what they called *a French reception;*

and began to clap their hands as soon as they saw us. Never have such acclamations been remembered at the Minerva! May we only deserve them! I tremble for myself."

Meanwhile the name of Piel began to get known; and success began to smile on him. His critical articles in the Reviews were favourably noticed. No one had higher views than he on the sovereignty of art; no one more vigorously supported the principles of the illustrious author of *Vandalism*. Besides his Church of St. Nicholas at Nantes, many important works were confided to him in various quarters. M. de Montalembert encouraged him, and asked him for the plan of a church for Franche-Comté. M. Vilet, to whom M. Guizot had warmly recommended him, when setting out for his embassy to London, gave him hopes of obtaining the next year the inspection of historic monuments. And was he to abandon a profession at once so Christian and so glorious? Must he throw up all his engagements, interrupt the labours he had begun, abandon his aged father, who was beginning to revive under these first few rays of prosperity, in order to shut himself up in a cell, and share the destinies of an undertaking which was still in its infancy? Such were the arguments urged by the friends of Piel, in order to detain him among them. Brother Peter, on hearing this, wrote to him: "As to the objections urged against your future vocation to the Dominican Order, they seem to me as weak as they ought to be. You have received certain talents from God; well, can you possibly do better than consecrate them to their Giver? I do not see that the rule and compass will be unsuitable at the girdle of a Friar-Preacher, if they hang there together with the Rosary. Let the world say what it likes, and let us follow the path traced out for us by God. I feel that God cannot separate during their future lives those who were twin brothers

16

in the faith. No, God will not separate two friends, whose only fear in entering the convent together was lest they should love one another too much.

" As for me, I am profiting by my abode here under the shadow of the cloister, to travel that long road which always remains to be passed by those who, having once left the Church, return to her by a by-way : I mean, the path which leads us back to the Church as a little child. I am learning no longer to take the cause for the consequences, nor the consequences for the cause; no longer to adhere to religious doctrines on account of their conformity with social doctrines, but rather to deduce social doctrines from religious doctrines ; no longer to love Jesus Christ because I love the poor, but to love the poor for the sake of Jesus Christ. It is an immense work, and one impossible without the help of grace. O my dear friend! how far easier it is to demonstrate the falsehood of rationalism than entirely to cease to be a rationalist ! Another advantage of the year of trial is to show whether one is capable of persevering in the truth in the midst of the most dangerous circumstances, that is to say, in solitude, abandoned to one's greatest enemy—one's self. In a state of struggle, whatever fatigue we experience, we are always sustained by the very act of struggling; pride also has its share in keeping us up ; but in solitude all the strength which we formerly displayed against the exterior enemy is now turned against ourselves, and the interior struggle which succeeds is more terrible, more dangerous, and I may also add, more glorious. I now perfectly understand the necessity of exterior action for society as well as for man ; and it seems to me quite certain that, with rare exceptions, every nation and every man who does not seek some exterior field of action is destined to succumb.

" Every day I see with pain how unworthy I am of being called to so heavenly a life as that which a good religious leads on earth. Happy he who always feels

his heart inflamed with love in the House of God!
Happy those moments when the kiss which he impresses on the crucifix kindles the lips and moistens
the eyes! But woe to those moments when, worn out
by the want of faith, of hope, and of charity, the eyes
remain dry, and the lips cold as they touch the sacred
emblem from which the meaning has passed away.
Alas! why are those unhappy moments so frequent
with me!"[1]

These letters, from which we regret to be only able
to quote a few passages, appeared so beautiful to
those who received them, that they thought proper to
publish them in a daily newspaper. Our readers may
judge of the surprise and pain of the humble Brother
Peter. He wrote at once as follows :

"MY GOOD BROTHER PIEL,—To our great astonishment, we have just seen my letters inserted in the
Univers, and I write to you in all haste, to entreat, in
the name of our friendship, that this publication may
immediately cease. In the course of my life, I have
too often burdened my conscience with rash judgments, to increase the heavy load any further by
unreservedly condemning the determination which
you have taken. But allow me to say, that I have
exhausted every possible explanation, and can find
none which appears to me satisfactory. It is really a
very grave decision thus to trample the privacy of our
correspondence under the feet of the public. I liked
to write to you as I would have spoken to you. I
liked to revenge myself for the absence which prevented me from pressing you to my heart, by pouring
out, without order or measure, all the thoughts of
my heart into yours; and you have been able to
discern some reason strong enough to prevent you
from respecting this confidence! You must have forgotten me altogether, not to reflect how much I

---

[1] La Quercia, May 19—June 6, 1839.

always dislike publicity. And besides, what is more serious, inasmuch as it is not personal to myself, you cannot have remembered that a religious no longer belongs to himself, that before all things he belongs to his superiors, and God grant that they may not be displeased at what has been done! However that may be, the only good result of the publication being accomplished — that namely, of making publicly known that, for His own wise purposes, God takes pleasure in mingling the ignorant with the learned, the man of genius with the poor in spirit, a Père Lacordaire and a Réquédat—this good result being accomplished, pray do not send another line to the newspapers. You never could be so cruel as to deprive me of the consolation of sometimes opening my heart to you."[1]

The year of noviciate was drawing to a close. To see France once more, to pitch his tent in the centre of Paris, to begin his apostolic life under the habit of St. Dominic, and to save souls—these hopes inspired Brother Peter with a joy which he sought not to conceal. He replied to his friends, who feared lest they should see Père Lacordaire establish himself in Belgium, where a home had been offered him, that they forgot how jealous he and his companions were of the name of Frenchmen, and that to them the proverb which says that "every road ends in Rome," meant that "every road ends in Paris." He begged them to have a novena of Masses said at St. Geneviève's, for their happy return to France. "Let us have St. Geneviève on our side," he said, "and we shall enter Paris, even if the gates be closed against us." This was the state of affairs when, in the February of 1840, Père Lacordaire decided on a step which was to prove to both of them a hard sacrifice, but which reveals the prudent slowness of the new religious called to direct his numerous family. This is how Brother

[1] La Quercia, July 6, 1839.

Peter announces this determination to one of his friends in Paris.[1]

" I have not forgotten that you are the protector of the Friars-Preachers, and on that ground I am bound to make you the following communication. After having thought much of it before God, Père Lacordaire has written to our most Reverend Father-General to beg his permission to remain in Rome for three years after our profession, in order that he may thoroughly study the theology of St. Thomas. As you will see, it is a very serious decision, but I think I may say, it is also one which is most wise and praiseworthy on the part of our dear Père Lacordaire. In the first place, the services which the Friars-Preachers may be able to render, however various, all reduce themselves to one, which may be expressed algebraically thus : *Rome—Paris*, and which I shall translate thus for you who know nothing of algebra : to unite France to Rome, the right arm to the head. Now for this purpose we must strike deep roots in the centre of Catholicity, and nothing will do this better for us than the time we propose to remain here, and the studies in which we shall be engaged. As to France, as we hope to give her our entire lives, she will, if God permit, have plenty of opportunities for making acquaintance with the children of St. Dominic ; and besides, it is time now to restore the study of theology in France. At present, almost everywhere they study nothing but the disciples and the commentators of St. Thomas. It is time to return to the great master ; and looking at it from this point of view, I do not know whether to say that my dear Father Dominic has given France the finest example by abandoning the path of honour in order to follow

---

[1] M. Amédée Teyssier, who wrote a Biographic Notice of Piel. On Réquédat's departure for Rome, M. Teyssier had said to him joking : " You shall write to me from Rome, thus : ' To M. Teyssier, Protector of the Order of St. Dominic in Paris.' "

that of poverty, or by resolving to become a schoolboy again for three years longer. I specially recommend to my good brother Piel, and to all our friends
often to pray God that I may live and die a humble
and faithful Friar-Preacher."

The prayers and holy counsel of Brother Peter,
meanwhile, had borne their fruits. Piel, renouncing
his passion for Christian art, and all his prospects of
success and human glory, resolved to follow the attraction which drew him to the religious life. He
hesitated for a long time; but when once he had
made up his mind, he advanced with a firm step to
the sacrifice, and displayed all the energy of his character. He wrote to the Curé of the Church which
he was to have built at Nantes, that he would be-
queath all his plans, and all his rights, to a skilful
architect. "I can do nothing in this business," he
said, "unless you authorise me. Do so then; for I
repeat it, whether the plans be accepted or rejected,
I am equally dead; nothing, neither gain nor glory,
can move me from the obedience which I have promised."

"Do you remember," he wrote to one of his friends,
"the gratitude which I expressed to our Lord, for the
graces with which He has never ceased to load me,
specially of late years? I only told you part, for my
tongue was not free, and my friendship held me back.
Now I can open my whole heart to you. I purpose setting out on the 20th of April (Easter Monday) to join
M. Lacordaire and our dear Hippolytus. Nothing will
be an obstacle to this plan except the holy Will of
God. I firmly believe in the truth of my vocation, and
therefore I am going to follow it. You are not so
lukewarm as to believe that I am disposed to unite
myself to the children of St. Dominic out of the hope
that I may serve them by putting at their disposal
what I know of my art. They call me, and they well
know why. I have but my obedience to offer them,
and they have accepted it; I need not concern myself

about the rest. God is my witness that in binding
myself more closely to Him, I accept the conditions
He may impose, in all simplicity. I would I had
more to sacrifice to Him ; if I have not been able to
give more it is because He has not willed it, and I
must adore His holy Will. I trust that you will not
think of putting before my eyes my interests, or my
glory, or the so-called services I might have rendered
in the world to Christian art, and by that means to
the religion of Jesus Christ. At this moment I know
nothing but the interests of my soul, which tell me to
follow a vocation which I believe to be a true one ; I
know but one glory, that of God, which I am about
to seek, together with my salvation, in poverty, chastity, and obedience. As to art and religion, our Lord
will provide for that. His servant has no consciousness of having any mission, nor of being a master of
these things, in the world he is quitting. He goes to
Rome to obey Him, and if, in His adorable design,
He intend to employ him worthily in the restoration
of religion by means of art, His servant is ready to
obey Him in that, as in all else."

Such was Brother Piel, and such he showed himself
to the end—a lofty soul, a heroic heart, incapable of
being divided, and aspiring from the very first moment to the highest perfection. Accompanied by
Hernsheim, he quitted France on the 1st of May with
the presentiment that he should never see it more.
The evening before he started, he wrote to his father,
"I bid you adieu once more, before leaving this land
of France, where my heart will remain as long as
obedience permits. God has always given me the
grace of having loved my country, and I thank Him
for it at this moment when I feel it my duty to quit
her. I leave behind me a beloved family, and friends
who are very dear ; above all, I leave some precious
graves. I have not been able to offer my prayers
over them as I should have wished to have done, but
you will discharge this debt for me. When you see

strangers in want, help them in the name of Jesus Christ, in memory of my absence."

Piel once more embraced his friend at the Convent of Santa Sabina, on Mount Aventine. The two first French Dominicans, Père Lacordaire and Brother Réquédat, had pronounced their vows on the 12th of April, before the Madonna della Quercia, and for the first time for fifty years France was represented in the Order of St. Dominic. Returning to Rome immediately afterwards, they were living at the Convent of Santa Sabina, where they continued to receive new recruits. Nothing had yet been decided as to the place where the newly-arrived Frenchmen were to make their noviciate; they were waiting there, praying, studying the theology of St. Thomas, making pious pilgrimages to some martyr's tomb, and strengthening their faith in that atmosphere of Christian Rome, so well known to all those who have once breathed it. We must hear Piel, the architect, telling his impressions in the masculine and nervous style which so admirably reveals the man. He is writing to a lady at Lisieux, who had patronised him in his artistic career: —" I beg of you never to read any of those wearisome accounts of journeys to the Eternal City. Those who write them have not heard the voice which spoke to Moses, saying, ' Undo the latchet of thy shoes, for the place on which thou standest is holy ground.' Had you ever trodden on the dust of the saints, you would feel how much such writings are wanting in the perfume of Christian recollections which that dust awakens within us. If you have never made this pilgrimage to the tomb of the holy apostles, you must choose the best Christian among your friends to make it for you. The ruins of Rome have taught me nothing about the architecture of a people who, great as they were, had neither heart nor pity at the time when they cultivated the arts. I only understood, as I beheld them, how much pomp and majesty these old stones add to the bloody history of our fathers in the faith. Each one is an altar on which the purest blood of the just has flowed ; and this renders them more precious to the convert who speaks to you at this moment than the chisel of the sculptor could render them to the architect whom you have perhaps forgotten. I see from the *loggia* of the convent, the whole city of Rome, and principally her historic quarter ; it is a view of surpassing beauty."

Hardly had he arrived at Rome when Piel had to undergo a trial worthy of his great character, and which shows the progress which grace had made in his souL His plans for the Church of St. Nicholas were criticised and cut up, and his friends conjured him to defend himself. "You tell me that they have criticised me," he replied ; ".well then, my dear friend, I am justly punished in the way wherein I have most sinned. Even now when God has called me to a life of meekness and charity I feel the old blood boil within me, the same which rendered me so severe in proclaiming the faults of the works which I examined, and so slow in doing justice to their good qualities. My flesh is not yet conquered, and I thank God for allowing me to feel something of the cruelty which I have so often exercised on others. May my hand dry up, O my God, before it writes a single line of criticism. Your letter pierced me like a sharp dart ; but God by His grace soon consoled me. If I were truly to compassionate the sufferings of my God, who was far more despised, in spite of His majesty, than I shall ever be in my baseness, can I ever feel any disquietude at what Peter says, or Paul thinks of me ? Peter, and Paul, and I, shall all be one day judged, and there will be no question of architecture at that hour. The law of the flesh is too much alive in me still to allow me rightly to bear these humiliations, which would make my treasure before God, did I bless Him for them with something more than the lips."[1]

[1] *Notice sur Piel*, p. 85.

In the little group of religious, or postulants at
Santa Sabina, Piel, by the energy of his character,
and the ardour of his ascetic aspirations, obtained a
kind of influence from which Père Lacordaire himself
could not always defend himself. He was indeed
formed to become a great orator and a great saint.
One of those who knew him best, said of him, " His
style recalls that of Pascal."

The strictest union reigned between the new
brethren ; but sacrifices, the necessary basis of everything which is destined to last, soon began. " It is
now nearly three weeks," wrote Père Lacordaire,
" since our little French colony has been installed at
Santa Sabina. We have had time to become acquainted with one another, and I am thoroughly satisfied with our experience. We have all truly but one
heart, and are but too happy. But the hand of God
must needs strike on some side or other ! The very
day but one after our installation, Brother Peter had
a violent attack of spitting of blood. The physician
was at first much alarmed. Since then he has judged
more favourably of the malady. He has acted in
consequence, and thanks to his care and the goodness
of God, our dear invalid is now quite convalescent."[1]
This was unhappily an illusion of friendship. Père
Lacordaire acknowledged it himself three months
later in a letter, in which he is led to speak of the
testamentary dispositions of his friend. " You cannot
have supposed that I had acquired the estate of St.
Vincent, or that I had millions in my coffers. As to
this estate of St. Vincent I never so much as heard of
it, and have not one sou to purchase it. And were
Providence to put millions into my hands, I should
look on my undertaking as accursed. Providence has
done this much only : seeing that we have to pass
several years out of our own country, and consequently
without any means of interesting charity in our favour.
It has provided for our wants during this time of exile.

[1] Santa Sabina, May 3, 1840.

It was even owing to me that Réquédat gave up the half of his patrimony to his family, as well for the present as for the future. But, alas! will there be a future for him? His health does not improve, and I often feel the most painful anxieties about him. He has, by my advice, informed his family of his state. This is our *wound;* without it we should have been too happy."

Brother Peter had, in fact, been attacked by pulmonary consumption. During his long illness, Père Lacordaire nursed him as though he had been his child. At the end of the month of August the last symptoms appeared. On the 28th, the feast of St. Augustine, he recovered hope, and became, what he usually was, gay, lively, and confiding. " I never saw anything so sad as that joy," said Père Lacordaire. The following day the invalid understood that he had been deceived, and prepared himself for death with the most calm and simple resignation. " Père Lacordaire," he said to Piel, " assures me that our good God treats me with great kindness; if He chooses to have me now, let Him take me ; if He wills me to remain, I beg Him to suffer me to serve Him well under the habit of St. Dominic." On the evening of the 30th of August, he begged Père Lacordaire to give him a little instruction on the Sacrament of Extreme Unction, which he was to receive next day. Thus prepared, with the whole community assembled around his bed, he humbly asked pardon of his brethren for the scandal and pain he had caused them, and slept in the Lord on the morning of the 2nd of September.

It was a severe wound to the hearts of those who loved him, and specially to that of Père Lacordaire. " He was the first friend I had lost," he wrote, "and the most necessary. No one had given themselves to me with more devotedness, no one had promised me more joy, no one united more natural qualities to more Christian virtues ; and he is taken from me ! Ah, the ways of God are impenetrable ! Nothing has ever yet struck me so deep as that premature death, and the certainty I have of the invisible presence of my friend cannot fill up the void he has left by his loss."[1] Nor did Piel feel the grief of this separation less sensibly. When the moment came for laying the body of his beloved brother Peter in the coffin, he could no longer contain himself; he threw himself upon his friend, covering his body with kisses and tears ; then convulsively grasping the hand of one of his brethren, he uttered a loud cry before all the astonished community. "Oh! God is a jealous God!" he wrote, under the influence of this terrible grief. "We are paying him to-day our tithes and first fruits ! . . . . Could a better Frenchman have given his life for the re-establishment of the Friars-Preachers in France ? Who ever loved his country better ? who was ever more ready to sacrifice himself for her ? and now he has done it ; and his death will bring a blessing on our work."

A year afterwards, Père Lacordaire caused the remains of Brother Peter Réquédat to be exhumed from the vault where they had been laid, and placed them under a brick sarcophagus at the extremity of the left aisle of the Church of Santa Sabina. He himself composed the inscription which is to be read on the marble tablet, attesting *the undying regrets which he left behind him.*[2]

Eight months after the death of Réquédat, a new victim was offered to God for the success of the infant

[2] Hic Dominum expectat
Fr. Petrus Réquédat
Ordinis Prædicatorum
Piissimæ memoriæ juvenis,
Quem mors,
Anno Salutis MDCCCXL.
Instaurationi Sancti Dominici in Gallia
Immature rapuit,
Ut nuncius operis ascenderet
et primitiæ,
et numen.

work ; it was Piel, whom his friend seemed to be
drawing to heaven, after having already drawn him to
the faith, and to religion. The French postulants had
quitted the Convent of Santa Sabina for that of San
Clemente, where it was intended that they should take
the habit and make their noviciate. It was then the
month of May, 1841. The ceremony of taking the
habit was preceded by a retreat during each day, of
which the future religious went in silence to visit
some one of the Sanctuaries of Rome, and to pray
there for the common undertaking. The Friday of
this week they went to the Scala Santa ; and as, according to the pious custom, they were ascending on
their knees those steps which had first been ascended
by the Divine Victim, Piel, who was the last behind
the others, felt himself inspired to offer his life for his
brethren. Perhaps he had a presentiment that his
offering was accepted. What is certain is, that being
seized a few days later with the first attack of his
malady, he met death with a calm serenity which
surprised every one.

Père Lacordaire, who had gone to see him at the
Convent of Bosco, where he had been sent, thus describes his impressions : " In four months the malady
has made frightful progress, and I find him changed
in everything except his soul, which is still lively,
calm, serene, resigned and even gay. Brother Peter
was as resigned as he, and like him he had made the
sacrifice of his life to God ; but there was something
austere about his peace ; whilst Piel, on the contrary,
seems to sport with death, and to have no more
regrets than he has temptations. It seems that all
his life he has expected to die young, and at the precise age at which he is dying."[1]

He was happy to die for the Order which he had
loved so well, and for the expiation of his past faults.
He confessed every day, and often with abundance of
tears. One of his friends having come to see him

[1] Bosco, Sept. 26, 1841.

from Paris, he embraced him, and told him he had only a few days to live. "I have been expecting this for the last six months," he said, "and see what a grace! I have come to die in a convent, and in the Order where they pray most for the dead. Listen! Those are the Fathers saying the *De Profundis*: they have to recite it each time they pass through the cloister; you may hear it every minute."

When the Order for which Piel died was re-established in France, Père Lacordaire recalled the memory of this second victim in these terms before the brethren assembled in the Provincial chapter: "Already an eminent architect, an eloquent man, a vast and creative genius, Piel promised to become one of those souls destined by God to sustain a rising work. But he deceived us by the shortness of his career. Death took him from us at the very moment when, dispersed far from Rome in consequence of orders which we were bound to respect, he was the more necessary to us that he might have fortified and consoled us. The same malady which had attacked Brother Réquédat suddenly attacked him between Rome and Bosco, which was the place destined for his exile and his noviciate. He entered Bosco, a celebrated monastery founded by St. Pius V., whose name he bore, already smitten with his fatal malady. His death was to be the second holocaust offered to God to expiate our faults, and to prepare us by adversity for blessings which should be greater than our misfortunes. Piel expired on the 19th of December, 1841. His body was placed in the funeral vaults of the convent, where our memory will never cease to follow him."

Piel had brought a companion with him from France; it was Hernsheim, whose name has been already mentioned. Born at Strasburg in 1816, of Hebrew parents, converted and baptized when very young, he had again lost his faith in the course of barren studies, when, as he was about to take possession of a chair of philosophy, on leaving the Normal

School, he was attacked by an illness which restored to his soul the divine light of religious truth. He himself thus relates how this sudden change was wrought within him : "At the approach of death the world appeared nothing to me ; I all at once loved God more than the most beloved of creatures ; I embraced the crucifix, calling to mind the Passion of our Lord ; I prayed with a fervour which I had never known before to the Blessed Virgin and the saints, and repeated with a kind of ecstasy the simple and consoling words, ' Hail, Mary, full of grace.' And specially I repeated the last words with a kind of rapture, ' now and at the hour of death.' I felt, in fact, that I stood in need of all His mercies, for I had been very guilty before Him. Whoever had then spoken to me of any philosophic system would have seemed very poor in my eyes, yet I had my note-books there, filled with all the doctrines that had been devised since the beginning of the world : but all that abandoned me at the hour of death ; it seemed no more than so much smoke and wind. When a man at the moment of death shall quit faith for philosophy, and when I shall have seen that with my own eyes, you may then sing me the praises of philosophy if you will."[1]

Saved from the abyss, he sent in his resignation to the university, and came to the little colony at Santa Sabina to ask for a sounder and safer philosophy. The *Summa* of St. Thomas delighted him. " I have at last found," he cried, "a true philosophy, which is not at the breath of every system, and which is the tradition of the Dominican Order. My dear friend, I have as yet read but half a volume ; but the blush rises to my cheeks, and I am ashamed of our age, when I think that it neglects such books as these, that it contradicts their teaching, and pretends to refute them without having ever known them."[2]

[1] Notice sur le P. Hernsheim, par R. P. Danzas, p. 33.
[2] Ibid., p. 30.

We shall not follow his life through every detail. Père Lacordaire has resumed it in a few lines of touching simplicity. " Hernsheim," he says, "was one of those who had to endure the unforeseen storm of San Clemente, which separated our little flock. The convent of La Quercia was assigned to him as the place of his noviciate, and he had the grief of leaving it without pronouncing his vows, on account of the doubt raised by his state of health. Afterwards being assigned to the convent of Nancy, the first which Divine Providence suffered us to found in France, he lived there for several years, making continual progress, both in piety and in apostolic eloquence. He had a firm, profound, and ingenious mind, which from time to time gave birth to the most beautiful ideas, always clothed with the sweetest unction. We already thought ourselves sure of possessing in him an excellent preacher, when the same malady, which seven years before had brought him to the brink of the grave, now opened it to him once more and for ever. He died on the 14th of November 1847, esteeming himself one of those humble foundation-stones which the hand of the architect hides in the depth of the earth, and which, all hidden as it is, nevertheless contributes its share to the solidity of the edifice. His body was buried at the Chartreuse at Bosserville, near Nancy, and he was the first of all our departed brethren who found his last resting-place on the soil of his native land."

It is still from Père Lacordaire's Memoirs that we must take the account of Père Besson's entrance into the order. "The history of young Besson was very singular. Brought to Paris from the valleys of Jura by a poor mother, he entered with her into the household of the curé of Our Lady of Loretto. This generous man placed the boy at his own expense in a school in Paris, where he did not get on very well; and appeals were sometimes made from the heart of the good curé to his reason, on the subject of this child. But he always replied with a sort of prophetic presentiment, 'Have patience, something tells me that this unpromising scholar will one day become an instrument in the hand of God.' He felt this so strongly that when he died he left the mother a legacy of 40,000 francs, which was, I believe, his whole patrimony. The presentiment of the good curé was fulfilled; and Santa Sabina, in admitting young Besson into its little French colony, received in him an increase of piety and grace, which was equivalent to a benediction."

We shall say nothing here of the life of Père Besson. This life, which deserves a place to itself, has happily found a worthy historian in M. Cartier. The intimate friend of the holy religious, from his first entrance into the artist's studio up to the time of his death, no one was better qualified than he to portray the beautiful character of the Fra Angelico of France. He has done this with an eloquence of style, an elevation of sentiment, and a charm of narrative, which carry along the mind and the heart from the beginning to the end of the book. M. Cartier, who had already rendered such precious services to the *Bibliothèque Dominicaine*, by his numerous publications, has worthily crowned his labours by this book, which is at once a pious homage to the holy memory of his friend, and an imperishable title to the gratitude of the Dominican Order, and of the public at large.

Of the six Frenchmen who lived for a year at the Convent of Santa Sabina, the four first are dead; we have told our readers their names, and the principal features of their lives. The sixth was to survive them all, in order to fulfil the high mission to which God destined him : it was the Abbé Jandel. He became acquainted with Père Lacordaire at Metz during the station of the winter of 1837. Superior of the little seminary of Pont-á-Mousson, about six leagues from Metz, he went to hear him, and like so many others, fell under the charm of his eloquence, and received a

17

visit from him at Pont-à-Mousson. "As I had been dazzled and subjugated," he says, "by the power and brilliancy of his preaching, so was I also edified and charmed by the novelty, the candour, and the simplicity of his conversation. Thus he left in my soul, on his departure from Metz, a profound impression of affectionate sympathy and respectful admiration."

When, in the spring of 1839, the *Memoir to the French People* appeared, the Abbé Jandel was deeply moved by it. "He was captivated by all that was generous in this enterprise, and the important results likely to ensue to the Church of France ; and with something in it, moreover, that savoured of the bold and the adventurous." Having himself decided on entering among the Jesuits, he resolved to go to Rome during the vacation of 1839, in order to confer with Père Lacordaire, and gain light on the subject of his vocation. It was a father of the Society of Jesus, the reverend Père Villefort, who sent him to Père Lacordaire, saying, "You are called to be a Dominican; offer yourself to Père Lacordaire, and to-morrow, when you say mass, thank God for the grace He has shown you by fixing your vocation."

Père Jandel was then one of the first generation of Santa Sabina ; he took the habit at La Quercia, on the 15th of May, 1841, made his profession the year following, and set out for Bosco. Returning to France with the others, after filling the first offices in several houses, he was soon to be called, through the confidence of the Sovereign-Pontiff, to the eminent dignity of Master-General of the whole Order, in which office the Chapter-General, held at Rome in the year 1862, confirmed him for twelve years. This life of such well-known holiness, which will have rendered such immense services to our Order throughout the entire world, cannot yet be related; it would require greater liberty to speak its eulogium, and to do so with perfect impartiality.

· Such, then, were the men whom it pleased God to

give to Père Lacordaire as his first companions. All were men distinguished by the qualities either of their minds or their hearts. But more than this, all of them were men of rare faith. They believed in what as yet had no existence, in what was taxed with folly by many Catholics both at Rome and Paris. They not only believed in the power of God—in that there would have been no great merit—but also in the man of His choice. They believed that this man, who still remained an object of suspicion to many, in spite of his words, his acts, and his whole life, was an instrument designed by God for the accomplishment of a noble and perilous enterprise; and they therefore gave themselves to him with generosity. Dispersed by a severe and unexpected trial, and decimated by death, their faith and hope remained unshaken. We bless them for it, but we cannot pity them. Workmen of the first hour, like the Apostles of the early Church, if they had their catacombs, they had also their Cenaculum. They knew that spring-tide blossoming of the faith which is found in hearts devoted to a difficult undertaking; they knew those transports of self-sacrifice, those moments of holy enthusiasm, that gaiety in suffering so well expressed in the words addressed by Père Lacordaire to Père Jandel, who appeared surprised at the austerities of the Order. "Oh!" he said, with a moving accent, "when once the soul is united to God, and the heart is satisfied, everything becomes easy." They knew those holy ties of friendship and mutual confidence, those warm emotions of loving hearts knit together in Jesus Christ, which gives such a charm and fragrance to life, and which made one of them say, "Do you remember that morning at Santa Sabina, when all three of us, you, and I, and Brother Piel, were talking together of God, and when Brother Piel threw himself weeping into my arms, and embraced me so tenderly? It seemed to me as if we all had but one heart, and that our good God had united us in that spiritual embrace, to bring

17—2

us nearer to himself, and render us capable of greater sacrifices."[1]

No, we do not pity them; we rather envy them their lot, and their crown. Let us revere their memory and imitate their example. They are our Fathers, and their lives shall be had in eternal honour. Would that we could also preserve and do honour to their tombs! Unhappily, none of them repose in France under the feet of their brethren. Réquédat, Piel, Hernsheim, Besson, even Père Lacordaire himself, all sleep in what is more or less foreign soil. Let us hope that the day will come when the justice of our country will insure us a less precarious existence, and thus permit us to gather together within our own walls the precious remains of those in whose hearts God and their country were never separated!

[1] Père Hernsheim to Père Besson.

CHAPTER XII.

PÈRE LACORDAIRE, as we have said, pronounced his solemn vows on the 12th of April, 1840, at the convent of La Quercia. Of all the disciples who were to join him at the commencement of his enterprise, and of whom we have given a sketch in the foregoing chapter, he had at this moment but one with him, and that was B. Peter Réquédat, then dying of a chest complaint. He had therefore to enter the lists almost alone, and his liberty was gone for ever. Whether he succeeded, or whether he failed, his life remained irrevocably united to the destinies of his Order, to be crowned and applauded, if success, in spite of all sinister prophecies, should eventually justify his confidence; and to be stigmatised with the disgrace of failure if this confidence should prove fallacious. Of all the difficulties which he had foreseen when pondering over his design at Rome, none had failed to realise themselves, whether on the part of his own nature, his enterprise itself, the French Government, and even the Roman authorities. Yet at the decisive moment he felt no hesitation; on the contrary, he entered cheerfully on

his path of sacrifice. And in reward of this simple
obedience, God was pleased to give him for one year
a sort of happy foresight and foretaste of the joys he
was one day to receive in the religious life under the
shelter of his restored cloisters.

The day after his solemn profession he started for
Rome, carrying with him the picture of the Madonna della Quercia, as the ancient Romans carried
with them their household gods. At the Ponte
Molle, just outside the gates of the city, he found
several young Frenchmen waiting to receive him with
honour.

The convent of Santa Sabina was assigned as his
habitation, and there his first companions successively
came to join him, whilst waiting until something
should be settled as to the place and manner of their
canonical noviciate. Père Lacordaire, in his " Life of
St. Dominic," thus describes the convent which was
the first asylum of the French colony :—" The church
of Santa Sabina is built on the Aventine Hill. Its
walls are on the highest and most abrupt part of that
hill, just above the narrow shores against which the
Tiber murmurs as it flows away from Rome, and
dashes with its waves against the ruined bridge which
Horatius Cocles defended against Porsenna. Two
rows of ancient columns, supporting a roof, the beams
of which are visible, divide the church into three
naves, each terminated by an altar. It is a primitive
Basilica in all the glory of its simplicity. From the
windows of the convent the eye wanders over the interior of Rome, and stops only at the Hill of the
Vatican. Two winding paths lead down to the city;
one conducts to the Tiber, the other to one of the
angles of the Palatine Mount, near the Church of St.
Anastasia. This was the road which St. Dominic had
to take in order to go from Santa Sabina to St.
Sixtus. No path on earth has preserved more vividly
the traces of his footsteps. Nearly every day for
more than six months he descended it or climbed its

steep ascent, carrying from one convent to the other
the fire of his charity. Since then a colony of his
children has never ceased to live within the walls of
Santa Sabina. The convent possesses the narrow
cell where the Saint sometimes withdrew, the hall
where he gave the habit to St. Hyacinth and Blessed
Ceslaus, and in a corner of the garden an orange tree
planted by himself extends its golden fruit to the
pious hand of the citizen or the pilgrim."[1]

It was from the old stock of this tree that, during
this very same year, there shot forth a strong new
sucker, which is still vigorous and covered with
flowers and fruit. It was looked on as a happy pre-
sage of returning strength in the Order of St. Dominic,
and as a prophetic encouragement to the founder and
to his new children.

They were in all seven Frenchmen living together
as religious, although only the two first as yet wore
the habit. All had but one thought and one life.
Their time, divided between prayer and study, flowed
on in a delightful peace, which no rumours from without had the power to trouble. From time to time, a
few Frenchmen, attracted by curiosity, climbed up to
Santa Sabina, and went away wondering at what they
had seen and heard. There was a fragrance of antique piety in these young souls so enthusiastic, so
devoured by that new fire which God kindles in the
heart of those generations whom He designs to save.
It was the family life of which Père Lacordaire had
so often thought, and the reality of which he was
tasting for the first time. "Nothing," he writes, "can
describe these good young men, or the life which
we are leading together with God." Their frequent
visits to the chief sanctuaries of Rome, the holiness
of the miracles of St. Dominic and his first companions, the memory of which was recalled to them
by the very stones of the convent—all this inflamed
their courage and urged them to those holy follies of

[1] Vie de St. Dominique.

love which are to be found in the glorious beginning
of every monastic resurrection. One day Père Lacordaire was walking with Père Besson in the Roman
Campagna. They were conversing on the love of our
Lord Jesus Christ for us, the favourite theme with
Père Lacordaire. As they came near the wood of the
Nymph Egeria, Père Lacordaire stopped before a
thorn-bush, and showing it to his companion, "Will
you," he said, "suffer something for the sake of Him
who has suffered so much for us?" And without
waiting for reply, both immediately cast themselves
into the midst of the thorns, and came out covered
with blood, thus renewing, in order to appease their
thirst for self-immolation, what other saints had done
to quench the flames of concupiscence. Without
wishing to attach more than their proper value to incidents like these, we yet mention them, because, far
from being isolated, they held the foremost place in
the spiritual life of Père Lacordaire. Our only difficulty would consist in knowing where to choose, and
how to say all that might be said. He himself wrote
of his friend Réquédat : " I possess all the secrets of
his spiritual life ; but I should hardly dare to tell all
I know of it, so incredible would it appear." Shall I
dare, in my turn, to tell all I know of the master who
formed such disciples ? God grant that I may be able
to do so !

After having led this sweet and holy life with his
brethren for eight months, it seemed time for him to
revisit France, and "to unite activity to the laborious
preparation of retirement." This was also the wish of
his friends ; they feared lest too long an absence
should hinder the success of the work. He was happy
also to be able to show himself to his country, still
her devoted servant, remaining the same he had ever
been, now that he wore the ancient habit of the
middle age. It was time, too, for him to see the new
archbishop of Paris, to reappear, if possible, in the
pulpit of Notre Dame ; in a word, to reconnoitre his

ground, like a prudent man, before coming to pitch his tent.

He left Rome on the 30th of November, 1840, and travelled through France, wearing the religious habit, which she had not seen for fifty years. Here and there he met with a few marks of astonishment, and sometimes of hostility. At Paris, where he was expected by no one excepting his most intimate friends, many rejoiced to see him. His former enemies had no time to think of their old rancours, nor the lawyers to bring forward their musty statutes. Everything else gave way before the sentiment of curiosity. All the world wished to see the friar, the spectre of past ages, the son of *Dominic the Inquisitor ;* and specially to know what he was going to do and to say. Mgr. Affre, the new archbishop of Paris, received Père Lacordaire with delight, saw no difficulty in his preaching at Notre Dame in his new habit, and only begged him to name whatever day he liked. We must leave Père Lacordaire himself to relate the story of this bold adventure :

" I appeared in the pulpit of Notre Dame with my white tunic, my black mantle, and my tonsure. The archbishop presided, the keeper of the seals, and minister of public worship, M. Martin (du Nord), was also present, as he wished to observe for himself a scene of which no one could tell the issue. Many other distinguished persons concealed themselves in the assembly, in the midst of a crowd which filled the church from the doors to the sanctuary. I had chosen for the subject of my discourse the *Vocation of the French Nation*, in order to veil the audacity of my presence under the popularity of my theme. In this I succeeded, and next day the keeper of the seals invited me to a dinner-party of forty persons, which he gave at the chancellor's mansion. During the repast, M. Bourdian, formerly minister of justice under Charles X., leant towards one of his neighbours, and said, " What a strange turn of events ! If, when I was keeper of the seals, I had invited a Dominican to my table, my house would have been burnt down next day.' However the house was not burnt, and no newspaper ever invoked the secular arm against my *auto-da-fé.*"[1]

This was, in fact, one of his happiest strokes—one of those surprises which he was fond of, and which suited the adventurous side of his character. The effect of this reappearance was immense; the religious standard had been planted in the very heart of the stronghold ; but the victory was not yet completely gained, and many of those who had been dazzled and disconcerted by the brilliancy and unforeseen character of the attack, were not long ere they turned against him, and demanded an explanation of his illegal triumph in the name of the state.

At the same time that the religious was for the first time displaying the habit of his order in France, the historian was likewise presenting her with a Life of his new Father. He had written this Life during his year of noviciate ; it was published during the winter of 1841. It had all the success which it deserved, and which has only been confirmed by time. M. de Chateaubriand, whose opinion we have already quoted, spoke of it with delight : "Nobody else," he said, "was capable of writing the pages in it which I most admire. It displays not merely talent of the first rank, but a unique kind of talent. Its beauty, like its brilliancy, is immense ; in fact, I do not know a more beautiful style."[2] We were then considerably poorer than we now are in good saints' Lives : almost the only one of any merit was M. de Montalembert's recently published Life of St. Elisabeth of Hungary, a model of hagiography never surpassed. Père Lacordaire, without imitating him, but with equal talent, resolved the difficult problem of reproducing the life of a saint out of the legends of the middle ages and

[1] Memoirs.

[2] Correspondence du Père Lacordaire avec Madame Swetchine, p. 346.

the dry discussions of modern historians, and placing
him once more vividly before our eyes, so that we can
see, hear, and love him, not as a saint only, but as a
man, surrounded by friends and brethren, possessed
of human feelings, a delightful simplicity, and an almost
maternal tenderness. Through his spiritualised body
we seem to discern the soul radiant with light, sweetness, and love ; and as we read this life we feel ourselves transported into a purer atmosphere, filled with
better desires, and a more ardent trust after God and
perfection. The great merit of the book is the spirit
of love with which it is written. A writer must love
the illustrious departed in order to have any right to
speak of them to the living. It is precisely this which
makes up the charm of these pages ; we feel that it
is a son who is writing of his father, an artist who is
painting on his knees, in the same way that Fra Angelico painted that portrait of St. Dominic that forms
the frontispiece of the volume. The Life of St. Dominic is in everybody's hands, and we shall therefore
give neither its analysis nor any long extracts. We
may, however, be permitted to quote two pages, one
of which shows us what St. Dominic was, and the
other what was his Order : they will thus serve to
make us better acquainted with the religious family
into which Père Lacordaire had just entered :

"Dominic journeyed on foot, with a staff in his
hand, and a bundle on his shoulders. So soon as he
had left inhabited districts behind him, he took off his
shoes and walked barefoot. If his feet were wounded
by the stones on the road, he would say, smiling,
'This is our penance.' He preferred to lodge at
monasteries, not stopping according to his own caprice, but according to the fatigue or the wishes of the
brethren who were with him. The journey never interrupted any of his practices of piety. Every day,
unless unable to reach a church, he offered the Holy
Sacrifice to God with abundance of tears ; for it was
impossible for him to celebrate the Divine Mysteries

without emotion. When the course of the ceremonies announced to him the approach of Him whom he had loved from his earliest years, it could be perceived by the emotion of his whole being ; and the tears coursed each other down his pale and radiant countenance. He pronounced the Lord's Prayer with a heavenly accent, which, as it were, rendered sensible the presence of the *Father Who is in heaven.* He observed silence, and caused it to be observed by his companions, in the morning until nine o'clock, and in the evening from after Compline. In the interval he prayed to God, whether in the form of conversation or theological controversy, and in every other imaginable way. Sometimes, specially in solitary places, he begged his companions to keep at a certain distance from him, gracefully saying to them, in the words of the Prophet Osee, 'I will lead him into solitude, and I will speak to his heart.'

" He preached to all he met on the road, in the cities, villages, and castles, and even in the monasteries. His words were like burning fire. Initiated by his long studies at Palencia and Osma into all the mysteries of Christian theology, they flowed forth from his heart with floods of love, which made known their truth even to the most hardened. One young man, charmed by his eloquence, asked him in what books he had studied. 'My son,' he replied, 'in the book of charity more than in any other ; for that teaches us all things.' In the pulpit he often shed tears, and in general he was full of that supernatural melancholy which is derived from the profound sentiment of the invisible world. When he perceived from afar the crowded roofs of a great city, the thought of the miseries and sins of men plunged him into sad reflections, which expressed themselves on his countenance. Then he rapidly passed through all the varied manifestations of love ; and joy, trouble, and serenity succeeded themselves in turns on his brow, giving to the majesty of his bearing an indescribable power and charm.

" He devoted the day to preaching, to travelling, and to business; and when the setting of the sun disposed every one to rest, quitting the world, he sought in God the refreshment of which soul and body stood in need. He remained in choir after the community had gone out, taking care that none of the brethren should imitate his example, both because he did not wish to overtax their strength, and because a holy modesty led him to fear lest they might discover the secrets of his intercourse with God. But these precautions were baffled by curiosity; some of the brethren concealed themselves in the darkness of the church in order to watch him during these vigils, and thus these touching particulars became known. When, then, he found himself alone, protected in his love by darkness and silence, he entered into the most ineffable outpourings of the heart with God. The church, the symbol of the city of the angels and saints, became to him as a living being, that he moved with his cries and groans. He made the circuit of it, stopping to pray before each altar, sometimes inclining profoundly, sometimes prostrating, and sometimes kneeling. Tears alone did not satisfy him : three times every night he mingled his blood with his tears, thus satisfying, as far as possible, that thirst for self-immolation which is the generous part of love. They heard him striking his body with iron chains ; and the grotto of Segovia, which witnessed all these excesses of penance, has for centuries kept the traces of the blood which he shed there. In his heart he divided this blood into three parts ; the first was for his own sins, the second for the sins of the living, and the third for the sins of the dead. Often he even obliged one of his brethren to scourge him, in order to increase the humiliation and the pain of his sacrifice. The day will come when, in presence of heaven and earth, the angels of God will place on the altar of judgment two full chalices : a

hand of infinite justice will weigh them both, and it
will be known, to the eternal glory of the saints, that
every drop of blood shed out of love, has saved a
deluge."

"The time was come for creating the legislation of
the Dominican family; for it is necessary that laws
should support customs in order to preserve their
tradition. Dominic, already a Father, now became a
legislator. After having given birth to a race of men
like himself, he was going to provide also for their
fecundity, and to arm them against the future with
the mysterious power which produces duration. Now,
one question presented itself in the first place : Ought
an Order destined to the apostolate to adopt the monastic traditions? or should it not rather be made to
approach more nearly to the greater freedom of the
secular clergy, by giving up most of the usages of the
cloister? As to the three vows of poverty, chastity,
and obedience, these of course could not be made
subjects of doubt; for without them no spiritual
society can be conceived as possible, any more than
we can imagine a nation without the poverty of taxa-
tion, the chastity of marriage, and obedience to the
same laws, under the same head. But would it suit
the end of the apostolate to preserve such customs as
the public recitation of the Divine Office, perpetual
abstinence from meat, long fasts, silence, the chapter
of faults, penances for breaches of the rule, and
manual labour? Was this rigorous discipline, so fit
for forming the solitary heart of the monk, and for
sanctifying his days full of leisure, compatible with
the heroic liberty of an apostle, who goes forth sowing
the good grain of truth to the right and left? Dominic
believed that it was. He thought that by exchanging
manual labour for the study of sacred science, by
mitigating certain practices, and using dispensations
in regard of those religious who were more strictly
employed in preaching and teaching, it would be
possible to unite apostolic activity to monastic ob-

servance. He therefore required that the Divine Office should be said in church briefly and succinctly, so as not to diminish the devotion of the brethren or hinder their work; that the brethren when on a journey should be exempt from the regular fasts, except from Advent, on certain vigils, and on the Friday of every week ; that they might eat meat when out of the convents of the Order; that the silence was not to be absolute ; that communication with seculars might be allowed even in the interior of the convents, women only excepted ; that a certain number of students should be sent to the most famous universities ; that they should receive learned degrees; and should open schools ;—all which Constitutions, without destroying the monastic character of the Friar-Preacher, raised him also to the rank of an apostolic man.

" As to the administration of the Order: every convent was to be governed by a conventual prior; every province, composed of a certain number of convents, by a prior provincial ; and the entire Order by one only head, who afterwards bore the title of Master-General. Authority descending from above, and binding all to the throne of the Sovereign Pontiff himself, confirmed the various degrees of this hierarchy, whilst election ascending from below, united the spirit of fraternity to that of command. Thus a double token shone on the brow of each one who held power : the choice of his brethren, and the confirmation of superior power. To the convent belonged the election of its prior ; to the province, represented by its priors and a deputy from each convent, that of the provincial ; to the entire Order, represented by the provincials, and two deputies from each province, that of the Master-General ; and by an inversed progression, the Master-General confirmed the prior provincial, and he again confirmed the conventual priors. All these offices were to be held only for a time, except the highest, in order that the providence of stability might be united to the emulation of change.

General chapters held at near intervals of time, acted as a counterbalance to the power of the Master-General, and provincial chapters to that of the provincial priors ; and a council was given to the conventual prior to assist him in the most important duties of his office. Experience has proved the wisdom of this mode of government. By its means the Order of Friar-Preachers has freely accomplished its end, equally preserved from licence and from oppression. It maintains a sincere respect for authority, united to a certain frank and natural character, which at first sight reveals the Christian set free from fear by love. Most religious Orders have undergone reforms, which have split them into different branches ; but that of the Friar-Preachers has existed for six centuries without losing its unity. It has extended its vigorous branches throughout the entire world, without one of them ever being separated from the parent trunk."[1]

After reading this sketch of the Dominican Constitutions it is easy to understand why Père Lacordaire preferred this Order to any other, and why he judged it best adapted to certain minds in the present day. Had he attempted, as he was advised to do, to found some new Order, it may be doubted whether he would have done so on such advanced principles ; and I have more than once heard the founder of the *Ere Nouvelle* express his astonishment at the daring liberalism of the so-called founder of the Inquisition.

After a two months' residence at Paris, Père Lacordaire returned to Rome on the 7th of April, 1841, with five new brethren. The little colony had just been transferred from Santa Sabina to the old convent of San Clemente. This convent, with its beautiful Basilica, had been given to them to make their noviciate in. Ten Frenchmen were shortly to take the habit; they only waited for the Congregation of Regulars to decide when the noviciate should be canonically erected. From his entrance into the Order up to that

[1] Vie de St. Dominique, ch. viii. and xiv.

moment, everything had succeeded admirably with the new religious, and during his recent journey he had been welcomed with the warmest encouragements, and testimonies of ever-increasing sympathy. At Paris the inter-Nuncio had invited him to dinner. At Genoa, Cardinal Tadini had said to him—" Go on and do not allow yourself to be alarmed." Detained ten days at La Quercia by the small-pox, he had received a visit from the cardinal archbishop of Viterbo, as well as from the delegate-governor; the Holy Father had caused his compliments of condolence to be conveyed to him, and received him on his return to Rome with the greatest kindness. Everything, therefore, appeared to smile on him, and yet, nevertheless, a sharp and most unexpected trial was at hand. He had a sort of presentiment of it, for, on the day before, he wrote :—" I am sensible of all those marks of esteem and affection ; but what most reassures me is, that I never felt more able to refer all to God, and to realise my own misery. *I see how little it would require to make the whole thing crumble to pieces around me*, and the insufficiency of my own means, whether natural or spiritual, for the work I have undertaken. I am here the father of a regular household! with seventeen persons to feed, clothe, and answer for before God." This tranquil glance at God and his own misery was shortly to give him strength to meet contradiction without trouble or discouragement, and to find in it what was as yet wanting to his religious life—the aureola of misfortune.

On the 29th of April the Congregation had given in its reply, according to which the French religious were free to choose some convent of the Roman province in which to go through their novitiate. They agreed with the Master-General to choose the convent of La Quercia. Before leaving San Clemente, they prepared for the taking of the habit by a general retreat. The churches were adorned with flowers

18

and foliage; joy and peace reigned in all hearts; every day the French community visited in silence one of the churches of the city to make the devotion of the Stations, which is so touching and so popular in Rome. One evening as they were returning to the convent of San Clemente, Père Lacordaire received an order from the Secretary of State, which enjoined him to remain at Rome alone, and dispersed all his little colony : one-half were to repair to La Quercia, and the other half to Bosco, in Piedmont. It was a thunderstroke. Humanly speaking, the work was broken up by the dispersion of its members, their separation from their head, and the manifest disgrace into which they had fallen. Happily, however, the hopes of Père Lacordaire were placed higher. He replied that the order should be at once executed. He called the brethren together, and after having declared to them with perfect calmness that his own duty was clearly traced out by his religious obligations, and that he should therefore obey simply and without reserve, he reminded them that, not having as yet contracted any engagements, they were still perfectly free, and had only to take such a decision before God, and their own conscience, as they might judge most suitable, bearing in mind the uncertainty of the future, under existing circumstances. All of them showed an admirable spirit, and replied with one heart that they would obey like him, and remain for ever constant to the vocation which they believed themselves to have received. This being settled, the retreat continued with the utmost tranquillity, and a few days later, on the 13th of May, Père Lacordaire, left alone in Rome, wrote the following lines, full of sadness and resignation :—

"I write to you from San Clemente, which is now deserted. This morning, at six o'clock, those of our brethren destined for Bosco set out; the others who were assigned to La Quercia had preceded them by thirty-six hours. I am now all alone, after seeing myself surrounded by a dear and numerous family. We separated from one another with mingled sorrow and joy, full of confidence in each other, loving each other, and hoping one day to be reunited in France. Yesterday was my birthday, and to-day is the anniversary of my baptism."[1]

Had he any thoughts, whilst linking together these two dates, of associating the ideas which they suggested? In truth it was a second baptism which he had just received forty years after his first, the baptism of religious manhood, that which *buries a man*,[2] according to the energetic words of St. Paul. As a simple priest, Père Lacordaire had known how to keep silence and submit to the Church, when certain of his ideas had not been exempt from blame; but now that he is a religious, will he also know how again to submit when she appears to reject him at the very hour when he has done everything to please her, and when an order, signed by the hand which only yesterday was raised to bless him, is to strike the shepherd and scatter the flock? Will he cast a glance backwards, or ask the Church her reasons for thus distrusting her most submissive child at the very moment when he is renouncing everything in order to serve her? He does neither one nor the other:—he obeys, and is silent.

The world, perhaps, may call this weakness. Nevertheless, who can tell the strength of which this one act may have been the germ and beginning in the life of Père Lacordaire? His character lost nothing of its manly temper on this account. He did not become less constant in his opinions, less firm against every seduction of pride, less opposed to all that was base, less frank and sincere in presence of truth, less a man in his entire life. We ought rather to say that this trial, and those that followed, formed part of the very conditions of his greatness, and of the success of his work. Père Lacordaire, like every

---

[1] Letters to Madame Swetchine.   [2] Col. ii. 12.

one else, and more perhaps than any one else, had need of something to correct that leaven of pride which lies at the root of every human heart, and is the bane of all moral progress. It is within us, far more than without us, that lies the obstacle to our real development, to the perfection of our actions, and the success of our enterprises. To believe and to obey none but ourselves is the most fruitful source of miseries and errors, and it is the capital sin of this century, many of whose principles Père Lacordaire loved so much. Has anything great ever been done in the world by a man who has not often consented to abase his own reason before the lights of others, and sometimes to believe without understanding? And what more noble use can a great intellect make of itself than to distrust its own strength, and humbly to bow before God? Called to command others, Père Lacordaire had need more than any other man to learn the difficulties and the merit of obedience, and it was only just that he should give his children the example of those duties and virtues which he was afterwards to require of them. Thus, at the moment when his whole design seemed about to fall to pieces, he was really laying the corner-stone of the edifice, and establishing among his followers the most essential of virtues—respect for authority; for it is of the religious life, in a very special way, that may be repeated that eulogy which is so true of the Catholic faith, that it is the greatest school of reverence.

In presence of this religious deference to the orders of his superiors, we feel less curious to inquire the reasons which could have caused such a storm to burst over the head of Père Lacordaire. Had he in any way incurred just disgrace? No, thanks be to God; and his silent and sincere obedience were so much the more admirable, from the fact of his being entirely innocent of the accusations brought against him. Some letters and a pamphlet had arrived in Rome from France, denouncing Père Lacordaire as one who upheld the doctrines of De la Mennais in a more skilful and subtle form; his attempt to establish a religious Order had no other object, it was said, than to restore in an underhand way the school which had been destroyed by the Encyclical of 1832, and to spread among the French clergy the idea of the separation of Church and State. By his prompt and filial submission, Père Lacordaire gave the best reply to these odious calumnies which only came to his knowledge at a later period, and he thus regained at once the favour and esteem of those whose confidence had for a moment been shaken.

Separated from those whom he called *his children*, and retired in the Convent of the Minerva at Rome Père Lacordaire resumed, with his accustomed tranquillity, his habits of solitary labour. " My time," he writes, " is divided between the study of St. Thomas and the preparation of my Conferences. The passage from activity to contemplation, from community life to solitude, is less painful to me than it would be to many, thanks to long habit. I suffer for the first few days, and then I settle into the new bend ; without such flexibility, I should have been dead long ago. I have passed years without seeing anybody, or being mixed up with anything; and I remember them now with a kind of terror, for I am no longer the same that I was ; the waters have sunk, and the time of repose will come in the midst of brethren and children. Then I shall be astonished at many things connected with myself, as an old soldier is when he can no longer use his sword. Our children at La Quercia and Bosco are happy. The Noviciate at Bosco and the whole house is in a great state of fervour and regularity. We have found there all that we wanted."[1]

At the end of the year 1841, he asked and obtained permission to return to France in order to resume his course of preaching. He set out in the month of

[1] Letters to Madame Swetchine, June 5, 1841.

September, and visited on his way his poor exiles of
La Quercia and Bosco. He was charmed at the
peace and union which reigned among the brethren,
and with their progress in the spiritual life. At La
Quercia Père Jandel had rapidly gained the confidence of the other French religious. He was the
only priest among them, and it was to him that the
brethren addressed themselves, as to a father, for
counsel and direction. He thus justified what Père
Lacordaire said of him a year later : " Père Jandel is
admirable ; he is just the man I wanted. I shall be
the man for outside, and he will be *the man for within ;* for although I make some progress in the spiritual
life, the old fire still peeps out."[1]

. At Bosco he found Brother Piel dying ; but, accustomed to recognise the goodness of God in afflictions
even yet more than in favours, he raised his heart to
Him, and said : "This will be a great loss to us from
a human point of view, but God knows what He is
about. He doubtless wishes to give us protectors in
heaven capable of supporting us in the difficulties
and adversities which await us. May His Will be
done to the end !"[2]   Later, in a letter to M. de
Falloux, he gave his recollections of this first visit to
Bosco, and his children there. It is a cheering sketch
that is little known, which our readers will therefore
thank us for reproducing in these pages :—

" MY DEAR FRIEND,—You ask me how much is
remaining of the famous convent of the Holy Cross
at Bosco, founded by our dear and holy Pope, Pius V.
What remains of it, my dear friend, is precisely the
whole of it. General Bonaparte having lodged there
for two or three days, in 1796, left an order, written
with his own hand, that it was not to be touched. In
the subsequent wars a company of French veterans
was posted there, who conducted themselves with as

[1] Letters to Madame de la Tour du Pin, 89.
[2] Letters to Madame Swetchine, Sept. 28, 1841.

much regularity and gentleness as if they had been a body of religious. They took particular care of the church, which is rich in marbles and valuable pictures, not one of which was taken away. They assisted there at Mass on Sundays, and every day some of these old soldiers were to be seen at all hours kneeling there in prayer. Nevertheless, this happy state of things was disturbed for a moment. Napoleon having resolved to make an immense arsenal of Alexandria, the engineer employed coveted the bricks and building materials of the convent, and sent an order for the purpose of obtaining them. The officer who commanded the veterans at Bosco was a Protestant; he replied that the convent was under his protection; that if any harm were to happen to it, he should be responsible; and that the Emperor having formerly left a written order forbidding it to be touched, he could not give it over to destruction without direct reference to him. Accordingly, at his own expense, he sent a courier to Paris. The day the courier returned he found standing before the doors of the church a number of conveyances sent from Alexandria to carry away the marbles and other valuables. The despatch was opened; it contained an imperial order to the effect that not one stone of the convent of Bosco was to be touched. Thus Napoleon saved the work of Saint Pius V. There is still at the convent an old lay brother, who waited on him during his residence there in 1797, and who is fond of relating how one day when he brought him his coffee in the morning, he found him sitting by the fireside supporting his elbow on a shovel, awake, but wrapt in such profound thought that for some moments he did not perceive the presence of the brother.

" In the month of September, 1841, after having for some time followed the road which leads from Alexandria to Novi, I turned to the right, and after proceeding for three-quarters of an hour, I saw before me, in the bosom of a plain surrounded by thick woods, an edifice imposing by its size. I descended from the little carriage in which I was, and entered with emotion ; a religious whom I met conducted me to a small door, above which were inscribed the words, ' *Domus probationis ;*' it opened, I went up a staircase, and found myself in the arms of five or six Frenchmen, clad, like myself, in the habit of St. Dominic. One of them, an artist of well-known merit, and a man of thirty years of age, was lying on the bed from which he was never more to rise. As we had left at Santa Sabina the remains ot one even yet dearer, so we were to leave at Bosco, as a memorial of our stay there, our beloved brother PieL We were afterwards all assembled there, being joined by the brethren from La Quercia and Viterbo, and by others who came to us from France. After La Quercia, Santa Sabina, and San Clemente, Bosco was the fourth asylum of the French Dominican colony; St. Pius V. had prepared and kept it for us. In the midst of the kind hospitality of our Italian brethren, we had but to raise our eyes to see before us the shining peaks of the Alps, the frontiers of our native land. O Bosco ! a time will come when we shall no longer rest in your cloisters, no longer kneel in that church which was saved from destruction by French soldiers, when we shall no longer gaze on that deep and brilliant girdle of poplars and willows which surrounds you, nor follow the course of those innumerable limpid rivulets which water those meadows, where we leave under your protection our beloved dead ; but even our native country will never make us forget your piety and hospitality, the increase which we received within your walls, and the joy of re-union granted to us there. And it may be that your image will return to our memory when we are about to breathe our last sigh !"

CHAPTER XIII.

He Preaches at Bourdeaux and Nancy — Struggle with the Government for the Liberty of Religious Orders—First Foundations at Nancy and Chalais.

ATING from the epoch of his return to France, with the exception of the events of 1848, the drama of Père Lacordaire's life consisted henceforth of only two acts—his preaching from the pulpit and the re-establishment of the Dominican Order. Before saying what he was as a religious, and penetrating deeper into the secrets of his intercourse with God and with souls, let us continue to follow him in his public life during the two or three first years of his return to his own country, which were the most fruitful years of his apostolate, and those which had the happiest results, both to his work and to the Church in France.

He left Bosco in the autumn of 1841, and went to Bourdeaux to preach there during the winter. This station lasted four months, from December 1841, to the end of March 1842. It was a great event for the city of Bourdeaux. Two immense tribunes were raised in the cathedral to enlarge the nave, already of vast size. All the official bodies, without exception, those of the courts, the bar, and the army, etc., had reserved places assigned them. The emotion and enthusiasm displayed by this immense audience carried the orator beyond himself, and several times he had to repress the plaudits which were on the point of bursting forth. There was a kind of frenzy throughout the city; in the saloons and cafés, and in the public streets, nothing was talked of but the Sunday conferences. This favour shown by the public continued constantly increasing up to their close. The effects produced were very great. Many souls were converted, and many more felt their doubts shaken; but what is too important to be forgotten, and what requires to be emphatically put forward, is the result of this triumph on public opinion, and the cause of the Church.

We were then entering on the period of our glorious struggles for liberty of teaching and of association. Whilst the inveterate hatred of the Liberals of the Restoration joined its resistance to the terrors of the university and of the Government, the clergy and laity made common cause. They ranged themselves in order of battle, and never, for many a long day, had so gallant an army been beheld; for, united under the standard of Christian liberty, all kinds of self-devotion met together, and all minor differences were forgotten. They were resolved to recover either by goodwill or by force the most holy, the most imprescriptible of all liberties—religious liberty. They desired to be free to bring up their children in the faith, and to choose masters for them of their own belief. They desired to be able to serve God under whatever form of devotion was accepted in the Church, without on that account being put under the ban of their country's laws, and treated as strangers, outcasts, or rebels. Liberty of teaching, and liberty of religious association, made up therefore the *Dieu le veut* of the new crusade. The numbers of the combatants were reckoned up, and the leaders chosen, or rather the leaders found themselves made such in the course of the struggle—and illustrious, eloquent, indefatigable leaders they were. The bishops pre-

pared to raise their voices ; powerful orators charged
themselves with the task of replying to their adversaries in both chambers ; the press gave back the
echo, and committees were arranged to direct and
keep up the movement. It was at this moment that
the orator of Notre Dame reappeared in France.
Now, who was this man who for four months held the
city of Bourdeaux captive under the magic of his
words? the man who was in like manner about to
fling his charm over Nancy, Grenoble, Lyons, Paris,
and so many other cities? the man, who for the first
time for so many ages had drawn around the sacred
pulpit audiences more numerous than those that had
flocked to listen to Bossuet or Bourdaloue? He was
a proscribed man, a friar, a descendant of the in-
quisitors ; his head was shaven, and his white woollen
frock was scarcely concealed under the lace of his
rochet.[1] His mere presence there was a crime ;
crowds applauded him ; but he had against him I
know not how many articles of an obsolete statute.
He came with the *prestige* of the purest glories
gathered round his single head ; with a burning eloquence, a brow illumined with genius, with the fame
of many services rendered to the Church in past
times, and of many errors which he had repaired, and
which did him even greater honour than his virtues ;
he stood there an object of the almost exaggerated
homage yielded to him by his age and his country ;
with the soul of a saint in the heart of a great man ;
but—he was a friar. Still he had no fears. It even
seemed to him that he had only quitted Paris and
France in order thus to reappear in the thick of the
fight, and shelter his new habit under the popularity
of his name and the splendour of his matchless eloquence. What stronger argument could there be in

[1] The Minister of Public Worship had written to the Archbishop to
beg him not to allow Père Lacordaire to preach in his religious habit.
It was therefore agreed that he should cover it with the lace rochet of
an Honorary Canon of the Cathedral.

favour of religious liberty than to be able to point to
such a man? If his presence was an infraction of the
law, was not this itself a sufficient demonstration that
the law was an absurd one? It was in this sense that
he called himself *a liberty ;* it was from this height
that we must look at and judge of those prodigious
triumphs of his eloquence, which were less the triumphs of *a man* than of *a principle.* This was the
way in which he himself regarded them, and he was
therefore able to speak of them without either pride
or false humility. " It is God," he said, " who pre-
pares men when He intends to use them, and who
gives them just what they require for their work, and
that by a marvellous succession of events, the connexion of which can only be seen when we examine
the whole chain. As I glance over my own life, from
whatever side I view it, I see it all converging to the
point where I now stand."[1] It was an admirable disposition of the Divine wisdom which gave to France,
at the very moment when the cause of the religious
Orders was in debate, the two greatest monastic characters of the age, Père de Ravignan and Père Lacordaire, and which presented them side by side in the
pulpit of Notre Dame, raised, as it were, above the
heads of the combatants, who were thus enabled to
judge of the tree by its fruits. M. de Montalembert,
whose name justly holds the first place in this immortal struggle, and who has acquired a title to the
gratitude of the religious Orders which we on our
parts shall ever feel it an honour to acknowledge,
thus appreciated the share which his friend's influence
had in this great debate. " Do not let us forget," he
says, " that it was he who gained the cause of the
religious Orders ; he gained not only that of his own
Order, which had been thought to be for ever crushed
under the unpopularity of the Inquisition, but that of
all religious institutes in general, even that of the
Jesuits themselves. The latter were for a moment

[1] Nov. 2, 1838.

threatened by a famous edict, and they were for one moment apparently dispersed by an order from their own General ; but anti-monastic hatred did not venture to go further. And why ? because Père Lacordaire had dared to appear in his friar's frock in the pulpit of Notre Dame, and boldly and frankly appealing to that liberty of conscience established in 1789, he had won over to his side that floating mass of public opinion by which such questions are always eventually decided."[1]

The station of Bourdeaux was reckoned among the best of those given in the provinces. A distinguished advocate of that city thus wrote to Père Lacordaire some time afterwards : " You have left behind you at Bourdeaux as many friends as admirers. As I have sometimes had the honour of telling you, you have found out the secret, so difficult nowadays, of conciliating all suffrages, of confounding all shades of political opinion, and of absorbing all minds in one subject, and that the greatest of all."

From Bourdeaux, which he quitted in the month of April, he went by Paris to Bosco, to see his brethren, spending there the whole summer of the year 1842. The time of their dispersion was drawing to a close. The religious of La Quercia had finished their year of noviciate. Three of them pronounced their solemn vows on the 15th of May, 1842 ; the fourth, Père Hernsheim, not being able to do so on account of his state of health. All four now came to rejoin their brethren at Bosco. They were seven professed, and three novices. Thus the little family, which a year before had been dispersed by the storm of San Clemente, was once more united under its common father. No obstacle was placed in the way of this : the falsehood of the accusations brought against him had made them fall to the ground of themselves ; and the holy lives of his religious had pleaded their cause better than all the rest.

[1] *Le Père Lacordaire*, p. 127.

The Reverend Padre Morassi, master both to the Italian and French novices, has left us an account of the time spent by Père Lacordaire at Bosco, in a letter from which we shall transcribe a few passages.

"He was," he says, "a most exact and edifying observer of the rule. I was then master of novices, and consequently had under my care the young Frenchmen who were admitted to go through their noviciate. Whenever he had occasion to consult me on important affairs, I always observed in him a magnanimous soul, which unreservedly abandoned itself to Providence, and judged all human events from that elevated point of view. Twice I gave way in his presence to great affliction of mind! I had just lost two subjects, as capable as they were courageous, in consequence of sickness and other unforeseen events, and I deeply regretted them, as I saw in them the future props of the rising edifice. But, with his usual calm confidence, he said to me : 'Let Providence act as It sees best ; let things take their course.'

"He could not endure any singularities or distinctions. Those who did not know him would have confounded him with the humblest of the other religious, so much familiarity and respectful amenity was there in his intercourse with all. Honour and respect were things indifferent to him; and the visits he received from illustrious personages, who came from a distance to see him, were only a burden to him.

"In recreation time he did not go out walking, but preferred remaining in the convent, where he worked in the garden with the novices, dug up the ground, or performed other similar labours. The affability and simplicity of his manner made strangers take him for a simple student. His thin figure, the vivacity of his countenance, and a certain transparent look, which reflected all the emotions of his soul, gave him, moreover, a singular appearance of youthfulness.

"A distinguished ecclesiastic had come from a distance to see Père Lacordaire, and pay him his respects. Hardly had he arrived when he went to the superior, and explained to him the motive that had brought him there. The superior invited him to dinner, the hour for that repast being just at hand ; and in order more fully to enable him to satisfy his desire, he placed him, without saying anything, by the side of Père Lacordaire, who was himself at the head of one of the tables. The ecclesiastic, impatient to know which was the man whom he was in search of, leant towards his neighbour, and begged him in a low voice to point out to him the Reverend Père Lacordaire. ' It is he,' replied the father, with that adroitness which he so well knew how to use, ' who sits at the head of the table.' The ecclesiastic, not suspecting his neighbour, thought that by this he meant to indicate to him a religious who was at the top of the table in front of him. He therefore set himself to observe him, and as far as courtesy permitted, carefully studied his every movement. When dinner was over, he hastened to greet him, and to express his joy at being able to pay his respects to a man whose fame and merit were so well known. The religious saw his mistake, and replied smiling, ' I am not Père Lacordaire ; you have been sitting next him the whole of dinner time.' But meanwhile Père Lacordaire had slipped away.

" He treated his body with so little care, that he seemed to make no account of it at all. All food was alike good to him ; he never asked for anything, and if he showed any choice, it was for the coarsest kind. He had a passionate love for the austerities of the Order, and held every sort of comfort and delicacy in absolute horror. . . . . He accustomed his young disciples also to lead a rude and austere life, to sleep on hard beds, and wear coarse habits, etc. He wished to inure them betimes to the hardships which must necessarily be entailed on them in the course of their re-establishment in France, and by the rigorous observance which he purposed to establish ; and he required that they should be ready, like himself, to overcome all obstacles.

" He did not like to take a prominent part in general conversation, he preferred listening to the discussions of others ; but he replied to their questions in an agreeable manner, and always in a low tone of voice. When in the course of conversation any subject of interest was touched on, he gave his opinion with so much grace and skill as to charm all who heard him.

" The theological *Summa* of St. Thomas was his favourite book ; he constantly read and meditated on it, and made this study his delight.

" General de Sonnaz, the governor of Alexandria, twice asked him to preach to the brigade of Savoy, then in garrison in that city. His extreme readiness to oblige induced him to accept the invitation. He chose subjects suited to the occasion, and his sermons had the success which might have been expected.

" Such was the Reverend Père Lacordaire during the time that he resided in our convent, and such did he appear in the eye of the religious who knew him there together with myself. I have much pleasure in sending you these recollections."

Bosco remained the noviceship house for the French religious until 1845, when it was exchanged for the convent of Notre Dame de Chalais, near Grenoble. The year of trial which had just passed, instead of shaking the courage of any, had only confirmed them in their vocation, and Père Lacordaire, now sure of the instruments he had in his hands, was soon about to set foot in France, by the foundation of his first house at Nancy.

He left Bosco in the month of November 1842, and went at once to Nancy. Madame Swetchine complained of his not having turned out of his way to see his friends in Paris. He replied to her gaily, that he was bound now by his vow of poverty, and that he

owed his time and his money to the simple requirements of duty. " I am," he writes to her, " a simple
mendicant ; both I and my brethren are living on
alms, and consequently I can no longer do anything
merely to gratify my affections or my pleasure, but
must act only out of duty and necessity. Every expense which I cannot justify to myself in the balances
of the sanctuary is blamable. Every state of life
has its rigorous obligations. I might, had I chosen,
not have become a mendicant; but having taken that
step, I must not give occasion to the public to say,
' Père Lacordaire consumes the money which we give
him to gratify his own pleasures.' All my steps must
be clear and capable of being justified. When we
are in the presence of God and of the public we
must not trifle. My conscience and public opinion
alike require that I should be in the convent with my
brethren whenever I am not employed in apostolic
functions ; the convent and the pulpit, these are the
two places in one or other of which the eyes of my
friends and of my enemies ought always to find me.
Anywhere else I should be liable to be called to
account, and should justly fall under suspicion. This
is har‚d I grant : but it is what I have voluntarily
chosen."[1]

The station of Nancy lasted five months, from
December 1842 to May 1843. "This city was far
from showing the same ardour as Bourdeaux," he
says, "nevertheless Providence had chosen it as the
site of our first foundation. Among my hearers
there chanced to be a young man at liberty to dispose of his own person, and the master of a fortune,
which, though not very considerable, gave him,
nevertheless, freedom to gratify his cultivated and
generous tastes. An artist and a traveller, endowed
with qualities which remarkably fitted him to shine in
society, and possessed of agreeable manners, which
delighted every one who knew him, he had lived up

[1] Correspondence avec Madame Swetchine, p. 338.

to that time in the enjoyment of the innocent but useless pleasures of the world that loved him, and a stranger to the more serious thoughts of religion. Yet he was marked by the invisible sign of predestined souls. A few months before, returning from a tour in Italy, he entered by chance into a church at Marseilles, and there received the first call from God. From that moment his soul bore the fatal dart within it, and wandered on those burning confines where the world and the gospel strive together in mortal conflict with one another. The light was clear enough, but as yet it had gained but an imperfect empire over its new conquest. M. Thierry de Saint-Beaussant, as he was called, was soon numbered among those youths of Lorraine who made my sermons an affair of the heart as well as an affair of faith. Uniting circumspection of character to a lively imagination, he charmed me at once with his ardour and his solidity, but it was long before I foresaw the design which occupied his mind. All the disciples who had up to that time joined me from among the laity, had been carried along by an enthusiasm of which they were hardly masters; but M. de Saint-Beaussant possessed the most admirable power of self-command. At last he confided to me his wish to establish us at Nancy, and, agreeing in our plans, we sounded the head of the diocese, who was at that time Mgr. Menjaud, coadjutor of the see, with the right of future succession. He had the courage to give us his word without consulting the Ministry, foreseeing, however, very well that our project would not be realised without many difficulties, both on the part of the public and of the Government.

"M. de Saint-Beaussant therefore purchased a small house, capable of lodging at the most five or six religious. Our friends provided the most indispensable furniture. An altar was put up in one room; and on the Feast of Pentecost, 1843, I took possession. Everything was as poor and modest as possible; but reflecting that for fifty years we had not had so much as a foot of ground in France, nor a roof over our heads to shelter us, I felt an indescribable happiness. A few days later we received a magnificent library of 10,000 volumes, which the Abbé Michel, Curé of the Cathedral, had bequeathed to his nephews, with the express orders that they were to bestow it on the first religious body who should establish themselves at Nancy. Later, M. de Saint-Beaussant himself completed his foundation by adding a chapel, a refectory, and a few cells for the use of guests. He was the first who occupied them, living among us as of old illustrious founders passed their lives under the shadow of the cloisters they erected. Although his health was very weak, and required extreme care, he chose to restrict himself to our fare, and little by little tried his strength for the austerities which he hoped one day to embrace.' I had the happiness of seeing him a novice. This great change in his life made none in the charm of his intercourse ; he preserved under his habit all the graces of his brilliant nature,—which was so gay, simple, and fascinating, making one both love God and him together. But we did not keep him long with us. He died in 1852, at our college of Oullins, and was buried in the chapel of that establishment. I, placed an inscription over his tomb, as I had done over that of Brother Réquédat. Both of them were, in different ways, the first fruits of our restoration. Brother Réquédat gave me the first soul of the edifice, and Brother de Saint-Beaussant the first stone."[1]

The care of this first foundation kept Père Lacordaire at Nancy during the whole summer of 1843. He remained alone until the month of June, not without sending many wistful looks towards his dear community at Bosco. His heart drew him powerfully towards that community-life in which he had found so much strength and consolation. "I bitterly

[1] *Memoirs.*

regret being alone," he wrote to Père Besson, "I
should wish henceforward always to have a companion, in order, at least, to be able to edify and
support myself by his example; alone one is always
weak and powerless in a thousand ways. You know
all I am for you, and all you are to me. My only
regret is not to be able to tell you this in writing, or
to believe that I shall be with you to-morrow."

In the month of June he summoned Père Jandel to
him, and informed the brethren at Bosco of this step
in the following letter, written with the simplicity of
ancient Christian times :

"MY DEAREST BRETHREN,—Père Jandel is about
to quit you in order to join me at Nancy, where
Divine Providence has given us the first house which
has been inhabited in France by the Friar-Preachers
for fifty years. Greatly as both you and I must
rejoice at thus beholding the first stone laid of our
re-establishment at France, it nevertheless necessitates a separation, which I for my part deeply feel.
God has doubtless prepared us for it by the other
separations which have gone before; but this is more
complete than the others have been, and I cannot
therefore resist telling you the pain it causes me.
The day will come when God will re-unite us all in
our own country, and there we shall all form but one
heart and one house; but He alone knows the hour
that He has fixed for this in His eternal decrees.
Our business is to work on from day to day without
troubling ourselves about to-morrow, resting sure that
He watches over us like the most tender of fathers.
You have already had many proofs of this, and the
one He is now giving us ought to penetrate us with
boundless gratitude. We are now possessors of a
house and a library in one of the largest cities of
France; a house given to us by a man, who three
years ago was not even a Christian; and a library
patiently collected during forty years, the rich and

rare materials of which we could not have gathered together ourselves at any price.   Do we not here see verified in us the words of our Lord, when He said that whoever should abandon for His sake father or mother, brethren or sisters, or house, should receive here below fathers and mothers, and brethren and sisters, and the hundredfold of all he had left, even in the midst of persecution?   Let not our hearts then be troubled, or give way to discouragement; let us constantly remind ourselves of the trials we have gone through for the last five years, of the brethren we have lost, the calumnies with which our enemies have sought to ruin us, the dispersion we have endured, and the many predictions that have been uttered, that we should never set foot in France.   All these things have purified us, without casting us down, and it will be the same for the future, and even yet better, because the further we proceed, the more, please God, shall we gain of the merit of our perseverance, our prayers, our mortifications, and our other good works, according to the measure of the spirit given to us.

"After these words of encouragement, my dear brethren, I must fulfil another duty, by providing one to take the place among you of Père Jandel.   I naturally turn my eye on him who, next to Père Jandel and myself, is the eldest among us.   I mean Brother Besson, whom God gave me as a companion three years ago, who was one of the brethren of Santa Sabina and San Clemente, who witnessed the death of both our brothers, Réquédat and Piel, and who has shared in every one of our past troubles.   I therefore present to you Brother Besson, as holding all the authority which I am permitted to exercise over you, as well by the will of my superiors, as by the disposition of Providence.   It is he who will preside at your chapter, and who will correspond with me on all the affairs of your little community. I am sure that you will render his government easy to him by your obedience, as he will render it agreeable to you by the fraternal spirit with which he is filled. This will be a great consolation to me, engaged as I am in unceasing labours, in the midst of which, however, I never cease to think of you, telling myself that it is for you that I labour, and that you will one day gather the fruit of that laborious seed-time, to which it has pleased God to call me first. Père Jandel will come at present to help me; let each one of you aspire to render himself worthy of one day co-operating in our feeble efforts. France is hungering for the word of God; her return to the faith is visibly being worked out in spite of every contradiction. Already the enemy, astonished at our progress, seeks to revive all the old rancours; but they will doubtless be of no avail; they should but warn us to redouble our cares and our fervour, in order that we may one day become good workmen in the rich harvest of the future.

"I earnestly recommend myself to your prayer, my dearest brethren, and am yours from the bottom of my heart."

On the same day he wrote to Père Besson: "This charge is a great burden for you, my dear friend; but you will bear it as imposed on you by our Lord, for the good of an undertaking that is useful to His Church. I recommend you, my dear child, to practise great gentleness towards the brethren, and great respect towards the Fathers; in conversation avoid speaking in too peremptory and absolute a manner; try to put up with and to comprehend the opinions of others; make yourself all to all, in order that the yoke of obedience may always be welcome. In government we must use firmness, no doubt, but also much flexibility, patience, and compassion. I only say these few words to you, my dear child, and place in the arms of our Lord, and of His holy Mother, embracing you myself with all my heart."

Meanwhile the foundation at Nancy had not been

made without a lively opposition on the part of the Government and the local authorities. This opposition was renewed at Paris on occasion of the recommencement of the Conferences, and at Grenoble on the foundation of Chalais: and there is no doubt but that Père Lacordaire must have given way, had he not found a providential and all-powerful support in the esteem in which he was held by the public.

Hardly had the rumour spread that the house at Nancy had been taken possession of than the Minister of Public Worship, that same M. Martin (du Nord) who in 1841 had invited Père Lacordaire to dinner on the day after his sermon at Notre Dame, took alarm, and wrote letter after letter to Mgr. de Joppé, Coadjutor to the Bishop of Nancy, urging him to refuse his consent, telling him that it was a very serious affair, that he appealed to his good faith, and that he was being deceived as to the real nature of the work in which Père Lacordaire was engaged. The prefect, in long visits to Mgr. Menjaud, repeated and amplified the same things. The Coadjutor, firmer than ever, replied that he had no power to exclude from his diocese a priest whom he loved and esteemed, specially at the moment when he was fulfilling in that diocese a sublime ministry, at once consoling and fruitful, not only in a Christian, but also in a social point of view ; that he should therefore leave him to do as he liked, and that if later on there was any question of a real convent being founded he would communicate with the Government. Thus repulsed on the side of the ecclesiastical authorities, they took another course, and tried to appeal to the anti-religious public, in order to force Père Lacordaire to quit Nancy. But this only showed how little they knew him.

He had delivered a discourse at the Lyceum of the town, after the conclusion of which the rector of the academy, yielding to the fear of compromising himself should he permit a religious ostensibly to preach

in a house belonging to the state, had forbidden his
subordinates to hold any intercourse, public or private, with Père Lacordaire. The odium of this
arbitrary measure had been yet further increased by
the declamations of the *Patriot*, a newspaper of
Nancy. For more than a month this paper, encouraged by the conduct of the rector, attacked the
person and the opinions of Père Lacordaire in violent
terms. Summoned by the Coadjutor to do justice to
the religious who had been thus insulted, the Minister
of Public Worship opposed himself to this, not being
sorry to see evil passions lending him a helping hand
in his unhappy campaign against the religious habit.
But Père Lacordaire was not a man to allow him this
too easy satisfaction. He resolutely took the offen-
sive, and set on foot an action for defamation against
the *Patriot*, which indirectly involved the rector and
the Government. The public was stirred ; the majority of the city took part with the orator, whom
they had been applauding for five months, whom
they were proud of having among them as a fellow-
citizen, and whom they beheld thus publicly calumniated in the grossest manner. The first advocate of
Nancy pleaded for Père Lacordaire, who was himself
to speak, and defend the legality of the religious
Orders in France. He saw in this occurrence a stroke
of Divine Providence, to deliver religious associations
from the miserable meddlings of Government, and to
place them under the more equitable protection of all
honest men. He therefore prepared himself for it as
a good religious as well as an intrepid soldier. In
this purpose he asked the prayers of his children at
Bosco. " Our cause will be pleaded," he writes, " on
the 25th August. On that day I beg of all the
professed to say for us the Litany of the Blessed
Virgin and the *O Spem Miram !* On the preceding
Sunday they will offer the Holy Communion for the
same intention." The Government saw that they
had gone too far, and that whatever might be the

issue of the lawsuit, things would turn against them. They therefore agreed to hush up the affair, put a stop to the invectives of the press at Nancy and Paris, and made up a reconciliation. Mgr. Menjaud, in a public letter, declared that Père Lacordaire had been calumniated, that his doctrine had always been as pure as his life, that the rector had exceeded his powers, and that he reserved to himself the right of demanding satisfaction of him, in so far as regarded the person of the chaplain of the Lyceum. No one protested against all this, and Père Lacordaire, believing himself sufficiently justified, and yielding to the advice of a prelate to whom he was under too many obligations to refuse him anything, consented to withdraw his suit.

Hardly had he recovered his freedom of action than he profited of it to hasten to Bosco to embrace his brethren, give them news of France, encourage them, and regulate everything regarding their studies. He only remained there three weeks, and then hastened back to Nancy for fear of a new storm. He arrived there on the 28th of October, and found everything as he had left it—that is to say, in the most profound tranquillity. The battle was over in that direction; it had been fairly gained, and he was able to bring another father to Nancy without exciting any other feeling than an increase of popular favour.

The little house at Nancy therefore now numbered three religious—Père Lacordaire, Père Jandel, and Père Hiss. But Père Lacordaire did not remain there long. A month after his return from Bosco he was obliged to remove to Paris for the Advent Station at Notre Dame. New and more serious struggles there awaited him.

Père de Ravignan had not caused Père Lacordaire to be forgotten at Notre Dame. The more the audience admired the lofty and pathetic eloquence of the former, the more also did they long for the sovereign, unique, and inimitable oratory of the latter ; and it was rightly thought that if France were rich enough to produce at the same time these two incomparable masters of sacred eloquence, there was room enough for both of them in the first pulpit of the world. Mgr. Affre had several times solicited Père Lacordaire to continue his Conferences, which had now been interrupted for seven years, and he had promised to do so during the Advent of 1843. Père de Ravignan was still to keep the Lent Station.

It was a solemn moment. For six months the struggle had been going on between the university and the clergy on the subject of liberty of instruction. On one side, all the privileges of the university monopoly were threatened ; on the other, were the hopes which had been so often deceived, of liberty officially promised and obstinately refused. On one hand, the firm determination to yield nothing, and to defend themselves to the uttermost ; on the other, a cry for war without either truce or peace till full victory had been obtained. On one hand, all the resistance of long possession ; on the other, all the energy and talent, which had sprung to life again within the bosom of a Church which, for the first time for fifty years, reclaimed its ancient rights. The utmost and united efforts of all the heads of the religious party were required at such a moment, and Mgr. Affre well knew what a powerful auxiliary he was giving himself when he summoned Père Lacordaire to Paris. Every one else understood it as well as he. The Government was terrified ; the king sent for the Archbishop to the Tuileries, and there for an hour, in presence of the queen, endeavoured to induce him to withdraw the promise he had given to Père Lacordaire. The Archbishop replied to him with much firmness, "Père Lacordaire is a good priest ; he belongs to my diocese, and he has preached in it with honour. It is I who have voluntarily recalled him and publicly passed my word to him ; I could not now withdraw it from him without dishonouring myself in the eyes of my diocese, and of all France." The king, unable to overcome his courage, ended by saying, "Well then, Monseigneur, if any mischief comes of it, understand that you will not have a single soldier or national guard to protect you."[1]

Meanwhile, whilst resisting with an energy which cannot be too much praised, the Archbishop desired one concession touching the religious habit. He requested Père Lacordaire to exchange his friar's frock for a *soutane*. The more firmly he had persisted in maintaining the orator in his pulpit of Notre Dame, the more he thought he had a right to press what he considered a mere question of detail, and a concession calculated to prevent serious disturbances. This incident brought out all the elevation of views, the indomitable courage, and above all the nobleness and greatness of Père Lacordaire's character. Where his best friends perceived nothing but an unimportant concession which secured the Archbishop and the future, he makes us see, and that with a crushing power of reason and of style, that there was a question of principles involved, and that in it alone lay the true courage and the true safety both of the Archbishop and himself, of the clergy and the religious Orders. In order more certainly to obtain what he sought, the Archbishop had begged Madame Swetchine to write to her friend, and she had done so, though with a trembling hand. "Reflect," she said to him, "that in refusing your consent to what may perhaps be enforced, you will be abandoning the Church in one of the most lamentable crises which has yet occurred, and that you are taking from us our only remaining hope. Reflect too that immense and important responsibilities weigh on you : the interests of the religious Orders which will suffer from your acts, and the blame which will fall on the Archbishop if you refuse to preach here." She drew out

[1] Memoirs.

these considerations in a long letter, and conjured him to come without delay to Saint-Germain-en-Laye, where, whilst conferring with Mgr. Affre and herself, he would be able to form a juster idea of the gravity of the circumstances. On this, Père Lacordaire replied in a magnificent letter, which we must quote entire, and which reveals to her alone what a heart—the heart of a man and of a priest—beat under that religious habit, which was regarded with so much alarm.

"It was impossible, my dear friend, that you could have given me a greater proof of attachment than that which your letter of the 6th of November expresses in so lively a manner, and if I were only to consult my desire to testify my gratitude to you, I should at once obey you without reflection, and without reserve. But you would not desire me, on so serious an occasion, to yield to a mere sentiment of friendship. There are other interests at stake, which, in your eyes as well as my own, are of higher value, and which command both of us to forget ourselves. I shall therefore have no fear, my dear friend, of giving you pain, and will explain to you with the greatest sincerity the motives which will not allow me to give you or the Archbishop the least hope that I can ever make a concession which I feel is prohibited to me.

"I shall not go over the past, nor examine whether, in publicly assuming the religious habit, I have added to the obstacles which oppose themselves to the re-establishment of my Order in France. I have done it; I have worn this habit in the pulpits of Paris, Bourdeaux, and Nancy. I have travelled through France six times in this costume; everywhere I have obtained for it respect; and I have preserved it in spite of the official pursuits of the ministry; all this is an accomplished fact. And now, to what am I to sacrifice it? To the clamours of the irreligious press! To the fears of the Government! To minds irritated against us by three months of an implacable war! I am to go to Notre Dame and give our enemies the spectacle of a religious who is afraid, after having proclaimed himself courageous, who hides himself after he has once shown himself in the combat, who begs for mercy in consideration of his voluntarily disguising himself! This is impossible. The graver the crisis, the more Catholics look for consolation and encouragement from my preaching, the less is it possible for me to give them such a sorrowful surprise. They want to prove to France that their hearts have not grown weak, and that their · words preserve all their former liberty. A hundred times better were it to keep silence than to betray their hopes. Religion has no need of triumph, it can very well do without my preaching at Notre Dame; God can support her and maintain her in the midst of opprobrium; but she does require that her children should not themselves humiliate her, and should not do dishonour to her trials. Whatever comes to her on the part of her enemies is good for her; the shame which comes to her from her own children is the only thing capable of causing her discouragement.

"As to His Grace the Archbishop, you know what I feel for him; I love him out of gratitude, from a full appreciation of his noble qualities, and from a sort of familiarity which enables me to comprehend his uprightness, goodness, and elevation of soul; and I should be unhappy at the thought of causing him the least pain. Nor will I do so. In the position in which his spirit of impartiality has placed him, the Archbishop stands in need of a solemn occasion for proving to all his episcopal independence. He finds it in me. I am for him at this moment one of those rare pieces of good fortune which Providence sends to those whom it loves. The Archbishop knows very well that no one will insult me in the pulpit of Notre Dame; he knows that an immense audience will shield me from every attempt at insult; he knows

that I shall not so much as give all the crowd the
time to look about them, and that at my third phrase
I shall have gained a sacred asylum in their hearts.
Nobody can do anything in the face of popular enthusiasm. Curiosity alone will keep hatred immovable, and the very audacity of my act will touch
those who do not wish to be touched. France has an
instinctive sense of honour which charms her wherever
she sees even the shadow of it. If anything could
crush me at Notre Dame, it would be my appearing
there in borrowed costume. Astonishment, distrust,
contempt, regret, would take possession of everybody,
and nothing would preserve me from it. The
responsibility of the Archbishop is, therefore, quite
protected ; he ought to know that he has nothing to
fear, and that to save Notre Dame he needs nothing
but the desire which the public have of seeing me
there. No doubt the Government does not feel the
same confidence, but what is that to us ? The event
will reassure them. We must have courage and
presence of mind for those who have not those gifts
for themselves. On the other hand, if I were to
yield, I should do the Archbishop the worst service
in the world. It would be said that he had granted
me leave to preach, at the price, on my part, of an
act of cowardice, and the humiliation of Catholics
would fall entirely on him.

"Moreover, there is another bishop to whom I am
under infinite obligations, and to whom I owe even
more than I do to the Archbishop. Mgr. de Joppé
has not only allowed me to found a house at Nancy,
but he sacrificed his own peace in order to support
me against the rector of Nancy. And what was it
that the rector of Nancy attacked ? What, but the
religious habit ? After, then, having engaged Mgr.
de Joppé in a struggle which is not yet terminated,
and which may embitter his whole episcopate, I am
now, by lying under my habit, to decide the cause in
favour of our common enemy, of the rector of Nancy

of the irreligious newspapers of this country, and of all those of the capital which have loaded him with abuse. I am to go and give him up to ridicule in reward for his courage and devotion in my regard! I ask you if this be possible?

"To conclude, after other questions mixed up in the affair, I may be permitted to consider those that are personal to myself. What we must preserve before everything else is—*character;* it is that which makes a man's whole moral force. Now do you not see, my dear friend, you, whose mind and whose friendship have so quick an eye,—do you not see the depth to which I should degrade my character by stripping myself of the religious habit in order that I might appear in the pulpit of Notre Dame? Who could doubt but that, after having assumed it out of vanity, I had laid it aside for the petty glory of preaching in the Cathedral of Paris? Who would see in me anything else than a weak, frivolous, and inconstant mind, altogether governed by the love of making a noise in the world? No, rather let us show the world that I do not accept preaching and glory at the price of dishonour. Let me show the world that I know how to keep silence at a time when my speaking would draw on me notice and importance. Let us put dignity and duty first of all. The older I grow the more I feel that the grace of God works in me detachment from the world. I care for nothing any longer save to do the Will of God. If it please Him that I should preach at Notre Dame, I shall preach there; if He close the doors against me, I shall preach elsewhere: if all the pulpits of France are successively prohibited to me, as is perhaps the purpose of the Government, I shall wait for better times, and shall do whatever other good remains for me to do. Perhaps, even, I shall do none, if none remain possible for me to do. The present is worth very little, the future is all in all. But, my very dear friend, even if all these reasons were of no value, one would yet remain, which would suffice, and render all argument useless. I have no *right* to put off my habit ; it was given to me with the obligation of never quitting it unless deprived of it by superior strength, under pain of incurring excommunication. Now here there is no question of superior strength. My General, even, has no power to authorise me to lay it aside ; that faculty is reserved to the Holy See. All discussion is therefore useless, for the shortness of time will not allow of our applying to Rome.

"I shall reach Paris on the morning of the 15th, and shall stop at the Rue Chanoisse, No. 11, near Notre Dame, at the house of the mother of one of our brethren, who places an apartment and her table at my service. This arrangement keeps me at a distance from you, which I deeply regret ; but it offers me many advantages which I am bound to accept. It is better that I should not go to hotels more than can be avoided. Whatever happens, my affairs will keep me in Paris until the 25th of January. I shall come and see you and the Archbishop at St. Germain's the day after my arrival. My determination, which is perfectly made up, will explain why I cannot accept your appointment at St. Germain's ; the pleasure it would cause me would be destroyed by a useless argument. I prefer making an end of it at once. It will give me great happiness if my reasons convince you. They will at least prove to you that I have studied the question, and that I feel its importance as much as I do the interest which your dear and inestimable friendship has taken in it."[1]

What most surprises us after reading the above letter is, that it did not satisfy Monseigneur Affre. Such was then the agitation of the public mind, and so great were the fears entertained by the Archbishop, that he thought it his duty to write to the Sovereign Pontiff, begging him to remove the scruples of Père Lacordaire, and to enjoin him to lay aside the reli-

[1] Correspondence du P. Lacordaire avec Madame Swetchine.

gious habit. In fact, he received a few days later, through the intervention of the Archbishop and the Apostolic Nuncio, a letter from the Master-General, authorising him to preach *as a secular priest.* It was accordingly settled with Mgr. Affre, that whilst preaching he should wear the canon's rochet and mozetta over his habit. Things being thus arranged, the Dominican reappeared in the pulpit of Notre Dame on the 3rd of December, 1843. What would take place? All the world was there, and the immense nave was too small to contain the crowd, from whom there issued a suppressed murmur. The Archbishop from his seat manifested a visible emotion. Several young men had placed themselves armed at the foot of the pulpit, in order, if necessary, to defend their great orator. One might have thought one'sself at Florence in the troublous times of Savonarola. What was the new Father Jerome going to say? Would he bring peace or war under the folds of his mantle? When he appeared there was a profound silence. He slowly threw his glance over those dense ranks, among which he could distinguish wolves mingled with the sheep—the *Piagnoni* and *Arrabiati* of his turbulent Florence—and thus began : "After the battle of Arbela, Darius, king of Persia . . . . " Every one was listening : they had no time to look about them, and, as he had foretold, " at his third phrase he had gained their hearts." There was no noise, no disorder. The press was either silent or favourable, and even the *Siècle* itself contained a flattering article, "although," said Père Lacordaire, "I cannot imagine how that should have come into its mind."

That year he treated of the effects of the Catholic doctrine on the mind, and of the opposition shown to the Church by statesmen and men of genius. It was treading on volcanic ground, with the living flames bursting out over the parched herbage, to speak thus in the midst of the tremendous struggle then agitat-

ing the Church of France. But never, perhaps, was
he at once greater or more moderate. He knew how
to keep within the region of general principles, and
never descended to those wounding personalities
which injure the best cause. This gave his words a
more complete success, a more universal empire. He
earnestly desired to rouse the hearts of Catholics
to courage in the contest, and confidence in the future;
but he had not one word of bitterness or rancour for
his adversaries. On the contrary, he took pleasure in
magnifying them in the eyes of everybody before he
attacked them. He addressed them in that tone of
amicable and gracious courtesy which so well became
him: "The question is serious, gentlemen; it is delicate.
But, be quite at your ease: I will treat you as Mas-
sillon treated Louis XIV. in the chapel of Versailles.
Whatever may be your necessities and my good will,
I cannot do better by you than to treat you as the
great century treated its great monarch."

Who does not remember that portrait of the statesman, at once so skilful and so original? "A man,"
he said, "is loaded with the gifts of birth and fortune;
he may, if he choose, live in the midst of every
domestic enjoyment, surrounded by friendship, luxury,
honours, and ease; but he does not choose it. He
shuts himself up in his cabinet, and there is pleased
to heap up for himself a mass of labours and difficulties. He grows grey under the weight of affairs
that are not his own, having no other reward than the
ingratitude of those whom he serves—the rivalries of
men as ambitious as himself, and the blame of the
indifferent. Any boy who has just left school may
draw his pen against him; and writers alike destitute
of talent, ancestry, or reputation, who may think
themselves obliged to the world if it pardons their
presumption, attack the statesman who, instead of
enjoying his wealth and renown, has hardly left himself a moment's leisure. Yet he does not care; he
passes from his cabinet to the field of battle; he

watches by the side of Alexander in order to counsel him ; he signs treaties for which the public will call him to account ; and at last he dies, his life cut short by care, calumny, and labour ;—he dies, and whilst awaiting the verdict which the future will pass upon his fame, his contemporaries commemorate him in an epigram."[1]

Having thus saluted the enemy, he turned to the phalanx of priests who were listening to him, and exclaimed, " To us Catholic priests has been given the power of resisting you ! Martyrdom is no great thing ; there is something far more difficult than to be a martyr. It is to be called on to resist a power which does not persecute us, to oppose the wishes of statesmen often most worthy of esteem, and to have to struggle with them hand to hand, day after day. When a priest wishes to be at peace, and to enjoy himself, his path is easy enough : he has only got to give way before the powers that be. If any serious juncture should arise, let him only act as a pagan, and not as a Christian priest, and honours, public respect, the credit of being tolerant, and the favour of the world, will all be showered on him ; it will not even cost him much to veil his weakness, and save the appearances of priestly and Catholic dignity. But if a poor priest hold to his conscience more than to his life, if he defend it against the attacks of power, then begins the really painful martyrdom—that of opposing those whom we love and esteem, and of drinking the cup of a hatred so much the more un-deserved because we are labouring and suffering for those very persons who are persecuting us."

Sometimes he would turn in a familiar way to the more sympathetic part of his audience, his dear young men, and would exclaim, "Oh you, my friends, the hope and crown of the Church at this moment, God alone knows what may be your future destiny ! but, above all things, wonder not whatever may

[1] Conference xvi.

happen. Catholic Christianity is like Milo of Crotona
on his oiled disk; no one can make him slide, and no
one can tear him from it. When, therefore, you see
the winds rise and the clouds gather, remember that
if it belongs to you to prove the truth of Catholic
doctrine by your constancy and your love, your
adversaries will be no less compelled to prove it, in
spite of themselves, by the very violence of their
hate; and remember also, that it is the perpetual encounter of these two opposite principles—the crossing
of these two swords over the head of the Church—
which will form her eternal arch of triumph. In the
second place, let your virtues be always greater and
more visible than your misfortunes, in order that if
you fall, it may be as soldiers who fall with their face
to the enemy, proving even by their death that they
were worthy to have conquered, if victory always fell
to right and courage."

If such accents as these move us even now, at this
distance of time, when a chill slumber has fallen over
us, the reader may guess what effect they produced
on minds heated by struggle, and in the very thick of
the conflict. If this were the eloquence of a democratic tribune, as was said by some at the time, and
as has been often since repeated, we can only wish
that the Church might produce many tribunes of a
similar stamp.

From this time up to 1851, Père Lacordaire continued to explain the Christian doctrine from the
pulpit of Notre Dame; but he did not on that
account discontinue preaching in the provinces, where
he was able to sketch the outline of his more important Conferences, and found opportunities for
beginning his chief religious foundations.

Here he had to endure a final assault from the
vigilant M. Dessaurat[1] against the religious habit:
" I have preached in my religious habit, without any
disguise," he wrote to Madame Swetchine; "it re-

[1] Director to the Ministry of Public Worship.

mains to be seen whether the vigilant M. Dessaurat, who for the last three or four years has been in pursuit of this poor habit of mine, will not send us a thundering letter." They had not long to wait for the letter: and we shall quote it, in order to do justice to so much excellent zeal for the interests of religion, and to the ungrateful indocility of the refractory friar. The letter was addressed to Mgr. Philibert de Bruillard, bishop of Grenoble, "a little old man of more than eighty, full of life and full of smiles, firmer and more courageous than many a bishop who does not carry the weight of half his years."[1]

"PARIS, *February* 4, 1844.

" MONSEIGNEUR,—I have just been informed that the Abbé Lacordaire has set out for Grenoble, doubtless with the intention of preaching in that diocese. I have hitherto felt it my duty to write to all the prelates of the diocese visited by that ecclesiastic, to inform them that his persistence in appearing in France in the costume of an Order not legally authorised is of a nature to disturb the public peace, and calculated to raise serious difficulties. I have, in consequence, successively requested their Lordships, the Archbishop of Bourdeaux, the Coadjutor of Nancy, and the Archbishop of Paris, only to permit the Abbé Lacordaire to preach in their dioceses on the condition of his wearing the dress of a secular priest, and observing a great reserve and extreme prudence in his language. The prelates to whom I have addressed myself have perfectly understood my warning, and have all required M. Lacordaire to comply with these conditions. Thus, quite recently, he has only been able to appear in the choir of the cathedral of Paris by assuming the costume of an honorary canon of the chapter.

" I feel every confidence, Monseigneur, that if M.

---

[1] Letters to Madame Swetchine.

Lacordaire preaches in your diocese, you will impose on him the same conditions which have been required of him at Paris, at Nancy, and at Bourdeaux. You know the sentiments of the Government in regard of everything which is connected with religious feeling; but neither can you be ignorant how important it is to those sacred interests which you are so specially called on to defend, not to furnish any pretext which may suffer popular passions to raise their voice. I reckon, Monseigneur, on your discretion and firmness, and desire to be informed by you of the course which you judge proper to take in consequence of this communication.—I have the honour to be, etc.,

" The Keeper of the Seals,
" Minister of Justice and Public Worship,
" MARTIN."

The good bishop, in *his discretion and firmness,* judged it proper not to reply at all, and M. Dessaurat went no further. But a few weeks afterwards his zeal was again roused by a much more serious affair. Père Lacordaire had just purchased an old ruined convent, situated among the mountains about three leagues from Grenoble. The Minister of Public Worship and his secretary had no difficulty in understanding the meaning of this audacious act, and were of opinion that the result would be *essentially to injure the interests of religion.* So they wrote as follows :

" PARIS, *April* 10, 1844.

" MONSEIGNEUR,—The Abbé Lacordaire has on different occasions vainly endeavoured to re-establish the Dominican Order in France, and his attempts for this purpose, whether at Paris, Bourdeaux, or Nancy, have always found the Government immovable in its resolution on this subject. In reply, therefore, to your letter of the 1st instant, which informs me of the project conceived by him of establishing a house in the ancient Carthusian Convent of Chalais,

I hasten to inform you that the authorities can give no consent, tacit or expressed, to its realisation. If up to this time a very few religious establishments, which have already existed for a considerable time, have been allowed a certain amount of tolerance, we must nevertheless oppose any new foundation, which would be an actual and flagrant violation of the law. Although the Abbé Lacordaire is not ignorant of the dispositions of the Government, since they have been already made known to him by several of your colleagues in the Episcopate, I beg of you to notify them to him afresh.

" He cannot establish himself as a religious in your diocese without your lordship's authorisation, and I rely on your wisdom and firmness under these circumstances.

" Enough prejudices already exist against the clergy, and the encroachments attributed to them ; enough irritation has already been produced, even among the best disposed minds, to induce the chief pastors of the doceses to use every effort to frustrate or suppress erterprises which can have no other result than essentially to injure the interests of religion.

" Your pacific intervention, Monseigneur, being sufficent to prevent M. Lacordaire from proceeding further in his designs, I continue to hope that I shall not have to prescribe coercive measures, to which I should certainly otherwise have recourse.

"I have sent a copy of this despatch to the Prefect of Isère, begging him to watch the proceedings of the Abbé Lacordaire, and to keep me informed of whatever he may attempt, in case he should, contrary to my expectations, disobey your advice. I feel it my duty to inform you of this.—I have the honour to be, &c.,

" MARTIN."

The excellent and intelligent old prelate, very little moved by all this solicitude on the part of the Minister, and perfectly at ease as to the interests of religion in his diocese, replied as follows :

"MONSEIGNEUR,—I have communicated to M. Lacordaire the contents of the letter which your Excellency did me the honour of addressing to me on the 10th of the present month.

" He has confirmed what he before told me, that in purchasing Chalais in his own name, and that of four of his friends, three of whom are priests, he proposes to use it for them and for himself, from time to time, as a place of retreat and study.

"These gentlemen are therefore proprietors and residents in my diocese. M. Lacordaire has only two more Conferences to give, after which he will leave Grenoble.—I have the honour to be," etc.

A few days previous to this Père Lacordaire had thanked the bishop in the following terms, for the support which he hoped to find from his pastoral firmness and kindness of heart :

GRENOBLE, *April* 1, 1844

" MONSEIGNEUR,—I have the honour to return to you the Prefect of Isère's letter, which your lordship has been so good as to communicate to me. I should have returned it to him myself if my first journey to Chalais had not been fixed for to-day. From motives of prudence I deferred this for ten days ; but now that the whole affair is public, there is no reason for waiting longer, specially as I am every moment expecting our four Dominicans. They will certainly be here before your lordship will have sent your reply to the Minister of Public Worship. We have arranged to receive them in the house of M. Gaime, my notary : they will set out for Chalais at nightfall in a private carriage, not to escape publicity, for that is impossible, but to avoid a disturbance.

" I need say nothing, my lord, of the corresponence

which has passed between your lordship and the Minister. Your lordship knows better than myself the position of affairs, and the real value of this sort of opposition. Less than ever, in the present state of things, will the Government be disposed to adopt any violent measures, which would be equally opposed to its own interests, our national habits, and all precedent; and which would only create more partisans for us in Grenoble than we have at present. All that I hear convinces me that the whole city, the clergy, laity, magistrates, and young men, all look on our establishment with pleasure. Your lordship, by maintaining this struggle, will only draw on yourself fresh respect, and confer greater glory on your Episcopate, already so illustrious. The clergy have in their hands all the weapons necessary for conquering their rightful liberties; they only require to use them. And no one is better fitted than your lordship to contribute to the emancipation of religion in France.

" I trust myself absolutely, therefore, to your lordship's heart and firmness. It will be my part to render your task more easy, by my prudence and moderation, and also never to forget what our Order will owe to you in the matter of its restoration in this country. The name of your predecessor, St. Hugh, is eternally linked with the foundation of the Carthusians: yours, my Lord, will remain for ever united, associated with the restoration of the religious Orders in France, and particularly with that of St. Dominic.—I am, &c."

Everything happened as Père Lacordaire had foreseen. The government, so threatening in its words, was much less so in its acts; it knew how to intimidate, but was unwilling to proceed to violence. It did make the attempt indeed, a year later, against the Society of Jesus; but whether it was that the project of the Dominican leader caused less alarm, or that the authorities were overawed by his popularity, and by the victories he had recently gained in his conflicts with the press and the law courts, certain it is that he was suffered to live in peace in his eagle's nest at Chalais. For the rest, Père Lacordaire's resolution was taken. He was determined to seize, and to defend by every legal means, the right of living according to his conscience—a right which had been solemnly guaranteed by the charter. "To allow himself to be dragged by force out of his house, to return so soon as the force was withdrawn, to protest publicly, and claim through the law the unmolested enjoyment of his own property, and when that enjoyment was restored, to return with all those who belonged to him;" this was the course he had traced out for himself, and which he recommended to every other community that should be threatened in a similar way.[1]

The Convent of Our Lady of Chalais, raised from its ruins and hastily repaired, was destined to become the first regular convent of the Order in France. The size of the buildings, their original destination, and the quiet solitude of the locality, allowed of the novices and students being soon transferred thither from Bosco, and enabled them to make this house the first in which monastic observance and community life were fully carried out. On all these accounts Chalais became the favourite place of residence of Père Lacordaire; and there, in the silence of that sweet retreat, in the midst of his brethren and his children, he loved to rest from his apostolic labours. It is there also, that we shall presently more closely study his religious life, properly so called. Let us first, however, allow him, with his own pen, to sketch the picture of this magnificent solitude, and hear how he recalls, on his deathbed, the memory of his first arrival on that holy mountain in company with his brethren.

"About the same time that St. Bruno was raising the great Chartreuse in the midst of savage mountains, separated from the Alps by the course of the Isère, a few monks of the Order of St. Benedict wished to

<hr>

[1] *Le Père Lacordaire.* Montalembert, p. 125.

establish in the same neighbourhood a reformed branch of their Order, which had, however, neither great celebrity nor long duration. Instead of concealing themselves in the most inaccessible part of the desert, they chose a level plain looking towards the south, of a sunny aspect, surrounded by rocks, meadows, and forests, whence, through two large hollows, the eye beholds on one side the valley of Graisivaudan, and on the other the broad plain where the waters of the Saône and the Rhône flow round the city of Lyons. In this beautiful solitude they built a convent, to which they gave the name of *Chalais*, whence they themselves were called *Chalasians*. After remaining there about two centuries, they gave it up to the monks of the Great Chartreuse, who made use of it as a warmer residence for some of their old religious who were no longer equal to the austerity of St. Bruno's cloisters. At the time of the Revolution, the lands were separated from the rest of the patrimony of the Great Chartreuse, and sold in the name of the nation. I bought the property, after obtaining the consent of the bishop of the diocese, Mgr. Philibert de Bruillard, an old man, (eighty-two,) who, in spite of his great age, hesitated not to expose himself on our account to a struggle with the government. The contract was signed with the utmost secrecy. No preparations were made for taking possession, for fear of awakening public attention, and attracting the notice of the Prefect. I still remember the day when, having met some of our young religious, whom I had sent for from Bosco, in a country house outside the gates of Grenoble, we set out together to that dear mountain of Chalais. The carriage set us down at the foot of the mountain, at the side of the high road ; and it took us a walk of three hours to climb the rocks and winding paths from thence to the house. We arrived about sunset, exhausted with fatigue, without provisions, or furniture, or utensils of any kind, each one having only his Breviary under his arm. Happily, however, the farmers had not yet gone out of the place, and we had reckoned on their assistance. They made us a great fire, and we sat down gaily to dine off some soup and a dish of potatoes. That night we slept soundly on a little straw; and rising next morning at daybreak, were able to admire the magnificent retreat which God had given us. The house was poor enough; the church, with its massive walls of the middle ages, was now nothing better than a hay-loft; but what majesty there was in the aspect of those woods! What sublimity in those rocks that rose above our heads! What a magical charm in those plains and meadows which stretched all around us with their verdure and their flowers! Some long alleys, shaded by trees of unequal size, led to all sorts of hidden spots—along the brinks of precipices, by the side of torrents, under thickets of firs and beeches, through younger plantations, and at last to the mountain summits which crowned these enchanted regions. It took some time to repair the house and set it in proper order; but all privations were sweet to us in the midst of that beautiful scenery, which had been marked for seven centuries by the grace of God, and where the ruins of a few years had not effaced the perfume of religious antiquity. The old bell of the Benedictines and the Carthusians still hung on its beam, covered over with fir planks; and the clock which had chimed the hours of prayer for them, called us, in our turn, to the same duty.

"It soon became known that the desert of Chalais had blossomed again under the hand of God. Guests came to us from all parts; and that which a while before had only been the dwelling of foresters and wood-cutters, became a favourite pilgrimage for devout souls. In the evening we sang the *Salve Regina* in the half-restored chapel, according to the custom of the Order; and it was an inexpressible joy to hear on those hills, in the midst of the murmurs of the mountain winds, the psalmody which seems to carry up to the angels the echo of their own voices."[1]

[1] Memoirs.

CHAPTER XIV.

N 1845 the convent of Chalais having reassumed its old religious aspect, Père Lacordaire wrote to Rome for authority to remove into France the noviciate which had hitherto remained at Bosco. The Master-General, whilst sending him full powers for that purpose, joined to them a diploma creating him *Master in Theology*, the highest learned degree granted in the Order. On the 4th of August 1845, the Feast of St. Dominic, the noviciate was therefore canonically erected in the convent of Notre Dame of Chalais, and thus the work of the restoration of the Order in France became solidly established after six years of laborious preparation. Père Besson was appointed first novice-master, and Père Jandel the first prior.

It had always been the purpose of Père Lacordaire to re-establish in France the observance of the rule in all its rigour as soon as possible, and only to introduce such dispensations as were authorised by the constitutions or required by the necessities of preaching. In Italy he had painfully felt the absence of the religious and apostolic spirit, and wrote from La

Quercia :—"When we Frenchmen become religious, we do it with the intention of being religious *up to the neck.*" The following were the chief points of observance established at the first foundation of the French province, and still preserved. After several experiments as to the best hour for rising at night, three o'clock in the morning was fixed upon, and adhered to, and at that hour the community went into the church to sing matins. After matins they were allowed to go to rest again until six. At six there was meditation, followed by prime, and the choral Mass, which was heard by all the religious, even the priests. From this time till half-past eleven, the morning was devoted to study. At half-past eleven followed the other little hours. At noon, dinner, followed by recreation. At a quarter to two, vespers, after which the time until seven was given up to study or the duties of the ministry. At seven, supper, followed by a short recreation. Then compline and meditation, and at nine the community retired to rest. In the interior of the convent perpetual abstinence from meat was once more established, except in case of sickness ; the use of woollen garments and sheets ; the great fast, which consisted in taking nothing before noon, and only a small collation at night, and which lasted from the 14th of September until Easter day. The chapter of faults was also re-established ; that is to say, that every week all the religious had to accuse themselves in presence of the community of the smallest exterior faults against the rule, and to hear themselves accused by their brethren of the faults which they had themselves forgotten or omitted ; and the least irregularities of this kind were punished by the hardest and most humiliating penances. We shall presently see what importance was attached by Père Lacordaire to this public acknowledgment of exterior faults, and in what way he directed the chapter to be held. A very few points of the rule were considered incapable of being observed, some on account of the small number of the brethren, as the chanting of the Office both by day and night; others from their state of health, already weakened by the labour of preaching, as the abstinence from eggs, butter, and white meats during Advent and Lent, and on some other fast days. But to make up for this, they followed the instincts of generous penance in other points, and made it a duty to exceed the strict precept, by way of a kind of compensation. Thus the custom was introduced of sleeping on boards, although the rule permitted a less austere kind of couch; and whereas it only required a quarter of an hour's meditation, they made it for half an hour, which, added to the choral Mass, gave them an hour of meditation in the morning, and a quarter of an hour in the evening.

This mode of life, which the world will doubtless consider austere, and which our best friends regard as beyond the strength of men nowadays, would have been yet more so had Père Lacordaire followed the generous desires of his first disciples without any modification. But he possessed in a super-eminent degree that spirit of true sanctity which is so severe to itself whilst it is so indulgent to others. He knew, moreover, that at the beginning of a religious foundation, as of a conversion, he ought to distrust those ardent aspirations after a too lofty ideal, which often fail with the ephemeral sentiment that has inspired them, and give place to lassitude and discouragement. He was not ignorant that what is quite possible to certain souls chosen by God to a special mission, and favoured by particular graces, is not so to the greater number, and ought not therefore to be imposed as a universal rule. Providentially charged with the office of re-establishing the Order of Friars-Preachers in France, he received the grace of keeping equally removed from a literal and impossible interpretation of the Constitutions, and of an excessive degree of liberty and relaxation; and thus he had the merit of giving a new proof of that spirit of moderation the enemy of all excess, which will continue to mark his acts and his ideas with that character of duration which is the special prerogative of truth. Thus the observance we have described, and which maintains all the grand outlines of the Dominican rule, has been preserved without any modification in the French province, and will subsist there as long as that province continues to cherish the memory of its holy founder.

The portrait of his religious life which we are now about to sketch, will best show whether the moderation with which he tried to inspire his first companions was the effect of the prudence of the flesh, or rather of a wisdom enlightened by a knowledge of human nature and ripened by experience. He was himself most exact in every exercise of the rule. Rising at the first sound of the bell, he came to the choir for matins with the rest of the brethren. He began the Office with an accent of grave and recollected piety which edified all. He regularly assisted at all the canonical hours, although he was dispensed from the obligation to do so in virtue of his rank as Master in Theology. His multifarious occupations and extensive correspondence were never made a pretext for absenting himself. The slave of duty, he did everything in its proper time, with the most perfect self-possession, and so soon as he was summoned by the bell, quietly laid aside his pen, put everything in order, and came out of his cell. At the convent of Paris he heard confessions in the church on certain days and at fixed hours. Exactly as the clock struck two the sacristy door would open; it was the Father going to his confessional. This scrupulous exactitude became remarked, and often excited a smile among the little group of his penitents.

He tried to inspire his brethren with the same love of regularity, hardly ever himself making use of dispensations, so that he who had the most right and the most legitimate motives for sometimes exempting himself from monastic observances, was one of those

who submitted to them with the greatest rigour. At
the beginning of the foundation at Toulouse, he
happened to be in that house alone with another
brother during the whole of Lent, the other Fathers
being absent preaching. The little community went
on with all its exercises as regularly performed as
usual. The fasts and abstinences were kept, and choir
and chapter were even held. One day during this
Lent the religious who was charged to awake the
Father at three o'clock, forgot it, and did not enter his
cell until four o'clock. The Father perceived that it
was past the hour, and said to him, "See that this
does not happen again; the rule before everything
else! Next day the same accident happened; the
alarum had not gone off, and four o'clock struck before
the religious presented himself. When the Father
became aware of it, "My dear brother," he said, "*the
community* cannot go on in this way, henceforth I
shall call myself."

But I feel that it is time to penetrate somewhat
deeper into the secrets of this religious soul; it is time
to tear away the veil, and to come to that which lay
at the root of all his virtues, which was the hidden
source of all his heroic resolutions, the explanation of
his whole life. I mean his love for Jesus Christ crucified. I know not at what hour of his existence the
thought of Christ crucified had first impressed itself
on his heart in characters of fire. But strange to say,
even before his conversion, this idea of the Cross of the
Son of God seemed already to pursue him. On the
15th of March, 1824, not being yet in possession of the
faith, he writes:—"*I should wish to be fastened alive
to a wooden cross;* I have even had serious thoughts
of becoming a village curé!" He has often related
how, in the early days of his conversion, this vision of
the Son of God, subjected for our sakes to the infamous
punishment of the Cross, left him no repose. He desired to suffer in public like his Master, his very dreams
were of the scourge and the gibbet. This idea pursued

21

in his own home, and wherever he went and when as he thought of his sins, the notion came into his mind of getting some little Savoyard, by sum of money, to scourge him in the eyes of Woman. A God, and a Cross! This among Christian dogmas was the one that pierced him and penetrated the deepest into his proud and sensitive nature. That divine Cross, illuminated on high, was a sort of revelation to him. It instructed his intellect at the same time that it warmed his heart. In the wounds of the Man of Sorrows he saw and comprehended the mystery of He saw the remedy for all our in humiliation and suffering, in pain of body His whole being was inundated with this and never lost the impression of it. He became in order to follow his adorable Master the his humiliations: he chose an Order in which penances were in use in order to animate the example of his brethren, and that he from them a service which he could not and God only knows to what an his whole life, he carried the heroic our Saviour's Passion.

We have long asked ourselves how we should make known all that we know on this subject. Should we be rather guessed than plainly told in Should we veil our narrative under a trans- of words and images, in order not to and fastidious minds? Or ought we not frankly to tell the truth at all risks? The last course appeared to us preferable; it seemed worthier of the man whose victories we are relating, and of the holy actions with which his life is filled. Why should not we have the courage to tell, and the praise to hear, of those things which he had the courage to do?

He had then an exclusive love for the Cross; it was a passionate, not a Platonic love, but a burning ardour which urged him incessantly to imitate the model exhibited on Calvary. All his mysticism reduced itself to this one principle, to suffer ; to suffer, in order to expiate justice, and in order to prove love. All his consequences flowed from this ; they lay in acts rather than in words. He had not received the gift of silent and tranquil contemplation at the feet of Jesus Christ ; but only that of proving his love for Him by generous actions. His thanksgiving after Mass was generally short ; in making it he most often experienced very ardent emotions of love to God, which he went to appease in the cell of one of his religious. He would enter with his countenance still radiant with the holy joy kindled at the altar ; then humbly kneeling before the religious, and kissing his feet, he would beg him to do him the charity of chastising him for the love of God.

Then he would uncover his shoulders, and whether willing or unwilling, the brother was obliged to give him a severe discipline. He would rise all bruised from his knees, and remaining for a long time with his lips pressed to the feet of him who had scourged him, would give utterance to his gratitude in the most lively terms, and then withdraw with joy on his brow and in his heart. At other times, after receiving the discipline, he would beg the religious to sit down again at his table, and prostrating on the ground under his feet, he would remain there for a quarter of an hour, or half an hour, finishing his prayer in silence, and delighting himself in God, as he felt his head under the foot that humbled him.

These penances were very often renewed, and those who were chosen to execute them did not resign themselves to the office without difficulty. It was a real penance to them, especially at first ; they would willingly have changed places with him. But gradually they become used to it, and the Father took occasion of this to require more, and to make them treat him according to his wishes. Then they were

obliged to strike him, to spit in his face, to speak
to him as a slave. "Go and clean my shoes; bring
me such a thing; away with you, wretch!" and they
had to drive him from them like a dog. The religious
whom he selected to render him these services were
those who were most at their ease with him; and he
returned by preference to such as spared him the
least. His thirst for penances of this description
appears the more extraordinary, from the fact that
his exceedingly delicate and sensitive temperament
rendered them insupportably painful to him. He
shuddered under the slightest blow, but his soul was
always firm, and he would entreat them not to mind
it; and they were forced to obey. Often when they
saw him thus crushed to the ground, trembling with
pain, and overwhelmed with confusion, they would
fall on their knees beside him, and with their eyes
filled with tears, ask his pardon for having made him
suffer so much, and beg him to require it of them no
more. "Ah!" he would reply, "this is nothing.
When you see me suffer too much, you stop, you
pity me; but when Jesus Christ writhed under the
blows of His executioners, they only struck the
harder."

He had a horror of ostentation; and only chose
witnesses of his austerities in order to add humiliation
to pain. Yet his desire of public humiliation would
have gained the victory over his natural reserve, had
his spiritual directors permitted it. But he was very
rarely allowed to perform public penances. Once,
however, at the Convent of Chalais, after having
made a touching address to the brethren assembled
in chapter on the subject of humility, he felt himself
irresistibly moved to add example to precept, and
entreated the brethren to treat him with the severity
he deserved. Then coming down from his seat, be
bared his shoulders, and prostrating before each of
the brethren in turn, he received from each of them
five-and-twenty blows of the discipline. The com-

munity was numerous, and the penance lasted a long time; all lay brothers, novices, and fathers were present at this spectacle, and were profoundly moved, and overcome by it. When the Father rose, he was pale and suffering. I leave the reader to judge how much veneration such scenes added to the love we bore him.

His office of provincial obliged him to take frequent journeys. Scarcely had he arrived at any convent, specially if it were a noviceship house, than he at once commenced his favourite penances, and this was one of his settled habits. He varied the forms of penance with a marvellous fertility of imagination, but he never omitted them. It would be impossible to repeat in detail the incredible industry, the thousand inventions of his love of the Cross. We shall do no more than indicate a few examples.

The chapter-room in the convent at Flavigny was supported by a wooden column. He made this his column of flagellation. One of his first cares when he arrived at that convent was to go to confession to the master of novices, and ask his permission to perform some penance. They then sent him two novices; he caused himself to be bound by them to the column in the chapter-room, with his hands behind his back, and his shoulders bare, and commanded them to scourge him severely. The novices, it must be owned, made but bad executioners; they hardly dared to touch him; but they gained nothing by that; he conjured them to have no pity on him, and remained bound there till he had obtained all that he desired. He loved this kind of penance, which in a lively way recalled to him the tortures of his Divine Master, and repeatedly made use of it.

At Paris, under the ancient church of the Carmelites, now served by our Fathers, there was a sort of crypt or subterranean chapel, which seemed admirably suited for the mysteries of suffering. Two rows of vaults extended on either side of a long corridor, filled with skulls and bones; and at the extremity of this corridor there was a larger chamber adorned with funereal sentences and emblems. It served as a chapel, and Mass for the dead was sometimes celebrated there. In these very vaults, on that ground formerly reserved for the burial of illustrious persons, had slept the yet more illustrious victims of the massacres of September, 1793; and many rooms in the convent preserved on their walls the traces of the martyrs' blood. No place could be better fitted for penance. Père Lacordaire thought at one time of transforming it into a Calvary. He wished to erect a great cross there, surrounded with all the instruments of the Passion. But as this crypt did not belong to us, he laid aside this project, and contented himself with descending into it from time to time, especially during Lent and Holy Week, and there alone, or with another religious, he would offer his body as a victim of love. One Good Friday he made himself a large cross, caused it to be set up in this subterranean chapel, had himself fastened to it with ropes, and remained suspended to it for the space of three hours. What would have been said by those crowds who flocked to hear his words, who listened to him with such enthusiasm as he preached during one whole Advent in that same church of the Carmes? what would they have said and thought of this man had they been able to witness the scenes which took place beneath that pulpit whence poured fourth the eloquence that so enchanted them? He knew so well how to conceal this sublime folly of love—the world was far from suspecting that under the orator lay hidden the religious craving after martyrdom! What has not been said, by ignorance or malice, of his vanity as a preacher, his desire of pleasing and being admired? Have not we ourselves even heard the incredible nonsense seriously affirmed, that after his Conferences Père Lacordaire was accustomed to disguise himself in order to mingle unobserved in society and gather up the praises uttered about him ! Let us now make known therefore, to the honour of one whose memory is so exalted by some, and so gravely mistaken by others, how those Sundays of the Conferences, those great days of Notre Dame, were really passed.

He remained during the morning in profound meditation. No one entered his room except one or two of his most intimate friends, who came to make sure that he wanted nothing. They came in and went out in silence, happy if there were any little service they could render him, but careful not to disturb his recollection. He breakfasted alone, at nine o'clock. As an exception he did not abstain on these days, but his repast was very moderate. If the weather were fine, he then went into the garden, and walked there slowly for some time, sometimes stopping before a flower, enjoying the aspect of verdant nature bathed in the morning light, and refreshing his mind by the sweet contemplation of the pure and beautiful works of God ; it was a kind of prelude by which his inspiration delighted in mounting gradually to a higher order of harmony. He set out at eleven o'clock accompanied by his friend M. Cartier. About three he returned, exhausted with fatigue, but with his brow transfigured, his countenance all on fire, his whole soul still burning and overflowing with faith, love and eloquence. In order to repair his exhausted strength he lay down on his bed, and, admitting into his cell one of his friends, a young layman, who then enjoyed his entire confidence, he would converse with him familiarly of the love of our Lord, and the happiness of the religious life. At the hour of supper they brought him his repast, exactly the same that was served to the rest of the community, two eggs and a salad. Then he resumed the conversation he had interrupted ; it always turned on the love of our Divine Lord, and the love of suffering, or something which bore reference to these subjects. He rarely spoke of his Conferences. To those who praised them to him he answered nothing ; but willingly asked his most intimate friends what they found to blame in them. The young friend spoken of above, told him one Sunday evening that several persons thought he studied effect in his oratorical action, and that he made certain pauses which were skilfully managed so as to provoke that movement of admiration which seldom or ever failed to follow.

The father appeared astonished, and, after having reflected for a moment, he acknowledged that he had never thought of this. "Then I can have very little of the exterior of humility," he added ; "but am I at least sufficiently humble in reality ?" "No, Father, not yet." "It is very true," he replied ; "but I will labour to become so. And you, my dear friend, must help me. You know me thoroughly ; well, you shall be my master ; you shall reprove me for every fault which you may remark in me. You shall *tutoyer* me, and speak to me as if you were speaking to a slave. When you come to see me, you shall impose severe penances on me. We must come to that point that the body shall accept at a moment and without dispute whatever the spirit of Jesus Christ may command."

The day always ended with a severe flagellation, which he obliged them to give him in spite of his extreme fatigue. Such were these days of Notre Dame, so splendid in their exterior before the eyes of the public, but in private so calm, so simple, so full of religious sanctity. And it was by this energetic reaction of the will that he held himself back on the slippery slope of his intoxicating success.

This constant look fixed on the Cross of Jesus Christ, on the innocent Victim discharging the debt of the guilty, inspired him, as he looked back on himself, with the passionate desire to know himself that he might correct himself, and with a kind of necessity for avowing his faults, and finding ministers of the justice of God against himself. He cherished to an incredible degree this sense of expiation by the reiterated confession of his most grievous faults. He desired to have many correctors and confessors. He had one, and often several, in each convent. They were not all priests, some were lay brothers. As soon as he arrived at any convent his first care was to go and find his Father corrector ; he humbly kissed his feet, sometimes he washed them, then acknowledged to him on his knees all the faults he had committed since their last interview, and asked him for a penance. One of these lay brothers, who had entered religion by his advice, and for whom the Father had a sort of veneration, was much surprised some time after his admission into the Order, to see Père Lacordaire come and kneel before him, saying, " My dear brother, one of the blessings of a religious is that he is surrounded by friends who will tell him of his faults. Every religious generally has one brother who is his corrector. You shall be mine ; and, in order that you may know me, I am going to confess to you the sins of my whole life." The brother exclaimed, " But, my Father, I conjure you not—it is impossible ;—I am not a priest." " I know that, my dear friend, and it is precisely for that reason that I choose you ; it is not the absolution of my faults that I ask of you, but the charity of hearing them, that you may humble me and punish me for them as I deserve." The brother had to yield to his wishes, and when it was over : " Now," he said, " you know me, and if you love me a little for the sake of Jesus Christ, you will tell me without sparing me whatever you notice blamable in me : you will treat me as the vilest of slaves, and will chastise me without pity." The brother ended by accomplishing, out of obedience, what his respect made him look on as impossible, and no pen could ever convey the smallest idea of the incredible ways invented by the holy religious in order to humble himself at the feet of the poor brother.

One day this same lay brother as he was serving in

the refectory, was the cause of some delay. The Father himself never made any one wait ; and he liked to see the same exactitude in others.   As the brother did not appear, Père Lacordaire could not repress a movement of impatience which appeared on his countenance.   In the evening, as soon as he was free, he went to find the brother, acknowledged his fault to him on his knees, begged his pardon, and entreated him to scourge him for it, and to send him away with the most injurious epithets.   These are only a few instances taken from a hundred of the same kind ; we name them rather to show what were his ordinary habits than for any singularity which they display.

It may well be imagined that what he asked from the lay brothers he did not fail to require from his real confessors.   At the convent at Paris his door, during his hours of reception, was besieged by numerous visitors, all of whom were not equally welcome.   He one day told his director that one of the things to which he had not yet been able to accustom himself was being interrupted over his work.   " Each time they knock at my door," he said, " I cannot prevent a first movement of vexation.   I want to correct myself of this fault, and if you approve, you shall enter into my cell at all hours, and without knocking.   If you perceive on my countenance the smallest expression of impatience, you will give me the discipline." " Yes, Father, I will do so."   And the same day, in order to put his penitent to the proof, he entered his cell abruptly.   The Father at once knelt down.   " But, Father, I observed nothing in your manner."   " You did not *see* my impatience," replied the culprit, uncovering his shoulders, " but I felt it."

That modest little chamber of the Carmes, what mysteries did it not witness !   Why cannot its walls repeat all that they have seen and heard !   It is a pious duty among us to surround with respect everything that was ever used by Père Lacordaire.   But this cell, which was given him by Mgr. Sibour, to-

gether with part of the convent of the Carmes, is
about to pass out of our hands into those of its former
proprietors. May they preserve it with affection in
memory of him who dwelt in it for twelve years !

We will mention another fact which took place in
the same chamber of the convent of Paris. We have
already said that his constant study of the Passion of
Jesus Christ inspired him with the ardent desire of
imitating that Divine Model in the two greatest manifestations of His love—humiliation and suffering—and
gave him a singular attraction for those expiations
which are at once hardest to pride and sensibility.
Hence his taste for general confessions. The confession of the faults of the week, which he never failed
to make, seemed to him nothing. He desired more
humiliating avowals and a keener pain. He generally
celebrated the anniversaries of his birth, his ordination
to the priesthood, and his religious profession by a
general confession, and was ingenious in varying the
forms of his penance. On one anniversary of his birth
he devised the following : He stripped himself of part
of his clothes, put a leather strap round his neck, and
agreed with his confessor that at every grave fault of
which he should accuse himself, his confessor should
drag him along the ground, or trample him under
foot, or give him a certain number of blows with the
strap. This confession lasted more than an hour.
When it was ended, he begged his spiritual director to
draw him along the floor of his cell, like something
not fit to be touched, loading him with the most humiliating epithets, spitting in his face, and treating him,
in short, like an unclean animal, as he would have desired to have been treated by God, whom he had so
grievously offended.

These irresistible outbursts of the fire that devoured
him, almost always ended with a spiritual conference.
When he rose all bruised and weeping, his soul would
give utterance to exclamations of love towards God,
which no language can ever render. "Do you love

me ?" he would say to him who had just inflicted these penances on him ; "do you love me a little ?" "Yes, Father, I do indeed love you ; I think I have given you a proof of it." " And yet, what have I ever done for you in comparison with what Jesus has suffered?... He caused Himself to be put to death for us, for you and for me, and we do not think of it ! . . . Ah, for my own part, how could I live if I did not love Him ? . . . I cannot fear Him. . . . I have never been afraid of hell. . . . I shall go to purgatory, I know ; but there at any rate I shall love God. . . . To suffer whilst one is loving God is not to suffer. . . . Ah, if the world but knew what a happiness there is in feeling oneself scourged for Him whom one loves ! Do you know in what I take refuge when some bad thought by chance comes into my mind ? I imagine myself on the scaffold, surrounded by executioners, and dying for the love of Jesus Christ. No happiness seems to me to be compared with that; and all the vain pleasures of the world disappear before that one image."

These sentiments astonish us,—this passion for suffering appears strange ; but it was this that lay at the bottom of his extraordinary soul ; it was the key to his secret life, the only reason of his love of penance, and in particular of his general confessions. He found united in this one exercise both suffering and shame, the very ideal of Calvary ; and what justly seems to most men a cruel difficulty, was to him on that very account an act of the greatest facility. He would have confessed to the first comer when this interior fire burnt within him. In the noviceship houses it was necessary to restrain him, in order to prevent his unveiling the sins of his whole life to most of the novices. He submitted to this, but without appearing to be convinced by the reasons urged against him. " And if they did know all the evil I have ever committed," he said, " what great harm would there be in that ? They will know it all at the day of judgment,

they and many more besides!" Thus when any
young man of the world was kneeling at his feet, and
he perceived him hesitate to acknowledge some grave
fault in confession, he would say, "What are you
afraid of? I have done much worse than you; and
if I had leave I would begin a confession to you of my
whole life; your own after that would seem easy
enough."

It is impossible to give, even approximately, the
number of general confessions which he made, whether
to priests or laymen. A great number of confidential
communications have been made to us on this point,
and we are far from having received all that could be
made. But this conviction has been left on our minds,
that could one know with exactitude the number of
these confessions, and the profusion of humiliating
circumstances with which he contrived to surround
them, we should probably not find a single saint in the
whole history of the Church who has carried this particular form of self-abasement to such a heroic degree.

What more shall we say? Must we add that every
kind of maceration in use among the saints—hair-
cloths, disciplines, scourges of every kind and description—were all known and practised by him! Shall I
say, on the testimony of those who observed him most
closely, and in spite of the extreme care that he took
to conceal what he did alone and in private, that he
flagellated himself daily, and often many times in the
day? Must I repeat that during Lent, and especially
on Good Friday, he caused his entire body to be
bruised and torn with stripes? Shall I say that this
supernatural gift of voluntary suffering which he had
received on the very first moment of his conversion
did not quit him till his last sigh; and that if one is
surprised to see him on the very day after his return
to God, pursued in the streets of Paris by the strange
desire of causing himself to be publicly flogged by a little Savoyard, there are no words to express what we feel
on learning that in the early part of October, 1861,

only six weeks before his death, when stretched upon his bed, wasted with sickness, no longer able to take any nourishment, and kept up only by the indomitable energy of his soul, he still desired them to give him the discipline, having no longer the strength to strike himself? At that time he received a visit from one of his friends, and his first words were. " Do you still love penance?" "Yes, Father." " Well then, will you do me the same service as of old, and make me suffer something for Jesus Christ?" And as his friend positively refused to do so, " At least," he said, " allow me to kiss your feet, that will always be a practice of penance agreeable to God!"

In unveiling this secret and delicate side of the life of Père Lacordaire, I cannot, I confess, avoid a painful feeling of doubt. I fear for myself, and I also fear a little for the public. I tremble before what I feel to be the soul of my subject, the soul of this great and holy life. I have placed my hand on the heart of my Father, and have laid it bare at that deep 'and mysterious spot where only the eye of God, and those of a few chosen friends, have ever before penetrated. I well know how jealous he was in keeping a veil over these secret practices, and I ask myself if his severe eye from the height of heaven will not blame me for what I have dared to do. Never, moreover, have I felt more keenly my own insufficiency to tell such things in suitable language, and hence I cannot but doubt the effect which they may produce on a certain part of the public. If the spectacle of this sublime martyrdom leaves my readers cold and insensible.— if it does not reveal the supereminent virtue of this great and humble religious, if they do not behold in what I have narrated the proofs of real sanctity, and of supernatural gifts far more rare and excellent than his gifts of genius,—if they cannot detect through this masculine vigour of will his exquisite tenderness of heart,—if, above all, they do not revere in this soul the bloody image of the Crucified, dug out by love in

characters of light and of fire,—shall I not have failed
in my object ? shall I not have undertaken a rash enterprise, and one above my strength ? and should I not
have done better to have kept a respectful silence, and
to have left it to others, or to God, to make known virtues, the real merits of which are known to Him alone ?

And yet how can one speak of this life without saying what was the soul of it ; without revealing what
was the hidden and powerful spring which gave
motion to all its virtues; to its tenderness, its eloquence, and its piety ? On the surface it was an existence embellished with peace, serenity, and unalterable
purity ; but at what price had those heavenly guests
entered his soul, and gained the right of citizenship ?
The pitiless justice with which we see him armed
against himself, must be our reply. Every other
remedy is powerless to give the soul the empire over
the body. God, it is true, planted in his path many
strong and beautiful friendships ; but friendship,
which is so useful by its counsels, its support, and its
consolations, does not give the victory over those
secret enemies the existence of which it hardly
guesses. There is needed for this the science of penance,—that science of which Jesus Christ came to
bring us the lesson and example. Of a lively, impetuous, proud, and gifted nature, Père Lacordaire had
ever present to his own mind the advice which he gave
to young men in general. " We have two great vices
to combat and to destroy—pride and voluptuousness ;
and we have two virtues to acquire—humility and
penance."[1] Where might not that ardent nature have
carried him without the bloody bridle with which it
mastered itself,—without the iron hand by which it
was subdued ? " I chastise my body," says St. Paul,
"and reduce it to servitude."[2] And every saint after
him has said and done as he did, because it is at this
price alone that the war between the flesh and the
Spirit is overcome, and that those souls are formed

---

[1] " Letters to Young Men," p. 61.   [2] 1 Cor. ix. 27

full of a holy jealousy to live for ever in friendship with God, and at peace within themselves.

But there was another motive for this antagonism of the mind against the weakness and infirmities of the body, a motive taken from the purely physical order. This severity to himself helped him to re-establish an equilibrium in his intercourse with God between a passionate soul and an exterior sensibility which was difficult to move. In fact, by an infirmity of nature which he shared with many others, there was an inequality and want of correspondence between the faculties of his soul, which were ardent and excitable, and the exterior covering, which was slow and hard to kindle. Whether it were carelessness or natural in-capacity, it was only with difficulty and reluctance that the interior passions found expression. He will-ingly concentrated himself in himself; and to strike the spark, to make him come forth from himself, re-quired an effort, a shock, a violent exertion. At the bottom of the vase lay floods of tenderness, but there was an unhappy incapacity of pouring them forth; these were treasures of the heart and the imagination, but they generally lay captives and in chains, or, as he himself expressed it, in words wherein the truth of the imagery is rivalled by the keenness of the analysis : " The heart of man, and my own in particular, is like a volcano from whence the lava only pours forth at intervals, and after the shock of an earthquake." And he added : " I am certain that I can love, nay, that I can love profoundly ! nevertheless it is true that there is a nameless something in me which causes pain to those whom I love. It is not harshness, for I am gentle; it is not coldness, for by nature I am passion-ate ; it is a certain something that is too positive, which has always too much either of *yes* or *no* about it—a habit of silence which everywhere pursues me without my being aware of it. What difficulty I have in speaking ! With my mother, who was accustomed to me, and who observed a great gentleness in her intercourse with me, I often remained for long without saying anything. I have never been tender in my expression of affection, even with her."[1] His mother and Madame Swetchine, to whom he thus spoke, knew him, and made allowances for this moral infirmity; but all did not guess the existence of this weak side of his nature; many suffered from it, particularly women, with whom he was, generally speaking, imperturbably laconic. The world knew not how to explain the contrast between the orator with his burning enthusiasm, who was so expansive in presence of his audience, and the man in private society, who was to be found in his own cabinet cold, impassible, and slow to move. The fact was, that whilst he was calm and disarmed in ordinary life, he had in public the sovereign resource of the excitement of preaching. He required the electric shock of four thousand glances fixed on him in order to enable him to take his flight upwards, and allow the pent-up waters a free course to pour out their swelling torrents. But what resource should he find in his communications with God against the slavery of the soul held in bondage under the jealous guard of his sensitive nature? How at the foot of the crucifix should he strike the spark which lay hidden in the marble? What door should be open to the fire which sought a vent? Our readers now know. He found his way to tenderness through the rugged paths of mortification; it was strength which opened the door to love. Where others pass long hours in the delights of prayer, allowing their souls to lose themselves as they feed in the wide pastures of contemplation, he went at once to action. He forced his body to unbind the captive soul; that body, an ungrateful, and too often a rebellious instrument, was compelled by him, as by a kindly hand, to minister to the desires of his heart; he taught it also to praise God after its fashion, and to sing with him the divine harmonies of

[1] "Letters to Madame Swetchine," p. 75.

the Cross. Happy were those who were able to gather some echoes of those chants of suffering which broke from his lips at such moments! Happy those who, as he came forth from that baptism of tears, have leant on the bosom of their Master, and have been able to drink at that ineffable source of a love *strong as the diamond, more tender than a mother!*

When once he had reached that point, everything else disappeared from his view. The joys of friendship, those even of eloquence, were only thought of at that moment in so far as they helped him to tell God how much he loved Him, and to receive the overflowing floods of His love in return. His devotion there found its centre, its nourishment, and its repose. Jesus Christ was truly to him "the way, the truth, and the life." Many must recollect the sublime exclamation which burst from his heart at the commencement of his admirable Conferences on Jesus. They will now be better able to understand it:

"Lord Jesus," he cried, "for ten years I have spoken to this audience of Thy Church. In reality, it has always been of Thee that I have spoken; but now, at last, I come more directly to Thyself, to that Divine Form which is the object of my daily contemplation, to those sacred Feet that I have so often kissed, to those dear Hands that have so often blessed me, to that Head crowned with glory and with thorns, to that Life whose perfume I have inhaled from my very birth, which my youth forgot for a time, to which my manhood returned, and which my riper years have adored and announced to the world. O Father! O Master! O Friend! O Jesus! help me now more than ever; because having now drawn nearer to Thyself, it is but suitable that all should be sensible of it, and that my lips should utter words worthy of Thy sacred Presence!"[1]

He could fearlessly appeal thus to the Heart of Him whom he called his *Friend*, for he knew Him.

[1] Conference xxxvii.

He had experienced His goodness; he lived with Him on terms of such sweet familiarity as in some sort made the shadows of faith to depart: *he saw Him.* We have endeavoured to show the road by which light once more found its way into his understanding; but if his understanding had need of light, his heart urged him yet more powerfully towards an ideal of beatitude which he well knew he could nowhere find complete save in God. Jesus Christ on His Cross appeared to him as the very Type of that superhuman felicity, and unveiled to him the mystery of a God who had become man that He might be loved by men, and who died of love in order that He might be loved by them passionately, nay, madly, if one dare so to say. From that touch of grace he received so piercing a light, so sensible an impression, that he preserved it through his whole life, and spoke of it with feeling that seemed ever new. This is what, in a describing the return of a soul to God, he called *the vision of Jesus Christ.* "He who has not known such a moment," he said, "has not really known human life." "One day, at the corner of a street, in some solitary path, we stop,—we listen, and a voice whispers to us in the centre of our souls, 'Behold! there is Jesus Christ!'—a heavenly moment, in which the soul, after gazing on a thousand perishable beauties, discovers at a single glance that one Beauty which can never deceive! Those who have never experienced this may treat it as a dream; but those who have once beheld what I speak of can never forget it more![1]

From that day he loved our Lord passionately; he no longer saw any but Him; he no longer had any love save in Him. "I can no longer love any one," he writes, "without the soul stealing behind the heart, so that Jesus Christ stands between us." Nothing made his Lord so present and sensible to his heart as suffering; and hence he could not do without it; he loved

---

[1] "Conférences de Toulouse," p. 165.

it to folly, as St. Francis loved poverty. It held the place of everything to him, and he preferred it to every other good. "When God bruises us under the rod," he writes, "is it not that our blood may mingle with His—His, shed long ago under yet sharper and more humiliating blows? Is it not that we may seek for no other head than the Bleeding Head of our Saviour, no other eyes than His Eyes, no other lips than His Lips, no other shoulders, on which to repose than His, furrowed with the scourges; no other hands and feet to kiss than His Hands and His Feet, pierced with nails for our love; no other wounds gently to bind up than His Divine and Ever-Bleeding Wounds?"[1]

This was his great devotion. One day he asked some of the young religious what was their special devotion: each one answered in turn. One said it was the Holy Eucharist; another, the Blessed Virgin; the third, the salvation of souls. "Well, for my part," he said, "my devotion is Jesus Christ crucified. I cannot go beyond that." And he added: "*Absit mihi gloriari nisi in cruce Domini nostri Jesu Christi.* That is the road of heaven and of love. Jesus Christ Himself knew no other road than that which led to the prætorium and to Calvary. I keep to that, and there I shall live and die."

Such was this true religious, such is the light in which we have longed to show him; for it was the side of his character which made him great in the eyes of God, and by which also, as we believe, he will be great in the eyes of men. He was doubtless endowed with many admirable gifts, but what is human genius in the sight of Infinite Wisdom? What is eloquence before the Eternal Word of God? But if genius be but a gift, the love of God is a virtue; carried to heroism it makes saints, the only great men who are recognised by God. Sanctity, in fact, consists in loving in the same way as Jesus Christ loved. The most holy are those who approach

[1] "Letters to Young Men," p. 107.

nearest to the Ideal of the Crucified. Such souls are rare in all times, for this love of a God overwhelms our weakness; it is a love strong as death, a love that slays. All have not a heart vast enough, a soul manly enough to receive it. But Père Lacordaire was of the small number of those to whom the Cross has no terrors; to speak in the language which he himself borrowed from Bossuet, he was of the number of those who bear with honour in their bodies the sacred stigmata of that love, who owe to those glorious wounds both their life and their death. That divine wound of love was his happy martyrdom and his greatest joy; he loved it to the end, sacrificed everything to it, even his life, and did not cease to suffer from it till he had ceased to live. Yes! this is the side from which God was best pleased to behold him, when he received into His bosom the generous champion of His love; and it is from this point of view, doubtless, that his disciples and friends, accustomed to admire the man, will henceforth love to venerate the religious. As to those who have too often encountered him in the troubled arena of our contemporary struggles, easily to forget that he was the constant opponent of their views, will they not at the touching spectacle shut their eyes to his frank, and at times perhaps indignant, advocacy of his age, and remember only the heroic virtues of the Friend of Jesus Christ ?[1]

[1] We cannot resist the temptation of adding to the text a quotation from Père Lacordaire's Conferences of Notre Dame, which illustrates in an exquisite manner the subject of the chapter. He is speaking of the empire of Jesus Christ, not only over the intellect, but over the heart. After touching, with that peculiar pathos of which none was a more perfect master, on the various forms of affection which subjugate the human heart, of friendship, of love, of the conjugal and the paternal ties, he thus continues : "Yet with all this we are forced to admit that as we journey through life in pursuit of affection, whatever we win, it is but in an imperfect manner which always leaves our hearts bleeding. And even if we were to obtain it perfectly in this life, what would remain to us of it after death ? Some friendly prayers would indeed follow us out of this world ; some kind voice would still preserve our memory, and occasionally pronounce our name ; but ere long heaven and earth would

take another step forward, silence and forgetfulness would descend upon us, and from the far-distant shore no ethereal breeze of affection would be wafted over our tomb. It is over—and for ever ; and such is the history of human love. But I am wrong. There *is* a Man over whose tomb love still keeps guard ; there *is* a Man whose sepulchre is not only glorious, as was predicted by the prophet, but even beloved. There *is* a Man whose ashes, after eighteen centuries, have not yet grown cold ; who is every day born anew in the memory of countless multitudes ; who is visited in His tomb by shepherds and by kings, who vie one with another in offering Him their homage. There *is* a Man whose steps are continually being tracked, and Who, withdrawn as He is from our bodily eyes, is still discerned by those Who unweariedly haunt the spots where once He sojourned, and who seek Him on His Mother's knees, by the borders of the lake, on the mountain top, in the secret paths among the valleys, under the shadow of the olive trees, or in the silence of the desert. There *is* a Man Who has died and been buried, but whose sleeping and waking is still watched by us ; whose every word still vibrates in our heart, producing there something more than love, for it gives life to those virtues of which love is the mother. There *is* a Man Who long ages ago was fastened to a gibbet, and that Man is every day taken down from the throne of His Passion by thousands of adorers, who prostrate on the earth before Him and kiss His Bleeding Feet with unspeakable emotion. There *is* a Man Who was once scourged, slain, and crucified, but whom an ineffable Passion has raised from death and infamy, and made the object of an unfailing love, which finds all in Him —peace, honour, joy—nay, ecstasy. There *is* a Man Who, pursued to death in His own time with inextinguishable hate, has demanded apostles and martyrs from each successive generation, and has never failed to find them. There is *one Man*, and one alone, Who has established His love on earth, and it is Thou, O my Jesus ! Thou Who hast been pleased to baptise, to anoint, to consecrate me in Thy love, and whose very Name at this moment suffices to move my whole being, and to tear from me these words in spite of myself."—*Conference* xxxix. *(Translator's Note.)*

CHAPTER XV.

Continuation of his Virtues—His faith in the presence of our Lord in the most Holy Eucharist—In the Scriptures—His Confidence in Divine Providence—His humility—His fidelity to duty.

ROM the tender and almost exclusive devotion of Père Lacordaire to Jesus crucified, from that holy " mountain on which he had planted his life," it will now be easy for us to descend to the study of his other virtues. They all flowed from it like so many rivulets from a common source ; and it is sufficient for us to have raised the veil which hung over the hidden sanctuary of this beautiful soul in order to see the thousand many-coloured flames burst forth like some golden fountain from this one furnace of Love.

That which is nearest to Calvary is the Christian Altar. The most living memorial of the great Victim immolated between heaven and earth in the midst of time, is that same Victim descending each morning into the hands of the priest, and offered by him, though in a different manner, to the same Father Who is in heaven. And it is as the priest at the altar, tenderly united to the Victim of Love, that we now have to make known Père Lacordaire to our readers. Hardly was he converted than his first thought, his first ambition, was to receive the priesthood. According to his way of understanding, and loving his Divine

Master, the power of calling Him down upon the altar, and giving Him to others, seemed to him the most natural and legitimate aspiration of a true and devoted love : it was the priest who must finish and complete the Christian. After loving the Cross so dearly, how could he fail to love the altar which placed in his hands and in his heart the Lamb slain from the beginning? He was, then, a priest; that is, in the highest sense of that word, a mediator—a Pontiff: he thought of and coveted the priesthood as the "immolation of man, added to that of God."[1] We know now whether he was faithful to this great vocation. In love beyond all things, with the beauty of voluntary martyrdom, he not only did not desire the honours of the Church, which were offered to him at the very opening of his career, but to his first sacrifice of himself he superadded that of the religious state, and carried this sacrifice to an excess capable of terrifying the most austere virtue. His whole life was a sacrifice to duty, and to the devouring ardour of his charity to God and souls. Thus prepared, he went to the altar to accomplish the sacrifice which had been begun by the expiatory penances of the preceding evening and morning: he went to sit at the banquet of the Lamb, to rest on the bosom of his Master, and to be united to Him in His ineffable embrace. This was his reward after labour, this was what gave him strength for new combats. He rarely said Mass without having first performed some of his favourite penances. If time failed him for this, he would take aside some lay brother—the first who came—into the inner sacristy, devoutly kiss his feet, remain for some time with his head bent down in this humble posture, and then, with his heart satisfied, and his brow illumined with joy, he would prepare for the Holy Sacrifice. With what imposing gravity, with what sweet majesty, did he not celebrate! He read the words of the Old and New Testament slowly,

---

[1] Panegyric on B. Peter Fourrier.

and with unction; and as the action of the Sacrifice
proceeded, what profound recollection was observable!
What self-annihilation! How profound an air of
reverence! What a transfigured countenance! All
those who beheld him received an impression of tenderness and devotion not easily effaced. "Never
shall I forget the Mass of Père Lacordaire," said one
witness to me; "I have never seen but one priest
who caused me similar emotion, and that was Pius
IX." Routine in an action daily renewed had no
power over him; there was nothing hasty or negligent
in his manner; he said Mass every day as he said it
on the first day of his ordination. He assisted at the
Holy Sacrifice with equal recollection. He never
read during the time, or even recited his Breviary.
At Sorèze, when some one expressed astonishment
at this, and asked him how it was that, overwhelmed
as he was with business, he did not take the time of
the student's high Mass for reciting his Office, he replied: "The Mass is too sublime and holy an action
for us to occupy ourselves at that time with anything
except what is said or done by the priest." Next to
our Lord present in the Tabernacle, he most loved to
study our Lord hidden in His Divine Word. After
his Mass, having retired to his cell, he read the Holy
Scriptures. This, with the *Summa* of St. Thomas,
was the only book that was always on his table. He
kissed its pages with respect, read a few verses, and
stopped at each thought that struck him, more desirous of meditating and penetrating the spiritual sense
than of making erudite researches. He earnestly recommended this study to others. Towards the end
of his life he said to his children at Sorèze: "I have
read this book for thirty years, and every day I discover in it new lights and new depths. How different
is it from the word of man! That is exhausted at a
single draught, but the Word of God is a bottomless
abyss!" He wrote on the same subject: "How much
are unbelievers to be pitied as they advance in life!

The light becomes so lively, so sweet, so penetrating
in proportion as we draw near to death under the
auspices of faith, and of a virtue which takes its root
in the gospel! We no longer believe—we see. In
the same way as the mystery of iniquity increases in
the unbelieving soul, and everything becomes to him
an enigma and a subject of doubt, so the light extends and envelops a soul accustomed to live in
God. When I read the Gospel, every word seems to
me like a flash of lightning, and gives me new consolation."[1] The Gospels were in fact his favourite
study; and in the New Testament his preference was
for St. John and St. Paul,—the Apostle of Love, and
the Doctor of the Cross. "The Epistles of St. Paul,
which I read by choice every day," he writes, "enchant
me more and more with the truth. They are an ocean,
of which God alone is the shore."[2]

For the rest, nothing in general could equal his
perfect indifference as to books. He never opened a
frivolous work; he did not even care to read *good*
books, but confined himself to *the very best*. "When
one is able to read Homer, Plutarch, Cicero, Plato,
David, St. Paul, St. Augustine, St. Theresa, Bossuet,
Pascal, and others like them," he said, "one would be
greatly in the wrong to waste one's time over the
rubbish of a drawing-room table. It is the misfortune
of people of the world, that they want to make their
whole life a distraction; whereas recreation ought
only to be a moment given to repose in order to re-
fresh the mind, and give its nerves new strength."[3]

The day being thus begun in union with God, and
in the meditation of His Word, he found no difficulty
in preserving the perfume of his first thoughts by the
exercise of recollection, and the remaining hours
flowed on peacefully and devoutly. He may truly be
said to have "walked with God." His pure and upright soul sought Him alone, and found Him without

[1] Unpublished Letters.　[2] "Letters to Young Men," p. 275.
[3] Unpublished Correspondence.

difficulty; His Divine Providence, amid the thousand accidents of his life, seemed to lead him on as by the hand. It was his favourite habit often to raise his heart to God, in order to offer Him his actions, his sufferings, and his work. "I abandon myself to God," he said. "His goodness fills me more and more with gratitude and adoration. . . . The presence of God is easy and natural to me, and I frequently feel my heart spring up towards Him. But it is hardly possible for me to follow any regular course of meditation, or rather any true contemplation. The love of the Holy Scriptures increases in me; and I seem to comprehend their sense better than I ever did before."[1]

He delighted in his little cell, where, as he said, there extended between his soul and God "a horizon vaster than the universe." It was a kind of sanctuary where peace, that tranquillity of order, to use the beautiful expression of St. Augustine, ever reigned. He liked to see it neat and well-arranged, and could not endure the least disorder. "If the eye of man does not see it," he would say, "it is nevertheless disagreeable to the eyes of the angels." There, alone with God, far from the world and its bustle, and seated at his writing-table, his soul, so naturally religious, was steeped in silence and love, and without effort, indulged in the holiest of joys. Who shall tell the secrets of those hours of sacred labour? of that life in his own cell, so simple, so full of work, so hidden in God? He spoke little of it himself even to his most intimate friends; but it was easy to guess by the fire which animated his countenance, and by the reflection of heavenly joy which shone there, where his thoughts were fixed. When in those moments of religious privacy and patient labour you entered his presence, it was impossible to resist a certain feeling of respectful fear; you felt yourself overcome as in the presence, not of a great man of this world, but of one invested with the Royalty

[1] Unpublished Correspondence.

of Intellect—nay, with a greater Royalty still—the Royalty of Virtue.

It was this in part that made up the charm of his intercourse ; the serene beauty of his countenance, the faithful reflection of the beauty of his soul, attracted and won the heart. You could not hear him speak without feeling better, and drawn nearer to God. His countenance which, in public, was ordinarily so cold and unmoved, had, in familiar intercourse, its moments of tender and ineffable melancholy. At such times it was impossible to resist the attraction which shone forth from his whole person. His soul filled with God, revealed itself in his flashing eye, poured itself out from his lips, and captivated you, even in his very silence. To judge of his power, one must have heard him at those moments pouring the super-abundance of his charity into suffering souls, weak hearts, or minds tormented with doubt. He first transported them to the mountain of Crucified Love, his only Thabor, in order to make them taste and see how sweet the Lord is ; and then he brought them back to the clear view of God, in all events of life, whether sad or joyous ; and this was his chief asylum of comfort, both for himself and others.

He found every one's way as straight and simple as his own. " If God wills to have it thus," he would say, " why should we trouble ourselves ? Is He not wiser than we ? All the rest is but a question of courage and filial abandonment to Him. Provided that we are humble, without party-spirit, truly and simply belonging to God, ready to die or to live, we cannot, either in success or in failure, fail to find the consolation of the Christian who has done all he can, and accepts all that God wills." This abandonment to the Will of God was his pole-star, his guide, his refuge. He saw that Divine Will everywhere—in his own life, in the life of the Church, in public and in private events. If, as he said before his conversion, he had a very incredu-lous mind, and a very religious soul, the mind had be-

come so wholly subjugated to the soul, that nothing
remained of its original tendency; for he had the
simple faith of a child. It had become second nature
to him to see God living and acting in the world, in
the human heart, and in history. If light ever failed
him to judge of certain obscure and equivocal events,
according to this rule, he would say, " Let us know
how to wait ; the hour of Providence will not fail soon
to show itself." When he received any unexpected
pleasure, or some happy news, the first movement of
his soul was towards God, the source of all good, in
order to offer to Him the first-fruits of his gratitude.
If he heard any grievous intelligence, he in like manner cast himself into the arms of his adored Master,
told Him his trouble, and rose restored to peace and
hope. From time to time it often happened that
he felt the attacks of sudden indignation at some
moral scandal or unexpected treachery ; and then his
brow became furrowed, and his looks were clouded ;
these were passing moments of sadness and even of
trouble, but they did not last long. God quickly regained His empire over that soul so docile to grace, so
incapable of bitterness, so eager for peace and concord.
" We must," he said, " have an absolute unlimited certainty that whatever comes from God is best, even if
from the human point of view it should seem to us to
be the very worst. I have seen that twenty times
during my life, and have always gained a more unbounded spirit of abandonment to God from my experience, which serves to arm me against the imperfections of a nature which is very quick and easily
moved to resentment."[1]

He learnt one day that a young man for whom he
entertained great affection had just failed in every duty
as a man and a Christian, and given grievous scandal
by his conduct. It was a severe and cruel blow to the
delicacy of Père Lacordaire's feelings ; and the sensibility of his heart as a Father and a Priest. He spoke

[1] *Le Père Lacordaire*, par M. de Montalembert, p. 173.

of this sharp trial shortly after the event in the following terms :—" The fall of poor N., of which you remind
me, was very great, and very unexpected. It is the
most complete treason of which I have ever been the
victim, and, at the same time, it is a sad revelation of
the instability of the human heart. But Jesus Christ
himself was betrayed by one of His own followers, and
that treason saved the world. God brings good out of
evil, and this thought is sufficient to make one endure
anything. In our hands they are poison, but in the
hands of God they are a medicine. Perhaps some day
the man over whom we thus mourn may become a
great saint, whilst without his terrible fall he might
have remained but an imperfect Christian. Mercy is
a fountain which flows from a profound abyss, and it
never rises higher than when it springs from the
lowest depths."[1]

A virtue which loves to abide on the calm summits
of faith, which finds God everywhere, in tears as in joy,
and in all things seeks only His glory ; such a virtue
easily forms a just and true view of self ; it is humble
naturally, and without an effort ; it loves to judge itself
with justice and equity, giving to each its due ; to
heaven the merit of all that it sees good in itself ; and
to earth the sad honour of what is bad. And it is precisely in this that true humility consists, which, according to St. Bernard, is " the perfect knowledge of ourselves and our nothingness."[2] And it was thus also
that Père Lacordaire understood and practised this
virtue. He had not that sort of humility which believes
itself the last of all in point of talent and merit. Nor,
certainly, had he that sort of humility which says as
much to every comer. He made no difficulty in
acknowledging the gifts he had received, and did not
believe himself to be either better or worse on that
account. "Humility," he said, "does not consist in
hiding our talents and merits, or in believing ourselves

[1] Unpublished Letters.
[2] De Gradib. humilitatis, cap. 1.

worse than we are, but in clearly knowing our own deficiencies, in not being puffed up on account of what we have, seeing that all we have has been gratuitously given us by God, and that even with all His gifts we are still very poor and little. It is remarkable that great virtue inevitably engenders humility, and that if great talent does not also produce it, it at least retrenches many of those asperities which generally cling to the pride of mediocrity. There is then no incompatibility between humility and real excellence ; on the contrary, they are twin sisters, who mutually seek and attract one another. God, Who is Excellence itself, the Supreme Excellence, has no pride. He sees Himself such as he is, but without despising anything which is not Him ; he is *Himself* simply and naturally."[1]

The virtue of Père Lacordaire consisted in always tending to this perfect knowledge of himself, and thus he was equally removed from pride and false modesty. In this he was powerfully assisted by the purity of his desires, his ardent and disinterested love of truth and justice, and his perfect sincerity with himself. He clearly saw his faults, and confessed them without difficulty ; but he did not on that account shut his eyes to the high position in which God had placed him in His Church. Without taking any vain complacency in it, he regarded it as a gratuitous vocation, entailing many perils and serious duties. Hence that equable tranquillity of mind which he displayed in the midst of the most prodigious success, that simplicity, that ease, that full possession of himself under the most various strokes of fortune. Free from all ambition, an enemy to every kind of falsehood, " he was *himself* naturally and simply." Moreover, he was able to defend himself against the fumes of vainglory by the energetic remedy of which we have already spoken ; the annihilation, namely, of the spirit through the humbling of the flesh. He rarely ascended into the pulpit without having first submitted to this kind of humiliation,

[1] " Letters to Young Men," p. 122.

without having first cast out the spirit of pride with
the powerful exorcism of the discipline.

It may perhaps be asked, how are we to reconcile
the apparent contradiction between so profound a
humility, and love of contempt, and the sallies of his
eloquence, which were sometimes so bold, so haughty,
so jealous of independence ; and also with the honours
which he consented to accept from more than one
illustrious body, and in particular from the French
Academy ? To judge of this side of his life, as he
did himself, we must see in him two different men,
and study him both in his private and public character. Before God and his own conscience he was
humble and simple as a little child, ever eager to turn
his friends into advisers to reprove, and masters to
correct him ; but when he had risen from the dust of
his self-abasement, he was no longer the same man ;
he resumed his position as a priest, and fearlessly
armed himself with the two-edged sword of his
apostolic eloquence. Far from seeking to efface himself, and suffering his arms to rust out of a false
distrust of his own powers, he feared not to appear
before the public, and to use all the resources of his
gifted nature in the service of truth ; the sallies of his
wit, the fire and keen edge of his originality, the
magic of his oratorical style, the irresistible fascination
of his passionate temperament, the mingled accents
of the poet and the apostle, of the priest and
the citizen, of the lyre of Homer and the harp of
David. He did not think that the humility of the
religious ought to interfere with the holy liberty of
the herald of the Gospel ; and the more little and
lowly he acknowledged himself to be in his own cell
at the foot of the crucifix, so much the more proudly
did he bear aloft the standard of truth before the
multitude ; like those knights of old who, prostrating
on both knees on the pavement of the church, humbly
offered their sword at the altar of the Lord of Hosts,
praying him to bless it, and vowing never to use it

save in a just cause, and then rose from their knees
animated by a holy ardour. Such was the humility
of Père Lacordaire, it was the humility of the warrior,
not that of the obscure artisan ; the humility of St.
Paul the apostle of the Gentiles, not that of St.
Anthony the hermit. Endowed with extraordinary
qualities, suited to an extraordinary crisis, he made
use of every weapon which fell into his hands ; and
set every engine at work which was capable of giving
him any hold over rebellious intellects, in order to
subdue them as captives to Jesus Christ. This war
of the outposts, in which he exhibited a bold and
novel system of tactics, hitherto without precedent,
which he had invented himself, and which was quite
appropriate to his peculiar genius, had its dangers
and surprises, from which he was not always able to
escape. He was reproached with using certain expressions unfitted for the pulpit, and somewhat
hazardous. He had no difficulty in admitting the
truth of these remarks, only caring to defend himself
from the charge of any preconceived and blamable
intention.

One of his friends once made some observations to
him on this subject. He thanked her, and hastened
to explain himself on the subject with his habitual
frankness. " I thank you," he wrote, " for your observations on some expressions which occur in my
Conferences. Those expressions are indeed a little
bold ; but since they escaped me at the moment, I
prefer leaving them as they are. . . The spoken word
leaves many gaps unfilled which cannot be excused
in the written word. As to my intention in uttering
those expressions, I had none, either good or bad ; I
was moved by the impulse of the moment, and that
was all. My style is not at all studied, and I am
more apt than others not to keep to what is noble
and grand, because one is always liable to run
into the very opposite extreme to one's natural
qualities. Those who suppose that I had any designs

23

hidden under such singular phraseology have not the remotest idea of my real nature, which is altogether spontaneous, and is incapable of foreseeing any such accidents beforehand. When once the harm is done I keep to it as to a *souvenir*, or a stain which reminds me of a past moment in my life."[1]

As to the honours conferred upon him by the world he accepted them, less for his own sake than for that of the cause which he defended. Certainly few men of the world have ever been rewarded with purer or more enviable success. An unrivalled orator in the pulpit, surrounded by enthusiastic popularity, and enjoying an unblemished renown, called by the votes of his fellow-countrymen, in spite of his friar's habit, to sit in the councils of the nation ; towards the close of his career he received the most glorious and most coveted of all literary distinctions from the hands of the French Academy. The more he shunned those honours conferred by the great, which are generally short-lived, because seldom the reward of real merit, the more was he pursued by popular favour, which bestowed on him that fame which is consecrated by time, because it is claimed by truth and justice. We do not mean to say that he was always insensible to this sort of glory (for insensibility to glory either has no existence, or does but argue a want of capacity), but we may safely affirm that he never sought it, that he was never dazzled by it, and that he always showed himself superior to it. When young he had a passion for fame ; but the more he felt the echoes of her trumpet trouble his soul, the more strictly did he impose it on himself as a law, when he became a priest and a religious, to fly from her seducing charms ; and as far as possible to keep at a distance from great towns where her poison is instilled in a more subtle way, and to love obscurity and retreat. Yet he did not on that account withdraw from the position rendered necessary by his providential mis-

[1] Unpublished Correspondence.

sion. The honours which he valued not for his own sake, were nevertheless not indifferent to him when he thought them capable of advancing the cause or the glory of the Church, his Mother. This was specially the reason why he consented to enter the Constituent Assembly in 1848, and the French Academy at a later period : two acts with which he has been often reproached. We shall have occasion hereafter to relate more explicitly the singular episode of his life during the revolution of February. As to the French Academy, it may suffice to make two remarks : in the first place, far from having been the first to entertain the thought, he hesitated some time before accepting it, and only decided to do so at last, at the solicitations of his most prudent and devoted friends, some of whom laid it on him as *an obligation of conscience.* And in the next place, he thought he could not properly refuse what he regarded as an extraordinary mark of homage, rendered less to his person than to the civil and religious principles to the maintenance of which he had devoted his life. All that he said and wrote at that period evinces this double sentiment : " You seem to suppose," he writes, " that I *desire* to belong to the French Academy, but this is an error. I never so much as thought of it ; they addressed themselves to me. . . . Madame Swetchine, when dying, thought that it would be wrong in me to refuse, because there was a certain homage to religion in this spontaneous movement of eminent men towards a religious. Now, ought we to reject an act of homage rendered to God in the person of one of His ministers, who has done nothing on his own part to seek it, and who can testify truly to himself that he never even felt such a desire."[1] And again : " They have made it *a case of conscience* with me not to refuse an honour which has been spontaneously offered to me, and which may turn to the glory of religion. . . . It is Providence alone that has con-

[1] " Letters to Young Men," p. 346.

ducted the whole affair, and made the result to
coincide with the present unfortunate state of the
Church.[1] My election seemed to me to be a kind of
protest against the violent and unhappy events which
are now afflicting all Catholic hearts, and from this
point of view it has caused me satisfaction. I believe
that this singular spectacle was designed by God, and
that it is a striking homage rendered to religion in
the person of a poor friar, the first who has taken his
place in the French Academy for the two hundred
years and more that it has been founded."[2]

This was his impression as early as 1845, when,
after his Lenten station at Lyons, which produced a
perfect frenzy of applause, he was admitted as an
associated member of the Academy of Arts, Sciences
and *Belles-lettres* of that city. He then wrote to
Madame Swetchine as follows : " It is certain that at
the very moment when the Church and the religious
orders are so hotly attacked, God seems to be pur-
posely surrounding me with greater sympathy than
ever." The same thought is also to be found expressed in great and noble words in the discourse
which he delivered to the Academy of Law at Toulouse, which bestowed on him the title of Associated
Member in 1854. "If I were only to consider my
own person," he said, "in the choice which has led
you to call me to sit in an assembly of jurists, I
should feel some embarrassment in thanking you, so
little real title have I to such an honour. . . . In
order, therefore, to be able heartily to rejoice in the
dignity you have offered me, I have to turn away my
looks from myself, and fix them rather on religion,
which you have thus chosen to sit beside you in your
councils. It is she whom you honour, and it is she,
in my person, who thanks you."

"In the midst of our social divisions the only hope
for the future lies in the hearty co-operation of all

[1] The usurpations of Piedmont, which followed on the war in Italy.
[2] Unpublished Correspondence, Sorèze, Jan. 4, Feb. 9, 1860.

ranks and all professions. There no longer exist among us any classes, properly so called, so much have our political vicissitudes ground and mingled men together; but there still exists differences of ranks, of services, and of duties ; and it is these which, by drawing near to each other in mutual esteem and a sense of mutual dependence, will one day lay the solid foundation-stone on which the human race will rest. For a long time in our country religion has been excluded from the hospitality of our hearts, and has been exiled from the councils of the public. She has been regarded as an importunate stranger rather than as a sacred portion of the rights and offices of the nation. This error is now at last beginning to disappear. France is beginning to understand that she has need of all kinds of self-devotion, capacity, and fidelity, and that nothing which God has done for man can be deemed super-fluous. You, gentlemen, by calling me to sit among you, have given a signal example of this reconciliation which the future bears in its bosom; and, considering it from this point of view, I reproach myself for having thanked you so badly for so great an honour, but the mind requires to be free in order to express itself freely, and nothing more deprives it of its liberty than gratitude."[1]

Such, then, was his rule of conduct in the midst of those tokens of popular favour which were showered around his person ; to accept, for the sake of religion, every honour not contrary to the spirit of his vocation. For the rest, this mode of viewing the subject was only criticised in France, and by Catholics whose zeal was more ardent than enlightened. At Rome, where religion, far from being *excluded from the hospitality of hearts*, animates and inspires everything, they had not the same scruples. "The Roman Academies," as was pointed out by Père Lacordaire himself, "are filled with religious ;" and he adds, "I know one

---

[1] Journal of Toulouse for the 19th of January, 1854.

Dominican occupying a high office at the Pontifical court, who is a member of the Academy of Arcadia, and bears in it the name of *Tityrus* or *Melibæus*. Much more reasonably might he therefore have been a member of the French Academy."[1]

It pleased God, six months after the death of Père Lacordaire, to allow his actions, and specially the two of which we are here speaking, to be approved and solemnly praised by the highest authority in our order—the Chapter-General, which is composed of all the heads of provinces throughout the world, enjoys sovereign power, promulgates laws, and causes them to be put in execution. In the month of June, 1862, thirty-eight provincials gathered together at Rome, under the presidency of the General; and after having drawn up ordinances, and provided for the necessities of the Order, they listened, according to ancient custom, to the panegyric of the chief personages who had died since the last Chapter-General, and among them that of Père Lacordaire filled the largest place. It is a clear, sober, historic abridgment, drawn up in a tone of warm and decided praise, as was suitable to brethren speaking of one who had been, to use their own words, "the pride and the hope of the entire Order." It is in the following terms that they speak of his entrance into the National Assembly and the French Academy :—"To the renown of his doctrine, which was his glory in the eyes of the French Episcopate, he united also a great intelligence of public affairs, which caused him to be elected one of the members of the National Assembly in 1848. The honour which he thought might thence redound to the credit of the Order, and the ardent desire of serving religion, induced him to accept an office, which was doubtless unusual, but which had already been conferred on several bishops and distinguished members of the clergy. He therefore took his seat in the Chamber. But events soon changed, and prudence counselled

---

[1] "Letters to Young Men," p. 342.

him to withdraw. In 1860, the French Academy,
which only chooses its members from the most illustrious men, inscribed among them the name of Henry
Lacordaire, as having deserved well of religion, literature, and his country."

It is with honours, as with everything else that is
passionately coveted by man ; it is easier to abstain
from them wholly than to enjoy them with moderation. And thus the more that Père Lacordaire was convinced that he ought not to reject a homage rendered
to him as the champion of a great cause, the more
he felt the necessity of supplying a counter-weight to
this glory by means of more profound self-abasement
before God. And this is, as we have already said, a
partial explanation of his astonishing courage in the
humiliation of his body and his mind. He trembled
before success as before his greatest enemy. If, before his conversion, he had said of himself, "that he
had loved glory and nothing else," we may say of
him after his conversion that he *feared* glory and
nothing else. A touching incident will show how
great this terror was. His Lenten station at Lyons
in 1845 was one of those which obtained the most
extraordinary success. Nothing like it had ever been
seen there before ; it was a perfect delirium. At the
very time when the Chambers and the press were
blowing up the flame of anti-religious passions, and
seeking to stifle every attempt at monastic restoration
under their contempt, a friar in his mediæval garb
was fascinating, by his eloquence, a chosen audience
among the population of Lyons, and renewing in the
19th century those marvels that had been wrought by
the great preachers of the ages of faith. From five
in the morning, an immense crowd besieged the doors
of the Cathedral. Hardly were they opened before
the waves of this impatient crowd burst into the
church, and purchased the happiness of enjoying an
hour of Christian eloquence by seven or eight hours
of waiting. And when this immense assembly, ex-

cited by the accent of the speaker, trembled under his words, respect for the sacred character of the place alone, and with difficulty, repressed the murmurs of their enthusiastic applause. One evening, after one of the finest of these Conferences, the dinner hour had passed, and the Father did not appear in his place. They waited for some time, but not seeing him come (he who was generally so punctual), an ecclesiastic went up to his chamber. He knocked, but no one replied. He entered and perceived Père Lacordaire kneeling before his crucifix with his head in his hands, absorbed in prayer, which was interrupted by his sobs. He approached, and folding him in his arms, " My dear Father," he said, "what is the matter ?" " I am afraid," replied the father, lifting his face bathed in tears. " Afraid ! Father, and of what ?" " I am afraid," was his reply, "of all this success."

He was no less humble with his brethren than with God, and knew how to unite what he owed to his obligations as superior to the gentlest form of paternal tenderness. In 1844 he wrote to Père Besson, who had made some observations to him on the subject of a point of observance on which their ideas did not coincide. " My dearest Father, I have received your letter, which gave me nothing but pleasure on account of the frankness with which you express your fears. You know that I have never shunned the advice, and even the correction, of others, and specially your own. My dispositions on this point are not changed, and I shall always remain such as you have seen me ; obliged no doubt to decide so long as God shall keep authority in my hands, but ready to listen to every-thing that may be said, and to humble myself before the least of my brethren if they have occasion to charge me with any fault. . . . I hope, my dear child, that the obstacle will not come from you, whom I shall love in life and in death, and to whom I have ever given proofs of confidence and love as numerous as they have been profound. Disposed in the spirit of faith and penance, to place myself under your feet, I cannot, nevertheless, renounce the duty of guiding you, and I ask of you the sacrifice of your own views on this point."

No one listened more readily than he did to the advice of others. In matters of business which were debated in council he expressed his own opinion clearly and simply; and if any one gave utterance to a contrary view, he listened to it with attention, and often adopted it with so much facility that one might have supposed he had maintained his own ideas less with the design of making them prevail, than in order to see them opposed by reasons which had already suggested themselves to his own mind. All he sought in discussion was truth; as soon as he recognised it, he defended it with warmth, without caring if by so doing he contradicted the opinion which he had maintained a moment before. He liked to consult others, and never engaged in any affair of importance without having for a long time previously prayed, reflected, and taken counsel. "I thank you," he writes, "for your good advice; do not spare me the expression of your opinion. You know that my soul is not rebellious to truth. Always, then, speak freely to me; you cannot better evince your affection for me." And again: "Never be afraid of telling me exactly what you think; it is the greatest proof of attachment you can show me, and one of those most rarely to be met with. God has given me the grace of being able willingly to receive reproof." And further on he adds: "You cannot better show your affection for me than by telling me truths which you think may be unpalatable."[1]

His whole correspondence manifests the same modesty and respect for the opinion of others. He once consulted one of his religious on a double plan of Conferences, asking him which he preferred. The

---

[1] Unpublished Correspondence.

religious excused himself, saying that the request humbled him. "But, my dear friend," replied the Father, "I assure you I do it in all sincerity; is there not always more light in two minds than in one?"

Out of respect for Jesus Christ, Whom he called *the first Servant in the world*,[1] he had a great love of servants, surrounded them with care and esteem, and multiplied his tokens of kindness toward them. He also loved their state, out of a spirit of faith and humility. He always discharged for himself every little necessary household office; or if he could not always contrive to be allowed to do this, he took delight in discharging the same offices for others. Nothing was more common than to see Père Lacordaire taking away the dust that had been swept out of the cells, and putting everything to rights in the courts, the corridors, or the guest apartments. He often went into the kitchen, specially in the early times of the foundations, put on an apron, and helped the cook. He flattered himself that he particularly understood how to prepare eggs, as they used to be dressed in his mother's house; but his genius on this point has been disputed. Some one seeing him thus engaged in the duties of the kitchen asked him if his age, and the more serious duties of preaching, might not dispense him from offices so good and humbling for novices. "No, no," he replied, "even in old age a religious ought to remain attached to the Cross of Jesus Christ, in order by his fervour and humility to be a model to the younger ones. If you but knew how much I should like to live buried in one of our convents, as a simple master of novices, labouring to sanctify myself in solitude, and in the fulfilment of all our vows of penance, forming our religious in the love of our holy Order!" In the noviceship houses, and specially in that of Chalais, he delighted in organising expeditions of labourers. They went out into the forests, with which the

[1] Conference on Humility.

mountains there are covered, to collect the dead wood, or to cut down trees for their buildings. The Father, with his tools on his shoulder, walked at the head of the column, and having reached the end of their journey, he would set to work in person, and fiercely attack the old pines of his domain, commanding his little troop as if he had been the general of an army. When they returned home, there was another office to be performed, which was no less sweet to him ; it was that of washing the feet of his tired soldiers, or cleaning their shoes.

One day when he was at Lyons, he begged some members of the Third Order to accompany him on a pilgrimage to Notre Dame de Fourvières. On coming out of the church, a torrent of rain obliged them to take refuge in one of these little shops for pious objects, which are to be found standing, one above the other, all up the hill, and the Father, joking, proposed to hold a chapter of faults, in order to pass the time. When the rain had a little abated, they set out again on their way to the quay of St. Antoine, where he was then lodging. He begged them all to come in, made them sit down, and said to them—"My brethren, if your shoes are in so deplorable a state, it is I who have been the cause, and it is therefore only just that I should repair the mischief." Then arming himself with some brushes and blacking, he knelt before each in turn, and cheerfully discharged the office of their shoeblack.

In 1853 the feast of St. Dominic was celebrated with great solemnity at the convent of Flavigny, in Burgundy. A new chapel was to be blessed there, of which the Father had been the sole architect, and which did more credit to his love of simplicity than to his taste for religious art. Among the numerous guests were their lordships the Bishops of Dijon and Autun, the Count de Montalembert, M. Foisset, and several eminent members of the clergy. The Father was to be seen from early morning sweeping the courts, picking up the dust and straw, dusting the furniture, laying the table, and lending a hand to every little preparation. After the ceremony he was doing the honours of the convent to his illustrious guests, when he perceived in a corner a young and timid ecclesiastic, who seemed to be waiting for something. He addressed him, and found that he had not yet breakfasted, so leaving his guests, he ushered the stranger into the refectory, made him sit down at a table apart, and standing before him with a napkin under his arm, he quietly waited on him during the whole of his repast.

At the end of the Lenten station at Lyons, he wished to go and see the venerable Curé of Ars. He always entertained the greatest sentiment of esteem and respect for priestly sanctity. He particularly admired in the old French clergy *that grand priestly air* which betokened, as he said, the union of two distinct qualities, the elevation of nature and of grace. He often prayed to God to give a saint to France. "My God!" he exclaimed in the pulpit of Notre Dame, "when wilt Thou deign once more to give us saints?" He therefore wished to see the Saint of Ars, to edify himself by his example, and doubtless also to question him as to the future of his Order in France. We shall borrow the account of this visit, which displayed the humility of both these illustrious souls, from the interesting history of the Curé of Ars, by the Abbé Monnin :[1]

"On the 3rd of May, 1845, the Curé of Ars had just finished the devotions of the month of Mary. The crowd of pilgrims were stationed around the church, waiting until the saint should appear, when they saw a modest carriage drive up, containing a priest wrapped in a great black mantle ; soon under the folds of the mantle there appeared a white habit, and every one began to cry out, 'It is the great preacher!' It was thus that our country people were accustomed to designate the orator who was then preaching at Lyons,

[1] Tom. ii. p. 321.

and producing an emotion altogether without precedent in the records of Christian eloquence. It was, in fact, the Père Lacordaire. The next day the inhabitants of Ars were able to contemplate the illustrious Dominican, as he sat listening to the sermon of the Curé of Ars with humble recollection, and in an attitude of respectful attention. Genius forgot itself in the presence of sanctity, appearing under its simplest form. M. Vianney was touched, and said to some one there, ' Do you know the reflection that occurred to me during Père Lacordaire's visit ? What is greatest in intellect has come to abase itself before what is meanest in ignorance—the two extremes have met.'

"Père Lacordaire was much moved by the warm exhortation with which he heard the man of God conjure his parishioners to invoke the Holy Ghost, and draw to themselves the plenitude of His gifts; he added, that he felt happy in being able to say, that had he been called on to treat the same subject, he should have done so, if not in the same terms, at least on the same plan. 'This holy priest and I,' he said, 'do not use the same language, but I am happy in being able to affirm that we feel alike, even if we express ourselves differently.' The orator had heard the saint, but the saint now wished to hear the eloquent religious ; he therefore announced that in the evening, at vespers, 'some one would talk better than he.' Père Lacordaire hesitated, and only consented when he was persuaded that to yield to the desire of the Curé of Ars would be to show him a mark of submission and respect. But he complained of being made to speak instead of listen. 'I came,' he said, 'to ask advice, and to be edified.' He placed himself at the feet of the servant of God with so profound and sincere a humility, that each one of the parishioners shared in the glory which they felt to be thus reflected on their saint.

"' Did you hear,' they said, as they came out of the church, 'did you hear the great preacher, how he put himself under the feet of our Curé ?'

" Every heart was touched as they beheld the most admired Christian orator of our times, with his head bent down, and with an air of profound humility and recollection, following the old man, from whom he had asked perhaps some prophetic word touching the future of that Order which he had restored in France. The holy Curé appreciated the greatness and the faith discernible in this conduct. Tears came into his eyes when, at the earnest entreaty of Père Lacordaire, he was obliged to give him his blessing. The elevation of his ideas, and the melody of his language, had produced the effect of enchantment on the mind and imagination of M. Vianney. ' I shall no longer dare to appear in my pulpit,' he said : ' I feel like the man who, having met the Pope, and made him mount his horse, never afterwards ventured to ride it himself.' As they spoke in his presence of the wonderful effects of the Conferences of Lyons, adding that, nevertheless, there were but few conversions ; ' Listen !' he said. ' it will be an immense result if the preacher has proved to the learned folk who go to hear him, that somebody knows more than they do, and if he convinces all our bright geniuses that they are not quite the cleverest people in the whole world—we must make them admire the beauty of the edifice before inspiring them with the desire to enter.'

" Thus the effect of this memorable visit was complete and reciprocal. The celebrated pilgrim appeared greatly edified by the holiness of the Curé of Ars ; he promised to return, and he kept his word. Without giving any account of the private conversation which he had held with M. Vianney, he acknowledged that he had received great light from him, and the most positive pledges of hope touching the restoration of the Friar-Preachers. He said, on the subject of the advice which he had received from the Curé of Ars, ' Learning creates a capacity in our life, but does not fill it up ; piety illuminates, elevates, and fills it.' "

Such, then, were the virtues of humility, simplicity,

and modesty, in Père Lacordaire. Did they narrow
or abase his character ? Would it be possible, in the
face of such a life, to maintain the incompatibility
of Christian humility with the highest nobility of sentiment ? Or does it not rather remind us of that principle of the divine morality which is expressed with
such rigorous exactitude, " He who humbleth himself
shall be exalted ; he who would be greatest among you,
let him be the servant of all." It was from his close study
and tender love of the Son of God that Père Lacordaire learnt that true elevation of soul of which the
gospel lays down the sublime laws. To us the secret
of his greatness is that of his profound humility. It
is, in fact, humility that sets the soul free, restoring to
her the liberty of her movements towards the Good
and the Beautiful—that is, towards God. The obstacle
to all greatness is Pride ; it is man stopping short in
himself ; held captive there by the pursuit of riches,
power or glory, and seeking in himself the principle of
an elevation as false as it is ephemeral. The honour
of man consists not in commanding, but in serving.
Now it is the virtue of humility that reveals to him
the meaning of this divine philosophy : it is she
who delivers him from the passion of making himself
talked about, and substitutes for it the passion
for doing good, and of rendering justice to all; it
is humility that delivers him from exaggerated attachment to his own opinion, the source of so many
errors, and which crowns him with glory by enveloping
him with obedience. What a difference, merely in a
moral point of view, between the obstinate apostasy of
M. de la Mennais, and the docile submission of Père
Lacordaire ! On the one hand, what a sad sterility ;
on the other, what magnificent fertility ! We will
not inquire where the proud genius of Père Lacordaire
might have led him had it not been for the salutary
chain of obedience ; but there can be no doubt that it
would have been very difficult for him to contain himself within bounds, to stop at the right moment, and to

avoid those shoals which are the ruin of even less impetuous natures. By taking refuge under the hand of
God, and binding his life to Him, he not only enfran-
chised it, and preserved it from the rock on which he
would otherwise have made shipwreck—namely, the
desire of being talked about ; but more than this, he
marked it for ever with the seal of true greatness. He
learnt at the foot of the crucifix how, whilst serving
God, to attain to the noblest of all royalties, empire over
himself, devotion to his brethren, and sanctity. Herein
lies all solid greatness : " To serve God is to reign."
When this royal service of God is united to talent, to
eloquence, to an upright and powerful character, and
to heroic virtue, it imprints on a man's life such a
reflection of divine majesty, that all mere human pre-
eminence is effaced by its splendour. Now the whole
ambition of Père Lacordaire was to serve and obey
God. His whole life was resumed in one word—*duty !*
Duty was to him not that stoical virtue in which there
often enters more pride than true courage ; but it was
the Voice of God, His justice, His truth, His law. He
made his ambition and his virtue to render himself at
all costs the slave of every sacrifice, even to his last
sigh. " I have never looked anywhere save to heaven
to read my duty there," he writes. " Duty is above
all things. No calculation, no fear, no skill, no desire,
ought to prevail over it, and I have long known from
experience that it is the sure way to succeed, even
though appearances may seem to preclude success."[1]

This fidelity to duty inspired him with a great self-
respect. He honoured in himself the gift of God, and
cherished it with scrupulous care. None knew better
than he how to keep his plighted word. None felt a
more instinctive horror of every violation of it. Had
he not passed his word to God, and henceforth would
not the slightest breach of faith have seemed to him a
treason ? Thus his nobility of soul contributed, as well

[1] Unpublished Correspondence.

as his intellectual conviction, to preserve the tranquil
purity of his religious belief. He did not understand
such things in a Christian as seductions of the will, or
weakness and division of heart. From the time that
he began to love God he knew not how to care for
anything else, and his only solicitude was to ascend in
his soul the mysterious degrees of that love. The
unity of his life in this respect was truly admirable.
He had been converted when very young, and no one
is ignorant that the most terrible struggles, the lingering glances cast backward on a world forgotten, yet
still alive, do not belong to the age of generous enthusiasm, but to that colder period when a man turns
back on himself, and begins to get a footing in life.
If Père Lacordaire knew anything of these later combats, they at least left no traces behind them, and
those who enjoyed his closest confidence can only
testify to the fact of his perfect indifference to the
most seductive fascinations, his constant ardour to
keep his soul pure from every stain, and his care to
render it more and more worthy of the Divine caresses.
He hardly understood in others those combats which
are, unhappily, so often followed by sad defeats. He
wrote thus to a young friend: "I am always astonished at the empire which the sight of external
beauty exercises over you, and at the little power you
possess of shutting your eyes. I pity your weakness,
and wonder at it, as at a phenomenon of which I do
not possess the secret. Never, since I have known
Jesus Christ, has anything appeared to me beautiful
enough to be beheld with desire. . . . . It is so contemptible a thing to a soul that has once seen and
enjoyed God !"[1]

He preserved the same fidelity through life to the
idea and opinions which made up his political faith.
He respected them in himself as a part of the Divine
Truth, and would no more have pardoned himself an
infidelity in this respect than he would have done in

[1] "Letters to Young Men," p. 44.

24

regard of religious truth. His religious and political creed was all of a piece, and the relinquishment of any principle of conduct, once admitted as such, was as incomprehensible to him as the abandonment of some truth of a higher order. "We must have convictions," he said; "we must reflect long before adhering to them; and once having adopted them, we must never change them." With him this fidelity to his *standard* was a sort of religion. He attached the honour of his life to it. "I hold above everything," he writes, "to integrity of character. The more I see men fail in this, and at the same time fail in the religion which they represent, the more I am determined, by the grace of Him who holds all hearts in His hand, to keep myself pure from anything which may compromise or weaken my honour as a Christian. Were there but one soul in the world that took any notice of my soul, it would be my duty not to grieve that soul; but since it has providentially fallen out that I am linked to many souls, who look to me for strength and consolation, there is nothing I ought not to do in order to spare them the weakness and bitterness of doubt."[1]

If this constancy of character was easy to him, we must remember that it was thanks to the precautions he had early taken to put himself beyond the reach of all temptations of ambition, or excesses of party spirit. Those sudden flights into retirement, that love of solitude which he so cherished, and those heroic aspirations after poverty and renunciation, contributed more than would be at first believed to the rare firmness of his character. He was truly *the great heart in a little house:* but to keep himself at this height he had to place his independence under the protection of the cloister, to forget himself, and to live with his eye constantly fixed on God and on duty.

This fidelity to duty was not the least admirable of the lesser details of his life. It is a virtue which is often more difficult than obedience to greater obliga-

[1] Correspondence with Madame Swetchine, p. 512.

tions; for the latter are, in the first place, rarer and more public, and carry with them a greater actual help; whereas the others occur every moment, are at the mercy of varying tempers and circumstances, and most often have none but God for their Witness and their Judge. Hence it is that the *prestige* of greatness will hardly ever bear the searching look which penetrates into its most private moments. But with Père Lacordaire it was quite otherwise; the nearer you saw him, the more you admired and venerated him. Nothing was more strictly regulated than the employment of his time. To accomplish our day's work (to use his own expression), to wear out one's groove, to get through one's appointed task, this was the virtue of every moment which he most frequently recommended to others, and most faithfully accomplished himself. Everything was done in its accustomed time and manner. He never put off till to-morrow what might be done to-day. Every morning at ten o'clock he sat down to his correspondence, and at the end of the two hours, which he generally gave to this duty, the letters were to be seen piled up at the corner of his table, folded and sealed with an invariable uniformity. Nothing ever tempted him to neglect this daily task. I have seen him bowed down by sickness, with his countenance pale and haggard, decline a walk which was proposed to him on a beautiful autumn morning in Provence, under the sun which so refreshed and invigorated him, and reply simply: "I cannot; it is my time for letter-writing." It was the voice of duty. At two o'clock his door was open to visitors, many of whom were often attracted rather by curiosity than necessity. Always eager to render any service to others, willingly entering into the explanations or discussions which were proposed to him by so many young men, he nevertheless discouraged the idle and indiscreet by observing an imperturbable silence. As soon as the hour had struck, he broke up the party, and took leave of his guests, unless in case of very

urgent affairs ; the *duty* had been accomplished. The
habit of thus regulating his least actions gave him time
for everything.   Thus, in spite of the accumulation of
business with which he was sometimes overwhelmed,
he was never seen hurried, slovenly, or impatient ; his
exactness, assisted by a prodigious activity, was sufficient for everything.   Even when pressed by an
unusual amount of work, nothing was ever changed in
his daily life.   He did not take any extra time from
his sleep or from any religious exercise ; but within
his usual time he would get through a task thrice as
heavy as his ordinary one.   Then he would appear at
the hour of recreation with a livelier colour, a brighter
eye, a more frank and expansive smile, a greater
vivacity in his words, like a man who, after a severe
tension of the brain, feels the need of unbending his
mind by diversion.

When he came home from a journey he generally
found on his table an enormous packet of letters in
arrears.   These were his first care.   Before thinking
of the rest which he so greatly needed he would sit
down to his desk, and without stopping, write often
very long letters in a fine and close handwriting, without erasure ; and the next day the packet of letters
had disappeared, and everything went on with its
usual regularity.   The body had to manage as it could
under this slavery to duty at the appointed hour.   He
took no heed of it ; it was a dumb and docile slave,
which he had taught to accomplish its task without
troubling himself much about its claims.   Thus, when
this poor slave, by dint of over-work, sank on the
arena before its time, like a horse under its rider, he
expressed his surprise, not understanding how such a
thing could be, and remarking with astonishment that
it was the first time his body had ever refused to obey
him.   " Let us crucify ourselves to our pen !" he wrote
to Ozanam ; who replied to him later : " I am killing
myself, I know ; but such is the Will of God."   Both
of them, like invincible warriors, died sword in hand,

truly *crucified to their pen.* When it dropped from the dying hand of Père Lacordaire, his mind, still vigorous, found strength to dictate those immortal pages, the offspring of a thought of duty which had been inspired by his friend, M. de Montalembert, who has thus acquired his right to a gratitude impossible ever to be discharged.[1]

Every one of his actions was in the same way regulated by duty, and subjected to the law of a conscience, more severe to itself than to others. Far from taking occasion of his rank as superior to grant himself any degree of independence, he made it his uniform practice to restrict himself within the limits which he allowed to his brethren. Duty was always the reason put forward for refusing the visits and journeys which he was continually urged by his friends to make. "It would be very pleasant to me," he writes, "to pay you another visit. The earnestness with which you press it would not be necessary in order to induce me to consent, were I really at liberty to do so. But although superior, I feel myself bound to do nothing which I would not permit to my brethren ; and as I forbid them to undertake any journey, unless in case of necessity, I am equally obliged to forbid it to myself. Henceforth all my actions must be regulated by duty. What you say of the use I might possibly be to some souls certainly touches me, and I would willingly undertake a long journey on such a motive if grave reasons did not detain me where I am. We cannot do everything here below ; we must choose the good that Providence sends us, and leave to others the happiness of accomplishing that which is prepared for them. Without this resignation to the Will of God, one runs the risk of failing in everything by dint of seeking to embrace too much. I am constantly obliged to leave undone

---

[1] The Abbé Perreyve, in bequeathing the Memoirs of Père Lacordaire to M. de Montalembert, only accomplished what was most suitably and justly his due.

some possible good, in order not to sacrifice another.
They say to me sometimes, ' Take your stick, and go
straight on, preaching to the right and left, until you
fall exhausted on the road.' That would be all very
well ; but God has given me another work to do,
which must be accomplished, and after that we shall
see what He may next demand."[1]

The voice of friendship, at other times so powerful
over his exquisitely tender soul, was of no force at all
against the claims of duty, and never shook the recti-
tude of his judgment or the inflexibility of his will.
What in general most injures high perfection of character is weakness of the heart. We fear to give pain,
and friendship is ingenious in discovering a thousand
motives for yielding to its advice. Then the character
softens, and the will becoming enervated, divides its
sovereignty, and too often ends by abdicating in
favour of feeling, which reigns as sole master. Or, it
may be, if there is not much heart, and strength of
will alone predominates, that the character becomes
stamped with a certain repulsive rigour. It is very
rarely that the two qualities of a tender heart and a
firm reason are found in such perfect equilibrium as in
Père Lacordaire ; like that Providence in which force
is to be found united to sweetness, he was *fortiter sed
suaviter*, " strong as the diamond, more tender than a
mother." He knew all the rights and the tenderness
of friendship ; no one ever more powerfully felt its
charm, but it was never to the prejudice of duty.
Friendship had its appointed times, limits, and rights
as exactly measured as all the rest, and it was never
allowed to overpass them. He did not bend his rule
or his time to his inclinations ; he refused every pleasure which would have gratified his heart at the expense of duty, and exacted the same sacrifice, and the
same empire over feeling, from his intimate friends.
One day a religious, for whom he felt a special affection, asked leave to go out of his way on a journey in

[1] Unpublished Correspondence.

order to visit his father and mother, whom he had not
seen for a long time. The Father refused. When he
saw this religious some day afterwards, " Well," he
said to him, " are you very angry with me ?" " My
Father," replied the religious, " I have suffered as
much from the want of feeling which I seemed to see
in you, as from the pleasure which you denied me."
" My poor child !" said the Father, with tears in his
eyes, as he pressed him to his heart, " I have suffered
from it more than you ; but it would have been a violation of the rule, and I was bound to obey my conscience rather than my heart. It is a hard duty,
against which my nature often revolts. But reason
must absolutely be the master. Without invariable
and inflexible rules, believe me, my dear friend, we
should fast sink into deplorable relaxation. Let us
from the first establish amongst us strong and generous habits of severity to ourselves, barriers that are
never to be broken through, even at the risk of making
flesh and blood cry out sometimes ; later on such a
work would be impossible, and the evil would then be
past remedy."

The effect of such virtue on those who witnessed it
may easily be believed. No one could long enjoy
the intimacy of Père Lacordaire without feeling the
salutary influence of a soul so perfectly well balanced in
all its faculties, so great, and so strongly tempered
throughout. Many of those who came to seek admission into his religious family were attracted in the
first instance by the splendour of his talents and the
popularity of his name. But when they more closely
studied the man whom they had at first only beheld
surrounded by the halo of his glory ; when they had
witnessed the equality and supereminent greatness
of his whole life ; when they beheld that power of the
will which governed every act without injury to tenderness, that constant generosity which made heroism
habitual to him, that insatiable thirst for the hardest
sacrifices, that passionate love for the Son of God on

His Cross, that simplicity and modesty in the most sublime outbursts of virtue, that type, in short of the true religious, a type which does not require that a man should grow *less*, but which rather perfects and elevates him high above all human glory — then the *prestige* of his genius faded away from their eyes before the yet greater charm of his virtue, and they felt disposed to imitate and to love, where at first they had only thought of admiring. Whatever care he took to conceal himself, to fly from the appearance of sanctity, he could not succeed in effacing the splendour of virtue from his lofty brow, or obliterating the gracious majesty which shone forth from his person, and which no one could approach without a sentiment of respect, which I have never seen any one excite in an equal degree.

Genius alone has no power to cast forth so bright a ray. Something more heavenly is needed, the reflection of God in the soul, the beauty of Christ on the human brow. But when coming down from heaven to form that sacred alliance, God finds an abode that is almost worthy to receive Him, a soul more closely formed after His image, a mind vast enough to comprehend Him, and a heart that is vaster still, ready to follow and to love Him, when, in short, He finds *a great man*, He lifts him to unmeasurable heights, and from that ineffable union of genius and sanctity He produces a superhuman splendour, before which all men bow, and which they love to contemplate as the highest ideal of greatness.

CHAPTER XVI.

FTER having spoken of Père Lacordaire as a priest and a religious, we should wish, in order to complete this part of our subject, to examine the influence on souls which he exerted as a priest and a religious.; in other words, to study him in the character of a *Spiritual Director*. Did the good which he effected in this respect bear any proportion to the eminence of his sanctity, and the heroism of his love of God ? We must acknowledge that the number of those who knew Père Lacordaire as a holy priest and an austere religious, devoured by the love of Jesus Christ, and consequently of those who were capable of receiving any powerful direction from him, was, comparatively speaking, limited. Certainly, if we consider the influence which he exercised, and will long continue to exercise by the power of his faith and the extent of his genius, by that assemblage of qualities which made him the most popular priest, and the most admired orator of his time, we cannot say enough of the immense good which he daily produced. Without speaking of his works, by which he continues to survive himself, and the ever-increasing authority of his character, his name, and his principles (all of them things as generally known and revered as his intimate intercourse with God remained unguessed), the mere book of his Conferences will long remain one of the most widely-spread manuals of Christian apology, and one which has been most fruitful in effecting serious conversions to the Catholic faith. The consoling and multiplied proofs of this which we continually receive enable us to judge of the yet greater number that are probably unknown to us. The period in which the influence of Père Lacordaire's life and works will have its full development is yet in its early days. As to his influence as a director of souls, it was, however, as we have said, much less extensive. A considerable number of young men, a few ladies of the world, some priests who sought his advice, and some religious who had given him their complete confidence, made up the little flock who sought and shared his pastoral care. Nor is this astonishing. In the first place, direction, which presupposes the continuous and daily knowledge of the actions, the state, and the habits of a soul, requires, for its extensive exercise, sedentary habits, and a fixed residence. An apostle can hardly be a pastor, and Père Lacordaire had in a special way received the apostolic mission. His life, with the exception of his last years, which he spent at Sorèze, was passed in continual journeys, which were difficult to reconcile with the assiduous cares of regular direction. And, besides this, there was another reason which made him unknown to almost all the world as a director, and that was his modesty. The care he always took to conceal the secret of his austerities and his piety permitted only a very small number to raise the veil under which he hid his sublime virtues. Many even of those who knew him the longest, or who saw him most frequently, never dreamt, and never dared to dream, of asking him to guide their souls. Perhaps they regretted it when it was too late. One of his oldest friends writes to us: " If we men of the world had asked spiritual advice from him, he would have given it to us with all his heart. But, alas! we did not ask it of him, and you know that he was not one to offer it of himself. It was entirely our fault, but so it was."

And further, it must be said that those who guessed him aright, and to whom he really opened himself, had not all the courage to follow his direction. It needed the exercise of a generous and intrepid will, a soul ready for every sacrifice, to remain faithful to his severe discipline. He knew no other road by which to lead others to God than that which he travelled himself; it was always the Cross, the strong and generous love of Calvary. He constantly repeated, "The way to arrive at the pure and disinterested love of God is that which our Lord traced out to us when going from the Garden of Olives to the Prætorium, and from the Prætorium to Calvary; it was love that traced the route, and love well knew the road which leads to itself."[1] And again: "We have two great vices to combat, pride and voluptuousness; and two great virtues to acquire, humility and penance." He never wandered from this theme. You went to him therefore with the certainty beforehand of what he would say, do, and command. You had in his hands to be a victim always ready for the holocaust. In this war without truce and without mercy, many lost courage and went away, saying with the pusillanimous disciples, "*This word is hard, who can bear it?* He has a language and laws beyond our strength."

He was more free and expansive with young men, finding among them more ardour and inclination to sacrifice; it was among their ranks that he found his most numerous disciples, and it was specially with them that he learned what he called *the true happiness of the priest*, the happiness of attaching them to himself by the tie of supernatural affection, in order

---

[1] "Letters to Young Men," p. 137.

afterwards to give them to God. His first title to their confidence was the friendship that he bore them; it was the best pledge of the success of his ministry among them. We can only do good to souls in proportion as we love them. Jesus Christ died out of love for us, and every good priest knows that noble passion of zeal which made St. Paul say : " I would give my very self for your salvation."

Père Lacordaire was born to be the chosen apostle of youth ; he took it as his peculiar inheritance. God had placed in his heart, and on his lips, the special gifts which have an irresistible charm for young persons, eloquence and virtue; the fire of charity mingled with the brilliancy of genius ; all the attractions of religion united to the moving accents that spoke of honour, poetry, and friendship. Thus, when he poured out over these beloved souls the treasures of his affection, it was impossible to resist him ; they acknowledged themselves vanquished, mingled their tears of repentance with those of joy which were shed by their father and their friend, and declared themselves ready for anything that would preserve that blessed peace which they had retained, and which surpasses all human happiness. The outpourings of his soul to his religious children can never be put into words. Besides the difficulty of translating into cold and colourless language those holy transports of his heart, we feel that there would be a sort of profanation in the attempt to reveal such sacred confidences. We will content ourselves with quoting one beautiful page, in which the elevation and the delicacy both of form and feeling allows us to guess at the richness and depth of his loving soul. He was writing to a young friend who had once more fallen into the darkness of doubt, after having for a moment laid hold of the light of faith.[1]

[1] The affectionate tone of this letter in the original escapes a translation, from the impossibility of rendering into English the significance of the French *tutoiement.*

"Your future, my dear friend, is hidden from me; but if it depended on my prayers and tears, the light which illumined you for a passing moment should once more appear on your brow. Do not despair of yourself! Truth may always be regained, however far we may have wandered away from it. Perhaps if I have yet much to suffer in this world, you may be reserved for one of those moments when a man, after thinking that he has done with joy for ever, finds joys granted him by God, so great that he feels as if he had never been really happy before. I shall still hope therefore some day to see you a believer, and to welcome you with double joy as a friend and a religious. Whilst waiting for this immense happiness, I shall continue to carry you in my heart as some dear wounded child, as the last fruit of my love on earth. I am too old now, in age if not in heart, to win the affections of those younger than myself; and destined as I am henceforth to cast my glances backwards, I leave you on the threshold of the past; you will be the first whom my eyes will meet there, as they look behind. And you, on your part, do not forget me! When you are sad, and out of heart with the world, cast a look towards the window of my cell, and think of the friend who so tenderly loved you! Adieu."[1]

How could any one resist appeals like these, which earned him the right to oblige those whom he addressed in such tender language to listen to him afterwards, when he spoke with the authority of a priest, thus enabling him by main force to rescue the victim from the deadly snares of evil! In a character at once so strong and so gentle friendship ran no risk of degenerating into what was mawkish and puerile; strength always prevailed over tenderness; the heart was only appealed to for the sake of the soul, and the *man* never made the *priest* forgotten for a moment. He made large use of the privilege of frankness, which is claimed by affection, and availed himself of

[1] "Letters to Young Men," p. 95.

the freedom which quickly sprang up between young hearts and himself to make his penitents hear the plainest and severest truths. He specially excelled in overcoming all pride and love of self, of family, or of fortune, the root of so many evils in rich and idle youths. He laid bare before their eyes their native misery, their incapacity, and their faults, with the crushing logic of a Pascal, and placed at their service a vocabulary of the severest and most humiliating epithets. Something of this, though in a somewhat softened style, found its way into his letters. He wrote thus to one of his penitents :

"You are vain, my dear friend. You like show ; you like your horse and your groom. You wish to be thought a very fine young fellow, and to be noticed. You are proud of your high birth : in short, you are a little animal, filled with a crowd of different sorts of pride, which are so natural to you that perhaps you do not even remark them. No one, therefore, has more need than you of humbling himself, and of being humbled. You see how I speak to you. But it is because I love you, and would gladly suffer much could I inspire you with the love of God."[1]

To the same friend he writes :—"You are luke-warm and languid in God's service. You have no regular habits. You live on the impulse of the moment, going to confession and Communion now and then, to Mass on Sundays, keeping the abstinence days of the Church, but not loving Jesus Christ ten-derly, or being ready every moment to suffer in your body pain or shame for Him, to be scourged and crucified for Him, as He was for you. . . . . And what is the result ? A void ! You are wandering in a dark and chilly tomb, haunted by frightful appari-tions. . . . . All this will only cease by your giving yourself in earnest to God."

Nor did he less excel in overcoming the senses than in mortifying the inflation of pride. We have

[1] " Letters to Young Men," p. 372.

seen in what way he understood the practice of penance for himself; he made use of the same means in his treatment of others. It was in his opinion a universal and infallible remedy. He did not believe that a young man could long preserve or recover innocence without making his flesh pay the debts of the flesh, without often chastising the real culprit, and maintaining the sovereignty of the spirit over the body by frequent acts of repression and salutary justice. "A young man," he said, "must feel the sting of pain, if he would not feel the sting of pleasure." If he met with any soul capable of understanding this language, he answered for his salvation and perseverance. Thus, among his penitents, this flagellation of the body, generally regarded as an exceptional kind of heroism in the lives of the saints, became an ordinary habit of life. He would allow of no practices likely to diminish the strength of the body, and never prescribed austerities injurious to health; but for all the rest (and the field was still ample), he showed a pitiless energy. They soon became used to these practices, which at first appeared so strange to them, and which, without losing anything of their efficacious power, were no longer surrounded with that vague unknown terror, which belongs less to their nature than to the religious enervation of our age. In this point of view, Père Lacordaire did not belong to his century. He had no confidence in those methods of treatment which profess to cure youth of the disordered love of pleasure by the external application of purely spiritual remedies, which are excellent in themselves, but are generally powerless, because they do not touch the root of the evil. When a young man, accustomed to the periodical avowal of his faults, has listened to the mild homily of the priest, and accomplished his yet milder penance, will his life have received any moral shock powerful enough to strengthen him for the most difficult and laborious of victories? Is it not rather to be feared that the routine of this repeated plastering of conscience, as easy as it is inefficacious, joined to the forgetfulness of the law of bodily penance, produces nothing but half-made Catholics, of a lame and indolent piety, always ready to come to a compromise with the world and with nature, studious of appearances, and wanting courage to put the axe to the root of the tree, adorning the outside of the cup, and neglecting to cleanse it within ?

Père Lacordaire had no settled plan for effecting a reaction against this system; he simply followed another which was more in harmony with his own principles, and his own instincts of piety, and which proved also more fruitful in its results. He belonged to that race of Catholics, so rare in our age, who take the gospel literally, and who learn it from the gospel itself, and not from that multitude of little books, which abound nowadays, of doubtful orthodoxy and sickly sentimentality, without sap, without force, without vitality ; in short, to use the happy expression of a young priest, his disciple and his friend, he was a *Christian* of the olden time, and a man of to-day.[1] How many young men owed their salvation to this skilful physician ! How many there were who, after dragging themselves along for years, weary and wounded in the unequal struggles between their unvanquished flesh and their feeble faith, arose under his manly hand, and once more seized the reins and recovered their peace, and "that hue of beauty which is derived from the union of youth and penance !"   It has fallen to my lot to become acquainted with several of the young penitents directed by Père Lacordaire.   And I feel bound to bear witness that nearly all have declared themselves to owe their salvation to his care, and consider themselves indebted for the recovery of their virtue to his burning appeals to the Cross of Jesus Christ, and his courage in applying fire and steel to their open wounds.

[1] The Abbé Perreyve.

He had also other resources for strengthening them in the practice of good. He appealed to all that is generous in the heart of youth; he often spoke to them of honour, friendship, self-respect, and magnanimity, and whilst showing them that virtue alone crowns and keeps alive these noble qualities, he persuaded them to become humble servants of God in order to be *true men*, to love the Church, in order that they might thereby the better serve their country, to preserve in themselves the dignity of human nature, because it has been bought at the price of the Blood of Jesus Christ; in a word, "to be of the number of those who maintain here below the esteem of God and man, which were united in order to save the world."[1]

We shall simply relate here the story of one of these conversions, in order to show how this true priest gained to Jesus Christ the souls of these young disciples who were so dear to him.

In the winter of 1854, a young man was called by his affairs to Paris. He was twenty-four years of age, and having by his intelligence become the head of an important commercial business, he saw every road to happiness and fortune open before him, and like so many others threw himself eagerly into the pursuits of all the enchanting and intoxicating pleasures of the world. Of a cultivated mind, with a taste for the beautiful, a generous heart, and great powers of conversation, much sought after, and surrounded by friends, joys flowed in upon him from all sides, and spared him the trouble of stooping in order to gather them up. Nevertheless this sort of life at length began to weary him; his lofty soul quickly sounded all these splendid miseries to their depths; a shade of melancholy clouded his most brilliant days, and began to disenchant him of his sweet illusions. Often in the midst of songs and feasting he found himself thinking of death, and of the poor who had no bread

---

[1] Discourse at St. Roch.

to eat, and asked himself sadly if this were the ideal
of which he had dreamed. Had his life been given
him that he should tear it into fragments, and fling it
away upon all these hungry monsters that preyed
upon it, and left him nothing but emptiness and
weariness? These were generous sentiments, noble
instincts of a Christian soul, which sufficed to show
him the gulf on the brink of which he stood, and the
way to escape, but which were not enough to give
him the strength requisite to follow it. He was
lingering in the midst of this sad struggle, on those
bloody confines where good and evil dispute for the
mastery of the heart of a youth of twenty, when one
day an idea seized him in the midst of the street;
he stopped a cab, and told the driver to take him at
once to the old Convent of the Carmes, in the Rue de
Vaugirard. This was the residence of Père Lacordaire,
whose name had flashed like lightning across his
mind; he trusted him, and resolved to have a word
with one whom he had heard spoken of as the great
friend of young men, on the strange grief that devoured him. He arrived at the Convent; it was the
hour when Père Lacordaire received visitors, and he
was introduced. What a spectacle was there! what
a contrast with his own life and luxurious habits!
Four bare whitewashed walls, a crucifix, a table, and
a few chairs; a plank, supported on wooden tressels,
with some white woollen coverings—such was the
bed and furniture, and such the cell of the great
orator, whose words held captive the ardent youth of
Paris. Five or six young men were seated around
the father, discoursing familiarly with him on the
subject of magnetism. "Sit down," said Père Lacordaire, "I shall be at your service in a minute, and we
will then become better acquainted." The affability
and simplicity of the Christian Socrates had already
touched his visitor more than an eloquent sermon
would have done. Three o'clock soon struck. It
was the hour when the time for receiving visits ex-

pired. The Father rose, and dismissed his guests with perfect kindness, and retaining the last comer, who was about to withdraw with the rest, he said to him : " No, no, *you* have something to say to me, come and sit down close to me." He had doubtless guessed the kind of service expected from him, and recognised on his countenance the signs of one *conquered by God.*[1] " My dear friend," he said, " what are you doing in Paris ? or rather, what are you doing in the world, and what do you intend to do there for the future ?" This one word broke the ice, and opened the whole question. The young man, deeply moved, felt himself able to open his soul as to a father, and gave him an account of his entire life, of all his faults, his struggles, and his aspirations after a better future. The father listened to him with marked kindness, from time to time raising to the crucifix his large eyes, moistened with tears. When he had finished, "I see," he said, "that you have within you either the soul of a ruffian or the soul of a saint. You wish to be a saint, do you not ? Well, then, listen to me. Leave Paris and go to Flavigny ; it is one of our houses, situated on a retired mountain in Burgundy. There in solitude, face to face with God and yourself, you will ask yourself what use you have hitherto made of the time which God has given for you to learn to love Him, and how you must henceforth dispose of your life. Our age is perishing because no one reflects. Were you only to give these eight days out of your whole life to serious meditation, you might die content, for you would have done the act of a reasonable man and a Christian. Adieu, my dear friend, or rather, *au revoir*, for I feel confident that you will one day call me your Father, and that you will indeed be my child." The young man

[1] " When a man, and particularly a young man, addresses me for the first time, I feel that he is *a conquest of God*, I recognise the unction of the Christian in his features, his voice, and his thoughts, and I have only been thus bold with you, because I have thus recognised you also."—*Letters to Young Men*, p. 90.

25—2

accordingly set out for Flavigny, but he had hardly
arrived there when a member of his family, terrified
at the thought of this eight days' retreat among the
friars, came to find him out, and persuaded him to
return to the world, and there think over his plan
more at leisure.   He remained thus for two years—
years of continual conflict between generous desires
and a feeble will.   One day he received a note from
Père Lacordaire, asking a service of him.   He arrived
at the time and place appointed.   Père Lacordaire
thanked him for his punctuality, and without saying
anything of the service he had requested of him,
began to walk up and down the room with a sad and
preoccupied air.   After a somewhat long silence he
stopped before the young man, and, looking him full
in the face, exclaimed, " How long are you going to
struggle against God ?   What have you done with
your vocation ?   Ah, how I pity you !   You must be
suffering very much, for one cannot refuse the sacred
debt of love to Infinite Love at a small cost.   What
is it that holds you back ?   Your family ?   but your
family are Christians, and their tears should no more
stop you than the tears of His Mother prevented Jesus
Christ from ascending Calvary.   Is it your friends ?
but you will not lose them ; you will find them all
again, for the Blood of Jesus Christ does not extinguish friendship, it only purifies by transfiguring it.
What then is the obstacle ?   Nothing, I fear, but the
cowardice and weakness of your own heart, the ignorance of what awaits you in this sacrifice ?"   He
paused, then with still greater animation he continued : " Would you know what God demands of
you ?   Would you know what that religious life to
which He calls you really is ?   It was for this that I
sent for you here ; tell me, do you desire this ?"
" Yes, Father, I do desire it !"   " Well, then, in the
name of Jesus Christ, my child, *on your knees !*"   " On
my knees, Father ?" replied the young man in consternation, unable to guess how this strange scene

was going to end. "Yes; on your knees! prepare yourself to suffer for the salvation of your soul, and for the sake of God!" So saying, he took in his hand a discipline of leathern thongs, and coming up to the poor victim who knelt there amazed and trembling, he began to strike without pity on his bare shoulders. His pride was vanquished, the flesh was mastered, and the will set at liberty; and the youth who a moment before, at the first touch of the scourge, felt ready to rise with wrath and shame on his brow, now humbled under what he acknowledged to be the Hand of God, gave thanks with tears in his eyes, and blessed his benefactor, and afterwards declared that this hour had been the most sacred in his whole life, inasmuch as it had decided his vocation and triumphed over his weakness. " Never," he himself protested, " had I felt before such contrition for my sins, never had I seen more clearly what God demanded of me, or felt more courage to embrace it." The Father clasped him in his arms, and spoke to him for an hour of the love of Jesus Crucified with extraordinary fervour. A few weeks from that time he was a religious. He took pleasure afterwards in declaring that he owed to that hour of sublime penance the power of breaking the links which bound him to the world, and the blessing of having never known throughout his religious career a single moment of doubt or regret.

This, then, was the manner in which Père Lacordaire placed the energy of his faith and the ardour of his charity at the service of hesitating hearts. We shall not dilate further on the advantage of his method of spiritual direction for the young. The publication by the Abbé Perreyve of the letters addressed by the ardent apostle to many of his disciples sufficiently reveals the affection he bore them, the wise advice with which he pursued them in their worldly course, and how constantly he brought them back to the ideas of humility, penance, the strict observance of a moderate rule, the avoidance of dangerous occasions, and the frequent avowal of their faults.

His method with the pious ladies whom he directed is less generally known. The two correspondences already published give no information on this head; neither Madame Swetchine nor the Countess de la Tour du Pin were his penitents; they were rather wise friends, double his age, on whose advice he chose to depend. His real letters of direction, should they ever be given to the public, would serve to complete our knowledge of his deep and tender piety, and those lofty views which were joined in him to such a rare practical spirit of detail in the guidance of souls. We must content ourselves here with a few extracts from this religious correspondence, which certainly shed a beautiful light on that private side of his character which we are here engaged in studying.

A lady, still young, begged his assistance in regulating her life so as to set it free from worldly engagements. He took her by the generous side of her nature, and hastened to dig out the solid foundations of the spiritual edifice in her soul, by establishing there a faith firm and ready for any sacrifice. " I rejoice to see," he wrote to her, " that you have not waited for the decline of life in order to abandon the love of the world and those vain frivolities which keep it in a state of perpetual childhood. There was reason to fear lest hard trials and severe heart wounds might have been needed to bring you to God, because your nature is deep and affectionate, and the more powerful the sea, the more need it has of rocks and shoals to break its waves. God has willed that it should be otherwise, and this is a great blessing. For you bring Him a soul still young, still susceptible of illusions, not yet rifled and faded. You know that Jesus Christ Himself died in the flower of His age.

" You could not do better than to begin by choosing a rule of life, and giving yourself time for serious study. Ignorance is one of the great enemies of the soul. How can we believe anything if we know nothing? How can we love if we have never seen? Daily reading feeds the mind, disgusts it with trifles, and forms within it an interior sap which nourishes the whole being. Your faith requires to be increased; for faith is the very principle of the spiritual life, since in this world, where we do not see God, we have no other way of knowing Him except by acquainting ourselves with what He has told us of Himself. Now, although it is true that you possess the Christian faith, you are, nevertheless, far from believing fully and ardently. If one drop of the faith of the saints were to fall on you, you would not be able to find tears enough with which to weep over your cowardly, self-indulgent, insignificant life, so full of vanity and the gratification of the senses. How many Christians *think* they believe, because they admit that there is a God in three Persons, that man is corrupt, that a Divine Person became Incarnate to enlighten and redeem us, that He died for us, and that we shall one day be judged according to our conformity to the life and death of Jesus Christ! They admit the truth of all this, I know; but these ideas merely lie on the surface of their minds; they believe, because they are afraid of hell, and want to make sure of not going there; they put their faith into their understanding just as we put a bit into a horse's mouth. But they do not believe in such a way as to make their faith and their understanding one and the same thing. There are certain moments with them when it is agreed upon to put faith into a corner of their brains; and there are others when they leave it *shut up in the pound*, in order that they may laugh and amuse themselves. But the true Christian, even whilst amusing himself, always has his faith present to his mind; he is still with Jesus Christ, who is like a part of himself, that never quits him. In a word, faith should become love or charity, and charity should kindle faith. The best means for arriving at this is *penance*, a thing which

most men love and understand even less than they do
faith."[1]

Penance! this was the subject to which he always
returned—of which he always spoke in his loftiest and
most eloquent language—because there was none more
familiar to his lips. "You ought not," he says, "to
regret the sufferings which, by separating you from
many sweet and pleasant things, have allowed your
heart to rise in earnest towards God. Be assured of
this, nothing is so incompatible with the enjoyment of
God as the enjoyment of worldly happiness. The
more I study happy people the more I feel terrified at
their incapacity for divine things that is, with some
few exceptions. And even what we take for exceptions may probably only seem such from our ignorance of the real state of the heart. Suffering has a
thousand unknown doors by which to enter, besides those grand ones which are seen by all the
world. It makes itself many a secret way, hidden
perhaps by flowers, and travels fast and far; for it is
the most active of God's messengers. It carries the
Cross of Jesus Christ; and humanity is so shaped as
to allow of that burden passing everywhere. Do not
complain, then, of the secret sufferings to which your
health condemns you; it is one of the conditions of
your moral and intellectual nature. What would you
have been without those sufferings?—a little spoilt
child, vain, capricious, pouring herself out over a
trinket or a pleasure, like so many other women of
your age and rank whom you see around you. Whoever attains to the knowledge and love of God has
nothing to desire and nothing to regret; he has
received the highest of all gifts, which ought to make
us forget all besides."

The dearer any soul was to him, the more he took
pleasure in humbling it and crushing its pride. The
distinctions of birth and rank, far from deterring him
from acting thus, only made him speak with greater

[1] Unpublished Letters.

firmness and severity. Writing to a lady of rank who had not yet succeeded in curing herself of a touch of haughtiness to her inferiors, he says : " I wish I could oblige you every day to obey without a word some peevish, *exigeante,* vulgar little woman; your pride would be well paid off! Be sure that you thoroughly deserve it, and act as if it were really the case."

In spite of his own special attraction to bodily austerities, he observed the utmost moderation when prescribing them to women, only allowing them such privations as suited their kind of piety and their physical strength, and that with extreme reserve. But the faults of the soul gained nothing by this greater indulgence to the body, and what, out of prudence, he dared not do in one way, he knew how to make up for in another. He accustomed his penitents to practices most humiliating to their self-love, making them sometimes ask pardon of their inferiors when they had been unjust to them, and requiring them to do this on their knees, if he knew that such an act of abasement were likely to be rightly understood on both sides, and received in the same Christian spirit as that which inspired it. " I am very glad," he writes, " that you begin to see in your housekeeper and your maid, sisters whom you ought to love and respect, by edifying them, and being edified by them. You cannot abase your pride too much, and that is only done by real practices of humility, by making oneself little, not only before God, which is natural enough, but also before men, our equals, and, above all, before our inferiors. A pious servant ought to be almost an object of worship to you, without, however, fostering her pride, or taking her out of her proper station. This was the reason why Jesus Christ washed the feet of His disciples ; He wished by this act to teach us to humble ourselves to our inferiors, and for God's sake to render them the lowliest offices. Often in spirit place yourself at the feet of the servants of your household,

... ... also sometimes, if you can do it ... ... We must always bear in mind the ... of others."

... ... in his hands to lay aside worldly ... regarding the distinctions of rank and ... ... to attain the holy equality of the ... ... and the humble simplicity of the gospel. ... ... that a Christian lady should expect ... ... as though she were a Roman ... and that she should ill-treat her servants, as ... pagan ladies did their slaves. He taught his ... ... to do without a multitude of those superfluities which have been introduced by our modern ... of luxury and to perform for themselves a number of services which, without appearing extraordinary or meeting the just requirements of social ... ... much more their patience, and are an excellent example in a family.

... traced out for them a rule of life, and if he had ... ... a lady who was mistress of her own time and fortune, would descend to the smallest details, showing himself severe in the matter of all unnecessary expenses, and dividing her day between the duties of her state, works of charity, and pious reading. "I am ... ," he writes, "that you begin to relish the 'Lives of the Saints.' They were the really great men of the human race, the loving hearts, *par excellence;* all our romances are cold in comparison with them. One surprising thing which strikes us in reading their lives is the prodigious variety that we find there, in spite of the general resemblance of ideas and sentiments. They are the *Thousand and One Nights* of Truth. But I am afraid you have only a few detached lives, or only such collections as that of Godescard, which contain nothing but abridgments which disgust by their dryness. The 'Lives of the Fathers of the Desert' by Arnauld D'Andilly, in seven or eight volumes, are very good, and the 'Acts of the Martyrs,'

[1] Unpublished Letters.

by Ruinart, are all one could desire. I wish some man of real merit would consecrate his time and his pen to the task, and give us a work on the saints, like Plutarch's 'Lives,' leaving out those that are least known, and not very interesting. In spite of the abundance of books which fill our libraries, we are every moment disposed to think that they are empty, and that this or that is wanting."

He combated ignorance and idleness as the two great enemies of the soul, and never failed to point out to the rich the dangers of worldly possessions. "People who are born to fortune," he said, "have more need than others of the counterpoise of religion to keep them steady. An unfortunate position does this by the very necessity of the case, but it is different when everything smiles on us! You are very fortunate to have escaped from the anathema which lies on riches, and you now begin to taste the fruits of a life directed by the light of God. There is a time when religion is only felt as a bridle that checks us; and then comes another time when it is a sweet and penetrating life-blood, which sets in motion every fibre of the soul, expands the understanding, gives us the Infinite for our horizon, and makes all things clear to us. You are then most fortunate, and you must not be astonished at the sort of interior fermentation which you experience. In the same way as a plant transported from a cellar into the sunshine feels all its pores open to the light and heat, so a soul transported from the atmosphere of the world into that of the gospel feels a divine germination within her, which lifts her out of herself."

It was thus that he raised the soul above self and the world, and by this road of entire detachment led her on to the impatient desire of her true country, and made her behold in death the angel that was to open the prison doors to the captive, and show her the fair vision of God. But at this height of perfection the voice of *duty* was still made to rule everything, and to subject everything to the good pleasure of the Master. "I would not have this calm and resignation," he writes, "make you neglect the care you owe to those who depend on you. When the soul has reached a certain degree of elevation towards God, she easily despises life, and then it is that God binds her to life once more by the ties of duty. Life is a very important business, though often enough we do not see its utility. Drops of water as we are, we ask what the ocean can want with us; and the ocean might reply that it is made up of such drops. Were it only for our faculty of praying and suffering, how many services may we not render to those who pray and suffer less than ourselves? Do not hate life, then, even whilst detaching yourself from it. Be like a lamb in the hands of God, equally ready to die or to live. Death is the beautiful moment of human life. Then it is that we regain all the virtues we have practised, all the strength and peace we have stored in the past, all the memories, the cherished images, the sweet regrets, and the glorious expectation of the vision of God. Had we but a lively faith we should indeed be fortified against death. But only think of it with such reserve as your own youth and the goodness of God ought naturally to suggest."

One of the charms of this direction was the freedom with which he gave expression to his own soul in speaking to those who inspired him with true confidence. He acknowledged to them his imperfections and spiritual joys with a delightful simplicity, asking them to help him with their prayers, and even with their advice. "Here is autumn close at hand," he writes, "and you will soon be going far away; but there is no distance between those who are united by the knowledge and the love of God. I have felt great interior joy since my return. Doubtless your prayers and your affection are in great part the cause. Souls who understand one another, and labour for their mutual perfection, have great power over the Heart of

God. Jesus Christ said, 'If two or three of you shall agree on earth touching anything they shall ask in My Name, it shall be granted to them.' What a promise! It seems to me that I have become better since you have done so. But be on your guard against excess. Do nothing to injure your health, or over-excite your imagination. No one is really calm and simple except God; imitate Him in this."

This freedom, however, never made him forget that mild and firm gravity of demeanour which he always maintained in his intercourse with women. He used the same reserve in his spiritual correspondence, in which we never find a word against which exception could be taken on this head, even when writing to persons for whom he felt the warmest affection. They sometimes complained of this. He replied, "Why do you complain of my severity? I am what I ought to be in your regard; grateful, full of esteem, and truly devoted; and if I do not express all this as much as I might, you can understand better than any one that all the thoughts and expressions of a religious ought to follow the habitual tendency of his heart, which must be all for God. The most austere religious rule does not *exclude* the affections, but it elevates and tempers them by mingling in our whole being a more than human element. You still incline too much to earth, and value good things without reflecting that there are yet better ones." And again, "I was surprised at your saying to me that *I had not shown you my soul.* I thought, on the contrary, that I had spoken to you with perfect openness of heart of all that concerned me, more than I had ever done before. It seems to me that by *showing you my soul,* you mean, making use in writing of a certain sort of eloquence, and that, I own, I rarely do. The more I love my friends the more simple I am in my relations with them, whether in speaking or writing, except on those natural occasions which necessitate another course. An Epistolary intercourse made up, as it were, of chapters out of a book, is to me a vain occupation, more akin to self-love than to friendship. Friendship simply confides its thoughts, asks advice, relates its affairs, consoles, reproves, advises, and talks familiarly; it does not attempt to write essays. The letters of Madame de Sévigné are nothing but witty gossip, yet they are too studied to be regarded as the work of a person who was either perfectly simple or seriously employed. One sees that she made the business of writing to her daughter her one important affair; and so one easily understands that she took time over it. But as to me I have no time, I write quickly, therefore, and without art; and I have an invincible repugnance to a fine style when it does not spring naturally out of the subject. Believe, then, that I really am showing you my soul when I tell you what I think; and do not ask for more. Christianity has not yet rooted out of you a certain influence of the imagination; you are true, and even simple, but you are not yet calm. Read the Gospels; what repose there is in their admirable simplicity! The style of the Gospels is that of the perfect soul; nothing in them aims at effect or surprise. That is what you must come to."

We are perhaps quoting somewhat too largely from this correspondence, but it seems to us, in its simple and unadorned style, in the variety of its lofty reflections, embellished with the rich colouring of the imagination, to present the most faithful picture of his attractive and fatherly charity. We may, therefore, be allowed to quote one more page containing some curious views on marriage, in a letter addressed to a mother who had just parted with a newly-married daughter.

"What you tell me of the happiness of your daughter gives me great pleasure. It is so rare to find a son-in-law all that one wishes, and in these matters solid qualities are so often sacrificed to financial considerations! Thank God, you have made a better choice, and can now tranquilly look forward not only to your daughter's prospects, but also to those of your future posterity. You ought to pray much for those future generations who are as yet hidden in the obscurity of time. It terrifies me, when reading history, to see what miserable beings have sometimes sprung from our greatest princes. The grandson of St. Louis was Philip le Bel, one of the most odious creatures who ever ruled over men, and his great-grandsons were not much better. It was the same with the descendants of Charlemagne. The degeneration of races is one of the most sorrowful mysteries in the world, and I know of none that more astonishes and afflicts me. What a misery to have to say to oneself that one may possibly, nay, even probably, have for one's posterity, impious, dissolute, or imbecile beings—if not worse. It gives one the vertigo to think of it. However, we can but do our best for those over whose connexions we have any direct influence, and leave the future to God. It is said in the Old Testament that God blesses those who serve Him *to the thousandth generation*, whereas He only curses those who despise Him *to the fourth generation*. We must then believe that in the alliances of blood by marriage there is a continual crossing of blessings and curses. What an abyss is here revealed! Who can see into it !"

It was thus he suffered his ideas to run on in this varied and easy train, never losing sight of his great object, namely, to impress deeply on the soul the divine image of Jesus Christ. His letters and his spiritual conversation bore the special seal of the Cross, a noble blazonry in which was resumed his whole apostolic and religious life. All his mysticism reduced itself to three heads : to destroy corrupt nature, to elevate what is good in us, and to graft therein Jesus Christ. Souls that had sufficient courage to suffer themselves to be thus fashioned to the end by his firm and skilful hand yielded him ever after-

wards the homage of their gratitude and veneration;
they felt it an honour to have been won over to Jesus
Christ by him, and engaged to serve Him in earnest
by the ardent charity of His apostle. He therefore
knew what it was to be a true spiritual father, and the
souls whom he brought forth to the Christian life
having been formed in some sort after his likeness, revealed their spiritual parentage by a certain inflexibility
in their convictions, by their intrepid love of suffering,
and by their complete detachment from the world.
There might be danger of indiscretion did we say
more on this subject, at so short an interval of time.
What we have said has been necessarily but an imperfect outline, which time may one day perhaps
enlarge.

We shall be more free in the rapid sketch which we
shall give of his relations with his own religious.
Here we find the same virtues and the same tendencies, but in a less timid form, and more strongly
developed; the same priestly and paternal heart, but
with a touch of deeper tenderness. In fact, it was here
that his character as a spiritual father was best discerned. How could it have been otherwise? How
could he fail to regard with peculiar affection that
chosen work of all his works, that religious family, the
sorrowful honour of his life, the crown of glory and of
thorns that adorned his brow? When first he beheld
this religious fraternity springing up around him,
made up of young men full of faith and courage,
whom a divine inspiration had gathered under his
standard, when he beheld his country once more
opening her doors to these generous children, wel-
coming them as brethren, and offering them houses of
prayer and study; and when he thought that day and
night praises would rise to God on that mountain
which had been abandoned for sixty years, his heart
dilated in thanksgiving to God and love for all these
new children, and he forgot the anguish with which
he had so long travailed with this new birth; he

forgot all the obstacles and contradictions which he had encountered before he had been able to bring his purpose into effect, whether from the government, from a portion of the public, or from his friends themselves. When therefore he saw this work before which he had so long trembled, daily blessed by God, he made it his principal thought, and lived for nothing else. Whether in the pulpit, or in his long and incessant journeys, it was the Order which he ever had in view ; it was for the Order that he preached, that he wrote, that he threw himself into the thick of the combat for religious liberty ; it was for the sake of the Order that he accepted honours, keeping for himself nothing but the burden of fatigue, and the severe anxiety of providing for the wants of his children, whose numbers were daily increasing. How then, I repeat, could he fail to bestow upon his brethren the treasures of his tenderness, that overflowing Christian friendship which up to that time he had never been able fully to pour out ? Let us hear his own words : " How I rejoice, my dear Father, once more to find myself with you and our spiritual family ! I hunger and thirst for them ! It is the greatest sacrifice of the life I lead that I am forced to be so much away from them ! I should like never again to leave Chalais, and to confine myself to assisting you in the education of our children. I am constantly with you in thought, and love you all better than ever,—you in particular, my dearest and sweetest Father." And again : " I ardently desire to see you all again. God is my witness how happy it would make me to pass my life with you, but our separation is necessary for the good of the work, and each time I have tried to make arrangements for remaining with you, God has broken them up. How I long to see you! Let us love one another, so as to be ready to give our lives for each other, so as to be willing to suffer death and ignominy for one another. For my own part, my

26

greatest happiness, next to dying for Jesus Christ, would be to die for my brethren."

All his letters belonging to this first period of religious restoration are filled with expressions of the tenderest devotion and affection. They are truly the tears of joy, shed by a father over the cradle of his child. "I write to you from Chalais," he says, "with my heart refreshed by the sight of our brethren. This holy mountain is indeed blessed, and I constantly picture to myself the praises of God rising to Him from these hills, which have been abandoned for sixty years." He writes to Père Besson: "You ought not, my dear child, and dearest Father, to trouble yourself about observing any form when writing to me. You know all I feel for you, and all that you are, and must ever be to me, and I leave you at liberty to use any expressions you like in addressing me, the tenderest or the most severe. Nothing can ever change the relations which the Cross of Jesus Christ has established between us. I am at your feet as your penitent; and no position in the world is so sweet and precious to me. At a fitting time kneel by the bedside of Brother Hernsheim, our dear invalid, and kiss both his feet affectionately for me."

This warm affection was not merely expressed in words; he constantly gave them proofs of it by his holy example when living among them, by a regular and minute correspondence, both with the superiors and the simple religious, and by the constant care that he took to form them in every virtue. Above everything else, he recommended to them union formed on charity. "I have learnt with unspeakable joy," he writes to them, "that union is more and more established among you: that is the grand point. If you love one another, if simplicity, kindness, openness, obedience, and penance every day bind you closer together, our work is founded."

He explained his ideal of Dominican life in many long letters to the Masters of Novices, which reveal at once the solidity of his religious spirit, the wisdom of his experience, and his indefatigable ardour to form his children into true disciples of Jesus Christ. We will quote one of these letters, which will give a better idea than any words could do of the nature of his direction.

"MY DEAREST FATHER, AND VERY DEAR CHILD. —I have received your letter, in which you ask my instructions with respect to the important office I have just confided to you. I will give them to you at the foot of the crucifix, beseeching our Lord, the Most Holy Virgin, St. Dominic, and all the Saints of our Order, to enlighten me as to what I ought to say to you, and to enlighten you also on the greatness of your present duties.

" What you must, above all, keep constantly before your mind, my dear child, is that your office as Master of the Novices is the principal business of your life, and that all the rest, whether prayer, study, or preaching, are but accessories. You must refer your whole life to your spiritual children ; you must meditate for them, read for them, prepare your sermons for them, pray for them, chastise your body for them, correct your faults for them ; in a word, you must have them present in your mind in all you do, even as a mother has her children in her heart all the day long. If your office be only the accessory of your life you will be in imminent danger of falling, and there would be no punishment you would not deserve for so cruel a betrayal of all your duties.

" This being granted, my dear child, in consequence of this great principle, which is the foundation of all, you will always be ready to receive your novices, to speak long with them, to receive their confidence, and even to anticipate them sometimes by visiting them, never allowing more than a week to pass without having seen each of them in private, whether in your own cell or in theirs, and that independently of their weekly confessions.

"You must be at once kind and severe, knowing how to chastise with the rod, and at the same time how to reach the very bottom of your children's hearts, so that they may love your very correction, as we see children feel in regard of their mothers. He who comes in order to obey, and sacrifice himself to Jesus Christ, himself desires to find a firm hand capable of correcting, reprimanding, humbling, and beating him into shape; without which he would suffer interiorly from not feeling the presence of a master, even though nature might feel a certain satisfaction at being left at liberty. Accustom your children willingly to kneel when they speak with you, even out of confession. This humble and penitent posture facilitates openness of heart, although it may at first be painful to pride. There are some Orders in which the inferiors are never allowed to ask anything of their superior except on their knees, because the superior stands in the very place of Jesus Christ, and it is therefore becoming that the religious should humble himself profoundly in the presence of Jesus Christ.

"You must not accustom your novices to a constrained exterior, or any affected casting down of the eyes, but rather to that simple, natural, frank, and attractive piety which is the foundation of the Dominican spirit, and which you have always seen expressed on the countenances of our Fathers.

"You will regularly hold chapter, and frequently inflict the penances agreed on; both you and I, and all of us, being fully persuaded that it is by these means that we shall preserve humility, mortification, and that sweet fraternal spirit which makes religious, who are accustomed to mutual correction, of one heart and soul with each other, each by turns becoming as a little child before the rest. By an immense grace we have re-established this point, which is the rock on which almost all restorations are shipwrecked, on account of the difficulties in overcoming human respect in the matter of humiliation undergone or inflicted; keep to it therefore as the apple of the eye, remembering the way in which I have so many times chosen to be treated by yourself.

"As to fasting, sleeping on boards, and all other penances likely to injure the health, you must on these points observe great moderation. Easily dispense with fasting, and do not let any one watch after matins who requires longer rest. Often study the countenances of your children, in order to see if there are any signs of a suffering state of health. Remember that their bodies are intrusted to your care as well as their souls: you must form both, without breaking them. If you love your children, if you live in them and for them, it will be easy for you to find out and anticipate all their necessities.

"After having read this letter, my dear child, place yourself at the foot of the crucifix, and having nine times piously kissed it, you will ask of our Lord the graces you stand in need of in order to become a good novice-master, and you will protest to Him that you are ready to spend your whole life in that office, if it should please your superiors always to leave you in it.

"I press you tenderly to my heart, my dearest Father, and most beloved child, and embrace you in our Lord."

The reader will no doubt admire the wisdom, the maturity, the prudence, and the constant mixture of sweetness and firmness, of strength and love, which breathes through these counsels. His affection for his children never made him forget the rights of justice; he could chastise them, and that severely, specially those whom he most loved; but his correction was always tempered with so much sweetness and union with the Cross of Jesus Christ, that no one could mistake the source of his rigour, and prevent themselves from loving him the more for it. One of

his religious having prolonged a journey beyond the
time appointed, Père Lacordaire, while acknowledging
the reasons which had induced the delay, blamed him
nevertheless for not having sought the necessary permission. He adds : "As I love you much, I prefer
treating you with severity, because you are capable
of understanding it, and turning it to your own ad-
vancement. You will, therefore, place yourself on
your knees before your crucifix after having read my
letter ; you will remind yourself that you have been
a disobedient child, and you will ask God's pardon.
Then, having prepared yourself to receive the penance
(that is, unless you are ill), you will go and acknowledge your fault to Brother Hernsheim, who will immediately give you twenty-five strokes of the discipline. You will then prostrate before him, and kiss
his feet as many times. If you are ill, you may
retrench from this penance that part of it which might
injure your health. I am persuaded, my dear child,
that you will acknowledge your fault, and that you
will feel the necessity of maintaining in yourself, and
in others by your example, the spirit of humble and
perfect obedience. If I did not love you, I should
not thus punish you. You have become the servant
of Jesus Christ of your own free will ; your soul and
your body no longer belong to yourself. You must
therefore carry that yoke which is so grievous in the
eyes of the flesh, but so glorious and full of sweetness
to the eyes of faith. I press you to my heart, my
dear and precious child, and shall be happy to see you
again."

He considered this obligation of punishing the least
failings as at once one of the most necessary and the
most difficult. He often insisted on it in his letters.
"One of the most sacred duties of religious superiors,"
he writes, "is to impose penances on those who deserve them, without which obedience, humility, and
every religious virtue, would soon disappear out of our
communities. It is cowardice in discharging this duty

which kills discipline, and destroys many houses which at one time promised well."

These instructions would have been much less efficacious had not those who received them known from experience with what rigour he first applied the rule to himself. He wrote to the same religious on whom he had imposed the above penance, " I greatly need, my dear child, to be once more under the convent rod a little, and under yours in particular. The Bishop of X—— is very pious and kind, but he does the honours of his house a great deal too much for me. Pray for me, that God may preserve me in the sentiments of a true religious, and that you may not find me worse than I was before."

This, then, was the light in which he understood the religious life, whether for himself or for others : it was to be a complete immolation—an absolute sacrifice of self for souls, and for God ; and this was the spirit in which he governed the French Dominican province during the sixteen years that he was its head. When in 1854 he ceased to be Provincial, a divergence of ideas was produced in the work, followed by a divergence of plans, of spirit, and of conduct. The history of the greatest saints, and the holiest foundations, is filled with similar facts. These passing trials, the ordinary baptism of all institutes destined to last during centuries, do but settle them more surely on their bases, let in on them the full light of experience, call forth a truer devotion, and form the safeguard of their future. " Men are so constituted," said Père Lacordaire, "that even the absence of those to whom they owe the most is one condition which reanimates their gratitude." And, in fact, the number of disciples who during his lifetime were devoted heart and soul to the restoration of the Order, according to his spirit and ideas, is far exceeded by those who have sprung up since his death. His work lives, and grows daily. His spirit abides in it. The mantle of Elias has been received by the Sons of the Prophet, and they will

preserve it with love and respect. They address to
their Father the prayer of Eliseus, "'Let a double
portion of thy spirit rest upon us.' May we obtain
as true a comprehension of the things of time and
eternity. May we, like you, love the Church and our
country, and never allow that zeal for God and souls
which devoured you to be extinguished in us!" A
glorious inheritance indeed! and one which those to
whom it has fallen will never suffer to decay!

And now, let me ask, are there many examples to
be found in history of characters in whom the man and
the priest, the citizen and the saint, are more harmoniously blended? Where shall we find a more
striking instance of a man as great in heart as in mind,
who concentrated all the energy of his faculties, all the
ambition of his life in the fulfilment of the hardest
duties and the highest virtues ; who was stirred with
all heroic passions, a passionate love of truth, honour,
and justice, with a horror of all hypocrisy, cowardice,
and everything that degrades the soul ; a passionate
devotion to the noblest causes, even when weak and
fallen, joined to an incapacity of understanding such
things as cowardice and treason ; and finally the
sublimest of all passions, the love of God reaching to
the contempt of self? The glory of this character has
scarcely yet shone over the present age ; time and
its contrast with our own infirmities will make it
gradually grow larger in our eyes. Many will desire
to study it yet closer, and to receive from it yet more
light and encouragement. It will have lessons for all
states, for men in public as well as in domestic life, for
the ascetic and for the humblest Christian. The life
of the illustrious Dominican, more eloquent than his
words, will continue his apostolic mission, and will
earn him more than the glory of surviving himself—it
will gain souls to the Church and Jesus Christ.
Defunctus adhuc loquitur ! "He being dead, yet
speaketh !"

CHAPTER XVII.

1845—1848.

AITHFUL to our plan of exhibiting the private and religious virtues of Père Lacordaire rather than of keeping to the chronological order and exact enumeration of facts, we have interrupted the course of events in order to take a nearer view of the priest and the Friar-Preacher. It seems to us that the light thus projected over the few events which mark the closing phase of his life will assist the reader in understanding them better, and will specially serve to explain the part he took in politics in 1848, enabling us to judge of it from the same height at which he himself was placed.

No important event distinguished the four last years which preceded the Revolution of February. He followed his course of preaching in Paris and in the provinces, and laboured in consolidating the establishment of the Friar-Preachers in France. All the French religious had been recalled from Italy, and the noviciate was installed in the Convent of Chalais, on the feast of St. Dominic, 1845. Studies were regularly organised there, and the two houses of Chalais and Nancy were slowly advancing in peace, unity, and work. Père Lacordaire considered that he had by this time earned the right to lay down the burden of authority, and to resume the far easier yoke of obedience as a simple religious. All the holy Founders of religious Orders have in their time felt this humble distrust of their own powers, and the desire of resigning into what they believed were worthier hands the government of the work intrusted to their care. Père Lacordaire, animated with the like spirit felt this noble desire *to descend.* Without informing any one therefore, he wrote during this same year 1848, to the most reverend Master-General, begging him to accept his resignation of his office, and to appoint Père Jandel in his place. The latter, informed of this unexpected step by a religious of Rome, hastened to make it known to the two eldest communities in France, and in union with them at once addressed a petition to the Master-General, conjuring him to leave at their head the man whom Providence had evidently raised up to found this difficult work, and who alone could secure its success. The resignation of Père Lacordaire was therefore not accepted. He had to remain in the first rank, which was due to him on so many titles, and his attempt or ? resulted in giving him a new claim to authority; for those only are worthy of commanding who know how to obey.

In the month of September, 1847, he went for the sixth time to Rome, in order to arrange some of the affairs of the Order. He travelled by the way of Turin and Bologna, and witnessed the enthusiasm felt throughout Italy in favour of Pius IX. "The Pope," he writes, "is at this moment the idol of the Romans, and of all Italy; you can form no idea of this enthusiasm, in which we see politics governed and consecrated by religion."[1]

This union between the people and their sovereign was doomed, alas! to be of short duration. It was the Hosanna, which preceded by only a few days the

[1] Unpublished Correspondence, 1847.

clamours and threats of death ; and when he beheld Pius IX., the peaceful deliverer, of whom his people were not worthy, about to be driven into exile, Père Lacordaire must have recalled his first impression on the accession of the new Pope, when he said by a sort of prophetic intuition, " It has come into my mind that Pius IX. is perhaps destined to be the Louis XVI. of the Papacy."[1]

He himself was now to be swept along for a brief space by the stormy current of politics, to touch on more than one rock, and to learn at his cost how little solidity is to be looked for in popular favour, for him who has no other ambition than that of self-sacrifice, no other tactics but sincerity, and who is " not a Richelieu, but a poor friar, loving only peace and solitude."

He foresaw the abyss into which the dynasty of 1830, through its own fault, was about to plunge. At the beginning of 1847 he had detected the storm on the horizon, attributing it to the obstinacy of the government in suppressing those Christian principles, which are the only foundation of power, and in refusing to the Church the liberty of teaching and of association, which offered the only effectual counterpoise to the ever-increasing flood of evil passions. " The horizon is dark with clouds," he said, " and if next summer does not repair the disasters of the last two years, I really do not know what will become of us with all the mischief which is everywhere fermenting around us. Poor Europe is threatened with terrible troubles, and, marvellous to say, none of those who are at the head of affairs seem to understand why their people are as they are. As blind as they were sixty years ago, they still reject the Christian system with the same prejudice and the same passion as before. They see the evil, and are terrified at it ; but to acknowledge that Jesus Christ is the only true Basis of society is beyond their strength ? Poor

[1] Correspondence with Madame Swetchine, 1846.

men! What hard lessons God has in store for
them!"[1] He blamed the victorious *bourgeoisie* for
having mistaken the reason of their triumph, and
kept civil and political liberty for their own profit
instead of rising superior to selfish interests; and he
pitied them "for not having found in the king of their
choice, the citizen king, who had issued from their
very bosom, a genius capable of lifting them above
themselves."[2]

He was, therefore, neither surprised nor troubled
when the popular movement broke out which swept
away, not merely the throne, as in 1830, but even
monarchy itself. Not that he was a partisan of the
republican form of government, as many thought, and
even still believe. His preference had ever been for
limited monarchy. He might perhaps, with other enlightened minds, have believed in the future triumph
of democracy; but he was never a democrat. He
was born a Liberal; and he lived and died faithful to
Liberal principles, above all parties and forms of
government. His words and his acts render abundant
testimony to the truth of this statement. "Never,"
he wrote in 1842, "never has *democracy*, or the
government by the people, for one moment entered
my mind. Never have I said or written one word
bearing that sense. But those who attack me because
I separate myself from them, like to believe that it
is my democratic tendency that is the cause of
my want of interest in their quarrels. One must
resign oneself to this. It would be in vain for me to
proclaim from the roof-tops that I am not a democrat;
they would make their voices heard above mine. In
all times and positions, we must have our cross, and
be careful not to break it."[3] Again about the same
time he wrote: "The opinion entertained regarding
my political opinions by certain persons has always
astonished me; because I have never spoken or written

[1] Unpublished Correspondence, March, 1847.   [2] Memoirs.
[3] Unpublished Correspondence, 1842.

a line indicating the slightest tendency towards the republican party.[1]   All my political ideas reduce themselves to this: apart from Christianity there is no possible society holding a middle place between the despotism of one, and the despotism of many. Secondly, Christianity will never recover its empire in the world except by an earnest struggle in which there must be neither oppressor nor oppressed.   In this belief I live, and to all the rest I am a stranger."[2]

He was not, therefore, what was then called *a republican of yesterday;* but without having any solid faith in the future of the young republic, he thought he ought not to refuse it the support of his sincere adhesion, in hopes of obtaining from it, for France and for the Church, those liberties and institutions so blindly refused by preceding governments.   He even plunged anew into the perilous struggles of the daily press, not certainly carried away by the enthusiasm of zealous youth, as in 1830, but from a sense of duty, and in spite of many personal repugnances. "For the first time perhaps," he said, *àpropos* of the foundation of the *Ere Nouvelle,* "I am making a great sacrifice for the sake of God; hitherto, everything I have done has been consonant with my own tastes; but at the present moment I go against my own feeling, and I abandon my life, in the full force of the term, against my own will to the Will of God.   This will be my consolation if I fail.   We must, above all things, resist fear, and shrink from no duty."[3]

He has laboured in his Memoirs to explain the position which he assumed at this solemn and important crisis : let us hear his own words :

"It was difficult to know what ought to be done, because it was difficult to understand in what safety consisted.   To restore a limited monarchy, after the two terrible failures of 1830 and 1848, was evidently not possible.   To found a republic in a country which

---

[1] Unpublished Correspondence, Jan., 1842.   [2] *Ibid.*, Jan. 1850.
[3] Correspondence with Madame Swetchine.

had been governed for thirteen or fourteen centuries
by monarchical institutions appeared equally impossible, but there was this difference between the two
alternatives, that the monarchy had just fallen, and
the republic was standing. Now what is standing has
just one chance more of life than what is fallen, and
even though there was little hope of firmly establishing
the new order of things, one might at least prop it up
so as to serve as a temporary shelter, which might
give France some of those institutions, the want of
which had evidently caused the ruin of two thrones
and two dynasties. This was the opinion of M. de
Tocqueville. He was not a republican, but he foresaw that the ruin of the republic must inevitably lead
to the establishment of arbitrary power. It was
necessary to choose between two extremes, and all
skilful politicians set themselves to labour either for
one or the other. All other projects were but illusions.
It is easy now to see this, but few saw it at the time,
and the greater part of the better order of minds
followed afar the phantom which promised them the
return of a limited form of monarchy on the breaking
up of the republic.

"For myself, I was very uncertain how to act. A
partisan, from my very youth, of parliamentary monarchy, I had limited my hopes and wishes to seeing
it firmly established among us; I hated neither the
house of Bourbon, nor that of Orleans, and only considered in them the chances which they presented for
the Liberal future of the country; I should have been
ready to support the first, had they respected the
charter of 1814; and I would have supported the
second also, had they allowed the charter of 1830 its
natural developments. Supposing these two great
houses could have formed a fusion so as at last to
give France a monarchy solidly based on institutions
not contradictory to themselves, no one would have
been more devoted to them than myself. But all this
was but a dream in the present as in the past. A man

of principles, not of parties, things and not persons had always ruled my choice. Now, if it be easy to follow a party here and there, wherever it goes, it is difficult to follow principles when one does not clearly see their application. As a Liberal, and a parliamentarian, I understood myself well enough ; but not so as a republican, and nevertheless it was necessary to decide.

" Whilst I was thus deliberating with myself, the Abbé Maret and Frederic Ozanam called on me. They spoke to me of the trouble and uncertainty that reigned among Catholics ; all old rallying-points were disappearing in what seemed likely to become a hopeless anarchy, which might render the new *régime* hostile to us, and deprive us of all chance of obtaining those liberties which had been refused us by preceding governments. " The republic," they added, " is well-disposed towards us ; we have no such acts of barbarity and irreligion to charge it with as disgraced the revolution of 1830. It believes and hopes in us ; ought we to discourage it ? Moreover, what are we to do ?—to what other party can we attach ourselves? What do we see before us but ruin ? and what is the republic, but the natural government of a society that has lost all its former anchors and traditions ?"

" To these reasons, suggested by the situation of affairs, they added higher and more general views, drawn from the future of European society, and the impossibility that monarchy should ever again find any solid resting-place. On this point I did not go so far as they. Limited monarchy, in spite of its faults, had always seemed to me the most desirable of all forms of government, and I only saw in the republic a momentary necessity until things should naturally take another course. This difference of opinion was serious, and hardly allowed of our working together in concert. Nevertheless, the danger was urgent, and it was absolutely necessary either to abdicate at this solemn moment, or frankly to choose one's party, and bring to the help of society, now shaken to its very foundations, whatever light and strength each one had at his command. Hitherto I had taken a definite position with regard to public events : ought I now to take refuge in a selfish silence because the difficulties were more serious ? I might indeed say that I was a religious, and so hide myself under my religious habit ; but I was a *religious militant,* a preacher, a writer, surrounded by a sympathy which created very different duties for me from the duties of a Trappist or a Carthusian. These considerations weighed on my conscience. Urged by my friends to decide, I at length yielded to the force of events, and though I felt a strong repugnance to the idea of returning to the career of a journalist, I agreed, in concert with them, to unfurl a standard on which should be inscribed together the names of Religion, the Republic, and Liberty."[1]

The prospectus of the *Ère Nouvelle* appeared on the 1st of March. A few days before, on the 27th of February, when the ruins of the conflict were still everywhere visible, Père Lacordaire ascended the pulpit of Notre Dame to continue the teaching of those unchangeable doctrines which, like the ark, float on the waters of the revolutionary deluge, and are even carried higher by those very waves which revenge the outraged rights of God. The audience was numerous, and awaited with evident anxiety for what the popular orator should say. Mgr. Affre presided, surrounded by his Vicars-General, and the Cathedral chapter. The Archbishop had been the first to give an example of confidence by publishing a Pastoral Letter on the 24th of February, in which he praised the people of Paris for their moderation in the hour of victory, and for the religious sentiments which they had displayed. His presence opposite to the pulpit of Notre Dame, in the midst of his clergy and his people, was another mark of confidence, and it was easy to guess that the thoughts of the orator himself on passing events, would declare themselves in the course of his address.   In fact, he could not restrain himself, and after having thanked the Archbishop for the example he had given in throwing open the doors of the Cathedral for religious instruction, on the very morrow of a revolution, in which everything seemed to have perished, having touched on the question of the existence of God, he exclaimed with redoubled animation, " But why need I demonstrate to you, gentlemen, the existence of God ?   Were I to attempt it, you would have a right to rise and thrust me out from among you!   If I dared to undertake such a task, the doors of this Cathedral would open of themselves, and would display this people, so proud in their anger, carrying God even to His altar in the midst of their respect and adoration! . . ."   At these words an irresistible emotion took possession of the audience, and broke out in applause.   The explosion was too sudden and unanimous to be repressed by the sanctity of the place.   " Do not let us applaud the Word of God," continued the orator, " let us believe it, love it, practise it ; those are the only acclamations which rise to heaven, and are worthy of it."[1]

[1] Conference 45, Feb. 27, 1848.   The following passage from the *Ami de la Religion* explains the incident referred to by the orator : "Last Thursday (Feb. 24), at the moment when the people had attacked the Tuileries, and cast all the furniture and hangings out of the windows, a young man belonging to the Conference of St. Vincent of Paul ran in all haste to the chapel, fearing lest it should be pillaged, and wishing to save it from profanation.   The chapel, where Mass had been said in the morning, had already been invaded, and some vestments were scattered about the sacristy, but the altar remained untouched.   The pious young man begged some national guards to help him in carrying away the sacred vessels and the crucifix.   They replied that they felt as he did, but that it would be better to have with them some pupils of the Polytechnic school ; two at once presented themselves.   They took the sacred vessels and the crucifix, and went out through the court of the Tuileries and the Carrousel to go to the Church of St. Roch.   In the court some cries were uttered against the men laden with the precious deposits, when he who bore the crucifix, raising it in the air, exclaimed, ' You wished to be regenerated ; well, do not forget that you can be so only by Christ !' ' Yes ! yes !' replied a great number of voices, ' He

27

It would be unjust at the present day to reproach Père Lacordaire for his sincere adhesion to the new order of things. He did not invoke the Revolution; but after the storm, as before, he beheld in it a severe lesson given by Providence to a power that had been unfaithful to its promises, and which had with one hand repressed all the efforts made by religion to rise from abjection, and with the other caressed every dangerous instinct; and which thus had only reaped what it had sown : " *Ventum seminabunt et turbinem metent.*"[1] This opinion was then generally shared by Catholics : all saw the finger of God in the facility with which the people had overthrown the monarchy and broken up the government.

Moreover, this Revolution exhibited none of the hostility to religion which characterised that of 1830. Not a single church, priest, or convent in Paris had anything to suffer. A thousand instances were cited of the sympathy existing between the people and the clergy during the insurrection, and the days that followed. One ecclesiastic related, in a public letter, how on the 24th of February he had crossed more than fifty barricades, everywhere meeting with testimonies of respect from the workmen, and cries of " *Vive la religion ! Vive les prêtres.*"[2] The Papal Nuncio himself bore witness to this happy symptom so new in the annals of our revolutions. In reply to the Minister of Foreign Affairs he wrote : " I cannot resist seizing this occasion of expressing to you the

---

is the Master of all of us,' and all heads uncovered, amid cries of ' Vive à Dieu.' The crucifix and a chalice without a paten were carried, so to speak, in procession as far as St. Roch, where they were received by the Cure.

" The honest men who formed this touching escort began by asking his blessing from the good Curé, who addressed them a few words, which were listened to with profound respect. ' We love God,' they cried ; ' we wish for religion ; we will have it respected ; *Vive la liberté ! Vive la religion de Paris !* ' Before returning, they again knelt to receive the Curé's blessing."—*Ami de la Religion,* Tuesday, Feb. 27, 1848.

[1] Os. viii. 7.　　[2] *L'Ami de la Religion,* March 2, 1848.

deep and lively satisfaction which has been excited in my heart at the sight of the respect shown to religion by the people of Paris during the great events that have just taken place." Finally, Pius IX. himself, in a letter to M. de Montalembert, gave the same testimony to France, and attributed this respect for holy things to the eloquence of the Catholic orators. "We heartily thank the Lord, in the humility of our heart," he writes, "that during this great Revolution no injury has been offered to religion or to its ministers. We take pleasure in the thought that this moderation is due in part to your eloquence, and that of other Christian orators, who have rendered our name dear to this generous people."[1]

We recall these circumstances in order to explain the attitude which Père Lacordaire assumed towards the new government. For the rest, this attitude had nothing servile about it. "He only saluted the victors with becoming respect," says M. de Montalembert ; "he spared the vanquished all recrimination and reproach ; he felt none of that cowardly ferocity against those who are conquered and proscribed, which is too often to be found among our triumphant party men."[2]

Another feature of this Revolution was its sending three bishops and eleven priests to the Assembly, which was charged with the task of re-establishing authority and liberty on a firm basis. Père Lacordaire was naturally pointed out, in the first place, as worthy the votes of Catholics. Without having presented himself as a candidate, his election was carried by seven or eight electoral colleges. At Paris the committee of his *arrondissement* requested him to appear at two public meetings in order to answer the questions which should be proposed to him on the subject of his candidateship. " I appeared, in fact," he writes, " in the great amphitheatre of the School of Medicine,

---

[1] *L'Ami de la Religion*, April 4, 1848.
[2] *Le Père Lacordaire.* Montalembert, p. 204.

and in the great hall of the Sorbonne ; and in both assemblies I frankly declared that I was not, to use the language of the day, a *republican of yesterday*, but a simple *republican of to-morrow.* At the School of Medicine my success was great ; they prevented its being renewed at the Sorbonne by tumultuous cries which came from outside. I obtained a great number of votes in both the colleges where my name had been proposed ; but it was at Marseilles that I had the honour of being returned as a representative."[1]

At Paris he obtained sixty-two thousand votes, in spite of the ferocity with which he had been opposed. At Toulon, where he had just been preaching the Advent station, he also obtained a great number of votes, and they wrote to him that he stood a good chance of success. " It would be very singular," he replied, " if it were to turn out that I had come to preach at Toulon merely to obtain a seat in the National Assembly. You will know the Will of God in this matter before I shall. If it be in the affirmative, kneel down and pray for your friend, for it will be a great trial."[2]

The city of Marseilles, which finally elected him, only knew him from having seen him during three or four days at the beginning of this very year, 1848. On returning from his station at Toulon he had delivered a sermon at Marseilles on some particular occasion, and had received incredible expressions of sympathy from the Catholic youth of the city. Deputations of three or four hundred persons had several times waited on him to express their thanks. These young men in their southern enthusiasm had literally thrown themselves upon him, all eager to press his hand. They had conducted him back to the office of the royal messengers, and there the Duc de Sabran, bidding him adieu in the name of all, begged him always to remember Marseilles, and to reckon on its faithful attachment. And, in fact, Marseilles gave

[1] Memoirs. [2] Unpublished Correspondence.

him a striking proof of her devotion two months later, and reserved yet further testimonies of regard for a more distant period, by calling him to found a convent of his Order within her walls, and by constructing for him and his children, at the foot of the Grotto of St. Mary Magdalene, a hostelry, to shelter the piety of the pilgrims who crowded thither.

He entered the Constituent Assembly, therefore, in his religious habit, and took his seat at the upper extremity of the first bench on the Left. "It was a fault undoubtedly" (he himself confesses) ; " I was too young a republican as yet to take so prominent a place, and the republic itself was still too young for me to give it so decided a pledge of my adhesion."[1] But this fault, the result of excessive confidence, was soon understood and repaired. He hastened to come down from the *Mountain* where he felt so ill at ease ; it was enough for him to have brought with him into the Chamber the liberties which he represented, and to have linked them to the triumphs of his popularity. The favour which he enjoyed with the public was manifested in a striking manner on the very day of the inauguration of the Constituent Assembly, and the proclamation of the Republic. The *Univers* of that date comments in the following terms on these enthusiastic demonstrations :

"Yesterday was a splendid day for Père Lacordaire, for the church of which he is the minister, and for the religious orders, of which he is our most popular representative. The Dominican friar appeared in the National Assembly, whither he had been called by the free votes of two hundred thousand Frenchmen. He entered clothed in that white woollen habit of the Friar-Preachers which he has restored among us. His election was acknowledged as valid without the slightest opposition, and his monkish costume did not excite the least murmur in the Assembly, which

---

[1] Memoirs.

nevertheless included M. Dupin and M. Isambert among its members.

"But this was not all. When the entire National Assembly came out on the peristyle of the Palais-Bourbon to proclaim the republic in presence of the populace and the national guard, Pére Lacordaire, accompanied by the Abbé de Cazales, Grand-Vicar of Montauban, came down to the railing, against which pressed the thick crowds of the Parisian populace. At the sight of the eloquent religious and his monastic habit, the generous people hailed him with acclamations. Père Lacordaire shook hands with and embraced a number of the citizens and national guards, and was led back in triumph to the doors of the legislative hall. At the close of the meeting, on quitting the Assembly by the Rue de Bourgoyne, he had to pass through the ranks of a company of the tenth legion, who, on seeing him, raised the cry of 'Vive le Père Lacordaire!'

"We may fairly say that, dating from this day, the oppressive laws against which we have so long struggled, and which have been enforced against the rights of conscience by each successive form of despotism, these laws, we say, have been virtually repealed. They have fallen, struck dead by the courage of one friar and the acclamations of the people. The second republic has this day repaired one of the most odious iniquities of its elder sister."[1]

During the short duration of his legislative career, Père Lacordaire only spoke twice; the first time to resist the motion for the direct nomination of the new ministers by the Assembly; the second to repel the charge of illegality raised against his religious habit by M. Portalis, Procurator-General to the Court of Appeal of Paris. He contented himself with pointing out the inopportune and unjust nature of this attempt to revive the old anti-liberal laws, and with thanking the republic for having abolished them. It was

[1] *Univers*, May 5, 1848.

regretted that he did not take occasion of the debate more energetically to defend the very principle of religious liberty itself which had been thus imprudently attacked by M. Portalis. But he was evidently influenced in the tribune by the wish to conciliate—a laudable sentiment, no doubt, but one which paralysed his strength, and made him sacrifice his oratorical renown to the desire of not increasing, by any warmth of language, the animosity of parties already too much excited. He very soon felt that his place was not in the midst of these political tempests, and that his life, since he had dedicated it to the service of God and the Church, stood in need of a calmer and holier atmosphere. Nor did he wait long before freeing himself from this false position. "On the 15th of May, 1848," he writes in his Memoirs, "only a few days after the solemn inauguration of the Constituent Assembly, a blind multitude invaded the hall of meeting, and we had to remain three hours defenceless in the midst of a disgraceful scene, in which no blood indeed was shed, and wherein the danger was not very great, but in which our honour had so much the more to suffer. The people, if the mob deserved that name, thus insulted their representatives with the simple view of making them understand that they were at their mercy. They did not indeed place the *bonnet rouge* on their heads, as they had done to the anointed head of Louis XVI., but they took from them their crown ; and whether it were the people or not who did this, the Assembly equally lost its dignity. During those long hours I had but one thought, which always returned in one monotonous form—*the republic is lost.*"[1] "I saw him," writes M. de Montalembert, "sitting passively on his bench, on the occasion of the invasion of the 15th of May, marked out to the threats of the mob by his white habit."

The next day he sent in his resignation. He knew

[1] Memoirs.

he should be accused of inconsistency, want of political skill, and perhaps even want of courage; but he found in the fulfilment of his duty what made up to him for a momentary failure, and he put his trust in the future. "We must know," he said on this occasion, "how to descend before men in order to ascend before God." He thought it right to explain the motives of his retirement to the electors of Les Bouches-du-Rhône.

"Yesterday," he wrote, "I resigned the post of representative, which you did me the honour of conferring on me; I restore it to you after having filled it for a fortnight without having done anything of all that you expected from me. My letter to the President of the National Assembly will already have informed you of the reasons of my retirement; but I feel bound to explain them more at length to you who chose me and thus gave me the highest proof of your esteem which it was in your power to bestow. You reckoned on me, and I have failed you; you hoped in my words, and I have scarcely so much as mounted the tribune; you trusted in my courage, and I have incurred no danger; you have therefore a clear right to demand an account from me, and I feel the necessity of forestalling your questions.

"I hold two distinct characters, those of the religious and the citizen. It was impossible to separate them, both in my person were called on to prove worthy of each other, so that the acts of the citizen should never cause any pain to the conscience of the religious. Now, in proportion as I advanced in a career so new to me, I began to see more clearly the nature of the passions and parties that surrounded me. In vain did I strive to choose a line superior to their agitations; in spite of myself I saw that it was impossible to keep the balance. I soon understood that in a political assembly, impartiality only leads to weakness and isolation, and that one must choose one's side, and throw oneself into it head-foremost. My retirement was therefore inevitable, and I have accordingly resigned.

"God knows, gentlemen, that it was the thought of you which most opposed my resolution. I feared to grieve you; I reproached myself for breaking in so rapid and unexpected a manner the ties I had felt happy in contracting with you. My only consolation is in thinking that in the very brief acts of my political career I have followed the dictates of a conscience which corresponds with your own. Elected without having sought that distinction, I accepted my post out of devotion to your service, I have held it without passion, and have retired from a fear of no longer remaining what I ought to remain in the sight of God and of yourselves. My resignation, like my acceptance, is therefore a homage which I render to you."

His private correspondence testifies yet more strongly the relief he felt at having quitted the Assembly. He was astonished himself at the *horror* he experienced of political life. "My position in the Assembly," he writes, "had become an intolerable burden to me; I could not sit there apart from democracy, and yet I could not accept democracy as I saw it there displayed. The convictions of my own mind, and the engagements resulting from my position, drew me one way; the realities present under my eyes drew me the other. And what is a man who has no ground, no clearly defined line of conduct? My retirement has cut the Gordian knot, but not without a great interior disturbance. It is hard to seem to be wanting in energy and consistency, but it is far harder to resist the claims of conscience. At last I have made up my mind, and I am now calm and satisfied. I am sure that you will have been much troubled about me, and will have prayed much for my intention. I never could have believed that I should have felt such a horror of political life; it is to a degree you cannot imagine. I found out that I was nothing but a poor little friar, and in no way a

Lacordaire—a poor friar, loving nothing but retirement and peace."

The certainty of having followed the right inspiration, rendered him more and more insensible to
the unfavourable judgments passed on his conduct.
"You may be assured," he wrote to the same person,
"that some day my retirement from the Assembly
will be one of the things for which I shall be most
praised. For the rest, whatever may happen, we
must look not to public opinion, but to duty. To do
one's duty at the risk of being blamed, is one of the
truest merits of which man is capable. I feel at this
moment like a man who had fallen into an abyss,
where he was about to perish, and who has been
miraculously drawn out of it. I have received several
very touching letters written with a similar feeling,
but the general impression has been most grievous.
Few men see into the future. I have only written
two or three letters, to justify myself in the opinion of
a few friends; it is better to wait for time to vindicate
our conduct. How many times, O my God! have I
been maligned! If you knew what is said of me at
Paris in the *salons* of the Regency Party and elsewhere, you would be actually stupefied.[2]   But there

---

[1] Unpublished Correspondence. Paris, May, 1848.

[2] The *Times* echoed some of these absurd reports, and several French
journals copied its article. The *Ère Nouvelle* replied to it in the following terms :—"The *Times*, an English newspaper, in its number of
the 21st of June, has made some ridiculous remarks on the subject of
Père Lacordaire's resignation, which several French journals have just
reproduced. According to the *Times*, Père Lacordaire had been a pupil
of Talma, and in his youth had pleaded some mysterious cause at
Carpentras, the consequence of which was his entrance into the Order of
St. Dominic; finally, the resignation of his seat in the Assembly had
been required of him by the Archbishop of Paris, after the latter had in
vain reminded that he should speak in the Assembly against the suppression of the Budget of the Clergy. It may suffice to say in reply,
that Père Lacordaire never spoke to Talma ; that he never saw Carpentras ; that he entered the Order of Preachers eleven years after
having received his ordination as priest ; that he is the author of several
articles published in this journal in favour of the Budget of Public
Worship ; and that, consequently, the Archbishop of Paris could not
have required his resignation on the grounds put forth by the *Times*."—
Ère Nouvelle, June, 1848.

are storms which we must suffer to blow over without being moved by them. Solitude has been for some time my best preservative ; and this causes me the greatest peace. I am only unhappy when I know not what part to take ; then I suffer much, first on account of my uncertainty, and then from apprehension of what will happen. But when my resolution is once taken, I become once more calm and serene."[1]

The same motives which had induced him to resign his seat in the Assembly, were not long in determining him to retire from the *Ere Nouvelle*. In founding this paper, he had plainly declared then it was to belong to no party, but to keep above them all, so as to be able to speak the truth to all with equal impartiality though always with moderation and charity. This generous attempt to produce a journal that should be Christian both in its spirit and its form, succeeded during the first few months, when the union of all the sincere friends of the new *régime* had not as yet permitted discontented parties to raise their heads. In less than three months the *Ere Nouvelle* reckoned 3200 subscribers, and published nearly 4500 copies. The Archbishop of Paris, Mgr. Affre, gave its editors a proof of his confidence and esteem by publicly supporting their work, which he had done to no other journal. He assured them "that Catholics would admire in their paper the frankness and uprightness which withdrew alike from all parties, knowing and desiring one thing alone, the wellbeing of religion and of the country."

For some time the *Ere Nouvelle* was one of the most widely-circulated and popular journals. The talent of its editors had created for it a place apart in the daily press, specially on all questions of civil or religious economy. Père Lacordaire contributed a series of articles, in which he defended the Budget of Public Worship, the suppression of which was then demanded. Frederic Ozanam published a remark-

[1] Unpublished Correspondence. Paris, June 6, 1848.

able article on the Law of Divorce, which some had
attempted to re-establish. It had a return of public
favour after the terrible days of June, when at the
same time that it energetically denounced the insurrection, the Christian journal endeavoured to heal the
wounds of the people, and to prepare the way for
reconcilation. Ten thousand copies of the journal
were sold in the streets of Paris, and the subscriptions
increased in the same proportion. This success drew
new fury on the head of the Catholic paper. It was
a pitched battle. " Some tell us," writes the chief
editor, " your journal is the most honest in the world;
we shall subscribe to it. Others cry out, your journal
is shocking, horrible, *sans-culotte*. . . . . I believe any
other man than myself would laugh at all the furies
that cast themselves upon us like wasps upon honey."[1]
But to him, the friend of peace and union, these struggles, which became every day more serious, soon grew
too much for his strength and courage. He began
to see the perils and impossibilities of the work of
religious pacification which he had undertaken.

"The difficulty of our work," he says, " is the application of the religious spirit to politics—that is to say,
of the spirit of peace and charity to the very thing
which engenders the bitterest hatred, and the most
terrible divisions. When one visits galley-slaves,
prisoners, the poor, and the sick, Christianity goes its
own road, and everybody understands it. But if you
try to apply it to politics, immediately a howl is
raised against you; your impartiality becomes weakness, your mercy a treason, your gentleness a desire
to please everybody. Nothing is so easy as to follow
a party created by faction, nothing so difficult as to
be just in the midst of factions."[2]

He felt at last the necessity of withdrawing; his
own interests required it no less than those of his
fellow-labourers, who wished to give to the *Ere*

---

[1] Correspondence of Père Lacordaire with Madame Swetchine, June 30, 1848.
[2] Unpublished Correspondence.

Nouvelle a more decidedly democratic colouring. The security which had to be advanced led to the remodelling of the proprietorship of the journal. Père Lacordaire took this occasion of giving up its direction without destroying the undertaking. "All has gone on well between us," he writes. "I never had any intention of remaining always at the head of the journal, nothing being more contrary to my tastes, if not to my duties. So far from my retirement weakening the paper, I believe that it will strengthen it, by allowing it to assume a more definitive character, and a more lively and decided line of opinion. In any case, I am tranquil, because I feel I have done my duty, both in founding or in abandoning the *Ere Nouvelle*. I have passed over in my own mind and before God the six months that have just passed, and, setting aside faults of detail, it seems to me that in these terrible circumstances I have done what religion and patriotism required of me. My vocation was never a political one, yet it was impossible for me not to touch for a while on this great rock, even were it only to reap from it a very sad experience. Now it is over, and not without some good results. You cannot think what peace I feel, and how much better I understand what God demands of me for the rest of my life. Even if I have lost something in the opinion of men, what is that if one loses nothing in the sight of God? It costs me less to descend than it does to some, because I have always lived so much alone, associated to a very small number of souls, drawing my life from my intercourse with God."[1]

It may be seen how profound was the sense of peace and repose which he regained after the storm. And it is on these expressions of gratitude to God, on his final return to the silence of his cell, that we love to dwell in considering the short phase of his political life. What we have said will, we trust, suffice to show those who are well disposed how little Père Lacordaire

[1] Unpublished Correspondence. Chalais, Sept. 7, 1848.

loved the passions and agitations of the Forum, to use
his own words, and how little he deserved the reproach
of taking pleasure in political strife. Those knew him
very little who believed him to be greedy of renown,
and of public life, and who charged him with seeking
occasions for being mixed up in such things, taking
part in them with passionate eagerness, and only
returning to the quiet monotony of the cloister with
regret. It was precisely the contrary. His real
crime in the eyes of those who knew him better, and
who would have desired to have drawn him into their
ranks, and to have made use of him for their own
political purposes, was that he did not choose to be
mixed up in politics, and refused to give in his
allegiance to any party. He knew very well that this
was to condemn himself to isolation, and to the unjust judgments which would be passed on his conduct;
but to this he had been long resigned. Already,
during the reign of Louis Philippe, when accused of
Jacobinism, he had replied, " I have been repaid with
ingratitude because I determined to be before all
things, and above all things, the man of God, of His
Gospel, and of His Church, because I would pledge
myself to no party, and was resolved to preserve the
right of speaking the truth to all of them alike, as is
my duty. They have been hurt by this religious
independence, and yet more so when I covered it with
the religious habit. Do not fear lest my influence
should be diminished under that habit ; it has rather
increased ; and henceforth, compelled by the circumstances of my position to aspire after nothing, I live,
as it were, in a citadel, secure alike from ambition and
from the possible mortification of feeling myself shut
out from everything. It is to this that I have consecrated my liberty and my life, and the disagreeable
consequences are simply just and unavoidable. Many
who but imperfectly appreciate my conduct and ideas,
form their notions of me from circumstances of which
they know nothing. It is always difficult to judge

aright a man who lives in the midst of factions, and belongs to none. Men want some precise definition of other men's views and tendencies in order to classify them ; they do not like to have to unravel the thread of an existence that holds itself aloof. The first question which every man puts to his neighbour is, ' To whom do you belong ?' and if one does not see very clearly what answer to give, one is judged on the strength of a phrase or hearsay. However, I feel no bitterness in consequence of the false judgments passed on me, and resign myself to them calmly enough. The final evidence must be drawn from a man's entire life; it is that which will show whether he has been ambitious or disinterested, simple or cunning, honest, or a hypocrite."[1] And, in fact, his life is now before us to give this testimony to his disinterestedness, and to the uprightness and elevation of his views. His death has judged his life, and justice is beginning to be done to his political virtues as well as to the gifts of the interior man. But prejudices do not easily give way. There are so few minds capable of distinguishing between the grand politics of the gospel and human politics—between that which consists in saying the truth to all—to the weak and to the powerful, to subjects and to sovereigns—and that which loves to engage in questions of social government, and to mix itself up in the ambitions of classes and parties. Was not our Lord Himself reproached with endeavouring to " stir up the people "? The first kind of politics was that aimed at by the eloquent apostle, whose powerful words were directed alike to kings and people : he never stooped to the second. It is thus he defends himself from the charge in a letter to a friend :

" I cannot think why it is that you are continually returning to this one idea, that *I meddle with politics.* The truth is that my crime consists in my *not* meddling with politics,—that is, in my remaining outside

[1] Unpublished Correspondence, 1842.

all parties, and taking occasion to tell them all in turn the great social truths of the gospel. No preacher desirous of following this line can fail to excite ill-will, because nothing is so displeasing to men as evangelical independence, and that interior strength which resists the passions of the day. Had I been a Legitimist or an Orleanist, I should have been loaded with praise ; I should have had newspapers flattering me and supporting me ; instead of which, the butt of every coterie, I have only found support from a few minds here and there, and that sort of vague sympathy which is excited in favour of men who stand isolated from everything. What people call my politics consist, in fact, in my speaking the most general truths to rich and poor, believers and unbelievers. I did not even touch on politics in the *Avenir*, for it is not to be a politician to demand the liberty of the Church, and to tell unbelievers to respect the rights of religious institutions, and believers to consent that error should struggle against them in open day. At one moment of my life alone have I ever been on the verge of playing a political part, and then I felt myself so unhappy, and in so false a position, that I very soon jumped down from my elevated post. Read my Life of St. Dominic, my Conferences, even my Funeral Orations, and where will you find in them any real politics? There are absolutely none; nothing but the accents of a soul that belongs to God, and desires only to give itself to Him. One day when I am read, if I am to be read, men will look with curiosity for any allusions to the politics of the times, and will be surprised to find so little of what the world at large believes my writings to abound in."[1]

But in justifying Père Lacordaire from the charge of *meddling with politics*, and in admitting of no other error in his brief political career than the error of self-devotion, do we mean to assert that he remained an indifferent spectator of the sad convulsions of modern

[1] Unpublished Correspondence, Jan., 1850.

society, and of the wounds of the Church, his Mother?
Assuredly not. The less importance he attached to
personal questions and political forms, the more did he
insist on those laws which lie at the basis of all society;
the less he was attacked by the social contagion of the
present day in which persons are everything and
principles nothing, and in which each man asks his
neighbour, "What is your party?" and never "What
is your faith?"—so much the more energetically did
he take his stand on the great truths of the gospel, and
make himself their defender and apostle. "Men die,"
he said, "dynasties become extinct, and empires are
restored, but principles remain unchangeable, like the
granite which bears up all those changing phenomena
of nature which we behold on the surface of the earth."
It was to this *granite* that he clung fast; he leaned on
the Cross which lifts itself immovable above all human
revolutions. Thence his tranquil eye glanced over the
future, and he consoled himself for present sorrows by
an invincible faith in better times to come. "I am,"
he said, "*a citizen of the future.*"[1] He believed in the
future reconciliation and alliance of religion with
society by means of a reciprocal respect for their
mutual rights. All his Liberalism consisted in this.
He believed in liberty, because he esteemed it equally
necessary to Church and State, according to the following formula; religion stands in need of liberty, and
liberty of religion. This was his only political creed.
He loved liberty no doubt out of a feeling of patriotism, because he desired the greatness of his country;
but he loved it yet more from a religious principle, out
of his filial devotion to the Church. He had a profound
and logical conviction that wherever despotism has
long prevailed, the Christian, and specially the
Catholic, spirit has gradually decayed. History
offered him proofs of this in all ages. He saw the
Greek empire ending in the Greek schism, whilst the
Western Church maintained its independence, and

[1] Conference 35.

inoculated the barbarian nations with its life, in the
midst of their incursions and feudal struggles. He
beheld Protestantism detaching a portion of Europe
from the Holy See at the very moment when civil
and religious liberties were disappearing, and when
the Church was about to be delivered up to the
miserable bondage of Gallicanism and Josephism. He
saw the faith condemned to ostracism or extinction in
every country subjected to the iron yoke of absolute
despotism, as in China, Japan, Russia, and Sweden;
whereas it revived and extended itself under the protection of free laws in England and the United States.
He concluded from all this that the Faith cannot long
exist without civil and religious liberty. It may
produce martyrs, no doubt, but martyrs only die, as
he said, in order to regain the liberty of faith. He
added: " Slavery eats into souls, and enfeebles them
in the religious order; it gave the vertigo to Bossuet
himself. It produces a cowardly episcopate, worshippers of power, who transmit to the rest of the clergy
a timidity, mingled with ambition—a double poison,
whence results baseness, and ere long apostasy. I
acknowledge that I should be fairly in despair did I
not believe that the present progress of the world has
no other end than the final enfranchisement of the
Church by means of the universal fall of despotism.
If God is not working to bring this about, I neither see
nor understand anything. To what are we pro-
gressing if not to this ?"[1]

This ardent conviction that the Church stands in
need of free air in order to breathe, and of independence and liberal views in order to prosper, far
from inducing him to mix himself up in politics, made
him rather dread the perils of such a course for the
clergy. " The French clergy," he said, " can never
expose themselves to the influence of political passions
without being injured by them. However eloquent,
courageous, and devoted they may be, they will appear

---

[1] Correspondence with Madame Swetchine.

far less great in the tribune than in the humble pulpit which the country curé adorns with the glory of his age, and the simplicity of his virtues. The truest sacrifice on their part would always be suspected as ambitious, and would be thought to conceal under well-sounding phrases a love of celebrity. France has for many ages formed so high an idea of the priest-hood, that she cannot endure anything that lowers that ideal, and brings it down even for a moment from the heights of Horeb and Calvary." It was thus that he spoke in an article in the *Ère Nouvelle*, in which, whilst inviting the French clergy to take part in the elections for the Constituent Assembly, and to give their aid to the nation in the serious crisis under which it was then labouring, he was careful to remind them that the part of mediator should not be pro-longed when the exceptional circumstances which had called for it should have ceased.

The more he felt the need that the people had of the priesthood, the less could he put up with anything which derogated from the priestly character, and diminished its religious influence. Thus the position assumed by a portion of the clergy under the new empire, and the unhappy attempts made by a certain school to revive the most unpopular ideas, filled him with bitter and inconsolable sadness. All the efforts that had been made since 1830 to persuade the nation that the clergy aimed at nothing more than common rights, that they respected the past, but did not seek to bring it back, and that they aspired to one thing only, namely, perfect freedom of speech, of action, and of teaching, whilst at the same time sincerely respect-ing the rights of others—all these efforts were defeated by evidence which seemed to prove the very contrary. We were condemned to hear Catholics reproached by the public with having attempted to practise a de-ception ; we had to witness the clergy in a short time losing the influence and popularity which they had gained during the preceding twenty years, and to behold old jealousies revived, and the old dread of the priest renewed ; he was now regarded less as a man of God than as a party-man, and we had once more to see him attacked rather as a political enemy than as the representative of religion. All this caused Père Lacordaire much pain. Hcw profoundly did it sadden and humble his great mind, his heart so enamoured with the twofold love of the Church and his country! His one great prayer was for the exaltation of the Church ;[1] this was his passion, and he now saw her interests compromised by the very men who pretended to defend them. He saw the priesthood losing little by little the respect, veneration, and confidence of the public. He was far from recommending a hostile attitude towards the existing government, and, for his own part, he was one of the first to applaud a war which he believed would tend to the profit of the Church, and the enfranchisement of a people ; but he considered that in a state of society like our own, where the reins of government pass with such frightful rapidity from one hand to another, and where the tendency is daily to a more radical democracy, there was no hope of progress and honour for the national faith save in an attitude of independence and dignity on the part of the clergy, by which they might hold themselves aloof from every party ; and he repeated with M. de Tocqueville, " Christianity is a living man attached to a dead body ; cut the bonds which bind them together, and the living man will rise and stand on his feet!"

Père Lacordaire was not permitted to see the hour of this future resurrection ; he died still suffering from the sorrowful spectacle which grieved his faith even more than his patriotism. But he never gave way to

[1] " I recommend you to pray continually for the welfare and freedom of the Church, particularly in the countries where she is most threatened. A Christian ought not merely to care for his own personal salvation, but for that of his brethren, and should ever be solicitous for the destinies of the Church. She is the only eternal work to which we can be associated ; everything else passes away."—*Unpublished Correspondence.*

despair, and he saluted from afar the dawn of that day invoked by so many prayers. He rejoiced in the thought that all his life he had laboured for it without having betrayed anything or denied anything, pure from all cowardice and all defection from his principles. He rejoiced in this thought, together with his illustrious friend the Count de Montalembert, one of the few combatants who remained faithful to the standard of their younger years, and said to him, "Whatever may happen in our own time, the future will dawn over our graves. It will find us pure from dishonour, from defection, and from all adulation of success, and constant in our hope of a political and religious rule which shall be worthy of Christianity.

"For the sake of our faith we have despised the support of despotism from whatever side it has come, and we have looked for the triumph of that faith only in the arms which were used by the apostles and the martyrs ; and if it is ever really to triumph in this world which is given up to so many disorders of heart and mind, it will only be by those means which once obtained its victory over paganism, and have up to this time saved it from the united attacks of false philosophy and unsound politics."[1]

[1] *Le Père Lacordaire*, by M. de Montalembert, p. 255.

CHAPTER XVIII.

1849—1854

*Foundations at Flavigny, Paris, and Toulouse—Canonical erection of
the French Province—Nomination of the Most Reverend Père Jandel
to the office of General of the Order—Conferences at Toulouse—End
of Père Lacordaire's Provincialship.*

PÈRE LACORDAIRE had discharged his
debt to his country in 1848 ; he had cast
himself into the fire, and, as he confessed,
had even *been a little scorched by it*, and had
thus acquired the right to retire and devote himself to
a less dangerous kind of service. He resumed the
ministry of preaching in Paris and the provinces, and
did not give it up till 1851. He had undertaken to
preach the Advent of the year 1848 at Dijon, the
town where he had passed his youth, and which had
witnessed his first college triumphs. An affair, which
was of importance to him, pressed him yet more
urgently to fulfil his engagement. Some ecclesiastics
of the diocese, owners of an ancient religious house in
the neighbourhood of Dijon, had offered it, almost
gratuitously, to the great orator of whom Burgundy
was proud, in order that he might turn it into a Convent of his Order. He came therefore, to Dijon, and
once more saw "those beautiful spires that Henri
Quatre had admired, those broad clean streets, flanked

by their mansions of the sixteenth and seventeenth centuries, the town and the palace of the Dukes of Burgundy, the park laid out by Lenôtre according to the directions of the Prince de Condé, and that magnificent girdle of mountains and hills where the Burgundian vines are first seen extending their rich branches. This scenery has always charmed me," he continues, "and nowhere do I breathe an air which makes me feel more thoroughly what it is to have a native country.

"About fifteen leagues from Dijon, towards the north-west, on an eminence at the foot of which several valleys branch out, and whence one discovers the summit of the ancient Alise, the last rampart of the liberty of the Gauls, rises, as on a promontory the little town of Flavigny. Formerly it possessed a Benedictine Abbey, a College of Canons, and a feudal castle ; and the Parliament of Burgundy held its sittings here in the time of the League. But nothing of all this splendour now remains. The Abbey Church has been destroyed ; that belonging to the canons is turned into a parish church, and the castle has been transformed into a humble Ursuline school. Among the ruins of this decayed glory you discover, on a sort of terrace, a modest building which formerly served the purpose of a little seminary to the diocese of Dijon. A few ecclesiastics of the diocese, who clung to the associations of their youth, piously purchased it, awaiting some opportunity of consecrating it anew to the service of religion. They now offered it to me, and after having consulted with Mgr. Rivet, Bishop of Dijon, I accepted it from them on conditions which did honour to their disinterestedness. Although the climate of Flavigny is rather severe, it is less so than that of Chalais, and hither therefore I removed our young novices, reserving the mountain of Dauphiny to be still the residence of our students. The beginnings of Flavigny were poor enough. I remember that at first we had only seven chairs in the whole house; each one carried his own chair about with him wherever he went, from his cell to the refectory, from the refectory to the recreation room, and so on. But this state of things did not last long. A committee of ecclesiastics and laymen was formed at Dijon, with the Bishop at their head, to provide us with necessary resources, and for several years, in fact, we received from this source a charity such as we have never elsewhere met with."

Flavigny was his third foundation. It had nothing of the painful circumstances which had attended the two preceding ones. Not only did Père Lacordaire find in his native province many kind friends who generously came to his aid, and who a few years later presented him with a house at Dijon completely furnished, but no opposition was raised on the part of the press against this new extension of the Dominican family, as had been the case both at Chalais and Nancy. The young Republic had the rare merit of repudiating the foolish fears of preceding governments on the subject of the extension of the religious orders. However natural and inprescriptible were the rights enjoyed by every citizen of living according to his faith and conscience, the governments which held power, both before and after 1848, have shown themselves so jealous on this score as to do the greater honour to those who, by a solitary exception, exhibited a larger and more intelligent spirit.

What would have been thought by M. Martin (du Nord), that watchful protector of the interests of religion in France, had he been told that Père Lacordaire was about not only to plant his Order amid the desert rocks of Dauphiny, but even in the centre of the capital itself? Yet this was what actually took place on the 4th of November, 1849. On that day Mgr. Sibour, Archbishop of Paris, solemnly installed Père Lacordaire and his religious in the ancient Carmelite Convent. They no longer hid themselves as in 1844; the doors of the church, thrown wide

open, admitted a curious and friendly crowd ; on this
occasion also the hostile press was silent, being occupied in pursuing elsewhere than among the friars the
true enemies of the Republic. The narrative of this
foundation, and of the events that followed, forms one
of the last pages in the Memoirs written by Père
Lacordaire on his deathbed.

" Mgr. Affre," he says, " before his glorious death on
the barricades, had entertained the idea of founding,
in the ancient Convent of *Les Carmes*, the scene of the
massacres of the 2nd of September, 1792, a school of
higher ecclesiastical studies, and at the same time of
placing a body of auxiliary priests there to serve the
Church. After his death, his successor, Mgr. Sibour,
offered me the church with a portion of the convent.
It was, it is true, a precarious situation, only secured
to me by a lease, renewable at pleasure ; but as the
diocese of Paris was under an obligation of conscience
to place some body of priests or religious in the
church, I accepted the offer of Mgr. Sibour, and took
possession on the 15th of October, 1849.

" We were then on the eve of one of the greatest
political and religious events that has taken place
since the edict of Nantes. The Revolution of 1848
had at last enlightened a considerable portion of the
French *bourgeoisie*, and made them understand that
300,000 men will not suffice to govern a nation of
34,000,000, unless that nation be ready to submit to
the laws which are imposed by conscience, and which,
together with respect towards God, give birth also to
the respect which men owe to themselves. This light
had been long in coming, but it had come at last, and
allowed M. de Falloux, the Minister of Public Instruction and Public Worship, to present to the
Legislative Assembly the project of a law for liberty
of teaching, which had been prepared by a committee
named by himself, and which by its very composition
manifested the progress of men's minds. In it the
name of M. de Montalembert appeared beside that

of M. Cousin, the Abbé Dupanloup was associated
with M. Thiers, and M. Laurentie with M. Dubois.
Catholics were mixed up with supporters of the
University, and altogether made up a group of men of
honour, belonging, however, to widely opposite parties,
showing that good sense, good logic, and common
justice were about at last to take this all-important
question into consideration. In fact, all these men,
differing so widely both in origin and faith, were
agreed on the principle of free education, without even
excepting the religious orders from the benefit of
their law ; and it was accordingly adopted on the
15th of March, 1850, by a large majority, after France
had groaned for forty years under the monopoly of lay
education. It had required three revolutions to break
this yoke of slavery, as in the sixteenth century it
had taken thirty-six years of civil and religious war-
fare to gain the edict of peace and toleration, which
was a greater glory to Henri IV. than all his victories.
The law on the liberty of education was the edict of
Nantes of the nineteenth century. It put an end to
the hardest oppression of conscience, established a
legitimate struggle between all those who consecrated
themselves to the sublime work of education, and
gave to those who held a sincere faith the means of
transmitting it incorrupt to their posterity. . . . As
the edict of Nantes formed for a century the honour
of France, and the fruitful source of her Church's
moral and intellectual elevation, so the law of free
education will be the sacred boundary where our
differences, instead of resulting in hatred and oppression, will only wage a friendly war which will
advance the natural progress of society. If any rash
hand, however powerful, should one day dare to touch
that boundary established by common consent in the
midst of our divisions and revolutions, let them
remember that Louis XIV. in the height of his glory,
when he revoked the edict of Nantes, did but dishonour his reign, and prepare for the eighteenth

century and the ruin of his royal house. There are certain points in the history of nations which ought to remain fixed ; the edict of Nantes was one, and the law of free education is another."[1]

During the first few months after his installation in the house of the Rue de Vaugirard, Père Lacordaire began a series of moral instructions given in the Convent Church, simpler in their form than the Conferences at Notre Dame, the subject being taken from the gospel of the day. He preached in the morning, in the middle of the mass, commenting for about half an hour on the sacred text. It was the first time that he had touched on the practical side of Christian life. He did it in a very familiar way, sometimes allowing himself to allude to passing events, and often making unexpected digressions, and giving narratives which engraved the truths he spoke of more deeply in the minds of his hearers. These homilies, which were begun in Advent, and continued until the Lent of 1850, produced much good. "Only think," he writes, "I am becoming a curé. Every Sunday after the gospel I deliver a *prône* for half an hour, or if you like it better, a *homily*, on the gospel of the day. Our church is full. This sort of preaching appears to be liked, and to do good, perhaps even more good than the Conferences of Notre Dame."[2]

Meanwhile, the Holy Father, who was aware of the progress of the Friars-Preachers in France, was contemplating a step by which he trusted that Italy and the entire Order would derive benefit from the renewal

[1] *Memoirs.*—The reader will form his own judgment on some of the opinions expressed in the foregoing pages, and while respecting the convictions of the illustrious orator, many no doubt will widely differ in their conclusions. The Abbé Rohrbacher, a former friend of Père Lacordaire, and like him a disciple of M. de la Mennais in his happier days, has characterised the edict of Nantes in very different terms, as an act torn from Henri Quatre by the Huguenots, who thus "formed a nation within a nation, a state within a state, a Genevese Republic within the most Christian kingdom."—*Rohrbacher, Histoire de l'Église,* vol. xxvi. p. 248. (Translator's note.)

[2] Unpublished Correspondence. Paris, Nov., 1849.

of life in the old Dominican stock. From the time of his first accession to the Supreme Government of the Church, Pius IX. had shown himself solicitous for the reform of the religious orders, and had seized every occasion capable of advancing that delicate and difficult work. He now cast his eyes on the Rev. Père Jandel, who had been pointed out to him as the man most likely to second his projects, and summoned him to Rome in the month of July, 1850. The choice made of him in preference to the restorer of the Order in France was differently interpreted by different persons. Madame Swetchine expressed her opinion to Père Lacordaire in the following terms :—" I can conscientiously tell you that the honour done to Père Jandel is more specially referred to you, and that nothing has appeared more simple than that the Holy Father, whilst having recourse to the French fountain-head, should be unwilling to incur the risk of drying-up that fountain by your removal. Père Jandel will do almost all that you could have done at Rome, but how could he have taken your place in France ?"[1] Whatever may have been the real motives which determined the Pope to choose Père Jandel, the honour which thus redounded to the French branch of the Order was felt by Père Lacordaire as a sweet reward of his labours. " It is a great honour to us," he writes, " who scarcely count a few years' existence, that the Vicar of Christ should proclaim aloud, by an extraordinary choice, that we are indeed a living off-shoot from the Order of St. Dominic. I feel it as the sweetest reward of all my labours. . . . Whatever may have been the motives determining this choice, I can see in it nothing but a wonderful mercy on the part of God, who has not seen fit to remove me from my apostolic ministry, and throw on me for the rest of my life the cares of an administration which would have left me no time to write a line or speak a word. Père Jandel is myself without the inconveniences of

---

[1] Correspondence with Madame Swetchine, p. 497.

myself. I assure you I feel no other sentiment than that of the deepest gratitude."[1]

The elevation of Père Jandel to the office of General of the Order met, however, with certain difficulties at Rome, and was delayed for some time. Père Lacordaire, who foresaw the obstacles which would oppose the work of reform in Italy, and feared them for Père Jandel's sake, set out for Rome in the month of September of the year 1850, in hopes of preserving for the infant province of France the services of a religious whose absence caused him great embarrassment. This hope, however, was not to be realised. Père Jandel, who would gladly have escaped the burden of authority, had to bow his head and submit. On the 30th of September he received the Brief, which appointed him Vicar-General of the whole Order, and took possession of his office on the 2nd of October following.

Père Lacordaire took occasion of his visit to Rome to solicit the canonical erection of the French province, and thus to make it enter in a more definitive manner into the machinery of regular government, and share in all the rights of the ancient provinces. It was necessary for this to have at least three convents: we already possessed four—Nancy, Chalais, Flavigny, and Paris. Père Gigli, then Vicar-General of the Order, and now Master of the Sacred Palace, showed himself eager to meet Père Lacordaire's wishes on this point, and on the 15th September, 1850, being one of the feasts of St. Dominic, he signed the act which restored the French province to all its ancient rights and privileges, constituting Père Lacordaire the first Prior-Provincial.

This journey to Rome gave him an opportunity of dissipating certain prejudices which had arisen there, the echoes of those which prevailed in Paris. He was accused of having given utterance in his Conferences to unusual propositions on the subject of

[1] Correspondence with Madame Swetchine, p. 495.

the origin of sovereign power, on the coercive power of the Church, and the temporal dominion of the Pope. It was not the first time that he had been met with these accusations, the source of which was, however, unknown to him. He had no difficulty in giving categorical and satisfactory replies to all these questions, and in thus recovering that position of esteem and sympathy which was due to him from the Court of Rome on so many titles. The Pope received him with the utmost kindness, and expressed to him on several occasions, in the presence of other Frenchmen, his interest and good-will.

He returned to France to resume the course of his Conferences at Notre Dame. He was to finish the explanation of the dogmatic part of his subject during the Lent of 1851. The moral section still remained to be treated, and this he purposed dividing into two parts, the Christian Virtues, and the Sacraments. " Here is plenty to fill up the future," he wrote ; " but what is a human future ?" He spoke truly : un-looked-for events did not allow of his commencing the second part of his proposed task, and with a sort of presentiment of what was coming, he this year took a solemn leave of his auditors. He could not descend from that pulpit, which was henceforward to retain so illustrious a character, without thanking those who had there given him their support. This farewell to the auditors of the Conferences gave occasion for one of those rare and eloquent out-pourings which remind us of some great captain who takes pleasure in glancing back on his past glories with the old companions of his renown.

" Even although a new career is prepared for me by God, and my devotion to you," he said, " I cannot resist speaking to you as though I were bidding you farewell. Permit me to do so, not so much out of any presentiment of the future, but as a consola-tion to my own heart.

" I say a consolation, because I feel within me at

this moment two contrary sentiments : one of joy
when I reflect that I have completed with you a work
which may be useful to the salvation of many souls,
and that I have finished it in an age too truly called
the century of *abortions;* and the other of sadness,
remembering that no work can ever be completed by
man, without his having left behind him the best part
of himself, the first-fruits of his powers, and the flower
of his years.   Dante thus begins his divine epic : ' In
the midst of the path of life I awoke, and found
myself alone, and in a thick forest.'   Gentlemen, I
have reached that middle point in the path of life,
where a man parts with the last rays of his youth, and
descends rapidly to the shores of infirmity and forgetfulness.   I ask nothing better than so to descend,
since such is the lot marked out for us by an All-
just Providence ; but at least at this point of separation, whence I can once more look back on the
times that have just come to a close, you will permit
me to invoke some of the memories which so endear
to me both this cathedral, and you who have been
the companions of my journey.

   " It was here, then, when my soul once more opened
to receive the light of God, that His pardon descended
on my sins, and I beheld the altar, where I for the
second time received the God who had visited me in
the first dawn of my youth, on lips now strengthened
with years, and purified by penance.   It was here
that, prostrate on the pavement of this church, I rose
by gradual steps till I received the priestly unction ;
and after threading many a winding way, seeking for
the secret of my destiny, I found it at last in this
pulpit, which for seventeen years you have surrounded
with your silence and your respect.   It was here that,
returning from a voluntary exile, I brought the religious habit which half a century of proscription had
banished from Paris, and presenting it before the eyes
of an assemblage, rendered formidable by the numbers and variety of those who composed it, obtained

for it the triumph of unanimous respect. It was here
that on the very day that followed a revolution, when
our public squares were yet scattered over with the
fragments of the throne and the signs of war, you
came to listen from my mouth to that Word which
survives all ruins, and which on that day inspired an
irresistible emotion, and was saluted by your applause. It is here, under the pavement near the
altar, that slumber my two first archbishops; he who
summoned me, when still young, to the honourable
task of instructing you, and he who recalled me to
the same task, when a distrust of my own powers had
for a time separated me from you. And it is here,
on the same archiepiscopal throne, that I have found
in a third Pontiff the same kindness and the same
protection. Finally, it is here that have sprung to
life all those affections that have consoled my life,
and that I, a solitary man, unknown to the great, and
a stranger to parties, ignorant of all that attracts the
crowd and binds fast the mutual relations of the
world, have met with those souls who have given me
their love.

"O walls of Notre Dame! sacred vaults that have
carried the echoes of my words to so many minds
from whom the knowledge of God was shut out;
sacred altars whence I have received so many blessings, I do not bid you farewell; I am but telling all
you have been to me, and pouring out my heart
before you, whilst I remember all your benefits, even
as the children of Israel, at home or in exile, still
celebrated the memory of Sion. And to you, gentlemen, in some of whom I may perhaps have sown the
seeds of faith and virtue, I shall ever remain united
for the future as in the past; but if one day my
strength shall prove too little for my courage, and if
you come to despise the feeble remains of a voice
that was once dear to you, know that I will never
be ungrateful, for nothing can prevent you from being

henceforward the glory of my life, and my crown throughout eternity."[1]

Such were his adieus to the cathedral of Notre Dame, which he used to call *his great country*. " I always salute it," he said, " as soon as on entering Paris I perceive its towers."[2] After the *Coup d'état* of the 2nd of December, 1851, he did not again return to the cathedral pulpit, in spite of the repeated solicitations addressed to him by the Archbishop of Paris.

He set out almost immediately after that event to visit the convents of Belgium and Holland, over which he was Vicar-General, and then passed into England, where the Dominican sap[3] had also penetrated. He only remained there three weeks, during which time, however, he visited three convents of our Order, and was able to form a general idea of the English people. The spectacle of the progress of Catholicism in that country inspired him with views as to the future of the world, which our readers will thank us for here reproducing.

" This journey, short as it has been, has greatly interested and consoled me. Our Lord is at work in this great country ; we shall not have the happiness of seeing it Catholic, but perhaps that spectacle may be reserved for our descendants. I cannot feel any despair on this head, or doubt that the gospel will reign one day over the entire universe, in spite of individual revolts, which, however numerous they may be, do not prevent nations from belonging to Jesus Christ. Thus, though there are many unbelievers in France, and many men equally licentious in life and

---

[1] Conference 73.   [2] Letters to Young Men.
[3] A slight liberty has been here taken with the text of the author, whose expression, " La sève dominicaine *française*," would lead his readers to infer that the English Dominican Province derived its origin from a French source. Such, however, is not the case ; the existing English Province being lineally descended from the Convent of Bornheim, founded in Belgium for English friars during the reign of James II. by Cardinal Philip Thomas Howard, in the year 1657.--*Translator's Note.*

in intellect, one cannot deny that France is a Catholic nation. The breath of the gospel animates the grand mass of her children, although many only submit a portion of their life to its influence. I do not believe that the order of things established in the middle ages with its methods of coercion will ever be re-established in the world ; but little by little, as all nations enter into more rapid communication with one another, and power no longer lends its support to error, schism, and false religions, two centres of unity will spring up, the one positive, which will embrace all Christians, and the other negative, which will unite all sceptics ; and from the struggle between these two colossal powers will result the combats of the last days. This is the light in which I regard the future."[1]

The days of his pilgrimage were now hastening to their close. He was only fifty—in the prime of his age and strength—and yet only ten years more of combat and labour remained for him before he was to sing the canticle of the dead : " My life is carried away from me, and folded up like a shepherd's tent." But God was preparing a noble crown for the remainder of his years, in a new undertaking, more humble, but not less rich in fruit, than all those of his former life. After having been occupied so long in the highest kind of instruction, he was to consecrate his last years to the education of youth ; he had sown the seeds of truth in the vast field of the intellects of his own generation, and now he was about to take the rising generation, and cultivate its heart. Could there be imagined a more enviable conclusion of a career which was already so full ? To use his own words, in speaking of his friend, Frederic Ozanam: " As there is in every great soul a sort of necessity of finishing the monument, the idea of which it has conceived, and which is to bear its name, so in the great soul united to God there is felt the need of

[1] Unpublished Correspondence. Flavigny, 1852.

finishing the work which has been begun for Him, and wherein its name is to be engraved beneath His own."[1] The education of youth appeared to him to form the natural completion of his life ; and he recognised and blessed the hand of God in those events which concurred to engage him in this new undertaking.

We shall relate more at length in the following chapter how the Founder of the Third Order adapted to the work of teaching,[2] understood and carried out the idea of education. We shall content ourselves here with saying that for a long time he had been urgently pressed to accept for himself and his Order the direction of a school established at Oullins, near the gates of Lyons. He decided on doing so during the summer of 1852, bought the college, and sent the first members of the Third Order destined for the work to make their noviciate at Flavigny.

He did not, however, on this account, give up the direction of the First Order. The new undertaking was merely an increase of his family, enlarging at once both his labours and his joys. Henceforth these two branches—the Teachers and the Preachers—were mutually to lend support to one another. A discourse delivered by Père Lacordaire on occasion of the translation of the head of St. Thomas Aquinas at Toulouse gave rise to the first idea of a Dominican foundation in that city; and it was Toulouse that gave Sorèze to the Third Order. Toulouse had been the first cradle of the Friars-Preachers ; there the holy Patriarch St. Dominic had raised his first house ; and that city, so rich in relics, gloried in possessing the body of St. Thomas Aquinas, the greatest doctor

---

[1] Notice on Ozanam.

[2] It may be well to remind the English reader that Père Lacordaire was in no sense the founder of the Third Order of St. Dominic, which dates its origin from the lifetime of the holy patriarch himself. But he was the first to establish convents of religious men of that Order exclusively devoted, not to apostolic work, like the Father of the First Order, but to the work of education.—*Translator's Note.*

of the Order, if not of the entire Church. Père
Lacordaire, therefore, eagerly accepted the proposals
made for commencing this new establishment. He
writes as follows, on the 24th of October, 1853:—"I
set out to-morrow for Toulouse. No foundation—
and this is our sixth including that of Oullins—has
ever caused me so lively a joy. I feel as if I were
returning to my own country, and as if St. Dominic
and St. Thomas Aquinas were about to receive me
into their arms." And a few days later: "Though
accustomed for ten years to receive from Heaven
blessings like these, this one has, nevertheless, sunk
deeper into my heart, and touched me more profoundly than any. It seems to me like the crown of
all the graces which God has granted me during my
life, and as if nothing could go beyond it, unless for
me to show myself somewhat less unworthy of what
I have so gratuitously received, during the few days
of life that yet remain.

"Each time that I pass through these streets and
roads of Toulouse, the thought occurs to me that
St. Dominic once passed there also ; and comparing
my own life with his, I am surprised that God should
have chosen as the instrument for re-establishing his
Order in France one so little resembling its founder.
Every Wednesday I go to St. Sernin to celebrate
Mass at the tomb of St. Thomas, for the intention of
our Order, and of the French province in particular."[1]

The installation of the Dominicans at Toulouse took
place on the 30th of December, 1853, and was celebrated by Mgr. Miolaud. Nowhere had they been
welcomed with more devout and profound sympathy :
every one seemed to look on them as brethren
coming back to their native country after a long
exile. Old men who remembered having seen
the former generation of Dominicans smiled on
them as on old acquaintances, and related a thousand anecdotes of their fathers of the days anterior

---

[1] Correspondence with Madame Swetchine, pp. 528, 531.

to the great Revolution. The following year Père Lacordaire resumed, in the Cathedral Church, and in the same pulpit from which St. Dominic had once preached, the course of his Conferences of Notre Dame. His plan embraced the whole Christian life, and, if completed, would have occupied six or seven years. He was only able to give the first series. These Conferences have been published, and form a continuation of those of Notre Dame. In them he displayed all his old eloquence, but with a certain diminution of physical strength, which did not allow of his voice reaching the further ranks of his audience with the same fulness and vibration as formerly.

During the course of the Conferences, a Joint-Stock Company of Toulouse, who had purchased the ancient school of Sorèze in order to prevent its falling into the hands of Protestants, came to offer its direction to Père Lacordaire, and to beg him to carry out their views and wishes, by founding and perpetuating in that illustrious house a solidly Christian system of education. They left him the entire and absolute administration of the school for thirty years, with power to apply its revenues to his own profit, so as gradually to extinguish the action of the proprietors, and thus to cause the proprietorship to pass into the hands of new directors without incurring any unfavourable risk. These conditions being submitted to the Master-General, and approved by him, were signed by Père Lacordaire, who took possession of the school at the distribution of prizes, on the 8th of August, 1854. His new functions as director of a great college were to fill up the remaining years of his life, and to withdraw him from every other occupation. He therefore gave up his purpose of continuing the Conferences of Toulouse, in order to consecrate himself entirely to the important work to which God was now calling him.

The Province had now been for four years canonically erected, during which time he had governed it according to the constitutions of the Order, but in reality he had been its head for sixteen years. He therefore convoked the first regular chapter at the Convent of Flavigny for the 15th of September, 1854, and, before resigning his power, desired to render an account of his administration to his brethren and children.

In this written memorial, he first of all recalls the history of the foundation of the five first convents of Nancy, Chalais, Flavigny, Paris, and Toulouse, without reckoning the two colleges of Oullins and Sorèze. Each step taken in the re-establishment of the Order had been purchased at the price of a death, and each new house had risen over some fresh grave. From this he took occasion to sketch in a few words the lives of those elder brethren who had now become our protectors in heaven. We have quoted these extracts when speaking of their history in its proper place. " May their tombs," he adds, "always devoutly visited by our posterity, be a constant memorial to those who shall come after us, of the great hearts who were given to us for awhile, and then snatched away !" He then sums up the apostolic labours of his children who had been permitted to bring back the Dominican habit to all the great towns of France, and there to gather abundant fruits of grace, testimonies of the assistance of the Holy Spirit of God, " Who alone opens, enlightens, and converts souls." He states the progress of the theological studies: " St. Thomas," he says, " is their star, as he has always been : taught with conviction, but without that superstitious idolatry which allows nothing to be seen outside of his writings ; so as to make them into a restriction, whereas they should be a vivifying fire." He invites his brethren to thank God with him for having enabled him to support eighty-three religious, not indeed without much difficulty and many privations, but without compromising the future, thanks to that pru- dent moderation and deliberation which he had made a law of his administration. "Our resources," he says, "have been derived from our work, from the patri-mony of some of our brethren, and, in a very small degree, from the pious donations that have been made us. It is remarkable that very little help has come to us from strangers to the Order. Many persons, however, with very moderate means at their command, have assisted us as much as was in their power, and if we do not here name them, it is from no want of gratitude, but only that we may leave their charity shrouded under the veil with which their modesty has covered it. Many prayers and good wishes have fol-lowed us in our trials ; many narrow purses have been opened to us, and the penny of the poor will one day be found to have contributed not a little to our foundations."

He reminds his brethren of the rule which he had traced out with regard to postulants entering the Order: "A rule," he says, "which we must never abandon ; first, to leave our religious before their profession full and entire liberty of heart on the subject of their wills ; secondly, to accept of nothing bestowed by them to the notable injury of their near relations, but to induce them to respect at one and the same time the rights of their family, and the honour of the Order."

He concludes as follows :—

" Here, then, my reverend Fathers, I bring to a close the account I owe you of my administration. I thank you, and in you I thank the entire Province, for the affection it has constantly shown me, and which has ever sustained me in the trials naturally inseparable from a foundation. At Rome, in Pied-mont, and in France, we have lived together as breth-ren, and by our union, in the midst of the hardest labours, have defeated the efforts of an enemy whose blows we have felt without ever knowing its name. Death, whilst striking down the best and dearest among us, has bequeathed us their virtues, which would have been our joy and our example had they gone before us on the way, and which have been our strength before Him Who withdrew those dear ones from our eyes that He might keep them before His own. We have lost much, but much has also been regained. Thanks to those who are dead, and those who are living, we may now put off our swaddling bands, and, though still young, lay aside the ties of an authority which has lasted four times as long as the time allowed by our Constitutions. In surrendering my powers, I could have wished to have made obedience more sweet and easy to you by practising it myself, and this, as it seems to me, would have been both most useful to you and most happy to myself. But without my having chosen it, another mission, closely connected with the first, calls me far from you. I accept it from the hands of God, whether it be that He wills, through my hands, to found the Third Order devoted to the work of education, or that He has other designs over me which escape our penetration. I go, therefore, without however quitting you, praying God to bless me together with you, to maintain in our houses, and in your hearts, peace, union, regular observance, faithful submission to authority, the spirit of our saints, and the apostolic life, and to make you increase and multiply 'as the stars of heaven, and the sand upon the seashore.'"

Tranquil with regard to this first and greatest work of his life, which he saw firmly established, and in a fair way to make progress, he was now able to turn his whole attention to this new family of the Third Order, which was yet in its cradle, and to lavish on it the cares and labours of that spirit of self-devotion which renewed its youth in the well-springs of his heart.

CHAPTER XIX.

Foundation of the Third Order, devoted to the work of Teaching—Oullins—Sorèze.

THE idea of the religious education of youth was one of very old date in the mind of Père Lacordaire. It may be remembered that when at Rome in 1838, at the time when he was settling the preliminaries of his project for restoring the French branch of the Order in concert with the Master-General, he had asked and obtained permission to establish colleges in connection with the Order. He always wished to make instruction from the pulpit and the education of youth march side by side in the front ranks of his work. He remembered how he himself had lost his religious faith and the innocence of his soul at the Lyceum of Dijon. He had entered the college pure in heart, praying, and loving the God of his mother; and he left it with his faith ruined and his morals blemished. This, he well knew, was almost the universal lot of young men. Was there no remedy for so monstrous an evil? The University doubtless possessed excellent masters; but all did not hold the same religious belief as that of the families who were compelled to intrust their children to their care. Religious faith was not sufficiently protected in these

schools, and Père Lacordaire himself, in spite of the
wholly exceptional care bestowed on him by his
excellent master, M. Delahaye, had not been able
to save his religious principles from a precocious
shipwreck. Here, then, was a gap not yet filled up,
and one deeply to be regretted. Moreover, besides
the supernatural gift of faith, the heart of a child
requires much care ; his moral nature has to be cultivated, and the real work of education, properly so
called, has to be carried out. The mere knowledge
of the dead languages, the acquirement of literary
tastes, even philosophy itself, will not suffice to make
a teacher; there must be the paternal sentiment, the
disinterested love of souls and of the young, the
spirit of self-sacrifice and devotion to this adopted
family, and the resolution to renounce every other
domestic joy. All preceding generations had been
educated by religious bodies of men vowed to a life
of celibacy, who understood their calling in this light,
and gave an equal care to the soul, the heart, and
the mind of the child. This was the tradition that
now required to be revived. Hardly had Père Lacordaire recovered his faith, and assumed the character
of the priesthood, then he presented himself before
the public as the intrepid champion of this idea of
education, but of an education that should be complete, and therefore free, since the only body which
then held the monopoly of instruction could do
nothing for the soul, and very little for the heart.

In concert with M. de Montalembert, he had been
the first to open this great question of liberty of instruction by the affair of the Free School, just after
the revolution of 1830; and before the Court of Peers
which tried that case, he proudly assumed the title
of *Schoolmaster*. Nor did he cease to maintain this
sacred cause with the weight of his words and his
name during the twenty years that the struggle lasted;
and when at last it was definitively gained by the
law of the 15th of March, 1850, he at once set him-

self to consider in what way he should make use
of this long-expected freedom, and became a schoolmaster in good earnest. It is true that the secular
clergy and the Jesuits already possessed a few houses
of education, and were about to open others; but the
same motives which had induced him to restore one
of the ancient nurseries of preachers in spite of the
co-existence of other similar Orders, satisfied him that
there was also room for a new teaching body in addi-
tion to the older ones already at work. In education,
in fact, as in every other human undertaking, it is
from the equal competition of many hands that there
arises that legitimate emulation which tends to progress and perfection. Moreover, each Order has its
own peculiar character, corresponding to the varied
needs of man, and to the thousand shades of opinion
and taste which must always be met with in every
Christian nation. There is now as ever, even among
Catholics, a great diversity of views and systems with
regard to things both human and divine; and this
is the natural result of that liberty which God has
left to man on all questions not affecting the integrity
of religious dogma; *in dubiis libertas.* It would be
madness to try and check this diversity of opinions,
and to pretend to make all diverging currents return
into the same monotonous channel. This, as we all
know, would be the wish of certain schools, both of
believers and unbelievers, who, under pretext of religious unity or State policy, would gladly see the
sceptre of education in particular engrossed for the
profit of their own exclusive doctrines, and withdrawn
from the hands of all those who do not think like them.
But Divine Providence breaks their clumsy efforts, and
at the right moment raises up the man and the work
which is to save more liberal ideas from the autocracy
of narrow dogmatists, and the oppression of mono-
polists.

Père Lacordaire was not long in perceiving that
his first idea of applying the Friars-Preachers in-

differently to the work of preaching or that of education was an impracticable one. The rule of the First
Order is too austere for men devoted to the wearing
duties of education. Fasting and perpetual abstinence
are incompatible with the exhausting labours of the
professor, and, moreover, the obligation of assembling,
at certain fixed hours, for the recitation of the Divine
Office in choir, would constantly have interfered with
the necessity incumbent on the masters of attending
to their pupils. He had, therefore, to resolve on
creating a new branch, under the wider and more
supple rule of the Third Order. The College of Oullins furnished him with an opportunity for making his
first attempt.

This house had been founded in 1833 by a society
of secular ecclesiastics, whose chief member was the
Abbé Dauphin, now Canon of St. Denis. These
gentlemen professed the same opinions held by Père
Lacordaire himself, which were indeed those of the
vast majority of Catholics. The school of Oullins was
therefore founded on principles at once Christian and
liberal. At its first establishment it had been placed,
by a kind of inspiration, under the invocation of St.
Thomas Aquinas, and the motto chosen for it consisted of these words of Holy Scripture, *Deus scientia-
rum Dominus*, which correspond so well with that of
the Friars-Preachers, " *Veritas.*"

The intelligence, self-devotion, and remarkable
talent of the first founders soon raised Oullins to an
honourable rank among the houses of free, secondary
education. But after a period of from twelve to
fifteen years, the college experienced the trial insepar-
ably attendant on every undertaking which depends
on personal and private exertions. When time, exhaustion, and death have taken away the first devoted
labourers, we ask ourselves with anxiety, What is to
become of the future? Into whose hand is the work
to descend? It was then that the thought suggested
itself to several of the younger professors of Oullins of

obtaining the support of some Religious Order, and thus securing the perpetuity of their common work. In 1851 they accordingly opened their plan to Père Lacordaire, who asked time for prayer and reflection ; after which they communicated with the original directors of the school, one of whom [1] replied to them as follows :—" I should die happy if I knew that Oullins was in the hands of the Order of St. Dominic." The next year the idea of filiation to the Order, blessed by God, had taken root and grown. The proprietors and directors of the school were inclined to give up the house into Père Lacordaire's hands on favourable conditions, and, on the other hand, four young professors of Oullins offered themselves to receive the habit of St. Dominic, and to return, after their year's noviciate, to take the direction of their beloved college. The contract was agreed to on these terms, and on the 25th of July, 1852, the day when the institution celebrated the feast of its patron, St. Thomas Aquinas, the Abbé Dauphin, in presence of Père Lacordaire, the masters, the pupils, and a numerous assemblage of friends and parents, solemnly announced in the chapel that the college had been made over to the Order of St. Dominic.

This was a day of real happiness to Père Lacordaire. He beheld Providence ministering like a tender mother to his most earnest desires, and he blessed its goodness with the simple joy that is known to pure and great souls. The evening before he communicated the good news to Madame Swetchine : " How I wish," he says to her, " that you could see this magnificent house of Oullins, standing on a hill which overlooks the Rhone, and from which you catch a view of Lyons, the mountains of Bugey, the Alps, and the plain of Dauphiny ! God spoils us in the matter of beautiful scenery : one marvel succeeds to another, and I am sometimes frightened, I feel so unworthy of all this. He treats me like a favourite child, with

[1] The Abbé Chaine, who died in 1860.

whom one may safely commit any folly. All things are to be found in God; even marks of tenderness which fill us with wonder because we cannot see their reason."[1]

On the 1st of October following Père Lacordaire took the four first novices, who were to become the corner stones of the new edifice, to Flavigny; they were the Rev. Fathers Captier, Cèdoz, Mermet, and Mouton. On the 10th of October, the feast of St. Louis Bertrand, he wished to consecrate the memorable date of the inauguration of the Third Order by a grand religious ceremony. They set out in procession from the chapel of Flavigny, and followed, singing hymns, the winding paths that had been cut by the religious in the woods on the side of the hill: and at the projecting corner of a rock, which stands over one of the terraces, they set up a small stone cross, which received the name of the Cross of the Third Order. Père Lacordaire delivered an address to the religious arranged in a semicircle around him, and they returned to the Convent in the same order, singing Canticles.

The Third Order adapted to the work of education was something of a novelty to the Dominican body. It was necessary, therefore, to lay down its principles, to harmonise them with the canonical rule of the Tertiaries, to study such special regulations as should form constitutions peculiar to the work of teaching, and finally to initiate the first labourers chosen by God for this noble mission into the religious life. Père Lacordaire applied himself to this task with his customary ardour. As soon as the novices had taken the habit, which was nearly the same as that worn by the Great Order, with the exception of the scapular, he installed them in some small cells prepared for them near his own, and became himself their novice-master. He assembled them in his own room three times a day. The morning meeting was

---

[1] Correspondence with Madame Swetchine. July, 1852.

held for the purpose of working at the Constitutions; these he prepared in private, and afterwards explained his views to them, asking the opinion of each one, and generally adopting the side of the majority. After this, notes were drawn up, on which the discussion might be resumed at the next meeting. This labour in common was based on the rule of the Third Order, the Constitutions of the Friars-Preachers, and the personal suggestions of the religious themselves, joined to those of the professors who had preceded them. Père Lacordaire had at that time no fixed programme of education. He knew that rules of this sort cannot be formed all at once, but can only be definitively settled by experience. The second, or afternoon's meeting, was devoted to the explanation of the rubrics and customs of the Order. This duty was always undertaken by Père Lacordaire himself; and in the evening, after collation, he took his recreation with his novices, and in free and familiar conversation completed that work of religious initiation, which is even more a work of the heart and of mutual confidence than of study and mental labour. Besides these regular meetings his door was always open to them, and at whatever hour they came to seek him he would interrupt his own occupations to listen to them, to lead them to God, and to devote to them as much time as they required. They found in him that firm and gentle direction, so austere, yet so paternal, so large and simple, of which we have elsewhere spoken, together with his profound love for Jesus Christ crucified, and his two grand means of sanctification, humility and penance. In the month of August, in the year following, he took his little colony back to Oullins, and the four religious who had all persevered, full of faith and hope in the success of their undertaking, pronounced their vows on the feast cf the Assumption, the 15th of August, 1853.

The first foundations of the work had been laid during this year of recollection and of interior pre-

paration, the basis of all the rest. The new directors
of Oullins would earnestly have desired to have kept
among them their natural head, him on whom the
future of the Third Order depended. But his duties
as Provincial, which were not to expire till the
following year, did not permit of his taking up his
residence at Oullins. He contented himself, therefore,
with frequently visiting them, and keeping up an
active and constant correspondence with his new religious. It was not until 1854, and when at Sorèze,
that he was able exclusively to devote himself to the
Third Order, and to study practically, on the spot,
the question of education, which was so new to him,
as well as so serious and complex.

Sorèze was an ancient Benedictine Abbey, founded
in 758 by Pepin le Bref, at the foot of the Black
Mountain, at the extremity of a fertile plain watered
by abundant streams. Like so many other abbeys,
Sorèze had very early a school attached to the
monastery, where the noble youth of the surrounding
country came to receive education. This school of
Sorèze obtained great renown towards the end of the
17th century, in consequence of a succession of
favourable circumstances, a slight sketch of which may
prove not uninteresting to the reader. The astonishing success it enjoyed during the 18th and the
beginning of the 19th century was owing to a con-
stellation of eminent men, who succeeded one another
as its managers almost without interruption, the catalogue closing with the name of its most illustrious
director, whose glory is reflected on those who went
before him, without, however, effacing it. The first
Benedictine who gave celebrity to this great school
was Dom Jacques Hoddy, Prior of Sorèze, towards
the close of the 17th century, about the year 1680.
Under his skilful management the pupils grew so
numerous that it became necessary to lodge them in
the town, and then to construct new and larger
buildings for their use. Dom Hoddy was the architect

of Sorèze. In the middle of the next century the Chapter-General of the Benedictines having assembled at Marmoutier, sent one of its most remarkable members, celebrated alike for his learning and the boldness of his ideas, to take charge of the school, which had at that time somewhat fallen off. Dom Fougeras well fulfilled his task; he it was who created the literary renown of Sorèze, as Dom Hoddy may be regarded as having laid its material foundations. In a very few years the famous school recovered all its former prosperity, thanks to a new system of studies introduced by Dom Fougeras, and continued by his successors. He was a man of universal learning, and repudiated the old method of the universities, in which he considered that the pupils wasted much time in the study of the dead languages, and were obliged altogether to neglect a number of other branches of knowledge not less useful in forming a complete education, and specially those of the arts and sciences. According to his system, instead of concentrating into one class, and under one master, the various studies of Latin, Greek, history, geography, and literature, each of these branches of study had separate hours and professors. Mathematics, both elementary and transcendental, and the arts, whether useful or ornamental, also had their place in this universal course. " Instead of being brought into communication every day in the year with only one professor, who was charged with informing him with a certain amount of monotonous intellectual culture, the pupil of Sorèze now saw and listened to six or eight professors every day, who by turns engaged his interest; and for private study he had only the time strictly necessary for developing the oral instruction he had received. If one master failed to gain the desired influence, another supplied his place, and under so many teachers it was impossible for a boy not, one day, to meet with that ray of illumination which was

30

to inspire him with the taste for learning, or reveal to him the mystery of his vocation."[1]

This plan of studies, so much less simple than the ancient one, required, it is true, a considerable staff of professors, and led to a somewhat complex entanglement of hours and engagements, which were perpetually crossing one another; but in the hands of one capable of directing all the various wheels of the machinery, it had the advantage of assigning a larger place to the sciences, which are ordinarily too much neglected at the universities, and, above all, of giving free room for the expansion and development of each one's personal attraction. The success of the new method of teaching was immense, and the celebrity thus gained by Sorèze drew thither numerous scholars from all parts. There was, of course, as will always be the case in such matters, plenty of opposition; people criticised the innovators who thought they could improve on the old method; they ridiculed the idea of monks giving lessons in *fencing;* but the opinion of the public was on the whole in favour of the new system over the old routine; and we may remark here that the first step in giving importance to the study of the arts and sciences in classical schools is due to the monks, and that the opposition was raised on the part of the lay university teachers of that day.

The work of Dom Fougeras was completed, and the glory of the school carried to its highest pitch by a third Benedictine, this was Dom Despeaulx. He undertook the management of the school in 1767, and kept it for twenty-five years. Not less learned than his predecessor, nor less partial to the cultivation of scientific studies, he formed a cabinet of natural history at considerable cost; he taught mathematics himself, and frequently exercised his pupils in measurement and land-surveying, and in taking plans of the surrounding country, in order that those among them who might afterwards be destined to serve their

---

[1] Père Lacordaire, Prospectus of Sorèze, Aug. 8, 1854.

country in the profession of arms, might not be ignorant of the different branches of knowledge necessary to them. Success crowned all these efforts; the pupils of Sorèze drew attention in every career which they embraced, and the college was at last erected into a royal and military school, a title confirmed to it by Louis XVI., on his accession to the throne. When the Revolution broke out, Dom Despeaulx went to Paris, where he hoped to be able to remain unknown. The Abbé de Montgaillard, who had been formerly his pupil, relates of him, that " having come to Paris to conceal himself and escape the scaffold, he managed to hide his poverty and his virtues, until he was at last denounced to the revolutionary committee of the section in which he lived. He was summoned to appear before the famous Payan, a friend of Robespierre. Payan was an old pupil of Sorèze, and, recognising his master, he fell at his feet, and gave him a ticket of safety and citizenship. After the 9th Thermidor, the virtuous and learned Benedictine earned his livelihood by giving lessons in mathematics, at the charge of twenty-four sous a lesson, and walked six or eight leagues a day to gain his bread."[1]

Such was the poverty to which this venerable man was reduced, when Napoleon, who so well knew the value of men, found him out in his misery, and rendered him the justice that he deserved. We shall let the Abbé de Montgaillard relate the anecdote. " Napoleon had charged Fourcroy, Councillor of State, to prepare a report on the organisation of the University, and the nomination of the inspectors. On reading over this report he was interrupted by Napoleon in the following terms :—' But I do not see among these names that you present me that of Dom Despeaulx. Have you never heard of the military school of Sorèze, which has produced so many pupils who have done honour to their country ?' ' Sire, I did not think that

[1] " History of France," by the Abbé de Montgaillard, tom. v. p. 191.

an old monk—' ' Sir, this *monk* is an illustrious man ; he has done great services to his country, and has brought up an entire generation ; he deserves to be assisted and honoured.' Napoleon then seized a pen, and inscribed the name of Dom Despeaulx at the head of the list of inspectors-general ; and at the first creation of the legion of honour he decorated him with the cross of the Order. Dom Despeaulx held his post until 1816 ; he was then ninety years of age, and died two years later."[1]

The Revolution did not cause the school of Sorèze to be closed. At the moment when all the Benedictines dispersed before the persecution, one alone had the sad courage to remain, unterrified at the guilty conditions imposed by the civil constitution of the clergy. Dom François Ferlus was professor of rhetoric and natural history. He now assumed the management of the school, and caused himself to be acknowledged its proprietor. But if, thanks to his capacity and to the talent of the eminent professors with whom he surrounded himself, Sorèze, under his direction, lost nothing of its former celebrity, as much cannot be said, unfortunately, for the spirit and tendency of the school, which completely changed, and repudiated the religious traditions of the first founders.

Let us add, however, that Dom François Ferlus was far from being an ordinary man. He was one of those men of great talents and great characters who, it must be owned, were at that time very commonly trained in the religious houses. In spite of heavy financial difficulties, which weighed on his administration for the first few years, he chose to keep and maintain at his own cost fifty pupils belonging to the Spanish, French, and English colonies, whose families, in consequence of the calamities of war, were unable to pay their pensions.

He died in 1812, and was replaced by his brother,

[1] "History of France," by the Abbé de Montgaillard, tom.[v. p. 191.

Raymond Dominic Ferlus, a former professor, whom he had associated in his work at the time of the dispersion of the religious orders. Dominic Ferlus, like his brother, kept up the Benedictine system of studies, and defended it with talent and energy in the *Journal des Débats* against the radical reforms which he was required to accept. He concluded by quoting those celebrated words pronounced on a somewhat analogous occasion — "*Sint ut sunt, aut non sint.*" He attributed the ever-increasing success of the school to this method, for he now reckoned under his direction more than four hundred scholars. He sent a great number to the Polytechnic School, where almost all took the highest degrees. The College of Sorèze, which under the Restoration had been in opposition to the government, lost its credit after 1830, and rapidly declined. In 1840 it was purchased by a Catholic Joint-stock Company, who confided its management first to the Abbé Gratacap, and then to the Abbé Bareille. These two eminent priests employed all their zeal to restore the school to the Christian and prosperous system of the ancient Benedictines. But the task was beyond the strength of men who depended only on their single efforts. It was reserved to Père Lacordaire, aided by his religious, to renew the sacred and glorious traditions of old Sorèze.

He took possession on the 8th of August, 1854, the day of the distribution of prizes. We may observe that he came to Sorèze with real pleasure. The prospect of passing the rest of his life within the walls of a college in the midst of a crowd of school-boys, far from repelling him, filled him with delight. His love for the young embellished his new retreat in his eyes, and peopled it with the most attractive images. He was going to live among them their own life, to initiate their young minds into the knowledge of all that was great and beautiful, to speak to their souls, to wean them from evil, and form them into men and Christians. He blessed God at the prospect before him, and expressed his satisfaction and his sanguine hopes to his friends. His holy impatience to serve those whom he loved so much did not allow him to foresee all the difficulties of the work he had undertaken, and, what was better, it gave him the assurance of final success.

Without this touch of priestly and paternal tenderness for the young, his genius would have been an obstacle rather than an aid. What children want is less great talent, than that amiable wisdom that knows how to be little with little ones, and a soul that is able to communicate itself to other souls. Too much light does but dazzle their minds, without penetrating them. Bossuet and his eagle genius obtained no influence over the mind of the dauphin ; whereas Fénélon, endowed with far less sublime gifts of intellect, but with a tenderer and more supple soul, became a true teacher, master and father to the Duke of Burgundy. Coming to Sorèze in his fifty-second year, after having up to that time exercised his intellect on the highest metaphysical speculations, and lived in intimate intercourse with a small number of chosen minds, with whom he had pursued profound and elevated studies on the providential government of the world, there was a possible fear that Père Lacordaire might have been wanting in that flexibility of character so necessary in college life, where metaphysics hold a very unimportant place, where conversation invariably turns on the progress of one pupil or the idleness of another, and where the whole policy is reduced to the infliction of punishment, or the distribution of rewards. There is nothing more grand and sublime than the *idea* of education, nothing more humble and obscure than the practical life of a *schoolmaster*, and nothing which requires a more complete and more constant abnegation of self. A man must be called to this office. Happily, Père Lacordaire had received that call. He felt the cost of the sacrifice, it must be confessed, and it was in this sense that he called Sorèze a tomb, *viventi sepulchrum*, but a tomb which gives rest and shelter, *beneficium ;* for he entered it willingly, in order that he might there complete the work that was dearest to his heart.[1]

Let us hear him during the vacation of 1854, in the great deserted college, counting the days that still intervene before the return of his children, and pleasing himself during their absence in embellishing their old Sorèze for them. " Our college," he writes, " is very beautiful. I like it extremely. I have already rubbed up the old place, by making some necessary repairs. I look forward with pleasure to receiving the pupils, who ought to return on the 18th of this month. I feel like the father of a family who has been beautifying the residence of his children, and is impatient until they can enjoy it. One begins at my age to cease to live for oneself. When I was young, I loved fame and glory; now the repose of a useful obscurity is the only thing that has any attractions for me."[2]

The father of a family : no words can better express what Père Lacordaire was at Sorèze. He had no fixed ideas on the subject of education ; but he possessed what was infinitely better than any system— the light which springs from tried self-devotion, and the infallible instincts of a paternal heart. He came resolved to labour at forming these children into men and Christians, and no one had a more noble and elevated ideal than he of those two grand creations.

He set out on this principle, that what forms the character and makes the faith take root is less constraint than persuasion, less fear than love. From the outset, therefore, he publicly announced to the boys that they would be left perfectly free as to the accomplishment of their religious duties. Each pupil was,

---

[1] He said of Sorèze: " It will be the tomb of my life, the asylum of my death, and to both a benefit ; *viventi sepulchrum, morienti hospitium, utrique beneficium.*"

[2] Unpublished Correspondence.

as a point of discipline, to present himself once a
month to the chaplain ; but neither at confession, nor
even at the Paschal Communion, was there any one
appointed to see that these duties were fulfilled. The
immediate result of this proceeding was that it became
necessary to restrain the ardour of the pupils for confession ; had they been allowed, they would have
presented themselves every day. It is not meant by
this that they all became little prodigies of virtue as
if by enchantment. Far from it. It even took many
years before the remains of the irreligious and undis-
ciplined spirit of the Sorèze of the Restoration was
entirely effaced. But they soon lost their repugnance
to religious practices : religion appeared to them what
it really is—the sweetest friend of man at every age;
and they felt drawn to her by an attraction so much
the stronger, because it was free and spontaneous.
During the first few years, when Père Lacordaire or
any of his religious appeared in the courts during the
hours of recreation, the boys hastened round them,
discreetly touching their white habits, as though they
possessed some mysterious virtue ; and, in fact, they
learned by this contact with goodness and virtue to
become better, and to love all that their masters
loved.

Père Lacordaire understood better than any one
how indispensable to the establishment of faith in the
soul is the spoken word of the priest, the ministry of
persuasive preaching flowing forth from the earnest
conviction of the preacher, *fides ex auditu.* It was the
want of this that he had so felt in the Lyceum of
Dijon, where the only preaching he had listened to
had been destitute alike of argument or eloquence ;
whilst, on the other hand, the masterpieces of pagan
antiquity were daily engaging the enthusiasm of his
young imagination. Things had greatly changed
since that time, and Sorèze in particular, whilst under
the management of the Abbé Bareille, had enjoyed
the good fortune of possessing as chaplain one of the

most distinguished priests, not only of the diocese of Albi, but of all the south of France—the Abbé Cavalier. Père Lacordaire had it greatly at heart to maintain the ministry of preaching in its place of honour, and to give it as large an influence as possible. He himself preached every fortnight throughout the year alternately with the chaplain, and every week during Lent ; and two other instructions were given by his religious. He treated this sublime ministry of the word of God with the honour and respect of an apostle, who feels all the importance of his mission. He made it a rule never to preach without previous preparation, even on ordinary occasions, and however much he might be pressed. At Sorèze his age and multiplied occupations, his constant habit of speaking in public, and the youthful character of his audience, never induced him to depart from this rule. He gave a week to the preparation of his college discourses, as he himself acknowledged to a young religious who showed too much facility in making use of his gift of speaking impromptu. But what dignity and power did his words possess ! How they stirred these young minds, subjugating them to the faith, and raising them to those divine heights where he had caught his inspiration ! The pupils were proud of their great orator ; they assisted at his sermons as at so many festivals, and came away from them electrified and transformed : and certainly of all those masters of rhetoric on whose immortal pages their attention was directed during the week, none left on their minds so luminous and profound a trace as he who thus interpreted to them that uncreated Beauty which they beheld through the rays of his eloquence. For seven years he continued a regular course of lectures on moral subjects, such as prayer, penance, the last end of man, the constituent elements of Christian life, faith, fear, hope, and charity. The general outline of these discourses has been found among his papers ; but unhappily this naked framework is wanting in all

the magnificent development which gave it life and
motion. Nor has anything been preserved by short-
hand; for, absorbed in the pleasure of listening, the
hearers never thought of gathering up anything for
the future. He mingled the most practical and
familiar advice with the most elevated instructions,
sometimes introducing historical anecdotes, which
were supplied by his prodigious memory as from an
inexhaustible mine. One day he related to them how
a curé in the neighbourhood of Sorèze, having come
to visit the school, had been struck by the marks of
politeness and respect which he met with on the part
of the pupils. Père Lacordaire thanked them for the
pleasure which this caused him, and took occasion to
inculcate anew a sentiment of profound faith for all
holy things and persons, and specially for the clergy.
"If Plato and Socrates," he said, "could have seen
this spectacle of a grave and learned man, the friend
of true wisdom, shutting himself up in a little village
to cultivate the minds and consciences of a few poor
peasants, to instruct their children, console them in
their troubles, and assist them in their death, they
would have been rapt in admiration. And yet such is
a village curé! Perhaps in such a way of life he may
acquire manners less polished and refined than are to
our taste, but under this rustic exterior there is far
more real self-devotion than is to be found in the
noblest circles of the aristocracy. It was the blood of
the barbarians which regenerated the Roman Empire,
and it is always the blood of the people which is the
organ of great things, and of that in particular which
saves the world—priestly devotedness. Napoleon I.
was one day surprised, while out walking, by a terrible
storm, which obliged him to take shelter in a cottage.
As he stood at the threshold of the door, he saw a
poor curé pass by, who was braving the storm with
hurried steps. The Emperor called to him, and
asked him where he could possibly be going in such
weather. 'Sir,' replied the good priest, who did not

recognise him, 'I am carrying the last consolations of religion to a dying man.' Napoleon, much touched, looked round on his companions, and said, ' See what stuff our French curés are made of !' "

Such was ordinarily his style in his college instructions; simple and familiar, but always full of a certain elevation of thought, which reminded you of the orator of Notre Dame.

He had another way of reaching the souls of his children yet more effectual than his preaching; it was the more intimate intercourse of the Confessional. He heard the confessions of a considerable number of the pupils of the first and second class. He saw them every week, or every fortnight. His door was always open to them, and none were ever sent away on the pretext of his being engaged. He lavished on them his time and his care with a liberality as boundless as the love he bore them. It is impossible to convey any idea of this devotion. His penitents were his most constant occupation; it was chiefly on their account, and in order to have them under his fatherly eye, and to be at their service by night and by day, that he finally established his residence at Sorèze; that he went away as little as possible; and that once, when at Paris, he took a journey of two hundred leagues, as M. de Montalembert relates, in order not to deprive his children of his spiritual assistance. His illustrious friend tried to detain him on some important matter of business; "No, I cannot stay," he replied after a slight hesitation, "it would perhaps make some of my children miss confession who have been preparing for the next feast. One cannot calculate the effect of one Communion less in the life of a Christian." The confessions were almost always followed by a confidential conference, in which the soul of the Father poured itself out with ineffable sweetness into that of the youth: he questioned him about his dispositions, his progress in study, his temptations and trials, painting to him in a lively

manner the beauty of virtue and the deformity of
vice ; and, above all, speaking to him of the love of
our Lord Jesus Christ, apart from which there is
neither peace, victory, nor happiness. This was, beyond contradiction, the means by which he effected
the most good ; the weakest souls yielding to the
power of that persuasive tenderness which was far
more irresistible than the studied eloquence of the
pulpit. And I cannot weary in repeating that the
secret of this ascendency was not in his genius, but
in the sacred attractions of the heart of the father, the
priest, and the friend. " I can only define the sentiment which we feel for our pupils," he said with an
accent thoroughly characteristic of himself, " by one
word, a word that is very famous, and yet very simple
—*we love them !* What will touch the heart of man
if the soul of a child does not touch it ! What will
ever soften him, if not the soul of youth, wherein the
mortal struggle is going on between good and evil?
We have no merit in thus loving them ! Love is its
own recompense, its own joy ; it brings its own riches
and benediction."[1]

How could souls thus trained fail to respond to the
call of such faith and charity ? How could such devotion to his noble ministry fail to be blessed by God?
The moral regeneration of the school by the spirit of
piety was visibly accomplished ; and on sending back
the children to their families at the end of the year,
the faithful pastor was able to say, " On their return
home, all these children, without a single exception,
will be able to join you in your prayers. Not one of
them has been tainted by that poisoned breath which
in our time attacks minds as early as their fifteenth
year, and deprives them of the light of heaven, even
before they have known the world. Religion has
regained an empire in this school, which she will never
again be deprived of. That empire has been estab-

---

[1] Discourse pronounced at the distribution of prizes at Sorèze. Œuvres
Complètes du Père Lacordaire, tom. v.

lished, not by constraint, or by the mere pomp of exterior worship, but by the sincere and unanimous conviction of the pupils, by duties fulfilled in private, by aspirations known to God alone, by the peace which is felt in virtue, and the remorse that is caused by vice ; by those solemnities in which all hearts meet together, and are united in an emotion which hypocrisy can never inspire, which is checked by no human respect, but is the generous fruit of true community of sentiments."[1]

This was, in fact, the kind of piety which he encouraged, leading his children to regard with equal horror both hypocrisy and human respect. He often repeated to them that, to be a good Catholic, it is necessary first to be *a true man*, to cherish all the natural virtues, such as integrity, uprightness, courage, and honour, without which piety is nothing better than a mask, concealing the most grievous wounds of the soul. "Whilst seeking the supernatural," he said to them, "be careful never to lose the natural." In order thus to cultivate their hearts as well as their souls, to *bring them up* according to the true sense of that beautiful expression, he also made use of the spoken word, but in a form less solemn than that of the pulpit, and less sacred than that of the Confessional,—I mean in his familiar conversations. He liked to talk with these young people, well knowing that it is in such intimate intercourse that characters come out and are corrected, that the intelligence is quickened, the imagination refined, and the heart opened to every generous instinct. Every evening after dinner he assembled the members of the *Institute* in the great hall. These were the elder pupils, the chosen members of his family, and he generally spent an hour conversing on all sorts of subjects with these young students.

In nothing did his devotion to his work at Sorèze

[1] Discourse pronounced at the distribution of prizes at Sorèze. Œuvres Complètes du Père Lacordaire, tom. v.

appear more admirable. as it seems to us, than in this
evening recreation. The idea was certainly good ;
but to carry it out demanded a patience and kindness
of disposition which love alone could inspire. The
collegian does not generally know how to converse.
The art of conversation, so difficult everywhere, even
in France, supposes a certain fitness of ideas, and a
method of seeing them and expressing them, of
which the schoolboy is quite incapable ; he does not
yet think for himself, and has no views of his own ;
he knows nothing of life, and nothing of the world ;
of what, then, should he talk, if not of his games and
his tasks, two subjects, one of which is not serious
enough, whilst the other is too much so ? It may
perhaps be thought that Père Lacordaire had in
sufficiently large measure what was wanting to his
young companions, in order himself to support all the
burden of the conversation. But then this would
have been to have made the talking a discourse ; and
he did not mean that it should be anything of the
kind. What he wanted was a real exchange of ideas
and sentiments between himself and his children. All
his attempts would have failed to make it so had it
not been for that gracious amenity which disposed
him to stoop to these minds so far beneath his own,
and which restored a certain sort of proportion between them. These familiar conferences in no way
resembled the studied dialogues of Socrates with his
disciples. It was not a class added to those of the
school-room, but a real recreation, a joyous intercourse, in which every one was at liberty to laugh
with all his heart ; and where the master's example
taught them that simple, cheerful conversation, full of
life and nature, is at once the most agreeable and
most profitable of all amusements invented to unbend
the mind. All stiffness was unscrupulously excluded
from these meetings, and he who should have taken
it into his head to wish to appear *fine* before his companions, would have been reproved for his affectation

by a sort of raillery which would soon have cured him of any desire to repeat it. The Father put every one at his ease, listening with interest to the smallest details, keeping up the fire of conversation, and always maintaining it on a level with the standard of the minds of his company. He related anecdotes, talked of his mother, of the Lyceum of Dijon, of his schoolboy tricks, and of everything, in short, except politics. He never touched on that delicate subject in their presence ; and this he made a law to himself.

One fête-day, during dinner, a professor, a Pole by birth, rose, and in the name of his country proposed Père Lacordaire's health as a toast, in gratitude for the sympathy which he had always evinced for Poland. The Father replied, "Although I have made it a rule with myself since I became the director of this school never to speak of politics in any public assembly, nevertheless, I cannot refrain from saying in reply to the kind words just addressed to me, that now and ever I shall heartily pray for the liberty of Poland."

Whilst becoming a child with his children, allowing their minds perfect freedom, and touching on a thousand subjects in the course of the evening, the skilful master knew, nevertheless, how to awaken reflection, and exercise a right judgment. One of the pupils once made use of a very simple word which he thought every one understood. The Father stopped him and asked him to define it. The young philosopher was embarrassed, consulted his companions, who were all equally puzzled, and greatly astonished at not being able to find a good definition for a thing they thought they perfectly understood. The Father then gave his own, and explained to them that to know how to make a definition is at once the most difficult of all mental exercises, and the one most calculated to make us reflect and master an idea. At other times he would give a phrase or a Latin verse to translate, and liked to exercise their taste in

the choice and arrangement of expressions. I remember, among others, the following line of Virgil :

"*Non ignara mali miseris succurrere disco :*"

which he thus translated : " I learnt from misfortune
itself to help the unfortunate."

Père Lacordaire read and recited admirably. He
had suppressed the theatrical representations which
were formerly held at the close of the year ; but he
wished to supply the advantage which they possessed,
in teaching the boys how to speak in public, by himself giving them lessons in reading. Before his conversion he had sometimes gone to the French theatre
to see the productions of the great masters acted.
He always experienced that disenchantment which, as
he says, is felt by every mind specially endowed with
any high sense of the beautiful. He relates of
Frederic Ozanam, that having gone to see *Polyeucte*
acted for the first time when he was twenty-seven,
his impression was that of disappointment. " He
felt," says Père Lacordaire, "as all do whose taste is
sound, and whose imagination is keen, that nothing
can equal that representation which the mind gives
to itself in the silent and solitary perusal of the great
masters."[1]

To give his pupils some idea of what good reading
is, and what it requires, he related to them an
anecdote of Talma. In a certain Paris *Salon*, the
great tragedian had been requested to read something from Bossuet ; and the first page of his funeral
oration on the queen of England was proposed to
him, beginning, " Celui qui règne dans les cieux."
Talma asked for eight days to prepare ; the eight
days passed, and they pressed him to keep his promise. Accordingly, he began to read ; but at the end

[1] Frederic Ozanam, by Père Lacordaire. (The English reader will be
forcibly reminded in this passage of the remarks of the late lamented
Cardinal Wiseman, in his last unfinished fragment on " William Shakespeare," wherein he speaks of the advantage enjoyed by those who read,
over those who witness, the acted representations of our great dramatist.)

of a few lines he stopped, and declared he could go no farther. " The thing was simple enough," added the narrator, " he broke down under the greatness of his subject." Accordingly, he was accustomed to assemble the higher classes in the Hall of Arts, and there the orator of Notre Dame would read a scene from Corneille or Racine. It was a sort of intellectual revelation. The young men who had perhaps just been learning these same verses in their classes thought they were listening to entirely new words, and assisted at these intellectual feasts in a stupor of admiration.

It is easy to imagine the results that naturally flowed from the presence of such a master, from his daily intercourse with the scholars, his words, his instructions, and his example. The standard of education sensibly rose ; the soul, the heart, and the intellect, were all naturally and without effort elevated under the influence of one superior soul. The state of the college studies had greatly declined since the time of the old Benedictines. From the outset Père Lacordaire employed all the resources of his creative genius to reorganise them, improve their character, and stimulate their progress.

The Benedictine plan of studies had undergone great modifications : some remains of it still existed, but the necessity of bending to the requirements of University programmes induced him to abandon the idea of thoroughly restoring it. Moreover, he had so decided a predilection for what was simple, accurate, and orderly, that the perpetual entanglement of hours and exercises in the Benedictine method was not at all to his mind. He had his own college recollections, and held to them ; he always liked to lean on his personal experience, and to be able to say, " At Dijon they did so and so." He therefore ended by simply adopting the ordinary University system.

The school had many good professors whom it kept. His presence at Sorèze attracted other ex-

31

cellent masters, who remained faithfully with him
to the last. He often assembled them together, inquired into the best methods of teaching, made them
give him detailed reports of the studies and progress
of the boys, and himself overlooked the classes, and
held the examinations. "Just imagine," he writes,
"I am sitting for seven hours a day putting questions
in Greek and Latin, explaining authors, and in fact
leading a regular college life. I am surprised to find
how much I preserve of my old studies, which nevertheless ended thirty-five years ago. This proves how
powerful is the first impression received in education.
Everything rests on that, without effacing or destroying that first furrow into which every seed is afterwards so laboriously sown. Thus I had never looked
at Greek since 1819, yet without being able to explain
Greek authors at sight, I find I am able to recall their
forms, and a multitude of words.[1]

He multiplied the means of emulation by a system
of rewards and degrees, which began with the lower
classes, and followed a boy even after he had left the
school. The detail of these would be too long. We
will only instance a few of his principal contrivances.
There was a literary academy attached to the school,
called the *Athenæum*, into which, on his entrance,
each member presented a written paper of a certain
value. The Father enhanced the importance of this
society by forming it out of the best scholars, and attaching to it considerable privileges. In order to be
admitted a member, it was necessary for a boy to
have obtained the first place for at least six times in
the first class, or twelve times in the second ; and,
moreover, to have a good character in point of conduct. The *Athenæum* held its sittings once a week,
and these were always presided over by Père Lacordaire. Two papers were then read on some question,
treated from two different points of view, and a discussion was held on the question, each one maintain-

---

[1] Unpublished Correspondence. March, 1855.

ing his own thesis against the objections which might
be brought against it. The Father summed up the
debate, and gave his opinion with his reasons. The
Athenæum was entitled to an annual walk ; but its
great privilege lay in the fact that it opened the door,
and was a necessary stepping-stone to the *Institute.*

The *Institute* was the highest division in the school.
Its members were withdrawn from the ordinary school
discipline, and placed in a position midway, as it were,
between the college and the world. They occupied
a separate quarter of the building, and had separate
halls and apartments. They dined at the master's
table, which was always presided over by the director,
and took their recreation in the Park. The three
chief officials of the school, namely, the sergeant-
major, the master of ceremonies, and the ensign,
were chosen from their ranks.[1] The members of the
Institute could not exceed the number of twelve, and
were exclusively recruited from the *Athenæum.* They
were directly under the superintendence of Père
Lacordaire ; and the sergeant-major, who held the
first rank among them, was held responsible for their
conduct. They were no longer regarded as school-
boys, and the only punishment that could be inflicted
on them was to be turned out of the *Institute.* The
nomination of a new member was an affair of some
solemnity. It generally took place on some feast-
day, either that of the college, or of the director.
The whole school was assembled, and the name of
the newly-elected was proclaimed aloud. The pupil
rose from his seat, and, accompanied by the sergeant-
major and the master of the ceremonies, came and
stood a few paces in front of Père Lacordaire. The
director then told him the reasons for which he had
been chosen. This public eulogium from the lips of

---

[1] The College of Sorèze always retained its character as a military
school. All the pupils, armed with muskets proportioned to their size,
were trained to the management of arms and military manœuvres, under
the command of an old military captain.

31—2

the Father, who was ordinarily so moderate in his praise, was the best part of the reward, and what the pupil enjoyed the most. The ceremony ended with this formula : " Do you promise to be a good and loyal member of the *Institute*, and as far as possible to promote the peace, good order, and dignity of the school?"—" I do promise."—"You are then a member of the *Institute.*" And then the Father gave him the *accolade* in the midst of general applause.

It would be impossible to describe the interest which was attached to this nomination, kept secret till the last moment, and with what incredible ardour the pupils looked forward to the hope of one day carrying off the golden palm, and becoming one of the fortunate twelve. And perhaps a greater happiness still was reserved, not for those who were elected, but for their families, who were able to say, " Our son is not merely under the direction of Père Lacordaire. but he enjoys his confidence."

There was, however, one more degree, which was even rarer and more envied than that of the *Institute;* t was that which bore the title of the *Student of Honour.* A pupil when about to quit the school, of which he had been the ornament by his industry and good conduct, might be chosen *Student of Honour.* Only one was chosen every year. His name was given out on the day of the distribution of prizes, in presence of the families of the pupils. The Father publicly praised him, making known the reason that had obtained for him this extraordinary distinction. and then embracing him, gave him a gold ring and a diploma. The *Student of Honour* had the right every year to spend a fortnight at the school, and was officially informed of everything of importance that was done there. At his death, his funeral elegy was pronounced in the college chapel, and a service was annually celebrated for the repose of his soul.

All these means of encouraging emulation would have been of little use, however excellent in themselves, had it not been for the life infused into them by Père Lacordaire. The success in education depends far less on the novelty of the method than on the devotion of the teacher. A college is formed after the image of its head, as a son is after the image of his father. The fame of the new Director of Sorèze of course did much to promote the prosperity of the school ; but, great as this was, it would not of itself have been sufficient had Père Lacordaire given himself less completely up to his work. He was, in fact, the soul of the college ; everything passed through his hands, and his influence was felt in the smallest details as well as in the most important circumstances. The pupil who was forgetful of his duty might be quite sure that his fault would not escape the vigilance of the director, nor the severity of his reproofs ; whilst the diligent scholar felt that he had a father's eye invisibly watching over him, and knew that all his efforts were known to him, and noticed with pleasure : this was his first reward, and his best encouragement. All these things required incessant activity, and a constant care to hold the reins of government with a hand at once firm and gentle. Nor did he fail for a moment in this duty, often so wearisome and overwhelming. His room, which was in the centre of the college buildings, was all day long full of professors or scholars. It was the heart of the whole establishment, and the seat of life.

Père Lacordaire was also the soul of the games, public walks, and holidays, as of everything else. He put an end to the Easter vacations, and granted in the place of them, a certain number of whole holidays, which were scattered over the year. On these days, he himself took the boys out, and delighted in conducting them through new paths to some of those beautiful spots surrounding Sorèze, all of which he knew by name, and the beauties of which he made them admire with him. They set out on these occasions at six in the morning, and did not stop till eleven. The Father, stick in hand, walked at their head setting them an example of ardour and spirit. About eleven they reached their journey's end, and sitting down on the grass soon forgot their fatigues while disposing of a repast seasoned with an excellent appetite. The Father also provided himself with his favourite dish, a salad and some hard eggs. After the dinner was over, seated at the foot of a tree, and surrounded by his children, he would chat with them cheerfully, telling them little stories, until, overcome with fatigue, he would lean his head on the shoulder of the one nearest him, and take a quiet *siesta.* He has not forgotten these pleasant walks in his letters to Emmanuel : " I was reminded by your letter," he says " of all those beautiful spots where we have wandered together in the forests of the Black Mountain, specially St. Ferréol, Arfons, Alzan, and Lampy, those dells and valleys obscure enough to the stranger's eye, but dear to the sons of Sorèze, and yet dearer to me than to any of you, because I bore into those solitudes the heart of a father."[1]

He excelled also in the art of getting up those little *fêtes* which remind a boy of his absent home-pleasures, and give him a greater love for his studies, his masters, and the walls of his college. Père Lacordaire formed the idea of celebrating the secular anniversary of the restoration of the school, and of its most glorious period, under Dom Fougeras in 1757, by a grand solemnity. The details of this memorable festival have been given in the *Correspondant.*[2] The Father pronounced an admirable discourse, and caused an obelisk to be erected in the Park in commemoration of this great day. On it he engraved the following inscription :

> " *Primum scholæ sæculum*
> *Post decem abbatiæ sæcula.*"

The renown of Sorèze daily increased. In a few

[1] First Letter to a Young Man. [2] Sept. 1857, tom. xlii.

years the number of scholars had risen from 120 to upwards of 300. This rapid prosperity was not effected, however, without some difficulties, both interior and exterior. A thousand absurd and ill-natured reports were circulated about the school. During the first few years it was constantly necessary to reassure the families of the boys, who were alarmed at rumours that Père Lacordaire was about to quit Sorèze on account of the failure of his attempts to set the college on a better footing. One day they were celebrating the Director's feast in one of the great halls. In the midst of a crown of flowers and foliage the pupils had placed the name of Ozanam, whose life had just been written by Père Lacordaire. The Abbé Perreyve, who had arrived at Sorèze a few days before, found himself seated at table on the right of Père Lacordaire. He could not resist saying a few words full of emotion, in which he mentioned with affection the names of his two friends, Ozanam and Lacordaire. On again taking his seat, he leant towards the Father's ear, and whispered something to him in a low tone. The Father rose : "Gentlemen," he said, with a smile, " it is reported at Toulouse that the pupils of Sorèze have hung their Director in effigy." The sergeant-major, M. Serres, immediately rose, and replied : "My Father, they know a great many things at Toulouse ; but what the public does not know, and what we should like to teach it, is that we would all willingly be hung for you."

It must, however, be acknowledged, that the first years were difficult enough, and that it was only gradually that the spirit of old Sorèze gave way. The Father was even obliged to decide on several expulsions, a step he did not hesitate to take, though it cost him bitter sorrow. One year, when it had been necessary several times to have recourse to this stern act of justice, he could not repress his grief when bidding farewell to his children on the day of the distribution of prizes ; and the violence he had done to his fatherly feelings by banishing from him these rebellious and ungrateful members, drew from him a complaint of touching eloquence. "On the day of the most joyful solemnities," he said, "the father of the family sees around him some empty places that ought to have been filled; he utters in secret the name of his absent child, whose presence is wanting to complete the festival. Alas! where is the earthly festival from which no one is absent? In vain do we arrange everything beforehand; in vain do we reckon and prepare our ranks; there is one who overthrows our calculations, an invisible hand that reckons after us, and who makes a sign, which we perceive too late, beckoning away some one from the place whom we least expect to lose, and perhaps the one whom we love the most dearly. When Œdipus, blind and aged, presented himself on the threshold of the temple at Colonna, in order to appease the Fates, he carried in his right hand an olive bough, and in his left another of cypress. Such is an image of man in his fairest days. And I, like Œdipus, carry these two branches in my hands to-day, and the table round which my family is seated is not filled. It is true that the gaps have been made by justice; but the justice of a father costs him tears of regret. I express these regrets to you, as a last remembrance of those I have lost, and as a homage to those who remain."

Those whom he thus regretted knew better than any one else how much he had loved them and how sincere was his sorrow; and the day when Sorèze mourned her lost *king*, many showed that they had never ceased to venerate the father after they had felt the hand of the judge; for on that day four of the pupils formerly expelled from the school followed the funeral *cortège* and mingled their tears with the rest.

The first difficulties having been overcome, Sorèze, under the powerful influence of its Head, soon became a model school. It could bear comparison in every respect with the best houses of education, and, moreover, acquired a certain great and elevated character that betokened the direction of a superior mind.. Every one, whether masters or pupils, were gainers by their daily contact with him ; everything, in some way or other, bore the impress of the master's personality, by that law of imitation which forms part of the nature of man, and especially of the boy. The pupils of Sorèze all had a deep and passionate love of the beautiful ; the old masters of style were read and relished by them with feeling and intelligence. In fact, Père Lacordaire, who has often been most unjustly branded with the epithet of a *sentimentalist*, was a severe partisan of the classics ; perhaps even too severely so, scarcely appreciating any contemporary writer, with the exception of Chateaubriand.

To that taste for the beautiful, which is the ornament of the mind, the pupils of Sorèze joined that love of simplicity which purifies the soul. Père Lacordaire waged implacable war against those habits of luxury and excessive delicacy which pass too often from the family into the college, and are as injurious to the purse as to the health of the boys. He banished all the vain superfluities which he found added to the military simplicity of the old school traditions.

Having observed that some wore girdles of silk or wool, " Henceforward," he said, " let no one wear anything but a leather girdle ; that is the only one to which one can hang a sword." One day he perceived that some of the boys had eider-down coverlets on their beds; he gave them a public rebuke : " Eiderdown !" he said, " for shame ! leave such things to women and sick people.' For my part, when I was at the Lyceum at Dijon, if I was cold, I put my trunk upon my bed." It was the custom at Sorèze to give little *soirées* from time to time, when the pupils of all the different classes assembled in the great hall, and by thus mixing together learnt to know one another, and to acquire those habits of politeness which are sometimes forgotten in the midst of school familiarity.

Père Lacordaire, aware of the advantages of these meetings, did not abolish them ; he even required the professors and religious to be present at them, in order to strengthen the ties of cordial intimacy between them and the pupils ; but he diminished the expenses of the refreshments and delicacies which it had become the custom to introduce on these occasions. He reminded them of the frightful distance which separates us from our ancestors in our manner of recreating ourselves. "Formerly," he said, "people used to invite their friends and neighbours to a table where the feast was celebrated, and heartily too, over home-made cake and old *vin du cru ;* and now-a-days, the son, a tradesman perhaps, as his father was before him, grows weary in finely-furnished chambers, over a banquet in which five or six different sorts of wine do not furnish the relish which is wanting to the feast. Formerly the same furniture lasted for many generations; but now the old furniture is changed with the old traditions, and the son no longer feels a pride in being able to say, ' There is the arm-chair where my father used to sit !' Now-a-days, the smallest tradesman thinks it necessary to refurnish his house at least three times during his life; but, on the other hand, his dwelling is small, and everything wants air, space, and good taste. The rooms are loaded with rubbish, often purchased at a high price, of which nobody can tell the use ; neither those who buy, nor those who sell, nor those who admire it."

An education based on principles like these was not merely Christian, but patriotic ; and by inspiring these young men with the love of simple and severe virtues, Père Lacordaire was, it is needless to observe, labouring efficaciously for their happiness, both in their family and in society. The contrary maxims have unhappily borne their fruits, and the most prejudiced minds begin to see the gulf dug under our feet by the Antichristian principles of the present day on the subject of luxury.

What, then, was wanting to this system of educa-

tion in order to make it complete? Sincerely, we
do not know. Based on the Catholic dogmas, immovable and fruitful; cherishing with honour the old
classical traditions, and giving to science and letters
their just, but not an exclusive place; opening the
minds of the boys to look to something beyond
the mere acquisition of Greek and Latin erudition,
and casting into the soul the divine seed of virtue;
teaching a young man to love his country and his
age, without concealing from him the wounds of
either; preparing for the family circle strong and
honest hearts, for society enlightened members, and
for the Church docile and generous children; forming,
in short, complete men and earnest Christians—this
glorious system, by which the young were trained
under a man of genius, had but one fault,—that of
being of too short duration. It lasted but seven
years. Sorèze had hardly risen from its ruins, and
been restored to its ancient splendour, when the architect died. And yet he did not altogether die. His
devotion had gathered others around him; a considerable number of young priests had been assembled, willing, like him, to consecrate their lives to the
grand work of education. The Third Order was
fairly founded. At the close of 1855, the first year
of the restoration of Sorèze, sixteen members of this
new branch of the Dominican family were gathered
around their chief. They had had their part in the
work of restoration, and on the death of Père Lacordaire they were able to carry on his undertaking, not
indeed at Sorèze, whence, unfortunately, circumstances soon obliged them to remove, but at Oullins,
at the gates of Lyons, and at Arcueil, near Paris, the
true sons of Père Lacordaire—the faithful heirs of
his spirit and his love for youth—they will go forth
thence to raise homes of education on the fruitful
soil of France, the character of which will be at once
Christian and national. Who will venture, then, to
complain of their work? Who would desire to check
it? The enemies of France and of the Church, it

may be, will do so ; but even if they have the will to
overthrow this work they will not be able to succeed.
Sooner will the germinating power be repressed in
the bosom of the earth than will the irresistible
strength of the Catholic life, produced and multiplied
by the spirit of religious devotion, be prevented from
bursting forth : " *Oaks and monks are immortal.*"

Wonderful fecundity of the apostolic spirit in the
Church ! So soon as a man has received this divine
vocation, he rises and goes forth, like the sower in
the gospel, casting the sacred seed broadcast into the
hearts of men, leaving it to God and to time to make
it grow and multiply through succeeding ages. Then
that seed strikes such vigorous roots that it acquires
almost indestructible perpetuity. Père Lacordaire
was the son of one of those heroic apostles who, six
centuries ago, peopled the world with innumerable
offshoots of his religious family. Swept from our
soil by the revolutionary tempest, all the old blossoms
had disappeared, and the sap, for us at least, seemed
exhausted, when suddenly it sprang up to new life in
one of the noblest characters of our time, who restored
its youth and its former fame,—and now we see it
once more extending its comely branches over our
land, under the shadow of which the children of the
coming generation may repose and find pasture.
When years shall have passed over the tomb of the
illustrious restorer of the Dominican preachers and
teachers, when his memory shall have become
dimmed, though not forgotten, in the minds of men,
his self-devotion will yet have lost nothing of its
vital energy. It will still call forth numerous voca-
tions similar to his own around his many colleges ;
and his future descendants will be raising new Sorèzes,
where youth will continue to be loved and educated
in all the great Christian and social virtues. Such is
the hundredfold of increase promised to those hearts
that are willing to sacrifice themselves. Such is the
fair immortality of virtue !

CHAPTER XX.

1860—1861.

Last Illness and Death of Père Lacordaire—Conclusion.

PÈRE LACORDAIRE was destined never to leave Sorèze. Advancing years, added to the cares and austerities of his life, had slowly diminished his strength and shortened his days. The end was close at hand, and yet nothing had as yet warned him of it. His faculties of mind and will, which remained full and entire, deceived him as to the shortness of the time which yet was his. Happy in the midst of his children, full of a tender care for their souls, which every day grew more intense, he loved his college ; free from all ambition, sought no other happiness than that of devoting himself to his work, no other reward than that of loving and being loved ; and was able peacefully to rejoice as he felt his heart growing young again, unsuspicious of the secret malady which was sapping its life.

" Religion," he said about this time, " is the true source of perpetual youth, and communicates to all our sentiments duration, brilliancy, and peace. For myself, I feel as if I should never grow old. The body changes, and the senses lose their energy ; but the soul floats on the surface above all these ruins, as the rays of the sun gild with their light the columns of a fallen temple."

In the month of September, 1858, he was again elected Provincial of the Great Order, to the sincere and enthusiastic joy of those among his children who could not accustom themselves to live deprived of his presence and direction. Four years of separation had only increased their feelings of tender and filial affection. His election called forth these feelings in a very touching manner. Letters came to him from every convent full of joy and congratulation ; and the welcome that he received throughout his dear province of France must have proved to him how deeply the remembrance of his devotion and fatherly goodness remained engraved on all hearts. He did not, however, on this account, resign either his office of Vicar-General of the Third Order, or the direction of the College of Sorèze. The time did not seem to him to be yet come when the school and the Third Order could do without his support. He therefore courageously accepted this increase of labour, in the hope that at the end of four years, the two works being both solidly established, he might at last be suffered to repose, and realise the dream of his life in writing for God and for souls.

"At the end of these four years of my Provincialate," he writes, "I shall be sixty years of age. It is a solemn epoch in life when one reaches that age. My greatest regret is in not being able to continue the publication of my *Letters on Christian Life*, three of which have already appeared, and produced good results. But God has not permitted this. May I at least, at the age of sixty, if I live so long, be able to find some place of retirement where I may consecrate my last days to the completion of this work for the glory of God." This retreat, and this active repose, he was, alas! only to find in God.

At the commencement of his second Provincialate he had the happiness of re-establishing his children in the neighbourhood of the tomb of St. Mary Magdalen, whence they had been driven away by the Revolution, after being its guardians for six centuries. The ancient church and convent of the Friars-Preachers at St. Maximin's, in Provence, had escaped from the revolutionary vandalism, and together with St. James's of Paris, and the Convent of Toulouse, formed the most illustrious houses of France. At a short distance from St. Maximin, in the midst of lofty upright rocks, which rise like a stone curtain, the eye discovers a habitation hanging, as it were, suspended, and at its foot a forest, the novelty of which arrests the glance. It is no longer the thin and odoriferous Provençal pine, nor the ever-green oak, nor any of the other kinds of foliage which the traveller has already met with on his journey. You would say that the north had collected all its most magnificent vegetation in this spot. If you penetrate into the forest, you are immediately enveloped in its majestic shadows, which remind you by their darkness and silence of those sacred woods which in old time were never profaned by the axe.[1] " This is the grotto and the forest of St. Mary Magdalen, the friend of our Lord, the converted sinner, the touching emblem of that fallen humanity which the Son of God came to restore by means of His love." It therefore gave Père Lacordaire a holy joy to take possession once more of places sanctified by such holy memories, and to re-establish the Friars-Preachers near the old Basilica and the sacred mountains.

In the summer of 1859, a few weeks after he had regained possession of the great Convent of St. Maximin, he hastened to bring thither the student-novices from Chalais, where they had become too numerous for that place, and to instal them in the vast cloisters which had just been reconstructed. After this he wished to discharge his debt of gratitude to St. Mary Magdalen by writing a little book upon her life, which is of consummate beauty. These pages, which form a sort of hymn on the friendship of the Son of God

[1] " St. Mary Magdalen," by Père Lacordaire.

for the poor sinner, and for that of St. Magdalen for Jesus, conclude with these words : " May these be my last lines, and, like St. Mary Magdalen on the eve of the Passion, may I break the frail and faithful vessel of my thoughts at the feet of Jesus Christ !"

His desire was but too exactly realised. These were indeed to be his last acts, and very soon afterwards appeared the first symptoms of that malady which was to take him from us. This was in the January of 1860.

In order to present the reader with the narrative of the last sad closing scene, we shall content ourselves with an almost verbal reprint of the pages we published a few days after the death of our Father. In default of every other merit, they will at least have that of being the faithful echo of a sorrow which time had not yet softened.

In the winter of 1860 he returned greatly fatigued from a journey to Paris, whither he had been summoned in consequence of his election to the French Academy. On his return to Sorèze he caught a cold, which he neglected to take any care of. He had enjoyed perfect health ever since he had assumed the Dominican habit. His constitution, which was up to that time weak and delicate, had become stronger ; and he never thought of taking any care of his health. In spite of his exhaustion, he would preach as usual each week during Lent in the college chapel. He did so, but only got through his task by dint of great efforts, and at the cost of much fatigue. During Holy Week he was obliged to keep his bed, and sank into such a state of weakness that we began to entertain serious anxiety. It was the first attack of his malady. He recovered from it, but not completely.

At the end of May he was to preach the panegyric of St. Mary Magdalen at St. Maximin's, on occasion of the solemn translation of her relics. He felt happy in being able to speak of her, as he had already written of her. Eight bishops were to assist at this solemnity, and many were coming from a distance to be present at it. It was so long since he had appeared in the pulpit—a sort of vague presentiment was generally felt, and many had come from Paris to gather up the last echoes of that voice which was so soon to be extinct. Before setting out, he consulted the medical man attached to the college, who, seeing how weak he was, tried to dissuade him from undertaking the journey. However, he made the attempt. Having reached Montpelier, and feeling unusually fatigued, he again took advice, and finding the same opposition and the same fears expressed, turned back, and once more reached Sorèze.

Once more in his dear college, he communicated to his children the warning he had received. "It is a great grace which God confers on a man," he wrote, "when a serious illness comes to warn him of the shortness and uncertainty of life. God has been pleased to give me such a warning, and I beg you to thank Him for it with me." He understood that his case was a serious one. On the 28th of May he wrote on the subject of the disappointment at St. Maximin's :—" It is the first time in my whole life that my body has refused to obey my will ;" and, again, writing to a friend,—" I often think of death, and am preparing everything so as to leave the Order in a good state, both morally and financially. If I should die, you will not abandon this work, the great work of my poor life. If I should last to the end of my Provincialate, all will be put in order, I hope ; our debts all paid, our seven houses fairly established, and St. Maximin's formed into the citadel of our Order in France. But if I die before that time, our poor brethren will find themselves somewhat embarrassed. They do not all of them know how much it costs to enable them to live, and to regulate all their affairs."

The day after his return to Sorèze, he wrote as follows to all the priors of the Order : — " Very

Reverend Father,—After having struggled for three months against a gradual loss of strength, I have been obliged, by the unanimous advice of all my physicians, to acknowledge that I feel incapable of fulfilling all the functions which my government imposes on me. By leaving the college of Sorèze, I should no doubt lighten my burden, but in a very slight degree, and I should at the same time seriously compromise the prospects of the infant Third Order, which I look on as bound up with the future destinies of our Order, and with the designs of God in its regard. Obliged, therefore, to seek for an alleviation of my labours in some other way, if I would not see my health give way yet more rapidly, I have resolved to appoint a secretary and a visitor ; a secretary to undertake part of my correspondence, and a visitor, that I may spare myself two months of travelling, and considerable fatigue, at the very moment when I might otherwise rest a little from the labours of the year.

"I feel persuaded, Reverend Father, that by thus using a right which is allowed by our Constitutions to the Provincial, I shall not give the Fathers of the province any cause of discontent, and that they will only see in this a proof of the desire I feel to serve them, in spite of the failure of strength caused by age and labour. It is now thirty years since I began my public career, during twenty-one of which I have consecrated my time, my words, and my every effort, to the restoration and consolidation of our holy Order in France. I may therefore be permitted, in my rapidly declining years, to retrench something from my burden, and thus, without cowardice, to obey the dictates of prudence."

The perusal of these lines will touch the reader as they touched us when we received them, evincing as they did the hesitation he felt in allowing himself the rest he so greatly needed, and showing how he who was to us more than a superior, a father, humbly asked his children not to be surprised if, in his failing health, which declined even more rapidly than he was aware of, he permitted himself in some degree to lighten his burden of anxiety.

He consented, therefore, to take care of himself. During the summer, he was ordered to go to Rennes-les-Bains. It was hoped that the waters might restore his strength. There he was joined by his friend, the Abbé Henri Perreyve. But even his affectionate care could not reconcile the Father to the wearisomeness of this visit.

The rules imposed on an invalid at the baths annoyed him ; he no longer enjoyed his regular and busy life, and his dear Sorèze, and he left at the end of three weeks. When he once more beheld the Black Mountain, he exclaimed, " Ah ! how I enjoy once more breathing the air of Sorèze !"

For a moment, a temporary rally caused him to be deceived with hopes of recovery. He imagined that his strength was restored. On the 12th of August he wrote: "My *machine* is still pretty well, but it requires to be *shaken* more than it used to do." In the September of the same year he went to Flavigny to preside at a meeting of the Priors of the Province, and to choose a Vicar-Provincial. He wrote on this occasion :—" Very Reverend Father,—The intermediary Congregation of the Province, assembled at Flavigny on the 1st of September of this year, has thought fit to take into consideration the weak state of health into which I have fallen for the last six months, which, by the unanimous decision of my physicians, necessitates perfect rest from work and great care. The Congregation has therefore authorised me to appoint a Vicar-Provincial, to whom I may intrust the government of the Province, until such time as it may please God to restore my health and strength. Without this previous authorisation, I should not have felt at liberty to impose on the Province for an indeterminate period the government of a superior not elected by yourselves; but the unanimous consent of the Fathers of the Congregation has left me no doubt as to the legality and fitness of this step. I shall thus, while relieved from the details of administration, be still able to watch over the wants and necessities, and the spiritual and temporal prosperity of the Province, which will never cease to be present in my thoughts."

In spite of his increasing weakness, and of our reiterated entreaties, he would not give himself absolute rest. This half measure of a Vicar-Provincial suited very ill with his notions of responsibility and his slavery to duty, which was a passion to which he sacrificed everything. In fact, he continued to govern the Province as before. He was only to lay down his arms when his strength was entirely gone, and he was on the eve of death.

On the 24th of January, 1854, took place his reception into the French Academy. A select and more than usually numerous audience crowded the Institute on this occasion, at which a Protestant, the most celebrated of our statesmen, was to reply to a friar, the orator of Notre Dame. When he appeared in that illustrious circle, and when he was seen, paler than his own habit, going to take his place in that chair, which he was only to honour that once, some might have supposed that he was feeling an emotion caused by so extraordinary a triumph. But it was not so; he came, the soldier mortally wounded in the service of the Church, to lay on the brow of his mother the crown which he had received from the hands of France. We have elsewhere spoken of the motives which led him not to decline the honour thus offered him. It will be sufficient to add here that France, with some rare exceptions, "applauded the joy and the pride of the spectacle offered that day by the Academy;"[1] and to observe that in receiving less for his own sake, than for that of his cause, suffrages the more honourable, because they had for the first time

[1] Discourse of M. Guizot.

sought for the object of their honour in the cloister, he placed the keystone on the edifice of his life; the reconciliation, namely, of his age, his country, science, and liberty, with the Catholic Faith; for he had only entered this temple of literary glory that he might stand there as the "Symbol of Liberty, accepted and supported by Religion."[1]

He returned to Sorèze so much fatigued as to be obliged to give up hearing the confessions of the boys. Nevertheless, this time also, he preached every week during Lent, according to his usual custom. He took for the subject of these Conferences, *Duty*. It was his favourite idea, not only because he had thought of it profoundly, but because he had himself practised it from his childhood. He made his young hearers comprehend that duty is the greatest and most generous of all ideas; the greatest, because it implies the idea of God, of the soul, of free-will, of responsibility, and of immortality; the most generous, because apart from duty, nothing remains but pleasure and self-interest. Duty is therefore the greatest of all powers, whether for action or resistance. It is the source of all true elevation, of which the successive degrees are —honest men, men of honour, magnanimous men, heroes, and saints. The sanction of duty lies in the justice of tribunals, conscience, and the final judgment of God. Finally, duty is the greatest source of happiness in childhood as in old age, in the state as in the family.

We may see by this brief outline the height to which he sought to raise his children's thoughts and aims, and how thoroughly his mind retained its mastery and vigour, in spite of the weakness of his body.

After Easter he wished once more to revisit his beloved Convent of St. Maximin, a foundation which he regarded as one of the most evident signs of the blessing of God upon his work. He wished once

---

[1] Discourse of Père Lacordaire.

more to see that young and numerous family in which lay the hopes of the future, to express to them his affection, to give them his last advice, and the special blessing which a patriarch bestows on the Benjamins of his love. It will be long before St. Maximin's will forget those evening instructions which were only too short, when the Father, surrounded by his snow-white crown of sixty religious arrayed along the walls of the great chapter-room, was able once more for their sakes to pour out those accents of unrivalled eloquence, and conjured them to fear the friendship of the world rather than its contempt, revealing to them, in inspired language, the eternal beauty of their vows, the ineffable espousals of the soul with God. On the 17th of July he wrote as follows to their Novice-Master :

" Very Reverend and very dear Father,—I have received the letter which you and your dear novices have written to me on my feast, and hasten to tell you in reply how much it has touched me.

" The foundation of St. Maximin's Convent has certainly been the most important work of my second Provincialate, whether we consider the grand and pious memories which are attached to the spot, or the number of religious which it is able to contain, which has enabled us to gather together all our young students under one head and under the same lectors, in a place as advantageous to health as to piety. The spirit which animates the community, and specially our dear professed novices, promises for our Province not only a large increase of supernatural life, but also of apostolic labour. God, who, amid many trials, has blessed the restoration of our Order in France, and has made it the door to admit the return of other bodies, has been pleased that the relics of St. Magdalen, one of the protectresses of our Order, should thus become the corner-stone of our edifice.

" I know not what He may decide as to my health

and my life ; but, whatever happens, I shall leave our beloved Province, after two-and-twenty years of labour, fairly established by the manifest grace of God. I beg you to read this letter to your dear novices, to thank them for their prayers."

His fatigue and exhaustion every month and every week increased. Our anxiety became greater as the malady made more rapid progress. At last he consented to have further medical advice. He had perfect confidence in the college physician, and of his own accord would never have sought any other advice or treatment. But M. Houlès, the doctor of Sorèze, was most anxious to be relieved from a part of the responsibility which pressed on him, and joined his entreaties to those of Père Lacordaire's friends, who pressed him to seek for further advice. The physicians who were consulted advised a change of air and of diet. He therefore accepted the kind hospitality of a friend at Becquigny, in the department of La Somme. Urgent as were the motives, and perfectly suitable as was the hospitality thus offered, it cost him much to quit his convent, and the fear lest he might thus be opening the door to relaxed habits constantly pursued him ; and he wrote thus on the subject to a friend in the world :

" This decision has cost me much, both on account of Sorèze, and on account of the example which it may give to our brethren. But I feel that I cannot shake off the languor which is undermining my health without some powerful effort. If this experiment does not succeed, I shall abandon myself to the grace of God."

It was under this impression that, in the month of April, he informed his religious, in a circular letter, of his departure for Becquigny. We shall quote this letter, which displays the true spirit of Christian authority, ever indulgent to others, and austere only towards itself :

"Very Reverend Father,—The weakness and indisposition from which I have now been suffering for more than a year had appeared, before the winter set in, to be leaving me ; but the severe weather, added to necessary fatigues, have caused its return, and the physicians consider it indispensable that I should have change of air and of diet, which appear to them to offer the only chance of success to any remedy they may prescribe. Their advice is so unanimous and so urgent on this point, that I cannot conscientiously oppose it. I have therefore agreed for a few months to accept the kind hospitality of a friend ; and I feel confident that this determination, which I have come to with great reluctance, will not cause dissatisfaction to our Fathers. This conviction will reconcile me in part to a change of life which is otherwise most distressing to me. I hope also that their prayers will accompany me into my temporary exile, and obtain from God the result that is most conformable to His holy Will and ulterior designs."

He set out for Becquigny at the beginning of May, but he only remained there six weeks. The change, and the delicate cares with which he was surrounded, obtained him some rest, and his appetite seemed to be returning. But these good symptoms were of short duration. On passing home through Paris he took the opportunity of consulting Doctors Rayer and Jousset. Whilst differing as to the original cause of the malady, they agreed as to its chief features, which were an inflammation of the bowels, accompanied by impoverishment of the blood. Doctor Rayer, knowing how disagreeable the mode of life at a watering-place was to the Father, prescribed the waters of Vichy, to be taken at home at the college.

His return to Sorèze was a regular triumph. The

prosperity of the little town depended on that of the college ; it rose and fell according as the school progressed or declined. Both interest and gratitude, therefore, bound the inhabitants of Sorèze to Père Lacordaire, who had restored their celebrated school, and commenced several benevolent undertakings for their benefit. They felt a pride in him who called them *his dear fellow-citizens*, and who was truly *a king* in their eyes—as one good woman said on the day of his funeral : " We had *a king*—and now he is dead !"

The pupils of the *Institute* came out a league from the college to meet the Father ; he was pale, and much fatigued with his journey. Having reached the parade he found a large crowd gathered together to receive him and do him honour. The school was there under arms ; and next came the Benevolent Societies and others, of which he was an honorary member, the Asylum, and other works that he had founded. They had erected a triumphal arch before the gates of the school ; and all along the Boulevard, inscriptions, hung between two poles, recalled the chief events of Père Lacordaire's life.

He was received at the gate of the college by the religious and the body of Professors. Conducted to the great hall, he thanked the town and the school, in a faltering voice, for this reception, and promised his fellow-citizens to live and die among them.

A few days later he received intelligence which overwhelmed him with sorrow, and carried back his thoughts to that image of death which was daily advancing and growing larger in his eyes. Père Besson, one of his first companions, had just died, the victim of his zeal and charity, in the missions of the East.

Père Lacordaire, desiring to do honour to the memory of one so much beloved, hastened to pour out his grief into the bosom of the Order in a letter addressed to his religious, in which he says : " Père

Besson was one of my first companions in the work of the restoration of the Order of Preachers in France, to which, more than any one else, he contributed by his boundless self-devotion, his great gentleness of character, and by a holiness of life which made itself apparent wherever he was, whether in France, Rome, or Mossoul. In him were to be seen from the very first, elevation of soul, a gifted and fertile mind, a solid and unselfish character, together with great moderation of views, and perfect justness of judgment. . . .

"His premature death in the distant countries of the East has united him to that chosen company of devoted souls on whose open graves our restoration to life has been founded—I mean the Fathers Réquédat, Piel, Hernsheim, and De St. Beaussaut."

Yes, their open graves—open too soon, specially for him who only a few weeks later was to complete our sorrow, and the joy of those whom he went to meet in heaven. A few days before his death, as we knelt beside his bed, we said to him : "Father, you are soon going to leave us. . . . All the sorrow is for us, but what a joy for your children in heaven! You are going to rejoin those you loved so much."—"Yes," he replied, "they are already numerous!" I named them : "Réquédat, Piel, De St. Beaussaut, and Père Aussant. . . ." He added: "And Père Besson!" And it was with an accent which seems even still to pierce my heart. A beam of light shot from his eye ; it was like a patriarch who, having reached the extreme boundary between the two countries occupied by his children, looks at them one after another, and consoles himself for the tears of those he leaves behind with the thought of the embraces that are awaiting him.

The heats of summer hastened the progress of his sickness, and prevented the medical treatment he was following from having any good results. In the month of August, 1861, his weakness increased, and his strength was entirely exhausted ; his digestion also became affected, and he was often attacked with fainting fits. He could not now rise before eleven o'clock. When it was fine he went out in a carriage, and so once more beheld those fields, and valleys, and country farms, the sight of which always refreshed him.

From this time the Father understood that God was asking from him the sacrifice of his life. Now and then, it is true, the old delusive hope of recovery returned ; the undiminished power of his mind sometimes deceived him as to the gradual decay of his physical powers ; but when he calmly questioned himself he saw the truth. He had given his life to God, and now he offered Him his death also. He offered it for the good of his Order, thus putting in practice the advice he had formerly given to the souls he directed. " The first foundation of any spiritual work," he was wont to say, " is *a detached heart ;* I constantly have a proof of this. Neither birth, fortune, talent, nor genius, exceed in value a detached heart."

On the 27th of August he sent in his resignation as Provincial of the Great Order to the most Rev. Master-General, who was obliged to accept it, not without expressing his regret to the Province. On the 12th of September, Père Lacordaire said to a friend : " I yesterday received good news from Rome : the most Rev. Père Jandel had had an audience with the Holy Father, whom he informed of my illness. The Holy Father expressed his concern, and desired the Master-General to forward me his apostolic benediction."

At this period began the farewell visits of his friends from Paris, and from all parts of France. They were very numerous ; we will only name a few. The Abbé Perreyve was the first to arrive. He was to return a second time, and to receive the last outpourings of a friendship which regarded not the difference of age but the sympathy of the soul ; for " the soul has no age."[1]

On the 25th of September he received the visit of M. le Comte de Montalembert. The Father advanced to meet his friend as far as the steps of the college. He was weak, and supported himself with difficulty, and the pallor which had spread over his features and his broad forehead gave to his wasted countenance an expression of indescribable beauty. The Comte de Montalembert, with his eyes full of tears, threw himself into his friend's arms. " Never in my whole life," he said to us, " did I experience such emotion! Never have I before seen such terrific beauty !"

This had, indeed, been an old and tried friendship— a friendship formed on the battle-field, and dating from 1830, which had lasted through good and evil fortunes, and which at the close of the day was now found fresh as ever, having never caused a furrow on the brow or a wound in the heart. M. de Montalembert came to behold for the last time in his friend the ideal of the two great passions of his life—Monks and Liberty.

He persuaded the Father to write his Memoirs. He quitted Sorèze on the 29th of September, and the next day the Father began to dictate a *Memoir on the Restoration in France of the Order of Preachers.* This Memoir, interrupted by his death, does not go farther than the year 1854. All those who read this last testament of our Father will be grateful to M. de Montalembert for having suggested the idea of this work, and encouraged him to undertake it. On the 10th of October, Père Lacordaire received the visit of his oldest friend, M. Foisset. They had studied together at Dijon, and had always since remained faithfully attached to one another at Sorèze. The Father loved to recall the days when he was full of an ardour for study and science ; " those days when," as

---

[1] " St. Mary Magdalen," p. 27.

he said, " he was wont to discuss the question of innate ideas with Foisset."

A little later he was consoled by a visit from M. Cartier. His name had been synonymous to Père Lacordaire with a devotion as deep as it was trustworthy. M. Cartier had accompanied the Father in nearly every journey he had taken for the re-establishment of the Order in France. He was something more than a *friend* to him; he was a *familiar;* and the Father loved him as if he had indeed been bound to him by family ties. A few weeks before his death, some one reminded him of this friendship, so tender, so modest, so unchanging to the last. He raised his arms, and murmured : " Ah ! Cartier ! Cartier !"

He wished that M. Cartier should be present at the Mass which was now daily said in his room, close to his bed. He also accompanied the Father in one of those carriage-drives which he was now but rarely able to take. He spoke to M. Cartier very much of Père Besson ; pressed him to write his life ; heard the explanation of the plan which M. Cartier had conceived of this work, and gave him much information respecting their common friend. Every morning, during the three last months, Mass was said in his chamber, and he communicated at it. He who writes these lines often had this consolation, and will never forget the expression of angelic ardour with which the Father received his God. The last time that I had this happiness, I was much struck by the words of the Office. " There were men full of mercy, whose godly deeds have not failed ; good things continue with their seed. Their posterity are a holy inheritance, and their seed hath stood in the covenants ; and their children for their sakes remain for ever ; their seed and their glory shall not be forsaken. Their bodies are buried in peace, and their name liveth unto generation and generation. Let the people show forth their wisdom, and the Church declare their praise."[1]

[1] Eccl. xliv. 10-15.

In the whole of Scripture there could not have been found words more in harmony with my thoughts and hopes at that moment.

The more the malady progressed, the more ardent and numerous were the prayers addressed to Heaven. In France there were few religious communities to whom the illustrious sufferer was not recommended, and where they did not offer prayers for his recovery. But more especially was he prayed for in the houses of our own Order.

At St. Maximin the young novices renewed all the holy temerity of the ages of faith. Some went barefoot over the flinty paths of the Sainte Baume to ask a miracle from St. Mary Magdalen; others passed entire nights before the Blessed Sacrament; and after the example of St. Dominic, tears were not enough for them, but they mingled their blood with their prayers, and generously offered their own lives to obtain that of their Father. On the evening of the ninth day of these prayers, all the religious went barefoot, and carried the relics of St. Mary Magdalen through the cloisters and interior of the convent. It was a sad and mournful spectacle to see those long files of religious advancing, by the light of their torches, through the dark cloisters, chanting verses of the most supplicatory of the Psalms, and pausing at intervals to raise anew their prayers, their sighs, and their chants. Almost the whole night thus passed amid ceremonies that can never be forgotten. They hoped for a miracle, and believed that St. Mary Magdalen would this time obtain the resurrection of another Lazarus.

When the Father was informed of all they had done for his cure at St. Maximin, he exclaimed, "O poor children! but it is too much!"

He loved St. Mary Magdalen tenderly indeed; if she did not obtain his cure, it was that the hour was come when he might have said with our Lord to His disciples, "It is expedient for you that I should go away." In a letter written towards the close of 1860, he says : " I think that St. Mary Magdalen will be the Patroness of my last days." He begged the religious who acted as his secretary to read to him every day out of the *Preparation for Death*, or in the *Acts of Abandonment to God* by Bossuet. For the rest, his great devotion to the Passion of our Lord Jesus Christ had long made the thought of death sweet and familiar to him. During the last days of his life, they said to him, as they presented him the crucifix, " You have always loved our Lord Crucified, have you not, Father?" " Oh yes, yes!" he replied, kissing it tenderly. Another time, pointing to the Crucifix which hung before him, he said, " I cannot pray to Him, but I can look at Him !"

He also made them every day read to him, according to his life-long custom, some passages out of Holy Scripture, particularly from the Acts of the Apostles, the Epistles of St. Paul, and the Gospel of St. John.

On Sunday, the 20th of October, the Provincial Chapter which was to elect his successor opened at Toulouse. The first care of the Fathers, before commencing their sittings, was to repair to Sorèze to visit their venerated invalid. He received us with his usual kindness, gave us his blessing, spoke to us of the affairs of the Order, and also of himself. " I did not think to have left you so soon," he said, " but God calls me to Himself. It is better that I should go away. . . . Were I to remain, it might be thought that the prosperity of our work proceeded from man ; I shall be more useful to you in heaven. Pray for me." The Fathers then went in pilgrimage to Prouille and Avignonet, that soil so rich in miracles, and so dear to the Dominican Order. A Novena of Masses was begun there, at the conclusion of which the Fathers returned to Sorèze to ask a last blessing for their new Provincial, and for every convent of the Province.

Ever since the malady had become serious, the

Master-General had desired that he might be kept regularly informed of the state of the sufferer. On the 9th of October he wrote from Rome to the Father's secretary : " Be pleased to tell him that in the audience I had last week with the Holy Father his Holiness inquired after his health with much interest, and expressed the most affectionate sympathy for his sufferings ; adding, that he looked on this long illness, which leaves him the perfect use of his mind, as a special favour from God, who is thus pleased to prepare him more perfectly to appear in His presence.

. " Tell him also that I have many times been tempted to set out for France in order to pay him a last visit. But our circumstances here are such, that I look on it as a duty not to quit my post. Assure him, however, that I am often with him in thought, and that I never cease to pray for him."

On the 30th of October the first crisis came on during the night. To his pains in the stomach were added rheumatic pains in the leg which caused him terrible suffering. About two o'clock in the afternoon Doctor Houlès, seeing how weak he was, said that he might receive the last Sacraments. " No," he replied, " not yet ; I will tell you when it is time for that."

In fact, during the following days he was better. He then received a third apostolic blessing from the Holy Father, together with a Plenary Indulgence for the hour of death. He expressed his gratitude for this, adding : " a Plenary Indulgence from the Pope is a good thing when one is about to appear before God !"

In the night of the 5th of November he had a second crisis. The vomiting and rheumatic pains returned more severely than before. At six in the morning he himself asked to receive Extreme Unction and the Holy Viaticum. All the religious and the pupils of the *Institute* assisted at the sad ceremony ; and all were in tears. He alone, calm in the midst of their grief, answered every prayer. He then took leave of all present, blessed the religious, and embraced them each in turn. He also embraced his nephew Frederic, who was the only representative of his family present, and who had not quitted him for several days. Then he wished to embrace each of the members of the *Institute*, saying, " Adieu, my dear friends ; it is for the last time. Be always very good." He received the Holy Viaticum at two o'clock.

He begged them not to abandon his servant Louis, who had attended on him since the beginning of his illness. He looked on Louis less as a servant than as a child, and was touched by the least services done for him. How, indeed, could he fail to be sensible of such devotion! Louis had not gone to bed for twenty days. To the last he bestowed on the invalid those delicate cares which spring only from affection. " My poor Louis," said the Father to him, "we must part ; God will have it so, and we must submit." When the violence of the pain drew from him some complaints, he at once looked at him kindly, and passing his arm round his neck, drew Louis towards him, and begged pardon for his impatience. The physician having entered just after one of these occasions, " I felt great pain in turning," said the Father, adding, "and I must confess I was a little impatient."

After having received the last Sacraments, he remained absorbed in recollection, which was only interrupted now and then by a few words to the most intimate of his children who came to see him. The Fathers of the House of Oullins, who had been summoned by telegraph, now arrived. On the entrance of the Fathers Captier and Mermet, who had been the first to give themselves to the Third Order, the Father evinced the joy he felt in seeing them again. He spoke for a long time about the House of Oullins with Father Captier, Prior of the College. He inquired about the unfinished buildings, the plantations, and the rest. The House of Oullins had been the cradle of the Third Order of Teachers. He had not been able to do for it what he had done for Sorèze, but he never forgot that the first idea of the undertaking had come from thence, and that from thence also his most intelligent and devoted fellow-labourers had been given to him. He also gave his blessing with much feeling to Doctor Houlès, a sincere Catholic as well as a skilful physician. All that science, united to the most constant and delicate care, could do, had been done by this good and devoted friend. The Father was touched with the anxiety he displayed, and we often heard him express his astonishment and gratitude.

In the evening of Sunday the 10th he seemed unexpectedly better, and a gleam of hope and joy appeared on all countenances. " Perhaps, if it please God," I said to him, as I kissed his forehead. He made a gesture of doubt, as though to say, " I have no such expectation !" The improvement could not last, for the Father took no nourishment, and his strength was every day failing. On Wednesday the 13th he spoke a few words, which showed where were his thoughts and his heart. A lady from Marseilles had come to see him ; he blessed her, and thanked her for all she had done for St. Maximin and La Sainte Baume, and begged her always to continue her interest in them. She promised to do so. He added : " St. Maximin and La Baume—they are my last thoughts !" St. Mary Magdalen was indeed the Patroness of his last days. He had desired " with her to break the frail but faithful vessel of his thoughts at the feet of Jesus," and his wish was accomplished.

During these long hours of his agony nothing disturbed his recollection. A few of the oldest and most intimate of his friends entered his room from time to time to pray before the little wooden altar, and after receiving a kind glance from him they would retire in silence. That glance rested now on one specially-beloved friend; it was M. Barral, the *Emmanuel* of the *Letters to a Young Man*, and the *honour of the school of Sorèze*,[1] who was too worthy of the regard with which the Father always wrote and spoke of him for us to hesitate in naming him here.

At the end of the week he became still more feeble, and his weakness continued to increase until the crisis, which took place on the evening of the 20th, and which was the last. For two days he had taken nothing, his stomach refusing all nourishment. He hardly spoke at all now, and if he asked for anything, it was with difficulty that he could make himself understood. God was thus gradually withdrawing from him, by the hand of death, the magnificent gifts which He had bestowed on him, leaving him, however, the perfect use of his mind, and the merit of being able to say, at each new sacrifice, " Father, let Thy Will, not mine, be done !" Those eloquent lips, which had in old time stirred the listening throngs, rousing or soothing them at his will ; those words of fire, which possessed so marvellous a power, a kind of sacred magnetism, which had communicated to us its superabundance, inspiring us with his own love of justice, and his own indignation against all that was unworthy ; that eloquence that penetrated the souls of his hearers with an emotion so ardent, that long after its echoes had died away, they still felt the magic of its charm, saying, " Has any man spoken like this man ?"—those lips were now stammering feebly like the lips of a little child. We experienced a sort of humiliation, mingled with fear, as we listened to those inarticulate sounds escaping from such lips ! But as for him, calm in the midst of the shadows of death, like one who is always a king, even amid the bonds of slavery, when he could neither by words or signs make himself understood, he thanked

[1] First Letter, p. 1.

the good-will of those who surrounded him with a look, and then sank back into his former state of repose.

On the evening of Wednesday the 20th he was attacked by a crisis the most painful and agonising of all, and one which was also his last. He was seized with that agony which is the near precursor of death, and which casts the soul into inexpressible torture. He raised himself on his bed—he, who before could not so much as move without the assistance of Louis. One would have said, by the efforts that he made, that he wished to speak, but was suffocating. His breathing, which up to that time had been quite regular, became short and difficult—the last struggle was beginning. It was terrible. We were all there kneeling, and repressing our sobs for fear of increasing his sufferings, with our eyes fixed on that agonising spectacle of our Father. We saw him stretch his wasted arms around him like a man who is trying to feel his way in the dark, sometimes opening his large eyes, which he generally kept closed, and slowly directing his glance to each one of us—looking now at the walls of his room, now towards heaven, as if, having already reached the shores of eternal light, he could hardly believe that he was still standing on the borders of darkness. Then, in a powerful voice, and raising his hands, he exclaimed : "My God ! my God ! open to me ! open to me !" They were his last words. Our sobs broke forth ; a moment after the faltering voice of the Father Provincial was heard above our tears ; the last prayers were beginning. The Father seemed to have been waiting for this, for he at once sank back on his bed, and was still able to command his sufferings. No cry, no complaint interrupted our prayers ; he listened absorbed and recollected in God. He struck his breast, and not being able to make the sign of the cross on his body, he made it over his heart. At the twice-repeated invocation of St. Dominic's name, the voice of the priest arose in a firmer and more supplicating tone. It was so natural for us to think that St. Dominic was there, close to the Father of his new family, close to him whom he had doubtless himself obtained from God to restore his children to that old soil of France, whose inexhaustible fecundity he knew so well ; that he was there, in that country of Albi, the battle-ground of his own apostolic struggles, in those same plains where his first convent had been founded ! For so it had pleased God to bring together in death those whose life had had the same destiny.

They now presented him with the Crucifix ; he took it and pressed it in his hands, attempting to carry it to his lips. But his arms refusing him this service, they held it for him to kiss ; and then the image of him whom he had so much loved rested on his heart. He looked at it, and doubtless exclaimed with his Lord, " Father, into Thy hands I commend my spirit !"

Having reached those solemn words, " Depart, Christian soul, from this world !" the Father Provincial paused. He hesitated, I could well understand— although it is not a formal command on the part of the priest, for death knows no other master save God alone, nevertheless we know how often it appears to wait until those words are pronounced by the priest ; and if it is always hard for a mortal to tell any soul to depart and quit this world, his family, his parents, and his children, how much harder is it for a son to utter those words to a father ! How shall he dare to bid such a father depart, to return no more, to quit his children, and never to see them more ! I asked myself if I should have had the courage to have done this, and if the priest would have been able to overcome the sorrow of the child.

The anguish of the last agony meanwhile continued ; there was no death-rattle heard, for his chest was perfectly sound—only stifled and half-uttered groans. At each shock we feared to hold nothing in our arms

but his lifeless form. I made a sign to the Provincial
to proceed, and with a slow and solemn voice he pronounced the words, "*Proficiscere, Anima Christiana,
de hoc mundo.*" What gave me courage to do this?
What inspired me with this fear lest my Father should
expire without those words? It was that the priest
does not only say, "Depart!" but also, "Come!" He
summons to meet the departing soul the Father, and
the Son, and the Holy Ghost, the Angels and Arch-
angels, the Patriarchs, the Prophets, the Apostles, the
Martyrs, and the Virgins—and all the shining throng
of the saints. He prays that the soul may receive
the sweet and joyous welcome of Jesus Christ : "*Mitis
atque festivus Christi Jesu tibi aspectus appareat.*"
With what an accent did not the priest address to
this great soul those words : "Go, and behold thy
Redeemer face to face, and, ever present at His side,
contemplate with thy happy looks the ever-resplendent
Truth." And did not that eternal truth which he
had so often and so eloquently announced to men
owe him indeed a more splendid revelation of itself?

The prayers were now over ; and the crisis had
ended with them. The dying man appeared to be
sinking, not yet into his last sleep, but as if into a
state of profound recollection. He did not again rally
from this state of drowsiness, and so the night passed.
Towards morning the religious retired to take a little
rest. A few only of the elder Fathers of both branches
of the Order remained in his antechamber. From
time to time they could with difficulty catch the
sound of some gentle sigh. The body had not even
strength left to suffer ; but the soul alone still held
out.

The 21st—the Feast of the Presentation of Our
Lady in the Temple—was the last day of a Novena
which had been offered, not merely at Sorèze, but in
all the convents of the Province. It was also to be
the day of his presentation to God by the hands of
Mary. It was a beautiful feast on which to die. God

does not always hear our prayers according to the sense of our desires, but according to the decrees of His own infallible goodness. The day passed without any change. In the evening, with that instinct of cleanliness which he used to call half a virtue, he made a sign to them to change his linen. About nine he had with him his Confessor and Louis; and in the next chamber were the Provincial and the Novice-Master of St. Maximin's. Louis, no longer hearing the sound of his breathing, brought the light which he had taken away to give him a chance of sleep, and he was the first to become aware that our Father was no longer with us. A few instants before he had uttered a slight groan, which we had hardly noticed; it was the soul of our Father taking its departure.

"The Father is dead!" Those words soon brought us to the foot of the bed, still almost unable to believe it. Death had so long hesitated to strike its great and holy victim that we wished to hope against hope. We bent over that dear head; we kissed his forehead, and sought to meet his glance, and once more to feel his burning breath. When our loss was but too certain, we closed his eyes. The Provincial closed one eyelid, and one of those whom he best loved closed the other.

Then the prayers recommenced. Both rooms were now full; the religious, the Professors, M. Barral, the pupils of the Institute, the Curé of Sorèze and his Vicar, were all there responding to the invocations. They recited the whole Rosary, that sweet prayer which must be heard by Mary, especially on such a day, and which had suggested to him those celebrated words, " Love has but one word to utter; and whilst it is ever *saying* that word, it never *repeats* it."

What a scene was this! How can I describe it? But I will not even make the attempt; for where would be the use? Those who knew him only as the great orator would see in it nothing worthy of his fame. As to those who valued his gifts of grace more than all his gifts of nature, his simple and Christian end has already told them all that they desire to know. They know that he is dead, the father of a numerous family, surrounded by his children ; a man of genius, whose only ambition was to hide his glory within the walls of a college as in a tomb, in the hopes that there it would be even yet more forgotten than in the cloister ; and he found there what he sought—simplicity in death—*Moriamur in simplicitate nostra.* He died in a poor cell—he who had been sought by the most illustrious men of his age, who gloried in his friendship—he died far from all human glory, in poverty, humility, and simplicity ; worthy in death as in life of the Master he had chosen, and the Cross that he had loved so well.

The Angels, as they bent over the lips of the Father to receive his soul, had left on his countenance an expression of heavenly joy that cannot be expressed ; we could not take our eyes from it. The contractions of the last agony were no longer visible, but only the serenity of sleep, and that sweet majesty which the angel of death impresses on the bodies of the saints. The rest of the night was spent in preparing to take the body into the little chapel of the Sisters, where it was to remain exposed as long as possible. He had forbidden them to embalm his body, and had left express directions that the coffin should be of simple oak. As soon as the body, clothed in its religious habit, was exposed, the Masses began, and were continued throughout the morning. During the Mass, which was celebrated by the Prior of Sorèze, the school-banner, veiled in crape, remained inclined towards the body, and all the officers of the college came to touch him with their ensigns of office —one with his sword, another with his *cordon*, and the others with their epaulettes.

It was exactly seven years since Père Lacordaire had taken solemn possession of the school, pro-

nounced his discourse, planted and blessed a cedar-
tree, and drawn up the *procès-verbal*, which had been
signed by all. Every one remembered that beautiful
festival day at Sorèze. And now these same insignia
that he had then blessed were brought to receive a
last consecration from his holy remains. The spectacle touched us deeply. These young men then
understood the sacrifice made to them of his last
years by a great man : " If my sword has grown
rusty, gentlemen," he had said to them a few months
before, "it has been in your service." I know not
if it had grown rusty, but at any rate it was at last
broken.

" The perfection of life consists in knowing how to
abandon ourselves. The number of those who really
do so is very small. I should esteem any man great
who could thus abdicate, even though he were only
to know some vulgar trade."[1] These were his own
words, and as he had spoken, so he had done. It was
for this purpose that he came to end his days at
Sorèze ; there he had found rest and a sweet reward
in the filial love of his children.

For the three days during which the body remained
exposed, the concourse of visitors was considerable.
They came from Revel, from Castres, and from all
the country round, to take a last look at the most
illustrious Director which that famous school has ever
possessed. They gazed long at that noble head that
had given light to so many others ; then they knelt
and prayed—often rather recommending themselves
to his intercession than praying for his repose. Some
brought objects of piety with which to touch the body.
During the whole day several priests were engaged in
satisfying these pious desires. Those who came were
for the most part simple country people, who thus
rendered the most touching homage to the memory
of one who bore so true a love to humility and simplicity.

[1] Panegyric on St. Thomas of Aquinas, by Lacordaire.

On Monday the 25th, at ten in the morning, it became necessary to lay him in his coffin. It was a painful moment for us all. For the last time we kissed his feet, his hands, and his forehead. Supported in the arms of his children, he was laid on his last bed of rest. Leaning over the coffin, we watered it with our tears, the only perfume with which he had not forbidden us to embalm him. It was amid renewed sobs and prayers that the attendants closed the lid, and shut him from our gaze; thus earth was taking him from us little by little, as though to bid us only seek him now in heaven.

The coffin being closed, it was covered with the pall, and the religious watched in prayer night and day until the hour of the funeral. On Thursday the 28th, we carried our Father to his last resting-place. We shall say nothing of the details of those magnificent obsequies, at which more than 20,000 persons were present. The manifestation of public sorrow surpassed all our expectations; it would be injustice not to acknowledge it, and ingratitude to be indifferent to it; but what could any one do to fill up the void in our hearts which had been left there by his death? The next day Sorèze resumed its accustomed aspect; and we quitted the village, carrying a wound in our hearts that was never to close : it is still bleeding, and will remain for ever open.

What most touched us in this great manifestation of feeling was the recollection of the vast crowd, the sorrow depicted on all faces, the tears of many, and such exclamations as, " He was a great saint! Why did not God demand two years from each of our lives that his might have been prolonged!"

The Archbishop of Albi, having been prevented attending by illness, his place was filled by Mgr. Desprez, Archbishop of Toulouse, who officiated, and gave the absolution. Mgr. Gerbet, Bishop of Perpignan, being also ill, was represented by one of his Vicars-General. At the conclusion of the Mass, Mgr.

de la Bouillerie, Bishop of Carcasson, pronounced the funeral oration. Having been called on suddenly, Mgr. de la Bouillerie gave himself up to the inspiration of his feelings, and lamented his illustrious friend in accents of sublime eloquence. He succeeded perfectly in making his audience understand, admire, and love Père Lacordaire, because more than any other he was himself formed to understand, admire, and love him. The ceremony began at ten o'clock, and at two all was over.

" But no, O Father, all was not over. You are no longer in the midst of your children, every year separates you further from us, and increases our sense of solitude and regret. But there remain your example for us to follow, and your promises never to abandon us, and we know that these promises will be kept. There remains the conviction that death has only taken from us a part, and that the least noble part, of our Father ; and that your soul, united to God, is but drawn closer to us. The God in whom you repose is not only the home of holy souls, but also the link that unites them. He is your Father, and He is ours also. He loves both you and us by the same title, and with the same love. What power has the tomb over that faith which makes up our Life Eternal ?

" Suffer us, then, to repeat to you, O Father, those great and consoling words, in which, shortly before your death, you prophesied your departure and your survival, ' *Vado ad Patrem ;* I have a Father, and I go to Him ; I have a tomb, and there I do not go ; for beyond my tomb is eternity that awaits me, and my Father Who calls me ; *Vado ad Patrem !* "[1]

It is impossible for us to close this book without a few words of conclusion, impossible to take leave of this great character, which is henceforward become an historical one, without for the last time examining what it was, to what great end it was predestined,

---

[1] Funeral Oration by Mgr. de la Bouillerie.

and what place it occupied in the religious movement of the age.

We know no man in France who has exercised a larger, more popular, or more decisive influence on the Catholic interests of the present epoch ; nor any who by his teaching, his writings, his works, or his life, has done more in our country for the cause of the Church, and for the happy solution of the great social crisis which has shaken the present century. If there is any fact evident to all those who study the signs of the times, it is that the evil from which we are all suffering is a religious evil, and that the great question to be decided is to know whether man and society can exist without supernatural faith, without any positive communication with God. In this lies the whole struggle of the day. On one hand, unbelievers, armed with the powers of reason, with the discoveries of science, and the progress of industry, would exclude from the life of man all divine intervention, and all positive religion, and aim at making humanity shake off for ever the yoke of revelation. On the other hand, believers labour to make the belief in God once more enter into all the normal conditions of human and social life ; but, whilst pleading the rights of faith, they often exaggerate them and diminish the range of natural reason : they are terrified at the bold investigations of science, and behold with anxiety the conquests of mind over the hidden forces of nature. Hence arises in both parties a mutual antagonism, which is not confined to difference of doctrines, but affects also questions of tendency and personal views ; and this renders the struggle more keen and passionate, and delays the hour of final reconciliation. Now Père Lacordaire seems to us to have been providentially sent in the midst of these grave disputes to dissipate misunderstandings and appease irritations, to defend true principles with moderation and impartiality, and hasten the hour when all minds should be united in truth. His chief mission was to show that, far from being radically opposed to one another, reason and faith, science and religion, society and the Church, might be harmoniously united ; and that outside of Christianity there is no complete life either for man or society. Hardly had he attained self-consciousness before he felt himself called to study and pursue this great work of the reconciliation of parties. A passionate lover of his age, he gloried in always remaining faithful to it within the limits of what was just and true ; and when he quitted the darkness of infidelity to enter the light of faith, he did not on that account think himself called on to chain his reason or to clip her wings, but rather to give her a wider freedom ; he sought not to narrow his heart, but to dilate it to an infinite Love. To use his own words, " The whole man remains; all that is added to him is the God Who made him."

It was this God, found once more after He had been lost ; the ocean of light and love, Whom it was his mission to preach to an age that had forgotten Him, but that felt His absence, and was already demanding Him from every echo that still gave back His name—from all the voices of nature, and all the harmonies of the world. What else is this great philosophic movement, this ardent and restless fever after certainty of reason, than the sign of God, absent from the thought of the age ? Whence proceeds all this incoherence of doctrine, all these newly-tried systems, all this uneasiness of minds, if not from the antireligious shock which has overthrown society, and displaced it from its natural centre, which is God, condemning it to labour for ever to recover its lost equilibrium ? " You thought to have cast God from off His throne," said the orator to this unbelieving generation, " and in spite of the mad attempt of your fathers, God is pursuing you without intermission. He is everywhere crossing your road, and presenting Himself in all shapes before your minds. In your philosophical deductions, in your studies of natural science, in your historical researches, in your attempts at social reform, the question of God is always the first to present itself; because it is, in fact, the first everywhere, and it is as impossible to do without God as it is to change Him. He is to-day what He was yesterday, and what He will be to-morrow. He presses you on all sides, and you do not see Him. Like the old pagans, you raise your altars to the *unknown God.* Now, the God Whom you seek without knowing it, Whom you invoke in secret, the God of Light, of Science, and of the Future, is He Whom I preach to you, the God of the Gospel, Jesus Christ our Lord, in Whom alone is life and salvation."

This kind of preaching was understood, and bore its fruits, because it corresponded to the profound evil which agitated the age, and urged it into the arms of God ; and because it aroused in the heart of the nation a generous sentiment, which may slumber for a time, but which can never entirely die.

This teaching did not oppose any legitimate progress or any praiseworthy aspirations. It combated error indeed, but without denouncing that reason which is the instrument with which error works ; it attacked false doctrines, but never branded individuals. It did not appear as a Jeremias lamenting over the ruins, but as a prophet of the future, ever pointing to the glowing dawn of the resurrection and to the rainbow, the sacred token of peace and reconciliation. It did not say, "*The gods have departed!*" as might have been said at the close of Louis the Fourteenth's reign; but rather, " *The gods are coming back to us!*" It believed in new and better days for the Church. It beheld in the universally negative results of modern philosophy, after such desperate and gigantic efforts, a salutary experience of the powerlessness of reason when deprived of a higher light, and a happy way leading to the necessary affirmations of faith. It hailed the discoveries of science and the progress of industry as auxiliaries of Divine Truth, as pioneers smoothing the way for the heralds of the gospel, and preparing, by drawing every part of the world nearer together, for the unity of one Church under one Shepherd. It said to unbelievers: You think to work against us, and you are but forerunners of the gospel, making ready for its yet vaster conquests. Historians, philosophers, and men of science, you are amassing on all hands precious materials for our use ; you are cutting out the stones of the edifice, of which Christ alone is to be the Architect, and in which you will one day enter together with us, that we may all together chant our eternal *Credo.*

To timid Catholics it said : Men of little faith, wherefore do you still doubt ? Instead of trembling and hesitating, accept the advancing tide of civilisation ; place yourselves boldly at the head of the movement ; you alone can lead it to Jesus Christ, and make it find in His bosom the salvation and the ideal that it pursues.

What this spirit of conciliation was to the mind of man disinherited of its faith, it was also to society, yet more dangerously wounded by its divorce from the Church. It presented the remedy with a friendly hand, and did not believe that, in order to save the sufferer, it was necessary to change his temperament and to destroy his vital powers. Modern society is suffering chiefly from two great evils : the absence of religion, and the excess of an unrestrained liberty. Liberty in the hands of a people without religious faith is like a sharp weapon placed in the hands of a child ; the least misfortune that can ensue is that he may wound himself. Virtue consists in making a right use of liberty. The danger of this liberty, without a sufficient counterpoise on the side of God, appears so great to some minds, that they do not hesitate to advise those in power to snatch this mischievous weapon out of the hands of an irreligious people. Père Lacordaire

belonged to that small number of Catholics who
believe that it is wiser to teach the people how to
make use of this weapon. He believed in liberty, as
he believed in reason and in science; he believed it
to be a civilising power, and not a scourge—a happy
consequence of the Redemption, not an enemy of the
Church. He saw that *the existence of the people* dated
from the gospel—that great charter of freedom—
which had broken the chains of slavery, and proclaimed the right of all to justice and truth; he saw
the people—that immense family of the little and the
abandoned, preferred and chosen by Jesus Christ as
His especial heritage, and the privileged children of
His love; he beheld this people, bequeathed by the
Saviour to His Church, elevated by her to enjoy an
equal love, growing up under her protection, gradually
attaining to political life, and at last reaching the age
of manhood, when, like a new prodigal, it chose to
abandon the hospitable roof of its Mother, to wander
through an adventurous life of independence, and
encounter a thousand misfortunes and reverses. He
saw this people, this modern democracy, extending its
empire in both hemispheres, accepting Christian
baptism, struggling in the crisis of slow transformation, everywhere taking root, never retreating,
but gradually acquiring a predominance which we can
no more refuse to acknowledge than we can seek to
check. "Its name," he said, "is on every lip; it is an
object of terror and hatred to some, of worship and
admiration to others. The Nile has beheld its soldiers,
the Tagus and the Borysthenes have heard the sound
of its march; and its arm is extended afar from the
valleys of the Andes to those motionless shores where
Confucius believed he had for ever chained up the
minds of future generations."

But the more he believed in the advent of this great
power, this era of full-grown liberty towards which all
nations are irresistibly hastening, the more did he feel

the necessity of raising on high over the heads of this triumphant democracy, the standard of the Cross, that sacred *Labarum* of every victory, without which liberty cannot fail to perish. Where God is not, he constantly repeated, the love of liberty can only engender anarchy and despotism. All history, whether ancient or modern, attests this fact. More than ever, then, is the gospel necessary to society, because it alone can produce that order which regulates and nourishes liberty ; and without it the people will necessarily fall under the iron rule of a master, or of many masters, who will enforce order with the sword.

Such for thirty years was the doctrine taught to France by the religious patriotism of Père Lacordaire. It was the teaching, not of a tribune, but of an apostle, understood by many, rejected by some, yet nevertheless sure of its final reward ; for it was the offspring of earnestness and self-devotion. Like his Divine Master, Père Lacordaire always preceded oral instruction with the instruction of example, which is the most eloquent of all : *cœpit facere et docere.* A humble son of the Church, he never hesitated to yield the prompt submission of faith, and thus gained the right to require similar sacrifices from others. He loved independence ; but he placed his own under the shelter of religious obedience. He loved the people, the humble and the poor ; but he had acquired the right to do so by first becoming poor himself, and for ever closing the door to honour by his vows. He often celebrated the glories of abnegation, and the joys of gratuitous service ; but his entire life was a model of the virtues of self-forgetfulness and fidelity to duty. To him it seemed the most natural thing that he should end his career in the humble but fruitful work of education, and he wondered that any should regard it as a merit. In a word, when we examine this life deeply, we find there one virtue which makes up all its beauty and

34

all its unity: it is the virtue of the Cross. It was from his love for Jesus Christ that Père Lacordaire drew the secret of a greatness which men will long admire, and of a sanctity which God alone has known how to recompense.

THE END.

R. WASHBOURNE, 18 PATERNOSTER ROW, LONDON.

R. WASHBOURNE'S
CATALOGUE OF BOOKS,

18 PATERNOSTER ROW, LONDON.

4 ———————— '78

NEW BOOKS.

OREMUS, A Liturgical Prayer Book : with the Imprimatur of the Cardinal Archbishop of Westminster. An adaptation of the Church Offices : containing Morning and Evening Devotions ; Devotion for Mass, Confession, and Communion, and various other Devotions ; Common and Proper, Hymns, Lessons, Collects, Epistles and Gospels for Sundays, Feasts, and Week Days ; and short notices of over 200 Saints' Days. Also short Liturgical Devotions for Holy Week. For greater convenience, the Latin has been given of all the Psalms, Hymns, and other Prayers, occurring in the ordinary services of the Church, in which the Faithful take more or less part. 32mo., 452 pages, cloth, 2s. 6d. ; embossed, red edges, 3s. 6d. ; French morocco, 4s. 6d. ; calf, 5s. 6d. ; morocco, 6s. ; Russia, 8s. 6d.

Are You Safe in the Church of England ? A Question for Anxious Ritualists. By an Ex-Member of the Congregation of S. Bartholomew, Brighton. 8vo., 1s.

Practical Hints on the Education of the Sons of Gentlemen. By an Educator. 8vo., 1s.

Prayers for Communion for Children. Preparation, Mass before Communion, Thanksgiving. 32mo., 1d.

The Child of Mary's Manual. Compiled from the French. Second Edition. 32mo., 1s. 6d.

The Church and Civilisation. By Cardinal Pecci (Leo XIII.) 1s.

Reeve's Compendious History of the Bible. New edition. Large size, 3s. 6d. ; small size, 1s.

Dr. Newman's Essay on the Development of Christian Doctrine. New Edition, 6s.

The Holy Sacrifice of the Mass. By the Bishop of Salford. 2d.

The Life and Passion of Jesus Christ. By the same. 2d.

Mary Immaculate, Mother of God ; or, Devotions in honour of the B. V. M. By Rev. T. H. Kinane. 2s.

The Angel of the Altar ; or, the Love of the Most Adorable and Most Sacred Heart of Jesus. By Rev. T. H. Kinane. 2s. 3d.

Daily Exercises for Devout Christians. By Fr. Monk. 3s. 6d.

** *Though this Catalogue does not contain many of the books of other Publishers, R. W. can supply any, no matter by whom they are published. All orders, so far as possible, will be executed the same day.*

School Books, *with the usual reduction*, Copy Books, and other Stationery, Rosaries, Medals, Crucifixes, Scapulars, Incense, Candlesticks, Vases, &c., &c., supplied.

Foreign Books supplied. The publications of the leading Publishers kept in stock.

The Belfast Man. Earlier and Later Leaves; or an Autumn Gathering. Poems and Songs. By Francis Davis. 6s.

Gaume's Catechism of Perseverance. Translated. In 4 vols., vol. i., 7s. 6d.

Sacred History in Forty Pictures. Plain, 5s.; Coloured, 7s. 6d. Mounted on cardboard, coloured, 18s. 6d. and 22s.

Recollections of Twelve Years' Residence (as a Missionary Priest) in the Western District of the Cape of Good Hope, South Africa. By Rev. James O'Haire. 8vo., 7s. 6d.

Recollections of Cardinal Wiseman, and other Memories. By M. J. Arnold. Second edition, handsomely bound in cloth, 2s. 6d.

Gathered Gems from Spanish Authors. By Mariana Monteiro, author of "The Monk of the Monastery of Yuste." 3s.

Contents :—The Rosary Bell—The Blind Organist of Seville—The Last Baron of Fortcastells—The Miserere of the Mountains—Three Reminiscences—A Legend of Italy—The Gnomes of Moncayo—The Passion Flower—Recollections of an Artistic Excursion—The Laurel Wreath—The Witches of Trasmoz.

Christ bearing His Cross. A Steel Engraving from the Picture miraculously given to B. Colomba, O.S.D., at Perugia. To which is attached a short account of Blessed Colomba. 6d.; proofs, 1s.

Life of St. Wenefred, Virgin Martyr and Abbess, Patroness of North Wales and Shrewsbury. By Rev. Thomas Meyrick, M.A. With Frontispiece, 2s.

A Month at Lourdes and its Neighbourhood in the Summer of 1877. By Hugh Caraher. Two Illustrations, 2s.

Grains of Gold. A small collection of Counsels for the Sanctification and Happiness of Life. 1st. series, 6d.; cloth, 1s. 1st and 2nd. series, cloth, 2s. 6d.

Incidents in the Life of Christ. A Series of 12 Illuminations. 4to., 6s.

The Catholic Hymn Book. Compiled by Rev. L. G. Vere. 32mo., 2d.; cloth, 4d.; Appendix, containing Hymns dedicated to Special Saints. 1d.

A Catechism for First Confession. By the Rev. R. G. Davis. *Nihil Obstat :* Johannes Can. Crookall, S.T.D., V.G. 32mo., 1d.

Manual of Devotions in Honour of our Lady of Sorrows. 18mo., 1s. 6d. Cheaper bound, 1s.

Tom's Crucifix and other Tales. By M. F. S. 3s.; or in 5 vols. each 1s.; or gilt, 1s. 6d. 1. Tom's Crucifix, and *Pat's Rosary; 2. Good for Evil, and Joe Ryan's Repentance; 3. The Old Prayer Book, and Charlie Pearson's Medal; 4. Catherine's Promise, and Norah's Temptation; 5. Annie's First Prayer, and *Only a Picture. (The tales marked * are not in the 3s. edition.)

To Rome and Back. Fly-Leaves from a Flying Tour. Edited by W. H. Anderdon, S.J. 12mo., 2s.

The Battle of Connemara. By Kathleen O'Meara, author of "Bells of the Sanctuary," "A Daughter of St. Dominick." 3s.

Industry and Laziness. By Franz Hoffman. From the German, by James King. 12mo., 3s.

The Two Friends; or, Marie's Self-Denial. By Madame d'Arras (Née Lechmere). 12mo., 1s.; gilt, 1s. 6d.

R. Washbourne, 18 Paternoster Row, London.

Stories of the Saints. By M. F. S. Third series. 12mo., 3s. 6d.
My Golden Days. My M. F. S. 12mo., 2s. 6d., or in 3 vols. 1s. each ; gilt, 1s. 6d.
Corona Lauretana. Twenty Litanies of the Blessed Virgin, with organ accompaniment. By Wilhelm Schulthes. 2s. nett.
The Holy Mass : The Sacrifice for the Living and the Dead. By Rev. M. Müller, C.SS.R. 12mo., 10s. 6d.
Pius IX., from his Birth to his Death. By George White. 6d.
Pius IX., his early Life to the Return from Gaeta. By Rev. T. B. Snow, O.S.B. 12mo., 6d.
The Faith of our Fathers : Being a Plain Exposition and Vindication of the Church founded by our Lord Jesus Christ. By Rt. Rev. James Gibbons, D.D., 12mo. 4s. ; paper covers, 2s. nett.

A DELSTAN (Countess), Sketch of her Life and Letters. From the French of the Rev. Père Marquigny, S.J. 1s. & 2s. 6d.
Adolphus ; or, the Good Son. 18mo., 6d.
Adventures of a Protestant in Search of a Religion. By Iota. 12mo., 2s. and 3s. 6d.
AGNEW (Mme.), Convent Prize Book. 12mo., 2s. 6d.; 3s. 6d.
A'KEMPIS—Following of Christ. Pocket Edition, 32mo., 1s.; embossed red edges, 1s. 6d.; roan, 2s.; French morocco, 2s. 6d.; calf or morocco, 4s. 6d.; gilt, 5s. 6d.; russia, with clasp, &c., 10s. 6d.; ivory, with rims and clasp, 15s., 16s., 18s.; morocco antique, with corners and clasps, 17s. 6d.; russia, ditto, ditto, 16s., 20s.
———— Imitation of Christ ; with Reflections. 32mo., 1s.; Persian calf, 3s. 6d.; 12mo., 3s. 6d.; mor., 10s. 6d.; mor. ant. 25s.
———— The Three Tabernacles. 16mo., 2s. 6d.
Albertus Magnus. *See* Dixon (Rev. Fr. T. A.).
Album of Christian Art. Twenty-three original compositions of Professor Klein, in Vienna. 4to., 7s. 6d.
ALLIES (T. W.), St. Peter; his Name and his Office. 5s.
Alone in the World. By A. M. Stewart. 12mo., 4s. 6d.
Alphabet of Scripture Subjects. On a large sheet, 1s.; coloured, 2s., on a roller, varnished, 4s. 6d.; mounted to fold in a book, 3s. 6d.
ALZOG'S Universal Church History. 8vo., Vols. i & ii, each 20s.
American Life (Forty Years of). By Dr. Nichols. 12mo., 5s.
AMHERST (Rt. Rev. Dr.), Lenten Thoughts. 2s. 6d.
Amulet (The). By Conscience. 12mo., 4s.
ANDERDON (Rev. W. H., S.J.), To Rome and Back. Fly-Leaves from a Flying Tour. 12mo., 2s.
ANDERSEN (Carl), Three Sketches of Life in Iceland. Translated by Myfanwy Fenton. 12mo., 2s. 6d.
Angela Merici (S.) Her Life, her Virtues, and her Institute. From the French of the Abbé G. Beeteme. 12mo., 4s. 6d.
Angela's (S.) Manual : a Book of Devout Prayers and Exercises for Female Youth. 2s.; Persian, 3s. 6d.; calf, 4s. 6d.
Angels (The) and the Sacraments. 16mo., 1s.
———— Month of the Holy Angels. By Abbé Ricard. 1s.
Angelus (The). A Monthly Magazine. 8vo., 1d. Yearly subscription, post free, 1s. 6d. Volume for 1876, cloth, 2s. 6d. 1877, 2s.

Anglican Orders. By Canon Williams. 12mo., 3s. 6d.
Anglicanism, Harmony of. *See* Marshall (T. W. M.).
Apostleship of Prayer. By Rev. H. Ramière. 12mo., 6s.
Are You Safe in the Church of England? A Question for Anxious Ritualists. By an Ex-Member of the Congregation of S. Bartholomew, Brighton. 8vo., 1s.
ARNOLD (Miss M. J.), Personal Recollections of Cardinal Wiseman, with other Memories. 12mo., 2s. 6d.
ARRAS (Madame d') The Two Friends; or Marie's Self-Denial. 12mo., 1s.; gilt edges, 1s. 6d.
Ars Rhetorica. Auctore R. P. Martino du Cygne. 12mo., 3s.
Artist of Collingwood. 12mo., 2s.
Association of Prayers. *See* Tondini (Rev. C.).
Augustine (St.) of Canterbury, Life of. 12mo., 3s. 6d.
Aunt Margaret's Little Neighbours; or, Chats about the Rosary. 12mo., 3s.
BAGSHAWE (Rev. J. B.), Catechism of Christian Doctrine, illustrated with passages from the Holy Scriptures. 2s. 6d.
———— Threshold of the Catholic Church. A Course of Plain Instructions for those entering her Communion. 12mo., 4s.
BAGSHAWE (Rt. Rev. Dr.), The Life of our Lord, commemorated in the Mass. 18mo., 6d., bound 1s.; Verses and Hymns separately, 1d., bound 4d.
BAKER (Fr., O.S.B.), The Rule of S. Benedict. From the old English edition of 1638. 12mo., 4s. 6d.
Baker's Boy; or, Life of General Drouot. 18mo., 6d.
BALMES (J. L.), Letters to a Sceptic on Matters of Religion. 12mo., 5s.
BAMPFIELD (Rev. G.), Sir Ælfric and other Tales. 18mo., 6d.; cloth, 1s.; gilt, 1s. 6d.
BARGE (Rev. T.), Occasional Prayers for Festivals. 32mo., 4d. and 6d.; gilt, 1s.
Battista Varani (B.), *see* Veronica (S.). 12mo., 5s.
Battle of Connemara. By Kathleen O'Meara. 12mo., 3s.
BAUGHAN (Rosa), Shakespeare. Expurgated edition. 8vo., 6s. The Comedies only, 3s. 6d.
·**Before the Altar.** 32mo., 6d.
Belfast Man (The). Earlier and Later Leaves; or, an Autumn Gathering. Poems and Songs. By Francis Davis. 6s.
BELLECIO (Fr.), Spiritual Exercises of S. Ignatius. Translated by Dr. Hutch. 18mo., 2s.
BELL'S Modern Reader and Speaker. 12mo., 3s. 6d.
Bells of the Sanctuary,—A Daughter of St. Dominick. By Grace Ramsay. 12mo., 1s. and 1s. 6d.; stronger bound, 2s.
Benedict (S.), Abridged Explanation of his Medal. 18mo., 1d.; or 6s. 100.
———— The Rule of our most Holy Father S. Benedict, Patriarch of Monks. From the old English edition of 1638. Edited in Latin and English by one of the Benedictine Fathers of St. Michael's, near Hereford. 12mo., 4s. 6d.

Benedictine Breviary. 4 vols., 18mo., Dessain, 1870. 26s. nett ; morocco, 42s. nett, and 47s. nett.

Benedictine Missal. Pustet, Folio, 1873. 20s. nett; morocco, 50s. nett, and 60s. nett. Dessain, 4to., 1862, 18s. nett ; morocco, 40s. nett, and 50s. nett.

BENNI (Most Rev. C. B.), Tradition of the Syriac Church of Antioch, concerning the Primacy and Prerogatives of S. Peter and of his successors, the Roman Pontiffs. 8vo., 7s. 6d.

Berchmans (Bl. John), New Miracle at Rome, through the intercession of Bl. John Berchmans. 12mo., 2d.

Bernardine (St.) of Siena, Life of. With Portrait. 12mo., 5s.

Bertha ; or, the Consequences of a Fault. 8vo., 2s. 6d.

Bessy ; or, the Fatal Consequence of Telling Lies. 12mo., 1s.; stronger bound, 1s. 6d.; gilt, 2s.

BESTE (J. R. Digby, Esq.), Catholic Hours. 32mo., 2s.; red edges, 2s. 6d. ; roan, 3s.; morocco, 6s.

——— **Church Hymns.** (Latin and English.) 32mo., 6d.

——— **Holy Readings.** 32mo., 2s , 2s. 6d. ; roan, 3s. ; mor., 6s.

BESTE (Rev. Fr.), Victories of Rome. 8vo., 1s.

Bible. Douay Version. 12mo., 3s. ; Persian, 8s. ; morocco, 10s. 6d. 18mo., 2s. 6d. ; Persian, 5s.; calf or morocco, 7s.; gilt, 8s. 6d. 4to., Illustrated, morocco, £5 5s. ; superior, £6 6s.

Bible History for the use of Schools. *See* Gilmour (Rev. R.).

Biographical Readings. By A. M. Stewart. 12mo., 4s. 6d.

Blessed Lord. *See* Ribadeneira ; Rutter (Rev. H.).

Blessed Virgin, Devotions to. From Ancient Sources. *See* Regina Sæculorum. 12mo., 1s. and 3s.

——— **Devout Exercise in honour of.** From the Psalter and Prayers of S. Bonaventure, 32mo., 1s.

——— **History of.** By Orsini. Translated by Provost Husenbeth. Illustrated, 12mo., 3s. 6d.

——— **Life of.** In verse. By C. E. Tame, Esq. 16mo., 2s.

——— **Life of.** Proposed as a model to Christian women. 12mo., 1s.

——— **in North America, Devotion to.** By Fr. Macleod. 5s.

——— **Veneration of.** By Mrs. Stuart Laidlaw. 16mo., 4d.

——— *See* Our Lady, p. 22 ; Leaflets, p. 16 ; May, p. 19.

Blessed Virgin's Root in Ephraim. *See* Laing (Rev. Dr.).

Blindness, Cure of, through the Intercession of Our Lady and S. Ignatius. 12mo., 2d.

BLOSIUS, Spiritual Works of :—The Rule of the Spiritual Life ; The Spiritual Mirror ; String of Spiritual Jewels. Edited by Rev. Fr. Bowden. 12mo., 3s. 6d.; red edges, 4s.

Blue Scapular, Origin of. 18mo., 1d.

BLYTH (Rev. Fr.), Devout Paraphrase on the Seven Penitential Psalms. To which is added "**Necessity of Purifying the Soul,**" by St. Francis de Sales. 18mo., 1s. stronger bound, 1s. 6d.; red edges, 2s.

BONA (Cardinal), Easy Way to God. Translated by Father Collins. 12mo., 3s.

BONAVENTURE (S.), Devout Exercise in honour of Our Lady. 32mo., 1s.

BONAVENTURE (S.), Life of St. Francis of Assisi. 3s. 6d.
Boniface (S.), Life of. By Mrs. Hope. 12mo., 6s.
Book of the Blessed Ones. By Miss Cusack. 12mo., 4s. 6d.
BORROMEO (S. Charles), Rules for a Christian Life. 2d.
BOUDON (Mgr.), Book of Perpetual Adoration. Translated by Rev. Dr. Redman. 12mo., 3s.; red edges, 3s. 6d.
BOUDREAUX (Rev. J., S.J.), God our Father. 12mo., 4s.
——— Happiness of Heaven. 12mo., 4s.
——— Paradise of God. 12mo., 4s.
BOURKE (Rev. Ulick J.), Easy Lessons: or, Self-Instruction in Irish. 12mo., 2s. 6d.
BOWDEN (Rev. Fr. John), Spiritual Works of Louis of Blois. 12mo., 3s. 6d.; red edges, 4s.
——— Oratorian Lives of the Saints. (Page 22).
BOWDEN (Mrs.), Lives of the First Religious of the Visitation of Holy Mary. 2 vols., 12mo., 10s.
BOWLES (Emily), Eagle and Dove. Translated from the French of Mdlle. Zénaïde Fleuriot. 12mo., 2s. 6d. and 5s.
BRADBURY (Rev. Fr.), Journey of Sophia and Eulalis to the Palace of True Happiness. 12mo., 1s. 6d.; 3s. 6d.
BRICKLEY'S Standard Table Book. 32mo., ½d.
BRIDGES (Miss), Sir Thomas Maxwell and his Ward. 12mo., 1s. and 2s.
Bridget (S.), Life of, and other Saints of Ireland. 12mo., 1s.
Brigit (S.) Life of, &c. By M. F. Cusack. 8vo., 6s.
Broken Chain. A Tale. 18mo., 6d.
BROWNE (E. G. K., Esq.), Monastic Legends. 8vo., 6d.
BROWNLOW (Rev. W. R. B.), Church of England and its Defenders. 8vo., 1st letter, 6d.; 2nd letter, 1s.
——— "Vitis Mystica"; or, the True Vine: a Treatise on the Passion of our Lord. 18mo., 4s.; red edges, 4s. 6d.
BUCKLEY (Rev. M.), Sermons, Lectures, &c. 12mo., 6s.
BURDER (Abbot), Confidence in the Mercy of God. By Mgr. Languet. 12mo., 3s.
——— The Consoler; or, Pious Readings addressed to the Sick and all who are afflicted. By Père Lambilotte. 12mo., 4s. 6d.; red ed., 5s.
——— Souls in Purgatory. 32mo., 3d.
——— Novena for the Souls in Purgatory. 32mo., 3d.
Burial of the Dead. For Children and Adults. (Latin and English.) Clear type edition, 32mo., 6d.; roan, 1s. 6d.
Burke (Edmund), Life of. *See* Robertson (Professor).
BURKE (S.H., M.A.), Men and Women of the English Reformation. 12mo., 2 vols., 13s.; Vol. II., 5s.
BURKE (Father), and others, Catholic Sermons. 12mo., 2s.
BUTLER (Alban), Lives of the Saints. 2 vols., 8vo., 28s.; gilt, 34s.; 4 vols., 8vo., 32s.; gilt, 50s.; leather, 64s.
——— One Hundred Pious Reflections. 18mo., 1s. and 2s.
BUTLER (Dr.), Catechisms. 1st, ½d.; 2nd, 1d.; 3rd, 1½d.
CALIXTE—Life of the Ven. Anna Maria Taigi. Translated by A. V. Smith Sligo. 8vo., 2s. 6d. and 5s.

Callista. Dramatised by Dr. Husenbeth. 12mo., 2s.

Captain Rougemont ; or, the Miraculous Conversion. 8vo., 2s. 6d.

Cassilda ; or, the Moorish Princess of Toledo. 8vo., 2s. 6d.

Catechisms—The Catechism of Christian Doctrine. Good large type on superfine paper. 32mo., 1d., cloth, 2d.; interleaved, 8d.

———— The Catechism of Christian Doctrine. Illustrated with passages from the Holy Scriptures. By the Rev. J. B. Bagshawe. 12mo., 2s. 6d.

———— made Easy. By Rev. H. Gibson. Vol. II, 4s.; Vol. III., 4s.

———— for First Confession. By Rev. R. G. Davis. 32mo., 1d.

———— Lessons on Christian Doctrine. 18mo., 1½d.

———— General Catechism of the Christian Doctrine. By the Right Rev. Bishop Poirier. 18mo., 9d.

———— By Dr. Butler. 32mo., 1st, ½d.; 18mo., 2nd, 1d.; 3rd, 1½d.

———— By Dr. Doyle. 18mo., 1½d.

———— Fleury's Historical. Complete Edition. 18mo., 1½d.

———— Frassinetti's Dogmatic. 12mo., 3s.

———— of the Council. 12mo., 2d.

———— of Perseverance. By Abbé Gaume. 12mo., Vol. I., 7s. 6d.

Catherine Hamilton. By M. F. S. 12mo., 2s. 6d.; gilt, 3s.

Catherine Grown Older. By M. F. S. 12mo., 2s. 6d.; gilt, 3s.

Catholic Hours. *See* Beste (J. R. Digby).

Catholic Keepsake. A Gift Book for all Seasons. 12mo., 6s.

Catholic Piety. *See* Prayer Books, page 30.

Catholic Sick and Benefit Club. *See* Richardson (Rev. R.).

CHALLONER (Bishop), Grounds of Catholic Doctrine. Large type edition. 18mo., 4d.

———— Memoirs of Missionary Priests. 8vo., 6s.

———— Think Well on't. 18mo., 2d.; cloth, 6d.

CHAMBERS (F.), The Fair Maid of Kent. An Historical and Biographical Sketch. 8vo., 6d.

Chances of War. An Irish Tale. By A. Whitelock. 8vo., 5s.

CHARDON (Abbe), Memoirs of a Guardian Angel. 4s.

Chats about the Rosary. *See* Aunt Margaret's Little Neighbours.

CHAUGY (Mother Frances Magdalen de), Lives of the First Religious of the Visitation. 2 vols., 12mo., 10s

Child (The). *See* Dupanloup (Mgr.).

Child's Book of the Passion of Our Lord. 32mo., 6d.

Child (The) of Mary's Manual. Compiled from the French. Second edition, 32mo. 1s. 6d.

Children of Mary in the World, Association of. 32mo., 1d.

Choir, Catholic, Manual. By C. B. Lyons. 12mo., 1s.

Christ bearing His Cross. A Steel Engraving from the Picture miraculously given to Blessed Colomba. 8vo., 6d.; proofs, 1s.

CHRISTIAN BROTHERS' Reading Books.

Christian Doctrine, Lessons on. 18mo., 1½d.

Christian, Duties of a. By Ven. de la Salle. 12mo., 2s

Christian Politeness. By the same Author. 18mo., 1s.

Christian Teacher. By the same Author. 18mo., 1s. 8d.

Christmas Offering. 32mo., 1s. a 100 ; or 7s. 6d. for 1000.

Christmas (The First) for our dear Little Ones. 4to., 5s.

Chronological Sketches. *See* Murray Lane (H.).

Church Defence. *See* Marshall (T. W. M.).

Church History. By Alzog. 8vo., 3 vols. each 20s.

———————— By Darras. 4 vols., 8vo., 48s.

———————— Compendium. By Noethen. 12mo., 8s.

———————— for Schools. By Noethen. 12mo., 5s. 6d.

Church of England and its Defenders. *See* Brownlow (Rev.).

Cistercian Legends of the XIII. Century. *See* Collins (Fr.).

Cistercian Order : its Mission and Spirit. *See* Collins (Fr.).

Civilization and the See of Rome. *See* Montagu (Lord).

Clare (Sister Mary Cherubini) of S. Francis, Life of. Preface by Lady Herbert. With Portrait. 12mo., 3s. 6d.

Cloister Legends ; or, Convents and Monasteries in the Olden Time. 12mo., 4s.

COGERY (A.), Third French Course, with Vocabulary. 12mo.,2s.

COLLINS (Rev. Fr.), Cistercian Legends of the XIII. Century. 12mo., 3s.

———————— Cistercian Order : its Mission and Spirit. 12mo., 3s. 6d.

———————— Easy Way to God. Translated from the Latin of Cardinal Bona. 12mo., 3s.

———————— Spiritual Conferences on the Mysteries of Faith and the Interior Life. 12mo., 5s.

COLOMBIERE (Father Claude de la), The Sufferings of Our Lord. Sermons preached in the Chapel Royal, St. James's, in the year 1677. Preface by Fr. Doyotte, S.J. 18mo., 1s. ; stronger bound, 1s. 6d. ; red edges, 2s.

Colombini (B. Giovanni), Life of. By Belcari. Translated from the editions of 1541 and 1832. With Portrait. 12mo., 3s. 6d.

Columba (S.) Life of, &c. By M. F. Cusack. 8vo., 6s.

Columbkille, or Columba (S.), Life and Prophecies of. By St. Adamnan. 12mo., 3s. 6d.

Comedy of Convocation in the English Church. Edited by Archdeacon Chasuble. 8vo., 2s. 6d. *See* page 18.

COMERFORD (Rev. P.), Handbook of the Confraternity of the Sacred Heart. 18mo., 3d.

———————— Month of May for all the Faithful ; or, a Practical Life of the Blessed Virgin. 32mo., 1s.

———————— Pleadings of the Sacred Heart. 18mo., 1s.; gilt, 2s.; with the Handbook of the Confraternity, 1s. 6d.

Communion, Prayers for, for Children. Preparation, Mass before Communion, Thanksgiving. 32mo. 1d.

Compendious Statement of the Scripture Doctrine regarding the Nature and chief Attributes of the Kingdom of Christ. By C. F. A. 8vo., 1s.

COMPTON (Herbert), Semi-Tropical Trifles. 12mo., boards, 1s.; extra cloth, 2s. 6d.

Conferences. *See* Collins, Lacordaire, Mermillod, Ravignan.

Confession, Auricular. By Rev. Dr. Melia. 18mo., 1s. 6d.

Confession and Holy Communion : Young Catholic's Guide. By Dr. Kenny. 32mo., 4d.; cloth, 6d.; red edges, 9d.; French morocco, 1s. 6d.; calf or morocco, 2s. 6d.

Confidence in God. By Cardinal Manning. 16mo., 1s.

Confidence in the Mercy of God. By Mgr. Languet. Translated by Abbot Burder. 12mo., 3s.

Confirmation, Instructions for the Sacramont of. A very complete book. 18mo., 3d.

CONSCIENCE (Hendrick), The Amulet. 12mo., 4s.
———— **Count Hugo, of Graenhove.** 12mo., 4s.
———— **The Fisherman's Daughter.** 12mo., 4s.
———— **Happiness of being Rich.** 12mo., 4s.
———— **Ludovic and Gertrude.** 12mo., 4s.
———— **The Village Innkeeper.** 12mo., 4s.
———— **Young Doctor.** 12mo., 4s.

Consoler (The). By Abbot Burder. 12mo., 4s. 6d. and 5s.

Contemplations on the most Holy Sacrament of the Altar; or Devout Meditations to serve as Preparations for, and Thanksgiving after, Communion. Drawn chiefly from the Holy Scriptures. 18mo., 1s. and 2s.; red edges, 2s. 6d.

Continental Fish Cook. By M. J. N. de Frederic. 18mo., 1s.

Convent Prize Book. By Mme. Agnew. 12mo., 2s. 6d., 3s. 6d.

Conversion of the Teutonic Race. By Mrs. Hope. 2 vols. 10s.

Convert Martyr; or, "Callista." By the Rev. Dr. Newman. Dramatised by Rev. Dr. Husenbeth. 12mo., 2s.

Convocation, Comedy of. By the Author of "The Oxford Undergraduate of Twenty Years Ago." 8vo. 2s. 6d.

CORTES (John Donoso), Essays on Catholicism, Liberalism, and Socialism. 12mo., 5s.

Crests, The Book of Family. Comprising nearly every bearing and its blazonry, Surnames of Bearers, Dictionary of Mottoes, British and Foreign Orders of Knighthood, Glossary of Terms, and upwards of 4,000 Engravings, Illustrative of Peers, Baronets, and nearly every Family bearing Arms in England, Wales, Scotland, Ireland, and the Colonies, &c. 2 vols., 12mo., 24s.

Crucifixion, The. A large picture for School walls, 1s.

CULPEPPER. An entirely new edition of Brook's Family Herbal, 12mo., 3s. 6d.; coloured plates, 5s. 6d.

CUSACK (M. F.):—Sister Mary Francis Clare.
  Book of the Blessed Ones. 12mo., 4s. 6d.
  Devotions for Public and Private Use at the Way of the Cross. Illustrated. 32mo., 1s.; red edges, 1s. 6d.
  Father Mathew, Life of. 12mo., 2s. 6d.
  Good Reading for Sundays and Festivals. 2s. 6d.
  Ireland, Illustrated History of. 8vo., 12s.
  Ireland, Patriot's History of. 18mo., 2s.
  Jesus and Jerusalem; or, the Way Home. 12mo., 4s. 6d.
  Joseph (S.), Life of. 32mo., 6d.; cloth, 1s.
  Lives of St. Columba and St. Brigit. 8vo., 6s.
  Mary O'Hagan, Abbess, Life of. 8vo., 6s.
  Memorare Mass. 32mo., 2d.
  Ned Rusheen. 12mo., 5s.
  Nun's Advice to her Girls. 12mo., 2s. 6d.
  O'Connell; his Life and Times. 2 vols. 8vo., 18s.

Duchess (The), Transformed. By W. H. A. 12mo., 6d.

DUMESNIL (Abbe), Recollections of the Reign of Terror. 12mo., 2s. 6d.

DUPANLOUP (Mgr.), Contemporary Prophecies. 8vo., 1s.

———— The Child. Translated by Kate Anderson. 12mo., 3s. 6d.

Dusseldorf Gallery. 357 Engravings. Large 4to. Half-morocco, gilt, £5 5s. nett.

———— 134 Engravings. Large 8vo. Half-morocco, gilt, 42s.

Dusseldorf Society for the Distribution of Good Religious Pictures. Subscription, 8s. 6d. a year. *Catalogue* 3d.

Duties of a Christian. By Ven. de la Salle. 12mo., 2s.

Eagle and Dove. *See* Bowles (Emily).

E. A. M. Countess Adelstan. 12mo., 1s. and 2s. 6d.

———— Paul Seigneret. 12mo., 6d., 1s., 1s. 6d., gilt, 2s.

———— Regina Sæculorum. 12mo., 1s. and 3s.

———— Rosalie. 12mo., 1s., 1s. 6d., gilt, 2s.

Early English Literature. *See* Tame (C.E.).

Easy Way to God. By Cardinal Bona. 12mo., 3s.

Ebba ; or, the Supernatural Power of the Blessed Sacrament. *This book is in French.* 12mo., 1s. 6d. ; cloth, 2s. 6d.

Edmund (S.) of Canterbury, Life of. From the French of Rev. Fr. Massée, S.J. By George White. 18mo., 1s. & 1s. 6d.

Electricity and Magnetism ; an Enquiry into the Nature and Results of. By Amyclanus. Illustrated. 12mo., 6s. 6d.

English Religion (The). By Arthur Marshall. 8vo., 6d.

Epistles and Gospels. Good clear type edition, 32mo., 6d.; roan, 1s. 6d.; larger edition, 18mo., French morocco, 2s.

————, Explanation of. By Rev. F. Goffine. Illustrated, 8vo., 9s.

Epistles of S. Paul, Exposition of. *See* MacEvilly (Rt. Rev. Dr.)

Ernscliff Hall. A Drama in Three Acts, for Girls. 12mo., 6d.

Eucharistic Year ; Preparation and Thanksgiving for Holy Communion. 18mo., 4s.

Eucharist (The) and the Christian Life. *See* La Bouillerie.

Europe, Modern, History of. With Preface by Bishop Weathers. 12mo., 5s.; roan, 5s. 6d.; cloth gilt, 6s.

Extemporary Preaching. By Rev. T. J. Potter. 12mo., 5s.

Fairy Tales for Little Children. By Madeleine Howley Meehan. 12mo., 6d.; stronger bound, 1s. and 1s. 6d.; gilt, 2s.

Faith of Our Fathers. *See* Gibbons (Rt. Rev. Dr.).

Fall, Redemption, and Exaltation of Man. 12mo., 1s.

Familiar Instructions on Christian Truths. By a Priest. 12mo. 1. Detraction 4d. 2. Dignity of the Priesthood, 3d. 3. Hearing the Word of God, 3d.

Farleyes of Farleye. By Rev. T. J. Potter. 12mo., 2s. 6d.

FARRELL (Rev. J.), The Lectures of a certain Professor. 12mo., 7s. 6d.

Father Mathew (Life of). By M. F. Cusack. 12mo., 2s. 6d.

FAVRE (Abbe), Heaven Opened by the Practice of Frequent Confession and Communion. 12mo., 2s. ; stronger bound, 3s. 6d. ; red edges, 4s.

Feasts (The) of Camelot, with the tales that were told
there. By Mrs. T. K. Hervey. 12mo., 3s. 6d., or in 2 vols. 1s. each.
Filiola. A Drama in Four Acts, for Girls. 12mo., 6d.
First Apostles of Europe. *See* Hope (Mrs.).
First Communion and Confirmation Memorial. Beautifully
printed in gold and colours, folio, 1s. each, or 9s. a dozen, nett.
First Religious of the Visitation of Holy Mary, Lives of.
With two Photographs. 2 vols., 12mo., 10s.
Fisherman's Daughter. By Conscience. 12mo., 4s.
FLEET (Charles), Tales and Sketches. 8vo., 2s.; stronger
bound, 2s. 6d.; gilt, 3s. 6d.
FLEURIOT (Mlle. Zénaide), Eagle and Dove. Translated
by Emily Bowles. 12mo., 2s. 6d. and 5s.
FLEURY'S Historical Catechism. Large edition, 12mo., 1¼d.
Flowers of Christian Wisdom. *See* Henry (Lucien).
Fluffy. A Tale for Boys. By M. F. S. 12mo., 3s. 6d.
Following of Christ. *See* A'Kempis.
Foreign Books. *See* R. W.'s Catalogue of Foreign Books. 3d.
Francis of Assisi (S.) Life of. By S. Bonaventure. Translated
by Miss Lockhart. 12mo., 3s. 6d.
FRANCIS OF SALES (S.), Consoling Thoughts. 18mo., 2s.
———— **The Mystical Flora ; or, the Christian Life under**
the Emblem of Saints. 4to., 8s.
———— **Necessity of Purifying the Soul.** *See* Blyth (Rev. Fr.).
———— **Sweetness of Holy Living.** 18mo., 1s.; levant, 3s.
Franciscan Annals and Monthly Bulletin of the Third
Order of St. Francis. 8vo., 6d.
FRANCO (Rev. S.) Devotions to the Sacred Heart. 12mo.,
4s.; cheap edition, 2s.
FRASSINETTI—Dogmatic Catechism. 12mo., 3s.
FREDERIC (M. J. N. de), Continental Fish Cook ; or, a
Few Hints on Maigre Dinners. 18mo., 1s., soiled covers, 6d.
Freemasons, Irish and English, and their Foreign Bro-
thers. 4to., 2s.
From Sunrise to Sunset. By L. B. 12mo., 3s. 6d.
GALLERY (Rev. D.), Handbook of Essentials in History
and Literature, Ancient and Modern. For the use of
Junior Pupils. 18mo., 1s.
Garden of the Soul. *See* page 32.
Garden (Little) of the Soul. *See* page 30.
Gathered Gems from Spanish Authors. *See* Monteiro.
GAUME (Abbe), Catechism of Perseverance. 4 vols., 12mo.
Vol. 1, 7s. 6d.
GAYRARD (Mme. Paul) Harmony of the Passion. Com-
piled from the four Gospels, in Latin and French. 18mo., 1s. 6d.
German (S.), Life of. 12mo., 3s. 6d.
GIBBONS (Rt. Rev. James, D.D.), The Faith of Our
Fathers; Being a Plain Exposition and Vindication of the Church
Founded by our Lord Jesus Christ. 12mo., 4s. Paper covers, 2s.
GIBSON (Rev. H.), Catechism made Easy. 12mo., Vol. I.
(out of print); Vol. II., 4s. ; Vol. III., 4s.

GILMOUR (Rev. R.), Bible History for the Use of Schools. Illustrated. 12mo., 2s.

God our Father. By a Father of the Society of Jesus. 12mo., 4s.

GOFFINE (Rev. F.), Explanation of the Epistles and Gospels. Illustrated. 8vo., 9s.

Gold and Alloy in the Devout Life. *See* Monsabré.

Good Reading for Sundays and Festivals. *See* Cusack.

Good Thoughts for Priests and People. *See* Noethen.

Gospels, An Exposition of. *See* MacEvilly (Most Rev. Dr.).

Grace before and after Meals. 32mo., 1d. ; cloth, 2d.

GRACE RAMSAY. A Daughter of S. Dominick (Bells of the Sanctuary, No. 4). 12mo., 1s.; stronger bound, 1s. 6d. and 2s.
——— *See* O'Meara (Kathleen).

GRACIAN (Fr. Baltasar), Sanctuary Meditations for Priests and Frequent Communicants. Translated from the Spanish by Mariana Monteiro. 12mo., 4s.

Grains of Gold. Counsels for the Sanctification and Happiness of Life. 18mo., 1st Series, 6d.; cloth, 1s. 16mo., Series 1 and 2, cloth, 2s. 6d.

GRANT (Bishop), Pastoral on St. Joseph. 32mo., 4d. & 6d.

Gregorian, or Plain Chant and Modern Music. 8vo., 2s. 6d.

Gregory Lopez, the Hermit, Life of. By Canon Doyle, O.S.B. With a Photographic Portrait. 12mo., 3s. 6d.

Grounds of the Catholic Doctrine. By Bishop Challoner. Large type edition, 18mo., 4d.

Guardian Angel, Memoirs of a. By Abbé Chardon. 12mo., 4s.

GUERANGER (Dom), Defence of the Roman Church against F. Gratry. Translated by Canon Woods. 8vo., 1s.

Guide to Sacred Eloquence. *See* Passionist Fathers.

HALL (E.), Munster Firesides. 12mo., 3s. 6d.

Happiness of Being Rich. By Conscience. 12mo., 4s.

Happiness of Heaven. By a Father of the Society of Jesus. 12mo. 4s.

Harmony of Anglicanism. By T. W. Marshall. 8vo., 2s. 6d.

HAY (Bishop), Sincere Christian. 18mo., 2s. 6d.
——— **Devout Christian.** 18mo., 2s. 6d.

He would be a Lord. A Comedy in 3 Acts. (Boys). 12mo., 2s.

Heaven Opened by the Practice of frequent Confession and Holy Communion. By the Abbé Favre. 12mo., 2s. ; stronger bound, 3s. 6d.; red edges, 4s.

HEDLEY (Bishop), Five Sermons—Light of the Holy Spirit in the World. 12mo., 1s.; cloth, 1s. 6d. Revelation, Mystery, Dogma and Creeds, Infallibility : separately, 3d. each.

HEIGHAM (John), A Devout Exposition of the Holy Mass. Edited by Austin John Rowley, Priest. 12mo., 4s.

Henri V. (Comte de Chambord). *See* Walsh (W. H.).

HENRY (Lucien), Flowers of Christian Wisdom. 18mo., 1s. and 2s.; red edges, 2s. 6d.

Herbal, Brook's Family. 12mo., 3s. 6d.; coloured plates, 5s. 6d.

HERBERT (Wallace), My Dream and Verses Miscellaneous. With a frontispiece. 12mo., 5s.
——— **The Angels and the Sacraments.** 16mo., 1s.

HERGENRÖTHER Dr., Anti-Janus. Translated by Provost Lobesm. 12mo., 6s.

BERTEY Eleanora Louisa, My Godmother's Stories from many Lands. 12mo., 3s. 6d.

—— Our Legends and Lives. 12mo., 6s.

—— Rest on the Cross. 12mo., 3s. 6d.

—— The Feasts of Camelot, with the Tales that were told there. 12mo., 3s. 6d.; or, separately: Christmas 1s.; Whitsuntide 1s.

HILL Rev. Fr., Elements of Philosophy, comprising Logic and several Principles of Metaphysics. 8vo., 6s.

HOFFMAN Franz, Industry and Laziness. 12mo., 3s.

Holy Childhood. A book of simple Prayers and Instructions for very little children. 32mo., 6d. or 1s.; gilt. 1s. 6d.

Holy Church the Centre of Unity. See Shaw (T. H.)

Holy Communion. By Hubert Lebon. 12mo., 4s.

Holy Family, Confraternity of. See Manning (Card.).

Holy Places: their Sanctity and Authenticity. See Philpin.

Holy Readings. See Besse (J. R. Digby Esq.).

HOPE Mrs., The First Apostles of Europe; or, "The Conversion of the Teutonic Race." 2 vols., 12mo., 10s.

Horace. Literally translated by Smart. 18mo., 2s.

HUGUET Pere, The Power of S. Joseph. Meditations and Devotions. Translated by Clara Mulholland. 1s. 6d.

HUMPHREY Rev. W., S.J., The Panegyrics of Fr. Segneri, S.J. Translated from the original Italian. With a Preface by the Rev. W. Humphrey, S.J. 12mo., 5s.

HUSENBETH (Rev. Dr.), Convert Martyr. 12mo., 2s.

—— History of the Blessed Virgin. Translated from Orsini. Illustrated. 12mo., 3s. 6d.   [Illustrated. 12mo., 5s.

—— Life and Sufferings of Our Lord. By Rev. H. Rutter.

—— Life of Mgr. Weedall. 8vo., 1s.

—— Little Office of the Immaculate Conception. In Latin and English. 32mo., 4d.; cloth, 6d.; roan, 1s.; calf or morocco, 3s. 6d.

—— Our Blessed Lady of Lourdes. 18mo., 6d.; with the Novena, 1s.; cloth. 1s. 6d. Novena, separately, 4d.; Litany, 1d.

—— Roman Question. 8vo., 6d.

Husenbeth (Provost), Sermon on his Death. By Very Rev. Canon Dalton. 8vo. 6d.

HUTCH (Rev. W., D.D.), Nano Nangle, her Life and her Labours. 12mo., 7s. 6d.

Hymn Book. Complete, for Missions. 32mo., 1d.; cloth, 2d.

Hymn Book (The Catholic). Edited by Rev. G. L. Vere. 32mo., 2d.; cloth, 4d.; Appendix (Hymns to Saints), 1d.

Iceland (Three Sketches of Life in). By Carl Andersen. 12mo.

IGNATIUS (S.), Spiritual Exercises. By Fr. Bellecio, S.J. Translated by Dr. Hutch. 18mo., 2s.

Ignatius (S.), Cure of Blindness through the Intercession of Our Lady and S. Ignatius. 12mo., 2d.

Illustrated Manual of Prayers. 32mo., 3d.: cloth, 4d.
Imitation of Christ. *See* A'Kempis.
Immaculate Conception, Definition of. 12mo., 6d.
———— **Little Office of.** *See* Husenbeth (Rev. Dr.).
———— **Little Office of, in Latin and English.** 32mo., 1d.
Indulgences. *See* Maurel (Rev. F. A.).
Industry and Laziness. By Franz Hoffman. From the German, by James King. 12mo., 3s.
Infallibility of the Pope. By the Author of " The Oxford Undergraduate of Twenty Years Ago." 8vo., 1s.
In Suffragiis Sanctorum. Commem. S. Josephi ; Commem. S. Georgii. Set of 5 for 4d.
Insula Sanctorum : The Island of Saints. 12mo., 1s.
Insurrection of '98. By Rev. P. F. Kavanagh. 12mo., 2s. 6d.
IOTA. The Adventures of a Protestant in Search of a Religion : being the Story of a late Student of Divinity at Bunyan Baptist College ; a Nonconformist Minister, who seceded to the Catholic Church. 12mo., 3s. 6d. ; cheap edition, 2s.
Ireland (History of). By Miss Cusack. 18mo., 2s. A larger edition, illustrated by Doyle, 8vo., 11s.
Ireland (History of). By T. Young. 18mo., 2s. 6d.
Ireland Ninety Years ago. 12mo., 1s.
Ireland, Popular Poetry of. (Songs). 262 pages, 18mo., 6d.
Ireland, Revelations of, in the Past Generation. 12mo., 1s.
Irish Board Reading Books.
Irish First Book. 18mo., 2d. **Second Book.** 18mo., 4d.
Irish Monthly. 8vo. Vol. 1877, cloth, 8s.
Italian Revolution (The History of). The History of the Barricades. By Keyes O'Clery, M.P. 8vo., 7s. 6d. and 3s. 6d,
JACOB (W. J.), Personal Recollections of Rome. od.
JENKINS (Rev. O. L.) Student's Handbook of British and American Literature. 12mo., 8s.
Jesuits (The), and other Essays. *See* Nevin (Willis, Esq.)
Jesus and Jerusalem ; or, the Way Home. *See* Cusack (Miss).
John of God (S.), Life of. With Photographic Portrait. 12mo., 5s.
Joseph (S.), Life of. By Miss Cusack. 32mo., 6d.; cloth, 1s.
———— **Novena of Meditations.** 18mo., 1s.
———— **Novena to,** with a Pastoral by the late Bishop Grant. 32mo., 4d.; cloth, 6d.
———— **Power of.** *See* Huguet.
———— *See* Leaflets.
Journey of Sophia and Eulalie to the Palace of True Happiness. From the French by Rev. Fr. Bradbury. 12mo., 1s. 6d.; better bound, 3s. 6d.
KAVANAGH (Rev. P. F.), Insurrection of '98. 1s. 6d.
Keighley Hall, and other Tales. By E. King. 18mo., 6d.; cloth, 1s. ; stronger bound, 1s. 6d. ; gilt, 2s.
KEMEN (Charles), The Marpingen Apparitions. 8vo., 1s.
KENNY (Dr.), Young Catholic's Guide to Confession and Holy Communion. 32mo., 4d.; cloth, 6d.; red edges, 9d.; roan, 1s. 6d.; calf or morocco, 2s. 6d.

KENNY (Dr.), New Year's Gift to our Heavenly Father.
32mo., 4d.

KERNEY (M. T.), Compendium of History. 12mo., 5s.

Key of Heaven. *See* Prayers, page 31.

KINANE (Rev. T. H.), Dove of the Tabernacle. 1s. 6d.

———— **Angel (The) of the Altar ;** or, the Love of the Most Adorable and Most Sacred Heart of Jesus. 18mo., 2s. 3d.

———— **Mary Immaculate, Mother of God ;** or Devotions in honour of the B.V.M. 18mo., 2s.

KING (Elizabeth), Keighley Hall, and other Tales. 18mo., 6d.; cloth, 1s.; stronger bound, 1s. 6d.; gilt, 2s.

———— **The Silver Teapot.** 18mo., 4d.

KING (James). Industry and Laziness. 12mo., 3s.

Kishoge Papers. Tales of Devilry and Drollery. 12mo., 1s. 6d.

LA BOUILLERIE (Mgr. de), The Eucharist and the Christian Life. Translated by L. C. 12mo., 3s. 6d.

LACORDAIRE'S Conferences. 12mo., On Life, 3s. 6d.; God, 6s.; Jesus Christ, 6s.

Lacordaire. The Inner Life of Pere Lacordaire. From the French of Père Chocarne. 12mo., 6s. 6d.

Lady Mildred's Housekeeper, A Few Words from. 2d.

LAIDLAW (Mrs. Stuart), Letters to my God-child. No. 4. On the Veneration of the Blessed Virgin. 16mo., 4d.

LAING (Rev. Dr.), Blessed Virgin's Root traced in the Tribe of Ephraim. 8vo., 10s. 6d.

———— **Descriptive Guide to the Mass.** 12mo., 1s. and 1s. 6d.

———— **Knight of the Faith.** 12mo., 4s.

Absurd Protestant Opinions concerning *Intention.* 4d.

Catholic, not Roman Catholic. 4d.

Challenge to the Churches. 1d.

Favourite Fallacy about Private Judgment and Inquiry. 1d.

Protestantism against the Natural Moral Law. 1d.

What is Christianity ? 6d.

Whence does the Monarch get his right to Rule ? 2s. 6d.

LAMBILOTTE (Pere), The Consoler. Translated by Abbot Burder. 12mo., 4s. 6d.; red edges, 5s.

LANGUET (Mgr.), Confidence in the Mercy of God. Translated by Abbot Burder. 12mo., 3s.

Last of the Catholic O'Malleys. By M. Taunton. 18mo., 1s. 6d.; stronger bound, 2s.

Leaflets. 1d. each, or 1s. 2d. per 100 post free.

Act of Reparation to the Sacred Heart.

Archconfraternity of the Agonising Heart of Jesus and the Compassionate Heart of Mary : Prayers for the Dying.

Archconfraternity of Our Lady of Angels.

Ditto, Rules.

Christmas Offering (or 7s. 6d. a 1000).

Devotions to S. Joseph.

Gospel according to St. John, *in Latin.* 1s. 6d. per 100.

Indulgenced Prayers for Souls in Purgatory.

Indulgences attached to Medals, Crosses, Statues, &c., by the Blessing of His Holiness and of those privileged to give his Blessing.

Intentions for Indulgences.

Litany of Our Lady of Angels.

Litany of S. Joseph, and Devotions.

Litany of Resignation.

Miraculous Prayer—August Queen of Angels.

Picture of Crucifixion, " I thirst " (or 5s. a 1000).

Prayer for One's Confessor.

Union of our Life with the Passion of our Lord.

Visit to the Blessed Sacrament. 5s. per 100.

Leaflets. 1d. each, or 6s. per 100.

Act of Consecration to the Sacred Heart.

Concise Portrait of the Blessed Virgin.

Explanation of the Medal or Cross of St. Benedict.

Indulgenced Prayers for the Rosary of the Dead.

Indulgenced Prayer before a Crucifix.

Litany of the Seven Dolours.

Prayer to S. Philip Neri.

Prayers before and after Holy Communion.

Revelation made by the mouth of Our Saviour to St. Bridget.

LEBON (Hubert), **Holy Communion.** 12mo., 4s.

Legends of the Saints. By M. F. S. 16mo., 3s. 6d.

Lenten Thoughts. By Bishop Amherst. 18mo., 2s.; red edges, 2s. 6d.

LEO XIII., The Church and Civilisation. 8vo., 1s.

Letter to George Augustus Simcox. 8vo., 6d.

Letters to my God-child. By Mrs. Stuart Laidlaw. 16mo., 4d.

Life in the Cloister. By Miss Stewart. 12mo., 3s. 6d.

Life of Pleasure. By Mgr. Dechamps. 12mo., 1s. 6d.

Light of the Holy Spirit in the World. Five Sermons, by Bishop Hedley. 12mo., 1s.; cloth, 1s. 6d.

LIGUORI (S.), **Fourteen Stations of the Cross.** 18mo., 1d.

————— **Officium Parvum.** Latin and English. With Novena. 12mo., 1s.; cloth, 2s.; red edges, 3s.

————— **Selva ;** or, a Collection of Matter for Sermons. 12mo., 5s.

————— **Way of Salvation.** 32mo., 1s.

Lily of S. Joseph : A little manual of Prayers and Hymns for Mass. 64mo., 2d.; cloth, 3d., 4d., and 6d.; gilt, 8d.; roan, 1s.; French morocco, 1s. 6d.; calf or morocco, 2s.; gilt, 2s. 6d.

Limerick Veteran ; or, the Foster Sisters. *See* Stewart (Agnes M.).

Literature, Philosophy of, An Essay contributing to a. By B. A. M. 12mo., 6s.

Literature, Student's Handbook. *See* Jenkins (Rev. O. L.).

Little Prayer Book. 32mo., 3d.

Lives of the First Religious of the Visitation of Holy Mary. By Mother Frances Magdalen de Chaugy. With 2 Photographs. 2 vols., 12mo., 10s.

Lost Children of Mount St. Bernard. 18mo., 6d.

Louis (St.), in Chains. Drama, Five Acts (Boys). 12mo., 2s.
Lourdes, Our Blessed Lady of. By Rev. Dr. Husenbeth. 18mo., 6d.; with the Novena, 1s.; cloth, 1s. 6d.
———— Novena of, for the use of the Sick. 4d.
———— Litany of. 1d. each.
———— Photograph, Carte de Visite, 1s.; Cabinet, 2s.; 4to., 4s.
Ludovic and Gertrude. By Conscience. 12mo., 4s.
LYONS (C. B.), Catholic Choir Manual. 12mo., 1s.
———— Catholic Psalmist. 12mo., 4s. [18mo., 2s.
MACDANIEL (M. A.), Month of May for Interior Souls.
———— Novena to S. Joseph. 32mo., 4d.; cloth, 6d.
———— Road to Heaven. A Game. 3s. 6d.
MACEVILLY (Bishop), Exposition of the Epistles of St. Paul and of the Catholic Epistles. 2 vols., large 8vo. 18s.
———— Exposition of the Gospels. Large 8vo., Vol. I., 12s. 6d.
MACLEOD (Rev. X. D.), Devotion to Our Lady in North America. 8vo., 5s.
Major John Andre. An Historical Drama for Boys. Five Acts. 2s.
MANNING (Cardinal), Church, Spirit and the Word. 6d.
———— Confidence in God. 16mo., 1s.
———— Confraternity of the Holy Family. 8vo., 3d.
———— Glory of S. Vincent de Paul. 12mo., 1s.
———— Independence of the Holy See. 12mo., 5s.
———— True Story of the Vatican Council. 12mo., 5s.
MANNOCK (Patrick), Origin and Progress of Religious Orders, and Happiness of a Religious State. Translated from the Latin of Rev. F. Platus. 12mo., 2s. 6d.
Manual of Catholic Devotions. *See* Prayers, page 31.
Manual of Devotions in honour of Our Lady of Sorrows. Compiled by the Clergy at St. Patrick's, Soho. 18mo., 1s. 6d.
Manual of the Cross and Passion. *See* Passionist Fathers.
Manual of the Sisters of Charity. 18mo., 6s.
Margarethe Verflassen. Translated from the German by Mrs. Smith Sligo. 12mo., 1s. 6d. and 3s.; gilt, 3s. 6d.
Margaret Roper. By A. M. Stewart. 12mo., 6s.; extra, 7s.
Marpingen Apparitions. From the German. By C. Kemen. 8vo., 1s.
MARQUIGNY (Pere), Life and Letters of Countess Adelstan. 12mo., 1s. and 2s. 6d.
MARSHALL (A. J. P., Esq.), Comedy of Convocation in the English Church. 8vo., 2s. 6d. *
———— English Religion. 8vo. 6d.,
———— Infallibility of the Pope. 8vo., 1s. *
———— Oxford Undergraduate of Twenty Years Ago. 8vo., 2s. 6d.; cloth, 3s. 6d. *
———— Reply to the Bishop of Ripon's Attack on the Catholic Church. 8vo., 6d. *
MARSHALL (T. W. M., Esq.), Harmony of Anglicanism—Church Defence. 8vo., 2s. 6d. *
        The 5 (*) in one Volume, 8vo., 6s.

MARSHALL (Rev. W.), The Doctrine of Purgatory. 1s.
MARTIN (Rev. E. R.), Rule of the Pope-King. 8vo., 6d.
Mary, A Remembrance of. 32mo., 2s.
Mary Christina of Savoy (Venerable). 18mo., 6d.
Mary Immaculate, Devotion to. By Rev. T. H. Kinane. 2s.
Mass, Descriptive Guide to. By Rev. Dr. Laing. 12mo., 1s., or stronger bound, 1s. 6d.
Mass, Devotions for. Very *Large type*, 18mo., 2d.
Mass, Life of our Lord in the. *See* Bagshawe (Bishop).
Mass, Memorare. By Miss Cusack. 32mo., 2d.
Mass (The). *See* Müller (Rev. M.), Tronson (Abbe).
Mass, A Devout Exposition of. *See* Rowley (Rev. A. J.).
Mathew (Father), Life of. By Miss Cusack. 12mo., 2s. 6d.
MAUREL (Rev. F. A.), Christian Instructed in the Nature and Use of Indulgences. 18mo., 2s.
Maxims of the Kingdom of Heaven. 12mo., 5s.; red edges, 5s. 6d.; calf or mor., 10s. 6d. Old Testament, 1s. 6d.; Gospels, 1s.
May, Month of. By Rev. P. Comerford. 32mo., 1s.
May, Month of. By M. A. Macdaniel. 18mo., 2s.!
May, Month of, principally for the use of Religious Communities. 18mo., 1s. 6d.
May Readings for the Feasts of Our Lady. By Rev. A. P. Bethell. 18mo., 1s. 6d.
M'CORRY (Rev. Dr.), Monks of Iona and the Duke of Argyll. 8vo., 3s. 6d.
———— Rome, Past, Present, Future. 8vo., 6d.
MEEHAN (M. H.), Fairy Tales for Little Children. 12mo., 6d. and 1s.; stronger bound, 1s. 6d.; gilt, 2s.
MELIA (Rev. Dr.), Auricular Confession. 18mo., 1s. 6d.
Men and Women of the English Reformation from the days of Wolsey to the death of Cranmer. By S. H. Burke, M.A. 12mo., 2 Vols., 13s.; Vol. II., 5s.
MERMILLOD (Mgr.), The Supernatural Life. Translated from the French, with a Preface by Lady Herbert. 12mo., 5s.
MEYRICK (Rev. T.), Life of St. Wenefred. 12mo., 2s.
M. F. S., Catherine Hamilton. 12mo., 2s. 6d.; gilt, 3s.
———— Catherine Grown Older. 12mo., 2s. 6d.; gilt, 3s.
——— Fluffy. A Tale for Boys. 12mo., 3s. 6d.
——— Legends of the Saints. 16mo., 3s. 6d. [gilt, 1s. 6d.
———— My Golden Days. 12mo., 2s. 6d.; or in 3 vols., 1s. ea.
———— Stories of Holy Lives. 12mo., 3s. 6d.
———— Stories of Martyr Priests. 12mo., 3s. 6d.
———— Stories of the Saints. 12mo., 3s. 6d.; gilt, 4s. 6d.
———————— Second Series. 12mo., 3s. 6d.; gilt, 4s. 6d.
———————— Third Series. 12mo., 3s. 6d.
———— Story of the Life of S. Paul. 12mo., 2s. 6d.
———— The Three Wishes. A Tale. 12mo., 2s. 6d.
———— Tom's Crucifix, and other Tales. 12mo., 3s., or in 5 vols., 1s. each, gilt 1s. 6d.
Message from the Mother Heart of Mary. 18mo., 4d. and 6d

MILES (G. H.), Truce of God. A Tale. 12mo., 4s.
MILNER (Bishop), Devotion to the **Sacred Heart** of Jesus. 32mo., 3d.; cloth, 6d.; gilt, 1s.
Miracles. A New Miracle at Rome, through the intercession of B. John Berchmans. 12mo., 2d.
———— Cure of Blindness, through the intercession of Our Lady and S. Ignatius. 12mo., 2d.
Mirror of Faith—your Likeness in It. By Fr. Hooker. [3s.
Misgivings—Convictions. 12mo., 6d.
Missal. *See* Prayers, page 31.
Monastic Legends. By E. G. K. Browne. 8vo., 6d.
MONK (Rev. Fr., O.S.B.), Daily Exercises. 18mo., 3s. 6d.
Monk of the Monastery of Yuste. *See* Monteiro (Mariana).
Monks of Iona and the Duke of Argyll. *See* M'Corry.
MONSABRE (Rev. Pere), Gold and Alloy. 12mo., 2s. 6d.
MONTAGU (Lord Robert), Civilization and the See of Rome. 8vo., 6d.
Montalembert (Count de). By George White. 12mo., 6d.
MONTEIRO (Mariana), Monk of the Monastery of Yuste ; or, The Last Days of the Emperor Charles V. An Historical Legend of the 16th Century. 12mo., 2s. 6d.
———— Gathered Gems from Spanish Authors. 12mo., 3s.
———— Sanctuary Meditations. *See* Gracian.
MULHOLLAND (Rosa), Prince and Saviour: The Story of Jesus. 12mo., Coloured Illustrations, 2s. 6d.; 32mo., 6d.
MULLER (Rev. M.), The Holy Mass. 12mo., 10s. 6d.
Multiplication Table, on a sheet. 3s. per 100.
MURRAY-LANE (Chevalier H.), Chronological Sketch of the Kings of England and the Kings of France. 12mo., 2s. 6d.; or in 2 vols., 1s. 6d. each.
MUSIC : Ave Maria, for Four Voices. By W. Schulthes. 1s. 3d.
 Cæcilian Society. *See* Separate List. Price 1s. or 2s.
 Catholic Hymnal (English Words). For one, two, or four voices, with accompaniment. By Leopold de Prins. 4to., 2s.; bound, 3s.
 Cor Jesu, Salus in Te sperantium. By W. Schulthes, 2s.; with Harp Accompaniment, 2s. 6d.; abridged, 3d.
 Corona Lauretana. 20 Litanies by W. Schulthes. 2s.
 Evening Hymn at the Oratory. By Rev. J. Nary. 3d.
 Litanies (36) and Benediction Service. By W. Schulthes. 6s. Second Series (Corona Lauretana). 2s.
 Litanies (6). By E. Leslie. 6d.
 Litanies (18). By Rev. J. McCarthy. 1s. 3d.
 Mass of the Holy Child Jesus. In Unison. By W. Schulthes. 3s. The vocal part only, 4d. ; or 3s. per doz. Cloth, 6d.; or 4s. 6d. per doz. [Schaller. 2s. 6d.
 Mass of St. Patrick. For three equal voices. By F.
 Ne projicias me a facie Tua. Motett for Four Voices. By W. Schulthes. 1s. 3d.
 Oratory Hymns. By W. Schulthes. 2 vols., 8s.
 Recordare. Oratorio Jeremiæ Prophetæ. By the same. 1s.

Regina Cœli. Motett for Four Voices. By W. Schul-thes. 3s. Vocal Arrangement, 1s.

St. Agnes's Eve. By Sister Clare. 2s.

The Bells of Kenmare. By Sister Clare. 2s.

The Morning Sacrifice. By Sister Clare. 2s.

Twelve Latin Hymns. By W. Schulthes. 1s. 6d.

Veni Domine. Motett for Four Voices. By W. Schul-thes. 2s. Vocal Arrangement, 6d.

Vespers and Benediction Service. Composed and harmonized by Leopold de Prins. 4to., 3s. 6d.

. *All the above (music) prices are nett.*

My Conversion and Vocation. By Rev. Father Schouvaloff, 5s.

My Godmother's Stories from many Lands. By Mrs. T. K. Hervey. 12mo., 3s. 6d.

My Golden Days. By M. F. S. 12mo., 2s. 6d., or in 3 vols., 1s. each ; or 1s. 6d. gilt.

Mystical Flora of St. Francis de Sales. 4to., 8s.

NARY (Rev. J.) Evening Hymn at the Oratory. Music, 3d.

Nano Nangle ; her Life, her Labours, &c. *See* Hutch.

Necessity of Enquiry as to Religion. *See* Pye (Henry John).

Ned Rusheen. By Miss Cusack. 12mo., 5s.

NEVIN (Willis, Esq.), The Jesuits, and other Essays. 12mo., 1s.; cloth, 2s. 6d.

NEWMAN (Rev. Dr.), Historical Sketches, 3 vols., 18s. ; Miracles, 6s.; Discussions and Arguments, 6s.; Miscellanies, 6s.; Critical and Historical Essays, 2 vols., 12s. ; Callista, 5s. 6d.; Arians, 6s.; Idea of a University, 7s. ; Tracts, Theological and Ecclesiastical, 8s. ; Loss and Gain, 5s. 6d.; Certain Difficulties felt by Anglicans, second series, 5s. 6d. Via Media, 2 vols., 12s. Development, 6s.

———— **Characteristics from the Writings of.** By W. S. Lilly. 12mo., 6s.

New Testament. 12mo., 2s. 6d. Illustrated, large 4to., 7s. 6d.

New Year's Gift to Our Heavenly Father. 32mo., 4d.

Nicholas ; or, the Reward of a Good Action. 18mo., 6d.

NICHOLS (T. L.), Forty Years of American Life. 5s.

Nina and Pippo, the Lost Children of Mt. St. Bernard. 6d.

NOETHEN'S (Rev. T.), Good Thoughts for Priests and People ; or, Short Meditations for every Day in the Year. 8s.

———— **Compendium of** the **History of the Catholic Church.** 12mo., 8s.

———— **History of the Catholic Church.** 12mo., 5s. 6d.

Novena to Our Blessed Lady of Lourdes for the use of the Sick. 18mo., 4d.

Novena of Grace, revealed by S. Francis Xavier. 18mo., 6d.

Novena of Meditations in honour of St. Joseph, according to the method of St. Ignatius, preceded by a new method of hearing Mass according to the intentions of the Souls in Purgatory. 18mo., 1s.

Nun's Advice to her Girls. By Miss Cusack. 12mo., 2s. 6d.

R. Washbourne, 18 *Paternoster Row, London.*

Occasional Prayers for Festivals. *See* Prayers, page 31.

O'CLERY (Keyes, M.P., K.S.G.), The History of the Italian Revolution. First Period—The Revolution of the Barricades (1796-1849). 8vo., 7s. 6d. Cheap edition 3s. 6d.

O'Connell the Liberator. *See* Cusack (M. F.).

O'GALLAGHER (Dr.), Sermons in Irish-Gælic ; with literal idiomatic English Translation, and a Memoir of the Bishop, by Canon U. J. Bourke. 8vo., 7s. 6d.

O'Hagan (Mary), Life of. By Miss Cusack. 8vo., 6s.

O'HAIRE (Rev. J.), Recollections of South Africa. 7s. 6d.

O'MAHONY (D.P.M.), Rome semper eadem. 8vo., 1s. 6d.

O'MEARA (Kathleen), The Battle of Connemara. 12mo., 3s.

—— *See* Grace Ramsay.

Oratorian Lives of the Saints. With Portrait, 12mo., 5s. a vol.
  I. S. Bernardine of Siena, Minor Observatine.
  II. S. Philip Benizi, Fifth General of the Servites.
  III. S. Veronica Giuliani, and B. Battista Varani.
  IV. S. John of God. By Canon Cianfogni.

O'REILLY (Rev. Dr.), Victims of the Mamertime. 5s.

——A Romance of Repentance. 12mo., 3s. 6d.

Oremus, A Liturgical Prayer Book. *See* p. 31.

Our Lady's Comfort to the Sorrowful. 32mo., 6d. and 1s.

Our Lady (Devotion to) in North America. *See* Macleod.

Our Lady's Lament. *See* Tame (C.E.).

Our Lady's Month. By Rev. A. P. Bethell. 18mo., 1s. 6d.

Our Legends and Lives. By E. L. Hervey. 12mo., 6s.

Our Lord's Life, Passion, Death, and Resurrection. Translated from Ribadeneira. 12mo., 1s.

—— By Rev. H. Rutter. Illustrated. 12mo., 5s.

—— Incidents. A Series of 12 Illuminations. 4to., 6s.

OXENHAM (H. N.), Dr. Pusey's Eirenicon. 8vo., 6d.

—— Poems. 12mo., 3s. 6d.

Oxford Undergraduate of Twenty Years Ago. By a Bachelor of Arts. 8vo., 2s. 6d.; cloth, 3s. 6d.

OZANAM (A. F.), Protestantism and Liberty. Translated from the French by Wilfrid C. Robinson. 8vo., 1s.

Pale (The) and the Septs. A Romance of the XVI. Century. 6s.

Panegyrics of Fr. Segneri, S.J. Translated from the original Italian. With a Preface, by Rev. W. Humphrey, S.J. 12mo., 5s.

Paradise of God ; or the Virtues of the Sacred Heart. By Author of "God our Father," "Happiness of Heaven." 12mo., 4s.

Paray le Monial, and Bl. Margaret Mary. 18mo., 6d.

Passion of Our Lord, Harmony of. *See* Gayrard (Mme.).

PASSIONIST FATHERS : Mirror of Faith. 12mo., 3s.
  Manual of the Cross and Passion. 32mo., 3s.
  Sacred Eloquence. 18mo., 2s.
  S. Paul of the Cross. 12mo., 3s.
  School of Jesus Crucified. 18mo., 5s.

Pastor and People. By Rev. T. J. Potter. 12mo., 5s.

Path to Paradise. *See* Prayers, page 31.

Patrick (S.), Life of. 1s.; 8vo., 6s.; gilt, 10s.; 4to., 20s.

Patrick's (S.) Manual. By Miss Cusack. 18mo., 3s. 6d.

Patron Saints. By E. A. Starr. Illustrated. 12mo., 10s.

Paul of the Cross (S.), Life of. *See* Passionist Fathers.

Pearl among the Virtues. By Rev. P. A. De Doss. 12mo., 3s.

Penitential Psalms. *See* Blyth (Rev. F.).

PENS, Washbourne's Free and Easy. Fine, or Middle, or Broad Points, 1s. per gross.

People's Martyr. A Legend of Canterbury. 12mo., 4s.

Percy Grange. By Rev. T. J. Potter. 12mo., 3s.

Perpetual Adoration, Book of. Boudon. 12mo., 3s. and 3s. 6d.

Peter (S.), his Name and his Office. *See* Allies (T. W., Esq.).

Peter, Years of. By an ex-Papal Zouave. 12mo., 1d.

Philip Benizi (S.), Life of. *See* Oratorian Lives of the Saints.

Philosophy, Elements of. By Rev. W. H. Hill. 8vo., 6s.

PHILPIN (Rev. F.), Holy Places; their sanctity and authenticity. With three Maps. 12mo., 2s. 6d. and 6s.

Photographs (10) illustrating the History of the Miraculous Hosts, called the Blessed Sacrament of the Miracle. 2s. 6d. the set.

Pilgrim's Way to Heaven. By Miss Cusack. 12mo., 4s. 6d.

Pius IX. 32mo., 6d.; 4to., 1d.

Pius IX., from his Birth to his Death. By G. White. 12mo., 6d.

Pius IX., his early Life to the Return from Gaeta. By Rev. T. B. Snow, O.S.B. 12mo., 6d.

Plain Chant. *See* Gregorian.

———— The Cecilian Society Music kept in stock.

PLATUS (Rev. F.), Origin and Progress of Religious Orders, and Happiness of a Religious State. 12mo., 2s. 6d.

PLAYS. *See* Dramas, page 10.

POIRIER (Bishop), A General Catechism of the Christian Doctrine. 18mo., 9d.

POOR CLARES OF KENMARE. *See* Cusack (Miss).

Pope-King, Rule of. By Rev. E. R. Martin. 8vo., 6d.

Pope of Rome. *See* Tondini (Rev. C.).

POTTER (Rev. T. J.), Extempore Preaching. 5s.

———— Farleyes of Farleye. 12mo., 2s. 6d.

———— Pastor and People. 12mo., 5s.

———— Percy Grange. 12mo., 3s.

———— Rupert Aubrey. 12mo., 3s.

———— Sir Humphrey's Trial. 16mo., 2s. 6d.

POWELL (J., Esq.), Two Years in the Pontifical Zouaves. Illustrated. 8vo., 3s. 6d.

PRADEL (Fr., O. P.), Life of St. Vincent Ferrer. Translated by Rev. Fr. Dixon. With a Photograph. 12mo., 5s.

PRAYER BOOKS. *See* page 30.

Prince and Saviour. *See* Mulholland (Rosa).

PRINS (Leopold de). · *See* Music.
Pro-Cathedral, Kensington. Tinted View of the Interior,
    11 × 15 inches, 1s.; Proofs, on larger paper, 2s.
Prophecies, Contemporary. By Mgr. Dupanloup. 8vo., 1s.
Protestantism and Liberty. *See* Robinson (W. C.).
Protestant Principles examined by the Written Word. 1s.
Prussian Spy. A Novel. By V. Valmont. 12mo., 4s.
Purgatory, A Novena in favour of the Souls in. 32mo., 3d.
Purgatory, Month of the Souls in Purgatory. By Ricard, 1s.
Purgatory, The Doctrine of. By Rev. W. Marshall. 12mo., 1s.
Purgatory, Souls in. By Abbot Burder. 32mo., 3d.
Pusey's (Dr.) Eirenicon considered. *See* Oxenham (H. N.).
PYE (Henry John, M.A.), Necessity of Enquiry as to
    Religion. 32mo., 4d.; cloth, 6d.
———— The Religion of Common Sense. New Edition. 1s.
RAM (Mrs.), The Spiritual Life. Ravignan's Conferences. 5s.
RAMIERE (Rev. H.), Apostleship of Prayer. 12mo., 6s.
RAVIGNAN (Pere), The Spiritual Life, Conferences.
    Translated by Mrs. Abel Ram. 12mo., 5s.
Ravignan (Pere), Life of. 12mo., 9s.
RAWES (Rev F.), Homeward. 2s. Sursum. 1s.
Reading Lessons. By the Marist Brothers. 12mo., 1st Book, 4d.;
    2nd Book, 7d.
REDMAN (Rev. Dr.), Book of Perpetual Adoration. By
    Mgr. Boudon. 12mo., 3s.; red edges, 3s. 6d.
REDMOND (Rev. Dr.), Eight Short Sermon Essays.
REEVE'S History of the Bible. 12mo., 3s. 6d.; 18mo., 1s.
Reflections, One Hundred Pious. *See* Butler.
Regina Sæculorum ; or, Mary Venerated in all Ages. Devotions
    to the Blessed Virgin from Ancient Sources. 12mo., 1s. and 3s.
Religion of Common Sense. By H. J. Pye, M.A. 12mo., 1s.
Religious Orders. *See* Platus (Rev. F.).
Rest, on the Cross. By Eleanora Louisa Hervey. 12mo., 3s. 6d.
Reverse of the Medal. A Drama for Girls. 12mo., 6d.
RIBADENEIRA—Life, Passion, Death and Resurrec-
    tion of our Lord. 12mo., 1s.
RICARD (Abbe), Month of the Holy Angels. 18mo., 1s.
———— Month of the Souls in Purgatory. 18mo., 1s.
RICHARDSON (Rev. Fr.), Catholic Sick and Benefit
    Club ; or, the Guild of our Lady ; and St. Joseph's Catho
    Burial Society. 32mo., 4d.
———— Little by Little ; or, the Penny Bank. 32mo., 1d.
———— Shamrocks. 6s. 2d. a gross (144), post free.
———— S. Joseph's Catholic Burial Society. 2d.
———— The Crusade ; or, Catholic Association for the Suppres-
    sion of Drunkenness. 32mo., 1d.
Ritus Servandus in Expositione et Benedictione S.S. 4to.,
    cloth, 5s. 6d.
Road to Heaven. A Game. By Miss M. A. Macdaniel. 3s. 6d.

ROBERTSON (Professor), Lectures on the Life, Writings, and Times of Edmund Burke. 12mo., 3s. 6d.

———— Lectures on Modern History and Biography. 6s.

ROBINSON (Wilfrid C.), Protestantism and Liberty. Translated from the French of Professor Ozanam. 8vo., 1s.

Roman Question, The. By Rev. Dr. Husenbeth. 8vo., 6d.

Rome and her Captors : Letters collected and edited by Count Henri d'Ideville, and Translated by F. R. Wegg-Prosser. 4s.

Rome, Past, Present, and Future. By Dr. M'Corry. 8vo., 6d.

—— Personal Recollections of. By W. J. Jacob, 8vo., 6d.

—— The Victories of. By Rev. F. Beste. 8vo., 1s.

—— (To) and Back. Fly-Leaves from a Flying Tour. Edited by Rev. W. H. Anderdon, S.J., 12mo., 2s.

Rosalie ; or, the Memoir of a French Child, told by herself. 12mo., 1s.; stronger bound, 1s. 6d.; gilt, 2s.

Rosary, Fifteen Mysteries of, and Fourteen Stations of the Cross. In One Volume, 32 Illustrations. 16mo., 2s.

Rosary for the Souls in Purgatory, with Indulgenced Prayer. 6d. and 9d. Medals separately, 1d. each, or 9s. gross. Prayers separately, 1d. each, 9d. a dozen, or 6s. for 100.

Rosary, Chats about the. *See* Aunt Margaret's Little Neighbours.

ROWLEY (Rev. Austin John), A Devout Exposition of the Holy Mass. Composed by John Heigham. 12mo., 4s.

RUTTER (Rev. H.) Life and Sufferings of Our Lord, with Introduction by Rev. Dr. Husenbeth. Illustrated. 12mo., 5s.

Sacred Heart, Act of Consecration to. 1d.; or 6s. per 100.

——————, Act of Reparation to. 1s. 2d. per 100.

——————, Devotions to. By Rev. S. Franco. 12mo., 4s.; cheap edition, 2s. [cloth, 6d.; gilt, 1s.

——————, Devotions to. By Bishop Milner. 32mo., 3d.;

——————, Devotions to. Translated by Rev. J. Joy Dean. 12mo., 2s. [12mo., 3s.

——————, Elevations to the. By Rev. Fr. Doyotte, S.J.

——————, Handbook of the Confraternity, for the use of Members. 18mo., 3d.

——————, Little Treasury of. 32mo., 2s.; French morocco, 2s. 6d.; calf, 5s. ; morocco, 6s.

——————, Manual of Devotions to the, from the writings of Blessed Margaret Mary. 32mo., 3d.

—————— offered to the Piety of the Young engaged in Study. By Rev. F. Deham. 32mo., 6d.

—————— *See* Paradise of God ; Kinane (Rev. T. H.).

—————— Pleadings of. By Rev. M. Comerford. 18mo., 1s.; gilt edges, 2s.; with Handbook of the Confraternity, 1s. 6d.

——————, Treasury of. 18mo., 3s. 6d.; roan, 4s.

Sacred History in Forty Pictures. Plain, 5s.; coloured, 7s. 6d.; mounted on cardboard, coloured, 18s. 6d. and 22s.

Saints, Lives of. By Alban Butler. 4 vols., 8vo., 32s.; gilt, 50s.; and leather, gilt, 64s.; or the 4 vols. in 2, 28s.; gilt, 34s.

—————————— for every day in the Year. Beautifully printed, within illustrated borders from ancient sources, on thick toned paper. 4to., gilt, 21s.

—————— Patron. By E. A. Starr. Illustrated. 12mo., 10s.

R. Washbourne, 18 *Paternoster Row, London.*

Sanctuary Meditations for Priests and Frequent Communicants. Translated from the Spanish of Fr. Baltasar Gracian, by Mariana Monteiro. 12mo., 4s.

SCARAMELLI—Directorium Asceticum ; or, Guide to the Spiritual Life. 4 vols. 12mo., 24s. Vols. 4, 3, or 2 sold separately, 6s. each.

SCHMID (Canon), Tales. Illustrated. 12mo., 3s. 6d. Separately :—The Canary Bird, The Dove, The Inundation, The Rose Tree, The Water Jug, The Wooden Cross. 6d. each ; gilt, 1s.

SCHOOL BOOKS. Supplied according to order.

School of Jesus Crucified. By the Passionist Fathers. 18mo., 5s.

SCHOUVALOFF [(Rev. Father, Barnabite), **My Conversion and Vocation.** Translated from the French, with an Appendix, by Fr. C. Tondini. 12mo., 5s.

SCHULTHES (William). *See* Music.

Scraps from my Scrapbook. *See* Arnold (M. J.).

SEGNERI (Fr., S.J.), Panegyrics. Translated from the original Italian. With a Preface, by Rev. W. Humphrey. 12mo., 5s.

SEGUR (Mgr.), Books for Little Children. Translated. 32mo., 3d. each. Confession, Holy Communion, Child Jesus, Piety, Prayer, Temptation and Sin. In one volume, cloth, 2s.

———— **Practical Counsels for Holy Communion.** 18mo., 1s.

SEGUR (Countess de), The Little Hunchback. 12mo., 3s.

Seigneret (Paul), Life of. 12mo., 6d., 1s., and 1s. 6d.; gilt, 2s.

Selva ; a Collection of Matter for Sermons. By St. Liguori. 12mo., 5s.

Semi-Tropical Trifles. By H. Compton. 12mo., 1s.; cloth, 2s. 6d.

Sermon Essays. By Rev. Dr. Redmond. 12mo., 1s.

Sermons. Irish and English. By Dr. O'Gallagher. 8vo., 7s. 6d.

———— By Father Burke, O.P., and others. 12mo., 2s.

———— **The Light of the Holy Spirit in the World.** By Bishop Hedley. 1s.; cloth, 1s. 6d.

———— **One Hundred Short.** By Rev. Fr. Thomas. 8vo., 12s.

Sermons, Lectures, &c. By Rev. M. M. Buckley. 12mo., 6s.

Serving Boy's Manual, and Book of Public Devotions. Containing all those prayers and devotions for Sundays and Holy days, usually divided in their recitation between the Priest and the Congregation. Compiled from approved sources, and adapted to Churches, served either by the Secular or Regular Clergy. 32mo., embossed, 1s.; French morocco, 2s.; calf, 4s.; with Epistles and Gospels, 6d. extra.

Seven Sacraments Explained and Defended. 18mo., 1s. 6d.

SHAKESPEARE. Expurgated edition. By Rosa Baughan. 8vo., 6s. The Comedies only, 3s. 6d.

Shandy Maguire. A Farce for Boys. 2 Acts. 12mo., 2s.

SHAW (T. H.), Holy Church the Centre of Unity ; or, Ritualism compared with Catholicism. 8vo., 1s.

Siege of Limerick (Florence O'Neill). *See* Stewart (Agnes M.).

SIGHART (Dr.) Albertus Magnus. 10s. 6d. Cheap edition, 5s.

Silver Teapot. By Elizabeth King. 18mo., 4d.

Simple Tales—Waiting for Father, &c., &c. 16mo., 2s. 6d.

Sir Ælfric and other Tales. *See* Bampfield (Rev. G.).
Sir Humphrey's Trial. By Rev. T. J. Potter. 16mo., 2s. 6d.
Sir Thomas Maxwell and his Ward. By Miss Bridges. 12mo, 1s. and 2s.
Sisters of Charity, Manual of. 18mo. 6s.
SMITH-SLIGO (A. V., Esq.), Life of the Ven. Anna Maria Taigi. Translated from French of Calixte. 8vo., 2s. 6d. and 5s.
— (Mrs.) Margarethe Verflassen. 12mo., 1s. 6d., 3s., and 3s. 6d.
SNOW (Rev. T. B.), Pius IX., His early Life to the Return from Gaeta. 12mo., 6d.
Soul (The), United to Jesus. 32mo., 1s. 6d.
SPALDING'S (Abp.) Works. 5 vols., 52s. 6d.; or separately: Evidences of Catholicity, 10s. 6d.; Miscellanea, 2 vols., 21s.; Protestant Reformation, 2 vols., 21s.; cheap edition, 1 vol., 14s.
Spalding (Archbishop), Life of. 8vo., 10s. 6d.
———— Sermon at the Month's Mind. 8vo., 1s.
Spiritual Conferences on the Mysteries of Faith and the Interior Life. By Father Collins. 12mo., 5s.
Spiritual Life. Conferences by Père Ravignan. Translated by Mrs. Abel Ram. 12mo., 5s.
Spiritual Works of Louis of Blois. Edited by Rev. F. John Bowden. 12mo., 3s. 6d.; red edges, 4s.
Spouse of Christ. By Sister M. F. Clare. 12mo., vol. 2, 7s. 6d.
STARR (Eliza Allen), Patron Saints. Illustrated. 12mo., 10s.
Stations of the Cross, Devotions for Public and Private Use at the. By Miss Cusack. Illustrated. 16mo., 1s. and 1s. 6d.
Stations of the Cross. By S. Liguori. 18mo., 1d.
Stations of the Cross and Mysteries of the Rosary. 2s.
STEWART (A. M.), Alone in the World. 12mo., 4s. 6d.
———— St. Angela's Manual. *See* Angela (S.)
———— Biographical Readings. 12mo., 4s. 6d.
———— Life and Letters of Sir Thomas More. Illustrated, 10s. 6d.; gilt, 11s. 6d.
———— Life of S. Angela Merici. 12mo., 4s. 6d.
———— Life in the Cloister. 12mo., 3s. 6d. [extra, 6s.
———— Limerick Veteran ; or, the Foster Sisters. 12mo., 5s.;
———— Margaret Roper. 12mo., 6s.; extra, 7s. [16mo., 1s.
Stories for my Children—The Angels and the Sacraments.
Stories of Holy Lives. By M. F. S. 12mo., 3s. 6d.
Stories of Martyr Priests. By M. F. S. 12mo., 3s. 6d.
Stories of the Saints. By M. F. S. 12mo., 1st Series, 3s. 6d.; gilt, 4s. 6d. 2nd Series, 3s. 6d.; gilt, 4s. 6d. 3rd Series, 3s. 6d.
Stormsworth, with other Poems and Plays. By the author of " Thy Gods, O Israel.' 12mo., 3s. 6d.
Story of an Orange Lodge. 12mo., 1s.
Story of Marie and other Tales. 12mo., 2s.; gilt, 3s.; or separately :—The Story of Marie, 2d.; Nelly Blane, and a Contrast, 2d.; A Conversion and a Death-bed, 2d.; Herbert Montagu, 2d.; Jane Murphy, the Dying Gipsy, and the Nameless Grave, 2d.; The Beggars, and True and False Riches, 2d.; Pat and his Friend, 2d.

Story of the Life of St. Paul. By M. F. S., author of "Stories of the Saints." 12mo., 2s. 6d.

Sufferings of our Lord. Sermons preached by Father Claude de la Colombière, S.J., in the Chapel Royal, St. James's, in the year 1677. 18mo., 1s.; stronger bound, 1s. 6d.; red edges, 2s.

Supernatural Life, The. By Mgr. Mermillod. Translated from the French, with a Preface by Lady Herbert. 12mo., 5s.

Supremacy of the Roman See. By C. E. Tame, Esq. 8vo., 6d.

Sure Way to Heaven. A Little Manual for Confession and Holy Communion. 32mo., 6d.; Persian, 2s. 6d.; calf or morocco, 3s. 6d.

Sweetness of Holy Living; or, Honey culled from the Flower Garden of S. Francis of Sales. 18mo., 1s.; French morocco, 3s.

Taigi (Anna Maria), Life of. Translated from the French of Calixte by A. V. Smith-Sligo, Esq. 8vo., 2s. 6d. and 5s.

Tales and Sketches. *See* Fleet (Charles).

TAME (C. E., Esq.), Early English Literature. 16mo., 2s. a vol. I. Our Lady's Lament, and the Lamentation of S. Mary Magdalene. II. Life of Our Lady, in verse.

———— Supremacy of the Roman See. 8vo., 6d.

TANDY (Rev. Dr.), Terry O'Flinn. 12mo., 1s.; stronger bound, 1s. 6d.; gilt, 2s.

TAUNTON (M.), Last of the Catholic O'Malleys. 18mo., 1s. 6d.; stronger bound, 2s.

———— One Hundred Pious Reflections, from Alban Butler's Lives of the Saints. 18mo., 1s.; stronger bound, 2s.

Temperance Books. *See* Richardson (Rev. Fr.).

———— Cards (Illuminated), 3d. each.   [3d. each.

———— Medals—Immaculate Conception, St. Patrick, St. Joseph.

Terry O'Flinn. By Rev. Dr. Tandy. 12mo., 1s., 1s. 6d. and 2s.

Testimony; or, the Necessity of Enquiry as to Religion. By John Henry Pye, M.A. 32mo., 4d.; cloth, 6d.

THOMAS (H. J.), One Hundred Short Sermons. 8vo., 12s.

Three Tabernacles. By Thomas à Kempis. 16mo., 2s. 6d.

Three Wishes. A Tale. By M. F. S. 12mo., 2s. 6d.

Threshold of the Catholic Church. *See* Bagshawe (Rev. J. B.)

Tim O'Halloran's Choice. *See* Cusack.

Tom's Crucifix, and other Tales. By M. F. S. 12mo., 3s., or in 5 vols., 1s. each; gilt, 1s. 6d.

TONDINI (Rev. Cæsarius), My Conversion and Vocation. By Rev. Fr. Schouvaloff. 12mo., 5s.

———— The Pope of Rome and the Popes of the Oriental Orthodox Church. An essay on Monarchy in the Church, with special reference to Russia. Second Edition. 12mo., 3s. 6d.

———— Some Documents concerning of the Association Prayers in Honour of Mary Immaculate, for the Return of the Greek-Russian Church to Catholic Unity. 12mo., 3d. Association of Prayers, 32mo., 1d.

Transubstantiation, Catholic Doctrine of. 12mo., 6d.

Trials of Faith. *See* Browne (E. G. K.).

TRONSON (Abbe), The Mass: a devout Method. 32mo., 4d.

TRONSON'S Conferences for Ecclesiastical Students and Religious. By Sister M. F. Clare. 12mo., 4s. 6d.

Truce of God. A Tale of the XI. Century. *See* Miles (G. H.).

Two Colonels. By Father Thomas. 12mo., 6s. [1s., or gilt, 1s. 6d.

Two Friends ; or Marie's Self-Denial. By Madame d'Arras. 12mo.,

Ursuline Manual. *See* Prayers, page 32.

VALMONT (V.), The Prussian Spy. A Novel. 12mo., 4s.

VAUGHAN (Bishop of Salford), Holy Sacrifice of the Mass. 2d.

———— Life and Passion of Jesus Christ. 2d.

VERE (Rev. G. L.), The Catholic Hymn Book. 32mo., 2d. ; cloth, 4d. Appendix containing Hymns in honour of Saints. 1d.

Veronica Giuliani (S.), Life of, and B. Battista Varani. With a Photographic Portrait. 12mo., 5s.

Village Lily. A Tale. 12mo., 1s. ; gilt, 1s. 6d.

Vincent Ferrer (S.), of the Order of Friar Preachers ; his Life, Spiritual Teaching, and Practical Devotion. By Rev. Fr. Andrew Pradel, O.P. Translated from the French by the Rev. Fr. T. A. Dixon, O.P., with a Photograph. 12mo., 5s.

VINCENT OF LIRINS (S.). Commonitory. 12mo., 1s. 3d.

Vincent of Paul (S.), Glory of. *See* Manning (Archbishop).

VIRGIL. Literally translated by Davidson. 12mo., 2s. 6d.

"Vitis Mystica " ; or, the True Vine. *See* Brownlow.

WALLER (J. F., Esq.), Festival Tales. 12mo., 3s. 6d.

WALSH (W. H., Esq.), Henry V. 8vo., 6d.

Way of Salvation. By S. Liguori. 32mo., 1s.

Weedall (Mgr.), Life of. By Rev. Dr. Husenbeth. 8vo., 1s.

WEGG-PROSSER (F. R.), Rome and her Captors. 4s.

Wenefred (St.), Life of. By Rev. T. Meyrick. 12mo., 2s.

What is Christianity ? By Rev. F. H. Laing, D.D. 12mo., 6d.

Whence the Monarch's Right to Rule ? *See* Laing (Rev. D.).

WHITE (George), Cardinal Wiseman. 12mo., 1s. and 1s. 6d.

———— Comte de Montalembert. 12mo., 6d.

———— Life of S. Edmund of Canterbury. 1s. and 1s. 6d.

———— Pius IX., from his Birth to his Death. 12mo., 6d.

WHITELOCK (A.), The Chances of War. An Irish Tale. 5s.

William (St.), of York. A Drama in Two Acts. (Boys.) 12mo., 6d.

WILLIAMS (Canon), Anglican Orders. 12mo., 3s. 6d.

Wiseman (Cardinal), Life and Obsequies. 1s. and 1s. 6d.

———— Recollections of. By M. J. Arnold. 12mo., 2s. 6d.

WOODS (Canon), Defence of the Roman Church against F. Gratry. Translated from the French of Gueranger. 1s. 6d.

WYATT-EDGELL (Alfred), Stormsworth, with other Poems and Plays. 12mo., 3s. 6d.

———— Thy Gods ! O Israel. 12mo., 2s.

Young Catholic's Guide to Confession and Holy Communion. By Dr. Kenny. 32mo., 4d.; cloth, 6d.; red edges, 9d.; French morocco, 1s. 6d.; calf or morocco, 2s. 6d.

YOUNG (T., Esq.), History of Ireland. 18mo., 2s. 6d.

Zouaves, Pontifical, Two Years in. By Joseph Powell, Z.P. Illustrated. 8vo., 3s. 6d.

PRAYER BOOKS.

Garden, Little, of the Soul. Edited by the Rev. R. G. Davis.
With Imprimatur of the Archbishop of Westminster. This book,
as its name imports, contains a selection from the "Garden of the
Soul" of the Prayers and Devotions of most general use. Whilst
it will serve as a *Pocket Prayer Book* for all, it is, by its low price,
par excellence, the Prayer Book for children and for the very poor.
In it are to be found the old familiar Devotions of the "Garden of
the Soul," as well as many important additions, such as the Devotions to the Sacred Heart, to Saint Joseph, to the Guardian Angels,
and others. The omissions are mainly the Forms of administering
the Sacraments, and Devotions that are not of very general use.
It is printed in a clear type, on a good paper, both especially selected, for the purpose of obviating the disagreeableness of small
type and inferior paper. Fifteenth Thousand.

    32mo., price, cloth, 6d.; with rims, 1s. Embossed, red edges, 9d.;
with rims and clasp, 1s. 3d.; Strong roan, 1s.; with rims and clasp,
1s. 6d. French morocco, 1s. 6d.; with rims and clasp, 2s. French morocco extra gilt, 2s.; with rims and clasp, 2s. 6d. Calf or morocco,
3s.; with rims and clasp, 4s. Calf or morocco, extra gilt, 4s.; with
rims and clasp, 5s. Morocco antique, 7s. 6d., 10s. 6d., 12s., 16s. Velvet, rims and clasp, 5s., 8s. 6d., and 10s. 6d. Russia, 5s.; with clasp,
&c., 8s.; Russia antique, 17s. 6d. Ivory, with rims and clasp,
10s. 6d., 13s., 15s., 17s. 6d. Imitation ivory, with rims and clasp,
3s. With oxydized silver or gilt mountings, in morocco case, 25s.

Catholic Hours : a Manual of Prayer, including Mass and Vespers.
By J. R. Digby Beste, Esq. 32mo., cloth, 2s.; red edges, 2s. 6d.;
roan, 3s.; morocco, 6s.

Catholic Piety ; or, Key of Heaven, with Epistles and Gospels.
Large 32mo., roan, 1s. 6d. and 2s.; French morocco, with rims and
clasp, 2s. 6d.; extra gilt, 3s.; with rims and clasp, 3s. 6d.

Catholic Piety ; or, Key of Heaven. 32mo., 6d.; rims and clasp,
1s.; French morocco, 1s.; velvet, with rims and clasp, 2s. 6d.;
with Epistles and Gospels, roan, 1s.; French morocco, 1s. 6d.;
with rims and clasp, 2s.; extra gilt, 2s.; Persian, 2s. 6d.; imitation ivory, 3s.; morocco, 3s. 6d.; velvet, rims and clasp, 3s. 6d.

Crown of Jesus. 18mo., Persian calf, 6s. Calf or Morocco, 7s. 6d.
and 8s. 6d.; with rims and clasp, 10s. 6d. Calf or morocco, extra gilt,
10s. 6d.; with rims and clasp, 12s. 6d; with turn-over edges,
10s. 6d. Ivory, with rims and clasp, 21s., 25s., 27s. 6d. and 30s.

Daily Exercises for Devout Christians. By Rev. P. V.
Monk, O.S.B. 18mo., 3s. 6d.

Devotions for Mass. Very large type, 12mo., 2d.

Garden of the Soul. Very large Type. 18mo., cloth, 1s.; with
Epistles and Gospels, 1s. 6d.; French morocco, 2s. 6d.; with
E. and G., 3s. 6d. Best edition, without E. and G., 3s. 6d.; with E.
and G., morocco circuit, 7s. 6d.; calf antique, with clasp, 8s.;
French morocco, antique, with clasp, 6s. 6d.

    Epistles and Gospels, in French morocco, 2s.

R. Washbourne, 18 *Paternoster Row, London.*

Holy Childhood. Simple Prayers for very little children. 32mo., 1s.; gilt, 1s. 6d. ; cheap edition, 6d.

Illustrated Manual of Prayers. 32mo., 3d.; cloth, 4d.

Key of Heaven. *Very large type.* 18mo., 1s. ; leather, 2s. 6d.

Lily of St. Joseph, The ; a little Manual of Prayers and Hymns for Mass. 64mo., price 2d.; cloth, 3d., 4d., 6d., or 8d.; roan, 1s.; French morocco, 1s. 6d.; calf or morocco, 2s.; gilt, 2s. 6d.

Little Prayer Book, The, for Ordinary Catholic Devotions. 3d.

Manual of Catholic Devotions. Small, for the waistcoat pocket. 64mo., 6d.; with Epistles and Gospels, cloth, 6d.; with rims, 1s.; roan, 1s.; with tuck, 1s. 6d.; calf or morocco, 2s. 6d.; ivorine, 2s. 6d.

Manual of Devotions in Honour of our Lady of Sorrows. 18mo., 1s. 6d.; cheaper binding, 1s.

Manual of the Sisters of Charity. 18mo., 6s.

Memorare Mass. By Sister M. F. Clare, of Kenmare. 32mo., 2d.

Missal (Complete). 18mo., Persian, 8s. 6d.; calf or morocco, 10s. 6d.; with rims and clasp, 13s. 6d.; calf or mor., extra gilt, 12s. 6d., with rims and clasp, 15s. 6d.; morocco, with turn-over edges, 13s. 6d. ; morocco antique, 15s. ; velvet, 20s.; Russia, 20s.; ivory, with rims and clasp, 31s. 6d. and 35s.

———— A very beautiful edition, handsomely bound in morocco, gilt mountings, silk linings, edges red on gold, in a morocco case. Illustrated, £5. [clasp, 8s.

Missal and Vesper Book, in one vol. 32mo., morocco, 6s.; with

Occasional Prayers for Festivals. 4d. and 6d.; gilt, 1s.

OREMUS, A Liturgical Prayer Book : with the Imprimatur of the Cardinal Archbishop of Westminster. An adaptation of the Church Offices : containing Morning and Evening Devotions ; Devotion for Mass, Confession, and Communion, and various other Devotions ; Common and Proper, Hymns, Lessons, Collects, Epistles and Gospels for Sundays, Feasts, and Week Days ; and short notices of over 200 Saints' Days. 32mo., 452 pages, cloth, 2s. 6d.; embossed, red edges, 3s. 6d. ; French morocco, 4s. 6d.; calf, 5s. 6d.; morocco, 6s.; Russia, 8s. 6d.

Path to Paradise. 32 full-page Illustrations. 32mo., cloth, 3d. With 50 Illustrations, cloth, 4d. Superior edition, 6d. and 1s.

Serving Boy's Manual and Book of Catholic Devotions, containing all those Prayers and Devotions for Sundays and Holi days, usually divided in their recitation between the Priest and the Congregation. Compiled from approved sources, and adapted to Churches served either by the Secular or the Regular Clergy 32mo., Embossed, 1s.; with Epistles and Gospels, 1s. 6d.; French morocco, 2s., with Epistles and Gospels, 2s. 6d.; calf, 4s., with Epistles and Gospels, 4s. 6d.

Soul united to Jesus in the Adorable Sacrament. 1s. 6d

S. Patrick's Manual. Compiled by Sister Mary Frances Clare. 3s. 6d

Sure Way to Heaven. Cloth, 6d.: Persian, 2s. 6d.; morocco, 3s. 6d

Treasury of the Sacred Heart. 18mo., 3s. 6d.; roan, 4s. 6d 32mo., 2s.; French morocco, 2s. 6d. ; calf 5s.; morocco, 6s.

Ursuline Manual. 18mo., 4s.; Persian calf, 7s. 6d.; morocco, 10

Garden of the Soul. WASHBOURNE'S EDITION.) Edited by the ... ... Late Secretary to the Archbishop of Westminster. Twentieth Thousand. This Edition retains all the Devotions ... have made the GARDEN OF THE SOUL now for many ... as the well-known Prayer-book for English Catholics. During many years various Devotions have been introduced, and, ... form of supplements, have been added to other editions. These have now been incorporated into the body of the work, and, ... with the Devotions to the Sacred Heart, to Saint Joseph, to the Guardian Angels, the Incarnation, and other important ad... ... render this at once pre-eminently the Manual of Prayer, for both public and private use. The version of the Psalms has been ... revised and ... conformed to the Douay translation ... ... with the concurrence of the LATE CARDINAL WISEMAN. The Forms of administering the Sacraments have been carefully ... from the Ordo Administrandi Sacramenta. To enable all present, either at baptism ... the administration of the Sacraments, to pay due ... to the sacred rites, the Forms are inserted without any ... both in Latin and English. The Devotions at Mass have been carefully revised and enriched by copious adaptations from the prayers of the Missal. The preparation for the Sacrament of Penance and the Holy Eucharist have been the objects of ... care to adapt them to the wants of those whose religious ... may be deficient. Great attention has been paid to the ... of the paper and to the size of type used in the printing, to ... that weariness so distressing to the eyes, caused by the use ... printed in small close type and on inferior paper.

... Embossed, 1s.; with rims and clasp, 1s. 6d.; with Epistles and Gospels, 1s. 6d.; with rims and clasp, 2s. French morocco, 2s.; with rims and clasp, 2s. 6d.; with E. and G., 2s. 6d.; with rims and clasp, 3s. French morocco extra gilt, 2s. 6d.; with rims and clasp, 3s.; with E. and G., 3s.; with rims and clasp, 3s. 6d.; Calf or morocco 4s.; with rims and clasp, 5s. 6d.; with E. and G., 4s. 6d., with rims and clasp, 6s. Calf or morocco extra gilt, 5s.; with rims and clasp, 6s. 6d.; with E. and G., 5s. 6d.; with rims and clasp, 7s. Velvet, with rims and clasp, 7s. 6d., 10s. 6d., and 13s.; with E. and G., 8s., 11s., and 13s. 6d. Russia, antique, with clasp, 8s. 6d., 10s., 12s. 6d.; with E. and G., 9s. 10s. 6d., 13s., with corners and clasps, 20s.; with E. and G., 20s. 6d. Ivory, 12s., 15s., 18s., 20s., and 22s. 6d.; with E. and G., 14s. 6d., 15s. 6d., 18s. 6d., 20s. 6d., and 23s. Morocco antique, with 2 ... clasps, 12s.; with E. and G., 12s. 6d.; with corners and clasps, 18s.; with E. and G., 18s. 6d.

The Epistles and Gospels. Complete, cloth, 6d.; roan, 1s. 6d.

"This is one of the best editions we have seen of one of the best of all our Prayer Books. It is well printed in clear, large type, on good paper."—Catholic Opinion.
"A very complete arrangement of that which is emphatically the Prayer Book of every Catholic household. It is as cheap as it is good, and we heartily recommend it."—Universe. "Two striking features are the admirable order displayed throughout the book, and the insertion of the Indulgences in small type above Indulgenced Prayers. In the Devotions for Mass the editor has, with great discrimination, drawn largely on the Church's Prayers, as given us in the Missal."—Weekly Register.

E. Washbourne, 18 Paternoster Row, London.